*Please turn the page
for more reviews . . .*

"GRIPPING . . .

From the opening pages onward, the story moves briskly along, with each of the chapters revolving around one of the key or secondary characters. In the process, Shaara gives us ringside seats at the Boston Massacre, the Boston Tea Party, the battle of Concord, and other turning points on the road to Independence. . . . A glowing tribute to Adams, Washington, Franklin, and the rest. Indeed, after reading it, you're likely to find that you have a new appreciation for our Founding Fathers."

—*Port Folio Weekly* (Virginia Beach, VA)

"Sweeping and turbulent, *Rise to Rebellion* rarely fails to satisfy the reader who appreciates historical fiction done with style, accuracy, sensitivity, and analytical skill. If there were questions about whether Shaara would live up to his literary pedigree, this should be the book to finally silence the doubters."

—*BookPage*

"As compelling as a novel . . . Shaara has done the historical research, but then he enters the mind of his characters as a novelist does, to let us know their thoughts and emotions."

—*Style Weekly* (Richmond, VA)

"Recommended . . . [Shaara] make[s] our national myths sing and our country's history come to vibrant life."

—*Library Journal*

By Jeff Shaara
Published by Ballantine Books

GODS AND GENERALS
THE LAST FULL MEASURE
GONE FOR SOLDIERS
RISE TO REBELLION
THE GLORIOUS CAUSE
TO THE LAST MAN
JEFF SHAARA'S CIVIL WAR BATTLEFIELDS
THE RISING TIDE
THE STEEL WAVE
NO LESS THAN VICTORY
THE FINAL STORM
A BLAZE OF GLORY
A CHAIN OF THUNDER

RISE

TO

REBELLION

Jeff Shaara

BALLANTINE BOOKS • NEW YORK

A Ballantine Book
Published by The Random House Publishing Group
Copyright © 2001 by Jeffrey M. Shaara

Published in the United States by Ballantine Books, an imprint of The Random House Publishing Group, a division of Random House, Inc., New York, and simultaneously in Canada by Random House of Canada Limited, Toronto.

BALLANTINE and colophon are registered trademarks of Random House, Inc.

ISBN 978-0-345-45206-1

Maps by Mapping Specialists Ltd.

Printed in the United States of America

www.ballantinebooks.com

First Hardcover Edition: July 2001
First Mass Market Edition: April 2002

OPM   20   19   18   17   16   15

Dedicated to the memory of
Dr. Richard B. Shaara
(Uncle Richey)—
you were always there
with a kind heart
and a
pat on the back

TO THE READER

THIS IS THE FIRST VOLUME OF A TWO-PART STORY OF THE AMERICAN Revolution, as told from the points of view of several of the key participants. This book follows the time line from the first bloodshed in Boston, in March 1770, through the summer of 1776. While the events and the people are real and true to history, this is not what you may have read in high school history class.

By definition, this is a novel. As painstaking as I try to be in telling you this story through the voices of the characters themselves, in their own words and through their own experiences, the dialogue and thoughts must be read as fiction.

I'm often asked about the source material, the research itself. Few subjects in American history are as well chronicled as the American Revolution. More specifically, some of these characters have been so focused upon that their names fill entire shelves in libraries. Wherever possible, my research takes me through their letters and memoirs, their diaries, their own written histories, or the accounts written by the people who were *there*. In telling you their stories from their points of view, it is essential that the research take me into their minds. It then becomes my task to bring those voices to you.

One immediate observation about this time in American history is the unique language of the era. As my father, Michael Shaara, noted in his introduction to *The Killer Angels*, in the 1860s "men spoke in windy phrases." Going back to the 1770s, the style of speech is windier still. Occasionally I have toned down some of the more complex language of the time, with significant exceptions: I have not changed any direct quote, nor have I altered the wording of any written document. I have made every effort not to pollute the characterizations by including any anachronistic words or inappropriately modern references.

This is primarily the story of this time as told through the eyes of Benjamin Franklin, John and Abigail Adams, General Thomas Gage, and George Washington. While I do not attempt to convey or explain every event, every important incident, every factor that carried America to the point of revolution, I have tried to show how each of these characters responded to his or her time, how they witnessed and experienced and impacted the enormous changes unfolding around them.

It has become fashionable in our modern, more cynical time to reexamine our history, to throw a supposedly new light on those who are famous for their accomplishments, to instead expose their faults, to topple the statue of the hero, to replace the honor and respect with the sensational and the shameful, as though it were the only meaningful way these characters can be relevant to today's world. I most adamantly disagree. That we know so much about these characters today is a testament to their accomplishments, their extraordinary achievements, and, yes, their astounding heroism. That they can so easily become targets is a testament to their humanity. They are, after all, so very much like us. Measuring their behavior with the crystal clarity of hindsight, with twenty-first-century standards and judgments, is a convenient and cynical shortcut to learning history, but it does little to help us understand their character and why they deserve to be not only remembered, but revered.

The American Revolution is not merely a story about great battles. The Revolution itself was about not just the power of armies, but the power of a people to decide their own future. This story allows you, the reader, to witness the very birth of our nation through the eyes of the wonderful men and women who by their integrity, sacrifice, and astounding courage caused it to happen. It is a story that belongs to every American.

JEFF SHAARA,
OCTOBER, 2000

INTRODUCTION

WHEN TWENTY-TWO-YEAR-OLD KING GEORGE III ASCENDS TO THE throne of England in 1760, he inherits an empire that is struggling financially, and worse, he inherits a war. The enemy is France, as for centuries it has always been. The war in Europe is called the Seven Years' War. But the conflict between the two great powers has spread well beyond the European continent for the first time. Both countries now have serious colonial interests in North America, and thus the war spreads there as well, involving soldiers not only from the two nations themselves, but from their colonies and from the native population. It is referred to by the colonists as the French and Indian War.

The war is ultimately won by the British, the largest spoils being Canada and the islands of the West Indies. To the American colonists, the greatest prize is peace along most of the Indian frontier. In England, the king and his ministers are desperate to shore up the British economy, to rebuild its treasury after the devastating financial cost of the war.

The king is essentially a decent, caring man who has been taught from birth that his first priority is to preserve his empire, to demonstrate a benevolent yet firm control over his subjects. He is said to have received a brief piece of advice that he will take to heart all his life: *Be* a king. Yet George is not an especially clever or resourceful man, and he is easily manipulated by the cunning and ambitious men around him. One of these men is George Grenville, who serves as chancellor of the exchequer (in effect, the empire's treasurer). Grenville is a miserly and hostile man whose narrow view of the world is punctuated by a sharpened pencil. To help solve England's financial woes, Grenville pushes through Parliament a series of acts aimed at raising money from the growing economy of the American colonies. The acts include new taxes on the importation of sugar, restrictions on colonial credit, restrictions on the importation of goods into the colonies from territories outside the empire, and the right of the British military to billet their troops in private homes without the householders' consent. But the most controversial of Grenville's acts, the tax that will impact the greatest number of colonists, is the Stamp Act, news of which arrives on colonial shores in 1765. The Stamp Act requires a royal tax stamp to be affixed on any newspaper, pamphlet, public document, or legal contract, and even on the tools of wagering, such as playing cards and dice. From the British point of view, the Stamp Act is a legitimate means of requiring the colonies to pay the cost of British military protection and their share of the cost of the French and Indian War. The British are astounded to learn that the colonies take a decidedly different point of view.

There are immediate protests in the colonies, claims that the new taxes will cause severe financial hardship. Then a sharp cry begins to spread throughout the colonies: "Taxation without representation is tyranny!" The phrase is taken from a famous speech given to King Charles I by John Hampden in 1638, but it receives a new and significantly passionate following. It has historically been regarded as illegal for Parliament to levy any tax in the colonies, the colonies being granted by the British constitution the power to tax themselves. But what further angers the colonists is that they are never allowed to send their own representatives to Parliament, that they have no one to speak for them on where or how these taxes might be used. No argument over this issue has been made in England for nearly forty years. In that time, the colonies have grown more populous and more prosperous and have formed a much stronger sense of identity separate from their English roots. None of this is understood by the officials in London who are charged with managing colonial affairs.

The colonists begin to hear of an organized resistance to what is being described as blatant abuses of colonial liberties. In Boston, the name of Samuel Adams emerges. Adams is the forty-three-year-old son of a respected deacon, church founder, and businessman. Adams is Harvard-educated but has never seemed capable of sustaining himself in either business or law; he is most notable for his huge personal debts. But Adams has a talent for rallying the citizens to a cause and is a principal founder of the Sons of Liberty, the name adapted from a pro-colonial speech given in Parliament by Isaac Barré. Under Adams' skilled hand, the Sons quickly evolve into an effective voice for organizing and mobilizing opposition to what they see as the abuses of the Grenville Acts. Adams understands the value of the printing press, and for the first time the newspaper becomes a valuable tool for propaganda. The impact of the Sons spreads throughout the colonies, and soon similar groups of the same name spring up in most of the larger towns along the Atlantic coast.

Adams and the other leaders of the Sons—Dr. Joseph Warren, John Hancock, and many others—begin a well-orchestrated and well-publicized manipulation of public opinion that results in outbreaks of violence against anyone in the colonies who might support the acts, including anyone who has accepted the lucrative position of royal tax collector. They tar and feather their opponents with relative impunity, instigate riots in Boston, and destroy the home of then lieutenant governor Thomas Hutchinson.

Pressure to repeal the acts comes from Parliament as well, and the colonial radicals learn they have support in that body. Besides Barré, other members of Parliament begin to speak out against the king's policies, notably John Wilkes, William Pitt, and Edmund Burke. Bowing to the pressure, Parliament repeals the acts in 1766, and Grenville's career is over.

The repeal has two effects: It spawns a growing resentment in England over the disrespect the colonies show their mother country, and it emboldens the colonies as they realize that they may in fact have an impact on their own future. The resentment fuels King George's efforts to find other ways to make the colonies feed the royal treasury. In 1767, Grenville's successor, Sir Charles Townshend, proposes what are known as the Townshend Acts, a clumsy attempt at levying another series of taxes on a long list of goods, including paper, ink, paint, glass, lead, and tea. In addition, the act calls for employees of the crown serving in the colonies to be paid out of colonial treasuries for the first time, thus eliminating any colonial influence in the management of many government offices. The Townshend Acts are as unpopular as the Stamp Act, and when Townshend dies soon after their passage, opposition both in America and in Parliament brings about their repeal as well. As a compromise, and an effort to placate the king, Parliament keeps only one small clause of the acts in effect: the barely noticeable tax on tea.

In 1768, King George appoints Sir Will Hills, first duke of Hillsborough, to serve as the first agent for colonial affairs. It is Hillsborough's job to manage and secure colonial cooperation with the king's government, but King George has chosen a man whose primary qualification for the position is his friendship with the king. Hillsborough responds to controversy and protest from the colonies with a heavy hand, prescribing military force as the most effective remedy for any unrest. It is his order that sends a large garrison of troops to Boston to support the beleaguered civil authority.

In Massachusetts, the civil unrest has so rattled the generally incompetent royal governor, Francis Bernard, that he sails to England, confronting the problem by simply abandoning the colony. In his place, Liuetenant Governor Hutchinson assumes control and agrees with Lord Hillsborough's deployment of British troops. The presence of the troops is incendiary at best, and the Sons of Liberty make the most of the public's fears of and antipathy toward such a visible military presence.

With King George's insistence on treating the colonies in any way that suits him, combined with the inability of either Hillsborough or Lord North, the King's prime minister, to comprehend the climate of their citizens three thousand miles away, the English government continues to impose restrictive and inflammatory laws on the American colonies. Despite the dire warnings of his political opposition in Parliament, King George begins to enjoy the heat of politics, begins to find sport in the conflicts, begins to believe the use of his army may be the most attractive solution to dealing with the annoying groundswell of protest and the gathering of angry voices from some of the most prominent men of his time.

BENJAMIN FRANKLIN

BORN IN 1706 IN BOSTON, FRANKLIN GROWS UP IN THE HOME OF A working-class family, and in his mid-teens, he apprentices in his older brother's printing shop. He develops a wanderlust and runs away from home; eventually he finds himself in Philadelphia, essentially broke and homeless, and talks himself into a job at a print shop. By age twenty-four he is half owner of the business, which includes a weekly newspaper, the *Philadelphia Gazette*. Though competition is stiff in the dynamic, growing city, Franklin takes his business straight to the hearts of the common people. When the streets are the busiest, and thus the audience the largest, he makes a show of delivering his papers himself, struggling with an old, heavily laden wheelbarrow. His printing business soon becomes the most successful in the city, and Franklin ultimately buys out his partner.

In September 1730, he marries Deborah Read, who gives birth to a son and a daughter. The son dies at age four, a sorrow of which Franklin will rarely speak. Franklin has one other illegitimate son, William, born shortly after his marriage, the product of a liaison that Franklin himself acknowledges in uncomplimentary ways: "That hard-to-be-governed passion of youth hurried me frequently into intrigues with low women that fell in my way." Though Deborah accepts William as a part of the family, their relationship is never as close as mother and son.

In 1732, Franklin begins his long odyssey as a writer, revealing a flair for humor, sarcasm, and biting satire. *Poor Richard's Almanac* is the most popular magazine of its time and appears regularly for twenty-seven years. It also makes Franklin a wealthy man.

He soon founds a debating society he calls the Junto, which eventually becomes the American Philosophical Society. He becomes one of Philadelphia's most well-known citizens by his acts of public improvement, including founding a library and the first fire department in Pennsylvania. In 1751, he recognizes the urgent need for education, and thus founds an academy that will eventually become the University of Pennsylvania.

Franklin displays an amazing talent for invention and an interest in scientific experiments, and in 1752, he embarks on his famous kite experiment, proving the direct relationship between lightning and electricity.

He enters government service for the first time in 1751, as a member of the Pennsylvania Assembly. He is appointed by King George II as postmaster general for the colonies, a position he holds for twenty-two years.

He visits England in 1757 and quickly develops a love affair for that nation that will keep him there for more years than he spends at home. His wife is desperately afraid of traveling on water, and so the Franklins will spend much of their later life apart. Traveling extensively throughout Europe, he impresses the elite of both government and academe with his intellect and charm, and by middle age, he is the darling of England and the Continent, with a considerable reputation for diplomacy and scientific knowledge.

His frequent presence in England makes convenient his appointment as colonial agent for the colony of Pennsylvania in 1764. Other colonies recognize the value of the man's celebrity, and within a few years, he receives the same appointments from Georgia, New Jersey, and finally Massachusetts.

On one trip to London he is accompanied by his son William. He succeeds in bringing his son to the attention of powerful friends, and in 1763, William is appointed royal governor of New Jersey. With the passage of Grenville's Stamp Act, Franklin's distance from the colonies blinds him to the inevitability of protests, and he even secures a position for a friend in Philadelphia as royal tax collector. When he learns of the violent outpouring of protest, Franklin begins to understand how much has changed in his absence, and, following the advice of friends in America, he works tirelessly for the repeal of the Stamp Act, for which he rarely receives credit.

As a friend to so many in high places, he begins to hear more and more of the blatant prejudice toward colonial citizens and the high-handed dismissal of colonial claims and concerns. He regularly observes that the British hierarchy is terribly removed from the reality of their policies' consequences. He contemplates returning to Philadelphia but cannot bring himself to leave London. He understands that his serious work on behalf of the colonies he represents may be just beginning.

John Adams

John Adams is born in 1735 in Braintree, Massachusetts, to undistinguished parents; his family, Adams says, "cut down more trees than anyone in the colony." His father's life as a farmer holds great appeal for the boy, who from his earliest days has a great love of the land. But his father is ambitious and sends the boy to school. Against his father's wishes, Adams' mother pushes him toward the ministry, and Adams considers that direction, but he changes his mind when he observes local church services and the fierceness of disagreement so inherent in the religion of the time. He finds immediate frustration in a career where the answers cannot be analyzed on paper, and he cannot take to a field where he finds himself "involved in difficulties beyond my power of decision." He continues to distance himself from the dominance of religion in the local culture, and in 1756 he writes, "Where do we find precepts in the Gospel, requiring . . . Convocations, Councils, Decrees, Creeds, Confession, Oaths, Subscriptions and whole Cartloads of other trumpery, that we find religion encumbered with in these days?"

Adams discovers a talent for science and math, but when he graduates from Harvard in 1755, he accepts the practicality of a more financially beneficial career in law. There are no law schools in the colonies at this time; he apprentices for three years and is finally admitted to the bar in 1758. He begins the arduous task of building a law practice in a field dominated by older, much more established lawyers, and actually comes to resent the time he wasted in all his former pursuits. He carves his path with a natural affinity for reading, study, and hard work, and accumulates the finest law library in the colony.

No matter his self-imposed workload, he never strays long from his beloved farmlands. He spends much time just wandering the open woods around his family's home; at one point he records in his diary, "Rambled about all day, gaping and gazing." As he puts it, "Exercise invigorates, and enlivens all the faculties of body and of mind. . . . It spreads a gladness and satisfaction over our minds and qualifies us for every sort of business, and every sort of pleasure."

In 1764, after a long and thoroughly charming courtship, he marries Abigail Smith, the daughter of a minister. Though without a formal education, which was often ruled to be illegal for women at this time, she has a hunger for knowledge and is a voracious reader, particularly of the classics and history. As events around Boston become more tumultuous, she is an unusually keen observer of the forces at work, and unlike so many of her female contemporaries, she is not afraid to state her opinion.

Because of Adams' law practice, he is in close touch with the politics of the day, and he begins to write for the local newspaper with a clarity of analysis that brings him to the attention of prominent members of the Massachusetts Assembly. In 1765, he joins the outcry against the Stamp Act and authors a resolution of protest to the assembly. Though he is second cousin to the older and much more well known Sam Adams, John never becomes active in the Sons of Liberty. He is consumed instead by the requirements of his law practice. In 1768, he buys a small house in Boston, a necessity for an aspiring young lawyer. He finds himself called to service in higher-profile cases, and he successfully defends the colony's wealthiest citizen, John Hancock, against charges of smuggling, a charge that everyone in Massachusetts knows to be true.

Torn between his love of the law and his love of the farm, Adams tries to maintain both lifestyles, often at a cost to his health. When the British send troops into Boston in 1768, his eyes are too focused on his law books for him to fully grasp the potential for disaster.

GEORGE WASHINGTON

BORN IN 1732 IN WESTMORELAND COUNTY, VIRGINIA, Washington lives as a young boy with his half brother Lawrence at Lawrence's estate, Mount Vernon, and later at his mother's home near Fredericksburg.

He receives little education, with no formal studies after the age of fifteen. Though he has a talent for mathematics, it is not attractive to him as a career until age sixteen, when his brother offers him an opportunity to serve as a land surveyor. This provides him a reasonable salary, which the young man desperately needs.

He grows into a huge figure of a man, described by a friend as "six foot two in his stockings, weighing one hundred seventy-five pounds . . . with well-developed muscles . . . wide shouldered . . . neat waisted . . . blue-gray and rather penetrating eyes."

In 1748, he accompanies Lawrence to the island of Barbados, where his brother seeks a cure for his consumption. Washington catches smallpox, recovers, and then spends most of the journey locked in the agony of seasickness. He vows never again to cross an ocean.

When Lawrence dies, in 1752, Washington inherits Mount Vernon and settles down to a new life as a gentleman farmer. As is customary throughout the southern farm country, Mount Vernon is worked primarily by slaves. As word reaches Virginia of a rise in hostilities between the British and French, both nations holding claim to the frontier of western Virginia, Washington joins the Virginia militia, receiving a commission as lieutenant colonel. In 1754, Governor Robert Dinwiddie instructs him to lead two companies of troops through hostile Indian territory to the French trading outposts, to communicate the king's warning to the French to vacate the area. The French dismiss the warnings, and on his own accord, Washington attacks and engages a French armed force, which he defeats at the Battle of Great Meadows. Thus in May 1754, he fires the first shots of what will become the French and Indian War. But his strategy is unwise, and his forces are easily cut off from their base. Two months later Washington's men are surrounded by a revenge-minded French army, and he is forced to surrender.

He is allowed to leave the wilderness, and returns to civilization to his first taste of the prejudice toward colonial soldiers from the regular British forces. His own reputation is thought by some to be tarnished beyond repair.

A year later, Washington is ordered to accompany British general Edward Braddock on a march to attack and drive the French away from their strong outpost at the head of the Ohio River. Displaying the arrogance that will hound the British military mind for generations, Braddock dismisses Washington's advice to prepare for the unusual tactics of the French and their Indian allies, and marches his men, in tight formation, straight into a trap. Braddock himself is killed, as are three-fourths of his officers, and it is Washington's coolheadedness in engineering a retreat that allows the few survivors to withdraw.

Upon his return to eastern Virginia, Washington is rewarded with a promotion to full colonel but still receives no respect from the British command and is denied a commission in the British regular army. For the rest of the war, he commands a few hundred militia along a loose boundary of the Indian frontier, a frustrating experience that teaches him a great deal about the uselessness of most local militias.

In 1758, he accompanies British general John Forbes in an advance against Fort Duquesne, what will later become Pittsburgh, and observes more British arrogance in their clumsy plan of assault. But before the poor British tactics have a chance to fail, the French withdraw; thus Forbes claims victory, and Washington's military accomplishments come to be regarded in Virginia with considerable respect.

In 1759, he greatly misses life at Mount Vernon and has tired of the high-handed arrogance of the British command, so he resigns his commission and returns home. He envelops himself in the joys of working the land and develops new farming techniques by experimenting with different soil treatments, including techniques he has observed being used by the Indians.

That year, he marries Martha Dandridge Custis, a widow who

has inherited an immense estate from her husband's death. The combination makes the Washingtons one of Virginia's wealthiest couples. Martha has two children from her former marriage, only one of whom survives to adulthood. The couple never produce their own child.

His new financial status is nearly an automatic ticket to a seat in the Virginia House of Burgesses, but he does not seem to have a flair for politics and has already been bruised by the arrogant dismissal and hasty judgment at the hands of the British. He settles into quiet political obscurity, rarely involving himself in the acrimonious debates that begin to roll through Virginia. Unlike his contemporaries Patrick Henry and Richard Henry Lee, Washington has no gift for oratory.

As controversy heats up in Boston and loud voices in Virginia begin to criticize royal policy, the governor dissolves the House of Burgesses, which begins to meet on its own accord. Washington awakens to the new crisis spreading throughout the colonies, and the debates take on new importance. As the talk grows hotter, the great minds who speak out with such eloquence turn their attention more and more to this huge, quiet, and unassuming man who, more than any of the rest of them, has already demonstrated he knows something of how to be a soldier.

LIEUTENANT GENERAL THOMAS GAGE

BORN IN 1720 IN FIRLE, ENGLAND, GAGE IS THE SECOND SON OF A moderately successful member of Parliament. His father's position allows the boy to attend the prestigious Westminster Public School, which opens connections into the royal military service. He receives his first commission as ensign in 1740, is promoted to captain three years later, and serves in a variety of posts in various conflicts in Scotland and the Netherlands.

In 1754, he is made a major and sent to America, where he serves under Edward Braddock. He is one of the few officers who survive Braddock's disaster, and by most accounts he is one of the bright lights for the British that day. Gage will recall well the heroic action of a Virginia colonel named George Washington. Though he and Washington establish something of a friendship, their lack of contact prevents it from deepening.

Ordered northward, Gage spends time in Albany, New York, as well as New York City, and does a brief stint in Halifax, Nova Scotia. In 1757, he is given his own regiment and promoted to full colonel. The following year he takes part in campaigns against the French up the Hudson River. He displays a talent rare in the British officer corps: compassion for the men in his command. He is enormously popular among his troops. To fight the constant plague of scurvy that affects men stationed in a land far from the benefits of fresh vegetables, he replaces their ration of beer with apple cider.

When his responsibilities allow, he makes frequent visits to New York City. His close friend General Jeffery Amherst, commander in chief for the army in America, is there, and Gage participates in the New York social scene, where he meets Margaret Kemble, the daughter of a prominent New Jersey political figure. They are married in late 1758, and she will bear him eight children. Margaret is an aspiring socialite, envies the cream of New York elite, and must endure their snobbery toward her New Jersey upbringing.

Gage returns to duty, accompanied by his new wife, and commands his regiment in the actions along the St. Lawrence River and the Niagara Valley. When the French surrender Canada in 1760, Gage becomes military governor and spends three years in what he describes as the misery of Montreal. He possesses the peculiarly English prejudice toward Catholics, who now comprise most of his constituency. Despite this, when he leaves the post, he is regarded in Montreal as having been extremely successful in governing a difficult situation.

He is promoted to major general in 1761, and when Amherst returns to England, Gage is named commander in chief of the British forces in America and promoted to lieutenant general. In 1763, he establishes his headquarters in New York City, where he will maintain his residence for most of the next thirteen years.

During the decade that follows, his role is that of a firm protector of British interests in a colonial land, and he is an efficient administrator. As the protests over the Stamp Act escalate, he begins to see the Sons of Liberty as an annoyance, but he gives little consideration to the growing tide of sentiment against the king's policies.

He is appalled when Parliament repeals the Townshend Acts, believing that if he had been given sufficient troop strength, he could have put down any protest by force and thus saved face for the king. But while Gage is an efficient officer, he will never initiate policy. He follows orders, which come via the agonizingly slow route from London. The messages go both ways, and to the sympathetic ear of Lord Hillsborough, Gage begins to champion the use of brute force and the hangman's noose as the means of restoring order and putting the Sons of Liberty in their proper place. But the politics of London is a morass of conflicting reports, inefficient and corrupt ministers, and an ongoing lack of awareness that Gage is actually facing the possibility of a significant uprising. Though Gage never really believes the Sons of Liberty pose a threat to his authority or to the general peace in the colonies, he begins to send requests to London calling for more troops to be added to the enormous scope of his command.

Despite all the turmoil of the political protests, the last half of the 1760s are the happiest years of Gage's life. He and his government in London are blissfully unaware that the angry forces in the colonies they so blithely dismiss are pushing them toward a series of shattering events, with an impact no one on either side can predict.

PART ONE
THE RIGHT AND
THE POWER

1. THE SENTRY

HE HAD BEEN IN BOSTON FOR NEARLY EIGHTEEN MONTHS, HAD come ashore with the rest of His Majesty's Twenty-ninth Regiment after a miserable journey down from Halifax. The troops had been summoned to the boats by their commander, General Thomas Gage, had been told only that they were going to the Massachusetts colony to maintain the peace. Few had any idea how that peace might be threatened, and nearly all saw the journey as an escape from the lonely isolation of the king's most northern port. When they finally marched out of the cramped warships, they moved into a town where the people did not welcome them, did not provide homes or hospitality. Now, after nearly two years, the conflicts between the citizens of Boston and the soldiers had become more than the unpleasant argument, the occasional barroom brawl. The discipline of the troops had begun to slip; men became frustrated by the hostility around them, the taunts and minor assaults, and when the officers were not close, many of the soldiers had begun to strike back. The citizens had responded to the anger of the troops with anger of their own, and gangs of young men armed with clubs and the occasional saber began to patrol the dark alleys outside the pubs and meeting places of the soldiers. The fights were more numerous now and were sometimes bloody. While the local magistrates were quick to arrest and prosecute, both sides protected their own, and no one had any illusion that the law could protect the innocent. Inspired by the newspapermen, who presented each incident in passionate detail, playing up the seething hostility, the citizens were more and more restless, fueling the growing anger toward the British troops. To many civilians, this military

3

occupation was oppressive, and even those most loyal to the policies of London recognized that the presence of the troops was dangerous; with the right spark, the minor disturbances could explode into a bloody disaster.

His name was Hugh White, and he had served in the Twenty-ninth Regiment for nearly three years. He had little ambition, had no particular designs on promotion, considered the corporal above him to be a far better soldier. He rarely spoke to the officers, was not a face or a name that anyone would ever single out. But today, he *had* been singled out, given a job that most in his company would dread. The duty was not for punishment of some indiscreet act. It was simply his turn. And so he stood guard in front of the Custom House, shivering against the sharp cold in a small wooden guardhouse, standing sentry to a place that would rarely attract attention.

He moved around as much as the cramped space would allow, touched the walls on three sides of him, felt the rough cold wood. His fingers were numb, and he flexed them, then pushed one hand hard inside his coat. He glanced out beyond the guard-house and saw only a few citizens moving quickly through the cold, ignoring him. He cast a glance down toward his hidden hand bulging in his coat, flexed his fingers again, worried about being seen. He thought of the drill the week before, the sergeant scolding the men to keep their decorum, maintain their dignity, especially on guard duty. That meant hands by your side. He eased his head outside the guardhouse, looked toward the door-way of the Custom House, saw no one, felt relief. Perhaps even that old sergeant would understand, he thought. It's just too cold. He put his other hand inside the rough wool, pulled his arms up tight. He blew out a sharp breath, thinking that if he stood up stiff the way they told him to, his fingers would probably fall off.

The musket leaned up against the wall close beside him, a light glaze of frost on the black steel. The guardhouse was really only a narrow box, not much larger than an upright coffin. But it kept away the awful bite of the wind, the sharp cold that blew deep into your bones.

Early that morning, the assignment of guard duty had made

him smile, and if the others laughed and teased him, he had only thought of relieving the boredom of the barracks. Now he imagined what the others were doing, playing cards, the profane talk. His father had warned him of the bad influences, and he could still see his mother's tear-stained face, watching as her boy marched away to join this army. She didn't want me to go, he thought. They expected me to work that land, still expect me to just come home and be a farmer, like them. They don't know anything else. He remembered the look on their faces when he had come home, the brief visit before the Twenty-ninth had boarded the great ship to sail West. He had stood tall, waited as his father moved around him, inspecting the uniform, even touching the dull red coat, could still see his mother's shock, her young boy now grown into this soldier. Their response had disappointed him. They had not seemed as proud as he had expected, seemed more worried instead, gave him more sharp scolding to keep himself clean, to avoid the awful deadly temptations that only a parent fears. I wish they could see me now, he thought. This is important, guarding the Custom House.

He hadn't even been inside the building, but he knew the rumors. There was supposed to be a huge vault filled with silver, the customs duties paid by the ships as they brought their goods into the port from England or from the islands far to the south. He hoped it was true, had no reason to doubt the importance of his duty, was proud of his responsibility, guarding the king's currency. If those chaps back in the barracks knew how much this post means to the king, they wouldn't laugh, they'd be out here, doing the duty. He glanced at the musket, then out again to the wide street, the hard-packed ice and snow, heard the stiff breeze whistling through the cracks in the crude wooden walls of the guardhouse. He wanted to drift away, tried to imagine the scene: Private White, holding away the bandits with his bayonet, ordering the riffraff to move away, and his mind spoke out, the voice loud and firm, *In the name of the king . . .*

He shivered now, and the image would not stay. He wriggled his fingers again, glanced toward the street once more. The locals didn't much care for them, he knew. He wasn't educated in politics; few of the private soldiers were. They had been surprised at the hostility from many of the citizens, and when they had marched away from the ships, they had been told that they would have to camp on Boston Common, since there were no open doors for them in private homes. But camping outdoors in tents could be deadly through the New England winter, and the commanders had struggled frantically to find accommodations. Finally, those in the town whom the officers called Tories and who did not seem so resentful of the troops began to open their doors, leasing buildings and warehouses, some even renting out their own homes. Now two winters had passed, and the duty was mostly monotonous, painfully boring. He had spent much of his time simply standing at drill in the common, marching in formation, parading in line down the side streets. He stamped his cold feet and wondered why so many of these people hated the British so. *All we do is march around.*

Many of the soldiers had begun to seek part-time work in the town, some spending their off-duty hours working jobs that would ease the boredom and provide a little more cash than their low army pay. But there was resentment for that as well, the citizens protesting that the troops were taking valuable jobs badly needed by the men of Boston. It was not long before the resentment turned violent. He had seen some of the fights, most inspired by strong drink, a sudden and accidental confrontation in an alley or outside a pub. But the violence had continued to grow, the fights larger, and men on both sides had seemed to organize just a bit, small gangs of citizens and troops, both looking for some satisfaction, some way to relieve the constant hostility. He had seen the man with the bloody wound, three nights ago, the first real wound he had ever seen. He thought of the man—John Rodgers, another young private—his skull split open. The anger in the barracks had brought the officers in, stern words, threats of punishment. But even the soldiers who had not been a part of the fights knew that there would be more violence.

He had endured the insults himself, knew better than to walk the streets alone, even off duty, out of uniform. He still didn't understand the anger. *We're just keeping the peace.* He said the words again in his mind, the first orders he had heard, even before they left the ship. Keep the peace.

He moved his legs, stepped in place, tried to relieve the numbness in his feet. He leaned out past the protection of the guardhouse, felt a stiff breeze on his face, pulled back inside. It's pretty peaceful tonight. Too cold for the officers, that's certain. They're all inside, probably eating their hot food. He could see the main guard building, and down the street the headquarters for His Majesty's forces. He felt a rumble in his stomach, began to think of the supper that waited for him back in the barracks. He could use a cup of tea right now. He tried to imagine the steam rolling up on his face, but the wind suddenly blew hard against the guardhouse, and now he could hear something else, voices, shouts. He leaned outside again, saw a group of men moving in the street, turning toward the Custom House. He watched them, counted maybe a dozen, then saw more men coming around a corner a block down the street. He had been warned about the gangs, all the troops understanding that they were targets for the bands of rough young men. He shivered again, made two tight fists inside his coat, watched the men moving across the street, coming closer to the Custom House. Now the voices were clear, and he saw one man point at him, felt his heart jump in his chest. They began to move straight toward the guardhouse, straight toward *him*. He pulled his hands from his coat, reached down, gripped the musket, leaned it up on his shoulder. Make a good show, he thought. No one will get past. They will not dare. He watched them move closer, realized they were young, teens perhaps, saw one bend down, scooping up the snow, rolling an icy ball in his hands. There were more shouts, and suddenly the boy threw the snowball at the guardhouse. White flinched, heard the dull smack against the wall, felt his heart pounding, said aloud, "Move along now. This is no place for play."

The faces were all looking at him, and he expected to see smiles, the playfulness of boys, but there was something new, unexpected, anger, and now more snowballs began to fly. The boys moved closer, their aim more true, and he felt a splatter of snow against his chest. The laughter came, but they did not move away, the fun was not over.

White stepped outside the cover of the guardhouse, felt his own anger rising, looked at the faces, the voices jeering, calling out to him. One boy suddenly lunged closer, and White watched his hands, expecting something, another snowball, but the boy said, "What kind of man are you? A filthy lobster-back!"

White tried to ignore the boy, glanced again at the door of the Custom House, saw the door open slightly, faces peering out, the door closing again. White began to move toward the steps at the doorway, but the boy jumped in front of him, close, reached out and grabbed at the uniform, began to shout, "Dirty lobster-back," and White swung the musket around, the butt striking the boy's face. The boy fell backward, a sharp cry, and now there was silence from the mob as White stared at the boy. My God, stop this. He moved up the steps of the Custom House, close to the doorway, saw the young faces watching him, could see out past the mob now, more men coming forward, older men, some in suits, staying back, watching. He felt his hands shaking, tried to grip the musket, shouted, "Leave this place! Move away!"

The injured boy was crying, shrieking, "You dirty scoundrel! I'll see you dead!"

The voices began to answer, more curses, the boys moving closer again. The snowballs resumed, hitting the door of the Custom House, and suddenly something dark flew past his head, a thick piece of wood, making a sharp cracking sound against the wooden door behind him. He shouted again, "Back! Stay back!"

He could feel his hands shaking, the icy numbness giving way to a rising wave of fear. The jeers from the mob were growing louder, and the officer's words suddenly came to him again: *Keep the peace.* He clamped the musket under one arm, his hands still shaking, reached inside the cartridge box at his waist. He felt the stiff paper with his numb fingers, fought through the pounding in his chest, the training taking hold, the fear giving way to the deliberate motion. He tore at the tip of the paper cartridge, poured powder into the pan at the breech, clamped down the lock. He set the butt of the musket down on the step, slowly slid the cartridge into the barrel of the musket, prodded it down the long barrel with the ramrod. Now he pulled out the bayonet, slid it hard on the barrel, a sharp twist, and lowered the barrel, pointed it out toward the crowd. His heart was racing, and he felt a surge of strength, the fear growing into raw excitement. He expected to see the fear in their faces, the respect for the soldier with the loaded musket, the great strength of the army, but the voices were louder still, and now another stick struck the door behind him. He could see more sticks, the crowd moving slowly forward, one voice shouting, "Shoot us! Go ahead, shoot us! You coward! Shoot us and be damned!"

He gripped the musket hard, still felt his hands trembling violently, the cold now deep in his chest. He wanted to say something, anything, to move them away. At that moment, he saw a man moving up to one side, well dressed, a familiar face, and the man said, "Soldier, easy now. Do you mean to shoot?"

"I will fire . . . if they assault me!"

The man came up the steps, said, "Easy, young man. Take care. There need be no killing here."

White glanced at the man's calm face. White nodded, felt a wave of relief, felt suddenly protected, heard a second voice, that of an older man, say, "Move away! Don't molest this sentry! There is no fight here!"

The mob began to quiet, some of the boys backing away, the curses now slowing. He took a deep breath, thought, Yes, move away. Let this end. Thank God.

Then there was a new sound, from a church tower, the sudden tolling of a bell echoing through the streets. Another bell began, farther away. The faces began to turn away, looking toward the sound, the fire bell. The voices began again, but the sounds were different. Far down the street, more men began to emerge, and he could hear shouting, one word flowing from place to place: *"Fire!"*

The sounds grew close, men suddenly moving out from a side street behind the Custom House, the word echoing all through the crowd, *"Fire!"*

Now the crowd pushed toward the Custom House, some moving toward him, some lining up on the street. In front of him, the crowd came to life again, the faces turning toward him, and the curses rose once more: "Dirty scoundrel! Lobster-back!"

He felt the fear coming back, the icy grip in his chest. He could hear sounds above him, men at the windows; he wanted to shout at them, but there were no words. His face still watched the crowd, and now the sticks were raised again, the snow and ice striking the walls around him, a sharp stab suddenly in his chest, the heavy stick punching him. He looked out over the heads of the men closest to him, could see the main guard building, fought the fear, suddenly shouted, *"Turn out the guard! Turn out the guard!"*

The people nearest to him began to move up the short steps, one man reaching out, grabbing at the musket. White jerked the gun to one side, swept the tip of the bayonet back and forth, forcing the men back. One boy shouted close to him, "Shoot us, then!"

White pressed his back hard against the door, still waving the bayonet toward the crowd, and said, "Damn you! I will shoot!"

At that instant, there were new sounds, and he turned, saw a line of red emerging through the crowd, saw the tips of bayonets. The man who led the soldiers held a sword high, the coat brighter red, the man's chest crossed with bright yellow, the uniform of an officer, a familiar face. White said, "Sir! Captain Preston! Sir . . ."

He wanted to say more, to thank the officer, felt the sudden flood of relief. The crowd seemed to pull away, the mass of men and boys watching as the soldiers repeated what White had done, loading their muskets. Preston moved up onto the steps, said, "It's all right, Private. Fall in. Take position with the troops."

White stepped quickly toward the line of soldiers, saw eight men, all huge, the handpicked elite, the grenadiers, all grim-faced. White moved among them, and the soldiers turned in quick rhythm, muskets held waist high, pointing toward the crowd. White stood between two of the men, felt their strength, their power. The fear was gone, the excitement filling him, and he thought, Now we will see. Now this mob will know.

He felt the snowball hit his stomach, and at once the sticks were flying again, the shouts coming as before. Behind the mob, more men were pressing forward, some still shouting, *"Fire!"*

Beyond, the bells still called to the town, the pealing growing louder, the sounds echoing, blending with the shouts of the mob. Captain Preston stepped out in front of the soldiers, glanced at White, then out at the crowd, said aloud, "We will march away from here! You will let us pass!"

There was a chorus of new voices, one man in front shouting, "Or you will shoot us? Go ahead, then! And damn you to hell!"

Preston looked back at the soldiers, waved his hand toward the wall of the Custom House, said, "Form here. Flanks anchored against the wall!"

The men moved back, White following the flow. Those on each end of the line positioned themselves close to the front wall of the Custom House, the others facing out in a short semicircle. Now Preston paced slowly in front of the troops, said to the crowd, "You will disperse! In the name of King George, I order you to return to your homes!"

White stood behind Preston, heard muttered curses from the soldiers on either side of him, their own anger building. Preston turned, said in a low voice, "None of that! We will move these people away! Do your duty!"

The crowd began to surge forward again, hands began to reach for the muskets. Preston shouted again, "Disperse!"

There were answers now, many voices, snowballs, more sticks. White saw something flash in the crowd, the bright brass of a saber. Suddenly a man lunged forward at the troops, grabbed one musket by the barrel, tried to pull it away from the soldier, who wrestled with his attacker. Another man stepped close, struck out at a bayonet with a long stick, knocking the musket from the soldier's hands. More men surged forward, tried to grab the musket, the soldier now on the ground, fists striking back. White fought the urge to help the soldier, held his musket straight toward the crowd, watched the faces, heard the voices louder still, the words flowing over the troops, the calls to fire, the screams of the mob, men powered by anger, hostility boiling into raw hatred, the sounds of the bells bursting in his ears, and now White looked to the side, saw the fallen soldier on his knees, pushing a man back, picking up the musket, screaming something White did not understand, a raw animal sound, and there was a blinding flash as the musket fired. White felt his heart leap, saw a man in the crowd go down, heard something from Preston, words, one word, "No . . ."

Quickly there came more shots, the soldiers losing all control, the fear and the anger giving way. White felt the growing horror, but then the crowd was there, close in front, the screams and curses, the violence flowing over all of them. He saw someone holding a thick piece of wood, waving it over his head, the man still moving forward, and White raised the musket to his shoulder, fought through the roar of sound in his ears, the church bells, the muskets now blasting smoke and fire on either side of him, the sounds of terror from the crowd. He gripped the musket hard, held it tight to his shoulders, the fear in his heart giving way to the madness now washing over them all. The man stalked toward him, brandishing the stick as some deadly club, shouting words, angry awful sounds. White watched him move close, and then the man stopped, stared at the muzzle of the musket, seemed suddenly calm, looked at White's face, deep into his eyes, and the sounds gave way to the man's words, soft through the chiming of the church bells. White could not hold back, the terror and the anger too strong, and as he pulled the trigger, he heard the man say, "You cannot kill us all. . . ."

2. ADAMS

HE HAD HEARD THE FIRST BELL, REACTED AS THEY ALL REACTED, responding to the awful threat of fire by moving outside, finding the flow of the people in the street, moving to help in any way he could. Fire was the greatest fear in a town with so many wooden buildings, and by now it was reflex as well as custom that brought the people into the street.

He was still pulling on his coat when he saw men running toward the center of town, and he shouted, "Where is the fire?"

One man slowed, seemed to recognize him. "There is no fire, Mr. Adams. The British have started a riot! The Custom House."

The man ran off, and Adams stopped, saw the people moving past him, many carrying sticks, clubs, one man with a pistol. He thought, The British? Soldiers don't riot. He began to move, following the crowd, could hear louder sounds now, screams, the bells still ringing above him. He turned a corner and was surprised to see people flooding toward him. He saw fear and terror in the faces. He pushed past them, but one man shoved him, nearly knocking him down, and so he stood aside, out of the street, waiting for the surge to pass by. A minute later, he made his way forward again, toward King Street, rounded another corner. The street was wider, and he could see the Old State House and, to one side, the Custom House. Now he stopped, saw the crowd thinning out, saw a mass of red, a thick line of troops spreading out around the Custom House, two small cannon moving into place. People still moved in both directions, some in a panic, some coming forward, as he was, to see what had happened. Another man ran past him, shouting, "They will kill us! They're going to kill us!"

13

Adams felt a sudden wave of confusion, looked toward the troops again, saw an officer guiding them, more officers now, one man on a horse. He saw muskets, bayonets pointing at the thinning crowd, the people moving away in a wave, saw the muskets pointing at him, felt the stab of panic. What has happened?

He felt his breathing in hard gasps, moved closer to the troops. There can be no danger here. They cannot just shoot us. They have commanders, they know the law.

The area close to the soldiers had been cleared, and for a brief moment there was little sound, the soldiers standing quietly, the shouts of the people muted, most of the crowd gone. He eased along the side of the street, looked at the officers, wanted to ask someone. This is no riot, it cannot be so bad. Now he heard a short scream, looked down a side street, saw a man being dragged by the shoulders, the man's face covered in blood, his shirt bloody, too, a smear of red trailing him in the snow. The man was pulled into a doorway, and now there was a woman kneeling, wiping with a cloth. Adams stared at the scene for a long moment. What did he do that they would shoot him? He turned toward the troops again, silent stares, no motion, and he noticed the dark red stains in the snow in front of them. He moved slowly toward the open area, ignoring the troops. He heard a voice, a soldier moving toward him, looked up to see a familiar face, the man's name not coming.

"Mr. Adams, this is no place for you. Go home now."

Adams stared at the dark smears on the snow, felt suddenly sick. "What happened here?"

"It is not your concern, sir. The situation is under control. I must insist you return to your home."

Adams looked at the man, wanted to ask again, felt a cold numbness. "There is blood in the street."

"It is not your concern, sir. I will ask you again—"

"Not my concern? You have shot citizens. This will concern us all."

HE SAGGED THROUGH THE DOORWAY, REMOVED HIS HAT, HELD IT for a long moment, staring down at nothing. He heard sounds, the quick footsteps, a small voice. His daughter burst into the front room, ran to him, grabbed him around the leg. "Papa, Papa, Papa . . ."

He looked at her, reached one hand down, touched the short curls, hair like fine silk, moved his fingers slowly, gently, could not push her away.

"There now, Nabby. Come. Leave your father be."

Abigail had come into the room, looked at him with dark concern, said again, "Here, Nabby. *Now.*"

The little girl released her grip, moved to her mother with a pout, and Adams watched her sink into Abigail's skirt, one thumb lodged firmly in her mouth. Abigail murmured, "Something terrible has happened. I can see it in your face."

Adams nodded slowly, blinked hard. "The soldiers have fired on the citizens. At least four are dead, maybe more. I heard it was a riot. But . . . I don't know."

Abigail moved to a small soft chair, sat slowly, clumsily, the roundness of her stomach obvious. Adams moved forward instinctively to provide a helping hand, though she said, "No, it's all right. I just need to sit."

"I'm sorry. I should not have gone out. I knew you would worry." He paused, glanced at his daughter, holding fast to her mother's leg, and he lowered his voice. "I saw the blood. It was . . . everywhere."

He moved close to her, closed his eyes. "I should not have gone."

She held out her hand, took his. "You had to go. It could have been a fire. And you know you would help. You would have to know what happened."

"I still don't know. We will hear the rumors tomorrow. Both sides will lay blame. There will be mobs, maybe more violence."

He knelt down, rubbed one hand gently on his daughter's back, said, "Perhaps you should return to Braintree. It is safer. We could be in some danger here. If things get out of hand—"

"No, John. There is no danger if we are together. I will not cower away like some weak and helpless damsel while you face the dragon alone. Where's my sword?"

He knew she was trying to cheer him up. He looked at her again, could not help but stare at the roundness under her dress.

"A pregnant woman fighting off the great evils of the world. It's an inspiring image. Do you need armor?"

She laughed, squeezed his hand. "You are my armor."

She rubbed her stomach again, suddenly seeming uncomfortable, and he backed away. "Are you sure you're all right?"

"Don't worry, John. There are no problems. He . . . kicked today. Hard."

Adams was curious. "*He?* Why do you say that?"

"I said he kicked *hard*. More than once. He's tired of being inside. Like his father. Only your son would be so expressive, so . . . stubborn. He is already strong."

The word hit him, rolled in his mind, *strong,* and he saw the sadness in her eyes betraying her smile. He thought of Susanna now, the frail baby gone barely a month. She had been their third child, had lived only two months past her first birthday. The shock had been extraordinary, the first great tragedy of their marriage. The death of children was a horror common in the town, but they had seemed to be immune, their first two children growing into healthy toddlers. But Susanna had never been healthy, and Adams had felt himself pulling away from the baby, as though he knew in some dark place that she would not survive. He could never have admitted that to Abigail, and he kept his sadness hidden away as she nurtured the weak baby, doing everything in a mother's heart to strengthen the infant's fragility. When the baby died, Abigail had been devastated, and Adams had begun to worry for her health as well. He had felt helpless, even afraid for her as she cried over the small grave, her hands self-consciously moving over the growing bulge in her stomach. He saw her own fear for the health of their new baby, still unborn.

He moved to the front window, looked out through the darkness at the open square, the courthouse across the street. He was used to seeing troops in formation there, right in front of his house, the constant drilling, the presence that even the most reasonable citizens had begun to dread, the annoying show of strength. Well, they have truly shown their strength now, he thought. It will be hard for the Tories to excuse this, to claim some conspiracy against the king. It could simply have been one mob facing another, and the men in the red uniforms were better armed. There are so many questions. I will know more tomorrow. I have to know. There is still law here. And no matter who is to blame, whether this disaster was born from evil intent or blind foolishness, if the mobs gain control, then God help us.

MARCH 6, 1770

HIS OFFICE WAS SMALL, NOT FAR FROM THE PLACE WHERE THE blood still stained the snow. He had gone to work as usual, surprised by the quiet in the streets. He had expected at least some reaction, some gathering of loud voices. But the people he had seen were calm, subdued, the mood more of shock than anger.

He had hoped for callers, official visitors, people with some real news. Now he sat at the small desk, staring at the front door, waiting for activity, anything, some motion from the street. He lifted his hand toward the small stack of papers on the desk, the cases he was working on. Get some work done. He tried to follow the words, some vague legal jargon written by a clerk who tried to impress, but the ink blurred into a black smear, and his mind drifted away. He glanced to one side, the sagging bookshelves filled with the dry tomes of law, all books he had read thoroughly. He let out a sigh, felt a wave of frustration. This will not do. I must know what is happening. He pushed the chair back from the desk. This is ridiculous, sitting here, waiting for what? Information? Go on, take a walk. You're bound to run into someone who has news.

Suddenly he heard voices, looked up, saw the door opening. He felt a quick rush of excitement, saw the young lean face of his friend Josiah Quincy. Quincy made a short quick bow toward him, said, "Excuse me, John. Are you busy at the moment?"

Adams reached out to the papers, pushed them away, a brief show. "No, certainly, it can wait."

Quincy nodded, moved into the office, and now Adams saw another man, older, thinning gray hair. Quincy said, "John, I believe you are somewhat acquainted with Mr. Forrest?"

Adams smiled at the older man, but there was nothing soft in his visitor's expression, his face hard, grim sadness.

"Yes, Mr. Forrest, how are you, sir?"

Forrest didn't answer, seemed to struggle for words, and Quincy hastened to say, "John, I believe you should hear Mr. Forrest's request. I will defer to your judgment about what we should do."

Adams was curious now; he had often shared cases with the younger lawyer, had always appreciated the sharpness of Quincy's mind, his instinct for the law. Adams motioned to the small chair, and Forrest sat down. Quincy moved over to the far wall, propped himself against the bookshelves. Adams waited, watched Forrest still searching for words. He glanced at Quincy, who was staring at the older man as well, patiently aware of Forrest's mission. Finally Forrest said, "I'm sorry for the intrusion, Mr. Adams. But I come on an important matter. Certainly you have heard about the events of last evening."

"Indeed, sir."

Forrest took a long breath, seemed to fight for control, anxiety tightening inside him.

"Sir, I am friends with Thomas . . . with Captain Thomas Preston, who was in the unfortunate position of commanding the king's troops. Captain Preston has been arrested, and we are being told he will be charged with murder. It is claimed that he gave the order . . . that he ordered his men to fire on the citizens. Sir, I know Captain Preston intimately. I can promise you he would not do such a thing. As God is my witness, Captain Preston is not guilty of murder."

Forrest was still anxious, moved about in the chair, and Quincy murmured, "Mr. Forrest, please continue."

"Yes, thank you. Mr. Adams, I have assisted Captain Preston in seeking counsel . . . legal representation. We can find no one who will listen, no one will agree to take the case. There is great fear of the mob."

Forrest stopped, visibly shaky, and Adams thought, I should offer him something, tea perhaps. But now the words burst out, driven by the older man's emotions.

"Mr. Adams, Captain Preston requires counsel. If he is not represented before the magistrates, there will be a great injustice done to a good, decent man."

Adams glanced at Quincy, asked, "Mr. Forrest, is Captain Preston claiming his innocence of these charges?"

"Sir, Thomas Preston has sworn to me that he did not order his men to fire. Sir, please. No one else will take his case. You . . . both of you have a reputation for honesty. You are highly regarded in the legal community. I don't know where else to turn. Captain Preston needs your help."

Adams looked at Quincy now, who said, "I could not do this alone, John."

Adams sat back in the chair. He thought of the senior lawyers, the distinguished old gentlemen who held tight rein on membership in their legal fraternity. He suddenly felt angry.

"No one would come to the captain's aid? This man's life is at stake. He should have whatever counsel he requests. He should not have to settle for a choice based on desperation."

Forrest was leaning forward, nodding, pulling in every word. At Adams' last statement, he shook his head.

"Oh, no, sir. Please do not be insulted. I assure you—"

Adams held up his hand.

"It's all right, sir. It was a poor choice of words. I meant that there is much more experienced representation in Boston. It angers me that none of our esteemed elders finds this case worthy of his time."

He shot a glance at Quincy again, added, "I have no doubt we would be risking more than the particulars of this case. But that cannot be the issue. If this man claims to be innocent, he is entitled, under the law and under the judgment of God, to be heard. He is entitled to an examination of the facts and the evidence. He is entitled to a fair hearing."

Forrest immediately responded, "Sir, Captain Preston asks for nothing more."

Quincy was slowly nodding.

Adams slapped the arms of his chair and said, "We are in agreement, then."

Forrest dug through his pockets, and Adams saw a small gold coin in his hand.

"Sir, please. I insist you accept this guinea as a first payment for your services. It is all I have at present."

Adams took the coin, rubbed it slowly between his fingers.

"This is more than adequate. Sir, you may return to Captain Preston and inform him that as of this moment, he has counsel."

"SO YOUR LOYALTIES WERE BOUGHT FOR ONE GUINEA?"

Adams did not respond. He had expected this from his cousin and chose his words carefully.

"My loyalties are to the law, Sam. I do not have to explain that to you. There is no need for excuses."

Sam Adams stretched out in the small chair across the desk from him, a strange smile on his face.

"A lot of publicity, you know. Here, all over the colonies, England, maybe all over Europe. The consequences could be . . . enormous."

"That's not why I am taking this case. It is not about notoriety."

"But it is, John. It can't be helped. Preston could have been carted off to England, safe and secure under His Majesty's wing, and nothing more would ever have been heard. But a trial here . . . not even the king can ignore that. No royal whim can change the verdict of the people. Once convicted, Preston cannot simply be spirited away."

Adams flushed with anger.

"So Captain Preston is already tried, sentenced, and hanged? You are quite happy with that?"

"Blame must be placed, Cousin."

"And what of the law?"

"Law? It was a massacre, John. Don't you see it? The troops lost all control. The officers did nothing to stop it. We're only fortunate there weren't more troops. The death toll would have been much worse."

The words seemed to drift past him as Adams focused on Sam's odd smile.

"What is there in all this horror that makes you so . . . happy?"

Sam shifted in the wooden chair, his eyes half shut, and said slowly, "Cousin John, you surprise me sometimes. For all your training in the law, for all your dealings with the political powers, you don't seem to understand what's really happening here."

"I'm not a politician. I'm just a lawyer."

Sam leaned forward.

"Yes, a lawyer. You understand the king's law, the colonists' law, even God's law better than anyone I know. But I'm afraid, dear John, you don't understand people."

Sam stood and moved slowly around the small office, pacing like a cat, the words forming.

"This is exactly what we needed, John. The people had begun to be bored with the issues. The anger simply wasn't there anymore. There is an awful danger when the people become accustomed to tyranny. If the people learn to accept small abuses, then larger abuses will follow. It is like a disease, crippling slowly, until the body is beyond repair. Think about our history, John. The times when we have risen up, protested the abuses, the Sugar Tax, the Stamp Act. When there are loud voices here, London hears them, and they back down. But when the voices are quiet, London grows brave again, bringing more abuses, stretching their own laws, reaching their fingers ever so slowly into our pockets, our homes, our rights. It has been five years since the Stamp Act protests. That's a long time, and memories are regrettably short. It's been nearly two years since they imposed those ridiculous Townshend Acts. We made so much noise about that, they sent the army here. But despite all those conflicts, the outrageous taxation, the meddling in our affairs by Parliament, even the military occupation, to most people it's all becoming normal. The people are getting used to being abused. That's an intolerable situation."

Adams felt a coldness in his stomach.

"Sam, are you telling me the bloodshed last night was . . . arranged?"

Sam straightened.

"Certainly not. You give me too much credit, John. I don't command the mobs in this town. They are driven by their own spirit, by their own intolerance for conditions here. They are inspired by the abuses that come across the Atlantic. And it was the soldiers who fired. Not the citizens."

"Sam, I doubt most of those people—those ruffians—know much about politics, or law, or the British Parliament."

Sam grinned. "No, perhaps not. *That* is my job. To educate. To enlighten."

"To inflame."

Sam seemed struck by the comment. Putting on a small display of hurt feelings, he murmured, "Such a harsh word, John."

But Adams could see through the act, and Sam knew it. He leaned on the desk now, serious.

"Do not underestimate the need, John. There is a powerful blanket cast over this colony, oppressive and deadening. It is much simpler for the citizens to simply endure, to obey the wishes of their king and those fools in Parliament and go about their own business. It is much easier for the government in London to move quietly, slowly, draw little attention to its policies, and before we are aware of it, the abuses become law. Your law. Right now, we are but servants to the merchants in England. We are not allowed to import goods from anywhere else. Our blood, our sweat, produces goods that enrich English merchants and their cronies here. We have no say in Parliament, and we get no respect from the king or his ministers. We are like children, without rights, without a voice, to be disciplined as the parent sees fit. Inflame? Yes, I will do whatever I can to inflame, Cousin. The people have become weary, drained of their strength. They need to remember *why*."

Sam was breathing heavily now, his face red with anger. There was a quiet moment, and Adams said, "Did you engineer last night's bloodshed?"

Sam stared at him hard, though Adams thought he detected a trace of a smile.

"No, John. But I am flattered by the question."

Adams looked down at the desk, the small pile of papers, the legal arguments forgotten now. He moved his hand along the edge of the dull wood, said, "Captain Preston deserves a fair hearing."

Sam seemed not to hear, had turned away, staring out the small window. After a long moment he replied, "Fair. Yes, fair. We don't need to give England a martyr. It could be an effective message. Your soldiers kill our citizens, and still we will follow the law. We are a civilized people. And all the other colonies will respect that. They will support us."

He turned now, looked at Adams.

"By all means, John. Fair."

Adams saw the odd smile again, thought, Sam is always planning, always beyond the moment.

"I will do what I can to delay the hearing. There will be a great deal of preparation. What will happen in the meantime?"

Sam raised his arms, said, "There will be an assembly where the people will urge—no, they will *demand* that Governor Hutchinson remove the troops from Boston. And certainly there will be a big story in the newspapers, both to inform the citizens here and to let the English people know what their soldiers have done. The news account will be on its way to England shortly. Very important to get the correct version to the London press before the army or the governor has a chance to make excuses."

"What exactly is the correct version?"

"They're already calling it the Boston Massacre. Five citizens, perhaps more, were massacred last night when Captain Thomas Preston of His Majesty's Twenty-ninth Regiment ordered his men to fire indiscriminately into a peaceful gathering of young boys who were guilty of nothing more than parading through the street, celebrating their own youth."

He stopped, waited for Adams' response. Adams felt a dull sadness, a helplessness.

"You will write that?"

"Already have."

"But . . . I thought you agreed . . ."

"That there should be a fair trial? Certainly. But you said

yourself that it will take a while yet. If they are not reminded, some people might even forget who Captain Preston is. Until the court decides one way or the other, all we can do is inform the people what happened. There is much more at stake here than the trial of one soldier. My God, John. The king has begun to shoot his subjects."

Adams stared at the grim satisfaction on his cousin's face, tried to understand what Sam was up to.

"How can you say that, Sam? Do you know what happened? Were you there? Did you see it?"

Sam suddenly moved toward the door, made a short bow, pulled the door open, and Adams felt the cold filling the small office. Sam said, "I have business to attend to. There is much work to be done. I'll be leaving you to your law books, John."

Sam pulled the door closed, then stopped, leaned in again.

"Be careful, John. Rely on your wisdom. These are dangerous times."

The door shut, and Adams felt suddenly irritated by the clumsy warning. So am I to fear the mob, too? I would stand beside you, Sam; I am not your enemy. He had always known that his cousin was the energy behind much of the protests, and even though Adams agreed with the principles, he had never been close enough to the violence to see so clearly that Sam Adams' methods were radical indeed. But now you are close, he thought. You are drawn in whether you like it or not. Then you had better understand what his warning means. The mob will hear no discussion; they will simply place their blame, magnify their enemy. Their anger will be focused, and they will talk of revenge. And they will not care about the rule of law. He had a sudden clarity, could still feel the energy for what lay ahead. I am not afraid of this. Sam knows I am not his enemy. There will be no mob around my home, there will be no harm to my family. Well, all right. You do your mischief, Sam. But I assure you: The law will guide us, the law will prevail. There will be no revenge in Boston.

3. GAGE

THE HOUSE WAS A SWARM OF ACTIVITY, MAIDS PLACING FLOWERS, laying out the linen and the silver with perfect precision. He had learned to stay out of the way of this kind of turmoil, knew when to retreat to his office, closing his doors even to the wondrous smells that drifted through the house. The routine was common now, another party, some elaborate dinner for some elaborate dignitary and his elaborate wife. He knew only the most basic rules of New York's social customs, had rarely felt the need to impress anyone on this side of the Atlantic. He had grown up in a family whose social status was always on the edge of aristocracy, and after much pursuit, his father had secured the title of viscount. It had meant more to his father than to him, and with his father's death, the title had passed to Gage's older brother, William. From his first days as a young lieutenant, his focus had been more on the prestige that came from rank, advancing in the army under the watchful eye of the ministry in London. To the officer who reached the highest ranks, retirement would often mean some precious title of its own. It would have gladdened his father's heart that Thomas Gage had been promoted to lieutenant general. In America, he had no peer. He was the commanding general.

The turmoil in the house was inspired by Margaret, and he had become used to that now, this need she had for entertaining, for making a grand show for the city's high society. He had no idea why it was so important to her, why the American wife of a British military commander would assume the airs of London's most energetic social hostesses. He would never say anything, of course, not even the whispered comment, the quiet grumble of a

25

man who treasured silence, who enjoyed removing the starched finery of his uniform as much as he enjoyed parading in military dress through the streets of New York. He suspected that much of her energy came from her own upbringing, coming out of the small town of Brunswick, in New Jersey. That alone could present a challenge to anyone trying to climb the city's social ladder.

She had never been to England, not yet, and he knew that somewhere in their future, sometime when he could settle into graceful retirement, she would finally understand what he missed. No matter how elegant the social circle, how abundant the finery at the parties, nothing in New York could compare to the grand atmosphere of official London. He had learned not to bring it up, as she was strangely sensitive to not being English. It was a distinction that many in the colonies simply ignored. They were all Englishmen, really, and if some insisted on adopting the absurd identity of "Americans," it was tolerated by the rest of the colonists as a mild affectation, a peculiar need to set oneself apart from the mother country. Gage himself rarely thought of anyone in his realm of command as anything but transplanted Englishmen, whether they were in fact transplanted or not. As much as he wished Margaret would cease her devotion to her roots in New Jersey, he knew better than to suggest it.

He stood at the open window, felt a chill, the daylight fading, the streets calm now, most of the day's business complete. Across the way, he could see the small shops that lined Broad Street, some of the merchants already shuttering their windows, locking their doors. He leaned to one side, put a hand on his stomach, felt the bulge, the tightness at his waist. This has got to stop, he thought. For all her frittering about, the glee that positively *infects* Margaret, the most profound effect these dinners have on me is the increasing bulge at my belt line. He stood straight, tried to relieve the pressure, pulling in his stomach. No use. I may have to order a new uniform. Again.

Now focused closer to the house, his eye followed the lines of green, new growth sprouting in the garden. Good, he thought. Fill that empty space with thick healthy plants, lots of flowers, even weeds. Especially weeds. Give her something else to do.

He knew the younger children would soon be gone, joining their brother and sister across the Atlantic. He had struggled to convince Margaret that the proper education could only be had in England. As each child had grown mature enough to withstand the difficult trip, each had gone to live with their uncle, his brother William. In the beginning, it was a long and stormy controversy, but she could not argue with his logic, that their future was best served by securing the credentials of an English school. He knew that when the younger ones boarded the ship, it would come again, the silence, the days of sulking anger before Margaret forced herself to resume the social routine. The children fought it as well, scenes he had come to dread, the long bouts of crying as mother and child said good-bye. He tried to be the example, stern yet smiling, sending them off on an adventure for which they would ever be grateful. He tried to see their faces, knew that when he saw them again, they would be so much different, so much more *English*. A soldier does not make for a good father, he thought. They will do better by what my rank can give them than by anything that comes from here, from any so-called advantages the colonies can offer. Even Margaret must understand that they cannot grow up here, that there is no future in America for a family with our station. Ultimately she has to accept that. It is always difficult, I suppose, a mother sending her children away. But each time she recovers, handles it all in her own way. It's better, perhaps, that she will not talk about it with me. Certainly it is her affair. I know better than to try to understand motherhood.

The last daylight was flowing into the dark walls of his office, the shorter days, the bleakness of winter pushed away now by the new spring. Here at least there *is* a spring, he thought. In New York the air actually warms up, flowers bloom. Nothing like Montreal. I do not miss that place. He felt another shiver, could not help it, never liked to dwell on the memories of his early posts, the three years of drab misery when he commanded the garrison in Canada after the war with France. No, not even the rabble in Boston can make me miss that life. If the worst thing I must endure is these dinner parties, that's not so bad after all. He felt his stomach again.

He heard a carriage, saw motion in the street, the carriage stopping outside the short walls of the garden. He watched the man emerge, standing tall, thin, almost fragile, wearing a fine dark suit, the ruffled silk billowing from the man's chest. Gage watched him, felt the usual dread slipping away. No, this evening may be quite different; there will be little of that awful mindless chatter so typical of these affairs. For once, the dinner is merely an excuse. He's here because I need him here.

He waited in the darkening room, the daylight finally slipping away, heard more carriages now, the rest of the guests. He didn't really care about them, knew they would be invited out of obligation, the *important* people who would be so insulted if they were somehow excluded. No, Margaret would not have that, would never slight the local peacocks. They must all come and coo and fawn and pretend to be so terribly impressed with Thomas Hutchinson. He is, after all, governor of Massachusetts. And Margaret will be watching me, that hard glint of steel in her eye, don't do anything clumsy, don't embarrass her, be patient. Hutchinson will be mine soon enough. He moved away from the window, put his hand on the back of a heavy chair as he heard the greetings. He knew he would soon be missed, that Margaret would begin to simmer if he hid in his office too long and she had to make excuses for his absence. That would be his costly mistake, would bring punishment from her later on, during those quiet moments when their blessed privacy would have all the charm of winters in Montreal. No, none of that. He tugged at his coat, smoothing wrinkles that were not there. All right, General, do your duty. And the sooner I can get through this, the sooner I can bring Governor Hutchinson into this room and find out just what kind of insanity has spread through Boston.

THE DINNER HAD GONE WELL, EVEN BY GAGE'S STANDARDS, WITH few of the annoying critiques of policy that tended to roll through the social circles. He always felt the need to defend, could not ever escape the feeling that, even in the idle chatter of small talk, he was somehow being attacked. He was the most visible protector of the king's interests, and by the third glass of wine even the most loyal Tory would become inspired to make some indiscreet comment about Gage's power or policy. The steely eye from Margaret always ensured he would be polite, enduring the opinions and petty gripes. But tonight, the attention had been focused elsewhere. The guests were clearly enamored of Hutchinson, handsome and prim in his ruffles, soft with his answers to the most ignorant inquiries. It had been a blessed relief to Gage, and he had even celebrated, filling his own wine glass more often than usual. And then it was over, another flurry of bows and compliments.

GAGE POINTED TO A CHAIR, WAITED UNTIL HUTCHINSON SAT. He looked out through the office doorway into the parlor, saw Margaret instructing one of the maids, already tidying up. Margaret looked at him, and he did not hide his smugness, the slight smile, the silent message he was giving her. You see? I am not such a beast after all. He waited for the response, and now she smiled back at him.

"Thank you, my husband. It was a wonderful dinner. Our guests were all quite enamored of Governor Hutchinson. And they even spoke warmly of you."

He made a short bow, still smiling, then turned back into the office. He could tell she was still watching him, a playful flirtation, and he felt a pleasing satisfaction, thought, No, it will not be Montreal tonight.

As Hutchinson settled himself, Gage moved to a small cabinet, opened a fragile glass door.

"May I offer you some port, Governor?"

Hutchinson seemed to hesitate, and Gage looked at him, saw the governor wrestling with the question.

"Don't feel obliged, Governor. We had quite a bit of wine already." He saw tension on Hutchinson's face, closed the cabinet. All right, I suppose port can wait.

He seated himself, saw Hutchinson glancing around the office, studying the dark bookshelves, the tall window that faced the garden, the great fat cabinets filled with the business of the army.

"Governor, despite how often you heard these words already tonight . . . welcome to New York."

Hutchinson seemed to loosen, replied, "Yes, thank you. Most cordial people, your friends."

"Not my friends. Margaret's." He saw a frown, told himself, Careful. He is, after all, a politician. "Not meaning disrespect to anyone, of course, Governor. I just don't find time to make personal relationships. Nature of being a soldier. My greatest responsibility seems to be to make sure they're not afraid of me. Well, perhaps a little bit."

He wanted to laugh at his own joke, but Hutchinson didn't respond. The governor glanced around again, self-conscious, the room filling with a stuffy silence. Gage said, "Governor, perhaps we should get down to the matter at hand. Has General Dalrymple completed the troop transfers to your satisfaction?"

"Oh, yes, General. Both regiments have settled into their quarters at Castle William."

"Good. You may already know that I have ordered the Twenty-ninth to leave Boston, to sail to the New Jersey coast. Since you have concluded the troops cannot remain in the town, Castle William simply isn't large enough for both regiments. If they can't be of service in Boston, they will be of service elsewhere."

Hutchinson seemed to slump in the chair, and Gage waited for some response. The silence continued, and Gage felt a sudden impatience, said, "I am still not certain this is the best course, Governor."

Hutchinson seemed to come awake.

"No, General, it is not the best course at all. But what choice do I have? You should have heard the protests. The town meeting was not a meeting at all, but a chorus of shouting, all of it aimed at . . . the authority of the crown. There are powerful forces at work in Boston, General. The unfortunate incident with Captain Preston simply gave them more power. Have you ever found yourself in command of a large gathering, and every one of those present is screaming into your face?" He stopped, the words seemingly choked off.

Gage said quietly, "No. That doesn't happen in the army."

Hutchinson appeared to gather himself.

"No, I suppose not. What else can I do, General? I did not call for the troops in the first place. It was my predecessor, Governor Bernard, who made the decision. It cost him his position. Now the responsibility is mine alone. The people know that by law, it is only the governor who can order troops into the town, that I am the only one who can order them out. After the shootings . . . nothing I could say had any effect."

Gage rose, moved again to the small liquor cabinet.

"You sure you won't reconsider, Governor?"

Hutchinson was staring down, nodded slowly.

"Actually . . . yes, General. Some port might be . . . helpful."

Gage poured the dark liquid into two small glasses, handed one to Hutchinson, who said, "I am prepared to do whatever is necessary to protect Captain Preston and his men."

Gage moved back to his chair. "I am pleased to hear that. Should we move them to Castle William? A fortified island in the harbor might be a safer place for them while they wait for their trial."

Hutchinson shook his head.

"With all respect, General, moving the prisoners would cause more trouble than it would save. Sam Adams would have the mobs out in force. We'd be accused of spiriting them away, ripping them away from the court's precious jurisdiction."

Gage stood now, suddenly incensed.

"Samuel Adams! How does he control so much? Where does his power come from? He's a traitor to the king, Governor. I have my own designs on Mr. Adams, and the rest of them as well. What are we talking about? Ten men? Five? Three? They make mockery of the king's law. They make mockery—" He paused. "Forgive me, Governor, but they make mockery of your authority as well. For what? Why? What noble cause lights such a fire in that . . . *faction* that they can so influence the affairs of Massachusetts?"

Hutchinson shook his head slowly, and Gage moved to the chair again, stood behind it, leaned forward.

"They don't believe they should pay taxes. It's that simple, isn't it? They want the protection of His Majesty's army, they want us to keep the Indians away, the French. But they aren't willing to pay for it. That was the point of the Stamp Act, and instead of obeying the law, they burned the stamps, and very near burned the agents sent by the king to enforce the law!"

Hutchinson replied, "I am aware of what the mobs can do, General. They destroyed my home."

Gage was suddenly embarrassed, thought, Of course. He knows better than I do. He reached for the glass of port, took a slow sip, calming himself.

"My apologies, Governor. You are certainly aware just why the troops were needed in Boston. And whether or not Governor Bernard lost his title, it was ultimately his courage that allowed me to station them there. With the army comes order. I doubt seriously if the mobs would have been so brazen in the face of the king's muskets. All the hue and cry about soldiers landing in Boston, all the rumors of great riots, armed insurrection. What happened? Instead of sword and gun, the mobs gave them gospel, great fiery speeches. *Words!* Those people are expert at that. But it's not enough. Their *cause* cannot be fueled by talk alone. Peace prevails after all, the soldiers become accepted, all is quiet, as it should be. So what then? Push the soldiers, push them again, threaten, assault, abuse. The soldiers are just men, after all. And everything I have heard convinces me their lives were in danger. If I had been in Captain Preston's place, I would have fired myself."

Hutchinson was looking at him with sharp eyes, absorbing his words, said now, "Yes. I would have fired, too!"

Gage stood straight, saw Hutchinson staring at the desk, an unfamiliar show of anger. Where was that anger when you faced your mob? Gage moved around the chair, sat down on soft leather.

"There is an old law, goes back to King Henry the Eighth. Anyone charged with seditious acts against the king can be arrested and sent to London for trial. It is not in my power to arrest those people or to order troops anywhere. Those orders come from Lord Hillsborough. But the statute is plain and can be exercised by the civil authority. That, sir, is you. Have you considered arresting the leaders of your mob?"

Hutchinson's fire faded, and he said, "Arrest by whom? Who will attempt to place chains around the legs of Sam Adams, or Joseph Warren, or John Hancock? I am aware of that old statute, General. But I am also aware of what the consequences would be for anyone who tried to enforce it. My office is accused of being an arm of British oppression. I am considered to be the enemy by the very people I am supposed to govern. My authority is checked every day by the State Assembly. We do not even function as two arms of the same government. They are elected by the people, and my authority comes from the king. There is no cooperation, none. We are simply adversaries. And they have the mob behind everything they do. I try to understand what must be done, what will heal this controversy . . ."

Gage grunted, the words flowing past him, Hutchinson's eloquence not able to hide his helplessness, his weakness. There was a pause, and Gage said, "You do not heal radicals. You hang them. I understand completely what must be done. With all respect, sir, I do not agree with removing the troops from Boston. You regard that decision as inevitable. I consider it a mistake. Your troublemakers are driven by a great deal of hot talk. But as long as the army has a presence, talk is all they will do. Your mobs do not have as much muscle as you seem to fear, Governor."

Hutchinson sat back in his chair, and Gage could see the sadness in the man's eyes.

"Forgive me, General, but you live in New York. You do not have to endure the threat."

Gage felt impatience now.

"Governor, I command an army that is charged with securing the whole coastline of the American colonies, inland to the Indian frontier. I am responsible for safeguarding the Bahama Islands, the island of Bermuda, and the seaports of Canada. Lord Hillsborough is firm in his belief that I can accomplish all of this with only five thousand men. Respectfully, sir, as serious as the problems in Boston seem to you, that is but one minor city in a vastly complicated area of command." He paused, but the anger had gripped him now, and he felt his voice rising, fueled by the wine. "To speak frankly, sir, if your citizens are unable to maintain their own peace, and your authority is ignored, I have little doubt that Lord Hillsborough will issue the instructions to this command that in my opinion are long overdue. If Massachusetts insists on shouting itself into open revolt, then the army is prepared to respond. And you may assure your mob, sir—we will not *shout*."

4. FRANKLIN

LONDON, MAY 1770

IT WAS ONE OF THE FIRST TRULY WARM DAYS, A GLORIOUS FLOOD OF sunshine filling the streets below him. With the warmth had come the clearer skies, the dark and filthy air swept away as the coal and wood stoves grew cold. He sat close to the open window, took in the air in long breaths, rubbed his hand on his chest, said aloud, "Marvelous. Springtime. Infirmities be gone."

He leaned close to the window, peered out into the street, could see the houses across the way still shut up, their dark interiors barred against the soft breeze. He shook his head, wanted to shout out, scold them, Why do you close out the fresh air? Why must you keep your sickness bottled up, your stale, deathly calm held tightly around your beds? He had come to believe that what the doctors had always insisted was simply false. The common belief was that disease must be kept isolated, that great evil was carried on the outside air, infectious and dangerous, worsening any ailment. Ignorance, he thought. You must feel it, feel the invigoration. Open your windows and let life inside. You cannot purge sickness by imprisoning it. You must wash it away!

He retreated from the window, rubbed his stomach, thought of food, could detect some marvelous smell from downstairs. Ah, yes, Mrs. Stevenson. What grand concoctions will you provide today? Something appropriate to this marvelous weather, something light, sweet perhaps. He was beginning to feel genuinely hungry, unusual for this early in the day. It had become his practice to rise with the sun, enjoying the first flow of activity in the street below, the first sounds of a busy new day, but after an hour or so he would return to bed, slip slowly between the cool sheets, the bed as refreshed as the day. Then would come the last bit of delicious sleep, another hour perhaps, the most restful time of the day. He glanced at the bed, thought, No, not just yet. Mrs. Stevenson has implanted a different idea.

He heard a shuffling sound in the hallway, and from beyond the door a small voice said, "Dr. Franklin, are you awake?"

"Quite, madam. Awake and ready to confront this glorious day!"

The door opened, and the old woman backed into the room, carefully holding a wide silver tray in her hands. She turned and made a sharp shriek.

"Dr. Franklin, you are undressed! Oh, my word!"

The old woman spun away, nearly losing the tray, stood in the doorway with her back to him. He glanced downward.

"Oh, my. Yes, my apologies. I quite forgot." He rose from the chair, pulled his robe around him.

Mrs. Stevenson still faced the hallway, said, "Really, Dr. Franklin. I wish you would take a bit more care. Even the neighbors are aware that you have no modesty. It is . . . embarrassing."

"Hmm, yes. The neighbors. They do tend to make somewhat of a fuss outside the window." He tightened the cord on the robe. "It's all right now, Mrs. Stevenson. I am now, by the neighborhood standards, quite decent."

She turned again cautiously, put the tray down on a small table. He examined the tray, could smell the tea, see the light dusting of sugar on the sweet biscuits. Folded to one side was a newspaper.

"Perfection, Mrs. Stevenson. It seems nearly as though you can read my very thoughts."

She shook her head, moved away to the door.

"That, Dr. Franklin, is more frightening than I care to imagine."

When she was gone, he slid the chair close to the tray, poured the tea into a small china cup. The steam rose toward him, and he breathed it in. Alive, that is what this is. Alive. Embrace the moment. He unfolded the newspaper, glanced toward the open window again. You have a great deal to learn, good neighbors. He reached for the teacup, felt the confinement of the rough cloth, so he stood, removed the robe, let it drop to the floor.

THE TITLE OF DOCTOR WAS AN HONOR GRANTED HIM FROM THE University of St. Andrews, Scotland. He rarely referred to himself that way, but never stopped anyone else from using the term either. It was a piece of formality that he had learned to stop protesting from Mrs. Stevenson as well, and he was aware that she paraded his presence in her home to everyone she knew.

He had been her boarder for over ten years, and though the gossips would occasionally whisper of some inappropriate relationship between them, Franklin continued to hope that his wife, Deborah, would someday overcome her deep fear of the sea and make the journey to England with him. It had been nearly five years since the last crossing, his longest stay yet away from his wife. He had not even seen their new home, had left Philadelphia just prior to its completion, though still he wrote long letters, instructions on both the structure and the décor of the new home, and all the while he had wondered if it was a place he would ever actually visit.

His children seemed to divide their loyalties to each parent. He had tried to be firm with Sally, insisting she accompany him to London, especially since he himself had engineered a potential match with the son of his good friend William Strahan. Both families had seemed to approve, but then Deborah had suddenly exercised the last word, and Sally had stayed in Philadelphia.

His son William had come to England for the first time years ago but would stay in the colonies now, appointed by the king to be governor of New Jersey. There was extraordinary prestige in the appointment, of course, and Franklin had been as proud as any father could be. But the air of politics was changing, and even in London, so far removed from the growing turmoil in the colonies, Franklin had come to understand that such a post meant absolute loyalty to the king. As governor, William was in fact one of the king's official arms, reaching into the affairs of the colonies themselves. Any colonial governor had to accept that his loyalty went first to England and a distant second to the people he governed.

In the years he had been in England, Franklin had drifted through all the emotions of a man whose family has made the choice to stay behind in the quiet place while he traveled the world. From the beginning, it had been the great difference between him and Deborah. Her fear of the sea, of taking any passage in the ships, simply reinforced what he had always known. His wife had no desire to leave their home. But rather than sit alone in quiet acceptance of his lifestyle, she had taken an active role in their livelihood, had learned how to manage their business affairs. To both their employees and suppliers she had become quite the stern and sharp-tongued supervisor.

As Franklin's notoriety grew, so did the need for and the usefulness of his travel, and the trips to England had led to other trips beyond, to Europe. His wide-eyed curiosity was served well by his reputation as both an entertaining philosopher and a scientist who knew the skills of showmanship. Doors were always open to him, from the subdued halls of universities to the great opulent ballrooms of royalty.

He wrote to Deborah often, relating the experiences, the pride of a man respected by important people. But her replies were mostly bits of news about home, business, and daughter Sally's social doings. He knew better than to scold Deborah, knew he could not draw from her what she would not give. He was never sure if she was angry at him for being gone so long, and he fought to resist the guilt of that. No, this is the life she has chosen, we have both chosen. There is no judgment, no right or wrong about it. It is simply who we are.

If he would not dwell on the guilt of his absence, he could not hide from those quiet moments alone, staring into the darkness, talking quietly to her—the extraordinary day he had just completed, perhaps, or the latest bit of notoriety he had received. He would explain silently whom he had met, his impression of some royal audience, would go into great detail as though she were there, watching over his shoulder as he concocted some new experiment, engineered some gadget. He could hear her pride, the touch of her hand, their laughter, and then the sleep would come, the night passing with pleasant dreams. In the morning, the image would still be with him, would inspire a new letter to her, certainly, but the written words were too slow. When he would hand the letter to the postman, he knew the response would take so long that the images would be long forgotten, replaced by some new, fresh experiences. It often took nearly two months for the precious words to cross the Atlantic, and sometimes she would not even respond at all, distracted perhaps by some crisis close to home. Or worse, he had begun to accept that she simply didn't miss him as she once had, that no matter how often he thought of her, imagined her there with him, it might simply have been too long. She had grown too well used to his absence.

If she did not respond to the letters as much as he would like, or if he could not be with his children now, the time was not yet ripe for leaving England. And since he was not ready to return to them, he would do the next best thing. He would send them gifts. That was another great service Mrs. Stevenson performed, and it only made the neighbors' gossip that much more ridiculous. Margaret Stevenson would spend long hours, and great sums of her tenant's money, shopping for those items that Franklin himself did not truly understand. But his wife and his landlady had formed an unmistakable connection, and so, on ships that would often pass each other at sea, the fineries of England would travel to Philadelphia, and in response, those uniquely American treasures would find their way to Mrs. Stevenson. The gifts *did* produce letters from Deborah. She was gracious, appreciative, though certainly she knew whose careful hand had chosen the presents. Mrs. Stevenson had accepted that this man in her home would only be her dear friend and often her provider. After all, he did pay his rent on time.

* * *

HE MOVED INTO THE STREET, MET BY FAMILIAR FACES, HEARD THE
polite calls from neighbors who were tending the gardens in
front of modest homes. He enjoyed this part of the day most of
all, and he walked with purpose, a quick stride. He would keep
up the pace until he felt his heartbeat hard in his chest, his
breathing sharp and deep, sweat dampening his clothes. On
colder days, the walk would last for perhaps an hour, but today
the sun was already moving high and seemed to block his path, a
bright fire in his eyes. It had only been a few minutes, and he
stopped now, let his breathing pour out in quick rhythm. He
glanced up at the sun again, thought, Wonderful and annoying at
the same time. There should be some way . . . He looked off to
one side, saw an old bottle under the low limbs of a bush. He
bent down, picked up the dull brown glass in his hand, held it up
toward the sun. Ah, yes, there. Block out the bright light, but I
can still see. He tossed the bottle aside, touched his pocket, felt
his glasses, thought, Why should all eyeglasses be clear? A
beautiful day such as today, and yet the sun is a brutal distraction. He glanced back at the discarded bottle, began to move
now, more quick strides, more bright sunlight. Yes, look into
that. When there is time . . .

There was no timetable for his stay in London, but there was
much business to be done. He had been appointed as colonial
representative to Parliament by three colonies now, Georgia,
New Jersey, and of course his home state of Pennsylvania. The
position carried complete authority to speak for colonial affairs,
yet Franklin understood, as many in the colonies did not, that the
authority meant little to anyone in England. As controversies
flowed in both directions across the Atlantic, he knew that it was
wishful thinking on the part of the colonies that their voice could
be heard with any influence in London.

He turned into a square, and he cast his eye up at the grand
spectacle of the Parliament building. He slowed, pulled out a
handkerchief, wiped at the wetness on his face. Show a little
decorum. That's what it's all about, anyway. Appearances. Can't
let them think I'm anxious about anything. He crossed the square,

moved toward the steps, more greetings, formal now, *Dr. Franklin*. He responded formally as well, polite nods, and began to climb the wide steps, but he heard louder voices behind him, and he stopped, looked back to the wide street. There was a small crowd gathering, more voices, some rising into shouts. Through the crowd he could see a boy holding a stack of newspapers, distributing them as quickly as he could pocket the coins. Franklin headed back down the steps, unable to recall anything in the paper that would incite much commotion. Must be some special edition. What on earth has happened now?

He made his way into the throng, tried to glimpse the papers that moved past him. Comments flowed all around him, people already locked in argument.

"Bloody fools! Damned bloody fools!"

"It can't be true!"

"It's right here! It has to be true!"

Franklin held out a coin, swapped it for a paper, the voices rising close around him. He moved away from the throng, held the paper up, began to read, his eyes immediately drawn to one word: *massacre*. He continued to read, then after a few seconds he paused, lowered the paper. More foolishness. Soldiers killing citizens. He looked again at the crowd of people, the newspapers spreading out in the square. We don't know what really happened, he thought. This is obviously slanted toward the colonists. Sounds like the hand of Sam Adams, Warren, the rest. *Bloodthirsty troops.* Not much impartiality there. The government will have their version in print, probably by the end of the day. They will have to. It's part of the game.

The damage is done for now, he concluded, returning to the Parliament building. Those people in Boston think they're doing their cause good service by writing this kind of inflammatory story. So troops fired on a crowd of citizens. If that is true, and some part of it must be, what do they expect to happen here? Do they believe that the king will apologize, change all the policies, give Sam Adams everything he demands? He reached the top of the steps and turned so that he could see out past the Thames River. It wasn't that far from here that troops killed citizens, too.

Some other cause about the downtrodden and oppressed. Mobs are rioting all over England. This isn't news, it's a way of life. The colonists still believe they can inflame the people here, but to what end? Parliament has already conceded the taxes won't work. And it wasn't only because of loud protests in Boston, but because the treasury realized they couldn't even collect enough to pay the cost of collecting.

He saw a carriage stopping at the base of the steps, men in black robes emerging, fresh powder on white wigs. He felt a sudden dread. Whatever else was to be considered today will all be set aside. They have a new distraction, a delicious new controversy. There will be loud voices of indignation, screaming back and forth their own party lines. The Whigs will take this story and parade it as pure fact, and the ministry's people will condemn the story as pure lies. The opposition leaders, men like John Wilkes, who so delight in tormenting the king's allies, who make their reputation by great earnest speeches in favor of anything that benefits the colonies—this story will give them energy for weeks of outrage. He stilled his thoughts, tried to push past the rising tide of cynicism. No, you old fool, we need those voices, Wilkes, Isaac Barré, William Penn, the others. Parliament must have a conscience, and some of those old fools should be reminded that they cannot simply run roughshod over anyone's rights without hearing about it from some of their own kind. But so much of that is self-serving, the stuff that builds careers, lofty positions. No one will even care about the *truth*, what might actually be happening in Boston to inspire such an event. He felt himself sagging, frozen to the spot. No, I don't really want to listen to all of that. It is too pretty a day.

"Dr. Franklin! Sir!"

He turned, saw the men in the robes now reaching the top of the steps, one man holding out his hand.

"Doctor, good to see you, sir! Will you be joining us today? Marvelous!"

He suddenly found himself trapped as another man moved up the steps.

"Dr. Franklin, have you some activity to attend to before the proceedings today?"

Franklin saw no robe, the older man dressed in a fine suit, struggling to reach the top steps, the thin face drawn, tired.

He glanced at the men in the robes, saw disinterest, the men already moving away, and tried to hide his relief.

"No, Dr. Johnson. I am merely observing today."

"Why would you want to do that?"

It was a strange question, and Franklin moved down the steps, saw more robes coming up, more carriages unloading the men who would fill the chamber.

He stood beside Johnson, could hear the older man's breathing, saw the rugged weariness in the man's face.

"Sir, are you all right?"

Johnson sniffed, nodded as the men in robes moved past, small formalities.

"None of us is all right, Dr. Franklin. None of us. You didn't answer my question."

"Sir?"

"Why are you intent on observing the chaos that will fill these hallowed halls? Surely you know what will happen today— indignation, righteous and strident and absurd. Condemnation, proud and boisterous and militant. It's all rather . . . tedious."

Franklin watched the older man carefully. *He's looking for an escape as well. All right, then.*

"Dr. Johnson, would you care for a cup of tea? I'm certain the Fox Glove would accommodate us."

"Tea, eh? Colonists still drinking tea?"

"Certainly, sir. This colonist might even be inclined to buy a cup for both of us."

Johnson began to move down the steps.

"In that case, I'll oblige you. Let those proper gentlemen keep their chaos to themselves."

Franklin followed Johnson down the steps, thought, *This is hardly an accident. He sought me out. Well, all right, let's talk.*

Samuel Johnson was a colonist as well, born in Connecticut ten years before Franklin. Johnson was a deeply pious man and combined his involvement in the church with a strong political instinct. He had served as a leader of the Episcopal Church in the colonies before traveling to England, settling there after becoming ordained as an Anglican priest. It was that position that gave Johnson the title of doctor. Now in his seventies, he had retired from active involvement in the church, filled his days observing the growing turmoil both in England and the colonies, writing long and thoughtful essays that articulated the positions supported by most in England who saw the king's policies as the only true course.

THE SMALL PUB WAS QUIET, EMPTIED OUT BY THE ACTIVITY NOW filling the Parliament chamber. Two cups of tea sat between them on the small dark table, and though Franklin was still curious, he said nothing. This was his idea. Let him speak first.

Johnson stirred his tea slowly.

"You have any word?"

Franklin wasn't sure what Johnson meant.

"Word? Of what, sir?"

"You just being cagey with me, or is this your official stance? Word about your *massacre*. What really happened."

"Sir, I assure you, I just heard about it this morning. I know nothing else."

"You believe it? You believe that some of the king's finest troops simply started shooting at townspeople? You think General Gage has decided to eliminate his problems by . . . *eliminating* his problems?"

Franklin hesitated briefly before responding.

"Sir, I have no idea what thoughts are traveling through the minds of General Gage or any of the people in Boston. Citizens are dead. That's the only aspect of this that seems to be uncontested fact."

"Correction, Dr. Franklin. *Colonists* are dead. That is a distinction important to a great many people. Are you familiar with the mob riots in Sulley Common? The troops shot into the crowd there too, killed four, five people. English people. In this country there's a mob just about every day unleashing some kind of violence on somebody they disagree with. When the military commanders hear enough squawking, they send out a company of soldiers, and the mob moves off somewhere else, starts all over again."

Johnson paused, drank slowly from the teacup. Franklin waited, knew there was more.

"Dr. Franklin, you have any idea why the people of Boston are so upset?"

"I am familiar with some of the issues."

"They're upset because we expect them to behave like Englishmen. That's a problem. Their safety is protected by the guns of Englishmen, their economy is sustained by the goods and currency of Englishmen, their behavior is governed by English law. But they're not Englishmen. They're *colonists*."

"Are they not to be granted the same freedoms as Englishmen everywhere?"

"Freedoms, Dr. Franklin? I would rather know how they feel about their own obligations first. Their responsibilities. The king rules over one kingdom, and there is no difference between Ireland, India, and America. Parliament passes laws and issues policy over all English territory. And yet it is only America that insists on being separate, beyond the very controls that hold this empire together. They strike out and bloody the very hand that provides comfort."

Franklin felt the walls tightening around him. There is no arguing this. Not with him. He will seek to debate, and he is too good at it.

"Sir, I cannot hope to dissuade you from your prejudice against the colonists."

Johnson laughed.

"Prejudice? I should be insulted, sir."

"I apologize."

"Don't. You're right, Dr. Franklin. The colonies invite prejudice. Look at them. Ruffians, farmers, the crudest of merchants, Indian fighters, scoundrels. How different from the Irish. After a bit of the proper influence, Ireland is now a peaceful addition to the king's empire."

Franklin felt a hot twist in his chest, fought it. *Influence?* What a strange euphemism for bloody repression.

Johnson continued, "Now, the Americans are wrapping their callused hands around the notion of politics, trying to rouse their rabble to defy the very system that nurtured them. They even have their advocates here, loud mindless voices speaking out in those very halls there, fools like Wilkes, spouting off about the virtue of the colonies. Daring to debate the king's own policies. Outrageous."

Franklin was becoming angry now. He told himself to stay quiet, reveal nothing. He glanced around, saw no one else save the pub master, sitting alone in one corner, drifting into a nap. He looked at the old man drinking his tea, saw the smugness of superiority, had seen it so often, the faces of the gentlemen in Parliament. He stirred his own tea, tried to calm himself, moved the spoon slowly, deliberately.

"How long . . . sir, how long has it been since you visited the colonies?"

Johnson lifted his narrow shoulders in a shrug.

"Don't recall. Many years."

"You have probably missed a great deal. The small towns along the coast have spread inland. The small boat docks have grown into major seaports. The population has grown to nearly three million people. And it continues to grow. Forgive me, sir, but the comparison to Ireland is inappropriate. Consider that the boundaries of the American colonies press against the enormous wealth of an entire continent. The population will double in our children's lifetime. Given time, the ability of the colonies to sustain themselves, to govern themselves, and perhaps, sir, even to defend themselves will become complete. The colonists are loyal to the king. But my understanding is that they have little patience with the heavy hand of Parliament."

"*Now* you are insulting me, Dr. Franklin. Look at this Boston incident, this so-called massacre. The colonists protest the policies of Parliament, and suddenly this wonderful massacre appears, this convenient tool for spreading their seditious cause. Loud voices cry out against the king, and driven by bloodlust and revenge, the voices grow strong. Accomplishing what, may I ask? The king will not just simply allow the hubbub to continue.

Parliament has virtually backed down on every issue the colonists find so odious. The Townshend Acts have been repealed."

"More or less."

Johnson seemed annoyed.

"Well, yes, Dr. Franklin, more or less. Surely even the most absurdly radical colonist would grant Parliament to maintain a bit of pride?"

Franklin absorbed that, took a slow drink of tea, sorted the words in his mind. Pride. That's all it is, I suppose. Keep one part of the acts in place, the tax on tea. Give the ministers their one small foothold on the issue of taxation. And ignore the principle.

All the arguments began to flood his mind, and he was suddenly weary, missed the sunlight, felt like a prisoner in the darkness of the pub. How can they not understand why this is so important? It's not about pennies or tea. His mind was swirling now, and he stared down into the golden liquid.

"The English constitution provides for assemblies of the people in each colony to determine for each colony how taxes are to be levied. Parliament cannot change that without altering the very charters that founded the colonies in the first place."

"Oh, please, Dr. Franklin. Are you next going to rely on that shopworn argument about taxation without representation? It makes for an effectively bombastic piece of oratory, but even the king has no patience for such an absurd notion. Colonists cannot be represented in Parliament. Never will be. They simply are not an equal part of the empire. They are not, nor will they ever be, *Englishmen*."

Franklin let out a small burst of sound, a quick laugh. He held it down but saw Johnson looking at him with mild disgust.

"I cannot dispute with you anything you say, Dr. Johnson. Your conclusions are poured into a mold that has hardened into inflexibility. All I can hope is that those who seek to squeeze the American colonies in so tight a fist . . . for the sake of the peace, I hope those people do not underestimate the depth of the resolve and the passion in the colonies."

"Dr. Franklin, here's what I believe about that resolve. What do you suppose would happen to all the loud protests coming from the colonies if a select few were suddenly silenced? Put a good stout hanging tree to work. It is pretty clear to me that once the most vocal of the rabble is subject to the noose, your unrest, your mobs, and your resolve will quietly fade away. I suspect that the king would be very pleased if suddenly America assumed her appropriate place in the empire, much as the Irish were convinced to do. All of this controversy would be quickly forgotten."

Franklin watched as Johnson sipped again from his teacup. Of course. This is what so many believe, that all the protests, the anger, come from the powerful words of a few malcontents. They have no idea of the depth of the differences, the power of the disagreements.

"Dr. Johnson, I regret your viewpoint. I am not certain why you have chosen to have this discussion with me. I'm afraid that perhaps America is too far removed from here for these issues to be taken seriously."

He stopped, saw Johnson staring at him blankly. No, there can be no useful debate. Not here. The debate will come soon enough, in the pages of the newspapers, in the arguments in Parliament, in the violence in the streets of Boston. No one who is three thousand miles away can be simply told what the American spirit is, or how the minds of the colonists perceive the world. The differences, the arguments, can only grow deeper. And this one old man speaks for so many.

"Forgive me, Dr. Johnson. I should return to my work."

Johnson seemed surprised.

"Only one cup of tea? I rather enjoyed our conversation. We should continue another time."

Franklin made a short bow, emerged into the bright sunlight. The sun was straight overhead now, and he glanced toward the Parliament building. I have always believed that talking would solve the problems, he thought. Even when faced with such obstinate disagreement, we must continue to communicate our differences. The alternative is unthinkable. He proceeded across the wide square, saw polite nods, heard brief greetings. Are these people so different from us after all? I do enjoy this place, the grand history, the dignity of this culture. He looked again at the Parliament building. *Perhaps that is the problem. This is your culture. We are not some primitive people who must accept your power, who have no choice but to kneel to your superiority. You have allowed us to grow strong, to build our own culture, to find our own identity and our own way in the world. You cannot suddenly decide to tax us, exploit us, drain our resources. You cannot do with us as you please. With your vast army and your great navy, you may have the power. But you do not have the right.*

5. ADAMS

BRAINTREE, AUGUST 1770

NEAR THE END OF MAY SHE HAD GIVEN BIRTH TO A BOY, AND THEY named him Charles. He was healthy and round, with an unmistakable resemblance to his father, and if the scars were still raw from the death of their baby daughter, the new baby's bright smile and the soft, happy squeals finally allowed both parents to let the awful memories, the quiet fears, fade away.

As the law practice had grown and Adams found the days suddenly too short of hours for the work he had contracted, he yearned for the proper excuse, the legitimate cause, to leave his office in Boston and return to the quiet of the family home in Braintree. As the birth had drawn closer, so, too, had the planting season. It was simply common sense that Abigail would return to the more peaceful place, closer to her own family, away from the turmoil that still infected Boston. He had finally persuaded himself to go with her, fighting with himself over his responsibility to the law, the practice, and his responsibility to her and the farm. As the time came for the carriage to be loaded, for the very pregnant wife and the two small children to gather together for the sad good-bye, it had taken only one look from her, one silent request, and the argument had dissolved. He had driven the carriage himself.

He had gone back to Boston several times, digging hard into the papers, the hearings before the magistrates, even attending some of the town meetings, something he had rarely done before. The mood of the town had improved a great deal since the soldiers had been moved away, and though one regiment still occupied the island far out in the harbor, Castle William was not Boston. Even the great violent energy that pushed for a quick trial of Preston and his soldiers had grown calm. The radical voices that inspired the mobs were reserved, patient, and Adams was grateful for that. The most influential men in the town—his cousin Sam, his friend Joseph Warren—were content to allow events to play out, and did not see the outcome of the trial as any kind of threat to their cause. But there were still others, friends and family of the men who had died in front of the Custom House, whose patience was tested by the delays. Adams would not be influenced by the discreet comments, the subtle glances he caught as he passed by them in the street. He knew that justice still meant different things to different people.

As the months passed, even the strident voices from the newspapers had begun to moderate, and the passion to put Preston's neck in a noose had become subdued. It was a relief to Adams that with the trial now scheduled for October, he had time to work with Josiah Quincy to prepare a case based on law and reason. And it meant he could spend time with his family and enjoy the wonderful peace of the farm.

It had been a mild summer, the farm prospering, the fields lush and green. He had left the house early, still felt a chill in the air, carried by a burst of energy that took him to the far end of the farm. He had increased the size of the farm whenever the opportunity arose, buying land from neighbors who had grown too old for the rigorous work, from others who wished to leave the land for the promise of the growing cities. Most of the land was cultivated, but there were still great patches of trees, thickets of brush and wild berries, small streams bridged by fat logs. In

Boston, his name inspired talk of ambition, his relentless drive to build his law practice. Few understood what strength these trips home gave him, what he drew from the energizing walks over the hills and through the fields of his beloved farm.

He had walked the fields all morning, climbing the hills slowly, slipping carefully through rows of cornstalks as tall as he was, through the dense thickets where the blueberry bushes grew wild. He had stepped through the mud of the creek bed, stopping long enough for a cold drink of the sweetest water he knew, enjoying a quiet moment under the great canopy of trees.

He could see the houses in the distance, two dark brown cubes, set side by side at an angle, the older home turned slightly, facing the side of the newer one. He had been born in the older, smaller house, the larger one now their home. The property had been in the family for fifty years, bought by his father. Deacon John Adams had always been a farmer but had seen beyond the world to a better life for his children. He had wanted his sons to move on, discover the world of books and education. Adams smiled now, climbed up on a pile of fat rocks, stared across a wide valley to the orchard that spread beyond the houses. He thought of his father, remembered the great challenge, his father testing the young John's will. All right, if you want to be a farmer, then by God, we will farm. His father had taken him into the village, made him load the wagon with hay, gave him a hard day's lesson in the use of a pitchfork. He remembered the blisters still. It was the hardest work he had ever done, and he had never felt so much pride in his life. My father thought he was convincing me how miserable this life was, he thought, he didn't expect me to say I *liked* it. He remembered the old man's frustration, his father's words. Well, boy, *I* don't like it a-tall. So *you* are going to school.

He looked east, thought of Abigail's family home, close to the water. So many had built there, and it had nothing to do with some connection to the sea. Most were neither fishermen nor sailors. It was as though they needed to see the watery bridge to the old country, that sense of connection, unbreakable. What no one could predict was the draw of the great wilderness, how many would begin to turn the other way, to look west. There had never been an opportunity like this for so many people, a vast rich continent. Even the Indian conflicts have grown quiet, he thought, the people learning to accept each other, lines of trade and communication opening. The colonies are growing in the only direction they can grow, inland. And now many people look at the sea not as a bridge, but as a barrier. The old country is a memory, and the children will never even know the bond, will have no loyalty to the old ways. The English must fear that, losing the loyalty, the allegiance. His mind focused sharply. Yes, fear. That's the word. There has been too much change. Even the trade laws were never really enforced. Right there, off this coast, goods were smuggled in all the time, still are. The law says we must import only English goods, and yet ships sail into these ports from all over the world, right past the offices of the customs officials. For more than a hundred years, we've been allowed to grow strong, prosperous, with few restrictions, few harsh laws. We've been allowed to elect our own assemblies, raise our own revenue. We have our own identity. So now in England there is fear. We're too strong, too prosperous, too . . . independent. And so, suddenly, they expect to dust off the old laws and pull us back to the way the empire was in 1680.

How many, English and colonists both, speak long and loud for a return to the old ways, as though nothing should change? But in all of God's creation change is the only certainty. He looked out over the green field again. It's all around us, every season, every blade of grass, every plant, every part of the earth. Mountains crumble, land is washed away by the rivers, forests and the animals in them grow and die. He could see the piles of rock lining the edge of each field, rock cleared from the soil to allow passage of the plow blade. We change the earth ourselves, turn these rocky fields into farmland, cut the trees to make more fields. It is the arrogance of men, of those who claim to have power, kings or lawmakers, who claim to hold things constant. Keep all things as they are or as they should be depending on the whim or policies of one man. God must find that . . . terribly amusing.

He had stayed away from most of the loud talk, but he had

heard enough from his friends to know what was going on in the town meetings. It had been the tax issue that had suddenly focused his attention. We have built this country, the farms, the businesses, changed this land from wilderness to bounty, and all the while England ignored us. Then suddenly some government minister wakes up and sees us as some great bountiful milk cow, just waiting to give buckets of money to their treasury. But I have never heard a Tory here ask the question, What of the consequences? What happens if a man cannot pay? What if any one of the absurd list of taxes puts a man into serious financial stress? He could lose that farm or that business. What does that do to our prosperity, to our spirit? And the suffering would spread. What would the English businessman feel if suddenly we stop importing British goods because we can't afford to pay for them? We are England's largest marketplace.

He felt the joy of the day's walk slipping away, was angry at himself for allowing the politics to interfere. He looked again toward the houses, tried to see if the children were outside, but it was quiet now.

He began to walk again, moved down the hill beside the rows of corn. You are not in Boston. This should be a time of relaxation. Am I unreasonable to have my own fear? You know too much of what man is capable of inflicting on himself. It is a strange aspect of being a lawyer. You see the darkest side of humanity, you become a pessimist. Captain Preston's men fire on citizens, and instead of grief or sorrow for this horrible affair, our first instinct is vengeance. An eye for an eye. Sam understands that—it's his most effective tool. But what happens when *both* sides seek vengeance? Reason is trampled. There can only be more violence. Pulling the troops out of Boston was good. For now. But the attitudes have not changed. England still sees us as something to be exploited. The Stamp Act didn't work, the Townshend Acts didn't work. So surely they will try to find another way to exploit us, to hold us tightly in their control. And we will keep fighting it. Every injustice will be met with protest, and the louder the protest, the angrier the response. An eye for an eye.

He thought of the sermon he had heard, the preacher calling for God to intervene, to set all things right. No, that is not what God does. God has given us the power to act, to change our own lives. He does not judge us on how we think, how pure we keep our thoughts. We are judged on what we *do*. If we believe that we are right, we must fight for that belief. If we lose the fight, we cannot be condemned for the failure. But if we do not fight, if we simply endure what we believe to be wrong, no piety, no sermons, no prayers will save us.

He was close to the houses now, and he saw Abigail coming out of the larger house, holding the baby in her arms. She waited for him as he crossed the last small field, thick with dense green hay. As he moved into the small open yard, he could see the tiny hands emerging from the blanket in her arms, touching her face.

"Was it a pleasant walk?"

He wanted to tell her all he had been thinking, knew she would have something helpful to say, some clarity to add. He stared at her for a long moment, then reached out, one thick finger touching the baby's hand, the tiny fingers wrapping around his, and he said, "Yes. Pleasant indeed. We'll talk about it later."

She was still looking at him, and he could see it in her eyes, the quiet understanding, so much happening around them, around all of them. He moved toward the house, Abigail close beside him, and for a short while, Boston was very far away.

BOSTON, OCTOBER 1770

THE WITNESSES HAD FLOWED THROUGH THE PROCEEDINGS IN A steady parade, nearly four dozen in all. The prosecution had been led by Robert Treat Paine, an earnest young lawyer who did not hide his association with the radicals, those strong voices behind the protests and outcries. Like Sam Adams, Paine had become public about his involvement in the Sons of Liberty. What had begun as a secret society had become much more bold, and now no one shied away from the label, from their association with the group. But Paine carried far more than a zeal for vengeance to the courtroom. He was an eloquent and proficient speaker, and for two days had performed his duty before the jury with prim efficiency. His case had been simple. His stream of witnesses sought to prove without any doubt or confusion that it had been Captain Thomas Preston who ordered the soldiers to fire into the crowd of civilians.

Adams himself had handled much of the cross-examination of the witnesses, and for the most part attacking the prosecution's case had not been much of a challenge. Paine's witnesses had been largely contradictory, with confused memories, uncertain recollections. But there had been a few damning witnesses, men who were completely certain in their identification of Preston as the man who spoke that one fateful word, the word that could send him to the gallows: the order to fire.

When Paine rested the prosecution's case, Adams had presented his own chain of witnesses. But now the testimony was much less confused, men adamant that Preston himself had never used the word. Adams had watched the jury carefully, knew that his case rested on that most important point: uncertainty. If there was even the slightest doubt that Preston did not give the order, he must be acquitted.

THE TESTIMONY OF THE WITNESSES WAS NEARLY COMPLETE, AND the court had adjourned for the noon meal. Adams stayed in the courtroom, studied his papers, refreshed himself on the words he had come to rely on, the wisdom, the rhetoric of so many great legal minds. He crumbled a piece of biscuit in his hand, focused on the papers, put his fingers to his mouth, but there was nothing left of the biscuit, the crumbs falling to the table. He swept the crumbs aside, still staring at the paper, and now Josiah Quincy was beside him, said quietly, "Here. Try this one."

Adams blinked, looked up from the paper, saw Quincy holding another biscuit, intact. He shook his head.

"No, thank you. I have one. Just finished it." He looked at the paper again, the names on the witness list, did not see Quincy leaning down behind him, looking at the mountain of crumbs under his chair.

"Whatever you say, John."

Quincy looked over the paper in Adams' hand, said, "John, I ask you again. Would you reconsider your objection?"

Adams did not look up.

"No."

Quincy sat back, frustrated.

"John, it can only help our case. If we establish that the citizens were in fact an organized mob, driven by the radicals . . . if we can establish in the jury's mind that pushing the troops out of Boston was a concerted and organized plan, it lends strength to the potential *threat* of the mob, a much more potent threat to Captain Preston than just a chaotic group of citizens."

Adams put the paper down, glanced over at Preston, who sat in a small partitioned area off to one side. He turned, said to Quincy, "Do you believe Thomas Preston ordered his troops to fire?"

"Certainly not."

"Then what else matters? If our testimony is convincing to the jury, it is not necessary to bring some political message into this proceeding."

"What can it hurt, John? You know as well as I do that the sentiment in Boston against the army was a threat to the peace. You know very well that the Sons of Liberty were looking for any excuse, any spark, to set off a violent incident. It is the best weapon the town had for pressuring Governor Hutchinson to remove the troops."

Adams glanced behind him now, saw Preston's friend Forrest leaning over the rail, listening carefully. Adams began to feel annoyed.

"Josiah, the prosecution has not proven its case. Nearly every witness has contradicted the one before him, and hardly anyone has been able to say that he heard Preston issue the order. If we establish that the captain commanded soldiers who were victimized by an organized mob and fought back in self-defense, we have to first agree that he ordered his men to fire. We would have to justify the very thing that we are trying to disprove."

"But John, it could strengthen our case. The atmosphere of this town—"

"Yes, consider the atmosphere. Thus far, the jury has seemed sympathetic to our witnesses. If you introduce the notion that mob rule is so threatening, you could suddenly plant the idea in their minds that any jury who acquits Captain Preston could be subject to the same threats. I cannot accept that we should pretend there is no rule of law here. Captain Preston is not guilty. That is our only focus."

He was angry now, pointed to the paper on the table.

"See here? Our next witness is Richard Palmes. If I cannot make our case with his testimony, if you are convinced that by introducing the truthful testimony of eyewitnesses, we have not established the innocence of our client . . ." He turned, looked at Forrest. "If you, sir, do not feel that I have performed with suitable competence in making the case for your friend, then I will step aside. Mr. Quincy, if the arguments of law are not acceptable to you, if mere truth is not satisfactory, you may try this case yourself."

Adams saw Forrest look at Quincy, wide-eyed, and Quincy put a hand on Adams' arm.

"Please, John. I will defer to your . . . strategy."

"It is not strategy, Josiah."

He saw faces watching him, realized his voice had carried. There was a stillness in the large room, and he saw Paine looking at him, the man's irritating smugness reflected in a slight smile. Adams glanced over toward Preston, saw the man staring at him with pale-faced panic. Adams stood, walked over to the prisoner's box.

"Captain, do not be concerned."

Preston tried to whisper, his voice cracking slightly. "Concern? Is there some problem of which I am not aware? Please, Mr. Adams . . ."

Adams put a hand out, touched Preston's shoulder.

"Captain, it's all right. I assure you. The testimony is in our favor."

"Mr. Adams, that one man . . . Mr. Calef . . . he said he was positive it was me. He identified me, said he saw me give the order. He was lying!"

Adams gripped Preston's arm tightly, said in a quiet hiss, "Calm, Captain. *Calm.* You must have confidence in your own innocence. You must have confidence in the testimony of our witnesses. One man's testimony will not convict you. Not if I can help it."

"But he was so bloody certain."

"Captain, a great many more are not certain at all. You must allow me to do my job. Do not show the jury you are afraid. The truth is on your side."

Preston sat back in the chair, nodded slowly.

"God help us, Mr. Adams."

Adams backed away.

"We don't need God, Captain. We need one more witness."

"MR. PALMES, WHAT IS YOUR POSITION IN THIS COMMUNITY, SIR?"

"I am a merchant, sir."

"Would you describe yourself as a Tory?"

There was a murmur in the courtroom, and Adams saw the defiant look on Palmes' face, waited for the man's answer.

"Sir, I would as soon be labeled a skirt-wearing nursemaid."

There was laughter now, and Adams waited patiently, heard one of the judges now, a sharp shout.

"Enough of that! There will be order!"

The room grew quiet, and Adams continued.

"Mr. Palmes, do you consider yourself a loyal subject of King George the Third?"

"Most definitely, sir."

"Then how can you claim such distaste for being a Tory?"

"Sir, Tories are blind followers of whatever England would have us do." Palmes seemed nervous now, glanced at the judges.

"It's all right, Mr. Palmes. No one is accusing you of any disloyalty. I am trying to point out to this court that you have no prejudice, no reason whatever to make statements here that would tend to free Captain Preston of the charges against him. You are not an agent for His Majesty, you have no agenda in seeing Captain Preston go free."

There was silence now, and Adams stood back. Now it will

come, he thought. If he has the courage to say it, to use the words, it will silence any objection. Palmes seemed to grow angry, defiant again, and Adams thought, Yes, good. Come on. Say it.

Palmes leaned forward. "Mr. Adams, I do not care a bit whether Captain Preston goes free or not. I have friends in this town—in this room, in fact, sir—who know my political leanings. I am no errand boy for anyone in England. I consider myself, sir . . ." He glanced at the judges again, then out to the gallery of onlookers, who were hanging on his words. He seemed to draw strength from the faces of his friends.

"I consider myself, sir, a . . . Son of Liberty."

There was a sudden whoop from the crowd, applause, and the judges again quieted the crowd. Adams felt a warm glow in his chest. Thank you, yes, indeed, thank you, sir.

"So, Mr. Palmes, if Captain Preston is found guilty by this court, you have some friends who would rejoice at that, certainly."

"I expect they would, yes, sir."

Adams felt a rush of strength, raised his voice, said slowly, each word echoing through the large room, "Then tell us, Mr. Palmes. What happened . . . what did you see on the night of March fifth?"

Palmes took a deep breath, glanced at Preston, then spoke. "I came into King Street, moved through the crowd of people in front of the Custom House. I saw Mr. Theodore Bliss, speaking to Captain Preston. Mr. Bliss asked Captain Preston, 'Why don't you fire?' And he said it again, with more . . . oath. He said, 'God damn you, why don't you fire?' "

Adams nodded slowly.

"Please continue, sir."

"I was close to Captain Preston. I wanted to speak to the crowd, to say something to calm the people. I looked at Captain Preston and saw his face, staring at them. He seemed afraid. I went to stand directly in front of him, thought maybe I could protect him from the sticks and such."

"Why? Why would you protect a soldier?"

"I said he was afraid. They were all afraid. The crowd was loud, shouting, throwing all manner of things."

"Go on, sir."

"Captain Preston looked straight at me, and I put my hand on his shoulder, and then someone shouted, *'Fire.'*"

There were sounds again from the spectators, and Adams did not hesitate.

"How close were you to him, Mr. Palmes?"

"I already said, sir. I had my hand on his shoulder."

"Do you have evidence of that, sir?"

Palmes raised his arm.

"I was wearing this coat, sir. If you see here . . . there is a burn mark. Black powder. It came from the musket of one of the soldiers. Captain Preston and I were standing right in front of them."

Adams stepped to one side, waited as Palmes held the scorched coat sleeve up for the court to see.

"Mr. Palmes, were you looking at Captain Preston, at his face?"

"Yes, sir."

"Directly at his face?"

"Sir, there was so much commotion, so much noise, you couldn't hear a man's voice. I was looking in fact, sir, at his mouth, in case he said something."

"Are you absolutely certain that Captain Preston did not say the word *fire*?"

"God may strike me dead, sir. He never said the word *fire*."

The crowd erupted, some cheering, some shouting angrily. The judges were trying to control the spectators, and Adams looked at the jury now, saw all twelve faces staring hard at Palmes, absorbing the moment, the man's words. He glanced at Paine, saw gloom, the man shuffling papers, avoiding the faces of the jury. As Paine lifted his head, Adams caught his eye, made a slight nod. All right, sir. Cross-examine him if you please. But you know it as well as I do, as well as everyone here. This trial is already over.

THE JURY REACHED A VERDICT IN THREE HOURS, AND CAPTAIN Preston walked from the courtroom a free man. Adams knew that Preston would not stay long in the town; there would still be a threat from the mob, someone whose anger would erase what any court might decide. Quietly, without any fanfare, or even notice from the town, Preston's personal effects were loaded on board a ship, and he made ready to cross the Atlantic.

"COME IN, CAPTAIN. I HAD THOUGHT YOU MIGHT HAVE SAILED already."

Preston slipped inside the office door, appeared self-conscious, and Adams said, "Relax, Captain. No mobs here today."

It was a feeble joke, but Preston seemed not to have heard, looked at him anxiously, unsmiling.

"I thought I should at least say good-bye, Mr. Adams. I only have a few minutes."

Adams pointed toward the chair.

"Have a seat, Captain. Enjoy your last few moments on hard ground. When do you expect to reach England?"

It was an attempt at pleasant conversation, and Adams could see that Preston would not participate, was glancing absently around the office.

"What's on your mind, Captain?"

Preston stared away, would not look at him.

"I felt it was my duty to come here. I am anxious to leave this place. I don't imagine I will ever return to these shores."

"No, I don't imagine you will."

Preston looked at him now, and Adams saw dark anger, a glint in the man's eye.

"It's bloody dangerous for me to even be seen on the streets here. I'm losing my command. The Twenty-ninth is already gone. None of the men I served with would speak to me before they left."

"Why not?"

"Because I can't even defend my own men. Your precious court . . . oh, bloody hell."

Yes, young man, Adams thought, this is the price.

"They wanted to try you with your men. One trial for all of you. Do you know what would have happened?"

"We've been through all that, Mr. Adams. If I didn't order them to fire, then they fired on their own account. If I'm innocent, they're guilty. If they're innocent, it had to be because the responsibility was mine. Legal gibberish, Mr. Adams. My men are no more guilty of killing that rabble than I am."

"I'll do what I can."

"Is that right? You planning on defending them, too, are you?"

"I thought you knew. Of course. Mr. Quincy and I will handle their case."

Preston's anger seemed to slip away.

"How do you think it'll go for them?"

Adams looked down at his hands.

"We'll do our best, Captain. The law still relies on truth, on proof of guilt. They cannot be convicted of murder if the court cannot prove to a jury that there was murder committed."

Preston shook his head.

"Murder. There was no murder, Mr. Adams. It was self-defense."

"We'll certainly explore that, yes."

Preston sat quietly for a moment.

"I didn't come here hating anyone, Mr. Adams. Didn't understand how much they'd hate us. Did we deserve that?"

Adams considered the question. It wasn't the soldiers, the men, faces and names. You were just a tool, a piece on a chessboard. And you may never understand that.

"Captain, when soldiers are sent to maintain order, it's because someone has decided that order has broken down. In Boston, there is a struggle for power. You were sent here to end that struggle. But the struggle is not over guns and strength and who has the most men. Governor Hutchinson represents the authority of England, and some would say the Sons of Liberty represent the voice of the people. It's about freedom and self-government, all the things this colony was guaranteed by its own charter."

Preston was staring at him with no expression. He doesn't understand, Adams concluded. And it's not his fault. It's not his job to understand.

Preston sat for a moment longer, then seemed to snap awake.

"What time . . . excuse me, Mr. Adams, but I'd best be going. The ship's sailing pretty quick. I hope . . . you'll do what you say. Take good care of my men."

Preston was on his feet now, and Adams leaned across the desk, held out a hand. Preston hesitated, looked at it for a brief moment, took the hand, a quick shake, said nothing, then quickly left.

Adams watched the door close.

"A thank-you would have been nice."

He sat down, leaned back in the soft leather of the chair. No, not the time for thank-yous. It's the true sign of an innocent man. Leave it to the guilty to gush and grovel their gratitude, bursting with relief that the good lawyer saved them from their punishment. All we did was ensure the truth was heard and that one man received justice. I shouldn't expect gratitude for that. I should be condemned if I fail.

DECEMBER 1770

THE TRIAL OF THE EIGHT SOLDIERS LASTED INTO DECEMBER. WITH Preston already on his way to England, the only testimony would come from many of the same witnesses, with many of the same flaws and confusion. Of the eight soldiers charged, six were acquitted, the eyewitness accounts failing to prove that any one of them had actually killed a citizen. Two others were convicted of manslaughter, and when the verdicts were read, the two men immediately pleaded the benefit of clergy, an arcane custom that removed them from the jurisdiction of civil punishment. The men instead would receive a branding on one hand, a symbol of guilt they would carry the rest of their lives.

As the trials ended, the voices of the mob had turned quickly toward Adams and Josiah Quincy, but it was not dangerous; the remarks were subdued, more of politics than violence, questioning loyalty rather than making threats against the home. Adams had heard the sharp words in the street, had come to expect it anytime he left his office. But it was the newspapers, the anonymous articles that attacked the acquittals, that sought to keep the public passion high with strange and inaccurate accounts of the trials. Adams read the articles with wonder, for their intent was obvious and clumsy. But as the articles continued, he could not help notice that his name was rarely mentioned, and finally he was ignored altogether. It was not personal after all.

Adams was still in Boston, would miss the first snow in Braintree, had begun to wait each day for the delivery of the packages and letters from the roads to the south. Abigail wrote to him nearly every day, newsy letters, the business of the farm, the children, always a self-conscious note about the growth of the baby.

He stood in the doorway of the small town house, held her letter, read it over again. She had never been very good at spelling, the disadvantage of a limited education, something of a sore point with her now. It was simply the custom that the girls might receive some formal tutoring in numbers, perhaps basic mathematics, but rarely letters, rarely the skills in reading or science. She had taken that upon herself, particularly reading, the ancient classics, novels, and histories. Her enthusiasm for learning was passionate, and she sought out other women who felt as she did, would correspond in long and thoughtful letters with new friends who believed with her that a woman could indeed find a place in a man's world. He would never argue with her, enjoyed her new discoveries, worked hard at finding unfamiliar books, opening new roads for her. Her letters were frequently filled with a wondrous exploration of some new philosophy, some historical event explored for the first time.

He glanced again at the letter in his hand, saw the first words, *Dearest friend*. She referred to herself as Portia, Shakespeare's cultured and educated woman from *The Merchant of Venice*. He smiled now, as it was an old joke between them: *My paper is very cheep, shall you lite your pipe with them.*

He shook his head at the amazing spelling. No, I shall never discard this. He thought of the reply, already forming in his mind. *No, I shall hold this paper as dear as the heart of my Portia.*

The words drifted away, would come back later that night, and he stood watching the fat snowflakes, the street now a blanket of solid white, deep enough so that even the horses would have a struggle. He thought of the ride home, knew the snow would stretch it out, a test of his patience. And I will return to Boston, probably too soon to suit my family. There can be none of the luxury of vacation, not yet. I am a long way from behaving like the old established lawyers, with their great staffs of workers, the hum of the office like so many bees. But if there are many more autumns like this one, that wonderful opportunity to do something in the courtroom that truly *matters* . . .

He was feeling very good, truly proud of the work he had done for Preston, the other soldiers. He knew his own reputation was growing in Boston, despite the controversy. He wondered about London, if anyone there had heard the details of the trial. Are they even aware of what we did, of just what those trials demonstrated? Do the British have any comprehension of how we conduct ourselves, that we are fully capable of exercising a system of law and justice every bit as civilized as their own?

He recalled the words he had used in the trial of the eight soldiers, his closing argument. He had practiced and perfected his speech, would probably never use the phrases again, but they stayed hard inside of him, drifting through his memory: *Facts are stubborn things. The law, no passion can disturb. It is void of desire and fear, lust and anger. It is deaf, inexorable, inflexible.* . . .

6. FRANKLIN

LONDON, JANUARY 1771

FRANKLIN HAD BEEN ENJOYING HIS MORNING TEA, BUT MRS. Stevenson had brought him a letter, and now the pleasant ritual was spoiled. The news had come from an unexpected place, from the hand of a young mother, a sadness presented with the matter-of-factness of someone who doesn't truly understand the grief felt by someone else, even her own child.

It had begun with an unusually strange gesture from Deborah, a gift uniquely American. Nestled into the hold of a great ship, packed tightly between bags and boxes, barrels and crates, a small cage that held one gray squirrel had survived the rough seas and haphazard care to be delivered to the pleasure of a little girl whose family was close friends with Mrs. Stevenson. The girl had named the squirrel Skugg, but despite Skugg's resiliency for travel, it could not compete with the ambitions of another pet, a dog, whose instincts were the hunt. The result was predictable. It was a deadly competition the squirrel could not survive.

Franklin could imagine the little girl in his mind, had seen the smiles, the joy in the young beauty. He had never quite understood why a squirrel would bring such squeals of delight, had thought the gift an odd one. But he had long ago stopped questioning Deborah's wisdom about what pleases the female. He glanced at the letter, the sorrow from the girl's mother more an expression of guilt, the regret that she had not taken more precautions to keep the dog away from the squirrel. He shook his head. So much attention to such an annoying little animal. But there is no explaining the affections of a young girl, especially when fur and whiskers are parts of the equation. Now they seek some comfort, some words of forgiveness, as though somehow, by the squirrel's death, they have wronged *me*. He thought a moment, reached for a pen, slid a piece of paper close. He raised the pen, searched for an epitaph, some lasting tribute, some words to grace a tiny tombstone. The small fellow shall leave a legacy, I suppose. He wrote:

> *Here Skugg*
> *Lies snug*
> *As a bug*
> *In a rug*

He frowned, thought of the little girl. No, that's a bit too coarse. I should pay a proper tribute. The creature was, after all, much more well traveled than most of its kind.

His attention was broken by the sound of a carriage. He shifted to his perch at the window, knew his friend Strahan would take his time, a leisurely stroll to the entrance of the house. It was done with slow purpose, and Franklin shivered slightly in the sharp cold air, peered out, tried to see Strahan's face. He waited for the self-conscious glance upward to the window, and Strahan obliged him, a quick furtive look, the quiet laugh. His friend was out of sight now, below him, at the front door, and Franklin listened for the knock. He is taking his time, as he always does. Well, go ahead, Strahan, she knows you're coming. He heard the squeal of the hinges, the faint voice of Mrs. Stevenson. He waited for the door to close, the squeal again, the creaky hinge he would not repair, too useful, a signal to alert him when someone visited the house.

He scrambled to work now, his clothes laid out in perfect sequence, pulled and tightened and tied, heard the footsteps on the stairs, Mrs. Stevenson's voice again, anxious, the ritual played out perfectly. He imagined their faces, her nervousness, concern that Mr. Strahan might arrive too soon, catch the eminent doctor in the embarrassment of his state of undress. He knew Strahan was well aware, and he could hear the small talk between them, a flow of words that meant nothing, passing the time, the last bit of delay before Franklin could put them suddenly at ease by appearing fully dressed. He tugged at the laces on his shoes, heard the silence outside the door, knew they had arrived, their self-consciousness complete. He moved quickly to the door, listening, heard one short mumble, one throat clearing, and now he stepped back, pulling the door open.

"Ah, Will, a pleasant surprise! Do come in!"

He watched both their faces, saw the visible relief, the quick scan of his clothing, the long exhale of breath. He was fully satisfied now, the ritual complete, saw Mrs. Stevenson moving away down the stairs, shaking her head, her mortification put away once more.

Strahan whisked past him into the room, went to the window.

"Really, Ben, do you mind if I close this? There's a bit of a nip in the breeze, even for you."

"If you must, Will. I do admit, these old bones are not standing up to the cold the way they used to."

Strahan pulled the window shut, shook his head slightly.

"Ben, you should exercise some care. If you won't listen to me, then be influenced by common sense. You just passed sixty-five years, my friend, and I'm right there with you. Old bones indeed. And even this rickety old typesetter has wisdom enough not to expose himself to the danger of the cold."

"You're as rickety as you choose to be, Will." They had been through this before; he knew that Strahan didn't agree with his theories about the benefit of fresh air, hot or cold.

Strahan said, "I suppose I choose to be as rickety as befits a man of my years. You, however . . . I imagine you will be swimming in the English Channel when the rest of us are too old to float."

Franklin rubbed the roundness of his stomach.

"I'll be floating awhile yet. And a swim in the Channel is a fine idea. But there's too much ice today. I'll wait for the thaw."

Strahan was smiling now, sat down slowly. He reached in his pocket, pulled out a small packet of letters, held them out.

"For you. I stopped by the wharf on the way over. There's a frigate just in. I assumed there might be mail for you."

Franklin looked at the letters, one with the flowery handwriting of his daughter, the other with the official seal of the governor of New Jersey.

"My children are quite efficient at fulfilling their father's expectations." He put Sally's letter on the small table, ran his finger over the wax seal on the letter from his son. "At least when it comes to letter writing."

Strahan sat back, held up his hand.

"It's long forgotten, Ben. Not even a hint of heartbreak. My son is doing quite well, you know. Made him a full partner. Hasn't married yet. I keep him too busy. I understand Sally has found a husband that she finds more suitable."

"Suitable to her."

It was a familiar joke, but Franklin still fingered the letter from his son, thinking, It bothers Will more than he admits. I couldn't make it happen, couldn't force Sally to marry the boy. Deborah didn't want it to happen at all, knew that Sally might have moved to England. And Deborah had more influence on Sally than either of them would admit. If I had been there, perhaps it would have been different.

Strahan was watching him, and Franklin tried to think past it, bring back the humor. He put William's letter on top of his daughter's. I'll read them both later. I already know what Sally's letter will say. There will be all sorts of flattery about her husband, how wonderful he is, how much I will come to love him, how we will be lifelong friends.

"Forget it, Ben. We've moved past all that."

"Oh, yes, I know. Of course we have. I wasn't thinking about that."

Strahan said nothing.

"I thought it was a father's prerogative to have some influence about these things," Franklin went on, to fill the silence. "I don't, you know. They've made it pretty clear."

"Give Sally a chance, Ben. She has enough of you in her. Trust her instincts. I'm sure her husband is a great deal more nervous about meeting *you*."

"I'm hardly nervous. I had just hoped she would allow . . . no, that's not right. I had hoped *Deborah* would allow me to play a greater role." He looked at the table again. "What do you suppose my son has to say?"

"Official business from the royal governor of New Jersey, I suppose."

Franklin picked up the letter.

"I should be pleased. *He* asks my advice. Nearly every time he writes me, he asks if I know the proper course for him to follow. He asks me to finish his letters for him. He has to send all sorts of reports to Lord Hillsborough, but he wants me to edit them."

"Does Lord Hillsborough know that?"

"Certainly not. Wouldn't help William's reputation at the ministry."

Strahan laughed, said, "Your son respects you, Ben."

"He's a royal governor. He's an agent for the king. My advice would be considered highly suspect in those circles."

"Let's just say . . . you have their attention," Strahan responded, more serious now.

Franklin knew that his friend was close to many in the king's circle of intimates, especially Samuel Johnson.

"Seems you have their attention, too, Will, even more than usual. I've heard rumors that your name is the only one on the list to become the king's official printer."

Strahan seemed surprised.

"Didn't know it was common knowledge. I have a few friends in important places. They've been recommending me to the king for some time now. Seems he's heard them."

"It was only a matter of time. Someone in the palace probably made note of how many books you've been providing *me*. You said I had their attention. This way, the king can keep track of what you're printing."

It was a joke, but Strahan's expression didn't lighten. Franklin felt the sudden strain, their relationship infected with this sudden formality whenever politics came up. He knew better than to bring up the subject of the difficulties in the colonies. He kept his work as private as polite conversation would allow, but Strahan had been his friend for thirty years, the two men corresponding through letters and business dealings long before they ever actually met. All the talk of wedding their children had been humorous at first, Sally barely eight years old when it began. But as the children grew, so did the wishful thinking of their fathers, and though there had never truly been a courtship, both men had seemed to take the talk more seriously than anyone else in their families. It was a strong symbol of the depth of their friendship, but now, watching Strahan turn suddenly uncomfortable, a slight frown, Franklin knew something was changing between them. But he would not give in to the mood, and tried a wide smile.

"I've had the attention of those fellows for some time. Talk gets back to me. They're concerned that their deputy postmaster for the colonies is in league with dangerous elements."

"Aren't you?"

Strahan let a smile cross his face, and Franklin was relieved, the humor returning. They had played this game before, and Franklin said, "I would tell you first, Will. You know that. They send me all those pamphlets, but I don't read them. And Lord knows you can't trust the newspapers. I'm just a simple servant doing my job."

Strahan reached into his pocket. "Oh, that reminds me. Forgive me, simple servant, there's one more letter."

Franklin saw another seal, different, no sign of the crown in the wax. He glanced at Strahan.

"Forgive you, indeed. You saving this one, what, for effect? Dramatic impact? I suppose you expect me to open it. Curiosity getting the better of you?"

Strahan could not hide the seriousness in his voice.

"Came from a different ship. A packet, just in from Boston. You probably *should* open that one."

Franklin turned the letter over in his hand, felt a small stab of nervousness. Strahan's attention was now hard and focused. Well, all right, then. How much harm can this do?

He slid his finger under the seal, broke the wax, unfolded the letter slowly. The nervousness was gone, replaced by surprise. He looked at Strahan, who was leaning forward, nearly off the chair.

"Anything interesting?"

"You might say that. It seems . . . the People's Assembly of the colony of Massachusetts has decided that I should represent them. They have appointed me as their agent."

THE ROADS WERE MUDDY, AND HE FELT SYMPATHY FOR THE MAN driving the horses, knew he would be filthy, miserable, the hooves kicking up an awful mess the driver could not ignore. The carriage slipped from side to side, lurched in a sudden jerk, one wheel finding a deep pothole. He tried to keep his focus away from the terrible road, stared at the crystal blue of the

January sky, unusual, the thick gray clouds swept away, a blessed break in the dismal London winter. The carriage jerked again, bounced him hard on the leather seat, and he heard the voice of the driver, a quick apology.

They had left the hardened streets of the city behind, rolled into farm country, larger estates, the homes of English high society. They passed through a patch of dense woods, skeletons of trees, a small brook running under the narrow roadway. The carriage climbed out of the thicket and the land flattened out, rows of neatly trimmed trees, a garden, the country opening up into a beautifully groomed estate. The driver turned the carriage into a narrow driveway lined tightly with thick bushes. There was very little beauty here, mostly dense clusters of brown, and Franklin saw a wide stretch of open ground beyond, bleak gardens, bare earth swept clean of last year's stems. There was no sign that there had ever been death and decay here, only fresh black dirt, waiting patiently for the warmth of the spring to return. The carriage ride was smoother now, the drive tended to by men with rakes and shovels. He adjusted himself on the seat, tried to undo the kinks put into his back by the ride. The carriage pulled up in front of the grand mansion, and he studied the architecture. Impressive, the tall columns, long narrow windows, black against the clean white marble. The driver was down now, opened the door, and Franklin stepped out, avoided the mud dripping off the side of the carriage. There was a quick flurry of activity from one end of the house, and a man appeared, adjusting his coat, hurrying forward.

"G'day, sir. Allow me."

The man reached for the bridle of the horse.

"Would you be staying long, eh, sir? I can stable the horse for you."

Franklin was still looking at the grandeur of the house.

"Not exactly sure. Give me just a moment."

He moved to the front entrance, wide twin doors framed by ornately carved wood. The door suddenly opened, and he saw a tall thin man staring past him with cold black eyes, bored annoyance.

"Yes, what is it?"

The voice faded slowly, and Franklin studied the man's face, deathly pale, etched with a permanent frown. The butler, I suppose. And very inconvenienced by my presence.

"Hello. This is an official call. Dr. Benjamin Franklin to see Lord Hillsborough."

The man sniffed, the door already closing, the man's voice trailing away as he said, "Lord Hillsborough is not at home."

The door shut with a heavy *thunk,* and Franklin stared into the dark wood. How wonderfully polite. He waited for a moment, expecting the door to open again, began to feel self-conscious. The longer I stay here, the sillier I will appear. He looked around, saw his driver and the groomsman watching him, hiding their smiles. How obnoxious of me to assume that anyone in this fine old home would appreciate a visit from a colonist.

He stepped carefully across the soft ground, moved to the carriage, the driver quickly in front of him, pulling the door open. The groomsman was close now, said cheerfully, "Well, now. Off you go. Drive him slow. The road's bloody awful. Could lose a leg."

Franklin climbed into the carriage.

"Thank you. I'll be fine." He saw a strange expression on the man's face, suddenly realized the man's concern was for the horse. Well, of course. In this neighborhood, even a mare has more stature than an American.

The driver climbed up on the carriage, waited, and Franklin said, "Let's go, shall we?"

The whip cracked, and the carriage lurched forward, and suddenly there was a shout, the groomsman running alongside. The carriage stopped, and Franklin looked back to the house, saw the butler standing in the door of the house, displaying an expression of painful impatience. The groomsman opened the carriage door, and Franklin leaned out, heard the butler announce, "His lordship will see you now."

Franklin looked at the groomsman.

"Apparently I don't understand the rules. Seems we weren't supposed to actually *leave*."

The man made a bow, smiled. He had seen it all before.

* * *

FRANKLIN MOVED SLOWLY INTO THE LARGE ROOM WITH DARK walls and high shelves. He was surprised to see several men, all dressed in the formal fluff and finery of political office. The activity ceased as the men became aware of his presence, slowly moving to greet him. He scanned the room quickly, always afraid of committing the faux pas of failing to acknowledge first the man with the highest title. He did not see Hillsborough, and one man was quickly in front of him, extending a hand.

"Why, Dr. Franklin, an unexpected pleasure!"

The man waited for Franklin to respond, and he searched the man's face, familiar, fought for the name.

"Ah, yes, Governor Bernard." There was a silence; Bernard's smile faded, and he seemed to hesitate.

"It's . . . no longer *governor*, sir. I'm sure you know that I have returned to England permanently. The king has graciously granted me a baronetcy. I won't be returning to Massachusetts."

The entire account flowed into Franklin's mind now, Bernard's amazing ability to alienate the people he was sent to govern, his replacement by Thomas Hutchinson. Bernard's recall was as much a rescue from the wrath of the Sons of Liberty as it was anything to do with the granting of some obscure title. Franklin forced his smile. Faux pas, indeed.

"Certainly, yes, I was aware. May I extend my congratulations on your good fortune . . . and, um, welcome you home."

Bernard seemed to slide away slowly, and Franklin was met by other hands, smiles, and cordiality, could glimpse Bernard pouring something from a crystal decanter. He saw glasses scattered around the room, some half full. Well, it's not all business. I should feel honored to be included.

He saw the butler again, the servant carrying a flat velvet pillow that cradled a small three-cornered hat, gold trim on dark blue silk. The voices in the room grew quiet, and Franklin looked toward the open door, saw Hillsborough now, a short, compact man, a tight round face clamped into a perpetual scowl. The butler stood to one side, and Hillsborough reached for the hat, set it gently on his powdered wig, adjusted it slightly, examined himself carefully in a small hand mirror.

"Very well, that will do. Have the carriage brought around."

The butler was quickly gone, and Franklin waited in the silence, glanced at the men around him. The decanter was being passed, and Franklin heard whispers, louder now, low conversation. They're not afraid of him, Franklin realized. It's all just politeness. Hillsborough still groomed himself in the mirror, and Franklin stepped forward gingerly. He may have no idea I'm here. Franklin remembered the smile on his own face, strengthened it, and now Hillsborough set the mirror aside, satisfied, and looked directly at Franklin.

"I'm on my way to court, Mr. Franklin. However, I understand you are a man who gets down to business, as they say. So when they told me you were at the door, I decided to see you immediately."

Franklin bent slightly.

"I thank your lordship. My business is brief. With all respect, sir, I wish to present your lordship my appointment, however unworthy I may be, by the Assembly of Massachusetts to be their agent here. I am pleased to be of service."

"Mr. Franklin, I must correct you. You are not agent."

The sounds in the large room had died away, and Franklin was confused.

"I don't understand, my lord."

"You are not appointed."

"Forgive me, my lord. I have the appointment in my pocket."

Hillsborough glanced around the room, the tight frown fixed hard on his face.

"You are mistaken. I have a late letter from Governor Hutchinson. He would not give his assent to the bill."

Franklin began to feel a cold pinch in his stomach.

"My lord, there was no bill. It was a vote of the assembly."

Hillsborough took a deep breath, his irritation now growing, a slight rise in his voice.

"There was a bill presented to the governor for the purpose of appointing you, to which the governor refused his assent."

Franklin felt the slow burn of anger. Something is wrong. This is a simple formality. Hutchinson has nothing to do with it.

"I cannot understand this, my lord. I think there must be some mistake."

Hillsborough motioned to one man, said, "Mr. Pownall, Mr. Franklin has the nerve to be skeptical of what I tell him. Do you have Governor Hutchinson's letter, in which he refuses his assent for appointing Mr. Franklin as agent?"

All faces turned to this man, who now stood, glanced at Franklin, said, "Uh, no, my lord. The letter relates to a bill calling for payment of salary to the previous agent. Governor Hutchinson had determined the amount to be excessive, and thus he refused his assent. It's right here, my lord."

Franklin could see redness on Hillsborough's face now, noticed his voice rising a note higher.

"Mr. Pownall, is there nothing in that letter regarding Mr. Franklin's appointment?"

"No, my lord."

Franklin was staring at Hillsborough. Yes, remember every detail of this. Something is going on here for which I will likely pay some price. He reached into his pocket, pulled out the appointment letter.

"My lord, my appointment was delivered by the most recent ship from Boston. Here is the authentic copy of the vote of the house appointing me, in which there is no mention of any act or any submission to Governor Hutchinson. Will your lordship care to examine it?"

Hillsborough took the letter, held it tightly in his hand, did not read it.

"What would you have me do with this, Mr. Franklin?"

"Sir, I am presenting this to your lordship so that you may enter my name with the Board of Trade. I have done this before, upon my other appointments."

Hillsborough seemed to glow dark red, and he held the letter out toward Franklin, said in an angry growl, "It will not be entered in any such place. Not while I have anything to do with such matters. We shall take no notice of any agents who are not appointed or approved by the royal governors."

So that's it, Franklin thought. It's all about who chooses the agent.

"My lord, I cannot conceive why the approval of the governor should be thought necessary for the appointment of an agent for the people. It seems to me that—"

"I will not enter into a dispute with *you*, sir, on this subject!"

Franklin absorbed Hillsborough's anger. Back up, you're on dangerous ground here.

"I beg your lordship's pardon. I do not presume to dispute the issue. I would only say . . ." The words were boiling up now, too many words, too much frustration. He paused for a moment, felt the anticipation in the room around him. "I would only say that it seems to me that every body of men who cannot appear in person and whose business is decided—whose fate is determined—by others should have the right of being represented by an agent. This is established policy for all the colonies. The concurrence of the governor is not only unnecessary, it is interference. The governor is an agent of the king. It is up to the people's assembly alone to choose who should represent their interests."

He stopped, saw Hillsborough shaking his head, the hot anger replaced by a patronizing smirk, waiting for Franklin to complete his speech. Franklin felt his own anger slipping into a muddle of confused thoughts, the words flowing together.

Hillsborough said, "I do not recognize this appointment. This is an offense to the principles set forward through my office. Mr. Franklin, when I came into this position, I found the administration of American affairs to be in great disorder. By my firmness, much of that is mended. And while I have the honor to hold the seals of this office, I shall continue with the same firmness. It is my duty to the king, and to the government of this nation. If they do not approve my conduct, then they may remove me from this office as they please. But I have heard no criticism." His voice began to rise again, the anger returning. "What I hear instead, Mr. Franklin, is that my firmness, my discipline, is a refreshing change of course. The administration of the colonies . . . the abuses that we have allowed to be inflicted on the king's subjects . . . I will not suffer the king's empire to be humiliated and abused by the rabble of Massachusetts." Hillsborough seemed to run out of words, was breathing hard, staring at him with raw heat. Franklin held the man's stare. Enough. This serves no purpose.

"I beg your lordship's pardon for taking up so much of your time. It is, I believe, of no great importance whether the appointment is acknowledged or not. I believe it is clear to everyone that no agent of the people can expect to be of any service to the colonies any longer. I shall therefore give your lordship no further trouble."

FRANKLIN DID NOT FEEL THE JOLTS AS THE HORSE POUNDED ALONG the muddy road. His mind was far beyond the bouncing carriage. He felt a strange calm, replayed his own words, the fiery anger of Lord Hillsborough. He is in charge of administering the affairs of America, of addressing the problems, solving the controversies, supporting and managing the policies of the king in a land where the king is moving farther and farther away. Why would he become so angry at me? It has to be, of course, because I am *here*. I come to him suddenly representing Massachusetts. I'm a symbol. Surely that wasn't lost on Governor Bernard. He's a symbol as well: failure. He lost control, the governor who could not govern. Now I stand before Lord Hillsborough and announce that if he wants to address the people of Massachusetts, he will do it through me. He can withhold his acknowledgment of that if he wants to, but it's not his decision. It's the decision of the people.

He looked out the window of the carriage, saw a dull red sunset, felt the rocking now, the sudden jounce from the bad road. So what will happen? I spoke a bit too plainly, that's for certain. I wonder how long it will take Strahan to hear about that. He'll come to me with that cautiousness, warn me about speaking out of turn. Words travel quickly here. And it is different now, something new. Words just might become dangerous.

He thought of the Stamp Act, an issue he had supported at first, had even used his influence to have a close friend appointed stamp commissioner for Philadelphia. I was too far removed from the mood of the people. I had no idea how the act would be received there. I didn't really understand it myself. They nearly lynched my friend, drove him from his home. Some of those people still don't believe that I changed my position, that I worked so hard to have the act repealed. I made a mistake, and mistakes aren't easily forgiven. Some people in Philadelphia still assume . . . they see me as too much of an Englishman. He sat back, looked out toward the last glow in the sky, laughed. So now the good folks *here* will see me as too much of an American. I was caught off guard by the hostility of the colonies to the Stamp Act. Found myself holding a precarious perch right in the middle of a lot of angry voices. Now it's happening again. But this time I'm not off guard. He thought of Strahan. Will, old friend, you're in the middle as well. I'm on one side, and the whole corrupt blindness of your government is on the other. He looked away from the sunset, stared into the darkness of the carriage, was suddenly uneasy, his stomach turning. He thought of the letter from his son, the careless remarks he had made to Strahan criticizing his son's habits of asking so many questions, seeking advice. To me, it's just somewhat ridiculous, and a little embarrassing. William is the royal governor of New Jersey; he should know what on earth he's supposed to think about everything that comes through his office. He should be asking my advice about raising his own son, his exercise habits, what to plant in his garden. But to them—to Hillsborough—William's letters could be interpreted as opening up the sensitive business of his office to an agent of those rowdy people in Massachusetts. And I made sure my friend Strahan knows all about it. Foolish. Dangerous. Remember, old man, the Italian proverb: He who is a sheep is eaten by the wolves. You are now a symbol. It is one thing to represent those quiet folks in Georgia or those Quakers in Pennsylvania. But now they know you will be in close touch with those *other* fellows, the ones who get their names in the newspapers. Certainly Hillsborough is paying close attention to how Governor Hutchinson handles his job. If Hutchinson makes mistakes, if he's as clumsy as Bernard, the Sons of Liberty will make him a target. And Hillsborough just might respond by making a target out of *me*.

7. GAGE

IT HAD BECOME HIS MORNING ROUTINE NOW, THE STROLL UP BROAD Street, the cheerful greetings to the people who enjoyed the energy of the city. It was that glorious time of year, the suffocating heat of August now forgotten, the leaves on the maple trees already showing the first golden glow. He would not yet wear an overcoat, enjoyed the crisp air, the first reminder that there would soon be a winter again, nature's subtle warning that autumn was something to be relished, enjoyed, and not taken for granted.

He was recognized, of course, the uniform certainly, and most would call him by name. The routine of the walk had come with the growing sense of peace, tranquility, the turmoil and hostility of the Boston winter long past. New York had suffered its own share of angry mobs, arguments over customs and taxes, fights between the Tories and those who saw them only as oppressors. It had not been as extreme as Boston or as violent. The angry voices were mostly behind closed doors, the turmoil of politics. The Tories, the staunch loyalists, were in firm control here, and protests did not have the inflammatory effect that they did in Boston. The displays of power were more subtle, the patronage and funding for pet projects. As the storm in Boston had diminished, the business of managing New York had grown calmer as well.

The change in mood, in the attitude of the people, was obvious to Gage. When news of the turmoil in Boston had filled the papers, even Margaret had seemed unusually tense, had begun to ask questions about his command, suddenly concerned about the affairs of politics. It was that peculiar American sensitivity, setting off some emotion in her, some unpleasant awareness that she was not quite the same as him, as his family. As the passions in Boston grew cooler, it was an enormous relief, easing the pressure in his home and on his command, weakening the threat that another Boston Massacre could occur anywhere the angry mobs patrolled.

He had been surprised at the impact of the colonies' "nonimportation" agreements, had considered the talk about them to be just more rabble-rousing instigated by the radical Sons of Liberty in Boston, an angry if impotent response to the Townshend Acts. But the talk had spread, and the result had been a surprising show of unity from the colonies. For a while the nonimportation policy seemed to be effective, with great shiploads of British goods simply turned away, and anyone who dared import against the will of the agreement was confronted not only by the mob, but by the wrath of the wealthier, more established merchants. The voices were loud, imploring the people to "buy American," rallying cries around a new enthusiasm for home manufacture, as though by simple will, the colonists could suddenly achieve the skill and artistry that the English craftsmen had perfected over centuries. In London, the economics of nonimportation were very real. The pressure began to affect the exporters and the manufacturers, and the ministers became nervous, surprised at the resolve shown in the colonies. Gage had assured them it would pass, that the energy would exhaust itself, the enthusiasm for the simple charm of sewing one's own clothes would give way to the reality that it was much simpler to buy than to create. His assurances were strengthened by what he saw in New York, the occasional odd sight, a woman self-consciously parading her homespun dress, strolling awkwardly through crowds of gawking onlookers as she tried to stay upright on shoes made by some local blacksmith. He had laughed as the crowd had laughed, ridiculing the man who paraded his new suit, the bold in the crowd pointing out to the man that his neck was turning dark red, matching the crude dye in his coat.

For a while, the shops had grown quiet, the merchants bending to the pressure of the radicals. But before any real damage could be done to the English economy, the patriotic fervor wore off. The people were simply too accustomed to browsing the shops, poring through vast selections of the finest products of English manufacture. Even Margaret did not argue, and he knew that despite her occasional lapses into the annoying loyalty to her family home, she enjoyed shopping for the fineries of English merchants as much as anyone in New York.

Gage had taken his walks through the markets daily, had felt the old energy returning. The fine weather brought the shop-keepers themselves into the street, and he could see it now, merchants bringing out bundles of cloth and finished clothing, heaping piles of color into outdoor baskets and bins, and all along the wide avenue there was the cheerful atmosphere of a festival.

He heard his name, quiet, respectful, nodded to an elderly couple, noticed the man's fine wool suit, English, of course. The woman walked close to her husband, her arm holding his, wore a scarf of frosty white lace. He smiled, said, "Beautiful, madam."

The woman put her hand to her neck, touched the delicate material.

"Brand-new, sir. He surprised me just this morning."

The old man winked at Gage, said nothing, and the couple drifted away into the crowd. He was feeling very good now, felt himself puff up, nodded and smiled at a pair of young girls who giggled past him. He began to walk again, Broad Street rising in a long hill. He could see the spire of Trinity Church. It was nearly a perfect day, and he lengthened his stride, surrounded by the glad tidings of a city celebrating all the advantages of a time when being English was as much as anyone could aspire to.

HE SAT AT THE WIDE DESK, READ THROUGH THE PACKET OF PAPERS, the newspapers, the official memoranda from Lord Hillsborough. He was not in the mood for work, and there was nothing in the correspondence from London that required any serious attention. He sat back in the chair, stared at the window, the garden beyond. All the violent talk, the outrageous protests, the damnable mobs . . . it has all collapsed into a marvelous heap.

Boston is quiet, New York is quiet. And now London is quiet. This could be a golden age, an era of peace and prosperity such as the empire has never seen. And I am in the center of it. Indeed. I should remind them, make sure they know. Lord Hillsborough, Lord North, even the king should know the good work I'm doing here. I should write a letter today, a prescription for continuing the prosperity. He had been considering the lessons of his experiences, did not want to be seen in London as a man who simply reacts to a crisis. No, we must *prevent*. If it is not yet in my power to hang the radicals, then we must do what we can to prevent their influence. So much of the competition to the merchants in London has come from the European settlers, their small factories here. The Germans, the Dutch—for whatever reason, they bring skills here that the English immigrants don't have. It is quite simple. Put a halt to European immigration. And any Englishman who demonstrates a skill, a craft, should be denied passage as well. The most effective way to ensure reliance on *English* manufacture is to make sure there is inadequate *American* manufacture. Yes, I will think on this further, draw up a specific policy for Lord Hillsborough. He should be aware that I am not merely a military man. I have a keen understanding of economics as well.

There was a knock at the door, and Gage saw the face of his young adjutant.

"What is it, Major?"

"Excuse me, sir. We have received a letter from the governor's office in New Hampshire."

"Have you read it?"

"Yes, sir. It is an urgent request for the king's troops to be sent to their western district. It seems there is a dispute with some people in New York."

"The boundary business again?"

"Quite so, sir. It's gotten a bit . . . nasty, sir. Muskets and whatnot."

Gage stood, moved to the window, could not hide a smile. So now they want my help again. They can't very well fight the king, so they fight each other. He turned now, watched as the young officer put the document on his desk.

"Major Kemble, what is a commander to do?"

"Sir?"

"One minute these Americans are trying to convince us that they are united as one people. They spit and bellow about their oppression at the hands of their English brothers. But, let the angry voices grow quiet, let the people return to their mundane lives, and what happens? They return to their age-old custom of fighting among themselves. Border disputes, all up and down the coast. New Hampshire fights with New York. Pennsylvania fights with Maryland, the Carolinas fight with Georgia." He turned to the window again, looked out beyond the garden, the people still flowing past in the street. "They are children, Major. They need a stern parent. But as every parent knows, you cannot wave the stick at every misbehavior." He paused. "You may respond to the governor of New Hampshire that local disputes are not a priority to this command. The colonists will have to learn to get along with themselves." He turned, saw the young man writing his words on a pad of paper. "You know what I think, Major?"

"Sir?"

"I think civilizing these people is a hopeless proposition. I think all their barbarism, their tendency to violence, has finally resumed its proper form. The very thought that they could stand united, that they could pretend to be one people, strike out at the king's authority, rid themselves of our influence, is truly astounding. But the sanity has returned. The power of the empire has prevailed."

8. FRANKLIN

THE TRIP WAS A LUXURY, THE OPPORTUNITY TO TRAVEL BEYOND THE pleasures of London, to absorb the experience of both place and people. His journeys had always been positive, even when they involved business, scientific lectures, and demonstrations. But this would be different, a vacation of sorts, a search for refreshment by a man who understood that at his age, these opportunities might never come again.

He had expected to fade into the background, to visit the sights of Scotland and Ireland without recognition or fanfare. It was not realistic. Immediately after he arrived in Dublin, he had been invited to attend a session of the Irish Parliament, and for long days, he was treated as an honored guest by anyone who could use their influence to affect his schedule.

THE TOUR HAD TAKEN HIM TO ALL THE LARGER TOWNS, BUT HE KNEW time was growing short, and despite all he had enjoyed, he was missing the familiarity of London. For the last few days before boarding the small ship, he accepted and obeyed the itineraries of the gentlemen who exhausted themselves entertaining him. His travels had followed all the recommended routes, and he had visited the mineral springs and pleasant resorts that all insisted were the cream of Ireland. As long as he stayed near Dublin, the invitations had been constant, and he had feasted at lavish dinners at grand estates of country gentlemen, hosted by enthusiastic ladies who gathered close to this charming American.

He had decided finally to ride alone in a small open carriage driven by a young man with shocking red hair. Franklin had given him only one instruction, to leave the city and the main roads behind, a long round trip to fill the entire day. If he was to see Ireland, all of Ireland, he knew that his tours would have to come from spontaneity, and not the careful planning of someone who had his own idea of sites worth seeing.

They moved through rocky hills and deep green valleys, past fat mansions and huge farms. The season was past now, the farms quiet, the traffic sparse. The roads were still rutted from the rush of activity that followed the harvests, and the carriage lurched and jerked as the young man fought to keep the ride smooth.

Franklin was staring out into a dark stand of trees when the carriage slowed, stopped, and the young man said, "Deep hole, sir. If you'd like to climb out, I'll feed her through slowly. Could be a bit messy."

Franklin peered out to the front, saw the narrow road washed out, a swift muddy stream plowing across. He climbed out of the carriage, limped for a moment, worked the stiffness out of his knees. He approached the rush of water, looked to the far side, rocks and mud.

"Mr. McCabe, I've not much of a mind to jump across. It seems the only way is to ride." He walked back to the carriage, put a hand on the horse's neck as the young man said, "Dr. Franklin, sir, it'd be a simple matter to turn back. If we stay out on the main road, the ride is much easier."

Franklin shook his head, moved to the carriage, climbed up, sat down heavily.

"This is the way, Mr. McCabe. I'm not interested in main roads. Proceed."

"As you wish, sir."

The carriage crept forward, the young man holding tight to the reins, easing the horse close to the water. Franklin leaned out, heard the young man speaking to the horse in a low calm voice, "Make it slow now, Katie, no jumpin'."

The horse stepped through the water, and Franklin held tight to the sides of the carriage, the wheels cutting deep into the mud, the water rolling hard against the side, spilling in. Then the young man slapped the horse, calling, "Go on! Move!" and the carriage jerked up and out of the water, climbed onto dry ground. McCabe turned around, saw Franklin lifting his feet above the deep puddle in the floor of the carriage.

"Oh, Lord, Dr. Franklin! I'm sorry, sir! We shoulda turned back."

Franklin wiped his stockings. With mud on his hands, he laughed and replied, "Nonsense, Mr. McCabe. Think nothing of it. It's only water. There's a small hole, it's draining out."

He looked at McCabe's face, was surprised to see wide-eyed horror.

"It's all right, Mr. McCabe. Really. Please, proceed."

The young man seemed anxious, strangely out of breath, shook his head, turned away to the front, and Franklin heard low words: "I'll catch it for sure."

The carriage began to move again, and Franklin stared at the back of the young man. *He's actually afraid. Surely it can't be of me; I've done nothing to make him uncomfortable.* He thought of the young man's employer, Lord Heaney. *A fine driver, he told me. Knows the country. Give him the whip if he gets lost.* The words rose in Franklin's mind like some awful beast. *The whip. I thought he was joking, some bad aristocratic humor. But the young man is clearly afraid. My God.* He wanted to say something to put the young man at ease, thought hard for the words. *No, there's nothing I can say. I can't change the way Lord Heaney might treat him. I never would have thought . . . Heaney seems like a decent sort of fellow. No, don't dwell on this. It's not my place, after all. It's their culture.*

He sat back now, felt a chill, the wetness in his shoes spreading a damp cold all through him. The carriage rolled up a long rise, began to slow again.

"Uh, sir. I suggest, with your permission, sir . . . we turn back now."

"Why, Mr. McCabe?"

"There's no need to go any farther. Nothin' to see here. And it'll be late. We haven't time."

"There's plenty of daylight. I know how far we've come. I'd really like to see some of the local farms."

There was a silent moment, and McCabe said, "Then we'd be there now, sir."

The carriage rolled forward to the crest of the hill, and Franklin could see a vast brown field dotted with tied bundles of grass. On the far side of the field was a long row of low dark mounds, and as the carriage moving closer, he realized, It's piles of . . . mud. Strange. What do they do with that? McCabe stopped the carriage.

"Please wait here, sir. Best let me explain who we are."

The young man jumped down, trotted away toward the mounds, and Franklin saw motion now, people suddenly emerging, and he thought, My God, they're coming up from the earth itself. The mud . . . it's their *home*.

He counted a dozen people, more, saw children, holding tight to the ragged clothes of their mothers. McCabe was speaking to one man, pointed back at Franklin, the discussion animated. Franklin wanted to climb down, move close, hear the words, but the people were staring at him, grim dirty faces, and there was none of the welcome, the kind hospitality he had become accustomed to. Now McCabe was coming back toward him, the people all standing motionless, watching, and McCabe climbed quickly into the carriage, said, "It's all right. We can pass."

Franklin still watched them.

"Pass? Can I talk to them? Meet them? I'd like to ask them about what they do here."

The carriage jerked forward, and McCabe did not answer him, slapped the reins hard on the horse. The faces followed Franklin as they moved past, and he waved.

"Hello . . ."

But in moments the carriage was past them, moving quickly, and Franklin was annoyed.

"Here now, Mr. McCabe. Is this really necessary?"

The young man did not answer him, kept slapping the horse, the carriage rolling around a long curve, the people now out of sight. They skirted another field, rocks and black dirt, great piles of sticks and grass, more of the strange awful homes, more dark stares as people stopped to watch the carriage pass by. He forgot about waving, understood now there was no friendly greeting in these people, no joy in their existence. He felt sick; he had never expected to see anything like this, such a beautiful land, but such poverty in the people. They moved past a thicket of brush, climbed another hill, and McCabe pulled on the reins, stopped the carriage, turned to Franklin.

"I'm sorry for that. With all respect, sir, I would not have come this way. They're not so used to visitors. The only carriages they see come from the landlords. Men with guns. They're good people. . . ." He paused, seemed nervous. Franklin waited, and the young man said slowly, "Begging your pardon, sir, but they just don't appreciate being gawked at by rich folks. They don't know much about fancy visitors, sightseers and such. They got nothin' but what you saw, work the fields all their lives."

"I don't understand, Mr. McCabe. Who are those people?"

McCabe seemed unsure of how to answer the question, thought a moment, said, "They're *Irish* people, sir."

FRANKLIN HAD EXTENDED HIS STAY A FEW MORE DAYS, A SIMPLE explanation to his hosts: sight-seeing. He insisted McCabe take him on a variety of routes, the young man obeying, silent and curious, wondering why this odd American would want to leave the comfort of the lavish estates of the gentry. Franklin could not explain it to the young man, did not try, kept his thoughts to himself.

They rode now into Dublin, the final trip complete, the city spreading out in front of them. He would leave the city tomorrow, an overland route to Belfast, and from there, the boat to England. McCabe had been unusually quiet, did not even offer the occasional commentary of the tour guide, seemed to understand that the points of interest to his passenger did not need explanation. Far beyond the lush estates, Franklin had seen the same sobering sights, people who owned nothing, who barely survived on a diet of potatoes and buttermilk, whose lives were played out in the cold despair of poverty. He had been affected most by the children, had seen a playfulness in the toddlers that twisted his heart. It was the only laughter he heard, but it faded quickly, dissolving into the faces of their older siblings, their future already etched there, their youth drained by the lives they would never escape.

The carriage began to wind through the streets of the city, and they passed near the vendors, some pulling their carts toward home, the shopkeepers shuttering their stores. He looked closely at the faces, as though for the first time, solemn, dark eyes focused on the day's end, the quiet time with family. He could see it everywhere now and was ashamed that he had overlooked it for so long. He thought of the loud voices in the colonies. Yes, they should come *here* for a while. Bring their righteous indignation from Boston to this place, see what oppression truly looks like. Here you will find all the inspiration for rebellion you will need. But not the energy. These people have had it strangled from them, there is no fight left. But there is a simple, sad clarity here. To all those in the colonies who dismiss any protest, who have such faith that the English way is the only way, who consider themselves so very civilized, look *here*. See what your civilization has done to these people. Boast of your Shakespeare, your Isaac Newton, your Walter Raleigh. Be fiercely loyal to your monarchy, recall with pride your Elizabeth, your Henry the Eighth. How easy it is to overlook your *people*. No wonder the Scots and the Irish despise you. They have one purpose to your empire. They *serve* you. They are simply your slaves.

He stared ahead, his heart pounding, boiling in raw anger. He tried to calm himself, thought, You should write this down, unburden yourself with pen and paper. His mind was forming phrases now, organizing, clearing. He began to relax, rocking with the rhythm of the carriage. He could hear small sounds from McCabe, quiet instructions to the horse. The word was still etched in his mind, and he closed his eyes, could see it spelled out on white paper. *Slavery*. He felt a cold stab in his stomach, his mind opening like some strange flower. So the English have taught us well. It has always been so simple for them to dismiss our protests, our noisy outrage about rights and liberties, simply by pointing a finger at the slavery we ourselves practice. Who are we to dare to make any claim for the proper rights of man when we enslave the Negro?

He had heard it before, from barroom argument to drawing-room sarcasm. There is no defense of slavery, no moral superiority to be had from any people who enslave another. His mind had wrestled with the argument, and there had never been a comfortable answer. No one quick to condemn the Americans seemed to consider, or care, that barely one family in a hundred owned slaves, or that from the beginning it had been the British traders who brought the slaves to America. No, even that is no excuse. We are, after all, responsible for our own sins, but there are many in the colonies who abhor the practice, who will fight to see it erased. Ireland is conveniently removed from view, however, and few in London are burdened with guilt, few consider the plight of the Irish with a passion for reform. Few would ever consider that what they have done to these people is no different from what has been done to the Negro.

I have never truly understood what drives King George, what inspires Parliament to such a passionate zeal that America be held so tight in the leash, no matter what the consequence. I always thought it was pride, or fear of our strength and our growing independence, fear that we would somehow turn the tide, dominate them economically. But it is far more basic than that. We are no different from the Irish or the Scots. It's there for all to see, the English attitude, from the ministers to the man in the street. The colonies' purpose is to serve. The child must give all to the mother.

The carriage turned into a narrow drive, passed between two close walls. At the far end, he could see the grand façade of the Heaney estate, the ornate entranceway framed by the yellow light of oil lamps. He glanced up at McCabe's back, the young man drawing back on the reins, gently halting the horse. Don't worry, young man, I will assure your master that the late hour is my fault, not yours. They already see me as some odd creature, this eccentric American who would wander off into the hell of their lower class.

McCabe jumped down quickly, held out an unneeded hand, helping Franklin to the ground. Then the young man backed away, head down.

"It was my privilege to drive you, sir."

"The privilege was mine, Mr. McCabe." Franklin stepped toward him, pulled a gold coin from his pocket, held out his hand, the coin discreetly hidden. McCabe hesitated, took the hand, and Franklin released the coin. McCabe seemed to flinch, jumped back, looked at the gold in his hand.

"Oh . . . it's not proper . . . sir, I was doing your bidding. It was my job . . . this is not necessary."

"It is entirely proper, Mr. McCabe. Of all the sights, of all the experiences from this entire journey, it is the last few days that have opened my eyes, that will stay with me long after I leave here. You have done me a valuable service, Mr. McCabe."

The coin disappeared, and McCabe said, "Thank you, sir. God bless you." He backed away, still looking at Franklin, moved close to the horse, put his hand on the bridle. Just then the door of the house opened, a flood of light spilling across the drive.

"Well, this would be our wanderer now! We were concerned, Dr. Franklin! Didn't want you abandoned to the wolves, as it were. Swallowed up by the monsters of the bog."

Franklin said, "Lord Heaney, I thought of bringing a few of them home with me. Might provide some entertainment."

Heaney was looking at McCabe, the stern expression a message the young man seemed to understand. Quickly he led the horse and carriage away, disappeared into the carriage house. Heaney turned his attention back to Franklin.

"What was that, Doctor? Wolves?"

"Never mind, Lord Heaney. I do apologize for subjecting your lordship's household to any concern on my behalf. It was probably not a good idea to be gone so late. I'll be rising early for the journey to Belfast."

Heaney turned toward the house, and Franklin followed, could see faces peering out through the windows, smiles and giggles from Heaney's young daughters. Heaney led him through the door, and Franklin caught a brief glimpse of female dress disappearing down a hallway, more giggles. Heaney said aloud, "Our guest has returned! See to whatever he requires!" He turned toward Franklin. "Oh, yes, Doctor, while you were out . . . a message came for you. Lord Hillsborough is presently at his estate outside Dublin. He has requested your presence."

Franklin felt the air pulled out of his lungs.

"Lord Hillsborough? *My* presence? Why?"

Heaney seemed surprised at the response.

"Why, I have no idea, sir. I would think . . . the invitation itself is an honor, to be sure."

Franklin pulled himself upright. Use some discretion, old man.

"Certainly, an honor indeed. Outside Dublin, you say?"

"Quite. It's on your route, actually, the road to Belfast. Should prove a marvelous conclusion to your visit to Ireland, I would say."

Franklin forced a smile, his jaw held tight, said quietly, "Yes. Marvelous."

HE WAS MET AT THE DOOR BY THE SAME BUTLER FROM HILLSBOR-ough's home in London. But there was no rudeness, the man's dour expression now twisted into a grotesque display of toothiness. Franklin had been led inside the grand estate, seated, offered port, sherry, and tea, scones and biscuits, and only after the butler had left him alone did he realize that what he had seen was the man's attempt at a smile.

He had been waiting only a few minutes, occupied the time studying an extraordinary portrait of a woman, a regal pose, white silk and satin, standing stiffly beside a large, overly hairy dog. Not a partnership I would have predicted, he thought. He leaned toward the painting, examined closely the expression on each face. No, clearly the dog would rather be somewhere else. Probably spends most of his time playing with this woman's maid's son, finds himself snatched from some joyful game of fetch-the-stick and dragged into some sitting room while an artist preens and prattles over this woman's amazing beauty.

"Recognize her?"

Franklin turned, saw the small figure of Hillsborough standing in the doorway.

Franklin shook his head.

"Your lordship . . . no, sorry. I don't."

Hillsborough shrugged, moved toward a small cabinet, retrieved a bottle of sherry.

"Me neither, I'm afraid. The painting came with the house. I have imagined that sooner or later someone will walk in here and suddenly exclaim, 'Well, my word, it's Lady Bathmere of Cowbottom' or some such. Until then, she will remain anonymous. Wonderful dog, though."

Hillsborough held out a glass of sherry, and Franklin stepped forward, took it gently. *Surely he will tell me what he wants. Don't presume anything.*

Hillsborough moved to a chair, motioned to a wide couch.

"Please be comfortable, Dr. Franklin. You're a guest in my home. I would prefer you relax, enjoy your stay."

Franklin rolled the word in his mind, *doctor. He never referred to me that way before. And he said . . .*

"*Stay,* your lordship?"

"Certainly. It is not often we receive such distinguished company here. There is much to see, much to do. Do you hunt? Ride? I am at your disposal, as is my son, Lord Kilwarling. We should have a grand time indeed!"

Franklin sat for a long moment, examined the smile on Hillsborough's face, something he had never seen before.

"I am honored that your lordship would consider me distinguished company. Forgive me, sir, but it is not an invitation I would have expected."

"Nonsense, Doctor. You are an important man. There is no reason we cannot be sociable or, for that matter, friends. We have much in common. We are both dedicated to the affairs of the colonies. Certainly if we make the effort, we will discover great similarities in our views. Little is to be gained from an adversarial relationship. Don't you agree?"

Franklin absorbed the man's smile again. *I'm in treacherous waters here. What does he want?*

"I agree, your lordship, that communication is always preferable to exclusion."

"Yes! Very well put! I look forward to hearing your thoughts, examining your insight. Relations between England and the colonies have never been better, and I intend to hold tight to that. We should be working together, not working apart." Hillsborough paused, seemed to drift off for a moment. "Working together, not working apart. Excellent, yes." He looked at Franklin again, held up the glass of sherry. "A toast to the future, Doctor. To His Majesty's health, to the prosperity of the empire, to lasting peace."

Franklin felt uncomfortable now, raised the glass.

"To lasting peace."

Hillsborough drained his small glass, and Franklin took a sip. How can I leave? He knew he had been manipulated, put in a position where nothing he could do would be correct. Hillsborough poured another glass, offered the bottle toward Franklin, who said, "No, thank you, my lord."

He felt helpless, waiting for the next move in this strange game. If I try to leave, I am rude, insulting his hospitality. If I stay, this might be viewed as some unseemly collusion, word going back to the colonies that Franklin and Hillsborough are allies. All right, nothing to do but accept the situation and simply be careful.

Hillsborough arose.

"We shall have a fine time, Doctor. I have already had your bags moved up to your room. Please, make use of all parts of the house. Any request, any requirement."

Franklin stood as well, saw the butler, the amazing smile planted again on the man's face. The man motioned for him to follow, and Franklin made a bow to Hillsborough.

"Thank you for your hospitality, my lord."

He followed the butler out of the room, paused at the entrance to a grand dining room, saw other servants now, a flurry of activity, setting the huge table, linen and silver, flowers and china. He tried to see the faces, but they would not look at him, kept their gaze low, focused on their work. He could not erase the image of the farm people from his mind, wondered if these people shared that experience, perhaps rescued to this place by some divine streak of good fortune. Surely they know that out there, spread all over this country, their people fight for survival. The butler was waiting for him, and Franklin followed again. Do what you have to do, old man. Pay attention. And be careful.

* * *

THE VISIT EXTENDED INTO FIVE DAYS, CARRIAGE RIDES AND GREAT dinners, sherry and conversation. On the sixth day, his own carriage was finally prepared, and his bags were secured for the final leg of the trip that would lead him to Belfast and the ship back to England.

He sat back on the soft seat, the carriage moving swiftly, the rhythm of the road rocking him toward a nap. He put his hand on his round stomach. *This is not good. None of my clothes will fit. Mrs. Stevenson will scold me unmercifully.*

Hillsborough's estate was far behind him now, and he still felt an odd confusion about the visit, had never been allowed to understand why he was so welcome there. He thought of the conversations, tried to recall some hints of intrigue, some prying into the secrets Franklin was presumed to carry. *It was really not like that. Not at all. Hillsborough seemed to want to erase all of that. He has made a great many enemies, and it must be causing him some problems in the ministry. But do not assume he is your friend. All the hospitality, all the pleasant talk was just that, talk. He does not like America or Americans. No platitudes, no patronizing kindness can cover that up. This whole affair was for his benefit, not mine. I feel like an orange that has been squeezed dry of juice. It was obvious it was time for me to leave. He was finished with me.*

The carriage climbed a long rise, rolled now into a long deep valley, wide black fields, small quiet villages. He thought of the red-haired young man, McCabe, the words Frankin had said to him. *I meant what I told him. My eyes are opened now, and I will remember this place. It is far more than just another experience, another chapter in a long life of observation. Everything that has happened to Ireland could happen to America. For all the high talk about economics and manufacture, all the complacency of this newfound peace, one thing has not changed. England is an empire, governed by people who see themselves as superior, all of them a part of the sovereignty over America. History is governed by inevitabilities. The English dealt with Ireland by brute force and succeeded in grinding this land under the king's boot. It is inevitable that these people will never forget that, never let* go of their hatred. It is also inevitable that as America continues to grow and prosper, England will respond in the only way that has worked before. All this talk about peaceful times will give way to the inevitability of competition and growth. Despite anything Hillsborough says about his concern for America, the English government will concern itself first with England. It is inevitable that America will continue to grow and strengthen and challenge, and perhaps even threaten. He had seen the newspapers from Boston, the plaintive cries from the Sons of Liberty to a people grown complacent. The enthusiasm for protest has faded away, the colonists have become bored with the radicals and their mobs. Enjoy this peace, these good times. But make no mistake. This empire still has claws, still has them wrapped around America. All it will take is one crack in this fragile peace, one sharp stab into English dominance, and the claws will dig in again.

9. ADAMS

RHODE ISLAND, JUNE 1772

THE SHIP WAS AN EIGHT-GUN SCHOONER CALLED THE *GASPEE*, commanded by a veteran naval officer named Duddington, a fierce and disagreeable man who pursued his orders with a blind eye to maritime law—or, in many cases, any law at all. The *Gaspee* had been sent to suppress what the British navy perceived as a hotbed of smuggling activity, and for three months the ship had cruised the peaceful waters of Narragansett Bay, stopping and boarding any ship it could intercept. Any ship, any boat that cruised the bay was Duddington's target, and then his prey. He began to seize cargo from any vessel that did not fly the British flag, and it made no difference if the goods were smuggled or clearly documented as legal. When the ship traffic was slow, Duddington sent his men ashore with orders to simply take from the farms along the coast anything the ship and its crew required. In the Rhode Island Assembly, the outcry against the *Gaspee* was loud, but the British authorities in Providence ignored the protests. As long as Duddington could justify his outrages by claiming a vigilance against smuggling, the navy and the governor's office paid little mind to the violation of the rights of the citizens. In the quiet back rooms of Tory influence, Duddington was a hero. In the town meetings, he was simply a pirate. But Duddington himself soon learned there was one more word to describe both his ship and its captain: *unlucky*.

There had been a rapid pursuit, a small sloop that had slipped past the *Gaspee* in the dull light of dusk. The sloop stayed close to the islands that spread throughout the bay, slipping in and out of sight of the *Gaspee*'s lookout. Duddington pushed the pursuit hard, the experience of a veteran helmsman closing the distance between the two ships. Duddington had already given the order to his marines to prepare to board, but the sloop stayed close to the shallow waters, and this time there would be no capture, no prize. This time the *Gaspee* ran aground.

Word spread quickly, and as Duddington waited with his ship helplessly perched on a sandbar, a makeshift fleet of eight small boats rowed close, manned by local citizens determined to gain their revenge. Duddington tried to fight, was wounded by musket fire, and finally the sailors could not stop the citizens from boarding the ship. The crew was removed and sent to shore, and Duddington and his first mate were set adrift in a small boat. Then, to the cheering delight of a vast crowd gathering on the shore, the *Gaspee* was burned to the waterline.

BOSTON, OCTOBER 1772

HE HAD RARELY ATTENDED THE TOWN MEETINGS, AND EVEN SAM had stopped inquiring if maybe, this time, he would come. The issues were always important, of course, but for a long while now, the meetings had been called more because of a mark on the calendar than any hard controversy. For years now, the people had become accustomed to rancorous debate, outrage against all the abuses from England or the governor's office, policy and politics. But as the nonimportation agreement had collapsed, even the most radical voices could not prevent their audience from drifting away. Throughout the past year, as the arguments and hostilities with England settled into the past, the attendance at the meetings had fallen off.

Adams shared the same concerns with many in Boston, but his cousin's rhetoric had often made Adams more uncomfortable than outraged. Despite gentle persuasion from Sam and their friend Joseph Warren, Adams had not made that next step, could not truly call himself one of them, a Son of Liberty. It was comforting enough to Adams that since the trials of Preston and his men, the peace had returned, the loud voices from both sides of the Atlantic growing quiet. Unlike his cousin and the other radicals in Boston, Adams had welcomed the calm, looked forward to enjoying the life of a respected lawyer, a prosperous farmer, settling into the comfortable routine with his family. Like so many, he wanted to believe that the quiet times were a look into the future, a constructive relationship with England that would actually endure. For many months now, the energy of the citizens had been focused less on turmoil and debate and more on the mundane, on fending for themselves, their farms and families. But then came the English response to the destruction of the *Gaspee*.

A council of inquiry was formed in Rhode Island to prosecute the crime against British authority, round up those responsible. But the council was not from Rhode Island. They were English, had come across the Atlantic to ferret out those citizens who were guilty of this outrageous assault. Neither Lord Hillsborough nor the military had made any effort to use the legal system already in place in the colony. The mission of the council was clear to all. Once the names were known and the arrests made, the citizens would be shipped back to England for trial. But despite long and tedious hearings, lengthy interrogations, promises of leniency and threats of swift punishment, not one witness came forward. No one doubted that the people who lived in sight of Narragansett Bay knew well the names of the men who had burned the *Gaspee*. But the council of inquiry exhausted its energy and returned to England with nothing to show for the effort except embarrassment. Bruised by the failure of the council, King George III had issued a stunning decree. All the judges in each of the colonies would now be given their position and their salary not by the colonies, as had been the custom for a hundred years, but by His Majesty himself. By an extraordinary stroke of the king's pen, the American judicial system had suddenly lost its independence.

Adams still stared out toward the carriage, the street nearly dark now. What had the English expected? Did they think the people of Rhode Island would happily reveal anything to these . . . intruders? It was a sad joke. No, it was far worse than a joke. For all their pomp and arrogance, their grand pronouncements about justice, they had found out nothing, had not one prize to haul back to England, to parade through the streets as some trophy to English dominance. All they had accomplished was resentment.

He turned away from the street, looked to the desk, the dim yellow glow from the small oil lamp. He felt his fists clench, opened his hands slowly, looked at them in the dim light. I have never been this angry before. It's as though some madness has infected those people. The English could not just accept that what happened to the *Gaspee* was an unfortunate incident. They don't seem to understand that this was not an event worthy of wiping away all the calm and sanity we worked so hard to maintain. It was simply one ship, and one overzealous captain abusing his authority. Duddington even survived; there was no murder. It was a crime against property. How often has that happened in the past? How many homes have been vandalized by the mobs? You cannot respond to this with such clumsy mindlessness. How important is the peace of the colonies, the relationship of the king to his subjects, the government to its people? Not every problem we face is easily solved. But we were building the cooperation again, we showed them that the colonies are not backward and barbarous. The courts . . . my God, if they require evidence that the colonies have lived up to the terms of their charters . . . look what our independent judiciary has accomplished, how we have maintained the high principles of the English constitution. They gave us a system and we made it work. Now they will just take it away. And for what? What do they think will happen now? Will His Majesty be surprised when the peace dissolves?

He leaned on the desk, flattened his palms against the wood. Madness. It's as though they *want* a war. They will push and push again, test our resolve until we fight them.

There was a knock, and the door opened slowly. He turned, saw the face of the young doctor, his friend Joseph Warren, who said, "I heard talk you were coming to the meeting."

Adams always reacted to Warren with a smile, and the young doctor's popularity as both a capable physician and one of the most vocal Sons of Liberty had made him a man of some notoriety in Boston. He was considered by his colleagues to be quite the prodigy, barely thirty years old, having graduated from Harvard before he was twenty. His closeness to John and Abigail was not so much because of his zeal for any cause as because of his service as their family doctor.

Adams stood straight, flexed his tense fingers.

"Yes. I thought I should attend tonight. Is it time?"

He could see out to the street now, small flecks of light, lanterns, people moving in one flow toward the meetinghouse.

"It's time, John. We should go."

Adams looked at his hands again.

"Will there be an opportunity for people to speak?"

Warren was smiling now.

"You have something to say, John?"

Adams nodded slowly.

"Perhaps."

"Well, good. A fresh voice is always welcome. You won't be the only one. The governor himself has agreed to attend. There's a bit of arrogance for you."

"Are you certain? Hutchinson? Why?"

Warren laughed.

"God only knows. He's a little too spoiled by all the quiet, I suspect. Nobody's been giving him enough aggravation lately."

Adams was curious.

"He doesn't usually attend the town meetings, does he? Is that strange?"

"No stranger than the fact that Mr. John Adams is angry enough to speak out himself."

Adams felt the need to make some sort of protest.

"I'm not usually . . . I have never been so . . ."

"It's all right, John. Sooner or later we're all angry. If it's not about taxes, it's about troops in the city. No matter what we do, the king always seems to respond by doing something . . . idiotic."

Adams felt as if he'd received a quick punch in his stomach, looked at Warren, saw the young man's face grim, unsmiling.

"It's gone beyond that, Joseph. This isn't an argument. The king cannot simply decide to remove our most fundamental freedoms—"

Warren held up a hand.

"Save it, John. Tell it to Hutchinson. He's probably coming to calm us all down with a bit of aristocratic wisdom. Might do him some good to hear a fresh voice as well."

Adams was beginning to feel excited.

"Yes. We should go."

He strode past Warren, out the door into the small sounds of the night. People were moving in the street, low voices, faces lit by the glow of lanterns. Behind him, Warren leaned close to the desk Adams had abandoned, extinguished the last flicker of light from the oil lamp.

IN THE GREAT HALL, THERE WAS A CHORUS OF CONVERSATION. Adams was at the front of the main level, close to the tall podium; when he looked back, toward the rear of the great hall, he saw the two rows of balconies, stacked high above the main floor. The roar of sound came from men and women, even some children, motion and energy spread out in every corner, every seat of the Old South Meeting Hall. He was nervous, his hands sweating. He had never felt so involved in this kind of energy. He looked to the side door and then to the main entranceway, saw more people pushing in, lining the wall in the rear, more people than seats. This is remarkable. It's as if the whole town—

There was a sudden hush, the voices nearest him falling silent, the quiet spreading out in a wave through the crowd. Behind him, a loud pounding of wood echoed from the podium, and he heard the voice of his cousin.

"Quiet, please! May we have quiet?"

He still stared out at the faces, saw their attention focusing to one side, and he followed the looks, saw the crowd part, saw the tall thin man move in a slow strut into the hall. The new entrant looked up to the podium, nodded unsmiling, began to move to the front of the hall. Adams watched him come straight toward him, the man's face staring grimly ahead. He came abreast of Adams now, a quick glance, surprised recognition, and Adams said in a low voice, "Governor . . ."

But Hutchinson had gone past him, moved around behind the podium, climbed up, and Adams stepped back, looked up at the two men now standing together. In the great hall, the quiet was complete, and Adams glanced to the far side of the podium, saw Warren taking his seat, looking at him, a quick nod, the tight smile, the silent message. Adams returned the look, waited with the vast crowd for his cousin to begin the meeting. Yes, you're right, Joseph. This should be interesting indeed. Now the voice came from above him, clear and distinct, the voice of Sam Adams.

"This town meeting will come to order. We are privileged this evening to share these proceedings with His Honor Governor Thomas Hutchinson."

There was a low rumble from the crowd, and Adams watched Hutchinson's face, no change in expression. Well, surely he doesn't expect them to cheer his every word.

Hutchinson came forward, seemed to ignore Sam, who stepped behind him, disappearing, climbing down from the podium. Hutchinson waited a long moment until the hall was quiet again, then said, "My good citizens, I am always eager to hear the voices of the people of Massachusetts, whom I serve with utmost dedication. It is your constructive contributions to the administration of this colony that allows the healthy interplay between our Royal Highness, King George III, and his subjects. It is the foundation upon which English law is based, and upon which it thrives."

He paused, and Adams could hear the respectful silence slowly giving way to something else, a low hum of dread.

"My good friends, we have enjoyed an extraordinary period of peace and prosperity these past months. Your governor's administration has enjoyed a renewed sense of cooperation and understanding with the citizens of this colony. Angry words have given way to words of reconciliation. The controversies of the past are replaced by a united sense of purpose for the future."

The words continued to flow in a deadening monotone, and Adams blinked hard, glanced to one side, saw a glazed stare on the faces of the people around him. He could see Sam walking away from the podium. Sam moved past him, staring down in silence, made his way out to the center of the seated crowd.

Hutchinson's voice reached a pause, and Sam said aloud, "Excuse me, Governor. With all possible respect, sir, this meeting was called to address our concerns about the king's most recent decree. The people have chosen a committee to address this issue. I have been nominated by that committee to address . . . you, sir. Governor, can you confirm for this meeting that the colony of Massachusetts will indeed conform to the royal order? Will you now pay our judges from the king's treasury?"

The voices rose around him, and Adams looked up at Hutchinson, saw no change in the man's flat expression. Hutchinson replied, "Your talent for confronting an issue is appreciated, Mr. Adams." Hutchinson seemed to wait for a lighthearted response to his comment, but the crowd was silent again. Hutchinson looked out over the room.

"The good citizens of Rhode Island are our neighbors. And like good neighbors, we should be interested in their welfare. When one neighbor poisons the pool, it is often an unfortunate circumstance that the entire neighborhood will bear the consequences. I dare not speak for the king, but I believe I understand His Majesty's concern."

Adams felt his stomach growing tighter. *So it is that simple? This is all about punishment? Vengeance?*

Hutchinson paused for the reaction to subside.

"I must admit, Mr. Adams, I am not accustomed to petitions from private committees, no matter how illustrious their spokesmen. It is not appropriate for me to comment to this gathering just what policy my office will enforce. The king's decrees are not open for discussion."

"Then, Governor, will you call the assembly into session, so that body may discuss this issue? Surely you recognize the right of the people's elected assembly to express their views on these important matters."

Hutchinson seemed to smile now, shook his head slowly.

"Must I remind you that it is solely the prerogative of the governor to decide when the assembly should meet? I have no intention of issuing such a call. I see no purpose in providing a forum, official or otherwise, so that your elected body may shout themselves hoarse protesting the king's decisions. I agreed to attend this meeting to express my desire to continue the amicable relations we have forged together. I am not here to debate. No committee, no spokesman, no representative of any gathering such as this has any influence on my decision to summon the assembly. It simply is not your concern."

Adams felt a fire spreading in his chest, words boiling up, watched Sam's face, the expression fixed, the eyes staring hard at Hutchinson. The crowd seemed to focus on Sam as well, and the voices began again, expectant, questioning, waiting for some sign. Sam smiled now, made a short bow.

"Governor, you have given us much-welcomed insight into the machinery of policy for which we have no say. Please accept our gratitude." Sam walked forward, headed around behind the podium, and the crowd understood the cue. There was a scattering of light applause, which slowly spread through the hall. Hutchinson seemed surprised, raised a hand to the crowd, then moved down off the podium as Sam climbed up. The applause quickly faded as Hutchinson made his way to a seat. Adams watched him, the anger pulsing through him still. He thought of Warren's word, *arrogance*. Indeed. His position is granted by the king, and he is everything his position demands him to be. And, like the king, he is making an enormous mistake.

He heard Sam's voice again above him, turned as Sam said, "I wish to invite someone to address this meeting whom we do not normally hear. If I may be allowed by those present, I request that Mr. John Adams be heard."

There was a flurry of sound filling the great hall, and Adams felt his stomach twist, the anger dissolving into nervousness. He looked at Warren, who smiled at him, motioned up to the podium. Adams glanced at his cousin's face, staring down at him, began to make his way around behind the podium. He climbed up slowly, wiped his damp palms on his pants legs, stood beside his cousin, heard Sam whisper, "Serve your colony well, Mr. Adams."

Suddenly he was alone, and he looked out to the balconies, the people leaning out over the railings, watching him intently, the quiet returning. He glanced up, saw the heavy sounding board hanging over his head. He tried to form the first words, could not erase Hutchinson's patronizing arrogance from his mind. Now he saw his cousin down in front of him, Sam looking at him with quiet confidence. He took a long, deep breath. All right, calm down. You've done this before. It's just like a courtroom. A *big* courtroom.

"I come here tonight as a humble servant of the law. The law provides guidance for all of us, through every difficulty, every conflict, every source of confusion in our lives. There is no issue that concerns the colony of Massachusetts, or Rhode Island, or the governor's office, or England herself that is not addressed by the law." He paused, closed his eyes for a brief moment, thought, No, don't give them a ridiculous lesson. This isn't school.

"To use Governor Hutchinson's words, since Rhode Island has poisoned our neighborhood, we should expect to share the punishment. It is evident that the governor's views reflect the views of Parliament and, with some certainty, even those of the king himself. I was taught, and I have come to believe, that it is important in any case that punishment be appropriate to the crime. I do not believe that the events in Rhode Island are responsible for the latest decree of the king. I believe they are simply . . . the excuse. It seems that in England, America is perceived as some quaint collection of backwoods settlements. It has been repeatedly decided that we are not yet competent, or worthy, or civilized enough to manage our own affairs. This time, our stern father has decided to remove our privilege of punishing our own criminals. Apparently we are not to be trusted. And further, we are not supposed to protest. We have been told tonight that it is not our concern." He looked down at Hutchinson again, saw the man glancing around, looking at the crowd. "With all respect, sir, I can think of nothing more . . . objectionable."

There was a sudden rush of sound, one quick breath inhaled by the crowd. Hutchinson was looking up, a dull stare, and Adams thought, Well, I have his attention now.

"Whether *you* agreed or disagreed with the acquittal of Captain Thomas Preston, the most important message that came out of that courtroom is that *we* are a people who rely on the law. The charter of this colony grants us the rights of English citizens to live under the rule of the English constitution. The verdict in the Preston case sent a strong message to everyone that we *agree* with those principles. We will abide by that law. The same constitution that gives legitimacy to English courts gives legitimacy to American courts as well. We have proven that we can judge ourselves. There is *justice* in our courts."

He paused, was feeling the anger again, the nervousness gone.

"What occurred in Rhode Island . . . the message sent to us all by the king's ministers was deeply disturbing. Our judicial system was simply swept aside, and we were told that only an *English* court would handle this matter. *English* counselors were sent to Providence, and if they had found one citizen of that colony who would agree to testify in such an outrageous proceeding, those counselors would have transported the accused person back to England for trial. The message is abundantly clear. The only justice that matters is English justice. But the people of Rhode Island would not cooperate with such an outrageous act."

He looked around at the faces, took another long breath, put energy behind his voice.

"Please, citizens of Boston, this is not just an argument about some arcane rule of law. Some of you have come to these meetings because you are outraged about something that affects you directly, your home, your business. Parliament puts a tax on paint or ink or tea, and some of you suffer. Some of you object when Parliament insists you open your homes, provide a place for soldiers to live. Some of you have protested in this room because you knew the men who died at the hands of English soldiers. Governor Hutchinson is correct when he says that the last year has been a peaceful time. But if you believe that anything has changed, truly changed, if you believe that there is a new respect for the colonies, that our rights and our concerns and our laws are regarded with legitimacy, I implore you, consider not just what happened in Rhode Island, but the result. The king's ministers were embarrassed. There was no one they could blame for the fire that destroyed the *Gaspee*. So we will *all* be blamed. When England exploits America, it is done by dividing us, by taking from each of us what we can best provide: cotton from the South, corn from Virginia, lumber from New England. But when they punish us, suddenly we are one people, united, subject to whatever rule of law they decide. They were taught a lesson by the people in Rhode Island. So what will happen next time? Will citizens be arrested at random?" He looked at Hutchinson again, the man's smugness gone, replaced by a look of silent dread.

"We have already experienced the heavy-handed blunder of soldiers marching past our homes. The result was bloody catastrophe. Now we have been shown that our courts are unimportant, our justice no longer prevails. All thirteen colonies are being punished as a response to what happened in Rhode Island. Perhaps it is time that all thirteen colonies recognize that we are in fact united. If we can be dismissed, disregarded, and abused as one people, then perhaps we should *stand* as one people."

He paused, felt the burn in his chest, the crowd silent, waiting for his words. He stumbled over the voice in his mind, looked down at Sam, who still watched him with a tight smile, and Sam raised his hands slightly, motioned to him, *Go on, continue*. Adams took another long breath, turned his gaze out to the sea of faces.

"I recall the night . . . the awful night I stood in front of the Custom House and saw the blood of our citizens spilled on the snow. I believed the horror of that would give us resolve that it would never happen again. If we do not unite, if we do not send a message to the king, to Parliament, to the royal governors of every colony, that we will not allow our rights and our laws to be trampled, then God help us, there will *be* more blood. There could be a great deal more blood."

The words stopped, and he sagged, held the podium with both hands. He was exhausted, his head dropping. That's all I can say, he thought. It's all I can do. He heard a sound, one man clapping. He raised his head, the motion catching his eye, saw Warren applauding. The motion began to spread, others around Warren now applauding as well. The sound spread through the hall, grew louder, rolling into a roar of hands and voices, one long chorus of cheers. He stared, stunned, his mind a blank, the words completely out of him, forgotten, and now he felt a hand on his shoulder, turned, saw the smiling face of his cousin close beside him, who said, "Well, John, I wondered how long it would take. Seems you've become one of the Sons of Liberty."

10. FRANKLIN

LONDON, DECEMBER 1772

HE MARCHED WITH PRECISE STEPS, COUNTED TO HIMSELF, ONE, TWO, three, four, turned sharply to the right, three more steps, turned again, four more, then three, back to the starting point. He did not stop, said aloud, "One . . . ," and repeated the routine, moving with a rhythmic pace, the steps taking him to each corner of the room, the sharp right turn at each wall. He was feeling the energy now, picked up the speed, counted aloud each time the circuit was complete, felt the floorboards bouncing slightly beneath him. He began to notice the looser boards, tell-tale squeaks as his heavy foot landed precisely on the same spot each time around. The sounds added to the routine, one more part of the rhythm. He began to breathe more heavily now, couldn't help but smile. Yes, it's working. He felt his mind wandering, fixed a brief gaze on the window, the heavy rain dark and dreary, turned past it, then back around, focused now, his mind scrambling back to the count.

"Let's see . . . seven . . ."

He could feel the sweat coming, thought, Good, good, yes, this is working better than I had predicted.

"Nine . . ."

He did not hear the knock at the door at first, but the sound distracted him, and now her voice broke the rhythm, muffled behind the door.

"Dr. Franklin! What in God's name are you doing?"

He didn't want to stop, his legs moving by themselves.

"Not now, Mrs. Stevenson . . . twelve . . . I'm indisposed."

"You had better be indisposed in a decent manner, because I will see what it is you are doing to my house!"

The door opened slightly, and he passed quickly, nodded, smiling.

"Fourteen . . . good morning, madam!"

She slipped into the room, and he motioned to the center of the floor.

"There, careful, watch yourself . . . fifteen . . ."

She looked at the furniture, all pushed together, away from the walls, his way clear for the circuit around the room.

"Sixteen . . . what may I do for you, Mrs. Stevenson?"

"You may tell me what in God's name you are doing to my house! The very walls are shaking!"

"Seventeen . . . I'm making my visit to Lord and Lady Barwell. Eighteen."

She stared at him.

"Barwell . . . ?"

"Yes . . . nineteen. I had planned on visiting there this morning, making the journey part of my usual exercise. Twenty . . . Because of the unfortunate turn in the weather, I thought it best to postpone the visit. However, being that I had . . . twenty-one . . . counted my paces to their home the last visit, I can approximate the distance . . . twenty-two . . . to be roughly four hundred sixty-nine circuits of the dimensions of this room . . . twenty-three . . ."

She sat now, cast her eyes down, and he glanced at her as he moved past, saw her shaking slightly.

"Dear me . . . twenty-four . . . are you all right?"

She looked up, put her hands on her face, and he moved past again, felt concern.

"Twenty-five . . . are you feeling ill? Is something wrong?"

She leaned back in the chair, her face turned toward the ceiling, her hand across her mouth, her eyes fixed on him as he moved by.

"Twenty-six . . ."

He suddenly stopped, leaned close to her, and now he could see she was laughing. The sound was faint, held in by her hand, but the small sounds became louder, and her small frame shook. He began to walk again, slowly, the rhythm destroyed, looking at her as he rounded the room. She watched him now, tears on her face, a bright smile, something he had rarely seen. He reached the starting point, his reflex telling him to count, the number erased, and she said, "Twenty-seven, Doctor."

"Yes . . . twenty-seven."

He tried to pick up the pace, resume the routine, could not take his eyes away from her, saw her shake her head slowly, and she pointed at the corner as he passed. He nodded.

"Yes, I know, twenty-eight."

She got up now, waited for him to move past the door, stepped quickly across his path, paused in the doorway.

"You know, if you continue to move in the same way, you may become dizzy."

It had not occurred to him, and he took a quick survey in his mind, his eyes darting around the room.

"Not to worry, Mrs. Stevenson . . . twenty-nine. Once halfway there, I shall reverse my course. Keep all things in balance."

She backed out of the doorway with one final comment.

"If the floor should collapse beneath you, I expect you to pay the bill."

She laughed again, closed the door. He strode past, the rhythm returning, found each noisy floorboard, the routine complete, focused his mind on the count. Her face was still in his mind, the marvelous sound of her laughter, and he could not help but smile.

MRS. STEVENSON HAD GONE TO THE COUNTRY, A VISIT TO HER daughter, and for a full week the house was strangely empty. He had kept up his routine, but the exercise, his attention to the newspapers, did not hide her absence.

When she departed, he had proudly announced his intention to fend for himself, but the quiet of the house had unnerved him. She had left him plenty of food, loaves of bread, biscuits, but he had insisted that anything beyond that, meat, vegetables, he would prepare himself. In only two days, the food she had provided was gone.

The table was set with her finest pewter, plates and flatware, and he pretended not to watch as Strahan began to unpack his basket.

"Quite a feast here, Ben. You sure you won't share? More than I can eat, for certain."

Franklin shrugged.

"No, you go right ahead. This mutton will do quite nicely. Been a while since I roasted a good cut of meat." He motioned to the low flame in the open hearth. "Right on the fire, right there, just like our ancestors."

Strahan sat, spread his own meal out on the table, and Franklin could see a bowl of green beans, fat rolls, a small jar of dark red jam. Strahan began to unwrap a linen cloth from a large bundle, and the smell began to drift through the room.

"Beef ribs, my good man. None finer. Horseradish as well."

Franklin felt his stomach twitch, swallowed hard.

"Don't eat beef much, you know. Makes my back itch."

Strahan spread the ribs on his plate.

"Have you told me that before? I recall seeing you eat beef many times."

"Yes, quite right. But always I had my ivory-tipped back scratcher close at hand. Seems the cat has done away with the ivory. All I have now is a stick."

"Pity." Strahan smiled, spooned a dollop of jam on one of the rolls.

Franklin looked at his own plate now, stared at the flat white bone, the blade of the lamb roast. He turned it over, poked his finger into a hard black crust, the remains of charred meat crumbling off the bone. He heard sounds from Strahan now, a mumble of pleasure, Strahan's mouth stuffed with his own dinner. Franklin tried to ignore him, stabbed at the lamb with his fork, but there was barely any meat on the bone. He set the fork aside.

"I will have a word with that butcher. Mrs. Stevenson claims he is an honest man, the best cuts of meat, all of that. But when I went to make this purchase . . . clearly he recognizes an opportunity to take advantage of the unwary. This roast is a bit . . . sparse."

Strahan leaned out over the table, examined Franklin's plate.

"It's more than sparse. It's naked."

Franklin looked toward the fire, studied the thick layer of ashes.

"It is possible I . . . burned away its clothes. I was occupied with other work." He paused. "It would be convenient if Mrs. Stevenson were to return a day or two early."

Strahan divided his meal, pushed a plate toward him, and Franklin looked at his friend.

"Pity accepted."

They ate quietly, and Franklin poured from a wine bottle, refilled Strahan's glass as well.

"What work?" Strahan inquired after a moment.

Franklin tasted the wine.

"Well, certainly the change of command, so to speak. I can't imagine the news caught you by surprise."

"Hillsborough?" Strahan sniffed. "Hardly. He was a man with an enormous talent for making himself unpopular. The king had heard enough, I believe. The word was all over; it was only a matter of time. You have any particular opinion of his successor, Lord Dartmouth?"

Franklin shrugged.

"There's a college in New Hampshire, started out as a school for Indians. He put up some of the funding, and they named it after him. He's a reasonable fellow, I've heard, not nearly as disagreeable as Hillsborough. Whether he has the ability to defuse all the difficulties between England and the colonies is to be seen. As far as I know, his most legitimate claim to the post is that he is the stepbrother of the prime minister, Lord North." Franklin smiled, but there was little humor in his words. "Another example, if you will, of the *English* way."

Strahan ignored the comment, raised his wineglass, suddenly held it away from him, stared into the red liquid.

"Oh, dear Lord. There's a . . . bug in the wine."

He put the glass on the table, seemed to shiver slightly, and Franklin reached for the glass, tilted it toward him.

"A fly. I wouldn't be concerned. They don't seem to eat living things." He reached into his pocket, pulled out a white handkerchief, spread it on the table.

"With your permission, may I retrieve the fly?"

"Of course. Why?"

"An experiment. I've seen this before. Let's see if it will work again."

He put a finger into the glass, retrieved the fly, carefully set the fly on the handkerchief.

"Now, let's see if he revives."

Strahan looked at him intently.

"You mean, he's not dead? He certainly looks dead to me. Forgive me, Ben, but it's rather . . . disgusting."

Franklin carefully prodded the fly.

"Never known you to be so squeamish, Will. But there is a point to be made here. This is a creature of God, no less than you or me. And God supposedly looks out for all his creatures."

The fly suddenly made a buzzing sound, rolled about on the handkerchief, and Franklin sat back.

"Ha! Observe. The little fellow will shortly regain his composure."

The two men stared at the fly, and the buzzing stopped, then began again, and suddenly the fly was gone, disappearing into the dull light of the room. Franklin sat back, satisfied.

"See? Told you I've observed that before."

Strahan looked at the wine bottle.

"I'm not sure just what it means, Ben. Was the fly dead?"

"Oh, I believe he was. But he was somehow preserved in the wine, held in some state that would allow his rebirth. I don't pretend to understand it, but it has caused me to study the properties of the wine. Can you imagine . . ." He felt the enthusiasm growing inside him, the joy of the successful experiment. "What do you suppose would happen if we tried this with a man?"

Strahan stared with wide eyes.

"You mean . . . drown a man in wine?"

"No, no, not drown so much . . . well, yes, that's one way to describe it. A man is suffering from a terrible affliction—smallpox, perhaps—his demise imminent. With his consent, of course, you immerse him in a vat of wine, allow him to come to rest, and seal the vat. At some future time, with advancements in medical science, there might be a cure for his ailment. At that time, perhaps, like the fly, he could be revived."

Strahan's mouth was slightly open.

"Assuming you are serious, and I know you well enough never to take that for granted, how long do you think a man could last in the wine? How much time could elapse before a successful . . . revivification?"

Franklin shrugged, reached for the wine bottle, filled his glass.

"I have no idea. There could be some basic difference between the fly and the man that would prevent it from working at all. And I suppose at some point time could become a factor. Leave the man in the vat long enough, he becomes a pickle."

Strahan blinked at him, a look of skepticism.

"Well, if I should fall prey to some illness, I would request you not attempt this experiment on me. I am quite content to go when my time has arrived."

Franklin sipped the wine, stared at the lamplight.

"Keep an open mind, Will. All great scientific breakthroughs begin as simply as finding a fly in your wine bottle."

Strahan eyed his wineglass but did not lift it.

"You going to waste a good glass of Madeira? Waste not, want not."

Strahan reached for the glass, a small hesitation, then suddenly downed the entire glass. He stretched his hand out for the bottle again.

"I believe we were talking about your work? Any other experiments taking place here besides your flirtation with the laws of nature?"

"A number of projects. I have considered undertaking the writing of an autobiography."

"*Auto*biography?"

"Yes, I know. It's considered terribly vain to tell your own tales, and all of that. But a concern for vanity has never stopped me from doing anything. I thought it might perhaps be useful to relate my own experiences, pass along the lessons of a long life. It is quite likely that if I don't do it, no one else will either."

"I can sell it. No doubt. There's an audience for something like this."

"Here or in America?"

Strahan laughed, took a sip of wine.

"America first. But you do pique some interest in England."

"I thought I would address it to William, shape it in the form of a letter to him. The tales of a father, passed to his son. It may be the only way. . . ." He stopped, and there was a quiet moment.

"He's still your son," Strahan said.

"And you are still my friend, Will, but the world is pulling us in all directions. Politics is a poison. Loyalties are being tested.

My son cannot speak openly to me, any more than I can speak openly to you."

"We serve our own masters, Ben. But the job is separate from the man. You work for the colonies, your son and I work for King George. That doesn't change who we are, how well we know each other. It doesn't change our friendship."

Franklin put a piece of bread in his mouth, thought, You may be very wrong about that. Whether you believe it or not, there are lines being drawn. And as the lines become deeper, the distance between us becomes wider. He sipped the wine.

"I have considered renewing my petition to Parliament."

"Which one?"

There was humor in Strahan's voice, but Franklin did not smile.

"The colony of Massachusetts supports my request that Parliament and the king's ministry allow representation from the colonies themselves. If we have a voice in those proceedings, if the colonies can send their own elected members, it will solve—"

"Ben, not again. You went through this a few years ago. Where did it get you? It's a closed door. Especially now, with Lord Dartmouth new to his position. This could embarrass him, plant him in the center of a controversy he doesn't deserve. The colonies will just have to be satisfied with virtual representation, the same as the rest of the empire. It's a system that works, Ben. Despite what anyone in Boston has to say."

The words dug into him. *Virtual representation.* It was the excuse, the dusty explanation unearthed each time anyone really examined the way Parliament was elected. He moved a fork around on his plate.

"One day that doctrine will rise up to bite this government pretty hard."

"Ben, I don't want to argue this with you now."

"I won't argue with you, Will. I'm not telling you that Parliament, or the king should change anything. But you had better recognize that there are an awful lot of people right here in England who have no say in their government. Parliament is elected by, what, three percent of your people? There are towns that are not represented at all, no membership. There are other places with barely a breathing population who have a dozen seated members. It's a corrupt system, Will."

"I've heard all of this, Ben. But it's the only system we have. The ultimate power still rests with the king. He will not allow any of your so-called corruption to injure this empire. He has our best interests at heart, yours, too. Parliament is a tool, one piece of the machine. How the members are elected, how any one man reaches his seat there, is of little importance. The whole body represents every part of the empire. Every subject of the king is virtually represented there, whether he votes or not, whether a citizen of every town sits there or not, whether or not a *colony* sends its own man. The Parliament's function is to govern. And governing means representing the whole."

Franklin pushed his chair back, felt a weariness, the dinner stirring in his gut. He stood slowly, moved toward the hearth, felt the warmth on his hands. It's a chasm, he thought, an irreconcilable difference. They accept the corruption in their system because it's too deeply implanted. They populate their government with the first men who can buy their seat, or who can grovel most effectively to the king. And across the Atlantic is a healthy, vibrant community that accepts nothing of the sort, that has a voice and a heart and a collective mind that will not tolerate the stale explanations. He turned now, looked at Strahan.

"There is no spirit here, Will. The empire is an ailing old man, empty of energy, of hope, of a future. What you do not understand is that America cannot suffer to live under the dominance of your decay. And the more they resist, the more they will be made to suffer for it. You govern the colonies by sending men over there who make their reputation by the loudness of their quarrels. The more controversy the governors achieve, the more the king applauds their loyalty. The division between England and America is now taken for granted. It is a fact of life. The more dissatisfied the colonies become, the more oppressive the king must be in response. The more oppression, the more dissatisfaction. How must this conclude?"

"I think you oversimplify, Ben. The king does not want open conflict with America. What is to be gained?"

Franklin turned back to the fire, and the word rolled through his mind. *Independence*. But I cannot say that to him. I cannot say it to anyone here. Any suggestion of revolution is treasonous.

"You're right, Will, there is little to be gained from any of this. What good comes from talk? What can one man do, after all?"

Strahan rose from the table, moved to the small cabinet across the room, pulled out a dark heavy bottle.

"I know where you hide the port, Ben. Join me."

Franklin moved away from the hearth, took the small glass from Strahan's hand. Strahan motioned to the chair.

"Sit down, Ben. Relax. You'll feel better once Mrs. Stevenson comes home. Good meals put you in a better frame of mind."

Franklin sat, stared silently at the dark red liquid in the glass. I love this place, I truly do. But I am not one of them. As long as change is so odious to these people, as long as they do not recognize that the world beyond the shores of this island is moving away faster than they can comprehend, then change will only come from one direction, from outside. I had so hoped they could be made to see, to recognize that the old ways cannot simply be imposed on everyone, that you cannot bludgeon the restless spirit out of an entire country and not pay a price. We just don't know what the price will be. Not yet.

Strahan held up the glass, said, "A toast. To one man's overwrought worrying."

Strahan laughed, and Franklin tapped their glasses together, said nothing. His friend leaned forward, scolding him, "Oh, come now, Ben. You said it yourself. One man's efforts are of little use in changing this world."

Franklin looked toward the fire. That, Will, is the difference between us. You place no value on the efforts of one man.

HE HAD SEEN THE MAN'S CARRIAGE STOP, HAD RUSHED DOWNstairs, waited by the door for the knock. Now he opened the door, looked at the man's fear, the eyes darting around, the head turning out toward the street. Franklin said, "Come in, it's all right."

The man reached inside his coat, pulled out the small parcel.

"No. I'll be going now. Here. This is what you wanted."

Franklin took the parcel, reached into his pocket, retrieved a small leather pouch, handed it to the man. The pouch vanished quickly, and just as quickly, the man was gone, the carriage rattling away down the street.

He closed the door, climbed the stairway, moved into his room, shutting the door behind him. He unwrapped the parcel, felt the paper, ran his thumb along the edge of the stack of letters. He looked up toward the window now, the weather clear and breezy, blue sky. Excellent. Good sailing weather. These should find Boston before the spring.

He spread the letters out on the small table, shifted them around, held one up, read the name on the cover page, *Hon. Thomas Hutchinson, Governor,* slid his finger under the wax seal, already broken, the paper worn, creased. He opened the letter, read, felt his heart beating in his chest, the words filling his mind, the anger now rushing through him. Yes, by damned. Here it is, plainly and directly, your arrogance, your disdain. Now we will expose the very heart of our troubles. One man's efforts, indeed.

11. ADAMS

BOSTON, MARCH 1773

ON THIS OCCASION I THINK FIT TO ACQUAINT YOU THAT THERE HAS lately fallen into my hands part of a correspondence that I have reason to believe laid the foundation of most if not all of our present grievances.

Adams read silently, then saw the signature, *Benjamin Franklin,* put the letter down, looked around the room. The men were all staring at him as he read Franklin's letter. Then he handed the letter to Warren, who said, "Dr. Franklin has sent us eighteen letters altogether. Six are directly from the hand of Governor Hutchinson. As you can see, the others are from Lieutenant Governor Oliver and two other quite prominent members of our most wise . . . *ruling class*. I make no apology for sarcasm. I would request that each of you read them and pass them along."

The letters were passed around the room, and Adams read a few, thought, There is little here of any real interest. I'm not sure I understand what all the drama is about. Dr. Franklin's concerns seem a bit exaggerated. He began to read another, glanced down at the signature, Hutchinson's familiar pen stroke, scanned the words, his mind coming to sharp focus now: . . . *there must be an abridgement of what are called "English Liberties"* . . .

Adams lowered the paper, looked at Sam, who was watching him carefully.

"My God, is he insane?"

"Read it all, John."

Adams studied the words again, and now the room seemed to come alive, the voices rising together. Warren raised his hands.

"Gentlemen, please. There is much to discuss here. Dr. Franklin has given our cause an extraordinary gift. It is up to us to make a prudent decision how it can be used."

Adams handed the letter to Warren, who gathered them all into a bundle. He looked at Sam now, his cousin's expression distant, his mind working furiously. Adams waited for a lull in the discussions, said, "The governor apparently believes that his office should no longer receive any input from the elected assemblies. Here, in this one, he actually insists that the governor should be independent."

"It's much more than that, John." Warren put a finger on the bundle. "It's pretty plain here that what Hutchinson and all these other men believe is that there is only one solution to the disputes between the colonies and England. Recall Hutchinson's words: 'a firmer hand.' That means one thing when a parent refers to the discipline of a child. It means something altogether different when one country seeks to dominate another. For all the talk, the patronizing attention he gives our concerns, here in his own words he reveals what he truly believes. If we disagree with the king's policies, we should be put down by force."

Adams looked around the room.

"If I may ask . . . how exactly did we come by these letters?"

Warren replied, "They were received by Tom Cushing. He is a friend of Dr. Franklin's and close to many in this room. Since he is speaker of the assembly and Franklin considers him a reliable friend, who would be more appropriate? I do believe that Franklin has placed himself in a somewhat vulnerable position. If word should spread in London that we have possession of these letters through his hand, he may well be arrested. He was quite specific to Cushing that these letters not be published, copied, or distributed carelessly. He also requested that eventually they be returned to him."

Sam reached out, took the bundle, turned it over in his hand.

"I'm sorry for Dr. Franklin, but his request is not terribly realistic. The comments made in these letters are more than just indiscreet musings for our entertainment. For years we have assumed that the policies of the ministry have come from the ministry. We have assumed that our struggle to protect our liberties has been with England. I am somewhat embarrassed that I did not think of this before. Consider this, gentlemen. They are three thousand miles away. Their information, all they know about what is happening here, comes from dispatches and letters, newspaper reports and pamphlets. We are all aware of the . . . questionable reliability of some of that." There was low laughter, and Sam put the letters down, leaned forward, his arms on his knees. "We have been fools, gentlemen. The ministry, Parliament, the king, they don't make their decisions blindly. They receive advice from the one source whose job it is to provide that advice. It is not Englishmen who create the threat. It is Americans. Thomas Hutchinson, a Harvard man, the good Bostonian. If there is to be a British army marching through our homes, it is because Thomas Hutchinson believes it is the right course of action."

Warren rose, moved around behind his chair, said, "It is one thing to be an arm of the king, to represent the king's interests, to be sure we follow official policy, obey the king's laws. It is quite another matter when a governor and his accomplices advise the king to do away with the law. Mr. Adams, you seem to understand that more than anyone."

Adams nodded, with a glance at the bundle of letters.

"Certainly. But I am somewhat troubled that we may be opening ourselves up to censure. These are private letters. Dr. Franklin may be quite right in his concerns. Is there no right of privacy that protects the governor from this kind of . . . invasion?"

"Cousin John, I admire your uncanny talent for serving as our collective conscience. You are certainly aware that there are often several definitions of the same law, more than one interpretation of the same event. These letters were written by public officials, men who serve their colony in an official capacity. I don't believe that anything they do or say or write is entirely their own business."

Warren leaned close to Adams.

"John, Dr. Franklin has written to me more than once of his certainty that his mail is opened and examined by someone in London. It has simply become a fact of life. For a time, he assumed it to be Lord Hillsborough or some of his people. The point is that both sides are doing whatever they can, legal, moral, or otherwise, to keep a close eye on the other."

"Is that how we think now? We are two sides?"

"John, you are an optimist. Despite all that has happened, you still want to believe that reason will prevail. Look at these letters again. What reason is here? Our own governor, our valuable connection to the king, is betraying us." Warren looked at Sam. "What do you think we should do with these?"

Sam shook his head.

"There is no such thing as absolute secrecy. Not anymore. As much as I respect the possible consequences to Ben Franklin, the contents of these letters are too important to keep sealed inside this room. Hutchinson's words are plainly and simply incendiary. This is a spark that could bring the people out of their complacency. I propose that these letters be read before the assembly. Public record. Let everyone know how the mind of their beloved governor works."

"What of Dr. Franklin?" protested Adams. "There's little anyone can do to protect him here. Is he to become a sacrifice?"

Sam glanced up at Warren, who said, "Franklin is a wise man. I believe he understands the risks he has taken, and he certainly has influence in London with people who can help protect him. This serves him quite well, you know. There has always been some speculation in Massachusetts about his divided loyalties. No longer."

Sam looked slowly at each man in the room.

"Does anyone object to the public release of these letters?"

Adams saw heads shaking. He turned to Sam now, said in a low voice, "No."

Sam picked up the bundle, stood.

"We will make copies. Distribute them to the papers. In a week's time, Governor Hutchinson will have discovered that his arrogance, his blithe disregard, his very *contempt* for the citizens he is supposed to govern will be unmasked once and for all. We are one step closer, gentlemen. We have identified the enemy."

BRAINTREE, APRIL 1773

SHE HAD PREPARED A HUGE BREAKFAST, GREAT MOUNDS OF FLAT cakes, fat links of sausage, bread, butter, syrups, and jellies. He pushed back from the table with a low moan, and she could not hide a smile.

"Did you get enough to eat? We have some bacon still."

He put a hand on his stomach.

"So may I now expect you to tease me about my eating habits? This feast was your doing, I believe."

She rose, began to clear away the dishes.

"You are innocent of the charges, Mr. Adams. The guilt is assigned to your wife. Overindulgence of cookery. What's my punishment?"

He rose, still feeling the roundness at his belt, watched as she finished clearing the table.

"No punishment. Conviction overturned, Mistress Abigail. Appears the evidence has vanished. Or at least, it's been well hidden under my coat."

The sounds of the children spilled over from the next room, but not what he expected, nothing of the infant.

They now had a fourth child, Thomas, born the preceding September, yet another responsibility for Abigail to manage in his absence. His eldest son suddenly burst in, crawled up on a chair.

"Papa! Are you all done? Can we go out to the hill? The big hill? I saw a fox!"

Adams looked at the boy, saw the bright excitement, a tumble of words welling up inside the five-year-old. He looked at Abigail, asked, "Where did he see a fox? What hill? Has this boy been allowed to run off by himself?"

Abigail still held the dish towel in her hand. She put it down on the table.

"Do you suppose we all just sit here by the fireplace and wait for you to come home? The children and I take a good long stroll around the farm whenever the weather allows. We were up behind the orchard, above the creek."

"We saw a fox!" The boy crawled off the chair, moved to Adams' side, pulled on his coat. "Can we go back? Come on, Papa."

Abigail slid around the table, took the boy's hand.

"Not now, John Quincy. We'll go later."

"But I want Papa to come! See the fox!"

She eased the boy away, said quietly, "Yes, we will. Later. Come now."

Adams watched them disappear into the next room. Soon Abigail returned, shaking her head.

"The mother doesn't count for much when it comes to affairs of nature, big-game hunting and all. He wants his father to handle all the dangerous things."

She laughed and picked up the towel. He just watched her, felt a strange gloom, and she said, "I was teasing, John."

"No, it is hardly a tease. I don't do those things with him. I'm so often gone."

She moved around the table again, close to him.

"No one blames you. I know you would rather be here. But your work is too important. It means too much."

He glanced toward the other room, could hear the voices of the children, and said, "Could we go outside?"

She knew the mood, made no protest, followed him to the front door, took his arm as the sunlight flooded the room. They moved out into the front yard, and quickly the two older children were there with delighted shouts.

"All right, you two," Abigail told them. "Leave us be for a time. Nabby, you look in on the babies. John Quincy, you find something else to do."

There were small protests, but the children stayed behind. She held his arm tightly, and said, "They are so fortunate to have this place. I wonder sometimes how much different it would be for them if they had only the city."

He began to walk slowly, Abigail close beside him. He led her past the corner of the house, stopped, stared up the long rise, the fields clean and brown.

"They are fortunate indeed. I have never doubted that. All my life, this was the most important place. It's all I ever really wanted."

She looked at him, curious.

"What's wrong, John?"

He moved apart from her, stepped close to the edge of the empty field, his hands resting on his hips. She followed, stopped close beside him again.

"It's happening faster than I ever imagined."

She said nothing, knew his words would come.

"I am proud of my profession, my practice. I suppose I have as much ambition as anyone else. I always wanted to be successful. I try to understand what drives other men, how their ambition is different from mine. Sam has a great need, a fire he cannot control. Men like Warren, Josiah Quincy, John Hancock . . . I never really understood what so inflames their fury, their passion for a fight against England. I have no quarrel living under the rule of the king. He's a good man, I think. He cares for his subjects, wants what is best for the empire. We have come such a long way since one man could simply have his way with his people, all the horror that seems to come from absolute power. But it is so much more complicated than that. The same way my life is so much more complicated than just enjoying my farm and my law practice. It's all connected, this place and Boston, Warren and Hutchinson, Sam and King George. Everything is changing. You can't hide from it. I can't just walk out into these fields and plant my seeds, play with the children, and pretend I'm merely a simple lawyer getting by in a simple world. Nothing is simple anymore."

He bent down, scooped up a handful of dirt, sifted it through his fingers.

"I've always appreciated that the law is so different from farming, so much more intangible. Here, it's dirt and seeds and plants, the children . . . you. In Boston, it's words, principles, ideas. If anyone should have understood what is happening to America, it should have been me. It's easy to confront soldiers marching by your house, or a ship like the *Gaspee*. It's tangible, real, something you can *attack*. It's much harder to attack an idea, to understand that there is a threat to something you can't touch. I haven't been paying attention. I've been too absorbed in my own ambition to understand how serious things have become."

She touched his arm.

"But you saw it for yourself when the king took the judges away. You spoke out. I was so proud of you then."

"It wasn't enough. I was angry because suddenly, there was an assault on me. My interests. It was selfish. And for all that anger, nothing changed. The king didn't listen to me. Hutchinson didn't listen to me. Sam did much more than anyone else. His idea about the Committees of Correspondence gave a voice to every town, no matter how small. All over Massachusetts, the people began to speak, town meetings, opening up communication with every part of the colony. It's spread to the other colonies, too, Virginia, Pennsylvania. He rallied the people, showed them that if they don't speak out now, they may never be allowed to speak at all. I don't know why it has taken me so long to understand what is going to happen."

"What do you mean?"

"Unless there is some radical change, unless some miracle brings these politicians to their senses, there will be a revolution. Sam has been talking about that for years. I thought he was a little insane. But he was only premature. And he was right. It's inevitable. There is no negotiation, no compromise, no reasoning. There are no rules. A lawyer looks for order, for rational, legal explanations, solutions to every problem based on law and logic and wisdom. But none of that is working now."

"Surely not everyone feels this way. I always thought your cousin was trying too hard, *creating* the turmoil, not responding to it."

He was surprised, said, "You've been paying better attention to all this than I have. Sam has been accused of a great deal, no doubt of that. But I'm closer to it now. I see what is happening. One by one, people I thought were removed from all this, the clear thinkers, are talking the same way, sounding the same theme. A year ago, hardly anyone would even have thought of using the word *independence*. Now everyone is using it. Even those most loyal to the king understand that something monumental is happening."

There was silence now, the soft whisper of breeze. Abigail pulled up close to him, a slight shiver. He clamped his arm tight on hers.

"I'm sorry. I should be here. My son is growing up. One day I'll come home and he'll have a musket over one shoulder and be dragging in a deer."

She laughed.

"Not just yet. He'll wait for you to show him how. He wants to do everything like you. When you're not here, he talks about being a lawyer. He doesn't even know what it means, but if you do it, he wants to do it."

"Then I had better give him something to be proud of."

12. GAGE

HER NAME WAS THE *EARL OF DUNMORE*, COMMANDED BY A STERN, crusty man named Effingham Lawrence. The ship had sailed from New York Harbor on June 8, and if the weather was not difficult and the currents were steady, they would reach England in a month's time.

Gage had planned the trip for several months, had begun to feel a restlessness not just with his command, but with the colonies in general. It went beyond simply missing the children sent home to school, beyond the obvious social airs that separated London from New York. Margaret's only experience beyond the borders of America was the difficult time they had endured in Canada, and he tried to nurture a curiosity in her, telling her stories of his youth, describing the English countryside with as much romance as he could muster. It was a struggle at best, and she had fought him in that awful silent way that wives know. He still could not understand her attachment to America, how any woman who was so fortunate to have the opportunity to travel to England would protest of all she was leaving behind. After days of silence, she had finally agreed to take the trip, as much to see the children as for any curiosity about gardens and green hills and meeting her in-laws.

His restless urge to leave New York had much to do with a growing frustration he was feeling toward his superiors in London. Since the *Gaspee* incident, there had been no policy coming out of England at all, no direction, no specific instructions for him on how to prepare for the conflicts that were certain to return. Lord Hillsborough was vocal and direct with his disdain for the rowdy behavior of the Americans, and Gage had always felt that Hillsborough shared his enthusiasm for a hard strike at the rebellious spirit. But if Hillsborough never said it to Gage, Gage believed that Hillsborough was held back by timidity in the ministry, the unwillingness of some to actually make a strong stand against the radical voices in Boston. The lack of conviction infuriated Gage, and now that Hillsborough was gone, replaced by a man who did not seem to share the hard-line attitude, the fading opportunity for Gage to exercise his troops at the expense of the rabble had made him question whether his position in the colonies held any future for him after all.

The farewell to New York had been dramatic and boisterous. There had been parties, the society women fawning over Margaret with poorly hidden jealousy for her visit to England, the source of everything civilized. Margaret had made the good show, allowed all the cooing to flow over her, the polite enthusiasm for the great adventure. Gage had been surprised at the outpouring from friends, long-winded toasts, firm handshakes from men with tears in their eyes. The salutes had been official as well, the city of New York sponsoring a lavish dinner, complete with gifts, and the strange offering of ceremonial keys to the city. There had been only silence from the Sons of Liberty, and Gage wanted to believe that to many of the rabble, those who stirred their unlawful rebellion, his absence was a relief. But the army would not be without a commander. In his place, Sir Frederick Haldimand would transfer up from the southern headquarters at Pensacola. Gage had made the choice himself, knew the Swiss-born Haldimand was both a good soldier and a no-nonsense officer. If the protesters believed they could make noise in Gage's absence, Haldimand would be the man to disappoint them.

For weeks before the *Earl of Dunmore* sailed, Gage had found himself daydreaming about the adventure of it, the journey on the great ship, then beyond, London, the old homestead, his brother, the children. He had no real idea how long he would stay, and it was a topic he avoided with Margaret. He knew that she expected to return as quickly as his official business would allow. But the surprising show of emotion from his friends told him that many did not expect him to return at all.

The sea had been calm for the most part, a steady westerly wind pushing the *Earl of Dunmore* smoothly over the rolling swells. Through the long quiet nights the ship rocked in a peaceful rhythm that helped keep the stomachs of even the most uninitiated travelers at rest.

THE DAY HAD COME AS MOST HAD COME, BRIGHT AND BLUE AND glorious. He stood beside Margaret's young brother, his aide, Major Kemble. Kemble was leaning out, staring down into the froth below them, and Gage said, "A bit of decorum, Mr. Kemble. There's enough of a competitive spirit between soldiers and sailors as it is. No need to demonstrate to them an unbridled show of curiosity."

Kemble pulled himself back, seemed disappointed.

"Yes, sir. Quite." He lowered his voice now, added, "But . . . I've seen fish, actually. Big ones, too."

Gage glanced behind him.

"I'm quite certain these sailors are considerably entertained by the gleeful sense of wonder shown by their passengers. But we are soldiers, Mr. Kemble. Need I remind you?"

Kemble was chastened now, nodded.

"Yes, sir. Won't happen again."

Kemble moved away, and Gage waited a long moment, then moved close to the railing again, peered out slightly. *Big* fish? He heard the voice of Captain Lawrence.

"Five degrees to starboard. Tighten her up."

Gage straightened quickly, looked around, saw the captain's lean figure, the man always on watch, always prowling the deck. Gage had tried to strike up some conversation with the rugged commander, but Lawrence seemed to be a man of few words. Gage watched him, thinking, He has that same arrogance I've seen in so many of the navy men. I'm simply a foot soldier, and no matter my rank or position, out here I'm just another passenger. If it was me, if this was my ship, I'd probably behave the same way. This is more than his home, his job. It's his wife, his friend, his life. I'm not sure why any man does this, leaves the land. It's dangerous, unpredictable. You can't hold tight to command out here. In the end, you're not really in charge of anything.

Lawrence was beside him now, looking out over the railing, and Gage said nothing, waited for the opening, saw Lawrence staring down into the deep blue water. Lawrence was silent, and Gage thought, He's not looking at fish. He seems to be . . . praying. Gage suddenly backed away from the railing, felt like an intruder. He had tried to guess the man's age, deep creases in his face, gray hair visible beneath the edge of his hat. The voice was hoarse from years of shouting commands, absorbing the hard weather on the high seas. So many of the ship captains were powdered gentlemen, men of title, of family, a long history of sailing in their lineage. He thought of many he had met, frail pompous men who came to the sea because they were supposed to, commanding by some supposed aura, the captain maintaining his perch like some glorious bird. And they probably never get their hands dirty. Not this one, though. There's nothing that happens on this ship that he doesn't control.

Lawrence pulled himself back, looked at Gage.

"Morning, General. We'll be reaching port today. The lookouts can see the coastline now." Lawrence caught Gage looking past him, toward the railing.

"You have your rituals, General? Last day at sea, I offer a little word of thanks. She was kind to us this trip. It's best we remember how many good men rode their ships to the bottom."

Lawrence strode away toward the bow, his crewmen standing aside as he passed. Gage went to the railing again, stared at the horizon, could see it now, the smooth line broken by a long low mound. He thought of Margaret, knew she was down in their quarters. Once they had left the prying eyes and talkative gossips of New York, she had grown sullen again, had rarely come up on deck. He had given up trying to bring her alive, to give her some reason why she should be enjoying this experience, not regarding it as a journey into the depths of hell. But he knew the door was closed, his efforts exhausted. He told himself, She is probably sleeping now, best just leave her alone. But I do wish she could see this. That coastline. *England.*

* * *

MARGARET STAYED BELOW DECK UNTIL THE SHIP REACHED THE wharf, would not join in the mass of passengers along the rails as the ship slid slowly into the harbor. There was excitement in all of them, businessmen mostly, families as well, watching with him as the great ship was pulled in tight to the wharf, secured by long fat ropes. The other passengers had treated him with respect, even distance, and Gage had been grateful there had not been too many indiscreet questions about Margaret. No one else knew of her silent protest of this voyage, and he had been rescued from his embarrassment by her obvious pregnancy.

She had rarely had difficulty with childbirth, and this child would be their seventh. Despite the arched eyebrows of many of the women in New York, and of some of the bolder passengers, Gage had shown no concern that her condition might be made difficult by the voyage. It was an arrogant dismissal of the dangers of weather and sea, but as the ship had rolled closer to England, even the most squeamish admitted that this trip had been as gentle and pleasant as any they had experienced, their arrival in Portsmouth less than a month after leaving New York.

He had wanted to be the first to disembark from the ship, to make some ceremony of his long awaited stroll onto English soil. It had begun to obsess him, and he was prepared to make a formal request to Captain Lawrence, the words chosen carefully, rehearsed: *As a senior officer of His Majesty's service . . .*

As the last ropes were secured firmly to the wharf, he had stepped into place at the rail, expected to find some competition, had his firm speech prepared. He would not admit it to Margaret, but he had imagined a brass band, some parade, a celebration of welcome, the soldier returning victorious to the land he left behind. But the fantasy soon dissolved, Captain Lawrence tending to other duties, and Gage felt a small tug of disappointment that no one seemed to care who was in fact the first off the ship.

He stepped onto the hard timbers of the wharf, the people crowding behind him, flowing off the ship to the cheers and arms of family and friends. The fantasy had vanished completely now, replaced by the practical, finding transportation, the handling of their luggage. Margaret was beside him now, her mood quiet, but he could tell that curiosity had replaced her sullenness.

Kemble was out in front, pointed the way now to a small building, the Naval Office, moved quickly away, stopping at the door. Gage saw the king's crest prominently displayed, felt a sudden sense of security, satisfaction. No protests here, no ridiculous tolerance for anarchy. Kemble pulled open the door, and Gage allowed Margaret to pass, then stepped inside. The room was dimly lit, the windows choked with dust, windowsills piled high with yellow paper. He blinked, fought the strange musty smell, saw no one.

Kemble stepped forward to a low desk.

"I say, anyone on duty?"

There was a shuffle of sound in a back room, and now a man appeared in the rumpled uniform of a sailor, frowning like a man whose peace has been disturbed.

"Aye, what can I do for you . . . uh . . ."

"*Major* Kemble. I am aide to Lieutenant General Thomas Gage."

The sailor seemed unimpressed.

"And I said, what can I do for you?"

Kemble glanced back at Gage, and Gage saw that his brother-in-law's face had already reddened. Kemble said with a low hiss, "Is that any way to respond to a superior officer?"

The man scanned Kemble, looked past him, studied Gage's uniform, seemed to see Margaret now for the first time, glimpsed the round protrusion at her middle, made a sudden show of toothy politeness, a short bow.

"Madam . . ."

Gage moved up close behind Kemble, could feel the young man's heat, said, "It's all right, Major. Excuse me, sailor. Is there an officer on duty?"

The man examined Gage's uniform more closely, eyed the gold epaulets, nodded slowly.

"Very nice, indeed. Yes, sir, that would be Ensign Phillips."

"Well, then, would you be so kind as to summon Ensign Phillips?"

"I hear my name? Bloody hell, this better be important."

The man came out of the back room, stopped in his tracks, stared at Gage with an open mouth. Gage saw a very young face, bad skin.

The man snapped to attention.

"Sir! My apologies, sir. I should not have kept you waiting."

The sailor looked at Phillips with amusement, slowly drew himself up to attention as well, and Phillips said, "Forgive me, sir, but I do not know you."

Kemble interrupted, seemed relieved by the show of protocol.

"Ensign, this is General and Mrs. Gage. We have just arrived from New York."

Phillips seemed to pale, glanced around the office.

"Oh, my word. Please forgive the conditions, General. We do not normally receive senior officers here. They usually have their own arrangements."

Gage said, "I did not expect any arrangements, Ensign. We are en route to London and require transportation."

The sailor leaned close to Phillips.

"The stage."

Phillips nodded.

"Yes, the stage. Sir, I will show you . . . if you will follow me . . . there is a stagecoach for London at the top of the hour."

Phillips moved quickly out from behind the desk, opened the door, made a bow to Margaret.

"If you please, this way."

Gage glanced around the office again, dust on every surface, looked at the sailor now, the man slouching under his own coating of grime, and the man suddenly smiled, said, "Welcome to England, General."

Gage stared at the man's dirty uniform, the rough beard, the brown teeth, felt a rising tide of disappointment, turned without speaking, moved out into gray daylight. Kemble was waiting for him, moved away now, matching the nervous paces of the young ensign. Gage looked back toward the ship, saw longshoremen silently unloading cargo, efficiency of motion. He looked up to the railing, saw Captain Lawrence staring down, a stern eye on every man. Yes, by all means, he thought. That's what it takes. It's the difference between this fine crew and that one absurd specimen in that office. And it's the difference between order and anarchy in the colonies. He picked up his pace now, Margaret watching him, waiting to take his arm. They moved together, following their guide, and his mind drifted away, thoughts of New York and Boston, all the turmoil so insignificant now. That's what all those colonists don't understand. They are so few, so . . . small. They live in their sheltered colonies, so far away from the authority of the king, from the power of real government. He could see more great ships, rows of tall masts lining the wharves, the quick bustle of activity, the trade and commerce of a great empire.

It's simple after all, even simpler than I had believed. He began to think of the meetings, imagined the conversations with the prime minister, Lord North, with Lord Dartmouth. He began to find the words, a rousing speech, fiery condemnation of the rebellious rabble, maybe even a speech before Parliament. Yes, of course, I should go there. There will certainly be an invitation, their appreciation for years of good service. It might even be a farewell of sorts, the prelude to a new position here. He was smiling now, looked away, hiding it from Margaret. He was suddenly excited, regretted that he had not been able to give plenty of notice of his arrival. It was all so complicated, Haldimand taking over, the travel plans, Margaret's concerns. Surely they are aware I'm here, or they will be when we reach London. He glanced at Margaret, saw exhaustion on her face, saw Kemble looking back at her as well, a brother's concern. Yes, soon. We will settle in with my relatives, at least for a while. She can give birth in a home that welcomes her as one of its own. It's all she needs, all it will take to convince her that this is where she belongs.

The excitement continued, a strange clarity in his mind. By God, we are *home*! The fantasy returned, and he felt himself strutting down the wharf to the sounds of a brass band.

13. HUTCHINSON

HE WAITED PATIENTLY IN HIS OFFICE, PASSED THE TIME BY THUMB-ing slowly through a fresh manuscript, his own writing, pausing on one page, studying his words carefully. Much of his work had been destroyed by the mob that had ransacked his house, one of the first true displays of violence from a people incensed with matters that he believed they simply didn't understand. That was eight years ago, the violence inspired by the Stamp Act, an out-pouring of viciousness that carried otherwise rational people far beyond the bounds of civilized behavior. His house had been a convenient target, the mob ripping through his personal belong-ings, terrifying everyone in the house. The family had escaped, but even now his daughter, Peggy, bore the scars, still suffered from the awful nightmares.

Hutchinson's wife had died nearly twenty years before, a victim of the dangerous horror that could accompany childbirth. His daughter had grown to fill her mother's place in the home, and it seemed to Hutchinson more than coincidence that before she had been born, his wife had been so adamant that if the child was a girl, she should bear her mother's name. The resemblance was, of course, nearly complete, and Hutchinson had come to re-gard his daughter as some kind of divine presence, the constant though sometimes painful reminder of the wife whose absence he felt as keenly today as he had twenty years before.

He paused, stared at the great rows of books spread along one dark wall, thought of the girl's nightmares, his helplessness, the pain of hearing her wake screaming in the night, the awful fear of violation, the mob destroying everything. They had no idea what they wanted, or even what they were so angry about. It was a fever, a rampaging disease that infested the entire colony. He put the manuscript down, stared at it a moment, could remember the awful sickness that struck him down when he returned to the scene of the destruction. The furniture, portraits, glass, all were scattered throughout his yard; his clothes and his daughter's wonderful satin and silk were ripped and muddied. But it was the manuscript that had dropped him to his knees, the written words on so many pages, scattered and torn and trampled beneath the boots of those who so brazenly invaded his sanctuary. The work was his life, far beyond politics, his service to the king's government. It was his first love, above all else, the careful, delicate descriptions, the research through so much of the old records, letters, and files. It was an ambitious challenge, assembling what could become the most complete historical record of the Massachusetts Bay Colony. It would be his legacy, his gift to the land that meant so much to him. In the time since the mob had destroyed his home and his work, he had somehow found the inspiration to begin again, reassembling the sources, writing each word carefully, some from memory, some with a fresh eye. He put his hand down flat on the top page, held it there for a moment. The work was far from complete, but the mass of papers was thick again, and he could not help himself from seeing the images of that terrible night. He rolled his fingers slowly into a fist, thought, It will not happen again. No one will come into my home. No one will take this away from me. Eight years ago, I was a target because I had no power to stop them. It was all about customs and duties and those infernal stamps, and I knew it was a bad law. But it was still the law, and I could not ignore that, could not just allow the king's own decrees to be shouted down. I would not yield to the mob, and when they could not intimidate me, they assaulted my family, destroyed my home. But now . . . He turned, moved to the tall window, stared out through fading daylight at a wide garden. Now I have the power. No mob dares to approach this place. Now the king is my ally, and I am part of the empire, immovable and strong. Their arrogance, Adams, Warren, all the rest, their subversion and rebelliousness will cease to be tolerated. I have no illusions, I know they will cross the line again, inspire their people to additional traitorous violence. It is inevitable and perhaps even for the best. Next time they unleash their mindless assaults, it might finally explode in their faces.

He had tried not to show any sign that the release of his private letters had any real significance to either his position as governor or his relationship to the people of Massachusetts. He had publicly tried to ignore the outcry directed his way, but privately he had been furious, another assault against him by the rabble, another violation from the crude and clumsy hand of Sam Adams' mob.

By now the letters had been read by anyone who cared enough to see what the fuss was about. He believed the impact of the letters had faded away through the summer months; in fact he could not really understand why they had created such a controversy. They had been primarily private correspondence to his friend Thomas Whately in London, written nearly four years before, and the passages the Sons of Liberty had pointed out with such venom seemed to Hutchinson to be opinions that were not only logical but self-evident. Of course I advocate the power of the crown, of course I favor a strong hand to deal with sedition and treason. Whately had died over a year ago, and Hutchinson assumed that it was the haphazard handling of his friend's estate that had allowed the letters to become public at all. It only proved one thing of any benefit to all the loud voices in the colonies: that they had friends in London.

He had never understood the formal opposition to the king's policies, the protests in Parliament made by men such as John Wilkes and Isaac Barré, even William Pitt. Is it simply ambition, that by making so much noise against your own king you can attract attention? Why can they not simply accept what *is*? Nothing can ever be accomplished by placing obstructions in the path of history. Not in London . . . not here.

His ambitious project to assemble a detailed history of the colony came from an enormous love of not only Massachusetts, but her place in the empire, the grand legacy of a whole culture and a people that would influence the world for all time. The writing itself was easy for him, a gift that matured even as he was very young. He had been accepted to Harvard when he was only thirteen and received a master of arts degree at nineteen. His professors had no doubt that the young man would be a man of letters. But he had surprised them, as well as himself, by becoming a man of politics as well. He had used his term as lieutenant governor as an apprenticeship, had watched the mistakes of the hapless Francis Bernard, made careful note of the man's weaknesses, his inability to confront the crisis at hand.

He stared out to the road now, saw no motion, the traffic quiet this time of day. He thought of Bernard, the great failures. The man had too much fear, simply could not confront the rabble. That is, after all, what is required. Any young child understands that he can only go as far as the parent will ultimately allow. Bernard allowed too much. I have been lenient as well at times, allowing the town meetings, permitting them to make their indiscreet pronouncements. Instead of respect and any attempt at cooperation with the government, they assault my privacy by publishing my personal letters. It is why those kinds of people should not be allowed into the royal service at all. They have no instinct for governing. It is certainly well established in England that the decisions for all are best left to the better sort of men, the aristocracy. We are bred for this sort of thing. When the common masses are given any allowance, any free rein, the result is chaos and corruption. And yet they insist they should manage their own affairs. Government by merchants instead of gentlemen. He laughed, a quick, sharp cough. Well, my common friends, you are about to discover what happens when your king's patience grows short.

He stared again out the window, was waiting for his sons, expected them around dark. They had best arrive soon, he thought, the supper must nearly be ready. He could smell the luscious fragrance of the evening meal drifting through the house. His two sons did not often share his supper, and he was suddenly in a good mood, all thoughts of mobs and treason replaced by the simple joy of having his grown children come home, if only for one evening, if only for a bit of business, and to share with him the lovely meal of a great roast of beef.

The carriage clattered into his yard now, and he didn't wait for them to emerge, moved quickly, closed the door to his office behind him. He adjusted the lace that billowed down his shirt front, put a hand gently on his wig, brushed his hands together, a trace of white powder swept away. The butler entered, bowed.

"Sir, your sons have arrived."

The two young men entered the room, each one stepping in front of the other, an adolescent race to be first, something they had done all their lives. Hutchinson hid the smile.

"Elisha, you know better than to impede Thomas. He will always find a way to prevail."

It was a childhood joke grown stale over the years, and Elisha seemed burdened by the comment.

"Yes, Father. He always makes a point of stepping on my foot."

Thomas junior spun around, faced his brother.

"Whatever it takes, Elisha." He looked back at his father.

"Isn't that the lesson, Father?"

Hutchinson was smiling now, saw so much of himself in both young men.

"We have some time before supper is served. If you can be civil to one another for a moment, I'd like to speak to you about a more . . . adult matter."

He made a show of sweeping open the door of his office, motioned for them to enter. It was a ritual he still enjoyed, the acknowledgment of their manhood, granting them passage into that most special of places. They had never been allowed into his private study when they were young, had been cautioned of great consequence if they trespassed into their father's most sacred lair. He knew they would remember that, knew it would give them a sense of their own importance that now the door was open.

They were both eyeing his great soft chair, and he slid between them, his back straight, pointed each one to his own seat. He would not let them decide where to sit, knew it would only erupt into another competition.

They both watched him carefully, expectant, and he sat himself, allowed the chair to caress him, a soft groan from the rich leather.

"I believe both of you will agree that supper can wait just a few moments. I have some business to discuss first. The king has made a decision. It will have a significant impact on this colony, and certainly on the other colonies as well. As you both know, the Townshend Acts were designed not only to raise revenue for the crown, but to symbolize to the colonies that despite their absurd protests, England has every right to levy any tax on the colonies that the king's government deems appropriate. However, there were problems with the Townshend Acts, and I recommended right from the beginning they be repealed. It simply wasn't going to generate enough revenue to offset the cost of collecting the taxes in the first place. Any tax that harms the merchants in England while producing little advantage here is simply a bad policy. Parliament agreed, and thus the Townshend Acts were repealed, but with one exception. There is still a duty on tea. The king always felt that to abolish *all* duties on the colonies would give the impression that the royal government was weak, abdicating its right of taxation. That the tea tax still exists is testimony to the toothlessness of the protesters. No one argues about a tax on the one commodity that everyone in this colony considers a necessity." He paused, the two young men hanging on his words.

"No matter how much shouting rises to the rafters of the meetinghouse, the ladies of Boston must have their tea. The noisiest of rabble must return home to their wives. Not even Sam Adams can change that." He paused again, saw Elisha glance back to the closed door, the aroma of supper finding him. Hutchinson cleared his throat, brought the young man back to attention.

"It has been widely reported that the British East India Company is in serious financial straits. It has been a mystery to some in England how this could occur, given the colonies' amazing ability to consume tea. The answer is simple: smuggling. Great warehouses of the king's tea sit rotting while men in this colony grow wealthy from smuggling. I have been urging the ministry to allow me to take a hard hand to the smugglers. But since the unfortunately clumsy affair with the *Gaspee*, the ministry has been reluctant to do anything that might give the rabble any more of a cause to celebrate. I must admit my surprise that they in fact have come up with a better idea. In order to both strengthen the East India Company and eliminate smuggling, the ministry has decided that India tea will be shipped directly to the colonies, eliminating the costly middlemen in London. The result is simply put: much cheaper tea. The price should be so low, in fact, that even the most efficient smuggler will not be able to compete."

He sat back, let the plan unfold in their minds. He saw a puzzled look pass between them.

"And so you are wondering what this has to do with you? Simple. It is my duty to designate those principals in Massachusetts who shall receive the tea as it reaches Boston. Those men will serve as agents for the sale of the tea, will see to its efficient distribution into the marketplace. These agents will have the formidable backing of the royal governor and thus will not likely be subject to any abuses from the rabble. In addition, I am supposing these positions to be profitable. At this moment, there are two such positions open. Would either of you care to offer your name before the governor's office for consideration?"

The two young men glanced at each other, and now Elisha stood.

"Father, I would like to offer—"

"Sit down, brother. He knows it already." The young Thomas was smiling, shook his head. "Forgive him, Father. He does not appreciate subtlety. Thank you. We accept the governor's generosity."

Hutchinson waved his hand, dismissing the gratitude.

"The right men for the right job."

14. ADAMS

THE OFFICE OF THE NEW TEA CONSIGNEES WAS CLOSE TO THE PIERS, within sight of the wharves where the English tea would be expected to unload. The first ships were already rumored to be en route, expected to arrive before the end of the month. The word had spread quickly, a sudden flurry of noise and activity. At first, some merchants actually welcomed the thought of cheaper tea, that no matter how commonplace the smuggling business had become, those with tighter connections to England could now compete for customers and avoid the risk of tainting their good names by dealing with "criminals." But it was soon clear that the issue went far beyond the savings of a few shillings.

The new agents had expected a great rush of business, merchants lining up to secure for their customers the first supply of the new cheaper tea. But business had been slow, the office of the two young men strangely quiet. Hutchinson himself had often stopped by the office, putting aside his daily business as a show of support to his concerned sons.

THE SIGNS OF WINTER WERE SPREAD ALL THROUGH THE CITY, THE stark bare trees rocking slowly under a sharp biting wind. The overcoats had come out, people wrapped in dark heavy wool, leaning against the wind in a slow struggle.

Adams pulled the coat hard against him, glanced up toward their destination, ducked his head down again, sheltering behind the thick shoulders of his cousin. Beside him, Warren sneezed, pulled a scarf up to his face, said in a voice of muffled misery, "Ridiculous. I should be in bed."

Adams stared to the front, followed his cousin's lead, thought now of his son, the tears, the boy actually begging him to come along. He had relied on Abigail's firm hand, could not explain to the boy why it was not a trip the boy should make. His mind had filled with plausible, logical explanations, and he had tried to stop his son's tears with a lecture of reason, telling him, It's a visit you will not enjoy, men talking about things you don't understand. The boy was oblivious, and Abigail had rescued Adams from his predicament, had told their son that it was so cold outside, his nose would fall off. The crying had suddenly stopped, the boy pondering the strangeness of that, one hand holding his nose safely in place. It had been the opportunity for escape Adams needed, and as he stepped out into the blast of icy wind, he had laughed, wondered how cold it actually was, put his own hand firmly on his nose.

There were six of them, shuffling together along the wharf. Adams could see past Sam's shoulder, the freshly painted sign over the ancient doorway, the wooden building leaning slightly to one side, a victim of many windy days. It had housed many offices before, some obsolete, some outgrowing its confines. Now it was part of the offices of the Custom House, something new, another creation of the governor to provide a lucrative position for someone close to him. It was a reputation Hutchinson had earned, and Adams glanced at the sign again, saw the two names hastily painted along the bottom:

AGENT: THOMAS HUTCHINSON JR., ESQ.
AGENT: ELISHA HUTCHINSON, ESQ.

Sam ducked into the door, and Adams thought, Esquire? Of course, the great need of the aristocracy, even American aristocracy. A title.

The men swarmed into the warmth of the office, a hot fire boiling in a large hearth at one end of the room. Warren and the others stepped that way, warming hands, scarves unwrapping, and Adams followed Sam forward, to the doorway that led to the back offices. They were met suddenly by a thin frail figure, all lace and curls, and the young man stared at Sam as if struck by some odd shock.

"Oh . . . yes, Mr. Adams. Both of you. What is it?"

The young man seemed to gather himself now, looked at the others, stepped out into the front room, as though protecting something behind him. Sam was pulling off his coat, said nothing, and the young man pressed, "Do you have some business here? Are you in the, ah, correct place?"

Sam hung his coat on a hook on the wall, said, "You would be Elisha Hutchinson . . . *Esquire*?"

Adams could hear heavy sarcasm in Sam's voice. He had noticed the sign as well. The young man smiled weakly, said, "Yes, quite."

The others gathered closer, a tight semicircle facing the young man, whose resolve began to fade slightly, the smile weaker yet.

"Is your brother here as well? The other esquire?"

"Um, no sir. He is with my father, but I expect them presently—" He looked past the men to a sudden burst of sound from the door, a cold blast filling the room, and now they all turned to see two more bundles of heavy wool, red faces emerging from colorful scarves.

"Oh, Father! Thank goodness . . . these men were just asking for you!"

The two men peeled off their warm protection, and Adams watched the eldest Hutchinson's face, locked firmly into a frown. Sam pointed to the other man, the younger Thomas.

"Actually, Governor, it's your sons we came to see. I assume they're allowed to speak for themselves?"

The newly arrived young man made a grunt, hung up his coat.

"I assure you, Mr. Adams, my brother and I are in complete charge of this office. Do you have business here? We are quite busy."

Sam glanced around the office, said, "Yes, I can see that. Hordes of people lining up to buy your tea."

Hutchinson's frown straightened into cold hard formality.

"Gentlemen, if you have legitimate business here, my sons are pleased to oblige. If not, you should perhaps make an appointment with my office."

Warren sneezed again, said, "Excuse me. Actually, Governor, with all respect, we have come here to speak to these . . . agents. We are appointed as a committee representing the town meeting. We are greatly concerned that these men understand what is happening as a result of your . . . the king's new policy."

The older son moved toward the back offices, stood in the doorway beside his brother, replied defiantly, "Dr. Warren, perhaps it is you who do not know what is happening. I know the reports have spread, and I can confirm them. Quite soon, at least three ships will dock in this harbor, fully loaded with His Majesty's tea. The same will occur in New York, Philadelphia, and Charleston. When the ships arrive here, this office will begin to distribute that tea to those merchants who have enough wisdom to purchase it." The young man seemed to puff up now, feeling his authority. "Gentlemen, do you wish to place your order for some of the king's tea? It's rather a good bargain, you know. Or perhaps you are here to plead for the sad predicament of the smugglers?"

Adams felt the men around him inhale in one quick breath, a short low growl.

"We are not here for a confrontation, Mr. Hutchinson. We bring news, actually. Something that may be of benefit."

The governor still stood near the door, inquired, "What news, Mr. Adams?"

Adams saw all the faces turn to him, and he stepped closer to the young man, who faced him with a defiant pose, hands clasped firmly behind his back.

"We thought this office should be aware that your counterparts in Philadelphia and New York have received the same advice we have come to deliver to you. The tea consignment agents in both cities have been asked to resign their posts. They have in fact done so. We are not yet certain what has taken place in Charleston, but we should hear within the week."

Hutchinson stepped past them now, stood beside his sons.

"There will be no resignations in this office, I assure you."

Adams could see the expressions changing on the faces of the two young men, and now Elisha looked at him with curiosity.

"Why did they resign?"

As he glanced at Sam, who was smiling now, Adams said, "Because they were asked to. The case was presented to them as we will present it to you."

Sam added, "You asked what our business was, sir. It is the business of rescuing this colony from yet another subtle attempt to undermine our liberty."

Hutchinson huffed and replied, "Rhetoric, Mr. Adams? Is that what this is about?"

Adams put a hand on his cousin's shoulder, could see bafflement on the faces of the two young men.

"What Sam means is that we never have accepted the lawfulness of the Townshend Acts. It has never become a serious issue because the tax on tea has for the most part been ignored here. There were . . . alternatives."

Hutchinson's older son had assumed his defiance again.

"Unlawful alternatives, Mr. Adams. Smuggling is illegal."

"Quite so, Mr. Hutchinson. But nonetheless, the merchants here made do quite well, regardless of the source of their tea supply. This new policy is meant to eliminate more than smuggling." He looked at the governor and continued, "Isn't it true that by unloading the tea at such cheap prices, the plan is to eliminate any competition for the East India Company?"

Hutchinson smiled.

"I didn't know you were so versed in business, Mr. Adams. But there is no plan, as you call it. It is a simple fact of life. Americans will drink their tea, and the British East India Company will supply it. You gentlemen know as well as anyone that your wives are not about to sacrifice their daily tea. So what is the harm?"

Sam said, "The harm, Governor, is that what you are attempting to do is make an unlawful tax palatable."

Hutchinson stared hard at Sam.

"That is a baseless accusation, sir. I would advise you to exercise care in what you describe as unlawful."

Adams put a hand on Sam's arm again.

"We mean no disrespect to your office, Governor, or to the

office of the tea consignees. But surely you must recognize that the people have a real concern that if a monopoly is established, it could ultimately threaten a great deal more than the marketplace for tea. There are many craftsmen and manufacturers here who would suffer ruin if, suddenly, goods from India or China were to flood into this harbor. The impact from that kind of interference, that kind of disregard for the interests of American commerce is unacceptable. It is the reason the agents in New York and Philadelphia were asked to resign, and why they complied. They appreciate the seriousness of the matter."

There were nods, hushed comments from the men around him, and Adams could see Hutchinson staring past him, his expression fixed. Hutchinson said, "All of you . . . your concerns are misguided. The tea is coming, the people will be quite pleased at the price. The smugglers will suffer, as will any merchant who does not exercise the proper judgment about which tea he will sell." He focused on Sam now, his face reddening. "I don't know what kind of coercion was used to convince loyal agents of the crown to give up their posts. But this is not Philadelphia or New York. You will not be allowed to impose your will in this matter. Your protest is as baseless and hollow as it has always been. England has always had the right to tax the colonies as she sees fit. There will be no discussion, no debate, and no backing down. Any retreat from this issue by the king would be fatal to the well-being of the empire."

There was a silent moment, the only sound the labored breathing from Warren. Adams could feel Sam's energy beside him. Let it go, say nothing, no anger, not now. This is not the place.

Warren cleared his throat. "I believe we should conclude our business here. I do wish to be clear on one point if I may. May we assume, then, that the two gentlemen who serve Massachusetts as agents for the East India Company do still intend to occupy their positions? Do you intend to land the tea and distribute it?"

Hutchinson turned to his two sons, and now Thomas straightened himself, said, "Doctor Warren, you may go back to your town meeting and inform them that no one in this office is resigning."

Adams moved toward the coat hooks, joined by the others, and the only sound was the rustle of heavy wool, the coats and scarves finding their place on each man. Adams looked at Hutchinson, saw the same smugness on the faces of both his sons. He wanted to say something more, to reason, break through the arrogance. Surely you must understand what is happening here. We are not some mindless mob. There is an entire colony out there, waiting to hear what happened in this office today.

The men began to move to the door, arms wrapping tight, preparing for the cold again, and now one voice broke the silence, the younger son, Elisha, calling out, "Enjoy your tea, gentlemen!"

The door closed behind them, and no one spoke, the six men moving again into the sharp wind. They crossed the street, moved along the wharf, and Adams heard voices, commotion, stopped, saw people gathering. Sam stopped in front of him, the men all turning to face the harbor, black water ripped by the wind. Adams could see it now, the tall masts, the thick billow of sails appearing from the east, moving past the walls of Castle William. The ship turned slightly, catching the wind as she tacked her way across the final stretch of open water, a slow silent sentinel, her bow slicing the dark water, easing closer to where the crowd of people was gathering on shore. The small harbor boats went into motion now, the harbormaster breaking the silence with a sharp command, his tugs sliding out to meet the new arrival, to guide her safely to the wharf. Adams could feel the crowd around him growing, the word spreading, people moving down to the wharf. They stood silently, braced together against the icy wind, watching together as the big ship dropped her sails, her crew scrambling through the rigging, quiet and efficient, the long journey finally complete. He saw the name, dark gold letters on her bow: *Dartmouth.* A new ship, perhaps, named for the man who was himself new to his position, the man who would advise the king, or obey him, eager to please. He wondered about the great speeches and parliamentary debates, decisions made in public, or private, by men so far removed from the consequence of their policies, so casual in their disregard for the passions of their colonies. And now we might see how deep that passion is, how much resolve we have.

He stared as they all stared, watched the ship settling securely against the thick wooden siding of the wharf, the ship's crew and their officers spreading along the rail, curiously watching the great throng of people who continued to gather, to see for themselves that the tea had begun to arrive.

15. ADAMS

BOSTON, DECEMBER 1773

THEY HAD COME FROM FIVE DIFFERENT TOWNS, EACH GROUP representing their own Committee of Correspondence, their own smaller version of Boston's massive town meetings. They came together at the Old South Meeting Hall, nearly five thousand people, an extraordinary show of support for those who opposed the landing of the tea, and all that the tea had come to represent. Two more tea ships had arrived, were tied up close to the *Dartmouth*, but there was no effort to unload their cargo, not yet. The ship captains listened to their superiors in the business offices along the wharves, and those men listened to the voices that spoke the unmistakable message of the town meetings. There had been a vote, a resolution that carried no legal or official muscle, but it was noisy and unanimous, and the message was delivered to the ship owners without bluster or threat, the language of the resolution clear and certain: No tea would be unloaded onto American soil until the duty was repealed, and anyone who ignored this resolution would be regarded as an enemy of the country. The resolution advised each ship to set sail with its cargo back to England.

DECEMBER 15, 1773

THE MEETING HAD ADJOURNED FOR THE DAY, AND THE COMMITTEE headed by Sam Adams had retired to a small office near the meeting hall. The men had settled into chairs, some sitting on the floor, and Adams waited with the others for Sam to join them. Warren stood by the door, peered out.

"Here they come. The ship captain, too."

Warren moved to a thick leather chair, and they all looked to the door as Sam entered, the other two men trailing close behind. Sam motioned to the last two empty seats, stood at one end of the room, said, "Gentlemen, by now you all are acquainted with Mr. Joseph Rotch, owner of the *Dartmouth*. Some of you may not know Captain Hall, the ship's master."

There were nods, small words of greeting, and Adams could see Hall glancing around the room, nervous, a slight twitch in one eye. Sam went on, "Mr. Rotch, please enlighten us on your dealings with the Custom House."

Rotch was a short round man, nearly bald, seemed calm, composed, spoke with the confidence of a successful businessman.

"Thank you, sir. I can assure you gentlemen that we have made no attempt to violate the spirit of your concerns. It is not likely that we would be successful even if we tried. Your people patrolling the wharf are quite vigilant, quite determined, and quite numerous." He laughed, and Adams thought, Yes, humor is in your best interests. There were a few small murmurs, and Rotch continued.

"If you will permit me to be blunt, gentlemen, I am in somewhat of a bind. According to law, I must enter my ship's cargo at the Custom House within twenty days of the ship's arrival. I have not done so, out of respect to the issues so poignantly expressed by your town meeting."

Adams glanced at Sam, could see quiet satisfaction, Sam returning the look. Adams thought, We know very well why Rotch hasn't taken his tea to the Custom House. He would have started a riot. A flow of words came from Rotch still, platitudes about the restrained behavior of the citizens, the righteousness of their cause. The men listened to the man's political droning, and Adams focused on Hall, the ship captain sitting stiffly in the chair, his eyes darting about the room, appraising each man. Sam followed his cousin's gaze.

"Excuse me, Mr. Rotch. John, you have a question?"

Adams still looked at Captain Hall, who glanced at him, then away. Adams said, "The twenty days has nearly expired, Mr. Rotch. Captain Hall, have you made a plan to sail? Is the *Dartmouth* going back to England with its cargo?"

Hall looked toward Rotch, would not speak for himself, so Rotch replied, "Mr. Adams, a very good question, sir. As you are all aware, Captain Hall understands the peril he and his ship face if he unloads his cargo. We have both made inquiry to the office of the tea consignees, requesting permission to return to England. Alas, they cannot authorize our leaving the harbor. That can only come from the Customs Office . . . or directly from Governor Hutchinson."

Sam made a short grunt, and Rotch said, "Quite right, sir. I made inquiry at the Custom House again this afternoon and was told that nothing has changed. However, it seems the governor has taken note of my specific dilemma. The customs officers said they were instructed by the governor to deliver to me this." He pulled a paper from his coat pocket, unfolded it slowly, read aloud, " 'Anyone who seeks unlawful exit from Boston Harbor will receive the most serious of consequences. All ship's masters are warned that the artillery batteries on Castle William will consider any ship's passage not approved by this office to be of hostile intent.' " He put the paper down. "The order is signed by Governor Hutchinson's own hand. I am well acquainted with the governor, gentlemen. This is a very specific threat. If the *Dartmouth* attempts to leave the harbor, she will be sunk by the artillery at Castle William."

Captain Hall spoke now, looking at Rotch.

"We spotted two men-of-war putting out anchor in the channel just beyond the castle. I'll not sail my ship into that sort of business."

Rotch handed the governor's order to Sam, who read it slowly, then started it around the room. After Adams read the paper, he said, "This is not a surprise. Hutchinson told us there would be no retreat. He means to hold his position on this."

Rotch watched as each man read the letter.

"Gentlemen, I have made every effort to have the ship released. As long as the cargo remains on board, the Customs Office will not allow me to move. If the twenty days expires, the law says they can board the ship, confiscate the cargo—"

"And do with it what they like." Sam scowled at Rotch now, who said, "Oh, no, not really, sir. They may hold it—"

Warren waved his arm, cut Rotch off.

"This is Boston, Mr. Rotch. The Custom House is under the tight control of the governor. If that tea is landed by them, I can guarantee you it will find its way into the pockets of his friends. It's a fact of life, sir."

Adams looked at his cousin.

"The twenty days is not yet past, Sam. There is still time to appeal to the governor. Surely he will not let this become violent."

Rotch pointed at Adams, wagging his finger, a sudden burst of enthusiasm.

"Indeed, Mr. Adams. Please, gentlemen, we have two more days. I will make a call directly to the governor himself. He is a reasonable man. I cannot believe he would make a sacrifice of my ship . . . of its crew. He is not a barbarian."

Sam sent his eyes around the room.

"There will be another town meeting tomorrow, gentlemen. Mr. Rotch, I wish you God's own guidance in finding that rare piece of reason that must surely inhabit our governor. Regardless of the outcome of your efforts, it is essential that you keep us informed."

"Certainly, sir."

They all stood now, and Adams saw Hall looking down, a look of pure misery on the man's face. He felt a sudden wave of sympathy for the ship's captain. He doesn't understand any of this. That ship is probably everything he knows. Now he faces the choice of having his ship either sunk by the navy or burned by the people. I hope to God there is another way.

DECEMBER 16, 1773

THE HALL WAS OVERFLOWING WITH PEOPLE, A LARGER CROWD than Adams had ever seen. He was pressed close to the podium, near the same spot where he had stood the night he had spoken out to the governor. There had been rumors that Hutchinson would appear, the ultimate show of both courage and arrogance, standing up in defiance to the enormous weight of public outcry. But the rumors weren't true, and when Rotch had gone on his last desperate journey, he found the governor had suddenly decided to take a visit to his country home in Milton, a few miles south of Boston, near Adams' own home in Braintree. But if Hutchinson sought a convenient escape from the turmoil, Rotch was determined to save his business, and with a final word to the meeting, he had quickly embarked toward the small town, a determined man caught between two sides of an argument that was rapidly heating to a conclusion.

Sam had adjourned the meeting for a while that morning, to allow Rotch his journey, but the people had not left the great hall, and the men who led the voices could feel the collective energy of a people who would not allow the governor to simply dismiss the confrontation.

Outside, where the great crowd spread into the streets, women had set up long tables, huge bowls and platters of food, and Adams had slipped out, knew he would find Abigail there, the children as well, the street alive with the sounds of a carnival. Even those who could never truly be counted as having interest in anything political had been drawn to the scene, and Adams had spent his brief dinner hour answering questions, speaking to strangers, some from the farms that spread well outside the city. He had wanted to take a quick walk to the wharf, to show her the men who stood watch, the calm vigil that lined the docks where the tea ships waited. But the crowd was dense, the streets nearly impassable, and so he had only been able to point to the church steeples, show her the lookouts that were posted still, prepared to give the signal if any attempt was made to unload the tea.

Gradually the people had filled the hall again, and Adams had moved back to his usual spot. Abigail had taken the children up to the highest balcony, joining the women and children already there. The mood was jubilant, strangers gathering from the small towns, many of them meeting the people of Boston for the first time. As the last few seats filled again, Sam had stood at the podium, the schoolmaster observing his students, and Adams watched him, caught the smile that passed quickly on his cousin's face. Yes, this is your show, Sam.

Someone called out, and Adams turned, could not see the man in the crowd behind him. Sam waved acknowledgment, then came down briefly, and Adams lost him in the throng, but now he appeared again, climbing the steps to the podium, held a piece of paper over his head.

"Attention! Please!"

The voices gradually grew quiet, and Sam held the paper out toward them.

"As you may know, our unanimous resolution to the ship owners was not only published in Boston, but sent to the other seaports as well. I am proud to inform you that we have received a reply from the Sons of Liberty in the city of Philadelphia."

There was a crash of applause, and Adams saw his cousin smile, waving the letter, his other hand now rising, quieting them again.

"If you will allow me . . ." He read slowly, each word booming across the upturned faces. " 'Our only fear is lest you may shrink. May God give you virtue enough to save the liberties of your country.' "

He lowered the paper, and the hall erupted into one long cheer. Adams felt himself pulled up by the sound, his own voice blending in with those around him. The crowd was a mass of motion, hands waving, handkerchiefs fluttering, and Adams saw Sam standing back, his face aglow, the emotion filling him as well. Yes, he thought, they are with us after all. They are all with us.

The sounds began to die down, and Adams saw commotion near the steps of the podium, saw Sam disappear for a moment, then reappear. Sam motioned behind him, and now another man stood beside him, nervous, unsure, staring out at the mass of curious faces. Sam was smiling broadly.

"I have been informed that our esteemed sheriff has been ordered to read something to this proceeding," he told the crowd. "Please allow him to do his duty."

The man stepped forward, looked at Sam, glanced out over the great hall, said something quietly to Sam, shaking his head, and Sam pointed to the crowd. Now the man stepped forward, held up a piece of dull yellow paper, read aloud, " 'To the . . . to the citizens of Massachusetts. You are warned that this meeting is construed to be against the public interest. You are ordered hereby to disperse. If this order is not complied with, the citizens herewith in attendance shall continue these unlawful proceedings at their . . . utmost peril. Signed, the most honorable Governor Thomas Hutchinson.' "

There was a moment of stunned silence, and Adams watched the man's face, waited for laughter, thought, A highly inappropriate joke. But the sheriff withdrew now, disappeared down behind the podium, and Sam came forward again, still beaming, waited for a long moment, and now from every corner of the hall a new sound erupted, a long low hiss rolling through the crowd, growing into a loud roar, men shouting words, catcalls, and curses. Adams joined in, shouted something meaningless, some sound that rose from his amazement, his utter speechlessness at Hutchinson's astounding lack of comprehension. The sounds continued for a minute or more, and now Sam was down off the podium again, the jeers of the crowd turning to animated conversation.

Adams looked around behind the podium, saw the top of a bald head, saw Sam speaking to the man, motioning him up the steps. Adams waited for them to appear, and the crowd began to quiet, all faces turning as the two men rose to the podium.

Sam said, "This assembly will come to order. It has been our purpose today to compel Mr. Rotch to make his most vigorous effort to secure the release of his ship, the *Dartmouth*, by petitioning our esteemed Governor Hutchinson directly. As we have discussed in this forum, this petition may in fact be the last resort. Mr. Rotch, could you please tell this assembly what the result of your meeting was?"

Adams saw weariness on Rotch's face, the effects of the brutal day, the long and rugged round trip that Adams knew well. Rotch paused a moment, seemed to gather himself, then spoke.

"Good people of Boston . . . of Massachusetts. Shortly after the noon hour, I met directly with Governor Hutchinson. He was gracious enough to allow me into his country home. I regret that my efforts today were without success. The governor respectfully declined to grant my ship a pass to leave the harbor. As of tomorrow morning, the customs officers are lawfully empowered to board the ship and remove the cargo. The governor has informed me that this will in fact occur."

Rotch backed away now, and the crowd began to hum, a roll of sound that Sam resisted with his open hands, arms raised.

"Please! Order, please!"

Gradually the voices grew quiet, and Sam said, "I wish to propose to this assembly a motion for your consideration. I would call for a vote from all those here gathered." He paused, and Adams saw something different in his cousin's face, the simple confidence he had seen so often now replaced by something else, fiery anger, his eyes staring down in a fixed glaze. Sam leaned forward on both hands, supporting himself on the podium, and Adams caught his gaze, his cousin looking at him in a quiet stare, the look of grim determination from a man who has worked so very hard, who has made the good speeches, who pushed and drove his cause deep into the hearts of the people. Sam stood straight again, looked out to the crowd, said, "Please give your assent by saying *aye*."

His voice was calm, and the hard stare now went out toward the people, fixed in a steely gaze, as though searching for the heart of each one of them.

"It is proposed that the people, as free citizens of a free land, at the risk of their lives and property, do whatever is in their power to prevent the tea on those ships from being landed on those shores. All in favor . . ."

The hall erupted again, louder than before, nearly seven thousand voices coming together, the roar rising as one great fire, the flame bursting beyond the walls of the hall, spreading through the buildings of the town, beyond, rolling out over the harbor. On the three ships, tied firmly together, the crews were finishing their day's work, the sun settling deep into the West. Gradually the men turned, faced the town, trying to make out the odd sound that did not stop, did not fade. It was the voices of those who knew that this time, with the arguments done, the debates exhausted, the talk no longer effective, it was time for *deed*.

16. CAPTAIN HALL

BOSTON HARBOR, DECEMBER 16, 1773

HE HAD NOT SPENT THE DAY TRAVELING WITH HIS SUPERIOR, THE rotund Mr. Rotch. The world of politics and intrigue, of Tories and Sons of Liberty, was far removed from this man, whose only love was the ship under his command.

He had paced the deck nervously, expecting at any time to hear the turmoil of the angry crowd. He had watched the men on the wharf as they watched him, had never been truly convinced that they would not suddenly turn aggressive, storming up the plank, swarming over his ship with torches. He knew well the details of what had happened to the *Gaspee*.

He had known its captain from early days as mates in the merchant service, very young men with a delicate hold over crews of derelicts, criminals, men who went to sea to escape the law. Duddington had never been his friend, was a man of very different personality, cold, driven. It was only natural for him to eventually join the navy, the man's military mind never at home in the undisciplined world of the merchant seamen. But Hall had not followed him, did not find any appeal in a life under the constant call to duty. He had heard little of Duddington in later years, but when the *Gaspee* was burned, and word spread of the abuses of its master, he had not been surprised to learn that it was his old acquaintance who had allowed his ambition to go unchecked, and so had paid the worst price of all. It was a crime against everything Hall believed in, more serious than losing your life. Duddington had lost his ship.

Hall had never been afraid at sea, did not share the fears that so often plagued the most ignorant of his crews, tales of great mythical beasts lurking in the darkness, all the well-worn stories of ghostly apparitions. Even during the darkest of nights, moonless, stormy, he would stare out through the black silence and focus on the strength beneath his feet, the hard ship rolling in soft rhythm, and her captain joined with her, a part of her, slicing through the marvelous vastness of black water, the only place he knew as home.

His had been a mundane voyage, nothing to compare with the disaster that had occurred to another of the tea ships, slamming into the shoals off Cape Cod, breaking apart with the sickening groan that Hall had heard only in his nightmares. That Hall had brought the *Dartmouth* into the harbor days ahead of the other three ships, a tribute to his efficiency and the good fortune of weather, had now become a curse. When he had arrived in Boston, he had not expected any controversy, had been stunned by the vitriolic anger toward his ship and her cargo. Because it was *her* twenty days that was now expiring, the angry clamor had been directed straight toward Hall, and Rotch, the man who owned her.

As the last bit of daylight faded, Rotch had stopped by briefly, the man exhausted and dirty. He brought a dark despair up the plank with him, told Hall of the hopeless visit to Hutchinson, enduring the miles back to Boston in a sweat of horror, imagining the worst fate for the *Dartmouth*. Hall had said nothing, let Rotch pour out his concerns, and then the man was gone, off to his offices, balance sheets, and ledgers, already calculating the loss of this ship in the only terms the man seemed to appreciate. Hall had stayed on his ship, watching the dying sunset beyond the hills west of town.

He stood against the railing facing the town, the darkness now nearly complete, the lamplights blooming slowly, spreading from the homes, the larger buildings, the pattern familiar. Rotch had been indiscreet with his despair, his words heard by the crew, and when he left, they had approached Hall carefully with questions, their own concerns. He could tell them nothing, knew only that all the anticipation of the past weeks was settling around him now into something new, a conclusion, a finality that he still could not grasp. He rested his hand on the cool brass rail, moved it slowly, leaned out, stared down along the side, studied the planking of the bulkhead, each joint catching a small piece of light, the lines neat and symmetrical. They would burn you, he thought. Right here, perhaps. Right where you sit. They would risk destroying their harbor, their wharf, scuttle you as some symbol of . . . what? He remembered the meeting, the words of that one man, the lawyer, Adams, something about keeping this whole affair from becoming violent. But Mr. Rotch seems to believe it's the only thing left. He looked down to his feet, thought of the cargo beneath him, the thick wooden chests. All because of this damned tea.

Something caught his eye on the wharf, a lantern, low voices, the fleck of light suddenly gone. He stared into the dark, heard one crewman near him, leaning out over the rail, call, "Halloo? What goes there?"

Hall moved closer to the crewman, and the man looked at him. "There's a goodly bunch of people down there, Cap'n."

Hall could see bits of motion, dark shapes, the street beyond a surging mass, one dense dark shape, more people moving down to the wharf. The man beside him said, "What do you s'pose they is wantin', sir?"

Hall said nothing, felt a cold sickness swirling inside him, and the man went on, "Should we be fetchin' out the muskets, sir? You want me to bring up your saber?"

Hall's fingers wrapped tightly on the rail, and he shook his head slowly.

"No. Too many . . . if they mean to come aboard, there's nothing we can do."

Another sailor hissed in a harsh whisper, "Captain! There's men coming up the plank!"

Hall felt his heart jump, the sickness now rolling over in his stomach, and he moved toward the gap in the rail, saw the dark shapes massing, flowing up toward him. Behind him, a burst of light suddenly washed over the deck, a lantern, the crewman stopping beside him.

"By Jesus, they's Indians!"

A deep voice rose from the plank, commanding, "Lights out! Dark! Now!"

Hall saw them now, more than a dozen men, wrapped in blankets, faces blackened by soot or grease, odd headbands, some carrying tools, hatchets, iron spikes. He felt an icy stab in his chest, thought, There are no torches. He shouted to the crewman, "Do it! Put out the light!"

The lantern was extinguished, and Hall blinked into the darkness. Now the shapes were around him, one man close to him, a quiet voice murmuring, "No harm will come to you. Your men are not in danger, Captain."

The voice was familiar, and Hall tried to see the man's face, saw only the dark shape of his head. The others were streaming past him now, and Hall said to the one man still in front of him, "Do I know you, sir? What do you mean to do?"

"There are no names here, Captain. We are Mohawks. If your men do not interfere, our business will be complete very soon."

There was a calm authority in the man's tone, and Hall backed away. He could hear more of his crew coming up on deck now, could feel the energy around him, the strange men swarming down into the hatchway, the only sounds small grunts, sharp whispers, the dull ring of tools. He moved to the open hatchway, could hear the sound of wooden chests being moved, more whispers, and suddenly he could smell the pungent aroma of tea. Now he understood what they were doing. He fought the sudden urge to laugh, the strain of nerves, said in a guttural whisper, "Crew! Do not interfere! No resistance!"

The men around him backed away with him, waited as the tea chests began to rise to the deck, one man turning a wheel, the hoist, the sudden squeal of old metal cutting through the muffled sounds. He could see the squat shape of the tea chest, close to him, hands moving it, a sharp crack of wood, the top of the chest broken away. Now the two men were groaning, lifting, the chest moving toward him. He moved aside, heard a crewman close to him whispering, "What are they aimin' to do?"

They lifted the chest up on the brass rail, balancing it carefully, and the two men made one last groaning sound, and suddenly the chest was gone, falling away, the black water receiving the impact with a hard splash. The men were back to the hatchway now, more chests rising, the sound of the hoist, then tools breaking the wooden chests, more chests rising, more men lifting them up, the splashes, and Hall began to laugh now, the sickly panic giving way to blessed, grateful relief for the safety of his ship. He tried to keep it quiet, heard the sound of men struggling, low curses, men stumbling in the darkness. He could hear the pulley tangling, forced by inexperienced hands, and Hall felt a cool wave of excitement, began to feel a part of some odd adventure, said now to the crewmen beside him, "Give them a hand."

IT TOOK THREE HOURS, BUT WHEN IT WAS DONE, 342 CHESTS OF TEA were spread out on the surface of the black water alongside the three ships, stirred by the current and the cold night breeze. The invaders were gone, disappeared into the night, absorbed by the crowd of silent onlookers who had massed on the wharf. Hall stared out at them, the crowd slowly thinning, moving away silently up the streets into the town. Beside him, he heard the sounds of his crew, lining the rail as he was, but there was little talk, the men as stunned as he was, their cargo suddenly gone, the great hold of the ship empty. He could hear some of their words, still in whispers: "They didn't touch nothing else. Didn't break anything."

Below him, in the water, the lights of the town reflected in a strange shimmer, broken not by water, but by the carpet of tea. The smell was thick in the cold air, and he looked up now, gazed into stars, was suddenly feeling very good. No matter what happens tomorrow, and it's certain something will happen to-morrow, this has been truly . . . remarkable. He could still see the people moving on the wharf, realized, It's not a mob, these were not criminals, there was no violence, no theft, no damage. That's not why they came. It was not mindless, and God bless them, they did not come to destroy my ship. He could see a few people still on the wharf, staring silently at the water, and he tried to count them, but lost them in the shadows. How many were there? It may as well have been the whole lot of them, the whole town. And they came out here just to prove a point. Someone had better damned well pay attention to that.

One sailor was close beside him now, and Hall could see it was his second mate, Hovey.

"Who were they, sir? You get a look at them?"

Hall thought of the familiar voice, the one who had seemed in charge, and he could finally picture the man's face, one of the men at the meeting with Rotch. He began to smile.

"You saw them, Kenneth. Every man here saw them, saw the same thing I did. No names, Kenneth. It was Indians, Mohawks."

Hovey was looking at him.

"Captain, you don't truly believe—"

"Mr. Hovey, they spared this ship. I saw Indians. No one else. Do you understand?"

Hovey looked at him for a long moment, said slowly, "Yes, sir. I saw Indians as well. We all did."

Hall scanned the wharf, saw no one there, the last of the dark shapes finally gone, drawn away into the town. He looked up at the small flecks of light, fewer now, but there were lights still, beyond where he could see, behind tightly locked doors, where men saluted each other, and excited voices toasted their success.

17. FRANKLIN

THE GRIEVANCES HAD BEEN READ ALOUD, AND NOW THE TWO MEN stood a few paces apart, separated by the hard chill of winter wind. They stared at each other with a growing uncertainty, all the voices quiet now, the fiery anger of their letters long gone, the words mute, the emotion now condensed into this one place, this one deadly moment. Both men could feel the strange emptiness, a blossoming fear emerging through the anger, brought by the sudden awareness, the voice whispering in each man's mind, Now is the time, and you are alone, absolutely alone. Each man felt the weight of the pistol in his hand, could hear the words of the man between them, meaningless ritual, the absurdity, as though anyone would need to hear anything about rules. The words stopped again, and the third man slowly backed away, out of the line of fire. They stared hard at each other's eyes, tried to see some sign of weakness, the other man's cowardice perhaps betraying itself, the slight tremble in the hand spreading to the man's mind. But both men kept their hard focus, and now there was an icy silence, the onlookers holding their breaths, each man hearing a hard thunder in his ears. Some of the onlookers felt tears, helplessness, the last bit of hope fading away. All the hot talk, the shame, the hostility, had finally brought these two men to this place, where each would summon the awful fortitude he would need to kill the other. Many had prayed it would not happen this way, that it was only talk after all, but these were men of pride and strength, and on this cold bright day, not even fear could dampen the muzzle of the guns.

The man in the middle was clear now, and there was a new voice, something about God, but neither man heard, each now staring hard through the red thunder in his brain. The pistols slowly began to rise, then there was a brief pause, the final bit of hesitation, the guns not yet aimed. But the flame would not die, neither man losing his determination, not while the other still faced him. With a slight waver, the pistols rose again, and each man looked into the eyes of the other, the last doubts now swept away, and they fired.

FRANKLIN COULD HEAR VOICES DOWNSTAIRS, MRS. STEVENSON, then a man's, an urgency that interrupted his careful examination of the newspaper. He stood, moved to the door, opened it, saw the man coming quickly up the stairs, Mrs. Stevenson below, sounding upset.

"Dr. Franklin, I tried to stop him. . . ."

The man burst past him now, into Franklin's room, and Franklin waved to her.

"It's all right, madam. No harm."

He closed the door, looked at his visitor.

"What has happened, Mr. Temple?"

The man was breathing heavily, moved in short lurches, pacing in quick turns.

"I nearly killed him! That damned stubborn fool! He brought it on, all his public ranting. The last thing I ever expected was a duel! But he wouldn't stop, wouldn't leave it be!"

Franklin felt suddenly deflated, sat down heavily.

"So you went through with the duel. I heard about the challenge, but I never believed . . ." He let his head sag, the air leaving his chest, stared down at the floor. "Are you injured?"

"By the grace of God, no. But I shot *him*. He'll live, they say. And now I hear from his people that he's still determined to see this through. He wants to do it again! William Whately didn't get his just revenge. His brother's honor is still violated!"

Temple stopped pacing now, and Franklin looked up at him, saw defeat in the man's face, thin shoulders slumping under his thick wool coat. Franklin felt a rumbling depression spreading through his mind.

"Mr. Temple, I truly never believed . . . you must be assured that if I had ever thought it would go this far . . ."

Temple sat.

"It *has* gone this far, sir. And it's bound to go farther. As long as William Whately believes I took those damnable letters from his brother's effects, as long as the whole of England is told that I am responsible for the treachery . . . have you seen the newspapers, sir?"

Franklin's depression pushed him into motion. He moved slowly to the window, stared out into the late gloom of the afternoon.

"Yes, I've seen them. I believed this whole affair would simply pass, the public would lose interest. I did not believe that Mr. Whately would bring such a passion to the matter."

"He has passion enough for us all, sir. And there is energy *behind* him as well."

Franklin turned away from the window, looked at Temple.

"What do you mean?"

"You know that I am one of the few Americans who work in the employ of the king's Customs Office. A great many men of prominence come through there, and no one seems to care if I hear what seems to be sensitive talk. There are quite a few who speak frankly that there is more than family pride prodding Mr. Whately, much more at stake than his damaged feelings over the theft of a few of his brother's letters."

"Gossip, Mr. Temple."

"Forgive me the insult, Dr. Franklin, but you are either a victim of arrogance or you are simply . . . naïve. Hutchinson's letters have become more than just the untidy musings of an unpopular governor. They have become a tool, an excuse for the ministry to make some response. There is talk of harsh measures, swift punishment. Whately claims the letters are stolen property, which makes the man who sent them to Boston not only seditious, but a thief. I have endured the accusations until now. I, too, believed this was simply an annoyance that would pass. But Doctor, I did not expect to end up fighting a duel! If I had killed him . . ." He paused, leaned forward, his hands on his knees, said slowly, "Dr. Franklin, I was willing to keep silent about your involvement with the Hutchinson letters because your service to the colonies is of enormous value. But I cannot have my name destroyed in the newspapers. And sir, did you not hear me? William Whately is insisting on another duel."

Franklin moved to his small desk, sat, turned the pen slowly in the inkwell.

"I heard you, Mr. Temple. Enough of this. I had no intention of making you or anyone else a scapegoat. Those letters are my responsibility, and mine alone. I do not need my friends to absorb the consequences that I alone deserve. You are involved in this matter through no fault of your own. Just because you had close dealings with the Whately estate, you came under suspicion. I never spoke out because it all seemed inconsequential, the newspapers moaning and groaning about private letters finding their way public. Mr. Temple, nearly every letter I receive now arrives to me opened. My mail has not been private for some time. The lack of privacy has become routine." He stared at the blank paper. "Your description is regrettably accurate. I have been both arrogant and naïve. Regardless, I have done you a great wrong, Mr. Temple. Mr. Whately is entitled to know the truth. They are all entitled to know the truth."

Temple regarded him, said, "I am grateful, sir. You do understand that if you admit your involvement, it is quite likely there will be an official response."

Franklin stared at the paper, raised the pen from the inkwell, rolled it in his hand. *If I had reason to feel like something of a target before, this will seal things properly.*

"Please excuse me, Mr. Temple. I have work to do."

The letter appeared in London's *Public Advertiser* on Christmas day, a frank and complete admission that it was Franklin alone who bore responsibility for securing the Hutchinson letters, and no one else. As the ministry pondered what action to take toward this increasingly troublesome man, the formal petitions arrived from the Massachusetts Assembly, carefully worded demands that Governor Hutchinson be removed from office. As with any petition from the colonial assemblies, it was the proper responsibility of the colony's agent to present the petitions before a hearing of the king's Privy Council. And the agent for Massachusetts was still Ben Franklin.

JANUARY 1774

THE TWO MEN WERE STIFF, FORMAL, SAT ACROSS FROM HIM LIKE two schoolmasters. He had not expected to need legal representation, considered that he had always been able to handle a confrontation with anyone in official government. But the advice had been unanimous, and even his friend Strahan had insisted that Franklin not face the wrath of the ministry alone.

Franklin studied the grim faces, focused on the older man, John Dunning, quiet, sober, having the confidence of vast experience from a term as solicitor general. Dunning said something under his breath, as was something of a habit for him, small comments meant for no one but himself. Beside him was the younger man, small, pale, by the name of John Lee, a man whose reputation in the legal community was still growing, whose deep ambitions were well hidden by a friendly, somewhat simple expression. Lee seemed to ignore Dunning's odd, nearly silent recitation, but Franklin studied the older man's mouth, tried to read the words, thought, I hope he doesn't give the impression that he's mad. That might not help my situation.

Dunning completed his private conversation and turned to Franklin.

"Dr. Franklin, they do not have the power to coerce you into revealing the source of the letters. This is not a criminal proceeding. There are no accusations of wrongdoing to which you must respond."

Franklin looked at Lee, who said, "Quite, sir. However, it is best left alone, you know. The letters themselves, I mean. I would not advise calling them into evidence in any way to support the Massachusetts petitions. It is best to allow the petitions to speak for themselves. The assembly has done its job. It is in our best interests for us to simply allow the ministry to do theirs."

Dunning brought his hands together, folded his fingers into one wrinkled mass.

"The letters serve two purposes, Doctor, quite at odds with each other. Governor Hutchinson's rather harsh viewpoint toward his subjects may have incited considerable wrath in Boston, but in London, his is a view held by many, especially many of those who will hear these petitions. I have no doubt that the outcome of this case has been decided behind closed doors even now. Governor Hutchinson is a loyal subject of the king, and the letters enforce that. As any kind of support to your cause, they are useless."

Lee nodded.

"Agreed. In fact, Doctor, the only case you can make is that the people of Massachusetts are discontented and find their relationship with their governor to be odious. The existence of the petitions themselves is proof of that. If you have any further function in the hearing, it will be to reinforce the suggestion that the king would be best served if the people of Massachusetts are content, and thus, to keep them that way, Hutchinson should be removed."

Franklin absorbed the logic, felt a strange weakness.

"Do I . . . do you believe I have any reason to expect some personal problems from the hearing?"

Dunning sat back, looked over his nose at Franklin.

"Hardly. They may not like you, but that's not a punishable offense."

There was a knock at the door, the faint tapping from Mrs. Stevenson, the small voice hesitating.

"Forgive me, Doctor. There is an urgent message for you."

What else can happen? Franklin wondered. He opened the door, and she handed him a folded piece of paper, the seal already broken, typical now with all his mail. There were other letters as well, and one fell into his hand, the blessed handwriting of his wife.

"Thank you, madam. I had hoped for some word."

He closed the door, scanned the others, would not read them yet, said, "Excuse me, gentlemen, but if you will allow me one brief indulgence . . . it is rare indeed for me to receive a letter from my wife."

"Certainly, Doctor. By all means."

Franklin read the letter, newsy, gossip and business, small tidbits of joy, tales of Sally, the goings-on of the neighbors.

"She is quite in a fine mood. I'm happy to see that." He glanced up at the two men. "One can never predict."

He kept reading, but the letter was complete, as brief as so many others, his eyes following her words to the very last, and now he laughed.

"Forgive me. No matter what else may occur, no matter how much news of the mundane, she never fails to bring a smile. She would never understand, of course." He held out the letter now, and Lee leaned forward.

"I'm sorry, Doctor. What . . . ?"

"Deborah is many things, gentlemen, but she is no master of letters. Her poor spelling is always challenging, if endearing. She concludes this letter with what must surely be a unique closing." He showed them the letter again, pointing out the closing: *your a feck shonet wife*.

Both men smiled, even Dunning breaking the stern expression.

Franklin sifted through the other papers, saw another one with a colonial seal, broken as well.

"Forgive me, this appears to be official. Boston, actually."

He unfolded the paper, read slowly, studied the words, felt them carving deep into his brain, working their way down, drilling through the calm, the quiet center of his confidence. He felt suddenly like laughing, but it was not humor; it was the only way he could react to something so unknown and terrifying. He felt his eyes fill, blinked hard, turned slowly, both men watching him. Lee was leaning forward, curious, Dunning more discreet, feigning disinterest.

"Gentlemen, I fear the climate may have changed somewhat. It seems that in Boston . . . a goodly amount of the king's tea was cast rather unceremoniously into the harbor."

Lee was suddenly wide-eyed.

"How much tea?"

Franklin studied the paper again, the laughter still pushing at him from inside.

"Apparently all of it."

Dunning held out his hand.

"If I may, Doctor?"

Franklin handed him the missive. Dunning read silently, then handed the letter to Lee. After a quiet moment, Lee said, "Indeed. At a cost of nearly ten thousand pounds sterling. Well, Doctor, if the ministry had to search for some reason to dislike you before, the task has become somewhat easier."

January 29, 1774

The hearing was called to take place in the Cockpit Tavern, a sprawling den of political wrangling and somber debate that sat close to the offices of Whitehall Palace. The most influential of the king's ministers and advisors, the Privy Council, had scheduled the event as the formal airing of the Massachusetts petition, but the enthusiasm and anticipation from those who were crushed into the tavern's limited space betrayed any semblance that this was just another official hearing. This was an opportunity for an official forum to finally strike back at the colonies by acting against the man who had become a symbol for all the disagreeable rumblings and traitorous outbursts London had so placidly endured.

He filed into the tavern's meeting hall close behind his two counselors, and the voices were all around him, a vast hum of barely disguised excitement. He wore his finest suit of Manchester velvet, and his most formal, if now somewhat dated, wig. He tried not to look around, stared ahead to the one long table where the ministers already sat. Dunning and Lee led him to the far end of the room, beside the rolling warmth from a wide fireplace. Behind the table, other men stepped into place, and Franklin tried to hide his reaction, was shocked to see the familiar faces, the extraordinary show of official presence. Behind the seated officials stood the prime minister, Lord North, speaking to Lord Dartmouth. He began to feel amazement, could not help but look at the faces in the crowd now, the men all standing, huddled together, their energy surging forward, the room pulsing with the pure power. His eye caught the burst of finery of church officials, and he was stunned now, thought, My

God, it's the archbishop of Canterbury and the bishop of London. The men were not looking at him, seemed engrossed in conversation, and Franklin scanned the crowd again, saw many were looking at him, saw one man now barely visible, the familiar flat wig barely disguising the bald head. The man struggled through the crowd, emerged behind the table, settled in behind the official panel, planting himself firmly in plain view. Franklin nodded to the man, polite instinct, said under his breath, "Lord Hillsborough . . ."

Hillsborough stared at him, did not respond, his face locked in a tight satisfied smile. Beside Franklin, Dunning was speaking to himself, and Franklin, feeling a wave of dread, fought the urge to nudge him, a slight jab of the elbow, thought, Not now. I need you here.

Now another man moved behind the table, carrying a glow of self-importance. He looked across at Franklin, and Franklin felt a sudden cold stab. Beside him, Lee leaned close.

"You do know Lord Wedderburn?"

Franklin nodded, and Lee said, "Bought and paid for, you know."

Franklin considered Wedderburn, who spoke briefly to the seated ministers, still watching Franklin with a cold stare. Franklin had never known the man socially, knew only that he was once a significant thorn in the side of the king's political interests, a vocal and effective speaker for the opposition. But suddenly Wedderburn was transformed, and the talk was pretty definite that his loyalties had been quite simply for sale, and the king's men had paid the price. But despite the cash value of his loyalty, Wedderburn had a reputation as a fearless attorney, a man any counselor dreaded to see on the opposing side. With a reputation for grand spectacle in the court and a disregard for both facts and evidence, he was considered more of a showman than a legal mind. As Franklin felt the man's hard glare, his dread increased to a dense wave of gloom, his mind clouded by the noise and the smoke and the fire beside him. So Wedderburn will provide the great show, the entertainment for this extraordinary audience. Franklin looked down now, thought of the advice from

Dunning. No, there is nothing they can really do to me, not here. This is about symbols, a show of strength from a government that has been unable to do little else. I have chosen to be in this place, after all. This is my doing. I cannot argue, I cannot protest, I cannot interrupt. Let them have their say. My greatest strengths will be patience and endurance. All right, Mr. Wedderburn. I am prepared.

FRANKLIN HAD BEEN IMPRESSED WITH DUNNING'S BRIEF PRESEN-tation, his soft voice carrying a powerfully dignified message to the assembled crowd, interpreting the formal request for Hutchinson's removal as a polite favor, not a demand. The milder formulation was put to the panel as being in the best in-terests of the king, not merely the radical complaining of a group of colonial malcontents. But Wedderburn responded by speak-ing for over an hour, and the rhetoric was just as Franklin had supposed. Wedderburn's argument was simple. How could a governor be removed if his greatest offense was that his subjects disliked him because he vehemently supported the policies of the king? But after the main issue of the petition was argued, Wedderburn had begun to aim his loud oratory toward the one man whom everyone in the audience had come to see.

There had been few quiet moments, Wedderburn not allow-ing his own momentum to flag, but now he stood silently, and Franklin stared at him as he had through the entire tirade, tried to maintain a calm, stoic expression. Wedderburn allowed the quiet to fill the room, the audience slowly leaning forward, expectant, and Franklin thought, Yes, very good, sir. So you know how to play the audience.

Finally Wedderburn said, "The petition against Governor Hutchinson is an exemplary piece of hostility toward a man who simply performs his good service. You are to consider removing this man from that service because his assembly . . . dislikes him."

There was laughter, a scattering of applause. Franklin did not look at the audience, stayed focused on Wedderburn, who waited for the distractions to pass. Now he leaned forward between two of the ministers, pressed his hands down on the table, said in a low hard growl, "All the ill will, all the turmoil and loss of confidence the crown has suffered, may be properly laid at the feet of the man who soils this proceeding with his presence."

There was a faint gasp from the crowd, and Franklin thought, All right, now we will have the grand show.

"We do not know how Dr. Franklin came to possess Governor Hutchinson's private letters. As his counsel has so ably pointed out, he is not obliged to tell us. Therefore, nothing will acquit Dr. Franklin of the charge of obtaining them by fraudulent or corrupt means, for the most malignant of purposes. If he did not steal them himself, then he most certainly stole them from the original thief. This sordid episode thus provides us with an enormous irony, this man being so very pleased to refer to himself as a *man of letters*."

There was more laughter, louder this time, and Franklin allowed himself to scan the audience slowly, saw a number of familiar faces who did not share the laughter of the high-spirited men and who stared at Wedderburn with undisguised outrage. He could see military uniforms now, a pair of high-ranking officers who had joined the crowd. He did not know them, but they were clearly enjoying Wedderburn's sharp tongue. The sounds began to diminish, and Wedderburn continued, "No possession can be more of consequence than the private letters of friendship. This property is as sacred and as precious to gentlemen of integrity as their family plate or jewels. Will Dr. Franklin avow the principle that he has a right to possess such letters by any means possible, and to make all private letters his own, to apply them to whatever evil he chooses? He dared to reveal these precious letters to six people in Massachusetts. Would Dr. Franklin like me to name the six? Privacy indeed!"

Franklin felt a short pinch in his throat, a burst of protest rising. He held it tightly, told himself, No, I cannot interrupt. But how curious that Wedderburn would know who received the letters if he did not in fact have access to my *own* private mail. He was feeling a wave of exhaustion now, the stamina that had allowed him to endure the hostile rhetoric slipping away. Get hold of yourself, old man. You can show them nothing, no reaction. Do not even consider trading barbs with a man who is so much a master.

"What purpose is served by inflaming the minds of the colony toward their governor? It is obvious. Dr. Franklin and his constituents desire no less than to remove the crown's influence and establish themselves into a tyranny greater than the Roman. This man desires nothing less than to find himself the successor to Governor Hutchinson! What a cruel miscalculation! To believe that this body would succumb to such a scheme, by carelessly removing one so loyal!" He leaned forward again, pounded his fist on the table. "I hope, my lords, you will mark and brand this man, for the honor of this country, of Europe, and of mankind. He has forfeited all respect of societies and of gentlemen. Into what company will he go now with an unembarrassed face or the reputation of honest virtue? Men will watch him with a jealous eye, they will hide their papers from him, lock their libraries. What cool and apathetic evil, what revengeful temper will this man, this wily American, bring to civilized society?"

Franklin blinked hard, the weariness complete. Yes, Mr. Wedderburn, you have gone far across any line here. But what does it matter? If he is trying to incite me into some kind of outburst, I will not give him—any of them—the satisfaction. Anger is simply momentary madness, and sometimes there is strength in silence. After all, he is only throwing words, not stones.

Wedderburn went on, calmer now, a brief, anticlimactic closing. Franklin's mind was swimming, and he fought to stay attentive, his energy all devoted to maintaining the expression on his face, which was no expression at all. Now Dunning spoke, surprising him, his attention snapping to the words.

"With respect to this body, Dr. Franklin declines to be examined directly."

Wedderburn was silent now, and the chairman of the council said, "There is no reason to delay. This body has reached a determination that the petitions of the Massachusetts Assembly are founded upon resolutions formed upon false and erroneous allegations, and that the same are groundless, vexatious, and scandalous, and calculated only for the seditious purposes of keeping up a spirit of clamor and discontent in the province of Massachusetts. This hearing is now adjourned."

The voices of the audience rose, some applauding the decision, some calling out in angry protest. Franklin felt himself pulled, his arms held by Dunning and Lee, felt himself moving through the crowd. His head was spinning, the heat and the exhaustion threatening to pull his legs out from under him. He could hear the voices close to him now, men shouting into his face, outrage, talk of revenge, some toward him, some toward Wedderburn. He felt a sharp coolness, was outside now, the two men guiding him up into a carriage, a sudden lurch of motion. There was no talk from the two men seated across from him, who watched him with quiet concern. The carriage moved quickly through the dark streets, the daylight already gone. He felt himself breathing heavily, his mind a chaos of words, the voice of Wedderburn, the vitriol and venom, the sarcastic rhetoric, the abusive accusations. He looked at the two men who were still watching him, managed a slight smile, said, "Difficult day."

JANUARY 31, 1774

IT WAS TWO DAYS AFTER THE EXTRAORDINARY HEARING, AND HE had spent the previous day entertaining a constant parade of well-wishers. Word was all over London, and even loyalists were outspoken about Wedderburn's abuse. The talk had been the same all day long, friends and acquaintances offering him kind words, many convinced that he should leave London immediately, some even encouraging him to challenge Wedderburn to a duel. He had met them all with graciousness, surprised at the general outrage, the anger toward the government on his behalf. The day had concluded with the arrival of a letter, the perfect capstone to the grotesque experience. He had been terminated as postmaster general for the colonies.

He had slept late, had calmly obeyed Mrs. Stevenson's insistence that he keep the visitors away today. He acknowledged what she clearly observed, that his graciousness was drained away. She had waited for him to rise at his own time, had brought him his tea, and he had seen a concern in her eyes, something unusual, something that seemed like fear. I must have looked a fright through this whole episode. He laughed quietly, thought of the spectacle of Wedderburn pounding the table. Have they no sympathy for a sixty-eight-year old man?

He sat at the small desk, sipped the tea. He stared into the cup, could not help thinking of salt water. It must have been extraordinary, men dressed as Indians. There will be no convictions, of course, the same problem for the law they had during the whole *Gaspee* incident. What do you do, arrest the whole town? But there is a case for restitution. Ten thousand pounds, an enormous amount of money, and someone will want it paid back. Still . . . I wish I had been there to see it.

He had thought of working, trying to write more of his autobiography, but the words were not there, the weight of the hearing had not left him. It wasn't exhaustion anymore, it was sadness, becoming deeper now, his mind sinking into a black pool of depression. It is not regret, he thought. You have performed an important duty. There is so little communication, so little understanding. They will probably publish Wedderburn's speech— edited, of course, leaving out the ridiculousness. But it will still be effective, will certainly defame me all over England, a good splash of dirt on my character. Wedderburn will crow about his great success, the ministers will congratulate each other on their wise vindication of Governor Hutchinson, and none of them will understand what has really happened, what the results of this will certainly be. He had begun to write a letter to his friend Cushing, his explanation of what had taken place, a warning that as the receiver of the letters, Cushing might come under some scrutiny of his own. But the sadness had flowed out of him with the words, and he thought of the real lesson of the hearing, what no one in England would understand. If the people have grievances, and the government is so closed to hearing them that the mere pipeline, the messenger who conveys them, is brutally censured, how are peace and union to be maintained? We are so far apart that problems are too easily ignored. Grievances and complaints cannot be addressed unless they are known, and they cannot be known unless petitions are heard. If the mere delivery of a petition is considered an offense, and the messengers are so abused, then who will perform the duty? It is a dangerous thing for any state to maintain its power by plugging up the vent of complaints, stifling the voices of the people. When complaining becomes a crime, hope becomes despair.

He finished the tea, looked around the room, saw his velvet suit still spread on a chair. At least I made a good appearance—the most important thing sometimes, an effective tool for standing up to abuse. After all, you're used to it, old man. It's part of the job, always has been. A public official must have a thick skin. If they believe their attack has harmed me, has somehow removed my resolve, they are mistaken. And this is no conclusion to anything, no completion of any task, no solution to any problem. This is one more symptom of the great illness that is still spreading between the crown and its colonies. All the bluster and rhetoric, and still no wisdom. And we must still answer for the tea.

18. GAGE

LONDON, FEBRUARY 4, 1774

HE HAD ENJOYED HIMSELF AT FIRST, CAUGHT UP IN THE SWELL OF emotion that had filled the Cockpit Tavern. The cheers had all been directed at Wedderburn, the response to the man's amazing command of language, turning the perfect phrase, the juicy insults aimed at deflating the lofty image of Benjamin Franklin. Gage had applauded, even shouted with the men who sat beside him, directing their taunts toward the round old man at the far end of the room.

He had always been outraged about anyone tampering with the mails, had never allowed it in his own command. It was the one pure sanctuary of privacy, a man's words, thoughts, emotions, communicated to an intimate. There was never any doubt that what a man wrote in a letter was never intended as public. No one should ever have to fear a sudden burst of light into the quiet darkness of one's own thoughts, no matter how indiscreet they were, no matter whom they might offend.

Unlike many in the noisy audience, though, Gage had come to understand that Franklin was only the most visible offender in regard to a practice that had become commonplace. Since Gage had been in London, he had learned that beyond Ben Franklin's amazing abuse of Governor Hutchinson's privacy, the opening of mail was actually becoming official policy. Whether someone was considered a potential threat to the government had become a judgment made by anyone from King George himself to the offices of Lord North or even, lately, the most junior clerk at the mail offices. Gage was immediately nervous about this sudden lapse of personal security, found himself editing his own letters, suddenly rereading his own words to ferret out any innocent reference that might be misinterpreted, any strong words that might cause indigestion in some bureaucrat. It had occurred to him with a stir of uneasiness that someone might possibly put some undue emphasis on his wife's being born an American. As much as he joined in the enthusiastic gloating over Lord Wedderburn's assault on Franklin, Gage held the thought in the back of his mind that Franklin might not have done something so terribly evil as to deserve all of this.

As the tirade from Wedderburn had begun to drone into its second hour, Gage had begun to focus more on Franklin himself, watching for a telltale break in the old man's composure, an impatient interruption, some reaction from Franklin to the amazing vitriol from the Scottish lawyer. But Franklin had remained perfectly stoic, respectful, even attentive. As the second hour drew to a close, Gage began to feel his sympathies shifting, was aware that many in the audience had begun to react negatively to Wedderburn's graphic hostility. Gage had been prepared to stand himself, make a statement, assist the panel in their consideration of the argument that had prompted the hearing in the first place, the petition to have Governor Hutchinson removed. But when the panel concluded the hearing by ruling immediately in favor of Hutchinson, Gage realized that the audience was paying much closer attention to the strange personal assault on Franklin. By the time Wedderburn wrapped up his remarks, many, Gage included, had heard enough.

In the taverns and meeting rooms around the Parliament buildings, there was still talk of the inappropriate abuse of Franklin, but the attention had shifted dramatically with news of the destruction of the tea. If Franklin was a symbol, the visible face who could somehow be blamed, called to task for the general unrest in the colonies, it was hard for anyone to blame him for dumping the tea. In England, the people had endured written abuse for years, the angry tirades in colonial newspapers, published pamphlets, all the mad pronouncements for which the Sons of Liberty had built their infamous reputation. But this was very different, a shocking bit of *action*.

The response in the British newspapers was confused at first, arguments over financial retribution, who should be made to pay and how. The destruction of the tea was an assault on private property, English property, and there were immediate calls for restitution, to find some means of forcing the colonists to pay the East India Company for the loss. But this was an economics problem, and the people were reacting more with emotion. Few of the voices in the taverns and on the street cared for economic solutions to anything. Finally the newspapers began to shout along with the people. In one great swell of English pride, the masses began to use a new word, formerly reserved for those most hostile to the annoying sounds from the colonial rabble. The word was *punishment*.

Gage had been supremely disappointed by the reception he had received in England. In fact, there had been very little reception at all. Margaret's pregnancy kept her close to home, the grand estate of his brother known as Highmeadow, while Gage's own time was spent mostly in mundane sight-seeing trips. Margaret had finally felt well enough to come with him to London, and it was then that the baby decided to surprise both parents by a sudden arrival. It was a girl, born in mid-August.

While Margaret and the baby spent the autumn months back at Highmeadow, Gage had tried to find a welcome in many of the ministry offices in London, had even been granted a brief audience with King George. But the visits were formal, stiff affairs of no substance, simply polite acknowledgment of the general's visit. There was no invitation to speak to Parliament, and for the most part, no invitations at all. The fantasy of the brass bands and great parades had vanished.

But with England's boiling response to the destruction of the tea, his frustrating invisibility had suddenly changed. He was after all, still the commander in chief of His Majesty's forces in America. And now there would be another audience with the king, and no one expected this meeting to be as meaningless as the last.

"YOU MAY ENTER, GENERAL. PLEASE CONFINE YOURSELF TO DIS-cussion of events upon which His Majesty addresses you."

Gage moved past the king's official greeter, nodded silently, peered ahead through the great wide doors of the king's official chamber. He didn't expect the meeting to be private, had experienced in his first visit the strange audience that spread around the vast room, government officials, military men. They sat as if they never moved, never left the room, were somehow designated as the king's official attendants. He saw the faces watching him as he stepped primly into the chamber, polite smiles, disinterested idle stares, one familiar face above the stark grandeur of his uniform, General James Paterson. Gage made a brief nod, returned by Paterson, and now in one single motion, they all stood, and at the far side of the chamber a door opened, and Gage saw a flurry of scarlet, the long coat draped over the man's shoulders, a final touch by a petite handmaiden, who was swept aside with an impatient wave. The king seemed to blow into the room, the bright red swirling around white silk. He ignored the audience, stared directly at Gage, moved to the great heavy chair, green satin and dark wood, sat heavily, rubbed his hands together, smiled.

"Shall we have a war, General?"

Gage made a deep bow, rose slowly, heard the men behind him sitting again.

"I am honored to be again in the presence of Your Majesty."

"Yes, yes. So? A war? Put this matter to rest once and for all?"

Gage glanced at the king's face, a brief look, knew the protocol, that it was highly insulting to look the monarch directly in the eye.

"Forgive me, Your Majesty, I'm not certain to what you refer."

The king grunted, waved his arm in a wide arc.

"Perhaps you should join the statuary here. I had thought you would be more . . . animated. You've lived with them long enough, I should think you would understand what is so plainly obvious to me."

Gage rolled the words over in his mind, suddenly realized the king was offering him an opportunity.

"Yes, Your Majesty. I believe I understand the problem with the colonies. My command is prepared to offer Your Majesty a solution, with your permission."

The king stared away for a long moment, and Gage glanced at his face, saw the pale softness bathed in a faint glow of light from a tall window across the room. The king seemed to converse with himself, his expression changing slightly, a small frown, and then he turned back to Gage.

"I rather miss George Grenville. He's dead, you know. A monarch requires the services of a man who understands numbers, who knows all about the most irritating details of commerce. He was chancellor of the exchequer for a time. The perfect man for the job. The Stamp Act was his idea, his plan. It was also his downfall. His problem was that he possessed an orderly mind, and he applied that to a disorderly situation. Chaotic, in fact." The king stared again at the window. "I would like some tea."

There was a small commotion through the far doorway, and a small man emerged carrying a silver tray, on which was balanced a small silver pitcher beside a round china cup. Gage watched the man pour the tea into the cup, saw the small wisp of steam, thought, Obviously he was prepared. He was impressed now. Of course. Good servants anticipate one's needs. As it should be. The man set the cup down on a small table beside the chair, withdrew silently, but the king ignored the cup, looked at Gage again.

"I have tried to govern this kingdom with wisdom, General. I have learned the value of persuasion and the value of force. In London, the ills of government are often best cured with the administering of gold pills. Spread the medicine properly, and the ills vanish. Persuasion. Doesn't work with colonials, General. I have heard all the tiresome metaphors. They are like children, they are merely farms to provide for the mother country, they are the ground upon which the polished boots of the empire tread. I tire so of newspapers." He leaned forward now, pointed a finger at Gage. "Until now. Now I rather enjoy the newspapers."

Gage waited for more, and the king sat back in the chair, blew out a short hard breath. "You're supposed to ask me why."

Gage bowed his head slightly.

"Forgive me, Your Majesty. Why does Your Majesty enjoy the newspapers?"

George's voice boomed, "Because they finally agree with me! The people are speaking out, and the newspapers are finally paying attention. The people have always understood the right course. You can always count on the English spirit, our resolve, to direct the empire on the right course."

Gage nodded, said nothing, hoped there would be an explanation.

"Who destroyed the tea, General?"

Gage rolled the possible answers through his mind, began to feel a bead of sweat on his lip.

"They call themselves the Sons of Liberty, Your Majesty."

"Sons of Liberty. Sons of insurrection, sons of barbarism! That was George Grenville's mistake. Apply a rational solution to an irrational problem. Impose a civilized policy on savages. Didn't work then, not going to work now. This is not about taxes.

We can impose taxes anywhere we desire. This is an issue involving nothing less than the authority of the monarchy over its subjects. That authority is not just being questioned, it is being overruled! Don't you agree, General?"

Gage sensed the opportunity again.

"Your Majesty, if I may be so bold. My command has requested the presence of troops in the colonies, a great many more troops than have been provided. This latest outbreak of lawlessness confirms that need. As long as the colonists have no fear of reprisal, they strut like lions, while we are seen as lambs. If we show resolve, all those traitorous voices will fall silent. With all respect to the soul of Mr. Grenville, my command believes there is only one method useful in defeating a rebellion."

The king bellowed again, "Rebellion! Yes! I have been saying that for some time now! Use the word, don't be afraid of it! So many of my ministers are hesitant to describe the situation for what it is. They fear the opposition, those absurd fools in Parliament who build their notoriety by speaking out against my policies, as though, by disagreeing with their king, they establish themselves as some sort of heroes. And until lately, the newspapers have played their game. Well, no more! We have a rebellion on our hands! The English people have united in the cause! The empire will prevail . . . and *you*—" He pointed at Gage, and there was a silent moment. Gage waited for more, felt his heart pounding, the rising excitement of the moment.

The king said quietly, "What do you think of Governor Hutchinson?"

Gage looked up, met the king's eye, immediately dropped his head.

"Forgive me, Your Majesty . . . I'm not sure to what Your Majesty refers."

"It was a simple question, General. All right, too timid to share your opinion? You're not alone. So I'll tell you what I think. He's an adequate governor, for the most part. A lot like George Grenville, actually. Orderly mind. Loyal, certainly. Puts the empire above all. I require that. An efficient bureaucrat." The king leaned forward again, pointed his finger close to Gage's face, said, "And, I regret to say, General, he is weak. Timid. Reluctant to offend the very barbarians who bark and growl at the walls of the empire. So now, General, do you have an opinion about Governor Hutchinson?"

Gage understood at last.

"Yes, Your Majesty. I feel that Governor Hutchinson is all those things as Your Majesty describes."

George sat back again, glanced at the tea beside him, said quietly, "I would like some hot tea."

The scene played out again, the small servant appearing with another tray, the first cup replaced by another, the slow rise of steam. The king ignored the cup, said to Gage, "How many troops?"

Gage felt relief, had hoped to hear that question above all others. He straightened himself, had prepared his answer well.

"If Your Majesty will authorize four regiments, my command will place them where they will perform the required service to the empire. The rabble in Boston will be brought under control again. The rebellion will be stopped."

"Crushed, General. It is not enough to stop it. It must be obliterated. Every element, every piece of inspiration, every voice."

"Yes, Your Majesty. Crushed."

"There are those in my ministry who feel we should bombard Boston with cannon. Inefficient. Destroying houses doesn't destroy rebellion. It is more about spirit, don't you agree?"

"Quite so, Your Majesty. There is a better way. I propose, with Your Majesty's permission, that we enact stronger measures, that we bring a swift and complete punishment not only on those rebels who shout the loudest, but on those who follow their calls. The punishment must be absolute!" He was excited again, and George was nodding, staring at the window. Gage waited, and the king rubbed his face with thick fingers, prodded the soft chalky roundness, then focused on Gage again, studied the man's uniform, as if for the first time. "Four regiments?"

"Yes, Your Majesty. That should be an adequate force to completely eliminate the insurrection as it now threatens Boston. My command does not believe the rebellion will receive assistance from the other colonies. There has been some contagiousness to the disorder in Boston, but once eliminated there, it will be eliminated throughout the colonies."

The king stared away again, closed his eyes for a moment, said, "I wish I could be there. I would enjoy watching the terror on their dirty faces, hearing their pitiful cries begging their king's forgiveness. What a joy to behold, to trample the unruly, to crush the spirit of rebellion from their simple minds, allow them to rise again in humble acceptance of their guilt. And then they understand who their king is, how he rules his empire. They will know that I have forgiven them, they will return to the empire cleansed. Their loyalty will never again be questioned." He glanced down at the teacup, sat back in the chair. "I would like some hot tea."

Gage watched the servant appear once more, and George was looking at Gage now, a slight smile.

"But I would starve them a little first."

APRIL 2, 1774

HE HAD MOSTLY STAYED AT HIGHMEADOW WITH MARGARET AND the children, had tried to find some way to work himself into the affairs of state, find access to the closed doors of government. But no word had come, and the frustration returned, the suspicion that he was simply being ignored, while the planning over the crisis in the colonies was played out by conferences of ministers and debates in Parliament. It had been two months since his audience with the king, and Gage still had no idea if anything he had said was taken seriously. He had become used to this in New York, hot talk and grand pronouncements in London, resulting in no action at all. It was more than distance, and now that he was close to the talk, he could see that despite all the outcries against the Americans, it might be the talk that would prevail after all.

He had begun to look for a home, a quiet fantasy that he might be allowed still to assume some honorary post, accompanied of course by a title, the reward for his years of good service. The longer he stayed away from the colonies, the less he wanted to return, and the fantasy of a long retirement in England was strengthened by the silence from the government. He was becoming more convinced each day that his role in colonial affairs was indeed coming to a close.

Margaret's health had been unusually fragile; the birth of the baby was now eight months past, but she had not yet regained her strength. Childbirth had not been difficult for her before, but the doctors seemed concerned about her age, knowing that as a woman grew older, the risks and the complications of giving birth increased. Gage had tried to bolster her strength with a show of optimism, trying to convince her, as much as he tried to convince himself, that this was the best place, the ideal place for all of them. She did not respond, and he knew that there was more to her sickness, something the doctors could not understand. It was not just the childbirth that had pulled her down, it was his talk, his dream that England would be their home.

If Gage could not reach her in that dark place in which she seemed to dwell, he had been more successful in insisting that she walk with him each day, enjoy the beauty of the gardens. With the warmer days of spring, it had actually seemed to work, the color in her soft face returning, her stamina increasing, the cold silence giving way to glimpses of kindness.

It had been another warm morning, unusual this early in the year, and the hills around Highmeadow were already deep green, a flat carpet of wildflowers appearing for the first time, small clusters of faint color. He had pushed the distance a bit, a wider arc across the low hills to the south, a new path she had not yet seen. Now, the walk nearly complete, they moved through the wide garden close to the grand house. She held his arm, and he could feel her sagging against him, moving in a slow rhythm, silent, with soft quick breathing. They had not spoken in a long while, and now she stopped, took one long breath, said, "Not another step." She looked around, spotted the small bench at one end of the garden. "There. Sit with me."

They moved together, and he sat her carefully down on the flat stone seat, eyed the narrow space beside her.

"A tight fit."

She glanced down to the side.

"You'll manage."

He smiled, slid himself down next to her, close against her, and it did not escape him that it was as near as he had been to her in a long while. The soft quiet returned, a light breeze rolling through a distant stand of trees. She took another deep breath.

"How much longer, Thomas?"

There was an edge to her voice, surprising him. He had heard the question before, had thought she was satisfied with the answer. He felt a surge of frustration, held on to it tightly, put a hand on her knee, felt the softness of the light wool.

"Are you not yet pleased? Is there nothing here that appeals to you?"

"This is not our home, Thomas. We are merely guests."

He heard the accent in her voice now, seemed to hear it most at times like this, cruel coincidence. It was the only American accent he had heard in months, and he could not escape it, the constant reminder that England was not her home.

"Please, Margaret. My brother has allowed us to remain here as long as we need to. Once we find our own estate, we will all be happier. Think of the children. . . ."

He knew immediately he had made a mistake.

"So *now* we think of the children? Did it not bother you to send them so far away from New York, so far from their parents?"

It was a familiar argument he knew he could not win.

"Margaret, we have been through this. You know that it was best. They had to be schooled in England. They would have little future if they took their education in the colonies."

She moved her knee, and he knew the sign, removed his hand. Her softness had changed, her back more stiff.

"I am not so certain of that anymore. There is so much angry talk, so much hostility. I am rather tired of being looked upon by your family as an . . . outsider. I don't relish the thought that my own children may soon regard their mother in the same way."

"Nonsense, Margaret. No one thinks of you as anything other

than the wife of General Gage. You need not worry that anyone will treat you with anything but the utmost respect."

"So I am to be pleased that I am . . . nothing but the wife of General Gage?"

"It's not a bad thing, my dear. Certainly."

He did not notice her looking at him, the glare in her eye; he was focused on the servant who emerged from the house. The man spotted them, made his way across the garden. Behind him, two children emerged from the house, running, passed the servant, a race, quick shouts, and the larger boy now pulled up close to them, piping, "I won!"

The smaller boy reached his brother's side, tried to stand straight as well, but the loss of the race overcame his attempt at stoicism, and he began to push the older boy, wrapped himself around his brother's legs, tumbling them both to the ground. The servant had reached them now, tried to avoid the chaotic scene erupting near his feet. Margaret was laughing.

"William, do not assault your brother!"

Gage leaned down, wrapped his hand around the smaller boy's waist, pulled him free, and the larger boy struggled to his feet.

"I did not hit him, Mum."

"Yes, Henry, you showed admirable restraint."

Gage released the smaller boy.

"I don't understand you, William. It does not hold much promise to pick a fight with your big brother. Your success is best gained by attacking a weaker foe, not a stronger one. A good general knows that."

The smaller boy now stood at attention, saluted his father, and the older boy said, "He's better today. I heard him coughing last night, but not this morning."

"William, come here," Margaret said, reaching out.

The smaller boy rushed into her arms, and she held him away for a moment, studied his face.

"You have good color today. Feeling all right?"

William squirmed free.

"I can run all the way around the house!"

He dashed away, and Gage said to the older boy, "Stay close to him, Henry."

The older boy made a bow, said to Margaret, "Mummy . . . ," and was gone in quick pursuit of his brother. Margaret watched them.

"He seems to be better."

"Don't worry, my dear. But don't you see? They love it here."

The servant stepped forward now, balanced a flat silver tray on his palm. Gage watched the boys disappear around the side of the great house.

"Sorry, Holt. What is it?"

The servant made a brief bow, held the tray out toward him.

"General, this just came for you. We were told it was rather urgent."

Gage picked up the folded letter from the tray, nodded toward the servant, the silent command, and the man backed away, retraced his steps toward the house. Gage glanced at Margaret, saw her staring down.

"Rather a grand seal on this one."

He began to feel the anticipation now, made a small show of breaking the wax, looked at her again, wanted her to share the moment. But she would not look at him, and his disappointment quickly passed, his attention now focused on the letter. He unfolded the thick paper, glanced at the bottom, felt a new stab of excitement.

"It's from Lord North himself."

He read for a long moment, felt the air slowly leaving him, his knees growing weaker. He sat down beside her again, lowered the paper, and she said, "So, are you a duke now?"

He sat silently, her words drifting past him. He began to shake his head.

"I did not think . . . I had thought the king . . ."

She looked at him now, a long quiet moment, her softness returning.

"What is it, Thomas?"

He stared at the paper again, the shock giving way to a bolt of anger, a sharp assault directed inside, at himself.

"It was foolish of me to believe they would allow me to remain here. A commander does not step away from his command in time of crisis. I thought the king was engaging me . . . I thought I was merely His Majesty's entertainment. I didn't know he was serious, that he would actually follow through."

"Follow through on what, Thomas?"

"I asked that my command be given four regiments, that the troops be sent to Boston to quell the unrest. I had thought . . . I assumed General Haldimand would manage the affair, as I had instructed him. But it seems the king has other ideas."

He stopped, felt an emptiness in his chest, straightened himself, took a long deep breath. He looked at her now, expected to see cold satisfaction, her wishes realized, the months of pulling away from this place finally successful. He wanted to be angry with her, blame her somehow, but she put a hand on his arm, and he saw only her deep concern. He shook his head, held up the letter.

"Lord North . . . it's official. I have been ordered to resume my post. But not in New York. I am to sail immediately to Boston. The ministry wants me in command of the troops. But that's not all of it." He looked at the letter again, fought through the disbelief. "Once in Boston, I am to assume control of the civil government. Thomas Hutchinson is being relieved of his position. I have been appointed governor of Massachusetts."

19. ADAMS

Braintree, May 11, 1774

BOTH HOUSES WERE NOW OFFICIALLY THEIR PROPERTY, THE smaller one, John's birthplace, purchased from his brother a few months before. It had always been theirs to use, the two homes so close together, but the title had stayed as his father's will had decreed. With his brother now willing to sell, Adams had leapt at the opportunity to increase his holdings, since the title to the house included over fifty acres of farm and pasture. Adams' pride had grown with the acreage, and when his business allowed him the pleasant stay at Braintree, his long joyous walks across the land had grown longer still.

Around the neighboring farms, the land was worked over by a swarm of laborers, some from the farms themselves, many more brought in from outside. While ships still brought their cargo into Boston Harbor, the numbers had gone down, nervousness over the destruction of the tea spreading to the merchants who traded in other goods. The town began to feel the effects of the slowdown in trade, and with the coming of spring, many of the workers had taken to the countryside, looking for work on the land.

Adams had been concerned about the planting of his own crops, had struggled with the long weeks in Boston. But Abigail's letters had calmed him, firm reassurance that the planting would be accomplished whether he was home or not. For a while now the smaller house had been sitting empty, but with the increase in traffic on the roads, the strong young men from the wharves who sought a new kind of work, vacancies all over Braintree had filled. Abigail had leased the house to an older man named Hayden and his two sons. Hayden was a stern, unsmiling man who assured her that his boys would do the work required. She was uncomfortable at first, had been told pieces of gossip about Hayden, his dismal reputation for argument, some even suggesting that his sentiments were strictly loyalist. Abigail had given that little thought, however, had signed the lease papers, counting more on the labor of three men to provide much value to the farm. She stayed away from any political discussion with the man, especially as the talk from the neighbors increased. She began to hear reports of Hayden's growing reputation as a man who could not visit a pub without spouting unpopular politics, inciting more than one fistfight. But though she had begun to feel uneasy about her new tenants, the young men had immediately taken to the wide fields, commanded by the fiery eye of their father. Within days, spreading out under a flurry of sweat and energy, the drab brown dirt had come to life, neat rows of furrows spreading far to the hills. If Hayden was a Tory, at least the farm had benefited from the strong backs of his sons.

She had kept John informed, sent letters nearly every day, but as the planting progressed, she stayed as busy as the young men who worked the plow. Much of her time was spent inside, the children always pulling at her, her attention never free of the silent fear as she watched the youngest child. She had to scold herself: Tommy is not weak, he is anything but. Charles was nearly four, had in fact grown into a healthy child, and Nabby was old enough now that she could manage the small chores. But if Abigail understood that no amount of attention could prevent the crying, the sound was still an alarm, bringing back the awful memories of the fragile little girl, and so brought the mother close to the side of the child.

The children were all napping, and she was amazed that even John Quincy had fallen asleep. She had been skeptical of the boy's silence, thought perhaps he was plotting some escape from the house. It was a common game now, especially with the two young men out working in the fields. She had snuck quietly to the door, trying to catch him putting on his shoes, perhaps, but there were only the soft sounds of sleeping children. She rarely had the luxury of her eldest son's silence. She welcomed the brief time alone, went outside into the warm spring air, closed the door quietly behind her, aware she was smiling. She moved between the two houses, curious, knew the two young men were in the field on the far hill, still planting the corn. Their father rarely went with them, and she could not recall if Hayden had actually done any of the work at all. She had not heard anything from him in several days, another blessed bit of silence. She knew Hayden was often away, some business in Boston perhaps, something he would never have discussed with her. She stopped, heard only silence in the smaller house, was embarrassed. What are you hoping to hear? she chided herself. She hurried past the house into the open yard, tried to see the young men in the field, but they were too far away, her view blocked by the roll of the hills. She glanced back to the smaller house. It is a strange thing,

men. They are so different. The young men had never been anything but kind, polite, always lowering their gaze when she was
nearby. But Hayden was different; nearly any comment could be
rude. She had heard the curses, the indiscreet mutterings, knew
he didn't care much to be working for a woman. His boys seem
almost afraid of him. He must be a terror when he's angry. She
felt a small shudder, a chill. Oh, for goodness sake, stop that!
You do have an imagination. He's just a bit strange, that's all. She
walked out toward the orchard, could see the clusters of white
flowers spread on the ground beneath the trees, the blossoms beginning to fall from the branches. She scanned the orchard, appraising. A good crop, certainly, for the apples. If it's not too wet
this summer . . .

She looked back toward the main house, listened for any
sound of waking children, still heard only the silence. She
turned, stared up toward the patch of far trees, thought of the
brook, that special place where John had taken her, the soft
trickle of water swirling into the one wide pool. They had knelt
down, stared at their reflections, and he had tried to touch her
face on the surface of the water, gently, trying not to disturb the
reflection. He was trying to be so careful, and she had suddenly
snapped her teeth together, her reflection biting at his finger,
startling him. The moment had changed from soft romance to
play, and he had reacted the same way, held his finger up, examining it in playful outrage. *You bit me, I'm wounded. . . .*

It could be another moment like that right now. The children
are quiet, and it is a glorious day. And John would know it, too,
would take me by the hand, and we would climb the long hill,
move down into the trees, laughing, the sly evil sound he makes
when we are being oh so naughty.

She smiled, began to walk out into the field, stepped between
the neat rows in the dark soil. Perhaps for a while I will stand
under the trees, maybe have a drink of water, look at my reflection. Yes, dearest friend, I am missing you.

There was a sound out on the road, and she turned, saw a
wagon rolling toward the houses, could see it was Hayden. He
reined up in the yard, a clatter of commotion, and her smile

faded. He was waving toward her, shouting something, and she raised a hand in acknowledgment, all the sweet thoughts gone now. She began to move toward the house, thought, The children will not sleep through all this. Not that he has any concerns.

He seemed animated, was moving toward her quickly, surprising her. She waited now, and he stopped, held out a piece of paper, uttered through sharp breaths, "Well now, there ya have it! Told ya all, I did! Told ya all!"

He was sweating, wiped at his face with a dirty handkerchief, flapped the paper toward her. "Told ya there'd be hell to pay, I did! Ya can read it yerself."

She moved closer, took the paper from him. He was staring hard at her, a sharp glare, the angry breaths pouring out in a hot smell of tobacco.

"Well, go on! Read it! All yer Sons a Liberty and such! Hell to pay! I dun told ya!"

She backed away, looked at what was in her hand, a printed pamphlet: *The Boston Port Bill! Outrage from London!*

"Go on, look at it! This is what yer protests have brought ya!"

"Please, Mr. Hayden! May I be allowed to read it in peace?"

He grunted, took a step back, locked his arms across his chest. She scanned the pamphlet again, began to read, and after a moment said, "Oh, my goodness. The king has ordered the port of Boston to be closed. No ships are to enter or leave. No trade. The army is to occupy . . ."

"I told ya. Keep readin' there, Mrs. Adams. There's a lot more."

"The charter of Massachusetts has been repealed. Our government has been annulled. No soldier can be charged with the murder of a citizen by any court in Massachusetts. . . . The town meetings have been abolished!"

"There! Ya see? Hell to pay! Ya happy about yer little Tea Party now, eh?"

She ignored him, moved toward the house. She could hear the children now, but focused still on the paper she held. She stopped, looked back at Hayden.

"Where did you get this, Mr. Hayden?"

"It's to be found everywhere around Boston, Mrs. Adams. It's the latest word from England, I assure you. Quite a bit of shoutin' goin' on."

"Did you see my husband?"

"Can't say as I did. I 'spect he knows more'n anyone else what's happenin'. Seein' how he's one of them who done brought all this down on us."

She moved toward the house again, saw Nabby standing at the door, and the girl backed suddenly away, saw the look in her mother's eyes. Abigail went inside, the other children waiting for her, and she suddenly slammed the door shut, startling them all. Charles began to cry, and Abigail sat down, held out her hand, and the boy hesitated, then rushed forward, pulled himself tight into her dress. She looked at them all now, saw the fear on their faces, and she gave them a smile, shook her head.

"It's all right. I didn't mean to scare you. Your papa should be home soon. Tonight, I'm certain. He has a lot of work to do."

The other two children moved close to her, and Nabby said, "Mama, what's wrong?"

Abigail shook her head, could not stop the tears.

"I'm not sure, dear."

She ran her hand gently across each face. The older boy backed away, went to the corner of the room, picked up a broom, the handle taller than he was, held it out in front of him.

"Don't worry, Mama. Nothing will happen to us here. I got my musket."

She tried to laugh, wiped at the wetness on her cheek.

"Yes, John Quincy, you may protect us."

She stood now, eased away from the children, went to the front window, looked out toward the road. She expected to see him there, jumping down off the carriage, knew he would have the same piece of paper in his hand, could hear his words, the hot anger, the outrage. She looked at the yellow sheet rolled up in her hand. Perhaps not anger; something else. Sadness. It is the loss of the charter that will upset him most, she thought, taking away our laws, just sweeping aside everything he holds so dear. And closing the port . . . the people are already without work.

There could be a panic. She was suddenly angry at Hayden. *You and your ignorance. What do you know of the Sons of Liberty? Your blind foolish loyalty, to what? A king who delights in punishing his subjects? To what end? All we want is to make our own lives in our own way. To live without fear of your soldiers suddenly telling us we're doing something wrong.* She stared at the empty yard, thought of Hayden's words: *hell to pay. We may all learn what hell is before this is through.*

20. GAGE

Boston, May 13, 1774

THE JOURNEY HAD BEEN FITFUL AND ROUGH, AND HE REACHED Boston Harbor in the grip of an impatience that bordered on outright fury. Through long nights on a rolling ship, he had pondered his career, his future, the dreams of peaceful retirement he had foolishly allowed to distract him from reality. When there had been a moon, he had cursed it, could not prevent the pale gold light from staring at him in bitter laughter, the shadows of thin clouds taunting him with the faces of his enemies. He was not even sure who the enemies were now, had tried to focus his anger on the most obvious, those traitorous serpents who called themselves Sons of Liberty. But he was angry as well at those he had left behind him, ministers and parliamentarians who accepted no responsibility for the catastrophe their policies had produced. *No, this is all up to me. And there will be nothing to be gained, no recognition, no advancement, no title. If I am successful and this ridiculous rebellion is crushed, the king and all his minions will crow and strut and claim it was the power of the empire that prevailed. And if I fail, then . . .*

Margaret had not come with him, would sail some time later. The excuse to their friends and family had been her frailty, but

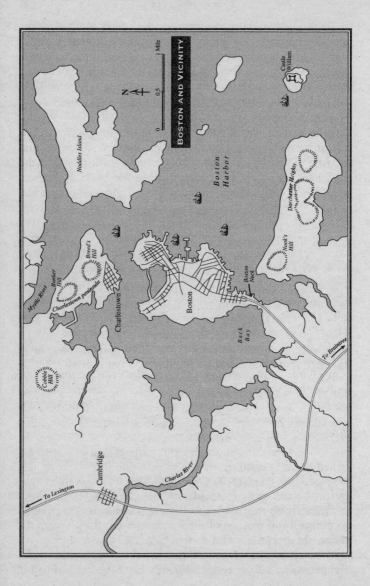

he could not hide from her that he was afraid for her safety. Boston is not the place for her, not now. In a few weeks she can sail to New York, go home for a while, until the situation in Massachusetts is somewhat more in control. She prefers that anyway, closer to her friends and family, the familiar social light. They will make quite a fuss over her return, and she will enjoy every moment of that.

He had not known what to expect when the ship finally docked at Boston, but he did not go straight into the city. He landed first at Castle William, the stronghold in the harbor insulated from the city's harsh chaos. He had been surprised to find the quarters nearly filled with civilians, those most loyal to the king, who had fled the city itself. They had greeted him with an urgency that had further depressed him. They spoke to him in grateful homilies, gushing appreciation that by his mere presence all their problems would quietly slip away, that Gage had brought to Boston all the power and virtue of His Majesty's empire. Even more than knowing the details of the king's new policies toward the colony, what mattered most was that the king himself knew of their crisis, and by sheer strength of will, all that had gone wrong would be set right again.

HE HAD BEEN AT CASTLE WILLIAM FOR SEVERAL DAYS, ABSORBING as much information as he could about the situation that would confront him in the city. The troops had arrived as well, the four regiments he had requested from King George. Castle William was now a madhouse of activity, many civilians seeking asylum under the protection of British guns. Anyone in Boston who was known to have Tory leanings was subject to extraordinary abuse, being the only tangible targets at which the citizens could aim their outrage. Gage had tried to stay behind closed doors, avoid the irritating stream of well-wishers, glad-handing loyalists offering their own simpleminded advice. When he forced himself to emerge from the walls of his small office, it was to move among the troops, an informal inspection, testing morale. He kept the officers at ease, would listen first to the soldiers, the comments and tidings of the men who would learn firsthand if the angry voices in the town would give way to violence. Each meeting in the barracks had been a source of strength for him, and as the time grew closer to when he would move his headquarters into Boston itself, his confidence was complete. He knew his new command was fortified by the finest soldiers of the finest army in the world.

There had to be some official ceremony, the passing of the governorship from Hutchinson to him. He was surprised Hutchinson had not been to see him sooner, but he would not push it, would allow the man to take his time, to remove himself from his royal perch in his own way. When the appointment was finally made, the meeting scheduled, Gage was relieved, an unpleasant task coming to a conclusion.

He waited in the small office, had put aside any work, a small stack of pamphlets brought to the castle by another cluster of frightened civilians. He glanced at the drawing on one, titled *The Massachusetts Calendar*, a caricature of Hutchinson being assaulted by two grotesque figures, symbols of death and evil. *Let the destroyers of mankind behold and tremble . . .*

He shook his head, made a small laugh. So we are the destroyers of mankind. They have skill with a phrase, no doubt. But does anyone truly read this absurdity and take it to heart? How can anyone not see this for what it is? Drama. Cartoons. Just like their voices, shrill and outrageous. How can this schoolboy nonsense inspire anyone to betray their king?

There was a knock, and slowly the door opened.

"Yes, what is it?"

"General Gage, Governor Hutchinson has arrived."

Gage arose, polite formality.

"Show him inside."

The door opened wide, and Hutchinson stepped forward, glanced around the small space.

"Not much to look at, Governor," Gage said. "But it's a headquarters. Do sit down."

He motioned to the one chair in front of the desk, but Hutchinson seemed to hesitate, and now Gage studied his face, saw something unfamiliar, the man's soft features scarred by a dark sadness. Hutchinson slowly sat, seemed to sink into the small chair, the sadness engulfing him. Gage noticed the man's clothes, all the careful attention to detail, the grand spectacle of the man's perfect presentation replaced by dowdiness, the shirt a rumple of unpressed silk, the burst of ruffles on his chest now flat and dingy. Hutchinson stared straight past him, waited patiently for Gage to finish his appraisal, until Gage sat as well.

"Welcome, Governor. Allow me to say, this is a most unpleasant occasion."

Hutchinson looked at him now, said nothing, his expression revealing only the dark mood. Gage felt suddenly uncomfortable, the light in the small room seeming to dim.

"Tea, perhaps? Anything at all?"

Hutchinson made a brief smile, said, "Tea." The word seemed to stick in his throat. "Thank you, no."

Gage folded his hands, had been prepared for a pleasant, polite conversation, typical of Hutchinson, all the business of the day. But Hutchinson sat quietly, waiting, and Gage felt a coldness in the room.

"Are you . . . all right, Governor?"

Hutchinson still looked at Gage, tilted his head slightly, seemed to contemplate the question. Then he said, "I suppose I will be soon enough. Once I am in England, there should be pleasant times indeed. All the proper courtesies paid, the respect of my . . . peers."

Gage could hear the bitterness in the man's voice, thought, Of course. I had not really considered that. He's leaving his home.

"You are well respected, Governor. I have heard that the king himself is eager to welcome you, certain to make some formal recognition of your work."

Hutchinson shook his head slowly.

"Forgive me, General, but what work is that? If you mean my obedience to the law, then, well . . . yes, certainly. If you mean my placing His Majesty's concerns above all else, his policies, carrying out the edicts of Parliament, doing the *good deed* . . ." He stopped, the words choked off, and Gage began to feel impatient with the man's misery.

"Governor . . ."

"Oh, do stop referring to me that way, General! I will endure that title from now on, every day of my life in England. I can join the crowd of pathetic men whose attendance at parties is made most notable by their careers concluding in whimpering embarrassment. I ceased being governor of this province the moment your ship landed. We hardly need a ceremony to establish what has occurred."

Gage was surprised by the volume of Hutchinson's outburst, the man now red-faced, the bleak sadness replaced by a fulminating anger. Gage felt his irritation growing, clamped it down.

"Mr. Hutchinson, I shall address you however you wish. But your volume . . . it would be best if we did not give audience to those beyond these walls. I am not your enemy, sir. I did nothing to undermine your position. I assure you, this is not a title I sought."

Hutchinson seemed to calm, the anger replaced by a sudden embarrassment.

"Forgive me, General Gage. I believe you, of course. I am familiar enough with the ways of London. In fact, I have received a letter from Lord Dartmouth assuring me of the king's affection. Whatever considerations were given weight for replacing me, I have been offered every assurance that it is not due to some particular hostility toward *me*. It is quite obvious that my administration has become ineffective. I'm afraid to say, my control, any control I had in the governing of this colony, is quite . . . gone."

Gage could see the sadness again, thought for a moment, then broached the question he had considered every day on the sea voyage.

"Governor . . . Mr. Hutchinson, I must ask you. Forgive me, but I must know your thinking. When the tea was landed here, why did you not summon the army to enforce its landing? Surely those who protested its presence were no match for even a small contingent of troops. If you did not intend to allow the tea to be returned to England, why did you not take the steps required to land it here?"

Hutchinson was not surprised by the question, seemed to expect it.

"It did not occur to me at the time, General. I was intent on enforcing the revenue laws. I am pleased to say that I accomplished exactly that. If I had called for troops, it would have been viewed as surrender, a defeat for the peaceful and civilized authority of the crown. If I made a miscalculation, it was in my use of the tea ships as a test, a necessary confrontation that would establish once and for all the final authority of the crown in this colony. I miscalculated the resolve . . . the willingness of the mob to take criminal action. When the tea was destroyed, any control, any government in this colony ceased to be. The law should have been sufficient. It is clear now that it was not. Your question implies that there was another option more appropriate to the situation." He put his hands up on the small desk, folded them slowly. "With a regiment of soldiers, the tea would have been successfully landed, that's certainly true. I was not ready to concede that the law of the land was completely eliminated. I was not prepared to govern by the bayonet."

"Well, Mr. Hutchinson, how is this colony to be governed now?"

Hutchinson sat back, spread his hands apart, turned his palms up, shrugged.

"That, General, is now entirely up to you."

There was a brief silence, and then Hutchinson slid his chair back, stood.

"I suppose, General, that we should make this meeting official. I do not require witnesses, if it's all the same to you. I hereby relinquish my position as governor of the Massachusetts Bay Colony. May God give His divine blessing to your judgment and to your policies."

Gage did not stand.

"Thank you, Mr. Hutchinson. By the decree of His Majesty, King George the Third, I accept the transfer of position, title, and authority." He motioned to the chair, said, "Please, sir, I had hoped we could discuss matters in the town. The meeting need not be brief."

Hutchinson backed away, close to the narrow door, seemed to fight his emotions.

"I beg your forgiveness, General. I am not currently disposed to offer you advice. Your arrival has certainly set into motion activities in Boston to which I for one am not privy. You come backed by military force and by legal measures that have only one possible outcome. I have read carefully the Port Bill and all its details. I imagine your first responsibility is to close this harbor to all civilian traffic. The people are aware of this, certainly. I must admit to being more than a little surprised by the harshness of the rest of the bill. By sweeping away the charter of this colony and eliminating the right of assembly, you have driven your enemies into the dark. I do not pretend to offer you advice, General. But little good emerges from dark places. I see you have a great many troops in your command here. If I may say, sir, you will likely need them."

Hutchinson made a short bow, pulled the door open, and moved away. Gage blinked at the light flooding the office, saw the silhouette of his aide, and Gage motioned to the door. The man pulled the door closed, and Gage stared through the dark gloom. I expected something different, he thought, but what? That he should be grateful his troubles are over, welcome me with parades? He got up, began to pace slowly in the small space. I expect I should feel sorry for him. He is a broken man in some ways, perhaps all the important ways. There is certainly no place for him here. After today, he is just a private citizen. And the most visible loyalist in the colony. They have already destroyed his house once. He can't live out his life confined to the walls of this miserable fort. So he will certainly go to England, leave everything behind him, find some consolation from the kindness of the king. But there is no place for him there either. He is, after all, an American. Just like Margaret, he will have to endure that prejudice.

He looked again at the pamphlet on his desk. Did he notice that? Well, certainly. Careless of me. But he has already endured this type of abuse. Now it is my turn. He did not think it appropriate to enforce the law with an army. That was a mistake that will not occur again.

He felt impatient, energized, sensed the need to walk. He

opened the door, saw the small courtyard filled with people, nearly all civilians. Faces turned toward him, voices began to rise, the sound grating on his nerves, and he held up his hands, said aloud, "Not now, please!"

He moved quickly through the crowd, saw soldiers coming to attention, guards along the wall above him, cannoneers manning their guns. He had a sudden need to see the water, stare into some vast openness. He climbed the short stone steps to the battlement, the soldiers moving aside, making room. Men saluted him, and he returned it out of instinct, did not look at them. He leaned on the fat barrel of a cannon, gazed out through a gun port in the thick wall, scanned the masts of the merchant ships along the wharf, the large men-of-war that now blockaded the channel. Yes, he thought, I am ready to leave this miserable castle. Tomorrow we will be in the town. We will see what there is to this duty. Hutchinson was wrong, he is still wrong. Gage put his hand on the cold brass barrel of the cannon beside him. There *is* law here. Right here. And those who reject that will be punished. It has been so long, so many years of enduring the protests, the ridiculous flaunting of authority. Now I am the authority. Driven them into darkness, have we? We shall see how long they can hide.

He could hear a low musical sound now, coming from the tall steeples of the town. He looked that way, and one man beside him said, "Bells, sir. We thought it was fire, you know, sir, the alarm. But it's been steady for a few days now. Ever since we arrived."

He looked at the man, saw the uniform of a gunner, stiff respect. Gage nodded, said nothing, thought, Bells? What kind of foolishness is that? The gunner cleared his throat.

"We been told, sir, it's the churches. Night and day, it's like a dirge. A funeral, sir. It's like the whole town's in mourning."

21. ADAMS

HE HAD GROWN TO THOROUGHLY DISLIKE THOMAS HUTCHINSON, had endured too much of the man's smug aristocratic superiority, the arrogant disregard for both written law and the collective wishes of the people. Hutchinson had made no public protest about the Boston Port Bill, and so all had naturally assumed he had not only favored it, but perhaps had some hand in its construction. But now Hutchinson was gone, and Adams could not find pleasure in the news.

He stayed in Boston while the family moved all their possessions out of the small townhouse. Many who had the luxury of two homes had done the same, leaving the sudden despair of Boston for safety in the country. Abigail and the children were settled at Braintree, and he hoped to be able to join them quickly. The office, after all, was dismally quiet, little work at all moving through the courts. Once the Port Bill went into effect officially on June 1, activity in the courts stopped altogether. No one would respect any decision by a judiciary controlled exclusively by the crown, and most of the judges had accepted the inevitable wrath of the citizens and would not preside at any hearing where a mob might suddenly appear. Even those judges who held tightly to their loyalty to the king understood that the Port Bill had eliminated the courts' usefulness in the colony. No one was comfortable risking a sudden bath of tar and feathers.

He could see up the street, an open square, watched the troops drilling in sharp formations, officers observing in bright clusters of red. The street was nearly deserted, typical now, and he backed away from the window, moved slowly around the desk, sat. The army is everywhere now, he thought, and this time there is open hostility. It is not like before, the order and discipline from officers who understand that keeping the peace is a priority. This time they have free rein, can quarter troops in any home at any moment, without explanation. If there is violence against the citizens, they are immune from prosecution here, can only be tried in England. He had read the Port Bill many times, the amazing rationale. He put his head down into his hands, wiped at the weariness on his face. They insist no soldier can expect a fair trial in Massachusetts. Can they truly believe that? How much more proof do they need than the trial of Thomas Preston? Four years later and Sam still insists on calling it the Boston Massacre, yet the soldiers were acquitted. There was justice. He dropped his hands down on the desk, sagged back in the chair, the sadness complete. You are being naïve again. It was never about justice. It's all about power. The die is cast, it was cast when the tea went into the harbor. He had cheered at that, described that extraordinary evening to his friends as a magnificent moment, had to admit to a keen jealousy that he had not been one of the "Mohawks." Beyond the outcry from the Tories, there had been no official attempt at punishment, nothing like the ridiculous hearings in Rhode Island. Hutchinson himself seemed paralyzed by the destruction of the tea, and they all knew that ultimately some response would come from London. Still, he thought, Hutchinson could not have ignored the message, could not overlook the direct assault on his arrogance. I would like to have been there when he heard the news, watched his soft puffy face turn bright red, as red as the uniforms of those officers . . .

He did not like thinking of the soldiers. We were warned of some dire consequence, sputtering Tories mimicking the voices in London, talk of restitution for the tea. This might have been an attractive solution to some, but once the matter poured out into public discussion, the Sons of Liberty had succeeded in convincing most people that the protest was not only appropriate, it was to be applauded. And the payment would have gone . . . where? To the East India Company? And who would have gained a benefit from that, besides the king's henchmen? So instead you will punish us by reducing us to noncitizens. If there was argument before about which rights, which privileges we expect to be granted, there is no argument now, no discussion about vague principles. We will have soldiers in our homes, our town is cut off from her source of survival, is plainly under siege. We will suffer the consequences of the removal of our courts. Even the capital has been moved; whatever form of government General Gage allows is now going to convene in Salem. Boston is to be regarded as simply nonexistent. Deny us food, deny us trade, deny us existence.

He pushed himself to his feet, moved again to the window. He did not look toward the soldiers, instead staring out at nothing, his eyes clouded by tears, anger mixed with the sadness. Stupidity. Blind, incredible stupidity! You don't slap an entire people across the face, put chains on a town, and expect . . . what? Sullen acceptance? Quiet regret? Who in England believes that this will be resolved by a renewed peace, an end to controversy? Starve us, enslave us, and then expect that we will be humbled into grateful obedience? How can they believe it will ever become normal again? Will the king and his amazing audience of buffoons ever consent to give us back all of what they have taken away?

He closed his eyes, clenched his fists, felt himself shaking. He blinked hard, looked into the street, saw a family passing by, two small children led by the hands of their parents. Yes, go on. Leave this place. It is no town for a family, not anymore. He tried to see the face of the father, young, barely twenty. He can work somewhere, find some way to provide. But there are so many others with no place else to go. The stores are empty now, shelves bare, nothing at all coming into the harbor. Those that must stay can only watch as their town collapses into rubble. It is about power, after all, bluster and passion from distant ministers who will never see the consequences. They are content to allow this colony to fall under the control of a government making laws from moment to moment, policy set down by the king and his single voice, General Gage. They will place soldiers in our streets and in our homes. Just so our king may make his point.

He took a deep breath, thought suddenly of Abigail, the farm. I should return; there will be much to do. How much can any of us do here? We have passed the river and cut away the bridge. The die is cast.

WORD CAME SLOWLY AT FIRST, REPORTS OF ANGRY MEETINGS IN other colonies, in Connecticut, Rhode Island. Then the written correspondence, the overland mail caught up with the faster flood of rumor, and now a growing number of official proclamations found their way into Boston, word from Virginia, the Carolinas. Some colonies' assemblies had been already disbanded by their royal governors, the typical heavy-handed response to the vocal outrage coming from the elected bodies. In New York, the moderates held control, but even those who typically hesitated to speak out were unable to keep their silence. Only the most outspoken of Tories tried to deny that what the king had done to Boston could just as easily be done to any other colony that exercised any legal protest against policies in London. In cities as diverse as the people who occupied them, from Newport to Charleston, Philadelphia to Salem, public gatherings swelled into riotous demonstrations. These were loud, symbolic ceremonies where the Port Bill was shredded and the ministers who had devised it burned in effigy. Despite the confident insistence from the king and Lord North that no colony would come to the aid of the criminals in Boston, the boundaries were coming down, and the people who maintained the pride of their uniqueness began to look outward and hear the words of their neighbors. All along the Atlantic seaboard, people who paid little heed to politics or the daily wrangling of petty affairs in their capitals were swarming into the cities, listening to the speeches, hearing the astounding terms of the Boston Port Bill. It did not take the eloquence of political craftsmen, there was no need for bombastic speech to communicate the message. The awareness was sudden and dramatic. They were all vulnerable, all subject to the sudden whim of a king who had become a dangerous threat to anyone's concept of freedom. As the boundaries between them fell, the people began to understand what Lord North and King George did not. There was a reason to become united. The alarm had been sounded. They had a *cause*.

JUNE 17, 1774

THE WAGON WAS LOADED, THE LAST OF THE BOXES FROM THE TOWN
house, some papers from his office. Adams scanned the bookshelves, tried to read the titles in the dull light of the oil lamp. He
paused, took one book from the shelf, placed it in a wooden box,
said aloud, "Yes, that one. Could need it." He bent low, ran his
finger along the titles on the bottom row, the light nearly blocked
by his own girth. He straightened, felt the strain in his back.
"That's enough." He lifted the box, turned toward the door, saw
motion, was startled.

"What? Who is it?"

The darkness gave way to a familiar shape, the small figure of
Joseph Warren. Adams smiled now through sharp breathing, set
the box on the desk.

"Joseph, you surprised me."

Warren seemed concerned.

"Sorry, John. I should have knocked. I saw you in here.
Leaving, I see?"

Adams glanced out at the wagon.

"Yes. Don't usually go to Braintree after dark. I'd just rather
not stay here another night." He put a hand on the box of books.
"I have about everything I'll need, at least for a while. No business at hand. The farm is the priority now."

Warren closed the door now, seemed to hesitate, looked down
at his hands, and Adams said, "What is it, my friend? Some more
good news for the citizens of Boston?"

Warren first seemed surprised at the sarcasm, then smiled.

"Well, actually, John, now that you mention it, I believe so.
Yes." Adams saw more hesitation, began to feel uneasy.

"What has happened?"

"I've just come from Salem."

"The assembly meeting?"

"Indeed. Quite a lively discussion. Sam wouldn't let anyone
leave. But the Tories couldn't just sit still, and so word got out
and Gage sent a deputy to shut us down. Didn't work. There was
a vote. One hundred seventeen to twelve, nearly unanimous. Always a few afraid to take a stand, of course. Not sure how anyone

can stay quiet these days. It'll probably be the last vote the assembly has. It was enough for today, though."

Adams knew that Warren was playing with him now.

"Vote about *what*, Doctor?"

Warren was still smiling.

"Well, you know that Sam attempted to push through his plan, the Solemn League and Covenant. He's still focusing on nonimportation, and his new covenant would have gone a great deal farther than the last attempt."

"He was urging citizens to abstain from buying from merchants who sold goods from England."

Warren nodded.

"A bit too radical, even for our assembly. When he sent word of his plan to the other colonies, he was met with something less than enthusiasm. But that's not important. What's important is that there was a response at all."

"What do you mean, Joseph?"

"We're not alone, John. The other colonies are bringing their people together to debate more than the issues in their own backyards. Once Sam accepted that he was being somewhat impractical, we discovered that most of the other colonies are willing to help us, willing to do something about the Port Bill."

"Before it becomes their problem as well."

"Certainly. We might suddenly learn of a Charleston Port Bill, a Norfolk Port Bill. In fact, it is our friends in Virginia who have confronted this crisis directly. You know much about Philadelphia, John?"

Adams was mystified.

"Philadelphia? Why? What's in Philadelphia?"

"Well, John, actually, as of September first, you are. Quite an honor. Virginia started this, issued invitations to all the colonies to come together in one assembly. There's Sam, of course, Tom Cushing, Robert Treat Paine, and *you*. You've been selected as one of the four delegates. You'll be representing us at the Continental Congress."

HE DID NOT LEAVE FOR BRAINTREE UNTIL MORNING, BARELY SLEPT at all. The sun rose on a town under siege, despair spreading through every home. As he rode out along the road through Boston Neck, the one overland passage out of the city, he could see troops marching in line, some building small guardhouses close to the road or other structures he could not identify. Just like the rumors, the greatest fear was coming true. The troops were beginning to construct the first barrier, the blockade to isolate Boston by land as well as by sea.

He slapped at the horse, tried to stare ahead, would not look at the faces of the soldiers, heard the calls, insults, comments, and curses inspired by the boxes piled high in the wagon as another frightened civilian ran away. His head was swirling with thoughts: Warren, Philadelphia, the farm, a lawyer in a town with no law. The trip home was already taking longer than he could bear, and he thought of Abigail now, could not keep her face out of his mind. How much time? he thought. How much time will I have with them? September is close, I will have to leave in August. Two months, all there is, all there will be. The farm . . .

He was jarred by shouts and shifted his attention back to the road, saw troops blocking the way. One man waved him aside, cursing, and Adams jerked hard on the reins, pulled the wagon off the road. He could see up the long hill now, blinked in surprise, thought, What . . . ? Where did they come from? All up the rise and beyond, the road was filled with wagons and carts, carriages and riders, some pulling livestock. He could hear the sounds now, the creaking of wheels, the slap of the whip, curses from the troops as they stood aside. He watched as they moved past him, a slow parade *into* the town, laden with piles of corn, other crops, grain, and salted meat. He looked at the drivers. Some smiled at him, polite waves, and one man shouted, "Come home, friend! It's all right! We'll be feeding you yet! No one goes hungry here!"

The man was quickly past him, and he looked up the long rise, could see that the road would be blocked for a while yet. He sat staring, did not think of moving, just watched each wagon, the incredible display, the outpouring of food. He heard a new sound, looked beyond the nearest wagons, saw a small herd of cattle, maybe a dozen animals, coming over the hill, driven by a man and two boys on horseback, whips cracking, the animals protesting, all moving forward. The man saluted him, tipped his hat.

"No reason to leave, sir! Come on back!"

Adams returned the greeting, a short wave, regarded the cattle pushing past him, wanted to explain, *I'm going home,* but the man was busy now, moving his horse quickly, herding a stray cow back onto the road. Adams felt helpless, frozen in place, still curious, wanted to ask where they were from, how this had happened. He tried to find words, something to say to these people, to respond to their compassion, their energy, their extraordinary generosity. There were more waves, more greetings, and he returned the kindness, said simply, "Thank you."

FAR BEHIND ADAMS, FROM THE WINDOWS OF TALL HOUSES, OTHERS could see this strange parade; people climbed up to rooftops, desperate for hope. Across a narrow strip of harbor, one man was enjoying his morning walk high on a hillside, his ritual in his new home as it had been in New York. But unlike New York, there was no kindness toward him; those few people who greeted him at all were kept at a distance by an escort of soldiers, and so their calls were faint, strained efforts at politeness: "Governor Gage . . ."

He had been enjoying the quiet dawn, the new routine, the walk becoming a brisk march through the countryside he commanded. He had moved with the satisfaction of a man who knows his own place, enjoys the power of his job, enjoys the triumph over his enemies. He had enjoyed every day of his new command, had watched the despair in the citizens of Boston with a delightful satisfaction, had written of it to his king: *Your Majesty, it is working. There is punishment here, there will be retribution. We will weed out the traitors, and in the end, no one will even remember their names.* Now he stopped, his stroll interrupted, stared out toward the heights to the south of the town. His escort stared out as well, and they could all see the wagons and the livestock, and his own troops standing aside as this strange procession, the head of an endless snake, wound its way toward the town. In the silence of his anger, he understood that the rebels were receiving an outpouring of aid from hundreds of farmers and merchants, shop owners and gardeners, sending help to those so desperately in need. It was an offense to his command, to his control, a disruption to his careful strategy. As he stood frozen in surprise and anger, he could hear sounds as well, somewhere in his mind, something no one in England thought they would ever hear: the sharp voices of thirteen colonies, coming together to speak as one.

PART TWO
LIONS AND LAMBS

22. ADAMS

AS JULY ROLLED INTO AUGUST, THERE HAD ONLY BEEN ONE thought, Philadelphia, and the final days at the farm had made his nights restless. In his waking hours, his mood was sharp and unpleasant. When he finally packed the wagon, a haphazard gathering of clothes and papers, there had been much silence, Abigail standing aside, avoiding his strange temper as he stomped and fretted his way through the house one last time. He had not invited her to come to Boston, had been putting off the goodbye, dreading the scene. He did not know that she had every intention of riding beside him to Boston, that she had already made arrangements for the children to be cared for by her mother. She was not yet ready to watch her husband ride away while he was still immersed in so much doubt about what the mission to the congress would involve. When the excuses for delay were exhausted and he had finally surrendered to the inevitability of good-bye, he had kissed each of the children, his mood finally softening, helpless against the rain of tears, passing them off one by one to the waiting smile of his mother-in-law. Abigail had not been there, and he had been curious why she did not stand with the little ones, holding tightly to her own tears. But then he had heard her calling him from outside, scolding him with impatience, her own excitement for the journey to begin. He had given one final good-bye to the children, emerged from the house to find Abigail already in the wagon. She was holding the reins out toward him, and her smile had lightened his mood. He had wanted to laugh. Thank you, dearest Portia, the company will be welcome. But there was a weariness to her playfulness, the sad reality that this time when he left them, it would not be for some

217

brief intrusion by his work, but a far longer distance and a responsibility for something far more uncertain.

THE DELEGATES CHOSEN BY THE MASSACHUSETTS ASSEMBLY were to gather in Boston in a purposeful symbolic gesture, would ride out on the first mile of their mission in a show of defiance to Gage and an inspiration to the townspeople. Adams had sought out the advice of many in his profession, had imagined the congress as a grand demonstration of the wisdom and practice of law. Despite all the calls from the Sons of Liberty, all the anguishing and pamphlet writing describing the inevitability of bloodshed, the urgency of striking back against what so many were calling a ruthless invasion of their soil, Adams tried to keep his focus on the one thing he knew better than most: If there was to be debate and conclusions to be drawn at the congress, even some plan of action for uniting the colonies, it should all be founded in the glorious and inarguable truth of law. But as the time to leave drew close, the doubts had come. He had spoken with the other delegates, knew of course that Sam was prepared to argue for complete independence, a total break with England. Thomas Cushing was more subdued, almost shy, a strange personality for the man who had been speaker of the assembly. Cushing had been the recipient of Ben Franklin's secreted Hutchinson letters, and his loyalty to Sam Adams was unquestioned. But he rarely spoke out with Sam's vigor, seemed to keep to a more moderate course. It was the main reason he had been voted to be a delegate in the first place. He was to represent Massachusetts, and many of the more conservative members of the assembly preferred at least one man who might not be so prone to lace his speeches with fire.

Robert Treat Paine was a different sort altogether, arrogant, prim, the man who had faced Adams in the courtroom for the trial of Captain Preston. But he had a fine legal mind, and Adams had been relieved to learn that Paine would be part of the delegation, another voice for the power of law.

The more Adams sought out comment and advice, the more he had realized how much genuine enthusiasm there was for the congress. Yet the more excitement he heard from the people he would represent, the more unsure he got.

The day was humid and gray, and he could not just stay in Boston, hemmed in by the narrow streets, the constant presence of troops. He had taken Abigail north, sought out the best view of the town, the heights that rose above the small stretch of harbor that led to the Charles River. The hills had a reputation for romance, riders courting their sweethearts in rich moonlight, staring wistfully out to sea or over the specks of light in the sleeping town. But the romance was gone now, the town stripped of the joy of a people who had sought the sunshine and the glorious view from the hills. Across the narrow strip of water, Boston was quiet, oppressed by the ugly exertion of England's power.

As he walked with her over the wide hills, his grip on her arm was firm and unyielding, and he did not notice that she had tried to loosen his hold more than once. They had left the wagon far back, behind Bunker Hill, the first of the three wide mounds. They had crested the second, lower rise, Breed's Hill, and finally he stopped, the nervous energy giving way to the sudden calm, the panorama of the harbor, the river, the far hills beyond the town. She slowly eased her arm away from his, rubbed her flesh, massaging, and he noticed her now.

"Did I hurt you?"

"John, you were simply . . . occupied. I know when your mind is off in other places. It's all right."

He stared away for a moment, could see out beyond the harbor, past Castle William, the broad gray ocean blending at the horizon into the dull of the clouds. He looked around, scanned the hillside, saw a cluster of rocks.

"Let's sit."

She followed him to a short fat ledge of gray stone, and he made a bow.

"My lady, your throne."

It was forced, a strained attempt at humor. She was looking at him, and he did not see a smile, shook his head now, said, "Sorry, I'm not in a very good humor."

"No, my husband, you have not been in a good humor for a week now. I would like to believe that you are anticipating how much you will be missing us. However, I imagine it is more to do with work?"

He stood close to her, put one hand on her shoulder, stared out toward the ocean again.

"Work does not bother me when I know what to expect. I am certain of those things I know well, such as the glad tidings I have received from so many of my friends, and even those who don't know me well at all. The people have such faith. There is so much confidence that what we will do in Philadelphia will be momentous."

"However . . . ?"

He smiled now, thought, You know me too well.

"Yes, there is that word. I have spent so much time pondering this during my walks over the farm; I muse, I mope, I ruminate. I plan what I will say, I try to imagine what others will say. Then I realize that outside of our small delegation, I don't know who the others are. I don't know what their colonies consider to be important. Do they place as much emphasis on law, or do they spout fire? Does South Carolina want a war, or rather some way to avoid one at all costs?"

"You will discover all of that in time, John. You cannot predict everything that will happen. Just by agreeing to this congress, the other colonies are showing they support Massachusetts. You must have a certain amount of faith."

"I am concerned that this dilemma is perhaps beyond us. Or at the least, beyond me."

She looked up at him.

"Why?"

"I have serious doubts if we are men fit for the times we are in. I wonder if what we hear from England may in some ways be true. We are deficient in education, in travel, in fortune. We are deficient in *genius*. It may be that simple. I stare and stare at the problems before us, and I cannot see a solution. I am at a loss, totally at a loss to know what we will do when we get to Philadelphia."

She made a strange grunt, then suddenly stood and faced him. He knew the look in her eye, said, "So, am I to be scolded again?"

She scowled at him, and he could hear the edge in her voice.

"Please, might you explain to me what great outpouring of genius has emerged from England? If our king and his ministers and their Parliament are so ripe with greatness, how have we come to this crisis? My dear husband, I am surprised that you of all people, you who are so versed in all things to do with law, you who are capable of mastering your world, you think you do not have the genius to solve all our problems! Well, perhaps it might be a fine idea to take your doubts to Philadelphia. Perhaps you will meet others like yourself who also have doubts, who fear that their minds are inadequate to the task. Perhaps all of you who are so inadequate should join your minds, combine all the little bits of genius into one that is capable of some accomplishment. Perhaps that is the purpose of this Continental Congress!" She paused. "Of course, I'm merely your wife. I don't know of such things."

August 10, 1774

The town had emerged from its gloom, the people swelling into the street in a fresh blossoming of enthusiasm. He had kissed her good-bye without embarrassment, and others had done the same with their loved ones, and finally, it was not just the wives, but the people of the town who released their emotion. As the carriage moved through the streets, led by an armed escort, the people gathered close, cheering, crying, calling out in a vast showering of affection and confidence for these four men who would bear their cause, and thus carry their fate, to Philadelphia.

As they moved out of Boston, farmers emerged from fields, women stepped out of small cottages, men on horseback moved aside, all saluting in their own way, offering their hope and guidance and faith that the journey be successful.

Each night, the carriage would bring them to a new town, a stopping place where the people surrounded them with questions. The farther they moved from Boston, the more uncertain the people were about what was truly happening there. The questions were tinged with alarm, people wanting to confirm the sensational rumors of citizens starving in the streets, horrible abuses by the soldiers. When the journey began each morning, the uncertainty was gone, the people left waving behind them understanding more of the issues, the importance of uniting all the voices of the colonies. And bit by bit, visit by visit, the four delegates themselves had their own trepidation stripped away by the good wishes and prayers of these people they were representing.

NEW YORK, AUGUST 20, 1774

THEY HAD REACHED THE CITY AT MIDMORNING AND IMMEDIATELY had an escort of local militia, armed men who rode beside them with the same good cheer as the farmers and shopkeepers from the open countryside. The muskets carried a cheer of their own, and Adams could not take his eyes from one man, the way the man's hands held tightly to the dark wood and silver of the man's musket. The militiaman had his sleeves rolled up, and Adams could see thick muscles, the hard arms of a man who knows heavy work, a blacksmith perhaps. The man rode upright, the musket resting across the saddle, a readiness that was more show than necessity. Sam was in another discussion with Paine, strategy and philosophy. Adams had enjoyed the stretches of silence, but they never lasted long, Sam's energy affecting them all. The quiet moments would pass quickly into some new burst of talk and debate, many of the conversations continued from the day before.

They crossed the Harlem River on a ferry, left their new escort behind with a solemn good-bye. When they reached the wharf, the carriage rolled onto the hard dirt streets of New York and into a world Adams had never seen. He stared at the bustle of activity, crowds of longshoremen, cargo being lifted from the holds of great ships. They all noticed the sharp ripple of the flags, the Union Jacks, sprinkled through the great cluster of masts. He tried to ignore the comments in the carriage, stared intently, thought, Yes, British ships. He began to feel something new, trying to absorb a culture that was unfamiliar. As they moved along the docks, the carriage was mostly ignored, a vast crowd of workmen tending only to their jobs. He glanced back into the carriage, saw Cushing close beside him, the man staring as he was.

"Awfully busy here," Adams commented.

Cushing merely grunted, but Sam, who had been staring out the other side, turned to the others and said, "*Here* is the challenge, gentlemen. This is a very different world. No oppression, no armed siege, nothing to inspire their own protests. Nothing has yet happened here to disrupt their tight hold on the skirts of England. They have employment, they feed their families. All is right with their world."

Paine had said nothing to this point, just pulled a paper from his pocket and read it. Now he handed the sheet to Sam.

"The list of the New York delegates. I assume they're already on their way to Philadelphia. I don't know much about them, except for reputation. Important names down here, so I've heard."

Sam glanced at the list, handed it back to Paine.

"They're not Sons of Liberty, are they."

It was a statement, not a question, and Paine shrugged.

"Not that I've heard."

"Well, I have heard. Very conservative. Duane, Jay, the others, Livingston, Alsop. All conservative. Some things don't change, gentlemen. We may not receive much support from New York."

Adams stared out at the street, the hustle of activity, said nothing. The names on the New York list had meant very little to him, though he was relieved to learn that two of the delegates were lawyers, James Duane and John Jay, with reputations for brilliant work. Of course, New York would send its best minds. Legal minds. It can't all be about politics.

They were away from the river now, rode deeper into the city itself. The energy in the streets around them was different from the activity on the wharves, the word preceding them about the identity of the men in this grand carriage, driven by the men with guns. Adams responded to the waves of the people they passed, heard the word shouted out by many, *Massachusetts*. They know who we are. They are very aware. Not like so many of the country people. Better news here, of course, better information.

The carriage rolled through a narrow street, then into an open square, a wide green park spread out before a gray stone building, unmistakably offices, some government place. The men in the carriage had grown quiet, the others absorbing this new city as he was doing, curious, all of them sharing Sam's awareness that the culture here was not like that of Boston. They moved now down a well-traveled street, passed through an intersection, and Adams saw the street sign, *Broad*. He could see a tall steeple, a grand church, more people stopping to point, wave at them. The carriage began to move downhill now, the street wide, sweeping gently to the left. At the bottom of the hill was a spacious square, and something caught his eye, a statue in the center of the green, the lush grass enclosed by a thin black railing. He leaned farther out the window, could see it clearly now, the statue tall, perched high on a massive block of marble, the sunlight reflecting in a brilliant gold sheen. It was a man on a horse, regal, a spectacle of grandeur.

Behind him, he heard Paine say, "Should we salute, gentlemen? Or perhaps bow down?"

Sam sniffed.

"Wonder how long that polished gilt would survive in Boston. A minute, perhaps."

Adams glanced back at the men, looked again at the statue, then suddenly understood. He made a short sound.

"Oh . . . yes. I see. That would be King George."

THEY STAYED IN NEW YORK FOR A FEW DAYS, HOSTED AND ENTERTAINED by several of the city's elite. The food was grand, daily tours of the city itself, and if the politics was subdued, at least the men from Massachusetts could feel confident that their mission, the journey to Philadelphia, was as important to New York as it was to Boston. But there was no escaping the presence of wealth, the grand spectacle of dinners served on silver and fine china, receptions at country palaces, all the trappings of a society that might not be eager to embrace change. Despite the polite words of respect and enthusiastic toasts for the success of their task, despite loud sympathy for the misery of Boston and the kindness that surprised them all, when the four finally pulled away from the city, it was with a great breath of relief.

THE CONVERSATIONS WERE MORE SUBDUED NOW, AND EVEN SAM seemed to understand that their energy was best saved for Philadelphia. Adams had left New York in a profound gloom, had tried to recall the cheers of the people farther north, the shower of enthusiasm they had received. New York had been very different indeed, and it was not the show of support that made the lasting impression, but the stain of politics that seemed close beneath every event.

Adams stared at a slow-flowing wide river, did not even consider the name, saw one small boat, a fisherman's, along the far bank. The New Yorkers are all so full of good cheer, all such fast talkers, boisterous, even a bit crude with their words. They all speak of this momentous event, this coming together of the colonies, but what do they truly understand? They talk of the Continental Congress as so important, a milestone in our history, and yet Sam is correct—there is no talk of the Sons of Liberty, no one seems at all interested in bringing up the subject of the king, or the problems we face. It could simply be politeness, not wanting to spoil their festivity on our behalf with the dirt of our crisis. But it is their crisis as well. Or do they not understand that? Why did they select delegates to attend this congress? Is the business of the congress to be nothing but a party after all? So much social banter: *How dreadful your situation in Boston must be, please pass the wine.* Are we so different? Is Massachusetts so isolated from the other colonies—

The carriage struck a rock, bounced sharply. The silence was broken now, each man reacting, small chuckles. Adams glanced at the others, saw the same expression, evidence of the same mood he was feeling. Sam shook his head.

"We are a pathetic lot. Are we now riding to our doomsday?"

The others responded, the mood lightening. Adams thought of Abigail.

"It is of benefit that my wife is not present. She has a talent for scolding me. I imagine she would find some way to look on the positive side. The people of New York at least seemed pleased to see us."

"It was certainly a kinder reception than the alternative," Paine replied. "We could have been ridden out of town, tarred and feathered."

Sam was laughing now.

"We haven't arrived in Philadelphia, sir. We may find that to be our fate yet."

Adams watched the fisherman again, the carriage rounding a bend, the road following the path of the river. He saw her face, began to speak to Abigail in his mind. Yes, I do recall the reception from the townspeople, the mass of citizens. They have surprising awareness, perhaps more than all those elite who presume to control them. I would rather have enjoyed a dinner with the crowd in an alehouse, heard what *they* had to say about the king. He had forgotten about the small band of militia who escorted them to the banks of the Hudson, rough men who seemed ready for . . . what? Was it all for show, some gesture of defiance against General Gage and an army that is, after all, pretty far away? Or do they feel the threat, understand that British troops in Boston can easily become British troops in every town? And if they are so aware of the danger, what then? Many are just like that fisherman, perhaps; others are farmers and shopkeepers. Will they truly be pulled away from their lives, their routine, the care of their families? And can they learn to stand up to a real army?

The fisherman was out of his sight now, and he saw buildings ahead, a small town spread along the banks of the river. He knew they would stop, the others now looking out, anticipating a break in the ride. He looked at the river, the name suddenly coming to him: the Delaware. This flows right into Philadelphia. Well, we are close. Tomorrow, perhaps. He saw her face again. Yes, dearest friend, then we shall see. Then our questions, our doubts will be answered. We shall learn if those men with the guns should be so prepared after all.

23. ADAMS

PHILADELPHIA, SEPTEMBER 1774

THE MEN FROM MASSACHUSETTS HAD BEEN INTERCEPTED OUTSIDE of Philadelphia, provided with wine and cautious advice from a small group of Philadelphia's own Sons of Liberty. The effects of the wine had passed quickly, but as Adams and the others had finally ridden into the city, the advice from their hosts had stayed firmly within all of them.

Adams had wondered how the Massachusetts group would be received, whether being so close to the controversy ensured they would be treated as special, however the definition might apply. The radicals in the Continental Congress surely would regard them as spokesmen for the martyrdom of Boston, treat them with humble respect, the bearers of so much sadness and sacrifice. The conservatives would react with shrill outrage, the reputation of Sam Adams irking them, their position being that the shameful energy behind the mobs of Boston would only stir up trouble and discontent.

The advice from their new friends had been simple and utterly direct: to exercise discretion with their choice of words. It would benefit the congress and anyone who leaned toward a break with England, who might be inclined to support the men from Massachusetts if the word *independence* did not find its way into the official proceedings. The expectation of so many of the other delegates was that the men from Massachusetts would roll into Philadelphia with fire in their speech, inflexible proclamations, and perhaps even try to bully the rest of the congress into the immediate acceptance of their outrage toward England.

They had arrived at the Stone House, a rooming house managed under the sharp eye of a matronly woman named Mrs. Yard, already home to several of the delegates. The talk had been mostly loud, boisterous anticipation, polite greetings, some giving way to enthusiastic backslapping. Other men had stayed back, withdrawn, appraising silently, extending their hands with hesitation. Adams had not been surprised at Sam's ability to reach out, his kind and gracious words, his friendly smile for the men from every colony. While Sam had toured his way through the gathering crowd, Adams had been among the quiet ones, more interested in serious conversation. As the first evening had stretched into late hours, the delegations had begun to separate, and Adams had withdrawn to his room.

He tested the bed, sat now, began pulling at the buckles on his shoes. There was a sharp knock, and Sam was in the room, closing the door firmly behind him.

Adams removed one shoe, said, "Lost? Well, no, at least you knocked."

Sam ignored him, was pacing, bursting with energy, finally stopped, faced him.

"John, this is . . . I never expected . . . we are in for a real time here."

"Do you mean that as positive?"

"Oh, my, yes! Indeed! It's the right strategy, you know. Keep quiet on the issues, don't burst out with all our demands. They quite expect that from us. But they are surprised, don't know what to think, find that we are actually . . . civilized. I hear the men from Virginia are quite behind us, can do quite a bit of talking on our behalf. This fellow Henry, Patrick Henry. Could easily mistake him for a Bostoner. And did you meet that fellow Richard Henry Lee? Another friend, for certain."

Sam seemed lost in thought, and Adams said, "You can't remember them all on the first night, Sam."

Sam looked at him, didn't seem to understand, and Adams thought, Well, no, he certainly can.

"What of the New Yorkers, Sam? And some of the Pennsylvania men? I met this fellow Dickinson. Seems friendly, but I understand he is quite the conservative."

Sam frowned.

"Yes, Dickinson. Flies in the ointment, those fellows. We shall see how this divides out, how many of them are of a mind to agree with us."

"It surely is not a competition, Sam."

"It surely is, John. In the end, it may come down to a simple vote, who can gain the most support. We cannot expect everyone to immediately come together and pour out a resolve, some document defining our plan of action."

Adams pulled at his other shoe.

"Well, yes, Sam, I understand that, of course. But we must hear every view, we must know how each colony perceives their role in this, how each colony interprets the rule of law."

"Yes, yes, John. You do exactly that. You speak about law. I understand what I must do here. I must remain discreet, I must speak quietly, without bluster. If I cannot convince men like Dickinson, then I must simply find allies to outnumber him. I must win them over one at a time, work in the shadows, influence from behind, not from in front. It is not my place to be an orator here, John. I leave that to you." He paused, his thoughts turning in his mind. "Did you know there's no one here from Georgia?"

"Yes, I was told."

"They didn't send any delegates. Not sure that's a problem, though. Mostly cotton farmers. They probably feel more than a passing affection for the British fleet. Too much wilderness down there. They'd rather have British soldiers in their towns than Indians."

"Their absence is unfortunate. They should be represented here."

Sam ignored him, moved to the door, lost again in thought. He stopped, looked at Adams.

"This your room?"

Adams smiled, glanced around.

"I believe so, yes."

Sam seemed to ponder this.

"Yes, good. Get some sleep. We begin tomorrow."

Sam was out the door now, shut it hard behind him. Adams sat back on the bed, leaned against the wall. He was exhausted, all the days of travel rolling over him. But Sam's energy was still infecting him, and he tried to see the faces, remember the names. So many just like us. So many not like us at all. But we are here. We are together. And we shall learn a great deal tomorrow.

SEPTEMBER 6, 1774

THE RUMOR HAD BEGUN AS MOST BEGIN, PANIC AT THE SIGHT OF troops, the expectation that bloodshed must surely follow, must surely be the only possible result. The troops were marching to Charlestown, the village north of Boston, just across the mouth of the Charles River. The local militia there had become too bold for the comfort of the British command, had accumulated a store of gunpowder and two cannon positioned where the local citizens convinced themselves they could be put to good use. More than one man had bragged indiscreetly about the town's arsenal, and more than one Tory had brought the news to General Gage. When his troops marched out of Boston, the countryside had surged to life, word spreading that the British had begun what so many had feared, a rampage of fire and death. When Gage's troops simply confiscated the powder and guns, the rumors grew bolder, fueled by embarrassment and anger at the loose talk of those who could not keep the existence of the munitions quiet. The rumors fed the fears of the people, and word spread quickly that the troops had actually fired on citizens, laid a path of widespread destruction, fire, and chaos. Across the countryside, the farmers and militia began to assemble, muskets held high at the sudden call to bloody revenge. Nearly twenty thousand men had gathered around the limits of Boston, surprising the British, who had already concluded the simple job of hauling and floating the munitions out to Castle William. As the truth about the British raid filtered through the region, passions subsided and the great mass of armed men reluctantly dispersed, returning to their farms, speaking in angry rumblings of what might have been. But word had traveled far, and before anyone had realized the power of the false rumor, the men assembled in Philadelphia received only the most extreme version, that Boston smoldered in ruins, blood in the streets. Before the great orations, before the fiery debate over the most incendiary issues of the day, the Continental Congress had first to absorb the horror that the rumors brought, that the worst fears of even the most devout Tories had come true.

THEY WOULD CONVENE IN CARPENTERS' HALL, THE HOME TO THE city's Carpenters' Guild. The site was an unmistakably stern message to the conservatives, who had favored another venue, something with more of an air of government. But the hall conveyed to any observer that many in this strange mix of delegates were far more interested in communicating an allegiance to the interests of the common people. As a compromise to the conservatives, the congress had elected Peyton Randolph as its first president. Randolph was an aristocratic Virginian and the most conservative member of that delegation. While the presidency was a parliamentary position and carried no real authority, the move was an appeasement to some who feared the radicals would make an immediate attempt to take over the business of the congress.

The rumors of the alleged catastrophe in Boston had come early, and the four men from Massachusetts had withdrawn from the opening of the congress, had requested a few minutes to meet quietly among themselves.

The room was small, attached to one side of the larger chamber. Adams stood close to Cushing, waited in black silence for Sam to join them. No one spoke, and Adams glanced at Paine, who leaned against a small table, staring glumly at the floor. Adams looked out toward the open door, could see the solemn concerned faces in the larger chamber. Then he noticed motion, heads turning, and he saw Sam moving through the larger crowd, then into the smaller room. He was trembling, his hands curled into tight fists, his breaths in sharp tight bursts.

"The only word I can get is that the warships suddenly lined up along the wharf and began to bombard the town. We are hoping to receive more details from some of the merchant ships coming down from Providence. More riders are expected as well."

Cushing was near tears.

"I cannot understand it. Is there no decency? Are they not civilized?"

Adams could feel waves of sickness, his gut twisting in cold knots, the vivid picture of a burning city lodged in his mind. Across the small room, Paine said, "We must know more. What happened? What prompted this?"

Sam seemed about to burst, prowled around the small room.

"I am not sure I believe it."

Paine seemed to come to life.

"What? Why?"

Sam fixed his gaze on Adams now.

"You should appreciate this, John. Proof. Evidence. Mr. Paine asks the correct question. What prompted this? There is no protest in Boston. Most of the citizens have gone. Why should the British destroy the city? Gage has control, has all the power. There is no one to oppose him. If he destroys the town, where will his soldiers sleep?"

Adams felt a spark, a piece of light cutting through his mind.

"Yes, surely, Sam. It is so . . . fantastic. It cannot be true. Not all of it. We must wait to hear from the ships. They will know more. They deal with the farmers, the merchants. There has to be some explanation."

Cushing rubbed his face with both hands.

"I hope to God your optimism is warranted, gentlemen. We have families to consider. I will not rest until I hear something."

It had been Adams' first concern, and he reassured himself again: They are all back at Braintree. Surely there was no reason for them to be in Boston.

"I agree, Thomas," Paine said. "Sam, we must consider the reports to carry at least some truth. And that means we have something important that we must confront right here. What will this news do to those men out there?"

Sam raised one clenched fist in front of him, regarded it.

"We will find out what kind of fortitude this congress has. We will learn if we are so alone after all. They're waiting for us."

Sam moved to the door, and Adams followed, heard a hum of voices in the larger room. Shortly the chamber fell silent, and Adams moved to one side, saw Randolph standing at a rostrum and saying, "There is no one man in this room who does not share the apprehension and the feeling of outrage that have befallen the gentlemen from Massachusetts. I was not prepared for this. I would appreciate a suggestion on how we should proceed."

Cushing raised a hand, said in a soft voice, "May I request a prayer, gentlemen? Mr. Randolph, if you will consider it acceptable, perhaps some devotional text to begin these proceedings."

Adams saw several hands go up. Randolph acknowledged one.

"Mr. Jay of New York."

"I deeply respect the feelings of the gentlemen from Massachusetts. However, how can we observe any moment of devotion that would be fitting to us all? This gathering is ripe with Presbyterians, Anabaptists, Episcopalians, Quakers, Congregationalists, and I have doubtless overlooked a few."

Randolph pointed again, said, "Mr. Rutledge, of South Carolina."

"I agree with the gentleman from New York. We must not offend anyone's prejudice here, not so early in these proceedings."

Sam stepped forward, close to Randolph, spoke up.

"If I may politely suggest, sir. I am no bigot, and I will gladly hear a prayer from any gentleman of piety and virtue who is at the same time a friend to his country. As you know, I am a stranger to Philadelphia; however, I have heard of a clergyman here whose character is well known. I believe his name is Mr. Duché. Might I move that this gentlemen be allowed to read a prayer to this meeting?"

There were nods, calls of approval, and Adams stared at Sam, had never heard the tone of his voice so intensely calm, so ingratiating. The motion was passed, and Adams caught Sam's eye, a quick nod. Well done, Sam. Despite what may have happened in Boston, here we are gentlemen still.

"CONTEND, O LORD, WITH THOSE WHO CONTEND WITH ME; FIGHT against those who fight against me. Take hold of my shield and buckler, and rise for my help. Draw the spear and javelin against my pursuers. . . ."

The man was gray-haired, bent with age, but read the Thirty-fifth Psalm with a clear voice to the bowed heads of the assembly. When the reading was concluded, Adams looked at the faces, saw many of them looking downward still, quiet reflection. Then slowly the gazes lifted, and he saw the eyes focusing on Sam, then him. Gradually there was motion, one man first, the sharp energy of the Virginian, Patrick Henry, who came straight toward him, held out a hand, said with urgency, "God bless you, sir! If there is a fight, then we will fight together!"

Henry angled toward Sam, said something Adams could not hear, the sharp voice muffled by the sounds of others who moved close to him, more hands, words of blessing and encouragement. Adams took the hands, wanted to respond, some bit of eloquence, but there was emotion rising in him, choking away the words. Men introduced themselves to him, so many names, and he nodded silently, tried to smile, felt the hands on his shoulders, heard the words, some soft and reassuring, others, like Henry's, already surging into anger, the anger that would carry forward into the great debates.

THE REPORTS FINALLY CAME SOUTHWARD, RELIABLE NOW, FROM men who had been in the town, who had seen Gage's troops. The rumors of Boston's destruction were completely false. While Adams felt a great release of fear and anxiety, the mood in the congress was subdued. For that one awful moment, the debates had been silenced, and though no one believed it would remain this way, they had put aside the animosities, rivalries, disagreements over politics and philosophy. They had reacted to the

rumors as one body, one people. The fictional destruction of
Boston had created an awareness in every delegate in the congress that the same reports could suddenly come to them from
Charleston or Norfolk. They felt the same devastating fear,
soothed now into a growing conviction that no colony, no matter
how distinct, should have to submit to any such outrage alone.

24. ADAMS

PHILADELPHIA, OCTOBER 1, 1774

THE PASSIONS AND CAMARADERIE THAT HAD BEEN IGNITED BY THE
rumors of Boston's destruction had faded, each man now settling
into one of the opposing camps, some exercising their skills as
speakers, others simply lining up with the viewpoint that made
them the most comfortable. As the discussions had droned into
long-winded debate, leaders had emerged, some by the strength
of their orations, some by their ideas alone. The conservatives
had begun to coalesce around the Pennsylvanians John Dickinson and Joseph Galloway. Galloway had drawn up a plan that
suggested a renewed effort at direct negotiation with the British
government, a pact pledging to secure the joint cooperation of
the colonies in a calm discussion of any grievance or controversy with the mother country. Galloway proposed a Grand
Council, a national legislature representing all the colonies,
which would serve as a subservient and miniature version of the
British Parliament, subject to veto by the king.

Galloway's plan had drawn surprising support, and Adams
had been distressed at the conservative mood of the congress.
He had begun to feel a deep frustration that all that was happening in Boston was being forgotten, that the immediacy of the
crisis was being replaced by the dull winds of politics. He still

did not know how long the congress would continue to meet, knew that the harvest was coming soon and that there was almost no chance that he would be home in time to tend to the farm. As his frustration increased, so had the length and frequency of his letters to Abigail, pouring out to her what he could not say out loud in the congress. But through it all, the discouragement came most from realizing that so many delegates seemed content with the terms of Galloway's proposal. As the more outspoken delegates found their resolve to break with England blunted by the conservatives, Adams began to fear that this congress would only conclude with a wordy resolution not to anger the king with any more talk of independence.

THE DINNER WAS AT THE HOME OF PENNSYLVANIA'S CHIEF JUSTICE Chew, who spared no detail in providing for the honored guests. When the call came for dinner, Adams was stunned by the display, a vast table spread with every kind of meat and bread, bowls of fruit, jellies and sweets. At one end of the table was a cluster of bottles, tall and thin, short and squat, wines, ports, and Madeira. He had almost become used to this kind of excess, knew that many of the delegates took full advantage of the hospitality of Pennsylvania's aristocratic hosts. As he moved along the table, sampling from the many dishes, Sam's word echoed in his mind, *feasts,* and he backed away, made room for the others moving in behind him. So, Sam, are we to feel guilty about this? Is it improper after all? The question answered itself, and he stared at the table again, his appetite slipping away. It was the fourth meal of this much grandeur this week, and while the men in front of him grunted and hummed their appreciation, he moved toward a chair at a small table to one side.

"Wine, Mr. Adams?"

The voice was unmistakable, and Adams smiled up at the Virginian, Richard Henry Lee.

"Thank you, yes. I seem to have forgotten."

Lee produced two glasses, poured them full, placed one beside Adams' plate, seemed to hesitate, and Adams said, "Would you please join me, sir?"

Lee sat, placed the bottle between them.

"Your cousin not joining us this evening?"

Adams shook his head. "He would rather work than eat."

"Yes, so I have learned. Energetic man, your cousin. Passionate in what he believes."

Adams felt uncomfortable eating while Lee merely watched him. He leaned back in the chair, put his fork down, looked across at Lee, and Lee raised his wineglass, took a slow drink. Lee was a few years older than Adams, from one of the most aristocratic families in the colony of Virginia. Adams had learned that Lee and Patrick Henry were the two most able orators in the congress, and both men were strong supporters of a complete break with England. Lee put the wineglass down.

"Forgive me. We should have had a toast. Salute our cause."

"Sam believes our cause may be in some difficulty."

Lee laughed.

"You mean our friend Mr. Galloway?"

"His plan seems to have a lot of sentiment behind it."

Lee sniffed. "Sentiment. But there is no power to the idea. Some of these fellows are very nervous about what we are doing in Philadelphia. Galloway offers an easy solution, and so the first inclination of the uncertain is to accept that which seems easy. You know it will not work. Worse, it is utterly ridiculous to believe that after all this time, after all that the king has proscribed for Boston, that he would welcome some . . . negotiation. Mr. Galloway believes we are still in some sort of partnership with England. He is wrong. And even the most timid who claim support for his plan know he is wrong. The plan will not prevail in this congress."

Adams was impressed with Lee's calm certainty, said, "I wonder about what the people will accept. Those of us from Massachusetts are prone to see things from a point of view of a people who have endured a great deal at the hands of the British. Most people in the other colonies do not have such experience. Mr. Caswell told me that in North Carolina, there are entire communities who welcome the hand of King George in their every affair."

Lee sipped his wine again, then added, "Mr. Chase says the same of Maryland. I'm certain there are many people beyond these walls who regard all of our doings here as dangerous talk."

Adams stabbed at a piece of meat on his plate.

"I wonder how Sam will tolerate this. He's used to getting his way, to running the show. I'm not sure he has patience for so many different points of view."

"Your cousin has his place here. He is the plow by which we all reap the harvest. I grow tobacco, Mr. Adams. I understand you do a bit of farming yourself?"

Adams nodded.

"On a small scale, but yes. I enjoy the land as much as I enjoy the practice of law."

"Which makes you the perfect man for this job. You and I have that in common: a skill in the law, a love of this land. Both are necessary to understand why our fight is so important, why it must succeed. And it will succeed. Perhaps not this year, perhaps not this congress. But we have taken the first step. We have broken ground."

Adams did not share Lee's optimism.

"Do you believe we will have to do this again? *Another* congress? Can we not complete the task before us?"

"What task is that, Mr. Adams? Convince the conservatives here to allow us to break away from England? Establish the independence of the colonies? Create our own government? I admire ambition, Mr. Adams. But Rome was not constructed in a day."

Adams had not considered there might be more than one congress. He was impressed with Lee, thought of Abigail now, her lecture on the bits of genius. I am certainly facing one now. He attacked the food on his plate, his appetite returning.

"These men are so divided, so many of them reluctant to embrace any notion of change. I must frankly admit to becoming annoyed by the long-winded speeches, by the oratory of so many men who seem to demonstrate only that they enjoy the resonance of their own voice. What began a month ago with such enthusiasm has settled into a tedious contest of endurance."

Lee chuckled again.

"Discouraged, Mr. Adams? I am surprised."

"I try not to be. But every deliberation is so spun out, and there is so much wit and eloquence, so much demonstration of learning and acuteness. I cannot help wondering if a resolution was to be offered that three and two equal five, we would be entertained with logic and rhetoric, law, history, politics, and mathematics, before two days later passing the resolution in the affirmative."

Lee sipped from his wineglass, pointed a finger at Adams.

"You may be right. And that is why some good is destined to come from this congress after all. So many of these gentlemen agree with your impatience. It is easy to overlook that not every man here is so impressed with his own talents. For every man like Galloway or Dickinson or Jay, there is a man like Colonel Washington."

The name was only vaguely familiar, and Adams said, "I don't know much about him."

"Hasn't said much. Doesn't breathe fire. But he's here because he cares deeply for what happens to Virginia, to all of us. He's paying attention to all of it, I assure you. Those are the men we must depend on. We must offer them an alternative to Mr. Galloway's simplistic solution. We require some infusion of passion, Mr. Adams. Something even the conservatives cannot debate."

THE DAY'S DEBATES HAD STRETCHED LATE INTO THE AFTERNOON, more of the same, the conservatives pushing for a vote on Galloway's plan. Voices had begun to speak out for holding off, delaying the final decision, and the words had grown hotter, each round of discussion increasing in volume with the weariness of the speakers.

They did not notice the man at first, the clothes ragged and dusty, moving into the gallery with hesitation, seeking out some familiar face. He had ridden hard, made the trip down from Boston as quickly as any man could ride, brought the precious piece of paper to the delegates who would need to know. Sam had spotted him first, a quick, solemn greeting, the two men slipping quietly to the smaller meeting room. Adams had seen them, followed, and now there was curiosity, questions from the other delegates. Adams saw Sam looking back toward him, saw Paine and Cushing gathering as well. He moved past the tall man, Colonel Washington, moved close to Lee, who said, "Should we know who that gentlemen is, Mr. Adams?"

"His name is Paul Revere. He is from Boston. Something rather important, it seems. A moment, please."

Adams was free of the questions now, moved into the room, where Sam was saying, "Let's see it, Paul."

Revere smiled through the grime and exhaustion of the long ride, slapped the paper against his thigh, a small cloud of dust. He handed it to Sam.

"Not sure if this will mean anything, but the assembly voted unanimously that you should be made aware of this, with all speed."

Sam read the paper, broke into a grin, nodded.

"Dr. Warren has been busy."

Revere continued, "Gentlemen, I have reports as well on the British activity. It seems General Gage is fortifying Boston Neck. It is quite likely that during the time it has taken me to reach Philadelphia, Boston may have been closed to any traffic."

Cushing took the paper from Sam, read as Paine spoke. "Gage's plan hasn't worked. Boston is not simply accepting her punishment."

Adams reached for the paper now, said to Revere, "Suffolk Resolves. Why Suffolk?"

"They convened the assembly there as a protest to Gage's authority. I can only tell you that patience has run out. Dr. Warren asked me to inform you that the reasonable citizens of Massachusetts realize there is no cure for what the British are trying to do, unless the chains are quite simply thrown off. It is hoped that by your communicating the Suffolk Resolves to the congress, it may help us in finding some sympathy from the other colonies."

Sam took the paper again, held it up in front of him.

"They declare that King George has violated the English constitution by the unlawful suspension of rights." He read for a few seconds more, then summarized, "A call for a refusal to pay taxes to any representative of the crown . . . the Port Bill is considered null and void . . . disregard the authority of British soldiers . . . take hostages if necessary to free anyone arrested on political grounds." Sam looked up with a broad smile. "I must agree, Paul, Dr. Warren is correct. This is just what this congress needs to hear."

OCTOBER 28, 1774

MANY OF THE DELEGATES HAD ALREADY LEFT PHILADELPHIA, AND if some felt the congress had failed in its mission, many more understood that it had been an extraordinary two months. Galloway's plan had been defeated, and in the end, the delegates had approved a Continental Association, a specific list of nonimportation and nonconsumption policies to be observed throughout the colonies. The congress understood that, ultimately, they could not effectively strike back at the king's policies except by the muscle of economics, that the only real punishment the colonies could inflict was on the pocketbooks of British merchants. If there was to be a war, the congress would not support aggression; it voted to support Massachusetts by military action only if the British were the first to open hostilities.

Adams had gathered his clothes, scanned the room for anything he had missed. In the hallway, he could hear good-byes, earnest salutes, respectful tidings among men who might not ever meet again. He heard one voice, sharp, distinct, went to the doorway, saw Patrick Henry speaking to a small gathering. Henry saw him, said something to the group, wended his way toward the open door. Adams backed away, but Henry stopped at the doorway.

"Mr. Adams, I had hoped to speak to you. Might I?"

Adams waved him inside, pointed to the one small chair, but Henry said, "No, I will stand. It's your room." Henry glanced at the leather bag on the bed. "You are leaving soon, then?"

"Yes. Sam might stay for another day, but we will be returning to Boston."

Henry rubbed his chin, seemed to be putting his words together.

"I truly hope your family stays out of danger. You as well. No one knows what you may find there."

There was a soft sincerity in Henry's concern, and Adams responded, "Thank you. We will do what we must. It seems the decisions are made by those who do not have much concern for the consequences."

"Do you think there will be any improvement in affairs? Did we accomplish anything at all?"

Adams was surprised at this question coming from the man who had led so much of the discussion, the man with the sharp words for every debate.

"We won't know that for a while. But if the British do not back away . . . if the king insists on strengthening his grip on the people . . . I am deeply afraid that there is only one appropriate response. We must fight."

Henry nodded.

"By God, Mr. Adams, I am of your opinion. I believe the next gale from the north will bring to our ears the clash of resounding arms."

Adams could hear enthusiasm in Henry's words, but he did not share the man's energy.

"I hope to God you are mistaken, sir. I so hope I can return to a quiet home. It is all any of us asks for."

He closed the bag now, tightened the wide strap. He did not know what else to say, could still feel Henry's desire to talk. There was a silent moment, and then Henry went on, "Whatever the result, this congress was momentous. The talk is pretty clear that we will convene again. I hope you will include yourself in the proceedings, sir."

"Perhaps. That decision will be made by others—my wife, for one. This is difficult for her. She has become quite the farmer." He smiled. "Farmeress."

Henry backed toward the doorway.

"Please convey my respects to your Mrs. Adams. And, sir, my deepest respects to you as well."

Henry moved away, and Adams could see Abigail in his mind

now, imagined her in the house, surrounded by the children, writing her precious letters: *Dearest friend*.

Yes, home again. Not so many stops this time. There is no need to tour the countryside. Our job here is done.

He had a sudden spark in his mind, thought, The date . . . today. The twenty-eighth. October twenty-eighth. He lowered his head, let out a long breath. Three days past, and it never entered my mind. He picked up the bag, slung the strap over his shoulder. I am sorry, dearest Portia. Ten years, our tenth wedding anniversary. And I quite forgot.

25. FRANKLIN

LONDON, OCTOBER 1774

HE HAD STAYED OUT OF THE PUBLIC EYE, HEARD ENOUGH TO STAY clear of the intense hostility toward him in the ministry. But to many he was still a symbol, if an unofficial one, and to those in the government who still could not quite fathom what was happening in the colonies, Ben Franklin was here, now, and would usually oblige their questions with a pithy answer about all the things gone wrong with the empire.

Strahan was the one friend with tight connections to the king's cabinet who would still risk a visit, not afraid to be seen by the gossiping neighbors. They had finished a long evening meal, left the fireplace to Mrs. Stevenson, climbed the stairs to Franklin's room. His knees had been bothering him, the long walks less frequent now, and he stood at the top of the stairs, a tight frown on his face. He looked away from Strahan, but his friend had already seen his expression.

"Something wrong, Ben? You're hurting."

"We're all hurting," Franklin replied. "Nothing healthy about anything these days."

He moved slowly into the room, eased into his chair, Strahan following, sitting across from him. Franklin picked up a letter. As Strahan watched him, he observed, "Hiding behind your papers won't work, my friend. I know you too well."

Franklin pretended to read still, his watery eyes blinking, the lines of black ink blending together into an unreadable blur. He had not wanted company, learned only when Strahan arrived for supper that he had been invited by Mrs. Stevenson, her quiet way of trying to lift Franklin from his awful mood. His attitude had grown more sour throughout the meal, and now he felt himself sinking to the bottom of some great black sea. Resigned to the inevitable conversation, he put the paper down and said, "Are we all in a state of decay? Are the infirmities of old age so infectious that not only the bodies of the people, their very bones, but everything they touch, everything around them, every institution must collapse into something rotten?"

"Old age? Is that what has you so bound up in misery? Forgive me, Ben, but you've endured old age for a good bit longer than many. It makes no sense to start worrying about it now."

Franklin did not smile at Strahan's joke, shook his head.

"No. It's not just growing old. My legs hurt, my knees are giving me some difficulty on the stairs . . . but I'm not in such bad condition. Better off than my son, certainly. At least my brain is functioning clearly."

Strahan smiled.

"Have you heard from William, then?"

Franklin gave the Englishman a hard stare.

"You should know very well how often I hear from my son. He writes to you more than anyone else. You have his ear now, his loyalty. You and your king. I hear from him when he lectures me about coming home. I hear from him when his finances require my assistance. He writes to me in these patronizing tones about how dangerous it is for one of my political persuasion to be roaming loose in London, as though I am some rabid beast."

Strahan looked down.

"He feels he can confide in me, Ben. It's no secret. William is a fine governor, a man true to his loyalties. He serves his king well. He is aware that his father does not approve."

Franklin sniffed. "He is not wrong about that." He paused, shifted position in the chair. "When I lost my position as post-master, I warned him to be careful, that he could easily become a target as well, probably was already the subject of talk in the ministry. I suggested, subtly, that he consider resigning. He did not take the advice. Once I understood that he intended to keep his post, I thought, All right, then, make your stand. But protect yourself, because there will be suspicions. It seems I worry too much. My son is perfectly capable of wrapping himself securely in the king's robes."

"Ben, there is no fault in an officer of the crown maintaining his loyalty. The duties of a royal governor are difficult in the best of times. These are not the best of times."

"He dares to offer me advice, Will. He preaches to me about my political indiscretions. He criticizes my writings, tells me not to inflame the passions that are already inflamed. Is that the offi-cial philosophy, the *royal* solution to our problems? Keep quiet and let things just . . . happen?" He was angry now, the dark mood rolling into fury. He felt his hands shaking, looked at them with tired eyes. "I am not accustomed to becoming this upset. My whole being is affected."

There was a silent moment.

"Have you heard from Deborah?"

"You know very well I have not. It's been too long. She is probably angry again. I've grown used to it."

"William wrote me that she has not been well. They all just want you to come home."

"She is busy with our affairs. The printing business is taking her every moment. Our son-in-law, Mr. Bache, is doing what he can, but she is always in command. By Christmas, the holidays, it will slow down. She will write then."

He did not like thinking about her when the letters did not come, could not help worrying. When he did not hear from her, he would write more often, trying to inspire a response. For sev-eral months he had hinted to Mrs. Stevenson that perhaps a gift was needed, and occasionally a package would come in return, but even then the letters had been brief, a curt acknowledgment, rarely anything else at all.

"I had thought I would go home this fall, November perhaps. But I must wait now. The Continental Congress will certainly issue some final document. If they petition the king or Parliament, it will be my job to communicate that."

Strahan stood now, and Franklin knew he had stepped onto uncomfortable ground. Strahan moved to the window, stared into darkness, mused, "It is all so . . . misguided. What would they have the king do? They destroy the tea, they spit in the face of authority. . . ."

"How can an entire people spit in the face of authority? Are not the people, ultimately, the authority themselves?"

Strahan turned, smiled.

"Ben, not this again. You know very well that if they had just offered to pay for the tea, none of this would be happening."

Franklin was taken aback by the smugness, the simple answer to all the problems of the colonies.

"I will not debate you, Will—neither you, nor my son, nor King George himself. Like a poor card player, you have shown your hand to the people. If you do not enjoy hearing protest, if you are made uncomfortable over some disagreement with your policies, you may depend on your king, who has no hesitation to take away everything of value. You have your army, your navy, your power. The message you have given the colonies is clear. They have nothing that is not granted at your whim. By assaulting Boston with such a clumsy sword, you have united your opposition. Don't you understand that? Don't you understand what the Continental Congress truly represents?"

Strahan shook his head, the smile not changing.

"Ben, the king must maintain a firm hand. I'm sure your congress will spout some formal document, yet another petition to the king to loosen his hold, change his mind about the punishment he has enacted in Boston. And what should he do then? Kneel down to this congress and say, 'Thank you for enlightening *me*. *I* made a mistake. I will manage the empire by *your* rules'?"

Franklin moved the stack of papers beside him, searching, found the article he sought, held it up. Strahan stepped forward, read the title: *Rules by Which a Great Empire May Be Reduced to a Small One.*

"Yes, I recall, Ben. A brilliant exhibit of sarcasm. You sent quite a few shudders through the ministry with that one."

Franklin looked at it, opened the first page, read, "I had hoped someone there would see beyond the sarcasm. This was very popular, you know. Even the English people understand folly." He read aloud, " 'Never believe that the discontents of the colonies are in any way justified. Listen to all the governors say, and to nothing from the friends of the people. . . . Invest the general of your army in the provinces with great and unconstitutional powers and free him from the control of your civil governors.' "

"Yes, yes, Ben. I printed some of these, remember? Admirable work, if a bit lengthy."

Franklin put the papers down.

"As I recall, you sold quite a few as well. More of this has actually come to pass than I ever expected. Some would suggest that the king misread the title and used this as a guidepost to his policies."

Strahan sniffed, and Franklin could see he was impatient, eyeing the door.

"All right, Will. You've accomplished your mission. As you can see, despite the fretting of Mrs. Stevenson, I am not close to my deathbed. Sadly, I can't say the same for your empire."

Strahan ignored him, moved toward the door, stopped.

"Any other visitors lately? Anyone I should tell the ministry about? Some seditious plotting, perhaps?"

It had been their usual joke for a while now, but Strahan was not laughing, the routine tired, worn.

"Let me think. Actually, last week I saw a gentlemen from the countryside, name of Thomas Paine. Desires to make a new start in America. I gave him a letter of introduction, told him to see my son-in-law in Philadelphia. He has an interest in writing, he says. Probably on shipboard already, conjuring up new offenses to the king. Slipped through your steely grasp."

Franklin tried to laugh, but Strahan was weighing his words, so he added, "Oh, really, Will. Mr. Paine is no threat. An unemployed bureaucrat with illusions of finding a voice among the oppressed."

Strahan still did not smile, opened the door.

"Thank you for the visit, Ben. Take care of those old legs."

He was gone now, and Franklin stood, closed the door, shuffled slowly toward the window, feeling the stiffness in his knees. He stared out into the darkness, could see motion in the dull lamplight, Strahan's carriage moving away. It is all so different now, he thought. Everything has changed. My wife has stopped writing me. My son has become a thorough courtier, a hollow mouthpiece for the king. I can't even entertain my friends. They've lost their sense of humor. Or worse, their sense of history. Just like their country, an empire who hides behind its army to justify its own mistakes. A deadly sign, to be sure.

DECEMBER 1774

THE HOUSE WAS EMPTY, MRS. STEVENSON AT THE VEGETABLE market. Franklin was tending to his mail, sat at the small desk in his room. He opened the envelope, saw an unfamiliar gold crest, thought, Another bit of wisdom, advice or criticism perhaps, brought forward on the gilded wings of someone's precious family title. He was surprised to see the letter was brief, an honest inquiry into the colonial mind. My word, they actually want insight. A plaintive cry for solutions. Unscramble the eggs for them. He scanned for the name, unfamiliar, Viscount Graddington. Not a government minister, just some bored aristocrat who doesn't understand what the fuss is about. He read the final line of the letter, a gracious invitation to explain what exactly might satisfy the Americans, avert the messiness of conflict. Well, at least he's inclined against a war. He set the letter aside, moved a paper on the desk, something he had been working on. This should do nicely as a response, he thought. Just complete the message. He took his pen, held it over the paper, said aloud, "All it requires is a few *r*'s."

He wrote now,

Recall your forces
Restore Castle William
Repair the damage done to Boston
Repeal your unconstitutional acts
Renounce your pretension to taxes
Refund the duties you have extorted

He stopped, thought. Require payment for the destroyed tea? Perhaps. Am I as naïve as Strahan, as the rest of them, to believe it may yet hinge on that? Would that be all it took to . . . *rejoice* in a happy *reconciliation*? He was annoyed now, put the note aside. They expect me to provide the answers, one old man with sore knees. What qualifications do I possess that makes everyone around here care so awfully much what I think?

There was a sound from below, a bell at the front door. Now a man called out, "Halloo? Dr. Franklin?"

He rose, went to the window, opened it, felt the sudden chill, leaned out, saw the man standing at the door below, huddled against the sharp wind.

"Yes, up here."

The man looked up, a short wave, said, "Dr. John Fothergill, sir. May I intrude? Only a moment."

Franklin backed inside, closed the window. He hurried downstairs, limping slightly, the one knee still aching. I sent for no doctor. Perhaps Mrs. Stevenson is caring for me behind my back. He opened the front door.

"My apologies, Doctor. Mrs. Stevenson is out. Sorry to keep you in the cold."

Fothergill moved to the hearth, the dull embers of a dying fire. Franklin hurried to one side, grabbed a short iron rod, began to stir the ashes.

"Sorry again. I neglected to feed the fire."

"Please, Dr. Franklin, no trouble on my account. I just came by to ask . . . if you would be interested in a game of chess!"

Franklin set the rod down, blinked at Fothergill.

"Excuse me? Did you say . . . chess?"

"Quite, sir. I come with an invitation for your consideration. I was asked to convey this to you by a friend . . . well, it's some-what convoluted. Are you acquainted with Lady Howe?"

"No, not really. I believe she is—"

"She is the sister of the two esteemed military commanders Lord Admiral Richard Howe and General William Howe. It has been requested of me that I offer you the opportunity of an eve-ning of chess with Lady Howe."

"Lady Howe wishes to play chess with me? Why?"

Fothergill seemed exasperated.

"Please, Doctor. There are great machinations at work here. I come only as a messenger. The lady made quite the point, was in fact most insistent that I communicate to you that your company is highly prized. Will you accept?"

"How can I refuse? You have my curiosity leaping great walls, Doctor."

Fothergill seemed relieved as he headed to the door.

"A carriage will call for you tomorrow afternoon, three o'clock, if that is acceptable."

"Fine. Three. Are you leaving already?"

Fothergill was already moving into the cold.

"Yes, sorry. Good evening, sir."

Franklin stared at the closing door, felt the chill filling the room again. I have not played chess in a while now. I must think about what this woman may expect. Is this simply a social call? Does she believe she can best me? Certainly she didn't invite me just to lose a chess game. Great machinations, indeed.

HE WAITED IN THE DRAWING ROOM, THE SERVANT GONE NOW. HE scanned the portraits, the glassware decorating the shelves, which lined an entire wall. He moved closer, leaned low, studied the ornate writing on one porcelain vase, Chinese, certainly. He eyed the artifacts displayed all along the shelves. Suddenly he realized, These are constructed as bookshelves, but there are no books. None. He looked all around the room. The fellow did say this was the drawing room. Not one piece of paper to be found. Not much *drawing* going on in here. At one end of the room, a chess set had been arranged, and he moved close, saw ornate pieces in rich ivory, one set of crusading warriors pearly white, the other with lacquered appointments, military insignia on each piece. The board itself was an inlaid pattern of blue lapis alternating with mother of pearl. He wanted to examine the pieces more closely, reached out, hesitated, thought, Not a chess set one would find in a Chelsea market. Perhaps this one is for show. Maybe they actually play with something more durable, a bit more utilitarian perhaps, like carved wood. I'd be more inclined to handle something a bit less . . . expensive.

"Please don't be shy, Doctor. It was my grandfather's favorite set."

He turned to see the doorway filled with a luscious gathering of rich deep red. The dress made a silky whisper as she swept into the room, a soft air of graceful delicacy. She was tall, held herself straight, the hair and jewelry perfect, a soft fragrance of something floral now blossoming in the room. He stared for a long moment, reflected, She is . . . amazingly beautiful. Then he remembered the rules, made a sudden low bow.

"Lady Howe, I presume. Your invitation honors me. I was not aware that chess was enjoyed by members of such an esteemed family. That you would accept the challenge of one so unworthy to grace these halls . . ." His mouth was pouring words like a spilling pitcher, and he stopped, suddenly felt ridiculous, had rarely lost his composure like this. He was still bent low, thought, Well, stand up, for God's sake. You're not her butler. He rose, saw a hand in front of her face, a spray of lace at her wrist. He heard the sound now, soft giggles. He wanted to say something else, told himself, Don't appear to be such a clown. She made a small curtsy now, an unusual gesture toward a commoner.

"I would hope you could be comfortable here, Dr. Franklin. Please, I would rather save the formalities of the royal court for . . . the royal court. Would you care for some tea? Brandy? Cognac?"

"Whatever your ladyship wishes, I will be pleased to oblige."

"What I wish is to converse with you over a game of chess, Doctor. May I hope for a long visit? I do hope my invitation has not interfered in your important business."

"No, not at all, Lady Howe. I am completely at your lady-ship's disposal."

He was still nervous, felt annoyed with himself, tried to avert his eyes as she swept toward the chess table. The red silk passed close to him, and he could not escape the generous display of ivory skin beneath her delicate necklace. She gave him a quick smile as she stood beside the table. He waited for whatever was next, realized suddenly she was waiting for *him*. He rushed forward, slid the chair out from the table.

"Oh, forgive me, Lady Howe."

She let out a small tinkly laugh.

"Please, Dr. Franklin, do relax. It will make this day much more pleasant if you accept that you are welcome here as my honored guest. This is rather a special privilege for me, not a formal occasion. Please, do sit down."

He moved to the other side of the table, enveloped by the scent of flowers, sat slowly, felt his mind suddenly go blank. He examined the chessboard, reached for the tallest piece, the king, cradled it gently in his hand, marveled at the detail, the fine workmanship of some long-dead craftsman. There was a long silence, and he wanted to speak, say something profound, provide some display of knowledge about ivory carvings.

"You . . . do know how to play chess, Doctor?"

Her voice brought him back to the moment, and he put the piece down, tried to steady his hand.

"Oh, my, yes, your ladyship. I was admiring the set. Extraordinary."

"You are white, Doctor."

He put a hand to his forehead, said, "I'm sorry, please forgive me, I just need a moment . . ."

"Doctor, the *chess pieces*. You are *white*. I believe that means you may move first."

He felt a rush of blood to his face, thought, Well, you are not white now. Get hold of yourself, man. She expects you to play chess, not fall about her like some schoolboy. You're old enough to be her . . . much older father. He reached for a pawn.

"Yes, well, I shall begin . . . here."

She responded to his move, and he moved again, another pawn. She leaned over slightly, and he felt the soft wisp of the floral scent. He blinked, tried to focus only on the board, watched her fingers slowly wrap around a knight, small hesitation, then she moved the piece forward, an aggressive tactic.

"You do not play defensively, Lady Howe."

"I prefer the assault, Doctor."

He moved again, immediately realized he had made an amateurish mistake, and she removed his pawn from the board.

"Was that carelessness, Doctor? I do hope you are not allowing me some advantage. I assure you, I do not require it."

"Oh, no, Lady Howe, I would not be so insulting. I will pay closer attention."

He scolded himself, Do not allow her to distract you. There is, after all, some honor at stake here. As he was pondering his next move, she said, "So what do you suppose is to be done with this dispute between Great Britain and the colonies?"

He looked up at her, saw her studying the board. She went on, "I do hope we are not to have a civil war."

She moved her knight a second time, again an aggressive move, and he tried once more to focus on the board.

"I would suppose, your ladyship, that they should kiss and make up. Quarreling can be of service to neither, but is ruin to both."

He moved a pawn again, an attempt to threaten her knight, and she reached out, swept the pawn away, another victim of carelessness. He frowned at his mistake, stared hard at the board.

"I have often said that I wish government would employ the services of one such as you to settle this dispute. I am sure no one could do it as well, " she said.

He tried to concentrate.

"I thank your ladyship for the good opinion of me, but the ministers would never think of employing me in that sort of good work. They choose rather to abuse me. It's something of a sport these days."

She sat back, looked at him.

"They have behaved shamefully toward you. And indeed,

some of them are now ashamed of it themselves. I know of one in particular who wishes to make your better acquaintance. Are you familiar with Lord Admiral Howe?"

The game had disappeared from his mind now, and he saw her looking at him with a blank innocence, a total lack of guile. Very good, he thought. Now we have come to the real game, the real reason I am here. She is quite the manipulator. The admiral cannot meet with me himself on any official basis. So this will be an *accidental* meeting, a chance encounter over a game of chess. Well, all right.

"Surely, Lady Howe, you don't mean that Lord Howe is . . . here?"

"Quite so, Doctor. If you will allow, I should be pleased to send for him."

"By all means, your ladyship."

She gave a quick wave of her hand, and he saw motion by the drawing-room door, had not noticed the servant who stood just beyond. He saw she was attending to the board again, seemed suddenly to concentrate exclusively on the game. He smiled, shook his head, thought, Why not just drop the pretense? Is there really a chess game now?

"Forgive me, Doctor, but . . . there. I believe this move would be checkmate."

"I ASSURE YOU, DR. FRANKLIN, NO ONE UNDERSTANDS THE PROBLEMS we face with the clarity that you bring to every subject." Franklin was still examining the details of Howe's uniform, the rich colors, lace, and silk.

"Your lordship flatters me."

"Nonsense, sir. It is plain truth. The ministry knows full well that you are the one man who can bring some sense to this ridiculous dilemma. It is ironic, of course, that those who speak so highly of you behind lock and key are the same men who have treated you with such violent disrespect."

"Excuse me, my lord, but no injury done to me compares with the injuries done to my country. I cannot consider my private affairs to be of any consequence when the affairs of the public are so grave."

"Your humbleness is well known, Doctor. In fact, there are many among the ministers who wish to open some communication with you. Since you are naturally assumed to find some discomfort with that, I am offering you my services."

Franklin sipped from the small crystal wineglass, studied the matter-of-fact confidence of Admiral Howe's expression. He set the glass down.

"Forgive me, your lordship, but in what way could your lordship be of service to me?"

"I propose to speak on your behalf to whomever you desire to reach. With complete discretion, of course. No one need learn about any conversation we may have."

"With all respect, your lordship, it has been my experience that three men may keep a secret only after two of them are dead."

Howe seemed set back by his words.

"Hmm, yes, quite so. However, neither of us is dead, and I assure you, no secret given my trust will escape."

"Forgive me, your lordship. I intended no insult. But please understand my lack of respect for official secrecy. My personal mail has become common reading material at the ministry, any conversation I have with even a casual friend is reported to someone in authority, and I am fairly certain my every move is watched by more than a passing glance. I must question why any of those gentlemen whose decisions are supported fully by the king would possibly care what advice I might suggest."

Howe studied his wineglass, slowly finished the contents, set the glass aside. He reached into his pocket, produced a tightly folded mass of paper, offered it to Franklin.

"I don't imagine you have yet seen this."

Franklin unfolded the thick paper, saw now the heading.

PETITION OF THE CONTINENTAL CONGRESS
TO HIS MAJESTY KING GEORGE III—THE
CONTINENTAL ASSOCIATION

Franklin sat up straight, a sudden burst of excitement.
"My lord, did this just arrive?"

Howe laughed.

"It is one of the privileges afforded those who hold the position of admiral. My statement was rhetorical, Doctor. I am quite certain you have not yet seen your congress' petition. You may have that copy for yourself. It was addressed, in fact, to you."

Franklin twisted in the chair, scanned the words quickly. So even the Admiralty intercepts my mail. I must know what this says . . . but not now. This is not the time or place. But I must know. . . .

"Doctor, my invitation remains open. I would suggest you prepare for the ministry a list of those conditions that you see as important to solving the current crisis. This is a unique opportunity, Doctor. You have an illustrious reputation in the arts and sciences. You may find this to be the opportunity to add to your formidable credentials a sterling reputation as a statesman. You may also discover the rewards that may shower upon a dutiful servant of his country."

Franklin dissected Howe's speech, one word lodging in his mind. *Rewards.* Surely he cannot mean . . . a bribe?

"Forgive me, your lordship, but I believe this document will contain exactly what you are requesting of *me*. That was, after all, the purpose of the Continental Congress."

Howe sniffed, let out a small laugh.

"Really now, Doctor, do you honestly expect that any document emerging from that spurious gathering of radicals will contain solutions? They have the nerve to issue a petition directly to the king! I can assure you that it is the view of most of the ministers—and, I might add, of the king himself—that the colonies are already in a state of rebellion. No government can be expected to give serious attention to demands made from such an outrageous assembly of criminals!"

Franklin stared at the papers in his hand, a dark cold spreading in his chest, his mind swimming with words. He tried to clear his thoughts, saw Howe now refilling his wineglass, said slowly, "But, this . . . represents . . ."

"I assure you, Doctor, what that document represents will be given little attention here. We are much more eager to know *your* thoughts, *your* plan for resolving this crisis. Dare I say again, sir, your very future could be secured by your willingness to serve your king and country. You are not so influenced by the criminal element in Boston."

Franklin stood slowly.

"Please, your lordship, express my pleasure to Lady Howe for her hospitality. I will consider your lordship's suggestion. Certainly any rational possibility of defusing this crisis must be entertained, no matter the source."

His carriage was waiting for him at the front entrance of the grand house, and he made his way slowly down the flat steps, climbed up into the carriage, rubbed the soreness in his knee. The wine had filled him with a strange uncomfortable heat, and as the carriage lurched forward, he sat back in the cushioned seat, rubbed a slow twisting in his stomach. He felt the papers in his pocket, the surging curiosity to learn the details dulled by a wave of depression. What does it matter? he wondered. If Lord Howe is so casual with his disregard of the congress, then the same will come from the others. Even the king. They might actually believe that I will somehow devise something that will miraculously end all of this, but surely ... *surely* they must understand what this document means for *me*. He thought of Howe's words: *criminal element*. Describe the congress as you will, sir. But if they are criminals, then you may as well arrest me now.

26. FRANKLIN

LONDON, FEBRUARY 1775

"MY WORD, DR. FRANKLIN, WE HAVE AN IMPORTANT VISITOR! MY word!"

Mrs. Stevenson was obviously rattled, nearly quivering.

"Doctor, do hurry! It is Lord Chatham himself! You mustn't keep him waiting!"

She seemed to be in some strange agony, fluttering like a bird, and he rose from his desk.

"It's all right, madam. I have been expecting him to call. Please, calm yourself."

"I will tell his lordship you will be right down. Do hurry, Doctor!"

She was quickly gone, and he smiled. *Not like her to be so enamored of celebrity. But I suppose Lord Chatham might be the man to inspire a collapse into some sort of lather.*

He had met William Pitt many years earlier, the man often credited with leading England to victory in the Seven Years' War with France. Pitt had always been a prominent member of King George's government, had established himself both in England and in America as the "Great Commoner," the one man who could always be depended upon to champion the cause of the people in addressing Parliament, including those causes that came from the American colonies. But power and influence had an unpredictable effect on Pitt, and he had secured a lofty position in the ministry, had taken the title of Viscount Pitt, the first earl of Chatham. The sudden affectation had alienated many whom Pitt had claimed to represent, and actually diminished his stature in the government. Worse, the man's health had deteriorated, for several eventful years keeping him from any active role in Lord North's cabinet. As the government's relationship with the colonies continued to collapse, Pitt, Lord Chatham, had found the strength to return to limited duty. Franklin had once again received an invitation to be of service.

He eased down the stairs, testing his knee, the tenderness not so bothersome, could hear Mrs. Stevenson begging Chatham if she could yet be of assistance, a pot of tea, wine. Franklin reached the bottom step, moved into the main room, the hearth alive with the roar of a well-stoked fire. Chatham was in Franklin's chair, did not stand, and Franklin said, "I am honored, Lord Chatham. Thank you for the visit."

The man held out a bent, discolored hand, and Franklin could see the man's age showing hard in his bones, every joint twisted, the man's face a mask of pain. Franklin took the hand, felt no strength, held it gently for a moment, as Chatham said, "Awful excuse for a visit. I had hoped to spend time with you on a more pleasant occasion."

The voice was soft, as frail as the man's body, and Franklin sat in the smaller chair.

"No excuse required, your lordship. You are always welcome here."

There were voices outside, and Mrs. Stevenson was at the door, then came close.

"Lord Chatham, your lordship's nurse is right outside in your lordship's carriage. If your lordship needs anything at all . . ."

Chatham raised a hand.

"Thank you, kind madam. I'm in good hands right here."

Mrs. Stevenson made a small sound, slipped quickly away, and Franklin waited, watched Chatham staring at the fire, could see now beyond the man's sickness, a deep sadness reflected in the glow of firelight. Chatham tried to straighten himself, and Franklin leaned forward, a silent offer of assistance.

"They thought I was dead and buried. North, Dartmouth, that troll Hillsborough. Even the king was surprised when I reappeared. I rather enjoyed that, rising from the depths of hell to bring a new plague on my king."

He laughed, a raspy sound. Franklin smiled, surprised at the man's humor. Chatham gave him a wry look.

"Impolitic words, eh, Doctor? A shameful lack of respect, wouldn't you say? Bah! They deserve no more. We have a proud history in this country, an extraordinary legacy. This is, after all, an empire! And it is being managed by clowns and buffoons, rife with jealousy and corruption, small men who have created a very large problem. It would be enormously convenient for them if people like me, and certainly people like you, would simply go away. Or better yet, die. But we're not dead yet, Doctor."

Franklin said nothing, waited for Chatham to catch his breath.

"There is still a chance, you know, Doctor. Still time to prevent a civil war. I intend to offer a petition to the House of Lords, calling for an end to the Boston Port Bill. I intend to ask the king to reinstate the Massachusetts charter and to recognize the Continental Congress as a representative body."

Franklin stared at the old man.

"You would do that? Excuse me, your lordship. Do you believe it will have an effect?"

"Oh, it will have an effect all right. It will show those twittering canaries that there is life left in the opposition. There are still men of reason who dare to have a voice in the government. There are some of us left who will not quietly allow the king to destroy his own empire without hearing why it does not have to be!"

Franklin tried to feel the man's passion, but the strength behind the words was missing, the fire of the man's oration barely there.

"I wish your lordship all the best."

"That's it? You think that's why I came here, to seek your good wishes? You have a role to play, Doctor. Some in this government are looking to you as the man they can either raise on a pedestal or lock in the Tower. They think if you can be brought forward as the symbol, a man who speaks for the colonies, then either of two things might happen. You might succeed, or you might fail. Assume you come up with a plan acceptable to both sides, settle this whole disastrous mess. If that were to happen, the king and his hirelings would suddenly be your good friends, Doctor. You could have any position in the government you desire, probably a title. You would be saluted in England and in America as a hero, a great savior. Ah, but if you failed! Then all the blame could be deposited squarely on *your* head. The king would wring his hands and say, 'If only Dr. Franklin had not interfered!' "

Franklin rubbed his chin.

"I have already been offered an opportunity to present some solutions. . . ."

"Of course you have! You are the ultimate colonist! They think you have the authority from your congress to negotiate. Doesn't matter whether you actually have that power. I imagine the invitations were discreet. Very secretive, no one wanting to actually associate with you. Did you comply?"

He thought of Admiral Howe, the ruse of the chess game.

"I have attempted to put some ideas on paper that might relieve the pressure. I can see, however, that your lordship's approach would have much more impact."

"I read your advice to the king, how to reduce the great empire to a small one. You have a sharp pen, Doctor. But we require more than wit and sarcasm. Which brings me to the reason for my visit. Parliament has every intention of ignoring the Continental Congress. But they will not ignore me. Trouble is, I haven't given a good speech in years. I want you to do it. The words, that is. You know the essence of what I want to say. Figure out how to say it."

"You . . . your lordship wants me to write your speech?"

"That a problem for you, Doctor? I have a surprise for you. I've read most of your other articles, some of the *secret* papers that are floating around the ministry. Pulled one or two out of the dustbin. Despite everything you may have been told, despite all the talk you hear about wanting to solve this dreadful crisis, no matter which, uh, admiral claims to be your friend, the truth is, this government is preparing for war. Lord North has already issued a request that more troops be sent over."

Franklin absorbed the words, felt suddenly a bit foolish.

"Why have they been so accommodating to me? Why do they claim to put so much stock in my involvement?"

"So they can say to history, 'Look here! Look how hard we tried! So much work, so many negotiations, so much effort at keeping the peace, keeping the empire intact, and to what end? The rabble would not be reasoned with. There had to be a war to bring the rebellion down, bring the wayward children home.' Problem is, Doctor, they don't understand what a war will do. They don't understand that they might, in fact, *lose*." Chatham paused, took a deep breath. "I love my country, Doctor. Believe it or not, I even love my king. I *must* try to convince them. It may be the only chance we have left. Will you assist me?"

Franklin stood.

"Excuse me, your lordship. Allow me to retrieve my pen."

* * *

HE HAD BEEN WORKING ON THE SPEECH FOR HOURS, THE PAGES spread over his desk, his energy manifest in the unstoppable flow of words and phrases, a fluency he had not experienced in years. He had tried at first to be kind, sparing the feelings of the more sensitive members of the audience, but then would come the barbs, the delicious sarcasm, and he would add more words, more paragraphs. Finally a cramp in his hand had brought him to a stop.

He actually felt optimistic, knew that Chatham still had influence, was still a force in the government, could sway those who might be quietly uncomfortable with the king's policies. That's all it might take. One voice, one influential man to turn the tide, persuade Lord North to turn back, at least for a time. There is so much at stake, and surely they must appreciate that peace is preferable to any alternative.

He closed his eyes now, tried to see it, Lord Chatham, the great orator, capturing the passions of the hall. It had once been like that, the newspapers quoting the man, the people gathering on street corners to read his words posted on the public boards. He opened his eyes again, stared at the papers. But now he is old. Not any older than I am, of course. But in many ways he is far beyond, so close to the end. No one knows it more than he does.

He gathered the papers into a neat stack, felt the thickness of the pile. This will require a great summoning of strength. Can he do it? Is he capable anymore? The empire may depend on it.

THE GREAT HALL WAS FILLED. EVEN THE VISITORS' GALLERY HELD no empty space. The House of Lords was more restrictive than the House of Commons, with entry strictly by invitation, and as Franklin was escorted to the place reserved for him, it was obvious that the day's agenda had excited the interest of official London.

There were polite greetings, everyone in the crowd around him recognizing him. He acknowledged them graciously, then stared forward toward the gathering of the men in their formal robes. He saw Chatham now, the frail man looking more able today than he had at any of their meetings. Chatham glanced up but did not acknowledge him as he moved to the speaker's table. Around him, the gathering of England's most prestigious gentry began to quiet down.

Franklin felt a strange excitement, his hands tightened into fists, cold butterflies in his stomach. Chatham began to speak, the words faint at first, the men at some distance from him leaning forward as they strained to hear. But his voice grew stronger, and Franklin watched the man's every inflection, every gesture, the earnest plea to reason, the simple and concrete answers to all the problems these men would still face if their government followed its disastrous course.

"The administration has repeatedly ignored the assertions and protests of the very people they claim to represent. Is not the ultimate purpose of government to facilitate the public good? Does not a government, even a monarchy, draw its strength from the approval and will of the people? His Majesty is no tyrant. He does not rule his subjects by fear and intimidation. Why then does the ministry employ such tactics against our colonies? Is it simply a matter of payment for spoiled tea? If that was all that was required to stop this calamity, I would offer to pay for the tea myself, as would any man of means who professes love for his king and his empire. But too much has transpired; we have taken a long road for which there may be only one means of turning back. The people of America know precisely the mistakes that have been made here. They have joined together as one voice, made an earnest plea for this government to acknowledge its mistakes. The response here has been . . . no response at all. Their petition, the united voice of their most learned and respected gentlemen, has been refused a hearing. When the voices are held silent, what must follow? We are witness to that, gentlemen. Government by the bayonet."

Franklin felt the impact of every word, and around him, there was silence, Chatham's energy pulling them all into his words. The old man concluded his speech, sat down, and the room stayed quiet for a long moment. Then slowly, the voices returned, a hum in the gallery, and now Lord Dartmouth stood.

"I for one appreciate that Lord Chatham's words carry great weight. His eloquence is to be congratulated. I must admit to being sufficiently influenced so as to suggest that his proposal be given serious consideration by this body."

Chatham rose again.

"I thank you, sir. I would have asked for nothing more."

Now there was a hand rising, another voice, and Franklin saw the man stepping forward. Dartmouth said, "Does Lord Sandwich have some comment?"

Lord Sandwich seemed to prepare himself, tugged at his robe, as though gathering in his audience. Franklin did not know John Montagu personally, but everyone knew the reputation of the man known as the fourth earl of Sandwich. He had served two kings as first lord of the Admiralty, a prestigious post that oversaw the management of the Royal Navy. But his reputation was much more for an extraordinary talent for corruption and greed, and an ability to spread his influence where it could bring him the most benefit. From the first rumblings of crisis in America, Montagu had spoken frequently in outrage against the rabble in Boston and what he described as their traitorous supporters in Parliament. He had been the loudest voice, triumphing against anyone who spoke in defense of the colonies, particularly if those spokesmen were popular with the masses, such as John Wilkes and, of course, Lord Chatham.

Franklin studied Montagu's face, the man's venom building, and Montagu began to speak.

"How dare this august body be subjected to the treasonous ranting of one who has so little regard for our beloved empire? Lord Chatham's claimed affections for His Majesty ring hollow and must be accepted only by their intent. We are being asked to ignore, violate, and subvert the very principles on which this empire thrives, the absolute right to govern by this Parliament. The absolute right to set policy by His Majesty King George. I am appalled that any gentlemen in this room would consider what we have heard to be of substance. Indeed, I reject the very notion that the words we have just heard have come to us from the mind of any true English peer." He turned slowly, and

Franklin saw now that Montagu was staring straight at him. "I have no doubt whatsoever that we have been subjected not to the words of Lord Chatham himself, but to the conniving influence of an American. Not just any American, mind you, but the one man I have in my eye, the most bitter and mischievous enemy known to this country! I do not hesitate in my denouncement of this outrage, and propose that Lord Chatham's proposals be rejected completely, utterly, once and for all, and with all the contempt those words deserve."

Montagu was silent, still stared at him, then Franklin saw a slight sneering smile. Chatham stood now, and Franklin could see the man's energy drained, his hand rising with a fragile quiver.

"How dare you, sir! I assure this body, the proposal is my own! But I should mention that if anyone should be called upon to address the affairs of the American colonies, it should be the eminent Dr. Franklin. . . ."

Chatham seemed to exhaust himself, his words trailing away. There were several individuals pointing at Franklin now, with words of support. He could see Lord Hillsborough speaking to someone beside him, and throughout the crowd, men were talking among themselves, some looking toward Montagu, Montagu moving slowly among them. Well, yes, Franklin thought. Influence. First lord of the Admiralty. He is a powerful man, someone no one in this room wants as his enemy. It is the way things are done here, the allegiances, the loyalties bought and paid for. Even when the opposition is allowed to speak, there is no opposition. The outcome has already been decided. By the very way the Parliament is assembled, the very corruption he supports, the king has ensured that his policies will be followed.

Franklin stared hard, tried to keep his expression firm, unchanged, knew many were still looking at him. He saw Dartmouth rising, his words breaking through the din.

"I apologize to this body for my hasty conclusion . . . I see now I was in error."

Franklin lowered his head, did not even want to hear the voices against Chatham, against the last hope for reconciliation.

The vote was tallied, the lords silencing Chatham's plea by better than two to one.

Behind him, the talk began to change, the men rising in voice as the vote against Chatham was secure. The politeness toward Franklin was gone now, the comments swelling in confidence and volume into something more hostile, menacing. They did not speak to him directly, but the words were loud enough so there would be no mistaking their intended audience. He still looked down, felt himself pulling away inside, wanted only to leave this place, silence the flow of noise around him. The vote was concluded, and there were cheers, and behind him one man said, "Now we shall settle things with a little cannon fire."

There was laughter, and another man exclaimed, "Send about forty or fifty dragoons into the countryside, scare up a few of their women. The Sons of Liberty will come crawling."

The laughter continued, more comments he forced himself not to hear. He looked toward Chatham, but the man was hidden by the robes of the victors, the men who had sealed their own place in history, the men who on this day had so pleased their king.

THEY STILL CAME TO HIM, EARNEST MEN SEEKING SOME WAY PAST the inevitable catastrophe. But there could be no plan now, no formal proposals. The Parliament had rejected any further attempt to even discuss the matter, and by now it was in the newspaper that Lord North had already issued the order for more troops to reinforce Gage's army.

Franklin had begun to feel utterly alone, a stranger in a foreign country, the only communication coming by post, frantic letters from men with not enough courage to be actually seen with him. He had begun to look into passage to America, realized that all his reasons for remaining in England over the years, the excuses he had made, were now simply washed away.

He thought of writing, his mind swirling with the names of friends, thought even of seeking advice, something he rarely did. But no words, no letters formed in his mind, and he sat at his desk, stared at old correspondence, the seals of royalty, the fine letterhead of the colleges. He had been thinking long and hard about Europe, the wonderful visits, Denmark, France, the grand opulence of royal courts, the prestige of the great halls of study. I am respected there, he thought. It would be a wonderful change. What duties have I here, after all? What job do I do now? I am representative of a country in rebellion. There is no longer a case to be made, no petitions to be addressed.

He heard the door downstairs, voices, and the footsteps of Mrs. Stevenson on the stairs. He waited for it, and she knocked.

"Doctor! A letter! It's from William, from your son!"

He rose slowly, said under his breath, "Dear madam, you are so full of hope." He had heard it from her before, scolding him tearfully, that no man should simply dismiss his own son. Well, then, what gem of advice has he for me today? He opened the door, and she was beaming, handed him the letter.

"There you are now. See there? He still writes his father. Tell me what he says!"

"Certainly, madam. There are no secrets in this family."

She followed him to the desk, and he slid his finger under the wax seal, felt it break.

"Curious. The ministry has seen fit not to violate this one. Well, of course, it's from one of their own."

He unfolded the paper, saw the date, Christmas eve, read, *I came here on Thursday last to attend the funeral of my poor old mother. . . .*

His hand suddenly shook, and there was a sharp cold shock in his chest. He stopped reading, said quietly, "Oh . . . dear, no . . ."

Mrs. Stevenson was close behind him now.

"What? What is it, Doctor? Is he not well?"

He tried to speak, the words locked in his throat: No, he is quite well. But Deborah . . . my wife . . .

He tried to read further, but his eyes would not see, and he stared at the blur on the paper for a long moment.

"What has happened? Is everything all right, Doctor?"

He suddenly felt her hand on his shoulder, and still he could not speak, tried to read again, the words on the paper clearing for a brief moment: *I heartily wish you had happened to come over*

*in the fall, as I think her disappointment in that respect preyed a
good deal on her spirits.*

He set the paper down, reached up, touched her hand for a
brief moment, now handed her the letter. She began to read, said
quietly, "Oh, dear God . . ."

She began to sob softly, sat down in the small chair, her face in
her hands. He tried to clear his mind, move past the moment. My
son is right. I have been away too long. There is only one home
now. He looked at her, thought, It will be farewell now. She
knows it, certainly. Dear madam, I will miss you.

He suddenly recalled Deborah's last letter to him, and he
leaned down, sorted through the papers in one drawer, saw it
now. He wanted to laugh again, as he had when he read it the first
time, nearly a year ago. He scanned the words. She could never
spell, was stubborn about learning. If I understood what she
meant, why did it have to be perfect? But I never . . . I could not
have known it would be the last thing, the final words she would
write to me. He came to the closing, managed a smile.

Your a feck shonet wife . . .

He had his certainty, knew the only place he belonged now.
He shuffled the papers, searching for the letter he had already
composed, booking the passage to Philadelphia. But he could
not escape, his emotions betraying him, pulling him back to the
moment, his son's words, and he felt his vision blurring again, as
the tears fell onto his cheeks.

27. GAGE

BOSTON, APRIL 1775

THE MAN LEFT GAGE'S OFFICE WITH THE OFFICIAL CADENCE IN HIS
footsteps, the rhythm in the march of an officer who knows how
important his mission could be. He made a short motion with his

hand, a silent command, his two-man staff climbing into the military carriage, six more men on horseback leading the way. They moved quickly, rattled through the streets of the town, past the salutes of the guard post at Boston Neck. They climbed a long hill, then turned off the main road, moved down a narrow country lane. They rode for several minutes, the few people they met standing aside, curious, some hostile, full of taunts and curses. But the men on the horses kept the way clear, and the officer knew there could be no slowing down, not this time, not for the gravity of his mission.

They reached their destination, a modest house, and the officer was disappointed, had expected something a bit more grand, some show of official opposition. The men on horseback did not dismount, spread out in loose formation, five of them scanning the other houses nearby, one focused on the open field that spread beyond. Inside the house, their arrival had inspired a flurry of activity, muskets pulled from discreet hiding places, powder and ball rammed into long barrels. The men inside moved up quickly beside closed windows, waited for the soldiers outside to make the next move. The house's occupant moved to the front door, took a deep breath, glanced to the man beside him, who would be hidden behind the door with two pistols in his belt and one in his hand. Slowly the occupant opened the door, faced the British officer, who said, "Good day, sir. You would be . . . Samuel Adams, then?"

Sam nodded, polite, a nervous glance toward the mounted soldiers betraying his show of calm.

"I am. What would be your business here?"

"Ah, Mr. Adams, I am Colonel Fenton, from General Gage's staff. Might we have a word, then?"

"Talk away, sir."

Fenton seemed disappointed.

"Out here? Well, if you insist, sir. I come with a message from the general himself. A proposal, actually." Fenton cleared his throat now, tugged at his coat. "Ah, General Gage wishes you to know that an adjustment of the existing disputes is most desirable. As you are aware, Mr. Adams, there are those who are somewhat active in the opposition to General Gage's enforcement of the legal measures of government. By law, General Gage is entirely within his power to secure these persons into custody, and in fact, under the law of King Henry the Eighth, General Gage may have these persons transported to England to stand trial. I am not here, sir, to make any personal accusations, you understand. However, you must certainly accept that your name has become associated with those who exhibit a conduct that the crown finds objectionable."

Sam crossed his arms against his chest, looked again at the soldiers.

"You said a proposal?"

"Ah, yes. To the point. Good. General Gage has authorized me to assure you that if you were to change your course, as it were, you would certainly find yourself in a position of considerable personal advantage. General Gage can be a most generous man. You would also find that King George would be pleased that you had, ah, come home, so to speak."

"Change my course?"

"Quite, sir. Change your course. Amend your vigorous opposition to the policies General Gage has been charged with enforcing. I speak frankly, sir, when I say your influence in this colony is considerable. Should you shift your sentiments and your message, the general is quite certain that the people here would respond accordingly."

Fenton had conveyed his message, the duty complete. Sam was smiling now.

"Does General Gage expect an actual response to this?"

"Well, I would think so, yes, sir. You may of course take time to consider the general's offer."

"Time is hardly required, Colonel. You may return to General Gage with this message. Tell him I am astounded that he would suggest in such a clumsy manner that personal considerations of any kind would induce me to abandon the righteous cause of my country. Tell him that Sam Adams offers him one bit of advice. I advise General Gage to no longer insult the feelings of an exasperated people." He paused, glanced again at the men on the horses, who were all watching Fenton. "Now, Colonel, you may depart, with your escort. Forgive me for saying so, sir, but you are currently trespassing."

"NO, I DON'T SUPPOSE I TRULY BELIEVED IT WOULD WORK. BUT WE had to make the attempt. There is always a chance a man's patriotism can be purchased. It's a regrettably common practice in London." Gage leaned back in the chair. "You are dismissed, Colonel Fenton."

Fenton saluted, backed away, moved out of the office, closing the door behind him. Gage shrugged now, looked at the other man seated to one side.

"So what else must we do, Major? Yours is the most recent arrival to this dismal situation. I'm available to fresh suggestions."

The man shifted in his chair, and Gage watched him. For a royal marine, he does not look at all like a soldier. He looks like he should be leading some grand ball.

Thomas Pitcairn commanded a contingent of four hundred royal marines, who had arrived as support for Gage's troops. He was a petite man, nearly Gage's age, fragile in appearance, who many described, not to his face, as strangely feminine. Gage could not help studying the man. He actually resembles my wife, he thought.

Pitcairn had made good use of his brief time in Boston, had taken advantage of being unknown to the Sons of Liberty to venture into the countryside, out of uniform, on intelligence missions designed to observe any military preparations the militia might be making. If there were any stores of powder or weapons, Gage was entitled by law to confiscate them.

Pitcairn stood now, smoothed his uniform, moved to one window of the office.

"We cannot simply allow them to form an army, sir. I am convinced that one active campaign on our part, one smart action, burning two or three of their towns, will set everything to rights. I have seen their alleged threat everywhere I have gone, General. Big talk, great broad pronouncements of what these farmers will do to our troops. Then we send a patrol marching through their little town, and all the big talk turns deathly silent. They are like sheep, waiting to be herded. When the shepherd is someone with a loud voice, like this Adams, or Hancock, or Warren, they follow dutifully along. When we appear, they scurry away."

Gage nodded.

"Nothing new, Major. I hear their insults daily, even in town, men who take their courage from a wine bottle, or from the fact that they can hide quickly. I am weary of the entire situation."

"It is as I have always felt, sir—the pride that comes from the uniform. The colonists feel it, too, no matter how much noise they make. When we march past, they can't help but reveal their true feelings. The protests stop, the loud voices grow quiet. They understand the grandeur, the might, the history, all that the uniforms symbolize. If the king himself could come here, simply *speak* to them, appear before them as the ultimate symbol of all that we stand for, this absurd talk of rebellion would simply dissolve. I am certain of it, sir." He paused, seemed to be caught up in some private parade. "Each time, as soon as the soldiers march away, these absurd militiamen regain their courage and prance about with muskets in the air, shouting treasonous epithets. Is that not cause enough to strip away their arms?" He paused, leaned on Gage's desk. "It has occurred to me . . . forgive me, General, but should we not be arresting their leaders?"

Gage felt the words gnaw at him. He had spoken the same words to himself for months. He stared down at the surface of the desk, the dark wood smoothed by long use, some businessman perhaps, or another officer, the former occupants of what was now Gage's headquarters. He thought of his meeting with the king, the great show of pomp that was really no show at all, one man sitting on one grand chair, speaking in absentminded phrases. And yet . . . so many of them believe Major Pitcairn is right. Just remind the colonists who we are, how wonderfully proud is our history, and they will forget all talk of rebellion. There was a quiet moment in the office, and Gage wanted to say something, felt strangled by the frustration. If you truly believe this twaddle, Major, you haven't spent enough time here yet. I hope to God you figure it out for yourself. This has gone far beyond symbols. Pitcairn was studying him, seemed to be looking for an appropriate opening for a delicate comment.

"General, forgive me, but Governor Hutchinson has been quite outspoken in London about the remedies required here. He is quite convinced that the rebellious spirit here will quickly disappear with the right show of force."

The name snapped in Gage's mind, and he leaned forward now, hands on the desk, a hard glare that backed Pitcairn away.

"Governor Hutchinson? So he speaks out *now*, does he? What was he doing here for all those years when his adversaries bullied him about this town like some schoolboy? I'll tell you what Governor Hutchinson has left behind him here, Major. Boston has become an asylum for magistrates. Loyalists pour into this town, escaping the wrath of mobs all over this colony. No man who tries to carry out his duty, no sheriff, no judge, no assemblyman is safe from the tar bucket. So they flock into Boston like . . . well, there are your sheep, Major. The royal government in this colony does not exist. My office controls, what? Everything inside of that guard post on Boston Neck. There is no authority anywhere else. We march troops through the countryside just to remind them that we can. But even then we must be careful, insist to the newspapers that it is drill, the common business of maintaining an army. Every town, every crossroads, they watch us, waiting for some mistake, some slip in discipline, some reason to strike out at us. While I hold a delicate balance in this colony between capitulation and civil war, the *former* governor, Hutchinson, sits safely in England spouting off his vast wisdom! Where were his grand ideas put into practice when he had the authority?"

"Sir, why cannot we do what the ministry wants us to do? I'm sorry, General, but I must request . . . will you please allow me to speak freely, sir?"

"You've done an admirable job thus far, Major. I'm not afraid of frankness."

"Sir, it is not just Governor Hutchinson. There is so much talk in London about your lack of resolve. There is much criticism. . . ."

"You mean like the Tories around here calling me an old

woman? I've heard criticism about my command my whole career, Major. What matters is one thing: We are soldiers. We follow our orders. No matter how much I wish to see the hanging tree decorated with those Sons of Liberty, I cannot act without the authority to do so."

"But sir, I only meant—"

"There's more, Major. You spoke freely, so will I. This is much more about passion than it is about symbols, whether you talk of the militia strutting around like so many puffed-up geese or the loyalists too afraid to stay in their homes. There is yet no *war* here. No blood is being shed. It's all about words. The first man who fires his gun is the man who changes everything. I am considerably more frustrated than you are, Major. But I do not want to be that man. When they had their celebration in March, the anniversary of what they insist on calling the Boston Massacre, they had their rally in the meetinghouse. They were all there, all the leaders, sitting in one room. There was a great outcry from the Tories here: 'Arrest them! Now's the chance!' Major, that hall was packed with people, thousands, all enraged with the passion for their cause, listening to that damnable Joseph Warren and his hot words. If I had marched in there with every soldier I have, what do you think would have happened? Do you think I could have arrested Warren and Adams, John Hancock, whomever, and just paraded them out like a Sunday stroll? All those who are so stupidly begging for a war, at that very moment, they would have had one. No mere riot, mind you. Full-out assault, both sides, all the musket fire everyone in London is so eager to hear. And no one would have been so impressed by . . . uniforms."

Pitcairn raised his hands, a show of frustration.

"Sir, I heard about your meeting with the king! The entire army was talking about it. The king's words were everywhere, every newspaper: 'Now General Gage will show them.' Sir, the talk in London is that you got your request. The king gave you everything you asked for."

Gage stood, moved to a map tacked to one wall. "Have you ever had an audience with the king, Major?"

"Uh, certainly not, sir."

"Your mind clouds up, you think of nothing but the expression on His Majesty's face. Make His Majesty smile. Make His Majesty happy. We shared a moment of blind enthusiasm, which has haunted me ever since. Yes, he gave me what I asked for. And I deluded myself." He ran his hand over the map, pointed to the sketch of the town. "We have four thousand men, Major, more or less. In this colony, there are tens of thousands of able-bodied citizens, who seem primed to jump to it."

"But sir, they're farmers, shopkeepers. They're no match for my marines."

"They're armed, Major. They have men leading them who understand how to inflame them. Since my foolish show of bravado for the king's entertainment, I have gained a bit more experience. I am now . . . *here*. I am now faced with the actual problem of putting down a rebellion in a very large colony, perhaps several colonies. I have made additional requests to London for troops. They sent me your four hundred marines. I requested twenty thousand. My critics claim that was a demonstration of my weakness. After all, Thomas Hutchinson says that all we have to do is rattle our sabers and Sam Adams will fall to his knees!"

"Sir, no one in London believes the rebellion will spread beyond Massachusetts. Surely you don't—"

"Major, it has already spread. I received regular reports from their congress, heard all I needed to know about how the Sons of Liberty are manipulating the people all down the coast. Not even the most strident loyalists can stop the tide."

"You said . . . a spy, sir? You had a spy in Philadelphia?"

Gage smiled now.

"Not bad for an old woman, eh, Major? I've been in this land for a long time, understand how they think, how they behave. They have weaknesses."

"Forgive me, sir, but can anyone in this place be considered reliable?"

"Right now, Major, I know where they meet, where they sleep, and, more important, I know where they hide their arms and powder."

Pitcairn was excited now, began to pace.

"We should make a plan, sir, a foray. They can't stand up to us if we attack their ability to fight back."

"In due time, Major. In due time. I have sent my reports and proposals to the ministry. They might publicly criticize my command, but privately, Lord Dartmouth and even Lord North know that I cannot move until *they* issue the orders. In the meantime, we do our jobs. We keep the peace. We drill the troops, and we give the frightened Tories a comfortable place to spout their complaints."

Pitcairn sat again, seemed to sulk.

"Sir, I can't help but feel that we're letting it all slip away. Our inaction may be interpreted as weakness."

"Major, our government has already shown a peculiar talent for weakness. Ten years ago we backed down over the Stamp Act. We have retreated time and again on issue after issue, principles and laws. It cannot continue. If the ministry backs down from the new policies, if England allows the colonies to have their way yet again, then the empire may well be lost. We might as well load up our ships and sail away, abandon them to their mobs and their congresses. And there's the challenge, Major. We cannot show the colonies our resolve by simply marching in here and burning cities. Simple military solutions are not always so simple. I will not start a war, Major. We will make our show of authority, we will march the troops through the towns on drill, but there will be no aggressive act. At least, not by *my* orders."

MARGARET HAD RETURNED TO NEW YORK SEVERAL WEEKS AFTER her husband had sailed, escorted by her brother, Major Kemble. Gage had insisted she remain in New York for a time, but she would not be separated from both her husband and her children and so had finally come to Boston in the fall. As she prepared to celebrate the Christmas season in yet another new home, she had eagerly awaited letters from her children, progress on their schooling, all the chattering words of expectation for the holidays. But when the mail arrived, there was another letter as well. Their son William had been stricken again with the illness that had so weakened him before. This time he had been beyond any treatment, and the boy had died in London.

The baby born in England was with them, of course, and Gage had hired a nursemaid to assist her. Margaret had settled again into a dark gloom, but it was different now, far beyond the frustration of being pulled away from home and family. She seemed to lose much of that soft instinct for motherhood, spent less time with the baby, left much of the daily care in the hands of the nursemaid. The talk from their friends was that she was hardened by the death of her son, a bitterness that showed itself even in the social times, the attempts from all the loyalists holed up in Boston to make some sort of good show during their forced togetherness.

She did not speak of the sadness, avoided all conversation with her husband, not a difficult thing, since his duties often kept him at his headquarters. She had taken to walking the streets, refusing any kind of military escort against the advice of friends. She seemed to ignore the concept that anyone might consider her, the wife of the most hated man in the colony, a target or a threat. She was, after all, an American.

For long hours, she would move along the wharves, staring at the great ships, rows of black cannon staring back from the men-of-war that protected the town. She would daydream, one ship perhaps newly arrived, bringing her children home for the last time, even William, the boy running down the plank to the arms of his mother. She could not even picture the estate in England now, beyond the miles of empty ocean. Instead she held the images of her own home, let her mind drift away to the green hills and farmhouses, the small town in New Jersey where her family would always welcome her, a place that would always have made a good home for the children.

Along the streets, soldiers knew to watch for her, an informal order from Gage's staff, men emerging from taverns, staring silently, respectfully as she passed. It was a town filled with sorrow, all varieties of sadness, despair, so much abandoned. Some could only suffer a future doomed to chaos and uncertainty. Others believed in hope, an escape, England perhaps. To

Margaret Gage, the daydreams drifted into the resolve that there could be no life with her husband and her children while the horror of siege and protest controlled everything around them. She had finally begun to speak to friends, and it was not about her son, about the sadness she could not avoid. It was about ending this turmoil, finding a way to bring this all to a peaceful end, a time when people like her would not have to fear for their children or their homes.

If the soldiers knew to watch for their commander's wife, there were others in the town who did the same. They were not a threat to this lone woman with the reviled name who stared at the ships. They were curious, and they were as motivated as she was to find an end to the plague of confrontation. At first came the casual invitation, a hot cup of tea, the comfort of a familiar face. She began to oblige, and the familiar faces soon gave way to those not so familiar. After weeks, her walks became less random, the visits to her new friends more purposeful. Gage had not worried about her, had received reports from the officers that she was never in danger, that she spent much of her time now safely behind the doors of her growing number of friends.

It was chance at first, Margaret making her determined way past a tavern where the officers often reveled in their raucous salutes to both the king and the women left behind. The tavern had been quieter, the younger officers subdued this night by the presence of more senior commanders. One man in particular had seen her pass, excusing himself to follow. He had not yet met her socially, had thought it might be the opportune moment. But she did not notice him, was already well down the street, kept her eyes to the front, focused on her destination. He followed for a short time, watched as she began glancing about, self-conscious, cautious. His instinct pushed him into hiding, a discreet doorway, and she crossed a street, made one last glance behind her, and disappeared into a narrow alley. The officer stepped again into the street, stared at the alley, more curious now, a professional appraisal, the mind of a spy suddenly at work. He tried to put it out of his mind, scolding himself, There is no intrigue here. She is drinking tea with friends. But as he turned away, walked back to the tavern, the doubt stayed with him, some strange nagging that there was something to be considered in her apparent show of nervousness. He reached the tavern now, moved back inside, saw the glasses raised on his behalf, the voices welcoming his return.

"Major Pitcairn . . ."

APRIL 14, 1775

GAGE HAD TAKEN THE TIME TO WALK THIS MORNING, WOULD INspect the new barracks himself. One of the wide green parks had been commandeered by his troops, and now the workmen had nearly completed their task. The carpenters had been brought in from Nova Scotia, the only source of the skilled manpower needed to construct the buildings. Boston simply didn't have the workmen, for nearly anyone with employable skills was long gone from the city. The new law had given Gage the power to move the soldiers into the homes of the citizens, but that was impractical. There were simply too many troops, and though the officers could usually find suitable accommodations, dividing the private soldiers into so many individual lodgings was a ridiculous inefficiency.

He had watched the new ships docking, had hoped to see troops, another addition to his meager strength, but they had not stopped at Castle William, the usual routine, had instead come straight into the wharf. There had only been cargo, but it was welcome nonetheless. He had seen the dispatch officer, and Gage stayed back, allowed the man to do his job, abide by his routine. The mail had been sorted on the ship, and any official dispatches would be given priority, distributed immediately to headquarters. Well, he thought, if there is something from the ministry, I will find out soon enough.

HE STEPPED THROUGH THE OFFICE DOOR, SAW THE STAFF SCRAMBLING to attention.

"As you were, gentlemen."

He could see the dispatch bag, the mail in small stacks, fought the urge to ask, did not look at Kemble.

"I'll be in my office."

He closed the door behind him, was breathing heavily now, not just the exertion of the walk. He stayed close to the door, heard the staff still poring through the mail, and he clenched his fists. There must be something, it has been so long. Suddenly the door behind him rattled, a sharp knock. He turned, backed away.

"Yes?"

"General, there is an official dispatch for you, sir."

He wanted to jump at the door, waited a brief moment.

"Oh, is there? Well, I suppose I will read it now."

The door opened, and Kemble handed him the thick envelope.

"Yes, thank you, Major."

He moved to his desk, felt his hands shaking, took a long deep breath, realized Kemble was still in the doorway. He said crisply, "That will be *all*, Major."

The door closed, and he cracked the wax seal, knew the symbol, Lord Dartmouth, felt his heart jump. Now we shall see. . . .

There were several pages, and Gage settled into the chair, read slowly, focused on each word. He read for a long while, studying Dartmouth's words carefully. Then he reread the paper, his shaking finger finding the passages that had shot into him like hot lead.

> There is a determination of the people of Massachusetts to commit themselves at all events in open rebellion. In such a situation, force should be repelled by force.
>
> The authority of this kingdom must be supported and the execution of its laws enforced. Since those who so vehemently give their support to the cause of rebellion in Massachusetts are determined to cast off their dependence upon the government of this kingdom, the only consideration that remains is, in what manner the force under your command may be exerted.
>
> The first and essential step toward reestablishing government would be to arrest the principal actors and abettors. . . ."

He was fully excited now, moved back to the opening page, read again.

> *In a situation where everything depends so much upon the events of the day, and upon local circumstances, your conduct must be governed very much by your own judgment and discretion.*

He put the papers down, wanted to shout, *Finally!* He tried to calm himself, put both hands flat down on his desk, felt his breathing, waited a long moment, found his composure.

"Major Kemble!"

The door opened quickly, and Kemble was there, the rest of the staff close behind him, all eyes on Gage.

"Major, I need a meeting of the senior commanders, including the navy. Be sure to send word as well to Major Pitcairn. He has been positively itching for a mission. Well, now he shall have one."

28. REVERE

Boston, April 18, 1775

HE HAD STAYED IN TOWN, CLOSE TO THE SUDDEN RUSH OF ACTIVITY around the British camps. All through the day, word had spread through Boston; the usual routine of several units of British regulars had been interrupted. The civilians who tried to enjoy their daily visit to a favorite tavern had become accustomed to the red-coated officers who monopolized the tables, peppering their boredom with loud toasts or profane participation in card games. But today the officers had not appeared, causing busy talk among innkeepers and their civilian customers. In the open greens, where sullen citizens usually went about their daily routines within sight of the formations of drilling troops, word spread as well. Today the greens were empty.

Revere had been working in his shop on the final burnishing of a small bowl, a gift for a friend. Business had been slow, as there was very little use for the hand of a fine silversmith. He had been sought out by the British officers, their wives seeking some memento to carry home to England, some souvenir of this dreadful duty in this dreadful place. As idle as the furnace in his shop had become, he would not comply, claimed a backlog of work. The disappointed ladies had continued to visit, hoping somehow to persuade this rugged man to accommodate them by attending some of the social gatherings. The wives did not concern themselves so much with politics and allegiances, whether Paul Revere was indeed one of those dreaded Sons of Liberty. They talked instead of this handsome craftsman, with the thick arms and broad chest, whose strong hands could fashion such amazing beauty. He would never have accepted their invitations, but there was one very good reason not to send them away. From the first occupation by the soldiers, the hierarchy of the Sons of Liberty had discovered that this man's attractiveness to the wives of British officers could be used to extraordinary advantage. For the wives' talk was not always strictly social. They might actually have information, some piece of news that might pass in casual conversation, something far more valuable than the women themselves might understand.

Revere had noticed another change in British routine. More than once a day, some officer, perhaps a small group of them, would happen by his workshop, pay their own compliments. He understood that they were on their own personal mission, finding out what the fuss was about, just who this silversmith was and what manner of threat he might be to the affections of their women. But today they had not come, the streets quiet, belonging only to the citizens, many with quickened steps, their sense of alarm driven by the feeling that something was already happening, some movement, some plan of the army that no one could explain.

At dark, he had been summoned with some urgency to a

meeting called by Joseph Warren. Warren was the only notable member of the Sons of Liberty still in Boston, having ignored the advice of Sam Adams and of many of his friends that his continued presence there could be a dangerous mistake.

Revere moved into the narrow alleyway, stopped for a long moment in the dark, listening, scanning the street, doorways, and black windows. He had passed the tavern where so many of the officers could always be found, was as surprised as the man who served the ale that the place was quiet, no discordant songs spilling into the street.

His eyes sought out the shape of the doorway, a few steps farther down the alley, and he moved that way, then waited one more cautious moment. Suddenly the door opened, dull candlelight splitting the alley, one man slipping outside. The door closed quickly, and Revere saw the man glancing about, adjusting his eyes to the dark. He recognized the man's stooped posture, the floppy hat. It was Will Dawes, who saw him now.

"Oh! Paul! Good, the doc's waiting for you."

"What's happening, Will? The meeting over?"

"It's all right, Paul. I'm off now. Doc Warren will tell you. I'm taking the long route, have to convince the guards at Boston Neck that I'm just a weary traveler, don't you see?" Dawes affected a thick English accent, laughed. "Got to be home afore me wife has me 'ead." Revere could hear the man's nervousness. "Well, then, Paul, I had better be off. Long ride."

"What's happening? Trouble?"

Dawes laughed again.

"Of course it's trouble, my friend. Only reason to go out on a night like this. Go inside now. The doc's waiting for you."

"Will, where are you going?"

"Same place as you, most likely. They aren't as likely to catch both of us. I'll run into you a bit later, if we're both lucky. Got to run now. It's a long ride in the dark."

Dawes moved quickly, farther down the alley, and Revere could hear the sound of a horse, hoofbeats now coming toward him. He stepped aside, his back against the rough wooden wall, Dawes now riding past, and Dawes stopped, leaned low.

"Take good care now. See you in Lexington."

* * *

JOSEPH WARREN AND PAUL REVERE HAD BEEN CLOSE FRIENDS even before Warren had begun his medical practice. Revere was a few years older than Warren, had built a reputation in Boston not just for silversmithing, but for engraving as well, from family coats of arms to portraits. In the earliest days of the organization of the Sons of Liberty, Warren had introduced him to Sam Adams, and Revere's skills at engraving political cartoons and caricatures were put to effective use. He had made himself useful in other ways as well, a talent that many tried to claim, but few had mastered. Sam Adams had employed him as the colony's official courier to the Continental Congress, and the reasons were clear to all. Paul Revere was an excellent horseman.

The fire was low, the windows covered, and Revere was surprised to see that he and Warren were alone. Warren had poured him a cup of coffee, set it on the table.

"Best I can offer. Hard to get much of anything else here lately. Haven't had a good bottle of Madeira in months."

Revere sat now, tested the coffee cup, his callused hands immune to the heat. Warren sat as well.

"I actually bring it into town hidden in my boots. They seem to watch me a bit closer than most. But after a day or two roaming over the countryside treating the sick, the guards don't seem much interested in checking me over too closely. Superstitious lot. I imagine some of them think a doctor's barely one step removed from being a witch."

Revere sipped at the coffee.

"Will Dawes mentioned Lexington. You want me to go to Lexington?"

Warren smiled.

"My apologies, Paul. I'm just rattling at the mouth. Coffee seems to have that effect. You'll be meeting a boat that will take you north, across the bay."

Revere was puzzled.

"A boat? I thought . . . I usually do my work on horseback."

"Oh, you will. But you have to cross the bay first. Dawes took the overland route, through Boston Neck. You need to go up through Charlestown. Can't risk having you both on the same trail."

Revere knew that information was typically given out in small doses, protection for the man who carried the message. He glanced around the room, looked for the papers, some document. Warren noticed and asked, "What is it?"

"What do you want me to carry?"

Warren shook his head.

"Forgive me, Paul. I thought you knew. You said you spoke to Mr. Dawes."

"He didn't say much."

Warren took a deep breath.

"The message you are taking is not on paper. You must reach Lexington as quickly as possible, and then move on to Concord. Sam Adams and John Hancock are in Lexington, and we have every reason to believe that the British will be attempting to arrest them tonight."

"Why them? Why tonight?"

"They're as prominent in this colony as any two men you can name, Paul. Gage has wanted Sam's head for years. And besides Hancock's prominence in the Sons of Liberty, he's been rubbing British noses in the trade laws for so long . . . well, I don't have to tell you, he's the richest man in the colony, and it's no secret that he's also the most accomplished smuggler. The timing is easy to explain. General Gage has had a burst of inspiration, in the form of official orders from London. For now, we know that several hundred British regulars will be on the move very soon. They'll be marching at night. That way"—he smiled—"we can't see them."

Revere ignored Warren's humor.

"Doctor, you think they'll put hundreds of troops on the road just to arrest two men? That's a mite clumsy, even for Gage."

"Arresting two men is only a small part of their plan. It's really just a case of coincidence. Our friends are staying at the home of Reverend Jonas Clark. It happens that the march of the soldiers will take them very close, close enough that stopping off to nab two of the most prominent Sons of Liberty is a simple matter. But Gage's main target is Concord, the powder and shot the militia has stored at Colonel Barrett's farm. It seems General Gage has eyes that see far beyond Boston. Apparently not everyone who comes to our meetings shares our sentiment."

Revere waited for more, watched as Warren rose, reached for the coffeepot.

"Forgive me, Doctor, but if you know so much about Gage's intent . . . sounds as though you have some pretty sharp eyes yourself."

Warren turned, looked at him, a slight shrug.

"We learn what we can."

Warren poured the steaming coffee into Revere's cup, put the pot back on the low fire.

"You must go to Reverend Clark's and alert them. It should be no problem reaching Lexington before the British. Putting several hundred soldiers on the march takes time, especially in the middle of the night. But we do not know which route Gage has decided upon. Before you leave, you must find out if the British troops are marching through Boston Neck, the land route, or whether they intend to take the shorter route, as *you* will, across the bay. There were a number of navy longboats assembled at the wharf today. These could be what they will use to cross, or they could be just a ruse to misinform prying eyes."

"What about you, Doctor? If Gage intends to arrest the others, are you not in equal danger?"

Warren chuckled.

"Probably so. I will be leaving the town before dawn, will try to reach Lexington myself. By that time, it should be evident which route the troops are taking. No army can disguise its tracks. I shall follow an alternative course."

Revere finished the coffee.

"I should be leaving, then. Once the soldiers begin to assemble, it will not be a good time to be in the street."

"The boat should be ready by the time you reach the wharf. There's a particularly good horse waiting for you in Charlestown. I believe you know her. Brown Beauty?"

Revere stood, felt the heat from the coffee, the strange energy rising in his chest.

"Brown Beauty. Yes, she's a real warrior, that one."

Warren stood as well, held out a hand.

"God be with you, Paul. You *must* warn them. Once the British reach Lexington . . ."

"Doctor, I assure you. I'll awaken every man in every farm I pass. By the time I get to Lexington, all of Massachusetts will know what is happening."

HE SLIPPED OUT TO THE MOUTH OF THE ALLEY, SCANNED THE DARK street. He could hear the sounds of a mass of men now, a few blocks away, metal and hoofbeats, an army coming to life. He stood still, pressed hard against the wall, looked for motion, waited for the perfect stillness, the time to move into the street. Across the way, the shops were dark, the only light a block away, the quiet tavern, the hope of the innkeeper that someone might still require a drink. His eye caught something now, a small shadow, betrayed by the light from the tavern, slipping along the storefronts across the street. The shadow crossed over now, coming straight toward him. He stayed frozen in place, flat against the wall, could see the shape more clearly now, outlined in the dimness. He felt his breathing, tried to hold it still, the shadow now close, the shape distinct, rounded. He could see a long coat, a hat pulled around long hair. He stared, amazed. A woman. She stopped only a few paces away, glanced behind her, then stared right past him down into the alley. He expected her to move on by, thought, It's all right, my dear, go on, attend to your . . . what? Some inappropriate late-night rendezvous, perhaps? There's nothing in this alley, no jealous husband, so just move along. She seemed to hesitate for a long moment, then she headed straight into the alley, quick and deliberate, passed within steps of him, her scent reaching him, the soft sweetness of lilac. He held his breath, watched her move to the one door, and she paused again, then a faint knock. Revere smiled now, understood, thought, Eyes indeed, Doctor. The door opened a crack, the candlelight freezing Revere again. She did not see him, slipped quickly into Warren's home. He heard the doctor's polite words, gracious: "Mrs. Gage . . ."

THE BOAT SLIPPED SILENTLY THROUGH BLACK WATER, THE OARS-man practiced at cutting the surface with no sound, pulling the boat in slow rhythm away from the wharf. Behind him, Revere could see the steeple of the church, framed against a starry sky. There would be no mistaking the light of the lantern against the darkness. The signal would come from the base of the steeple. He will be there, he thought. He is a good man. I know he understands the importance. Now he turned to the front, steadied himself with both hands on the rail of the small boat. The oarsman said nothing, kept steadily at his work, and Revere could see the moon, just rising out to the east, a bright spray of light across the harbor, broken only by the British warships. He felt the excitement now, and looked to the west, toward the mouth of the Charles, saw one shape looming large, the moon-light now reflecting off three tall masts. It was His Majesty's ship, a grand man-of-war called the *Somerset*. Revere glanced at the oarsman, could see a smile, a slow nod. Yes, young man, we are very close to a great deal of trouble. The small boat slipped slowly past the great ship, and Revere could hear sounds now, voices, the crew of the massive ship right above him, the night watch perhaps, enjoying the peaceful evening, guarding against nothing, nothing that could keep their army from crossing this bay. No, we cannot stop you. But we can make your secret no se-cret at all.

In moments, the *Somerset* was behind them, and he could hear the oarsman breathing, small grunts, the young man tiring. He wanted to help, but the man had been very clear: sit tight, no motion to alert the lookouts on the big ship. They reached the far bank now, and Revere was surprised to hear a harsh whisper, someone waiting for him.

"Aye, easy now. There you go . . ."

The boat slid to a halt against hard sand, and Revere stood, felt a hand on his arm, helping him from the boat, a face in the dark, a short, round man, the voice unfamiliar.

"Welcome to Charlestown, Mr. Revere."

Revere cringed at the volume, the man showing no fear of the sound, and the man now reached into his pocket, handed something to the young man, who still sat with his oars. The round man said something, a thank-you, and Revere wanted to quiet him, looked back nervously at the great ship, coming alive with the glow of moonlight. The man began to speak again, another enthusiastic greeting.

"Glad to have you here, sir."

"Sir! Please . . . lower your voice!"

The man turned, guffawed.

"Mr. Revere, you are not in Boston now. There's no danger here."

There was more laughter now, calls of greeting, and Revere looked up past the sandy bank, could see bits of reflection, glimpses of faces. He realized the shoreline was alive with men. And suddenly he saw one clear reflection, sharp, metallic. Yes, men with guns.

"Come now, Mr. Revere. We've got your horse right up thisaway."

Revere followed the man up the low slope.

"I must wait for the signal. There can be no mistake."

They crested the hill, and the man said, "Signal? From whom?"

Revere looked back across the water, could see the church steeple framed clearly in the moonlight.

"There, the church. I cannot leave just yet. I have to know by which route the troops are marching."

"Whatever you say, Mr. Revere. Here she be now. Your mount, Brown Beauty."

He moved to the horse, could tell she was tall, heavy, well fit for a good hard ride. He patted her neck, still stared at the distant steeple, thought, Please, don't fail me, sir. Surely he understands. . . .

There was a speck of light now at the base of the tall steeple, and he stared hard, the voices around him now falling silent. One man said quietly, "Is that what you been waitin' for? What does it mean, sir?"

He held up a hand, said nothing, waited, saw now a second speck, a second lantern in the high window of the church, like two small eyes in the dark, unblinking, staring out toward him in the cold moonlight. He felt a great burst of energy, climbed the horse.

"It means, gentlemen, that you had best advise your men here to stand away. With all respect to you, sir, this is not a fight you want. You could have several hundred soldiers landing on your shore. Two lights . . . the signal that the British are coming this way, by water."

THE MOONLIGHT OPENED THE ROADS IN FRONT OF HIM, A WIDE bright path. The horse took his every command, did not hesitate, and together they pushed past farmhouses, each one hearing his quick shout, to rise and be ready. All along the roads, doors opened, window curtains were pulled back, the farmers and villagers coming awake to the sharp call that a great force of soldiers was marching their way. As he passed, each house rolled into life, muskets were pulled down from stone hearths, slid out from under beds, retrieved from closets. The men had drilled and planned for this moment for many months, and now they dressed in the dark as their wives pulled together a knapsack, a bit of food perhaps, bread or dried meat, laid out on the table beside a powder horn. It took barely a minute, and with a last soft word, the men were out of their houses, moving into the road, following the tracks of the horseman who woke them, knowing only that the tracks led to Lexington.

29. PITCAIRN

THE SOLDIERS HAD BEEN ASSEMBLED NEAR THEIR CAMPS BEFORE midnight, forming as quietly as can be expected of six hundred men. They had marched the short distance to the waiting long-boats, expecting to cross the mile and a quarter stretch of the bay. But before the first oarsman began his work, Pitcairn was forced to accept what every officer learns, that not every military plan is destined to run with efficiency. As the troops crowded into the boats, Pitcairn realized that they were too many for the boats provided. No one had thought to check with the naval officer in charge whether they had the right number of boats for the number of troops.

He had reached the far shore, only to sit and wait on his horse with boiling frustration while the longboats had gone back to Boston, to load the men left behind. It had been the first great delay. The first troops who had reached the northern shore had been made to stand in formation for nearly two hours, and once the remaining men had arrived and the entire force was prepared to move, they were distributed a day's cooked rations. Pitcairn had watched the work of the quartermasters with outraged dis-belief, another delay caused by someone neglecting to handle this small but crucial detail, which should have been done while they were still in Boston.

When the order came, finally, for the troops to march, they had been ordered away from a plank bridge, their commander fearing that the sound of boots on wood would awaken the neighbor-ing citizens, giving alarm of the movement of the troops. The men instead had to push through the icy chill of waist-deep water, a slow and demoralizing beginning for a force of men

291

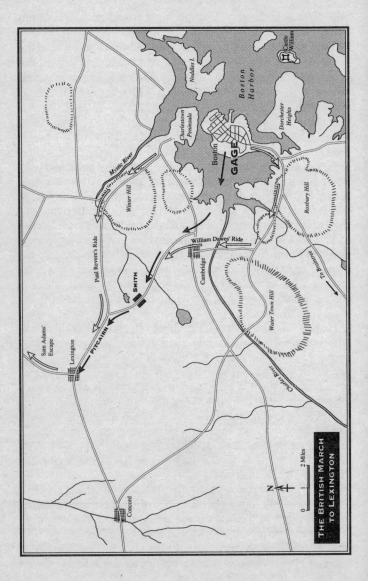

Castle William

Noddles I.

Boston Harbor

Dorchester Heights

Charlestown Peninsula

Boston

GAGE

Mystic River

Winter Hill

Roxbury Hill

Paul Revere's Ride

William Dawes' Ride

SMITH

Cambridge

To Braintree

Water Town Hill

Charles River

Sam Adams' Escape

PITCAIRN

Lexington

Concord

N

0   1   2 Miles

THE BRITISH MARCH TO LEXINGTON

who already understood that this night would pass without any sleep.

Pitcairn was still not completely sure why he was a part of this mission. He was the only marine present, and even the most discreet officers around him had commented that there were many officers who had a closer relationship with the units on the march, who could have performed the job with ability. The overall commander was Lieutenant Colonel Francis Smith, an older man whose ample waistline had given rise to many unkind nicknames. Smith was a reasonably capable man who inspired little actual enthusiasm, and Pitcairn had overheard one injudicious comment from a gathering of junior lieutenants that General Gage had sent the marine so that there would be at least one officer on the mission who could ride as quickly as the foot soldiers could march.

He was grateful for the moonlight, rode near the front of the column, kept an ear open for the instructions of the local guides. He had not seen Colonel Smith for a while, the commander content to allow his men to precede him, and as the troops moved deeper into open countryside, Pitcairn had focused more on roads and intersections than on his commanding officer, making sure the lead of the column marched in the right direction.

He crested each hill with a sharp eye, had moved farther to the front, away from the main body. The lead scout troops had spread out slightly off the road, moving quietly, with as much stealth as possible, seeking out anyone who might be attempting to block their march, or worse, some farmer with a musket who might decide that killing a British soldier made for good sport.

Even before the troops had boarded the longboats, word had come back to headquarters that Boston was alive with news of their mission. It had been a shock to Pitcairn, and one more symbol of the frustration of the duty in this miserable place. It was bad enough that so many of the citizens hated their existence. But it was intolerable to Pitcairn's pride in his professionalism that military secrets were paraded through town on the back of every newspaperboy. The order from Smith was still in effect: a silent march, as much stealth as possible, as though the element of surprise was an asset they could depend on. Pitcairn stopped his horse now, could hear sounds rolling across the dark hills in front of them, the men around him hearing as well, muttering their own comments. The first sound had been a church bell, a single chime, followed a minute later by several more. He had felt curious about that, odd that any church would be calling anyone to services this late. But as the same sounds echoed farther away, he had understood, of course; it was a signal. As they marched farther from Boston, there had been more church bells, long litanies, some even tolling as the column moved past them, whoever might be inside the church ignoring any threat that the soldiers might attempt to silence the chimes. On the far hills, he had begun to hear small bursts of musket fire, but the distance was far too great for them to be a threat to the column. It was another form of signal, protest perhaps, and he stared ahead to the moonlit road with a growing sense of dread. For all the trouble, the inconvenience, the inefficiency of marching at night, nothing at all had been gained. He tried to force himself away from his growing doubts, assured himself, It is of no consequence that they know we are here. We are too many, and too strong, and no matter how much noise they make from the protection of the darkness, it is just chatter, after all. Nothing will stop us from doing our job. They have never stood up to these soldiers before, and they will not stand up to us today.

He could hear a sudden flurry of voices out in front, and now a lantern was lit, and he saw a man pulled down from a horse, a brief fight. He spurred his horse, moved up, saw a civilian held by two soldiers, the man shouting, "By damned, you have no call . . ."

Pitcairn spotted the sergeant, said, "What have we here?"

The sergeant prodded the man, roared, "Answer the major! What brings you out on a lonely road in the middle of the night? Mischief, perhaps?"

The man struggled against the hold of the soldiers.

"I live hereabouts. I have a right to take a ride anytime I see fit!"

The sergeant looked up at Pitcairn.

"What do we do with him, sir? He was up to no good, that's a bloody certainty."

The man looked at Pitcairn with a hard sneering grin.

"Well, Major, you'll be finding out soon enough what mischief is. There's five hundred men up the road at Lexington Green, just waitin' for ya. You might as well turn this parade of lobster-backs and march 'em back to Boston."

Pitcairn said nothing, thought, Mischief, indeed. He knew we were out here before he ran into us, and he probably knows why we're here. The sergeant still looked up at him.

"Sir? Maybe we should tie him to a tree. Keep him out of trouble." There was laughter from the other troops, and the man said, "You'll be laughin' mighty hard once you run into Sam Adams!"

Pitcairn thought, That's what we're counting on, sir.

"Though it is within my power, I am not disposed to begin shooting spies this night. Sergeant, have your men escort this gentleman to the rear of the column. He will be our guest for the rest of the march. Sir, since you have been so generous in offering us information about what lies ahead in Lexington, I am pleased to return the favor. There is a great deal more on this road than a parade. There is the entire might of His Majesty's empire. Even if I believed your ridiculous claim, no five hundred men on this earth can stand up in the face of that. Once the sun has come up, you will be released. At that time, I would suggest you go on back to your home."

The soldiers led the man back to the tail of the main column. Pitcairn ignored the man's cursing, pointed now to the lantern, prompting the sergeant to say, "The light, Jenkins."

It was suddenly very dark, and Pitcairn warned, "Keep a sharp eye out, Sergeant. If they are nothing else, they are alert."

"Did you believe him, sir? Pardon me, sir, but you think there's five hundred waiting for us?"

"Five hundred *what*, Sergeant? Cows? Farmers with pitchforks? Move out now. Keep a sharp eye. Any more like him, make sure they're disarmed, then send them to the rear."

*   *   *

THE MARCH HAD GONE TOO SLOWLY FOR HIS IMPATIENCE, AND HE had finally gone back to find Smith. There was no effective way to simply speed up the column, so Pitcairn secured Smith's permission to move forward with a select few companies, about a fourth of the total force.

He had spoken to more colonists the sergeant had captured, and the amazing claims of the catastrophe that waited for them had grown, one man insisting that more than a thousand well-armed militia stood guard at the small town. The scout troops had grown used to the spectacular claims by now, treated the prisoners more as entertainment than any danger to the army.

Pitcairn glanced behind him more often now, expected to see the sky lighten, knew that the sunrise was close. The advance guard was still on the alert, and he rode up near them, the rest of his select force close behind. He heard the now familiar pattern, a single set of hoofbeats, the soldiers surging into the road behind the man, grabbing the reins, but the sounds were different this time—no lantern was lit, just shouts and curses. The hoofbeats came again, a hard gallop moving away. He spurred the horse, reached the troops in the road, and the sergeant said, "Sorry, sir. Missed that one. He must have gotten wind of us. His horse was spooky, turned away before we could get close enough."

Pitcairn stared ahead down the road.

"No matter, Sergeant. The guides say we're nearly at Lexington. It will be daylight soon. There's not much that man will tell anyone that they won't see for themselves. Keep your men in the road. Let's make good time."

He rode back to the head of the tight column, saw one of the guides, a loyalist farmer named Langston. Behind the column Pitcairn could see a soft gray glow, the road now visible by more than moonlight.

"How much farther, Mr. Langston?"

Langston pointed ahead.

"No farther, Major. We're there."

Pitcairn looked again to the front, could actually see the dark figures of the advance guard gathered in the road, looking back at him. He moved the horse, saw the sergeant waiting for him, and the man simply pointed ahead. Pitcairn spurred the horse gently, moved beyond the advance of the troops, could see the trees clearing away, after them a wide stretch of open ground. Out past the last of the trees, the road fell away in a gentle slope, then divided. On either side, the small buildings, homes, businesses, spread apart with the two branches of the road. He still moved forward, could see between the roads now, the dawn spreading a faint light on a wide patch of flat ground, a green wedge that grew wider as the roads led away. He stopped the horse now, could see motion, realized there was a line of men stretching across the center of the open green. Other men on horses were easing up beside him, and he said quietly, "Order the column to halt."

He could hear the horses moving away, the officers giving the command, the steady tramp of footsteps growing silent. He felt a knot growing in his chest, stared ahead, saw more men emerging from a building to one side of the road, running now, joining, lengthening the line. He could feel his men close behind him now, some officers, and he did not look back, still stared at the green.

"Inform Colonel Smith. We have encountered resistance. Order the column into battle line."

Beside him, he heard the voice of the sergeant, the man laughing.

"Not exactly five hundred, eh, sir?"

Pitcairn still watched the green, said nothing, thought, No, forty, perhaps. And forty muskets.

"Put your men into line, Sergeant. Mind them."

He turned now, saw some faces staring at the scene in front of them, some faces watching him. The officers began directing, the orders familiar from weeks of drill. The men began to flow out away from the road, three lines, one behind the other. He looked at the officers, each one waiting for his instructions.

"No one shall fire unless fired upon. Do you understand?"

The response was quick, precise.

"Sir . . . yes, sir."

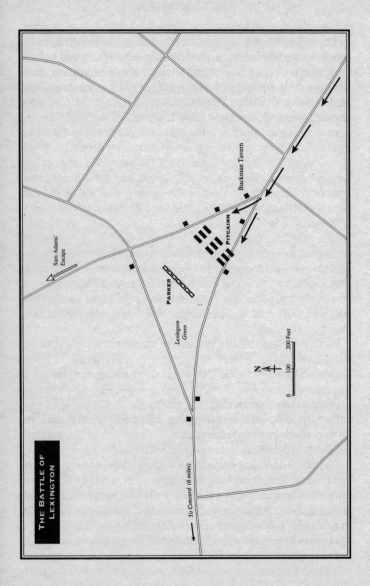

THE BATTLE OF LEXINGTON

Sam Adams' Escape

Buckman Tavern

PITCAIRN

PARKER

Lexington Green

To Concord (6 miles)

N

0   100   200 Feet

"Be sure the men understand as well."

He turned his horse, faced the green again, could hear the rising voices of his men, a roar of cheering, shouts, and calls as each man took his place in formation. It was the tradition, cheer your own, let the enemy know you're ready for the good fight. He stared at the line of civilians standing in tight formation across the green, could not help a smile, was suddenly feeling very good, the confidence of a professional who knows he commands the field, who knows his is the advantage. How long will it take? he thought. How much arrogance do they have to stand up there as though they intend to make a fight against this army? What do we call them? A mob? Rebels? He was still smiling, glanced up at the gray sky. No, they can see us, they know what we have brought. And still they stand there, defiant. It is almost . . . comical.

The lines behind him were now spread wide, and he looked out in both directions, saw the officers before their men, all looking at him. We do not have time for this, he thought. If Lexington knew to expect us, then Concord will as well. We cannot allow them time enough to move their arsenal. If these people will simply stand aside and let us pass . . .

He pulled at the reins, moved the horse out to one side, beyond his left flank, pulled his pistol from its holster.

"Forward!"

The lines began to move in precise sequence, no waver, the perfection of so much training, the cheers and calls of his men filling the dawn. He watched the rebels still standing in the green, his own men closer still, could see across the way, one man suddenly breaking out of the rebel line, running. His men picked up the call, the cheers louder, and now more men began to break away from the line of ragged militia. He did not cheer with his men, still stared at the uneven row of muskets, the rebels who did not run. He raised his arm now, and the officers shouted out, halting the troops. The two sides were barely forty yards apart, and Pitcairn saw one man standing apart, on the far end of the ragged line, older, staring back at him with grim anger. Pitcairn had a sudden curiosity. Perhaps he is their commander. He wanted to know who this man was, to talk to him, to ask him, Why? How did you come to be in command of this rabble? No, there will be time for that later, when he is in a cell in Boston. He scanned the line of civilians, appraised the muskets, saw the faces of each man, some looking at him, many more staring at the soldiers who faced them. He saw some fear now, but not in all of them, and he waited for the voices of his men to grow quiet, the taunts and cheers fading away. There was a moment of strange silence, both sides staring into the muzzles of the other, and Pitcairn felt a hard pounding in his chest, shouted out, "You will lay down your arms and disperse immediately!"

There were responses, shouts from the civilians, his own troops joining in, and he shouted again, "Rebels, disperse! Lay down your arms!"

He looked again at the man on the end of the rebel line, saw the man raise his hand, saw him speaking. He tried to hear the man's order, saw the rebels on that end of the line looking at the man, the muzzles of their muskets dropping down. Pitcairn's chest was still pounding, and he nodded toward the man. Yes, good, if you command them, then command them wisely. There must be no blood here.

More of the civilians were lowering their muskets, some beginning to move away. The line was broken now, the men in small groups, some standing alone, but gradually they were all spreading apart, moving toward the edge of the green. Beside him, his men began to call out again, a steady stream of taunts and curses, and he wanted to stop them, tell them, *No, it is over. If they disperse now, we can move on our way.* He watched several of the civilians moving away, some backing off, watching their enemy carefully, some dragging muskets behind them in dejected defeat. He noticed the onlookers for the first time, spectators spread all along the far side of the green, some women, even children, some embracing their men as they left the green. Beyond, he saw men standing in the doorway of a house, and suddenly there was a flash of light, and he could see the musket, one man aiming from the corner of the house. There was no sound of a shot, and he tried to see the man, thought, A flash in the pan, but we should pursue him . . . and now more sounds came, scattered and distinct, musket fire, from beyond the green. His horse suddenly staggered, and he looked down, saw a squirt of blood on the animal's neck, saw a man in line beside him go down. The voices had stopped, and even the civilians who still stood across from him seemed confused, men looking around, searching for the source of the sounds. Down the line, he heard a shout, an order, one of his officers, "Fire! Fire, damn you!"

Suddenly the line of British muskets exploded into flame and smoke, a solid burst, pouring their shot into the men who still stood across the green from them. His horse reared back, and he gripped the reins.

"Do not fire!" he yelled, but his voice could not rise above the screams from the men who fell on the green. Across the green, the onlookers began to scream as well, some running in panic. The fog of gray smoke drifted across, and he could only see glimpses of the civilians.

"No! Do not fire!"

But down the line, the officers were closer to their men, firing their own pistols, their men pouring out their hatred, the months of boredom and abuse from the colonists now exorcised through the muzzles of their muskets. The volley was uneven now, scattered, soldiers loading, firing at will. He began to ride, moving between the lines, could see one rebel lying in the grass facedown, blood on the man's back. Beside him, another man was sitting, bloody hands holding a wound. The musket fire slowed now, and the voices came back, and it was not the cheers and taunts, it was something new, women screaming, some running into the green, falling into the arms of their husbands, more voices, cries and curses from the men who were still trying to get away, to escape the blood spreading on the green. He shouted again at his men, waved his pistol high, and finally his voice was heard, the soldiers obeying, the muskets falling silent.

He had waited for Colonel Smith, the rest of the column finally arriving in Lexington, in time to push the march forward. The civilians had mostly stayed beside the roads, but there was no fight in them, just stunned sorrow at the death that spread across the green. At least eight men were dead; more were badly wounded. By the time Smith's column absorbed Pitcairn's men into their ranks, the bodies of the rebels had been dragged away, some to their homes, trailed by the devastating grief of their women, some into the tavern close by. With Smith organizing the troops and the townspeople focused on the tragedy, Pitcairn had quietly sent out a patrol, a discreet attempt to accomplish at least one part of the mission. But the reports came back as he expected: Sam Adams and John Hancock had long gone.

THE SUN WAS BEHIND THEM, JUST ABOVE THE HILLS, THE MORNING still holding the chill of the April night. He could see clearly now, and on hills on both sides of the road, on every crest, on every open spot of high ground, men were gathering, a hostile audience to the march.

The advance guard was out in the road, no need for stealth now. They were scanning not only the hills to both sides, but also the road in front, should rebels suddenly appear there. Each curve in the road, each slight rise might reveal a human obstruction, another row of muskets. Pitcairn moved close behind them, could feel the column pressing from behind. He probed the wound on the horse, found a second one, but both were minor, the blood already clotted dry. He thought of the soldier who had gone down, only a minor wound, the man still in the march somewhere, farther to the rear. He tried not to think about the chaos, the uncontrollable horror of an army whose discipline fails. They knew their orders, but no one could stop the instinct. He was certain the musket fire had come from beyond the green, a long distance away, the minor wound in the horse's side testament to that. The rebels were, after all, right there, right in front of me. There will be some questions, that is for certain. General Gage will want to know precisely what occurred. He remembered the flash of light, the misfire. That was it, he thought, that was all it took. One fool, one hotheaded coward who would not stand tall, who did not have the courage to march into the green, and a few others like him, back behind some tree, the coward's

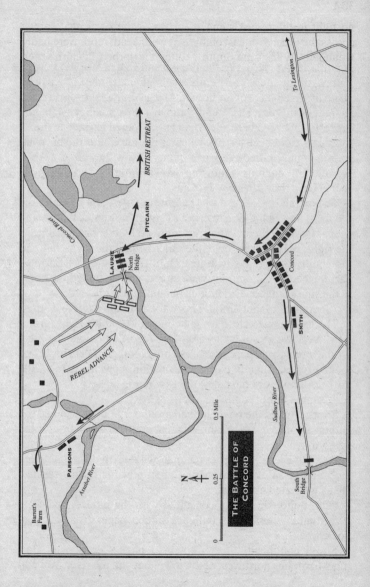

THE BATTLE OF CONCORD

BRITISH RETREAT

PITCAIRN

Concord River

LAURIE

North
Bridge

REBEL ADVANCE

Concord

SMITH

Sudbury River

PARSONS

Assabet River

To Lexington

Barrett's
Farm

South
Bridge

N

0   0.25   0.5 Mile

way. Well, it was not our doing, no responsibility will come to us for that skirmish. It was the work of cowards.

He had learned the name of the rebel commander, Captain John Parker, a veteran of the French and Indian War. So now he betrays all he fought for, leads a ridiculous band of rebels who stand up in defiance of the crown. At least he had the wisdom not to fight us this day. His friends probably do not believe it, but by his restraint he is a hero. He could have ordered his men to fire. If there had truly been a fight, whether the musket or the bayonet, we might have killed every one of them. Now they are out *there*, scattered on the hills, following us, watching us, and they must still believe they can stand up to us.

The march to Concord was barely six miles, and he could see the town now, another gathering of small buildings, homes and shops. Beyond, there was a river, crossed by two bridges, one to the right, north of the town, the other behind the town, more to the south. The guides had given him the location of Barrett's Farm, where the munitions were stored, and he pulled the horse to the side of the road, motioned behind him for his aide.

"Send for Colonel Smith. The officers should assemble here."

The troops were close by, the column keeping a tight formation, every weary soldier aware of the rebels who lined the hills. As the men moved past, Pitcairn waited for the officers to gather, looked for one man in particular, saw him now, the man's wide girth spilling over both sides of the straining horse.

"Colonel Smith, Concord awaits us."

Smith studied the town, looked around him now, scanned the gathering officers. "Captain Parsons, are you familiar with the geography here?"

Parsons was a young, eager man who carried the unhidden ambition of an officer expecting great rewards for his service. He exaggerated his salute.

"Oh, quite, sir. I have consulted with the guides, made my own map . . . here." He pulled a folded paper from his coat pocket.

Smith continued, "Yes, Captain, I have seen a map. Barrett's Farm lies northwest of the town, beyond the river. You will command three companies to search that place for the powder stores of the rebels. Any you may find are to be put to the torch."

"Yes, sir!"

"Captain Laurie, you will lead three additional companies and take up position at that north bridge, and secure the crossing for Captain Parsons' return. The southern bridge is of less concern, but I suppose one company should occupy that, to prevent any rebels from annoying us from that direction. I will lead the remainder of the column and occupy the town itself." Smith looked at Pitcairn now. "Anything you care to add, Major?"

"We must avoid bloodshed, gentlemen. Keep tight control on your men."

Smith sniffed.

"Perhaps, Major. But I am of a mind to teach these rebels a lesson."

"Sir, our orders were explicit."

"I know our orders, Major." Smith scanned the faces of the officers. "We will discuss this at another time. I do not expect any of His Majesty's soldiers to shirk from a confrontation. If the rebels insist on facing us in battle line, they should expect the consequences."

Pitcairn wanted to argue, but Smith turned his horse, the discussion over. Pitcairn nudged the horse gently, followed Smith, moved alongside him now, said quietly, "Colonel, if we engage the rebels, it could well start a war. It is not in our orders. . . ."

"Major, the war was started by the Sons of Liberty the first time they violated the king's edicts. It does not take blood to make a war. I am surprised at you, Major. A man with your experience—a marine, no less—should not even be questioning this. We are operating under instructions to seize and destroy rebel arms. Anyone who stands in our way is subject to immediate imprisonment. Capturing armed men must certainly involve using arms ourselves. What does war have to do with any of this? General Gage would quite agree with me, I'm certain."

"Yes, sir." Pitcairn stopped the horse, watched Smith move away, thought, I'm not so sure about that, Colonel. General Gage has done everything in his power to avoid a war. He turned, could see the other officers still gathered in place, waiting for the final order to begin dispersing the troops. He rode toward them, heard Parsons boast, "We'll be sitting pretty in Boston when this day is through!"

Pitcairn moved up close to the others, could not help a strange, nervous feeling in his gut.

"You have your orders. Proceed."

The officers moved away, instructions shouted out in crisp detail, sergeants pulling their men together. The column began to divide, the selected companies moving out in separate directions, the men on horseback directing the flow. He moved out to the right of the column, rode a short way into a field of green grass, could see the river clearly, a sharp bend away to the north, and just to the right of the bend an arching bridge. Beyond the bridge, a small group of rebels had gathered. He muttered to himself, "No. Move away, don't attempt such foolishness again. Can't you see us, the numbers, the strength? We will not be stopped."

Parsons was already on the move, his men in line, marching down the long slope toward the bridge. Behind them, Laurie was still forming the other troops who would hold position around the bridge. Pitcairn nudged the horse again, moved alongside the column, could see the rebels backing away from the bridge now, felt relief. Yes, use wisdom. His uneasiness had faded, the confidence returning. We will do our job, and no ragtag bunch of militia will slow us down.

He watched the rebels as they scampered away, up another long rise, a wide crest beyond the river. There were a few houses scattered along the crest, farm buildings spread out all along the higher ground. The rebels were nearly out of sight now, and Parsons' troops had reached the bridge, were moving across. The sound of boot steps now broke the quiet, and he watched Parsons waiting on the far side of the river, urging his men across, faster, the mission awaiting them. The column was soon clear of the bridge, moving away, following the course of the river. He thought of the map, Barrett's Farm, not far, they should be there in a few minutes. To find . . . what? It has taken too much time;

surely the rebels know why we're here, have already moved their powder. He shook his head. No, it doesn't matter. We will complete the job, march back to Boston by nightfall. He thought of Gage now, the man's frustration at doing this job. It is not my place to question his decisions. It is a fragile situation, and unlike Colonel Smith, I do not believe you can have a war with no bloodshed. Those men who died in Lexington . . . certainly they will have their hue and cry, but if we are fortunate, nothing more will come of it. Let us march these men back to Boston and try to forget this day ever happened.

The second column had reached the bridge, one company crossing over, moving out into the wide-open field, facing up toward the crest, the farmhouses. He began to move the horse closer to the river, then heard a shout, saw an officer pointing toward the town. He looked in that direction, saw a column of black smoke, pulled the horse that way. They must have found something. Well, very damned good. Let's find something worth burning and then leave this place behind. He crossed the road that led down to the bridge, climbed a short rise near a large house, saw faces hiding behind curtains as he passed. He reached a vantage point, could see out over the town. The smoke was still thick and black, and he could not yet identify the source. Colonel Smith is there . . . but perhaps I should find out just what they're doing.

He heard more shouts now, back at the bridge, turned, saw the men on the north bridge suddenly moving, scrambling into a tight line. He stared out across the river, beyond the wide field, up the long hill. All along the crest, there was now a solid line of dark motion, emerging from the farmhouses. He began to move the horse back toward the bridge, to where his men were now standing hard in a new line of battle, staring, as he was, at the mass of men gathering on the crest, gradually forming their own line. He tried to see details, the long line on the crest growing now, still too far away to see clearly, but now the sun caught the reflections, and he could tell there were muskets, a great many muskets. He felt an icy stab in his chest, saw the mass begin to move forward now, an uneven advance coming at them slowly down the hill, and now he heard new sounds, music, the fife and drum. All along the crest, the rebel line was still forming, massing more tightly as they moved forward, precise, an amazing display of drill and command. As they advanced down the hill, he could see the men themselves, and it was not like the green at Lexington, it was not forty men. It was four hundred.

HE WATCHED AS LAURIE'S SOLDIERS ON THE FAR SIDE OF THE bridge pulled back across, forming a battle line along the edge of the river. He knew Walter Laurie, knew the man's weakness could be the inexperience of an officer who has never seen an enemy. Now they faced him, and Laurie had placed one company, forty-five men, in position to receive the rebels should they attempt to cross the bridge. The other two companies were in close formation, right behind them. Pitcairn was still riding toward the bridge, saw an aide riding hard away, toward the town. Yes, good, it will be Laurie's request for reinforcements. The smoke still billowed in a black column in the town, and he knew that Smith might have some problems of his own, might be facing a force just like the one that was now forming up by the far side of the bridge. Still, if there is to be trouble, it might be over something as absurd as who controls this one bridge. But Captain Parsons is out there in the countryside somewhere, and we cannot just abandon him. We have to make a way for him to get back. He spurred the horse, felt more of an urgency now, saw nothing moving from the town. The three companies at the bridge were holding their ground, the only sound the strange fife and drum from the rebels. He could see the soldiers holding tight in line, motionless, thought of Laurie's inexperience. No, it's not a good position. He should back us away a bit, spread them out more, we're too bunched up at the bridge. Still, it could be a deterrent if the rebels try to cross. Suddenly the music stopped, and he held up the horse, a cold breath of deathly calm drifting over the open ground. He felt a twist of fear, glanced across the empty ground toward Concord, saw nothing, no reinforcements. There may not be enough of us if they mean to come across. . . .

Suddenly there was a burst of musket fire, and it was not the rebels, it was Laurie's men, the front line facing the bridge. Pitcairn felt a cold shock, paralyzed, a scream of horror in his brain—*No, you must not!*—and now the response came, a great burst of fire and smoke, the rebel line erupting in a volley of their own. The bridge was bathed in white smoke, and the soldiers fired again, another volley, but there was little precision, the shots coming in scattered bursts. The rebels fired a second time, some precision still, but then all order was gone, the scene engulfed in a vast fog, shouts and screams blending with the hard pops and chatter of the muskets. He stared at the great cloud of smoke, felt completely helpless, the battle roaring in front of him, could see soldiers suddenly flooding back away from the bridge, the order and precision of the troops wiped away by the sudden terror of a fight they could not win. He spurred the horse, raised his pistol, shouted, "No! Hold the line! Stand firm!"

The troops were rolling past him now, a panic he had never before seen, and he screamed at them to halt, to form and fire. Along the bridge, the smoke had begun to drift away, and he could see the rebels swarming across, the last of the soldiers now in full scrambling retreat, the ground at the bridge littered with grotesque heaps of red. He pointed his pistol at the mass of rebels now spreading out on the near side of the bridge, fired, the pistol jumping in his hand. His own voice screamed at him inside his head, Too far away! Do your damned job! Form the men!

The soldiers had slowed the retreat, some of the men coming back into line behind him, but not all of them. Too many were still moving away, pursued by their own shock, the awful horror of the unexpected, leaving their own dead and wounded behind. Pitcairn stared down at the bridge, saw the rebels were not pursuing, were content to hold their position. He backed away now, moved with the troops, glanced toward the town, saw nothing, no motion, the reinforcements not coming, saw the fat old figure of Smith in his mind. Damn him!

The musket fire had stopped, and now there was a new sound, coming from the bridge, the sound of men cheering, the rebels suddenly erupting in a wild celebration of their victory. Pitcairn began to wave his sword, but the energy was gone, the fight in his men drained away by the deadly shock that these rebels, this ragtag militia, had faced the king's soldiers and had driven them away.

COLONEL SMITH HAD TRIED TO BRING THE REINFORCEMENTS TO the north bridge himself, but the troops could only move as quickly as their rotund commander, and so by the time any British troops could be formed to face the rebels, it was clear even to Smith that there was nothing more to be done. All along the hills around Concord, rebel militia continued to arrive, some as well organized as the advance to the north bridge, the numbers growing by the hour. The rebels had moved away from the bridge itself, and Parsons' men had been able to pull back, recrossing the north bridge without opposition. The mission to Barrett's Farm had unfolded as Pitcairn had expected, with little in the way of munitions to be found. In the town itself, the troops had burned a blacksmith shop, accidentally setting fire to the small courthouse, but there was no armed resistance there either, and the officers themselves had wisely ordered their men to assist in extinguishing the fires. By midday, neither Smith nor Pitcairn had any reason to keep their troops at Concord. The only priority now was to make the return march to Boston. Pitcairn had placed a rear guard to protect the last of the column, and for the first mile away from Concord there had been no trouble, no close pursuit. The column reached an intersection, known as Meriam's Corner, turned southeastward, the road that would take them back through Lexington.

Pitcairn stayed back near the rear guard, the men marching with muskets ready, their faces staring down, not seeming to believe that this morning had truly occurred. He had tried to talk them up, words of encouragement, and they answered him in polite response, but he understood that these men were marching back to Boston wearing the awful shroud of defeat. He swung the horse out to the side of the column and looked up toward the front, could see a mass of woods narrowing in on the road, thought, Perhaps I should move up, ride with Colonel Smith. We should plan for some possible resistance again when we reach

Lexington. He glanced back at the guard to the rear, and suddenly there was a dull pop, then another. He looked for the sound, saw the soldiers up ahead breaking the line, a few spilling off the road. Now there were more sounds of musket fire, and he felt his heart jump in his chest.

Scattered through the woods, he could see flashes of fire, small clouds of smoke filling the spaces. He felt a raw fury exploding in his brain. Damn them! Enough of this! We will kill them right here! He began to shout, "Form in place! Advance into the trees! Use the bayonet!"

The men near him rushed forward, picking their way into the woods, and the cacophony of musket fire grew. His men were shouting on their own now, anger and frustration pulling them deeper into the woods. He spurred the horse, would follow them, the mind of the officer fighting through his own fury. We cannot get them all, but we can take prisoners, grab what we can!

He shouted again, "Capture them! Take prisoners!"

His men took up the call, pushing deeper into the woods, the rebels' muskets silent now. He ducked his head, passed under a low limb, was moving through his own men, could see motion in front of him, the rebels running away. He noticed the trees thinning out, the ground opening into a wide field. He surged out into the clearing, his men behind him, saw the rebels running across the open ground.

"Damn you! Now we will have you!"

His men took up the call again, but there were too few soldiers, most still back in the woods, the exhaustion slowing their pursuit, holding them closer to the road. The rebels disappeared over the crest of a small hill, and he let out a short cold laugh. No time for you to reload . . . I have you now. He stabbed with his spurs, the horse lunging forward, and he reached for one of his pistols, the pair of guns held tightly in their holsters on his saddle. Suddenly there was a blast of fire in front of him, the horse rearing up, his hands slipping from the pistols, and he grabbed for the reins, missed, the horse now surging forward again, driven by its own panic. He fell back, landed hard on the ground, a sharp pain in his side. He tried to see, shouted for the horse, but the animal did not stop, galloped past the rebels, and Pitcairn could only watch as the horse disappeared, the saddle empty of its rider, but still holding the prize of his two pistols.

His men were around him now, hands helping him to his feet. He tested his back, his side, the pain not crippling. He wanted to pursue the rebels, order his men to move forward, but the enemy was gone now, vanished into another patch of woods. He brushed away the helping hands, felt the fury again, saw the familiar face of the sergeant, who said, "Sir, we can get you a horse straight-away. But we had best get back to the road."

Pitcairn glanced toward the far woods again, to where his horse had disappeared, his demeanor shattered.

"Damn you! You fight like cowards!"

The sergeant waited a moment, repeated, "Sir, we'd best be getting back."

Pitcairn saw now that there were only a handful of troops, could hear voices back on the road, the column pulling itself back together again. He began to walk, the soreness in his side stabbing him, his own private defeat.

"Back to the road. Fall in line."

They rejoined the rest of the column, the men trying to find the rhythm of the march again, slowly moving forward, and sec-onds later he could hear the pops again, farther ahead, then sud-denly, from the other side of the road, another shot, much closer, one man going down near him. He pointed.

"There!" He wanted to order them out again to pursue the rebel in the woods, but there was only silence there now, the man already gone back into deep cover. The wounded man was being tended to, rose slowly to his feet, blood on his shoulder. The men of the rear guard were watching Pitcairn, waiting for his next order, and he looked toward the front, saw the column still in motion.

"We cannot pursue. We must keep moving."

All along the road back to Lexington, the thickets of woods were alive with rebels, men firing in quick bursts, then disap-pearing. From close and far away, the rebels continued to pick and snipe at the march of the soldiers, and if the aim was poor or the shots too distant, there was still a deadly effect, the unlucky soldier suddenly dropping in his tracks, a short scream perhaps, or worse, a man collapsing with no sound at all. The disciplined march of the army had become a chaotic horror, the men reacting to every sound, some firing their muskets against the orders of the officers, responding to the ghostly glimpse of a rebel's quick retreat. Pitcairn marched with them, heavy footsteps on a road where every rock, every tree, every farmhouse hid a new danger. By the time the column reached the familiar green of Lexington, exhaustion had blended with terror. Pitcairn had absorbed the mood of the men around him, knew that this could not continue, that if the rebels continued to pick at the column with such efficacy, there would be no column at all, these men would become a mob of their own, a panicked scramble back to Boston, to any safety they could find.

Beyond the green, the road was suddenly alive with a new sight, new sounds, cheers and calls from a new force. When Pitcairn crossed the open ground, pursued still by the hot zip of the musket balls, he could see a solid line of red, spread out as his own men had spread out in the dawn. He knew that early that morning, Smith had sent word back to Boston, a message that they had met armed resistance at Lexington. Pitcairn had disregarded its impact, knew that Gage had thought six hundred men more than up to the task, that Gage might simply consider Smith to be overly cautious. But Pitcairn realized now that he had been wrong. Gage had responded. He marched with a new energy in his steps toward the astounding sight and had to convince himself, No, it is truly not a mirage, an apparition. It is blessed reinforcements.

AN ENTIRE BRIGADE HAD MARCHED OUT OF BOSTON TO SUPPORT the retreat of Smith's column. But the fight was not yet complete. As the British resumed their march to Boston, the rebels still picked and prodded, sudden bursts of assault on men who rarely saw their enemy. The British panic grew slowly, began to change in ways that even horrified officers could not avoid. The soldiers began to strike back with animal viciousness, and each house became a target, the troops storming anyplace that might hide a sniper. The uncontrollable violence intensified with each shot from a hidden musket, and by the time the soldiers finally reached the safety of Boston, they had left in their wake a terror of their own, citizens who had no part of the day's fight murdered in their homes, houses and farms put to the torch. The rebels did not stop their deadly harassment of the troops until, at long last, with the sun setting over the hills that still held gathering masses of rebel militia, the devastated force of King George's army once again boarded the navy's longboats and were rowed slowly across the harbor to their camps in Boston.

30. GAGE

BOSTON, APRIL 21, 1775

THE SENIOR OFFICERS FILLED THE OFFICE, OCCUPIED EVERY SPACE. The talk had rattled on all morning, and he had stayed mostly quiet, had let them blow out their theories, great hot breaths of indignation, small bits of wisdom sprinkled among grand explosions of outright foolishness. He could not help noticing Pitcairn's silence, the man's mood obviously subdued, none of the brash pronouncements that came from the others. Well, of course. What depresses a royal marine most of all? The loss of battle? Or the loss of pride?

He could sense the conversation running out of energy, waited a moment longer, the faces beginning to turn in his direction.

"There you have it, gentlemen. Your own demonstration of the obvious. I bring you in here to expose your brilliance, to make the best use of His Majesty's most valued military minds, and what have we decided to do? What one principle have we agreed upon? Since no one advocated outright surrender, I assume we should consider an alternative. I would select one of you to provide a summary." He scanned the faces, saw no one poised to speak out. "What? No one to reveal how inept I have been? No one who carries the great weight of the empire on his back, the intelligence of centuries of triumph? No one to reveal the simple solution, or perhaps throw out on this desk the plan that could have averted our present dilemma?" He had run out of energy for his own sarcasm now, held up his hands. "Anyone?"

A man stood now, older, the naval uniform unique in the room. Gage glanced at the faces of some of the younger men, saw grimacing, telltale hints of dread that the old man should be the spokesman. The old man seemed to puff up, said, "General Gage, I have fought for the empire in wars that most of these younger men have only read about. I have felt the rage of His Majesty's warships explode in fire and flame beneath my very boots. The navy's tradition—"

"Admiral Graves, no one here is unaware of your long and valiant service to the empire."

Graves was silent for a few moments, then continued.

"As commander in chief of the navy's contingent in these waters, I would offer a suggestion." He pointed out toward one window, with a view of the harbor. "Before the enemy enables themselves to make a powerful defense, we must assault those hills to the north. The Charlestown peninsula must be cleared of rebels. The danger to the city is significant, General. Rebel artillery placed on those hills could make *this* position untenable. Since I assume the general does not wish his headquarters reduced to ashes, this action will eliminate that very threat. Once secured, your troops could then assault Roxbury, Cambridge, and any of the other towns where the rebels might make a stand. With the support of my ships, no rebel force near the coast could survive a coordinated assault. With your troops controlling the hills in all directions of Boston, and my ships controlling the harbor and any surrounding territory, Boston will be impregnable, a veritable fortress."

Graves looked around the room, weighing the impressiveness of his plan, then slowly lowered himself to a chair, his satisfaction complete. Gage looked at the faces, was amazed to see nods of agreement.

"Thank you, Admiral. So you would advise that we be absolutely certain to take the steps necessary to demonstrate that we are truly and without hesitation engulfed in a state of war." He scanned the faces again, saw a few frowns.

Now Pitcairn seemed to wake up, glanced at Graves, said, "What else can it be, General? Surely you have seen the reports. We suffered nearly three hundred casualties; nearly a hundred men died. I don't know how many rebels we killed. How can anyone say that we are not now engaged in a war?"

There was heavy sorrow in Pitcairn's voice, and Gage felt his sarcasm slip away. The mood of the room was somber.

"I am not convinced . . . I refuse to be convinced that we have but one course. I am not concerned that there are those of you in this room who disagree with me, because I am still in command. I *am* greatly concerned that *London* may disagree. About that I can do nothing but wait. I understand the value of the Charlestown peninsula, Admiral. I am grateful that the rebels do not appear to yet have much in the way of artillery to mount a bombardment on us from Breed's Hill. But I can tell you with absolute certainty that we do not have the strength of manpower to carry out any kind of general assault on any well-defended position. Major Pitcairn, you should understand that better than anyone in this room. There are other reports on this desk besides casualties, Major. One is an estimate of the rebel strength that now occupies the ground beyond this town. The rebels were not satisfied by merely harassing and humiliating the king's soldiers. They did not return to their homes, safe in the knowledge that this army dare not make any more forays into the countryside. They came to *us*, gentlemen; they are right out there, a solid line. I myself have heard them digging, and it has convinced me that they plan to stay awhile. Whether any of you care to admit it or not, our little contribution to the empire's history has had a change of course. *We* are now under siege."

THE MEETING HAD BROKEN UP, AND GAGE WATCHED THEM LEAVE the office with a profound sadness that he himself had felt since the disaster two days earlier. Colonel Smith had not even attended the meeting, had requested time to compose letters of sympathy to the families of the dead, a request that Gage had not wanted to grant. He had thought there should be some delay, some time to gather the emotions, to sort out the bits of truth from the loose and angry talk of the men. But then he had received word from up the coast. A fast packet boat had already sailed for London, and with it went the report from the rebel side of the events of April 19. It would reach an English people who would soak up the horror of what their soldiers had endured, and worse, the horrors of what the soldiers themselves had done, the animal response to the terror that followed their retreat. No mere military explanation would ever justify the atrocities against the civilians, and no official report written by his office could ever hope to offset the impact that the first accounting of the details would have, especially as written by anyone close to the Sons of Liberty.

He stared at the closed door, thought of London, the newspapers, the cries over the fresh bit of news, the scramble of the crowd to read the first words. But it is of no import, really. It can never matter to an army what the people read of death and the bloody hell of war. What matters to a commander is what is said in private, behind those thick walls of government, where men who have too much authority and who are too far away will decide who carries the blame. To anyone who has preached with such certainty how this annoying little rebellion will simply disappear under the heel of our boot, there can be no explanation except failure of command. The decision might already have been made. London is filled with men of great ambition, and whoever makes the best case will certainly find himself boarding a ship. He wanted to look toward the window, scan the harbor, but there was no energy. He still rested heavily in the chair, stared ahead, wondered, Who might it be? Who might announce his presence here? And will he do it with grace, as I tried to do with Hutchinson? Or will there be brass bands, an official parade, guards with bayonets to remove me, lest I attempt some resistance? He shook his head, cleared his mind of the ridiculous image. You are still in command, you still have a job to do. You still must convince the ministry that we need more men.

There was a faint knock on the door, and Gage stared at the source of the sound for a moment.

"What is it?"

The door opened, and he saw Kemble, the young man wide-eyed, one hand pointing discreetly toward the outer office.

"Sir, you have a visitor. . . ."

"Not now, Major. Have them make an appointment."

"Sir, it's Dr. Warren. Joseph Warren."

Kemble was still pointing, nodding now, as though Gage needed convincing, and Gage sat back in the chair, the surprise blossoming in his mind. He gave a small laugh.

"Well, now. Give proper credit to courage. Show him in, Major."

The door swung wide, and Kemble stood back, waited as Warren stepped inside the office. Gage motioned to Kemble, the familiar order, *out,* and Kemble's face curled into disappointment as the door closed.

"Well, the good doctor comes to visit. Is someone ill? Or are you here to surrender?"

Warren stood straight, held his hat in both hands at his waist, said, "Surrender whom, sir?"

Gage laughed, pointed to the closest chair.

"Of course. We are all innocent men. Please sit down, Doctor. Forgive my lack of graciousness. These are not the best of times. Or have you been so consumed by the business of medicine that you have not heard?"

Warren moved the chair close to the desk.

"I have heard of great tragedy, General. I feel the need to inform you, sir, that a great many people in Boston are of the belief that there is tragedy still to come. Many of the people here feel considerably endangered."

Gage stared at Warren, expecting a smile, but Warren revealed no humor.

"Endangered by whom, Doctor?"

"It depends, sir, on which people we might refer to. I would refer to several groups, actually, each in its own way."

Gage was curious now, began to feel a game brewing.

"I don't have the patience for riddles, Doctor. Would you care to give me an example?"

"Well, first, there are the private citizens, innocent bystanders, as it were. It may be true that . . . not all of us are as innocent as we would like. But the fact is, a great many people in this town are guilty of nothing but their choice of residence."

"You may be correct about that, Doctor. Is there another example?"

"Possibly, General, you have a number of soldiers who may feel somewhat endangered as well."

"By whom, Doctor? Those rebels out there in the hills? Or are you suggesting that under the right guidance, your innocent citizens might somehow cause some trouble of their own?"

Warren finally smiled.

"I would never suggest that, sir."

Gage's patience was thinning, and he said, "What do you want here, Doctor? I admire bravery, and you were brave to show up here. But I do not respect foolishness, and some in my command would consider your visit a foolish mistake, would not resist an opportunity to jail a recognized leader of the rebellion. So are you brave or foolish?"

"General, I am interested in preventing injury to the innocent. On behalf of no one but myself, I am asking that anyone in Boston who wishes to leave be given the opportunity to do so unmolested. You have sealed off the city, and that is a military decision with which, under the present circumstances, I cannot argue. But there is no need to endanger the innocent."

"And if I allow the citizens to leave, I reduce the risk that someone might be inspired to make an unwise attack on my men. I'm not sure it's a fair trade, Doctor. I rather like having the, um, *innocent* under my care. You have a large number of friends surrounding this town who might reconsider some reckless assault of their own if they knew the risk to the civilians. I would never use the word *hostage*, Doctor. But then, I didn't create this crisis."

He felt a growing smugness, expected Warren to show something, anger, a glimpse beyond the man's calm. Warren simply shook his head.

"*Hostage* is a horrible word, General, but I regret that it is certainly accurate in this case. But I must say, it is an equally appropriate description elsewhere."

The smugness slipped away, and Gage asked, "What do you mean?"

"I am only familiar with those citizens in Boston who wish to leave, who carry no blame of their own, who fear for the safety of their families. However, I have heard rumor, General, that there are a great many people beyond this town who share the same desire, the same fear, except that their particular sense of allegiance brings them to want to come here. Some refer to them as Tories. I have heard that a good many Tories feel the same fear for their safety as the citizens of Boston. You see, General? *Hostage* is hardly a word anyone should be using. I am referring to *all* of these people, whether in or out of Boston, only as refugees."

The game was over, and Gage understood that he held no advantage. He still searched Warren's face for some sign, some betrayal, but Warren had made his case, was simply waiting for Gage's response, a policy decision from the man who supposedly held all the power. He thought a long moment, tried to imagine the outcry in London if the Tories and loyalists outside of Boston were denied entry to the one place they could find safety. Does it matter if the danger is real? Are the loyalists any more likely than civilians in Boston to suddenly be dragged from their beds? Neither side would commit such outrageous brutality, and yet . . .

Warren leaned forward slightly, said, "General? Should I leave you to consider the question further?"

"The question requires no further thought, Doctor. I will allow passage out of the city to anyone who wishes to leave. I will expect the same from your friends in regard to anyone who wishes to come here."

Warren smiled again, a long breath of relief.

"Thank you, General. Frankly, sir, it was the decent thing to do."

"One more thing, Doctor. One rule. The guns stay here."

"Sir?"

"The muskets, pistols, anything else your innocent civilians might have in their possession. Leave them behind. What would *innocent* people need with guns anyway?"

Warren seemed to digest the point, got up, made a short bow.

"I will pass the word, sir. Thank you again."

Warren opened the door, and Gage watched him leave, saw Kemble peering in, desperate to satisfy his curiosity. Gage waved him away.

"Close the damned door, Major."

He stood now, his legs stiff with tension, moved to the window, stared out at the harbor, the masts of the tall ships, the might of His Majesty's navy. It will be soon, he thought. Someone will sail in here and announce that I haven't done the job. He will carry a fresh stack of orders from Lord Dartmouth, will be eager to relate how he received such good wishes from the king. He might even have the officers gather, just as I did today, and reveal with that arrogant confidence the plan of action, the answers to all our problems, the grand strategy that, this time, will actually *work*. Well, good luck to *you*, sir.

31. ADAMS

Lexington, April 30, 1775

His visit was official, to learn firsthand from the militia leaders there what preparations had been made, what could be done to prevent the British troops from marching so freely through the countryside, what the necessities might be for maintaining a well-equipped defensive force. But the official meetings would wait, something drawing him first to the wide green, some hand leading him in the footsteps of the men who had fallen there, a pull that was far beyond mere curiosity. Like so many in the colony who read the accounts or heard the talk, he could not yet simply accept that every hope, every bit of optimism, had suddenly been swept away, that in one awful day the last hope for resolving the crisis was shattered completely by musket fire. It would simply not be real until he could see it himself, walk the ground.

He walked the green in no particular direction, found himself searching for signs of the fight, the telltale stain of blood in the thick grass. From the moment when he had first ridden into Lexington, he had felt himself staring at the simple beauty of the wide green, and he knew it was unavoidable, he knew he would have to follow the footsteps, stand in the bloody tracks. He had fought it in his mind, did so now, stared out across the green as he left the carriage. Why must you do this? Are you so morbid? This is not what is important. But he could not keep the nightmare away, and as he crossed the hard road and stepped into the lush grass, he found himself reliving the horrible shock of another time, staring at the blood in the snow, that one awful night five years before. Then it had been called a massacre. Now, what? Sam will have his name for it, the story already written, making the best use of the horrible details, enrage and infuriate, manipulate the people to a frenzy of revenge. So much depended on the skill of the writer, the fiery speeches of the orator. But this time, we have much more than grand pronouncements, glorious pamphlets decorated with vicious cartoons. Now we have . . . this. Sam would call them martyrs, but that is only part of the story. This time there are dead on both sides. It should not be so easy to separate the two, as though we accept with such certainty that one side is completely evil, the other virtuous. And yet . . . this did not have to happen. This was brought about by the blind arrogance of a government that believes it can simply force its citizens to succumb to any punishment, any whim of their king. Where is the virtue in that? Does General Gage dare to sit in his office and claim that his men died because of *us*? He stopped walking, felt a sudden burst of clarity, imagined Thomas Gage sitting behind the grand desk, writing his reports, explaining it all to London. Well, yes, he *will* claim that. All the blame will be cast here, on these men, the citizens who believed they were simply defending their own. In London, the government will listen to Gage's version, rebels killing the king's soldiers. No matter who was right, who started it, who fired first, there can be no middle ground. And that is why there will be a war.

He looked out beyond the green, saw people watching him, some moving past. He studied the buildings, saw the tavern, the place he would meet the militia commanders, began to walk that way. He rolled the word through his mind. *War*. They will not want to hear that in Philadelphia. But I will make sure they do.

PHILADELPHIA, MAY 10, 1775

ADAMS HAD NEVER EXPECTED TO RETURN TO PHILADELPHIA, HAD shared the feeling with many of the more radical members of the First Continental Congress that for all the celebration of the very existence of that body, little had truly been accomplished. But even those who dismissed the importance of the debates and lectures, the numbing speeches and endless politicking had to concede that in some unexplainable way, the first congress had opened the door to something very new and unique. Despite the monumental differences in the delegates and their views, it had been a system that had actually worked. And none could say that it was some fluke, the cooperation born of a crisis that had now ceased to exist. Not only did the crisis still exist, but with the bloodshed at Lexington and Concord, it had grown much worse.

The second congress was called to meet on May 10, and Adams found himself selected again, had accepted with graciousness, surprised that anyone in Massachusetts could find something to admire in his service the first time around.

The other delegates from Massachusetts were appointed again as well, with one addition: John Hancock. Hancock was in all likelihood the wealthiest man in the colony, and some said the richest in all of New England. Though considered notorious by loyalists for his smuggling activities, much of his wealth was actually inherited from his father, who had been a most successful businessman. Hancock had taken to Sam Adams, drawn not only to Sam's personal magnetism, but to the power of his words and the power of Sam's talent for rousing the people. Hancock was known to have great ambition, especially when it came to his role in the Sons of Liberty. Though Hancock believed he had a potential for some lofty position in the scheme of things, Sam understood that Hancock's most useful asset was his wealth, that Hancock's willingness to underwrite many of the expenses involved in mounting the opposition to the crown made him an essential part of the organization. Hancock's selection to serve in the Second Continental Congress was more of a reward for his generosity than because of anyone's belief that he actually had much ability to get things done.

This time, the delegates did not make the journey together, their triumphant parade across New England and New York. Sam Adams and Hancock had made their way south shortly after their escape from Lexington. The others had followed soon after. As he had done before, Adams had first tended to the farm and tied up the loose ends of his law practice. After the visit to Lexington, he had made one final visit to Braintree, and had begun to journey southward suffering from the effects of some illness. He endured the long ride with bouts of fever and misery, passed through small towns that did not celebrate his passing, but met him with respectful salutes, town squares and open roads now alive with the drill and assembly of new militia.

The delegates had chosen a new, larger site for their meetings, the Pennsylvania State House. Many of the faces were familiar, the men still considered the most thoughtful and prominent in their colonies. The illness had finally given him relief, and he spent his first day shaking hands and sharing greetings both casual and serious. He had sought out the Virginia delegation first, had hoped their sentiment was still for unity with Massachusetts, was relieved to find Patrick Henry, Richard Henry Lee, the imposing figure of the one man who wore a uniform, the commander of the Virginia militia, Colonel George Washington. There were new faces as well, and if John Hancock was known outside of Massachusetts and thus did not always need introduction, some of the faces were new to everyone. Virginia had added one new delegate, a quiet young man, wide-eyed with his new responsibility. Adams had shaken the man's hand, saw the same look he had seen in so many of the others, a fire in the eyes that revealed a mind that would move quickly past the verbiage of endless debate, a young man who brought a fresh energy that Adams knew they would need. His name was Thomas Jefferson.

There were familiar faces who did not inspire pleasantries, the men from Pennsylvania, particularly the one man whose views had not changed, the one man who would still lead the opposition to what Adams saw as the prime mission of the congress. John Dickinson had taken Adams' hand with cordiality, had even expressed a deep sadness over the events in Massachusetts. But Adams could see beyond the man's patronizing show of sympathy. Dickinson was still a staunch pacifist who believed a reconciliation with England was the only course.

As Adams drifted through the crowd, he began to hear whispers, men pointing toward the door. He was becoming used to this, the sudden recognition of some new arrival, the outburst of greeting. But the men stayed back, no one calling out a name, and Adams was curious, slid between two men, heard the whispers still. He moved forward, could see the doorway now, one man standing alone, much older, short and round, peering out over tiny spectacles. Adams boldly strode forward, his usual shyness replaced by a quick stab of excitement. He held out a hand.

"Dr. Franklin. We have not met, sir. . . . I am John Adams, of Massachusetts."

Franklin seemed to perk up, took his hand.

"Ah, yes. Mr. Adams. Unlike so many, the man who *thinks* before he speaks. We find ourselves in interesting times, do we not?"

Adams could feel others moving close behind him, their hesitation gone now, men lining up to meet this one man who was known to them all.

*   *   *

THE PLACE WAS CALLED TICONDEROGA, A BRITISH FORT FAR ABOVE New York that guarded the geographically important juncture of Lake George and Lake Champlain. Despite the strategic importance to the British, the fort had been largely ignored, and few in Gage's command had considered that any serious threat existed to a place so far removed from the talk of rebellion. But besides the fort's geographic position, the colonists had discovered Ticonderoga's true importance. Contained within the fort's crumbling walls were nearly eighty cannon.

Two separate expeditions had formed, both targeting the fort, commanded by two very different kinds of men. Ethan Allen led the Green Mountain Boys, a ragtag group of mountaineers, while Colonel Benedict Arnold carried the official sanction of the Massachusetts Assembly. When the two operations learned of each other, there was conflict, and when Arnold attempted to exert his official seniority, the Green Mountain Boys made it clear they would accept no other authority than Allen. The compromise was reached, and in a cold night swept by the misery of wind and rain, Arnold and Allen stood side by side at the entranceway of the fort, backed by Allen's men. The stunned British command had no defense, and with barely a casualty, the strange assembly of rebels had captured not just a cornerstone of British pride, but enough artillery to provide a deadly new power to the siege of Boston.

PHILADELPHIA, MAY 28, 1775

THERE HAD BEEN OUTRAGE FROM THE CONSERVATIVE VOICES OF the congress when news of the capture of Ticonderoga had reached Philadelphia. But when a proposal was made to offer an official apology to the British, and a resolve was put forward calling for the return of the fort and its spoils to Gage's command, the outcry from both the radicals and the moderate delegates was long and loud. A compromise was agreed to: As long as the crisis existed with the government in England, the fort and its artillery would remain in colonial hands.

From the first days of the session, Adams had expected a great show of sympathy from the entire congress for the catastrophes of Lexington and Concord, but it was soon apparent that hesitation and timidity had replaced the fiery calls for action. Though nearly everyone agreed that the British had put events into unstoppable motion by the deaths in Massachusetts, many of the conservatives found their own ammunition for placing blame on the colonists themselves, evidenced certainly by the capture of Ticonderoga.

John Hancock was now the president of the congress, succeeding Peyton Randolph, who had been called back to Virginia on some pressing business. The Massachusetts delegation had applauded the selection, quietly aware that Hancock himself had vigorously worked the delegates for their consideration.

It had already been a long, drawn-out day, and Adams was feeling genuinely depressed, had endured a long harangue by Dickinson, the other Massachusetts delegates around him sitting silently fuming at the amazing speech. He endured Dickinson's words by staring at Hancock, could see grim impatience, the monotony of Dickinson's speech broken by sudden bursts of commentary, more speakers chiming in, some in support of Dickinson, calls for unity with England, for the astounding offer of an apology to King George. Adams glanced around, could feel the mood of the entire room, frustration, each part of the argument digging deeply into the patience of the men of both sides. Dickinson seemed to have finished his presentation, but he continued to stand silent for a long moment, and then Hancock quieted the room.

"Does Mr. Dickinson wish to continue?"

Dickinson looked straight at Adams, and Adams straightened in his chair as he felt the man's gaze.

"Forgive me, gentlemen. I am not one to occupy this congress with hollow oratory. I wish only to remind the honorable delegates from Massachusetts of one fact. Outside of this hall, in Pennsylvania, or Maryland, or New York, are the homes of men who still believe themselves to be Englishmen. Throughout the thirteen colonies, yes, even in Massachusetts, around the hearths of the vast majority of the people, the name of King George is still venerated. Prayers are said for His Majesty's health. Prayers are said for an end to this break with our mother country. The overwhelming sentiment in this land, in all of this land, is for the peace to return. Our brothers in England have made missteps, errors in judgment, errors in policy. But the same may be said of people on this side of the Atlantic. I am as outraged as any man here at the blood that was shed in Massachusetts. But it is not too late to resolve this matter with one simple plea. No matter your loyalties, no matter the depths of your anger toward the foolish policies of Parliament or the injustices that have been inflicted on all of us by the ministry, our allegiance is not to those foolish puppets of wrongheaded policy. Our allegiance is to His Majesty the king. We must trust in the king's wisdom, in His Majesty's understanding that it is not the colonies who betray him, but the self-serving power-hungry minions in his own ministry. I have no doubt that there are those in the king's own government who betray him with silence, who go to extraordinary measures to keep His Majesty in the darkness, unable to hear the cries of his own people. If we apply the energy of this body to one cause, to address the king without the censoring hand of Parliament, reach out directly to King George with the olive branch and allow the sword to fall from our hands, we will be welcomed once more into the loving family from which we have strayed."

Dickinson sat down, still staring at Adams. Others began to look toward him as well, expecting a response. He sat in a hot fog, words swirling through him. Hancock motioned toward him, and he wanted to stand, to confront Dickinson's astounding optimism, when a voice behind him suddenly broke the silence.

"Thank you, Mr. President."

He realized now that Hancock was pointing past him, and he turned his head, saw Franklin slowly rising. He spun now in his chair, had not heard Franklin say anything thus far, had begun to wonder if the old man spent much of these sessions asleep in his chair. Franklin wiped his eyes now, took a long breath, glanced at him, and Adams could see the old man's energy slowly lifting him, the face now full of light as he began to speak.

"I know Mr. Dickinson quite well. I know that he is a man of principle, a man who speaks his mind with a passion and an eloquence to be admired. I recall his opposition to the Stamp Act at a time when I myself did not truly understand what the Parliament was attempting to force upon us. With all respect to Mr. Dickinson, I submit to this congress my own experience. I have just recently returned from England after a stay of nearly ten years. In my capacity there as agent for the affairs of four colonies, it was my responsibility to deal directly with those very . . . *puppets* to which Mr. Dickinson refers. I do not dispute his description, and could add a few more epithets of my own." He paused at the scattering of laughter. Franklin adjusted his glasses, looked now at Dickinson. "I do wish to dispute, however, Mr. Dickinson's portrayal of King George as merely a helpless bystander, a man who has been ingloriously shoved aside while his ministers conduct their dastardly business. Perhaps it is the great disadvantage of distance that clouds your eyes, sir. I, too, shared your hope that all could be repaired, that surely His Majesty would not allow his very kingdom to slip away into a morass of chaos and anarchy. You propose yet another petition, I suppose, another address explaining our position, seeking to enlighten His Majesty's understanding of just what is happening to his colonies. May I remind you, sir, that half a year ago, such a petition from this very body was received in London. If the king had any interest in receiving it at all, I assure you, sir, he would have. In fact, the opposite occurred. In my dealings with every part of the government in London, I came to realize, sir, that despite all of your best wishes, and despite all of mine . . . no decision that floats across that ocean, no order to General Gage, no decree of policy to our governors, no scrap of paper whose design is to assault our very freedom, *nothing* springs forth from that place without the king's knowledge, and you may be sure, sir, *nothing* that has so assaulted us does not come here without His Majesty's very *blessing*. Hold tight to your olive branch if it suits you, sir. I believe it is prudent that we hold a bit more tightly to the sword."

Franklin seated himself, and Adams felt the weight of his

words, could feel the powerful silence engulf the entire room. It
was the first open comment Franklin had made, and Adams
looked around now, saw the impact, the others staring at the old
man, and slowly they began to stand, the silence broken now by a
slow roll of applause, the clapping growing, filling the hall.
Adams stood as well, could see that not all of them responded
to Franklin's words with enthusiasm, some remaining in their
chairs, their hands still, but it was not many. He saw Dickinson sitting as well, the man's thin frailty now magnified by his
despair.

JUNE 9, 1775

THE WORD HAD COME SEVERAL DAYS EARLIER. MORE BRITISH
ships had reached Boston Harbor, a sudden addition to Gage's
numbers. No one could be precise, but all the reports suggested
that the British now had better than ten thousand soldiers, a force
certain to press outward. While no one could be certain what
was taking place in Gage's headquarters, it was most definitely a
busier place than it had been before. The new arrivals were an
unmistakable sign that even before London knew of the disaster
on the road to Concord, the ministry had finally acceded to
Gage's pleas for reinforcements. Even the most optimistic delegate in Philadelphia understood that a gathering of fresh troops
meant something else as well: Gage would have every reason to
begin a new round of planning and strategy. There were simply
too many soldiers in Boston for even the conservatives to deny
that something dangerous was about to happen.

As the days passed, the delegates began to respond to their
changing situation with more than speeches of rhetoric and philosophy. The reality was heightened by rumor: troopships on
their way to New York, even Philadelphia, more occupations. As
communities from New England to Georgia continued to increase their militia, men continued to gather close to Boston,
joining the ragtag mass of colonial troops holding the British in
place.

Adams had received a letter from Abigail, sat alone in his room and read it with ice in the pit of his stomach. The British had begun to send raiding parties ashore, all around Boston. She had not heard of any bloodshed yet, the raids mainly for forage for horses, but he could imagine the terror of watching red-coated soldiers suddenly appearing on the quiet shoreline, the isolated roads, marching up to his own door, unstoppable, their power absolute, their brutal disregard for protest . . .

He put the letter aside, felt sick, noticed his hands shaking. The ice rose to his chest, and he stood up, paced the small room, felt anger, more, a raw black fury. He tossed her letter aside, both his fists clenched, could think of nothing but the horror, his mind racing with thoughts of soldiers in his house, the children screaming, John Quincy standing up to them, trying to protect his mother. He let out a sound now, a quick shout, no words, utter helplessness, dropped down on the bed, one fist punching the small pillow. The door suddenly opened, and he heard Sam, who said, "What is it? You all right?"

Adams lowered his head, his shoulders slumped, the awful vision swept away by helpless defeat. He wanted suddenly to cry, saw her face. God, I miss you, I miss all of you. . . .

"What happened, John?"

He fought for control, blinked away tears, wiped his eyes now, looked up at Sam.

"I'm sorry. A letter, news from home."

"Something wrong?"

"Oh, yes, Sam. Something is quite wrong." Adams slowly stood, said, "I must go outside, get some air."

He left the room, Sam close behind him, and they moved out through the rear of the tall house, the early morning still holding a chill. They moved through a garden thick with low green plants, the first signs of flowers. Sam stayed close behind him.

"You going to tell me what's wrong?"

Adams stopped now, turned, looked at him.

"We are all in grave danger, Sam. Our families, our homes. Everything we have, everything we hold dear. It can be taken away, just so easily."

"We have known that for a long time, John."

"But this congress . . . *they* don't seem to know it! We debate endlessly about whether or not we have the courage to break away from our beloved king, and all the while, his army grows stronger and bolder and more dangerous. How do we convince them, Sam? What must we do to show this congress that there is only one stand we can take?"

"What do you want them to do, John?"

"We must declare ourselves to be a free and independent country. We must establish ourselves with a government, we must invite alliances with foreign countries, build our own defensive forces . . ."

Sam laughed now.

"Why, cousin, you sound like some sort of radical! Do you have some plan for enticing this congress to accept these, um, proposals?"

Adams felt his anger slipping away, Sam's good humor disarming him.

"Well, I had thought of presenting these points. . . ."

"And what do you suppose will happen, John? The same thing that has always happened. The radicals will applaud, the conservatives will quiver in their shoes and blame you for blaspheming against everything sacred, and those in between will find a way to change the subject."

"I find no humor in that, Sam."

Sam was serious now, put his hands on John's shoulders.

"Neither do I. I have spent a good many days sitting in my room alone in darkness, wondering how, after all we have done and all that has happened, we can fight against timidity and stupidity. How can we make the blind see? How many more times will we give them *speeches*?"

He moved beside Adams now, began to walk farther into the garden, Adams moving with him.

"But this morning, something has changed. *You* are different," Sam went on. "What got you so upset? A letter from home. Your family is in danger. That had as much an effect on you as anything I have ever seen. That's the key, John. The same fear will affect everyone in that congress. But it cannot come from speeches. They cannot simply hear it, they must feel it. Every man must feel what I saw in your face, the impact of Abigail's words. When the fear is made real, they will respond."

Adams began to feel the excitement returning, the enthusiasm. Sam stopped walking, put a hand on his shoulder.

"You have a gift, John, a talent I do not have. You understand details. You would not make the same mistakes I would make; you do not have the impatience to attempt to thrust this congress into rebellion all at once. You must explain to them, show them wisdom, show them logic. A plan. They are like a team of six, the carriage moving only as quickly as the slowest horse. I am too impatient. It's too easy for me to just whip the team." Sam laughed. "It doesn't work with horses. And it won't work here."

Adams thought a moment, the names running through his mind.

"We have support from many. It will only take a few."

"The slowest horse, John. Speak to them."

"Gentlemen! A pleasant good morning!"

Both men turned, saw Hancock emerging from the house. He moved toward them quickly, skillfully balancing a small china cup.

"Have you sampled this coffee? Truly wonderful. I admit, it required some getting used to."

Sam glanced at Adams.

"Yes, had my fill earlier. You off to the hall?"

"Oh, quite so. Work to be done. Well, I don't have to tell either of you." There was a silent moment, and Hancock seemed to sense there was no conversation to be had.

"Well, then, see you in session!"

He spun away, the cup still perfectly steady, disappeared into the house. Adams stared at the motion of the door.

"Nice suit. Don't suppose it's English?"

Sam laughed.

"French. Maybe Chinese. He finds a way." Sam pulled out a pocket watch, studied it for a moment. "I suppose we should follow his example. They'll be arriving even now. And if I know John Hancock, he'll be cornering every one of them, putting in his plea for some kind of appointment. He wants to be a general, you know."

"General of what?"

"Whatever he can get. The Roman Empire is out of the question. That leaves Massachusetts."

Adams shook his head, a new wave of despair brewing.

"That's not what we need, Sam. Those men around Boston need leadership, someone who knows something about fighting. My apologies to Mr. Hancock, Sam, but the ability to accumulate wealth does not automatically ensure ability in everything else. Mr. Hancock has proven he is a capable leader of parades. I shudder to think how much pure glee would erupt from the headquarters of General Gage if someone like John Hancock was given command of an army."

"No matter, John. That opportunity exists only in Mr. Hancock's imagination. The troops will certainly elect their own commander."

Adams stared at him a moment, shook his head slowly.

"No. That is equally as dangerous. Sam, an army is not a democracy. No one miraculously acquires the ability to command because he receives the most votes. There must be other considerations—experience, for one."

"I don't know about that, John. If the troops don't approve the commander, they will simply go home."

"Sam, you're talking about a mob, not an army. If we are to defend ourselves against the British, we need more than a gathering of angry farmers. We need discipline and drill and regulations. We need regular channels of supply, food and powder, recruitment, organization. A commander must understand all of those things."

"Sounds like you may be the man for the job."

Adams shook his head.

"No. Oh, no. I could never . . . I don't have the first element: experience."

"All right, then, since you've clearly given this a great deal of thought, do you have someone in mind? Artemas Ward is up there right now, seems to be doing an adequate job. There's

Parker, Barrett . . ." Adams stared down, frowning, and Sam said, "What's wrong with them?"

"They're all from Massachusetts, Sam."

"But that's where the army is, John."

"It has to be an army of all the colonies. We need New Jersey and Delaware to send their own men to Massachusetts, we need whole companies marching up from right here. There will be great reluctance to making this fight, this army, a *Massachusetts* affair."

Sam thought a minute.

"This could mean professional soldiers. There is great danger in that. A standing army is a threat to liberty, John. We don't need to look at history to see that. We are experiencing it right now."

"There have to be concessions, Sam. One concession is that we are *facing* a professional army. Possibly the finest army in the world. We cannot fight them with lofty principles."

"I never thought I would concede an argument to my younger cousin. So, you have someone in mind to command this army?"

JUNE 15, 1775

HE HAD ENTERED THE HALL WITH THE FRESH CONFIDENCE OF A lawyer trying the case he already knows he has won. There would be no surprises today, and he took his seat knowing the men around him were watching him, many already aware that much of his work was done, committees already at work on the supply lines, word already going back to each colony to lend support to the military needs of the men in Massachusetts.

The debates and grand speeches had grown quiet in recent days, with more smaller meetings, the delegates dividing into specific committees. The larger presentations had become more practical, a growing clarity throughout the entire congress that such basic problems as communication should be addressed. Ben Franklin was appointed postmaster general, the same post he had held for many years under a different authority. One committee proposed a call for the colonies to adopt a state of military readiness, which was approved by the vast majority of the delegates, an extraordinary step considering the blunt language and the acknowledgment that war might not be avoidable no matter what resolutions Dickinson's friends might offer the king. Another committee began work on drafting the actual regulations for the operation and management of an army.

This morning the tone of the entire assembly was unusually businesslike, small conversation scattered throughout the room. He felt strangely nervous, had prepared himself to speak, rehearsing his key points in front of Sam early that morning. He knew Sam was still uncomfortable with the notion of a professional military, had tried again to convince him that the necessity outweighed the risk. Sam had listened to his points, had been stoic, only mild approval. He glanced over at Sam, saw him speaking to Patrick Henry, the two men often together, sharing the same hot spirit. Well, Sam, I suppose I can seek little comfort from anyone else now. Either they will approve or they will not.

He watched Hancock raise his hands, calling them to order, and Adams sat quietly through the brief convocation, did not even hear the prayer, his mind racing with the anticipation of his speech. He had already told Hancock of the importance of his remarks, had left the chairman enthusiastic with curiosity, and Hancock had assured him there would be no delay, that no one else had requested the floor.

The room grew quiet now as Hancock spoke.

"I open the floor this morning to the distinguished gentlemen from Massachusetts, Mr. John Adams."

Adams stood, felt the eyes on him, took a long breath, tried to grapple with the swarm of butterflies in his stomach.

"I would like to say, first, that those of us who come to this congress from the colony of Massachusetts are as grateful as any man can be for the support you have demonstrated for our plight. I believe that your support has arisen from your understanding that it is not, after all, *our* plight. What has already occurred there is tragic. What might yet occur could be catastrophic. I am certain that some of you believe that an army of thousands, coiled in waiting like some deadly snake, is a threat only to those who may tread upon it. I would suggest to you that we have been fortunate, all of us, that the snake has stayed within its own boundaries. That boundary, thus far, is the town of Boston. We already know that the innocent in Boston have seen suffering and deprivations worse than any of us hope to know. I need not detail that yet again."

He paused, felt the nervousness lessening, glanced over at Sam, saw a quick nod, a small sign of impatience, the message *get to it*.

"By your actions here, you have demonstrated not only to Massachusetts, but to England, that Boston is not alone. A valiant army has arisen, has gathered around Boston to contain the growing threat from the British soldiers there. But, in fact, it is not an army at all. It is simply *us*. It is private citizens who recognize that no man in this continent has the luxury of sitting home surrounded by the comforts of family, while close by his own countrymen are denied that very comfort. And so some of you have offered your own, men from great distances shouldering muskets, volunteering to fight if necessary, to fight because they know that if Boston submits to the outrages, is conquered by the enemies of our liberty, then nothing, *nothing* will discourage the snake from uncoiling, from winding its way into the heart of every city, every farm, every village, every home."

He paused again, felt the rising heat in his chest, saw them all watching him, the words pulling them toward him.

"I am concerned that the extraordinary gathering of what we must now call our own army is, by its very nature, destined to suffer. While we have men in Massachusetts who are rightfully appointed as authority over this army, their skills are not sufficient. It has already been suggested that this congress consider the adoption of the troops around Boston as an army of all the colonies. It is not reasonable to expect such an army, if it is to be made up of soldiers from the entire continent, to willingly submit to command only by those men appointed by one colony. If no army can exist without the approval of the men who must ultimately follow the orders, it is also true that no army can exist without organization, without equipment, without a means of subsistence. The more time we take to debate proper policy and procedure without implementing them, the more committees we have who deliberate details without fulfilling them, the greater the opportunity for the British to strike out of Boston. I therefore propose that this congress adopt as a genesis of a Continental Army those troops and commands now gathered around Boston. I further propose that this congress nominate a general to exercise absolute command over that army. I understand that there can be great concern on this point. It is a difficult decision. I have in my mind one gentleman for that important command. He is very well known among us as a man whose skill and experience as an officer, whose independent fortune, great talents, and excellent universal character would command the approbation of all America. I believe he would unite the cordial exertions of all the colonies better than any person in the union."

He paused again, scanned the room, saw the men looking around now, saw Hancock staring at him with a broad smile, leaning forward in his chair, preparing to rise. Adams felt a tight knot in his throat. My God, he thinks I'm talking about him. He saw the uniform now, Colonel Washington suddenly rising from his seat near the main entranceway, and Washington quickly and quietly slipped away, out through the door. Adams suppressed a small laugh. Of course he knows who I'm talking about. And he's too embarrassed to hear me say it. Well, all right, then. Fair enough, sir.

"I propose a motion to nominate before this congress a man from Virginia for whom we all hold the highest respect. I propose to nominate as commander of the Continental Army Colonel George Washington."

He could not help looking at Hancock, the man suddenly deflating, sinking down in the chair. There was a hum through the crowd, no one but Hancock showing any surprise, and now beside him, a voice rose. It was Sam.

"I would second the motion."

EVEN THE MOST CONSERVATIVE IN THE CONGRESS COULD FIND NO reason to object to the appointment of the large, quiet man from

Virginia to assume command of the army in its infancy. There could be no disputing that the army did in fact already exist and might be suddenly engulfed in combat the moment the British chose to burst out of Boston. Before there could be discussion over the selection of subordinate generals, proposals for the equipping and financing of the Continental Army, Washington himself had to be persuaded to accept the role, something no one had thought to question. He had stayed for a long time in his room, and Adams had been only one of those who had sought quiet conversation with him, surprised to discover that the man who so willingly wore his uniform might be so overwhelmed with the offer to command an army.

JUNE 16, 1775

THE CHAMBER WAS QUIET, AND WASHINGTON ROSE, PULLED A piece of paper from his pocket. Adams could not help a smile. So he does not believe himself to be an orator. I am not aware that should be a requirement for leadership. Washington looked out over the room now, the silence complete. He looked at the paper, slowly read from it.

"Mr. President. Though I am truly sensible of the high honor done me in this appointment, yet I feel great distress from a consciousness that my abilities and military experience may not be equal to the extensive and important trust. However, as the congress desire it, I will enter upon the momentous duty, and exert every power I possess in their service and for support of the glorious cause. I beg they will accept my most cordial thanks for this distinguished testimony of their approbation. But lest some unlucky event should happen, unfavorable to my reputation, I beg it may be remembered, by every gentleman in this room, that I, this day, declare with the utmost sincerity I do not think myself equal to the command I am honored with."

He stopped, glanced up at the faces watching him, studied the paper again, seemed to search for his place.

"As to pay, sir, I beg leave to assure the congress that, as no pecuniary consideration could have tempted me to accept this arduous employment at the expense of my domestic ease and happiness, I do not wish to make any profit from it. I will keep an exact account of my expenses. Those, I doubt not, they will discharge . . . and that is all I desire."

He sat down, the room still in silence. After a moment, men began to rise, gathering around the man in the uniform, who found his hand gripped and shaken, others touching his shoulder, the congratulations and well-wishing now infecting them all. Adams stood as well, saw Franklin close by, made way as the older man moved forward. The crowd thinned a bit, and Adams stood close behind Franklin, saw a scattering of smiles, a show of unbridled enthusiasm that had never before filled the hall. Washington was still shaking hands, wearing an embarrassed smile. Franklin reached out to him, and Washington sketched a bow.

"Doctor, I am not so sure about this. I am afraid that I am but an amateur in these affairs."

Franklin put a hand on his shoulder, and Adams heard the old man say with a laugh, "So are we all, Colonel. So are we all."

32. GAGE

BOSTON, MAY 25, 1775

HE HAD WATCHED AS THE FRIGATE SAILED IN PAST CASTLE WILliam. He had known immediately it was not like the others, the larger ships of the line, which carried the new regiments to reinforce his troops. He had not bothered to scan the ship with his spyglass, was not curious about her identity, had waited until it was brought close to the wharf, only then had seen the name *Cerberus*. She was vaguely familiar, a vessel that had done some brief work in and out of New York. He watched as she was pulled tight to the wharf, expected to see a mass of troops lining the rails, swarming in one great column down the plank, soldiers joyous over leaving the bowels of the cramped ship. But there had been no great flow of men, and he understood now. It was not a troop ship after all. But there had been soldiers, a few officers, and when he saw the first of the men in the familiar uniform, his eyes had closed for a brief moment, his head down. He had become numb to the anger, could feel only a faint sadness, had expected it for so long now, the ship that brought the man who had come to take his job.

He stayed close to the window, made himself watch again, saw a crowd of fresh uniforms emerging from the ship, more than he had expected, a flock of officers, a casual stroll down to the wharf, men gathering on solid ground again, grateful after the long voyage. But the scene was too different from what he had imagined, and he suddenly wanted the long spyglass. What was happening?

The office was empty, and he couldn't find the spyglass, it was put away somewhere, the tedious efficiency of Major Kemble. He turned to the window again, saw a carriage suddenly appear on the wharf. Of course, my brother-in-law doing his job. He watched them board, but only a few, the rest waiting for more transportation. The carriage disappeared, and he backed away from the window, felt the sadness deepen, moved slowly to the chair, sat. All right, come on. I'll just wait.

HE HAD NOT BEEN REPLACED; INSTEAD, THE MINISTRY HAD SENT three major generals. By rank, they were his subordinates, and even the quantity did not change the fact that Gage was still in command. But even if there was to be no direct change, the message to Gage was clear. The command might be his, but London was counting much more on these three men to actually do the job.

He knew them all, met them as they entered the office together, a great cluster of power, descending on him with the weight of all England.

William Howe was the most senior of their rank, his family

one of England's most famous, the brother of the admiral who had tried to befriend Ben Franklin. Henry Clinton was likely the most able commander, building a career through service in both the Coldstream Guards and the Grenadier Guards, and hard-charging service against France in the Seven Years' War. John Burgoyne was the oldest of the three, nearly as old as Gage, but by the date of his commission he had the least seniority. All three men were products of the aristocracy, all had been members of Parliament, all had risen to early prominence largely on the power of their family connections. Now all three had come to Boston, charged by the king and Lord Dartmouth to rescue Gage from what official London saw as an embarrassing predicament.

JUNE 16, 1775

THERE HAD BEEN ANOTHER COUNCIL THAT AFTERNOON, TO FI-nalize preparations for the first grand foray to break the siege holding the army within Boston. The meeting had been no different from the ones before, Gage deferring to the fresh strategy, sitting patiently, enduring the monologues, each man laying out his perfectly conceived strategy, the result of weeks of bored confinement on the *Cerberus*.

Gage himself had proposed the overall plan. It made the most military sense to march out of Boston Neck, to the southwest, occupying the hills at Dorchester Heights. From there, the British artillery might gain control of much of the rebel position, putting the heavier cannon to good use in breaking a wide hole in the siege.

Gage had allowed the men to state their cases again, knew that after all, it was the reason they had been sent here. He knew enough of ambition, was aware that each of these men had probably been disappointed to be only one of three and not the one and only to rescue Gage's disaster. Howe had made a good show of discretion, his genteel way of sparing Gage's pride, but he could not hide his disdain for Gage's apparent mismanagement of the entire situation. In nearly every conversation, Howe referred to the *embarrassment* of it all, as though to London, and to Howe himself, that was the most important consideration to be dealt with.

Clinton was a short, stout man who had stayed mostly quiet. It was obvious to Gage that Clinton had difficulty hiding his dislike for the other two men, and the more he spoke, the more obvious it became. Clinton had his own plan, of course, but would not fully discuss it, not yet, had grave concerns about the ability of Gage's headquarters to hold military secrets. He had no doubt that he had been sent across the Atlantic to be the one who ultimately replaced Gage. Gage ignored the drama and intrigue, had respect for Clinton as a strategist, but suspected that no matter how reasonable Clinton's strategy might be, the others would oppose it anyway.

Burgoyne was another matter altogether. Gage sensed that he didn't have any strategy at all, had spent the weeks on shipboard composing a play; Burgoyne had a reputation for a certain theatrical flair. Gage had seen from the first day of his arrival that Burgoyne was much about show, a man who placed great value in the parade. Oddly enough, his men had given him the nickname "Gentleman Johnny" because he chose to drill and discipline his soldiers with a gentle hand, unusual in the army. But if it made him popular with the foot soldiers, it caused serious doubts among his superiors whether he could ever be relied upon to put his men through a difficult fight. And if there was indeed a problem holding the details and strategy confined within the walls of Gage's office, it was the barkeeps and tavern owners who had learned that John Burgoyne loved to impress an audience with his knowledge of all that would soon happen.

Gage had spent much of the evening in the quiet of his den, but he had rarely been alone. He was surprised that Margaret had stayed so close, fixing him tea, fluttering about him like some devoted butterfly.

It had been quiet for a few minutes now, Margaret busy with some detail of motherhood, the harsh crying emerging from the baby's room, some difficulty from which he stayed far removed.

He sipped the tea, ran his finger along the page of an open book, a halfhearted attempt at reading. But the words were a blur, his mind wandering, and he put the book aside.

"Too much to expect . . ."

She was suddenly at the doorway.

"What? Did you call me?"

He smiled, waved her into the small room.

"I was just grousing. I had thought a nice quiet evening, one long night away from the office, just some time alone, might clear my head a bit. Hasn't worked."

She sat in the small chair, put her hands on both knees.

"And why does your handsome head need clearing?"

He could see playfulness in her, a rarity now.

"You are in a strange mood. Perhaps I should plan these evenings more often."

"Perhaps you should. Is that not what this time is for? To escape from all of that duty?"

His lightheartedness dissolved.

"Must it give you such joy? Do you take pleasure in seeing my career disappear before your eyes?"

He turned away from her, reached for the book again, and she slid the chair closer.

"My husband, what gives me pleasure is to have you home. What would give me greater pleasure is to have all of us together. There is nothing I want more than for you to be my husband and the father of our children."

He had heard it before, stared at the closed book.

"You will no doubt get your wish. I am engaged in little more than a performance, playing out the final scene, which I did not write. I am supposed to be elated that I am receiving so much . . . help. Lord Dartmouth expects that now, nothing but good news will flow out of here. We have the reinforcements I asked for, we have all of these *outstanding* generals at my disposal. And, of course, I have Lord Dartmouth's latest orders: Go to it! Make good use of all this talent and resource! Drive the rebels into the hills, bring peace and prosperity to our land!"

She put a hand on his.

"You have always known that they do not understand what is happening here. Now they will hear it from the other generals as well. Surely little will change. Then Lord Dartmouth will hear four voices, not just one. You will be vindicated. Even if they decide to replace you, you can retire with dignity."

He was surprised, stared at her now for a long moment, saw a soft smile.

"I have never known you to be so . . . concerned with such official matters. But my dear, I'm afraid you are wrong. Something will definitely change. They did not come over here just to observe, nor to repeat my failings, nor to write schoolboy notes to Lord Dartmouth. My orders from the ministry are more emphatic than ever. *Do* something. I have been given twice as many soldiers and three major generals. Today, we put our plan closer to reality, mapped out our strategy for breaking the constrictions around Boston. I regret to tell you, we are in some trouble here. If the rebels put cannon on any of the heights . . . even one gun up there above Charlestown would cause havoc here. When the rebels raided Ticonderoga, it changed the equation. We don't yet know what they have done with the cannon, where they might have taken them. But they'll not sit quietly. We must act to stop them from making our life here . . . well, suffice to say, if the rebels decide to fire their newfound artillery into Boston, it is unlikely we can stay. In fact . . ." He paused, leaned forward, his hands covering hers. "I want you to leave here. I have said this before. It is not safe, it never has been. Now it could become more dangerous."

"Is New Jersey any safer, Thomas? I have heard the rebels are forming their army in every colony."

"I was not suggesting New Jersey. I would like you to return to England. If we succeed here and crush this rebellion, you may return. If we do not . . . then I will certainly be joining you there in short order."

She sat back now, and he knew the look, the familiar argument.

"I will not discuss this with you, Thomas. I will not sail to England, certainly not without you."

He knew her resolve, a battle he could not win. He nodded slowly, put his hand on the book again.

"Perhaps you should go on to bed. I would like to do some reading."

She stood but did not leave, stared down at him for a long moment. He opened the book, made a show of finding his place. Slowly she moved to the door, then stopped.

"Why must you insist we are better off apart? Can you not just retire, accept all of that glory you always talk about? Your frustration is so apparent. You have said yourself that there is no satisfaction to be had here. Let us unite the family and enjoy what years we can. Can you not just . . . give the colonists their wretched town? Must anyone else die for your precious king?"

Her words struck him hard, and he tried to hold his calm, rubbed his fingers along the spine of the book, pushed the anger down hard inside.

"You are forgiven for your outburst, my dear." He took a deep breath, his words now tightly clipped. "You cannot be expected to understand. But you should know your observations are not accurate. If the army withdraws from here, there will be no glorious voyage home, no lofty rewards for your husband's service to the king, no grand retirement. No matter what may come, *my* fight is already lost. If the rebellion is crushed, those three generals will gain all the credit. If we lose, it is because of what I have already done, the mistakes the ministry believes I have already made." She said nothing, still looked away, and he sagged in the chair. "I am sorry. It is not appropriate for me to involve you in this. I should leave these matters in my office. I just wish you would consider your own safety, the safety of the baby."

She moved quietly away, and he looked up at the open doorway, thought of her anger. I should have reminded her, His Majesty is *her* king as well. She knows that, of course; it was an angry slip of the tongue. But it was unwise. I should caution her to be careful in what she says. She has too many American friends. It might reflect poorly. She must show respect, even if she does not believe we are doing right here. He felt his frustration rising, could suddenly picture Sam Adams in his mind. Is it not enough that he shames himself before the king? Must his blasted rebellion infest my very home?

He still had the book in his hand, tossed it aside now, pounded one fist hard on his desk. Damn them all! Lord Dartmouth has given me a chance, a final opportunity. There is honor to be had here. And, yes, my naïve wife, more men will die!

JUNE 17, 1775

HE HAD BARELY SLEPT, AVOIDED HIS BEDROOM BY STAYING IN HIS study all night, small naps breaking into his work. He had studied the troop alignments, the positioning of the regiments, which men would be best for the great push out of the city, even though it had already been discussed many times during the councils with the three generals. Even now he could not shake his anger that his own wife seemed not to care about his work, about why he must crush this rebellion.

It was nearly dawn, and he moved quickly, felt the need to be out of the house, back to his office. He pulled his hat from a hook by the front doorway, moved outside, the earliest light just finding the wider streets. He had neglected his coat, felt a chill, the cool breeze misting in from the harbor. The walk to his office was not long, and he drew in a deep breath, the salt air filling him. He saw troops, the night guard, still patrolling the street. He moved close to them, and they stiffened, saluted him, and one man said, "Sir! Have you seen it?"

He was not in the mood for conversation.

"Seen what, soldier?"

The man pointed out past the houses behind him, said, "Up there, sir. Across the bay. We heard it all bloody night, figured it was some crazy farmer. Excuse me, sir."

Gage was beginning to lose patience.

"What are you talking about, soldier? I don't have time—"

They all were staring out now, and he turned, could hear a strange noise, the dull ringing of metal, voices, drifting across the water, carried on the low breeze. He could see, out to the east of Charlestown, the gray light bringing the hills to life. He could make out motion, men going to and fro, the sounds still coming.

"What is it? Who . . ." He felt a rising knot in his chest, suddenly realized the odd noise was the sound of shovels, of men moving dirt and rock.

One of the soldiers said, "Appears to be rebels, sir."

He could see more men now, a column appearing over a crest farther back, above Charlestown, the line spreading out across the hills, then closer, more men moving in line around the fresh earth, the crest of the closest high ground, Breed's Hill, the place he had feared, the vantage from which the cannon of the rebels could destroy his army.

NO ONE WAS WAITING FOR HIM IN HIS OFFICE, AND HE WAS SURprised that all was quiet, not even Kemble had risen yet. He moved through the outer office with mild disgust. Everyone will sleep late. They were, after all, so very busy last night on a much more *important* mission. He moved into his own office, closed the door sharply behind him, had never been able to shake the anger over one of the key priorities of the three senior commanders. Gage had been astounded that one notation in Lord Dartmouth's official documents provided that each of the three new arrivees be allotted the sum of five hundred pounds from the army's accounts to provide each man with a new carriage. It was an extraordinary bit of luxury in a town where fineries had become nonexistent. Gage had been amazed further that each of the men had actually accepted this as perfectly routine, as though, of course, a general should ride in splendor, no matter what circumstance may face his army.

HE SAT AT HIS DESK IN THE SILENCE OF THE OFFICE, HIS MIND RACING with details, alternating between impatience and the excitement that this day might finally bring some serious confrontation with the rebels. He had waited for over an hour, spread out a map on the desk, marked with the supposed positions of the rebels' strength. He scanned the map yet again, knew every detail by heart, narrowed his focus to the Charlestown peninsula, where he had seen the rebels at work. The door suddenly opened, and Howe burst into the room, seemed surprised to see Gage there.

"Oh, forgive me, sir. I should have knocked."

Gage said nothing, made room for Howe at the map, and soon Clinton and Burgoyne came in as well, scurrying close, as though they might miss some vital piece of information. Gage leaned back in his chair.

"The shopping go well last night?"

Burgoyne jumped at the bait.

"Oh, quite, sir. There's a broker here who represents the most prestigious carriage maker in London. He claims they use only the finest inlaid ivory. . . ." Burgoyne stopped, and Gage saw Howe's hand on his arm as Howe said, "Perhaps we should focus on the purpose of this meeting. Excuse me, sir, but are you aware what is happening on the Charlestown peninsula?"

Gage acknowledged Howe's show of proper protocol with a short nod.

"I saw it myself. Seems the rebels intend to open up a new front."

Clinton leaned close.

"Forgive me, sir, but I have done a bit of observing on my own. The rebels have gone beyond intention. They have completed construction of a redoubt and a series of earthworks on the crest of Breed's Hill. There are fence lines extending away from the crest of the hill in such a way as to give cover to troops. I have observed a considerable number of muskets moving into position. I can only assume that their artillery is not far behind." He paused, then looked at Gage. "Excuse me, sir. I have avoided asking this question, but now seems an appropriate time. May I inquire as to why we do not have troops already occupying those hills? It seems a logical position, if not essential for the defense of Boston."

Gage pointed to the map, the mainland southeast of the town.

"Look at the map, General. Dorchester Heights. Another logical position. And of course there's Cambridge . . . Roxbury . . . Salem too. The fact is, gentlemen, prior to your timely arrival, we barely had enough troops in this command to keep the rebels from marching across Boston Neck itself. Not to mention keeping them out of Castle William. I had to make a choice—spread out in an ineffective front, or bring our forces in tight to Boston. The logic of that decision was pretty clear. General Clinton, how many muskets did you observe?"

"Several hundred. Perhaps more."

Howe went on, "No criticism intended, sir. If the rebels are marching out onto the hills on the Charlestown peninsula, it is obvious that our attention should be there as well. We all understand the value of those hills for artillery. While I'm sure we all commend General Clinton for his astute observations, no force of peasant militia is a threat, no matter how many their number. I have given this considerable thought, sir. Simply put, we must clear Charlestown peninsula of enemy forces completely. With the troop strength now in Boston, we can safely establish a formidable position there to prevent any further incursions. It can also be useful as a staging area for the final push inland against the main rebel positions."

Gage sat back in the chair. He's right, of course. If I had the troops, I would have done the same thing months ago.

"What do you propose, General Howe?"

Howe pointed to the map.

"Land two main bodies of troops, here . . . and here. If we move in tandem, it does not matter how the rebels may line up. We can assault them in two waves and easily drive them off their hills. Once the ground is clear, we should place field pieces in a pattern suitable to—"

Clinton interrupted.

"A frontal assault? For what purpose? The neck of the peninsula in the rebel rear is quite narrow. With the guns from one frigate close by, we can cover the landing of at least two regiments, who can sweep in behind the rebel position. The rebels would have nowhere to go and would probably surrender en masse. We might not have to fire a single shot."

Howe stepped slightly back from Clinton, looked at him with an air of disbelief.

"General Clinton, you propose to assault the rebels from *behind*?" The word was expelled from Howe's mouth like a spoiled oyster. He looked at Gage. "Sir, I will not debate General Clinton on the proper etiquette of war, but I assure you, if we form into

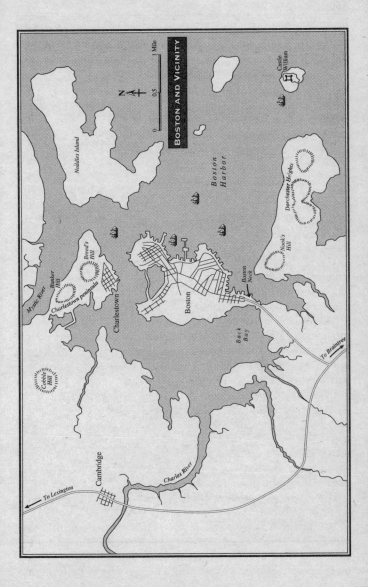

BOSTON AND VICINITY

0   0.5   1 Mile

Noddles Island

Boston Harbor

Castle William

Dorchester Heights

Nook's Hill

Mystic River

Bunker Hill

Breed's Hill

Charlestown peninsula

Charlestown

Cobble Hill

Boston

Back Bay

Boston Neck

To Braintree

Cambridge

Charles River

To Lexington

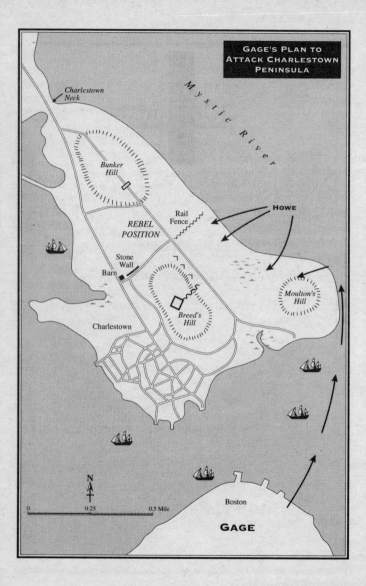

GAGE'S PLAN TO
ATTACK CHARLESTOWN
PENINSULA

*Charlestown
Neck*

Mystic River

*Bunker
Hill*

HOWE

Rail
Fence

*REBEL
POSITION*

Stone
Wall
Barn

*Moulton's
Hill*

*Breed's
Hill*

Charlestown

N

0   0.25   0.5 Mile

Boston

GAGE

the position I have suggested, the king's soldiers will present a demonstration like none seen on this continent. I am not concerned with how many rebels are in whatever ridiculous earthwork. Their rout will be complete. I do, however, agree with General Clinton on one point. It is entirely possible we may not have to fire one shot."

Gage looked up at both men, then at Burgoyne.

"Your thoughts, General? Do you favor General Howe's plan, or are you more inclined to favor General Clinton's?"

Burgoyne swaggered close to the desk, peered at the map, then straightened, seemed deep in thought.

"Well, sir, if I may . . . if the rebels choose to face us, then it seems entirely proper to oblige them. What a lesson! Rebels! We dare you to come out and oppose His Majesty's finest! I believe, sir, it might send the lot of them in a mad scramble to the safety of their wives' skirts!"

Clinton seemed resigned to the inevitable.

"Sir, at least consent to land a force of men, even one regiment, to block the rebel retreat. If they suddenly confront a solid line of soldiers damming up their one route of escape, we can capture the entire force!"

Howe held up his hand.

"General Gage, if you will allow me . . . it is best in this situation not to capture anyone. Would we not better be served by allowing them to flood back into their own headquarters, regaling their leaders with all the luscious tales of terror? Surely that will be a most advantageous weapon."

Burgoyne seemed to inflate.

"Oh, quite, sir! The sight of so much rabble fleeing for their lives . . . it could give the men quite a boost, sir! Something to remember to their grandchildren—the day the rebellion ceased to be!"

Clinton gave a slight shrug, looked at Gage.

"The decision is yours, of course, sir. You may place me at your service where you see fit. Despite the disregard for my proposals, might I offer one more? Speed, sir. The longer we allow the rebels to fortify themselves, the greater chance their strength might present a challenge."

Gage glanced at Howe saying, "I agree. We will put this into motion immediately. Delay could prove costly." Howe was still looking at the map, confident of his plan, and Gage thought, It should work, after all. And we need this, we need the land, we need the victory.

Howe continued, "The senior officers are already on alert. It will be no inconvenience to have their men moved to the boats and barges. They will be ready at your command, sir."

Gage was beginning to feel the excitement again.

"Yes, very well, General. They should be well rested and well prepared. They have had very little else to do." He reached into a drawer now, brought out a piece of paper. "Here's the tidal chart. The land along the peninsula is mostly shallow draft. The high tide will be at about two o'clock."

"The boats can be loaded by noon," Howe replied. "The daylight hours will eliminate confusion."

Gage nodded in silence, could not help but think of the embarkation for Lexington, the delays, the supposed advantage of the nighttime an absurd joke. He looked toward the window, the dawn now full across the harbor.

"We have a great deal of work to do, gentlemen. Let us now consider the specific deployment of the troops. I want the initial wave to be the finest men we have, the grenadiers, the royal marines. If this is to be a show, then let it be a glorious show!"

Now Clinton interjected, "Sir, I am concerned about Charlestown. We do not know what may await us there, if the rebels have located any sizable force. It could be a tedious mission removing snipers from rooftops."

Howe pointed to the map, the waterway beside Charlestown.

"A simple solution, General. One gunship could provide enough hot shot to eliminate that problem completely. We'll simply burn the town. Call it another good lesson for the rebels."

Gage thought of Admiral Graves, the impatience of the old seaman.

"I agree, General. But the warships can be of more practical use. Since we will have the entire morning to observe the enemy positions, with enough cannon fire directed there, toward the rebels themselves, we just might expose their greatest weakness." He laughed, caught up in the spirit of the plan, the enthusiasm from the others. "Once they have a healthy swallow of what the king's navy can serve them, they may have no appetite left to face the army. I will order Admiral Graves to move the appropriate vessels into position. He has been rather insistent on my making better use of his ships. This should delight him."

The papers began to appear, the lists of units and their commanders, the officers to handle the details. They worked quickly, the efficiency driven by the fresh enthusiasm, drawing up the orders, the timing, coordinating with the navy.

Each of the three moved out with the quick steps of men who know their duty. Gage was pacing the office, looked at the stack of paperwork, the drawings, rough sketches, the plan of attack, the list of companies. He did not try to read any more, the details hard in his mind. He thought suddenly of Pitcairn, remembered the look of utter despair on the marine's face, the defeat that had so crushed the man's spirit. Well, Major, today you shall have your revenge. Today we shall *all* have our revenge.

33. WARREN

CHARLESTOWN PENINSULA, JUNE 17, 1775

HE HAD SPENT THE MORNING IN A MEETING WITH THE COMMITTEE of Safety, a scrambled affair, arguments about overlapping commands, the selection of officers who had no ability to lead troops. The meeting had been energized by word of the British response to the entrenchments on the peninsula. If anyone ever believed Gage's plan was supposed to be a secret, every one of Warren's observers in the city had sent him the same report: The barges would carry as many as twenty-five hundred men, several cannon, would land them on the northeastern point of the peninsula. The objective did not have to be explained. By noon, nearly sixteen hundred colonial militia had spread out into a strong defense that extended from the north, a hard anchor behind a fence line that ran right to the water's edge at the Mystic River, all across the peninsula to a position down behind Charlestown itself, men securing themselves in a narrow ditch dug out behind a short stone wall.

Except for the town itself, the peninsula was primarily pasture, but there were no cattle; the farmers, Breed and Bunker, had removed their livestock to a safe haven behind the lines the rebels had constructed beyond Charlestown Neck. The cattle were too tempting a target for any British raiding party, and the assembled colonial troops required feeding as well.

When John Hancock had left for Philadelphia, Warren had replaced him as president of the Provisional Assembly and had found himself embroiled in the chaos of organizing an army. The militia units brought plenty of enthusiasm to the lines that encased Boston, but rarely did anyone consider the value of discipline or drill. Sitting tight in one dangerous place had little appeal for many of the men, whose expertise in waging war consisted of weekend marching in their own town squares, inspired less by patriotic zeal than by the admiring gaze of the town's feminine audience.

Warren had been delighted to meet some of the officers from Connecticut and Rhode Island, some who could actually claim to be soldiers, veterans from the French and Indian War. Even if they had difficulty convincing their men of the value of military discipline, nearly a third of the men who lined up around Boston had once shouldered a musket in that very real war.

The assembly had naturally assumed Warren would serve the fledgling army in a medical capacity, but his reputation for outright leadership had grown, and he had come to fill the essential vacancy left by the absence of both John Adams and Sam Adams as well as Hancock, Cushing, and Robert Treat Paine. The assembly had been wise in their choice of delegates to the congress. But with the delegates went the valuable experience the colony needed right at home. The motions for Warren to serve the army as chief medical officer were soon disregarded. Instead, he had been appointed as major general of militia, a title that technically elevated him to command just under Artemas Ward. Ward, another veteran of the French and Indian War, carried an old wound that plagued his health. Though Ward was sensitive to any suggestion that he was not fit for the command of an army of any real size, he received Warren's sudden appointment as a blessing.

Warren had left the meeting by late morning, rode hard from Cambridge toward the sound that drew the attention of every man in the ragged army. From the first hour of sunlight, the thunder of British artillery had rolled over the hills.

He reached Charlestown Neck, rode the horse past columns of men, all moving out along the narrow roads toward the peninsula. The rumble of the British guns had echoed both loud and soft, the sounds muffled by the roll of the land. As he moved close to the shoreline, the sounds suddenly changed, the air now punched sharply by a sound he had never heard, a rhythm of firing that seemed to come from everywhere at once. The horse was jerking beneath him, and he patted the animal's neck.

"Yes, there now. Easy. Let's take a look."

He moved out into a clearing, the narrow strip of land between the Charles and Mystic Rivers. The sounds came again, startling him, the horse responding as well, rearing back. He could see the ship now, just offshore in the Charles, bathed in a fog of its own smoke. The horse settled, and he felt his heart beating, heard a man shouting to him, "You! Get offa there! You're in the wide open!"

He still stared at the great ship, the smoke now gone except for thin gray ribbons that drifted out of each gun port. The man shouted something again, and Warren said under his breath, "Yes, certainly. I suppose we're in the open," but still he stared, drawn by the enormous power. Suddenly the gun ports erupted, perfect sequence, a sharp burst of flame from each gun, the ship hidden again by the smoke. He could hear the air splitting above him, a rush of sound, a sharp whine that suddenly stopped, the ground in front of the horse bursting in a great spray of dirt. The man shouted again, and Warren spurred the horse, could actually see the man now, huddled down behind a fat tree. The horse was still nervous, jerking him sideways, and Warren gripped the reins, moved along the road, looked again for the ship, could only see the tall masts, the ship now masked by a rise of land.

The man yelled at him again, "You some damned fool? They been takin' shots at anything that crosses the clearing. You was lucky. Just solid shot mostly. Lucky for sure. If that had been a hot one, you and your horse'd be blowed to pieces."

Warren saw the man had a musket but was alone.

"What are you doing here? Do you have a commander?"

"Oh, yes, I got me one gem of a commander. Old Put—General Putnam's up thataways. Left me back here as a guide. I'm supposed to make sure nobody gets lost. What you doing out here? You look like someone who's supposed to be somewheres else."

"No, I'm supposed to be up ahead. Can I find General Putnam?"

The man pointed.

"Follow this road, take the left fork up there. That'll take you straight over Bunker Hill. Leave your horse up ahead a ways, where you see the others."

He knew the route already, wanted to thank the man, but the sounds came again, the air alive with the strange whine. The horse jumped ahead, and he held the leather tightly, the horse moving him quickly toward the fork in the road. He knew the right fork went straight into Charlestown, but he had no reason to be there. And now he saw more smoke, different, black, tall columns coming from the town itself. He stared in shock. My God . . . the town is on fire. He pulled the horse to the right. I should be there, they will need help. But he hesitated, the road strangely empty, ghostly, no one leaving the town. No, they would have been the first to see the ships. From the first sound of the cannon fire, they knew what would happen. They're gone already. He stared, the columns of black smoke rising into one dense mass, then drifting away to the southeast, toward Boston. Now the thunder of the guns was far in front of him, another ship farther out in the harbor, beyond the town, and he could hear the impact of the shells, saw a sudden burst of flame, more black smoke, a new target struck. He tried to recall the town itself, the fine homes, the fishing boats, the people who wanted a life outside of the bustle and activity of Boston. But it was all wiped away now, the fires growing, spreading, and even if the people had stayed, they would only be able to watch their town collapse into black ash.

He gripped the leather straps in his hands, tight fists, the shock turning to violent anger, and he saw another blast of fire, one more shell, flames engulfing a church steeple. He shouted out, *"Why?"* as his eyes filled with tears. They have done nothing . . . there is no cause to do this. So, General Gage, you will destroy the entire town. It will just cease to be. He thought of the man, the perfect uniform, the decorum, the politely veiled threats. So now we see it. This is how you fight your wars.

He pulled the horse back to the other road, looked up the long hill, began to ride, galloped over a short rise, then down again, reached the base of the big hill. He saw a line of horses tied up along a hitching post, saw one man tending the animals, spreading hay in a shallow feed trough. The man waved to him, said, "This would be the best place for your mount. General Putnam said no horses beyond here. There's lead flying thicker'n bees up there."

Warren dismounted, handed the reins to the man, gave the horse a soft pat on the neck.

"She's yours, sir. I'll be back for her. Do you know where I might find General Putnam?"

The man pointed up the big hill.

"Somewheres up there. Don't sound much like any place fit for man *nor* beast."

He stared up the hill, could see streaks of red in the air, disappearing beyond the hill. The sounds had dissolved into his mind now, the shock gone, and he nodded silently to the man, began to move on foot up the road. Up ahead, he could see the rear of a column of men, ran to catch up with them, saw it was no more than thirty men in a double line, a musket on every shoulder, each man clothed in blue, the pants and short jackets lined with a narrow red stripe. Uniforms, he realized, and glanced down at his own plain clothing. Yes, we should consider that. It gives them something cohesive, more than just an identity. They actually look like an army.

He was breathing hard, slowed his steps, the column moving away from him. He began to look around, saw more men gathering in small groups, some lined up, others just a mass of disorganization. He pushed up on the hill, could see more men in line, more muskets, several hundred men, and he felt a hot rush of excitement. Yes, here we are! Marvelous! He was on the crest of the hill, could suddenly see it all, the harbor, massed with craft of every size, the great men-of-war spread along the shoreline, the massive clouds of white smoke drifting on the water. He saw other boats now, different, flat red barges, moving away from Boston, far out toward the end of the peninsula, but there were no guns, no smoke there, and he stopped suddenly, saw more of the strange boats now drifting away from the Boston wharf, moving out to the east as well. He could see more detail now. It was not the boats that were red. It was their cargo. They were filled with masses of British troops.

Men were shouting all along the crest of the hill, and he moved forward again, a slow run, saw one man pointing a sword, and he said, "Sir! I am looking for General Putnam."

The man said nothing, pointed the sword down to the right. Warren moved that way, was running straight at the awful scene pouring up out of Charlestown, could see the flames now, the houses and shops engulfed in one black mass.

"Dr. Warren!"

He looked for the voice, saw the short, heavy man, and Putnam waved him close, shouted through the steady din of sounds, "At your service, Doctor. Or should I say General? We're lining up here on Bunker Hill as a reserve. I am in command here, best as I can tell. I'm trying to hold these men together. Not too easy. They've never seen anything like this. Hardest thing we have to worry about is keeping these men from turning tail and heading for home."

Warren was absorbing the sights, motion everywhere. He saw two cannon now, pulled by a team of men, a small wagon behind, more men pulling a load of powder and shot. He could see the hill falling away on all sides, along the base of the rise only a narrow strip of land on either side before the rivers took over. This is an excellent place, he thought. The British would have to climb the hill, and unless they come in by water behind us, it would be nearly impossible for them to get past us. He stared ahead, the next hill, lower than where he stood, could see activity there as well, realized it was much more crowded, long lines of men, a fat square of fresh earth.

Putnam was shouting, pointing to a column of men, "Get them up there, move across!"

Warren grabbed his shoulder.

"Can you tell me, sir, why we are spread out on both hills? Should we not concentrate—"

There was a sudden rush of sound, the sharp whine of a lead ball, and he ducked down, instinct.

Putnam seemed impatient.

"Doctor, I have all I can handle right here. This is the reserve. Colonel Prescott is up there, on Mr. Breed's hill. That's the front line. I've been back and forth between these two hills so many times, I'm lucky to be standing. I will try to send up reserves if he needs them. We're prepared to hold a good solid line back here, but *that's* where the British will attack, you can depend on it."

Warren stared out east toward the lower hill, could see flashes of light all along the crest, scattered impact from the bombardment. Putnam was moving away from him, shouting something to the men with the cannon, and Warren said to no one, "Well, then, I suppose I should go on to Mr. Breed's hill."

He ran down the open face of Bunker Hill, the road dug out by the artillery shells, small holes now punched all across the flatter ground, some with wisps of smoke rising from the churned-up dirt. He could see a stone wall out to the right behind the hill, a barn to one side, men massing behind both in a thick line. Out to the left, the steepness of the hill flattened out into a gentle slope down to the shore of the Mystic River, and he saw a column of men moving that way, falling in behind a rail fence, some men hauling logs and rails from elsewhere to strengthen the fence itself. There were muskets in line all the way to the water, the shoreline itself a narrow beach just below a bluff of rocky earth. He looked up to the crest of Breed's Hill, then down to the left, studied the wide-open flat space, thought, We cannot defend that—if they send enough men, they'll just push right through, surround Breed's Hill. He looked behind him, the long rise up to Bunker Hill. That's where we should be. That's where the defense should have been dug. He began to move again, hard breaths, his heart pounding, and as he climbed the rise, he could see the fresh earthworks, thick with men, more men spread out on both sides. He moved close to the raw dirt, a large square cut into the ground, nearly fifty yards wide, lined by a wall of dirt nearly four feet high. On the far side, facing East, an extra trench had been dug, the bottom scattered with ragged fence rails, one more obstacle for anyone trying a frontal assault. At last he saw the older man, William Prescott, tall and thin, climbing up on one of the earthen walls, staring out toward the east. Prescott turned, looked back to the men who still worked with the shovels, shouted out, "They are putting ashore! Prepare for the assault!"

The shovels were cast aside, and Warren saw the men gathering around the stacked muskets. As each man took a musket, he moved to the dirt wall, lining up close to the man beside him. Warren stepped over the fresh dirt, closer to Prescott, who stared out through a long spyglass toward the end of the peninsula.

"Colonel Prescott. I am at your service, sir!"

Prescott looked at him, was suddenly wide-eyed.

"Well, Dr. Warren!" Prescott jumped down off the wall, saluted him. "Excuse me, sir. General Warren."

Warren was suddenly embarrassed, said, "That is not necessary, Colonel."

Prescott was not smiling.

"General Warren, you are the senior officer here. I turn command over to you. You should know that the British are landing out there, near Moulton's Point. They are already forming their lines along the shore. More barges are heading their way, some likely transporting field cannon. My best estimate is that they are landing near two thousand men. We have here about fifteen hundred, spread across this entire position. The reserve . . . I don't know the strength of the reserve."

Warren stared at the man's hard face, another veteran of so

many good fights. Prescott seemed to be waiting for Warren's response, and Warren thought, He wants *me* to command *him*?

"Colonel, I was given the appointment of major general two days ago. I am not . . . I cannot exercise authority here. This is your command."

"As you order, General."

"Colonel, I must ask. Why are we not dug in back on Bunker Hill? Forgive me, but is that not a stronger defensive position?"

Prescott stared at him.

"You are a better commander than you realize, General Warren. I argued that very point with Israel Putnam for better than an hour. As I understood General Ward's orders, we were to hold tight to Bunker Hill. It was a wise tactic. Even if the British came in behind us, from Charlestown Neck, they could never have driven us off that hill. General Putnam disagreed. His interpretation of our orders was to confront the enemy in the best possible position. General Putnam's concept of *best* is to be as far forward as possible. General Putnam insisted we be certain that Gage could see us up here. It's pretty clear by now that he can see us just fine. You might say, sir, that on Breed's Hill here, we are sticking our chin out a little farther than I would prefer. But here we are, and we have to make do with what we have." He turned, looked out toward the east, and Warren could see a spreading red stain on the tip of the peninsula.

Suddenly he felt a shock beneath his feet, heard the sound of men screaming, and Prescott shouted, "Order in the ranks! It's just shot hitting the wall! They can't hurt us in here!"

Others were shouting as well, junior officers pulling their men and themselves together, and Prescott said to him, "Been like this all morning. They complained like hell when we gave them shovels last night. But every time one of those balls hits that wall, they thank God for dirt. It still rattles them, though. Had a few come rolling right in here." He pointed, and Warren saw the round shallow hole. "Still there, just plopped down like some big fat raindrop."

The sounds of the shelling still cut the air, and Warren moved close to the wall that faced the harbor, could see the mass of black smoke from Charlestown now drifting eastward, along the shore below. Men were still loading their muskets, some coming in over the wall, leaving the shovels behind.

Now one man climbed up on the wall, held his musket high, shouted out, "Bring 'em on! Bring them lobster-backs!" There was a low sound, one sharp crack, and Warren saw the man still standing with the musket straight up beside him, and the man's head was gone, the body now collapsing, rolling back into the earthwork into a heap, the musket falling to the ground. Around the man's body, some cried out, one man backed away from the awful sight, others stared in shock. Warren could not avert his eyes, the fresh earth beneath the man now dark with blood. All through the works, there was a low moan, growing louder, each man feeling it in his own mind, the rise of panic.

Prescott shouted now, "Dr. Warren! Pull him back! Get him out of here! Get him buried! Now!"

Warren clenched his fists, pulled himself into control, leaned down, grabbed the man's coat, began moving him to the rear of the works, and now other men were helping, dragging the body out through the narrow opening. He looked around, saw the faces all along the fence line, some men doing nothing but watching the ghastly scene. He searched the edges of the works, saw a shovel.

"Back this way! Come on! Get the shovel!"

One man went for the shovel, then more appeared, and quickly the hole was dug, the dirt flying fast. In short minutes the man's body was gone, hidden beneath a mound of fresh earth. Warren moved back into the works, to the safety of the wall, felt his hands shaking, the emotion filling him. No, stop it. You cannot lose control. There can be no fear. He could not help himself, stared down at the stain in the earth, all that was left of the man now, the man who would be a soldier, who would never have the chance to fight his enemy. All around him, the men were crouched low, no one daring to peer out over the wall. Warren saw the man's musket, still lying where it had fallen, and he picked it up, saw the pan covered, the powder still in place. So you loaded your musket. Well, then, soldier, I will make good use of it.

Prescott was up on the wall, standing tall above them. Dangerous, Warren thought, stupidly dangerous. He wanted to say something, but Prescott shouted, "You can't see anything if you're hiding! And gentlemen, you should see *this*!"

Gradually, the men begin to peer over the wall, and Warren realized the whining and thunderous sounds had stopped. He shouted to Prescott, "Colonel! It's quiet! The cannon have stopped!"

The silence was broken again, this time by shouts, a great wave of blessed relief, cheers. The men now stood, some calling out with new courage, cursing the enemy. Below, the black smoke from Charlestown spread a complete fog over the bay, blotting out all but the tallest masts of the ships, drifting in a dense fog into Boston itself. Suddenly Warren understood.

"It's the smoke. They cannot see us! The smoke is blowing right back over them!" He felt a burst of satisfaction from that. Damn them! May they choke on their own brutality!

Prescott was still up on the wall, glassing out to the east.

"It's not the smoke."

"What do you mean?" Warren said, moving closer.

"That's not why they stopped."

He followed Prescott's gaze, stared down to the far point, saw that the red stain on the land's end was now different, pulled into two wide straight lines. They were much closer, one column coming forward down to the left, close to the shoreline of the Mystic, toward the fence line he had seen before. The other column was moving straight toward them, beginning the long climb up the rise of Breed's Hill, straight toward the earthworks. He felt his heart jump.

Prescott jumped down and, pulled his pistol, shouted, "Let them come. No one fires until my order! Only on my order! Save your powder!"

Warren rested the musket on the top of the dirt wall, sighted down the barrel, felt his hands shaking, blinked hard, tried to clear his mind. He watched them coming in silence, slow and precise, no wavering in their lines. Behind him, there was an occasional shout, more men reaching the earthworks, and different sounds, a man suddenly overcome by the fear, running away, the others shouting after him, cursing, even laughter. Warren did not

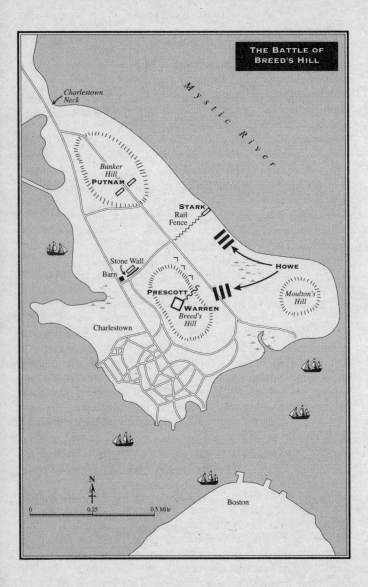

THE BATTLE OF
BREED'S HILL

Mystic River

Charlestown
Neck

Bunker
Hill
PUTNAM

STARK
Rail
Fence

Stone Wall
Barn

PRESCOTT
WARREN
Breed's
Hill

Charlestown

HOWE

Moulton's
Hill

N

0   0.25   0.5 Mile

Boston

look around, stared only at the great wide line of men, coming up the hill.

The line of soldiers was within two hundred yards now, a solid mass of red and white, the motion of their legs visible as they marched in step, plodding up through the grassy hillside. Suddenly, far down to the left, there was one great blast of musket fire, the British reaching the fence line below the hill, the far left flank. He wanted to look, but there was nothing to see, his mind screaming, No, look here! Ahead! And now Prescott was shouting again, "No firing! Wait for my order!"

There was another blast from the far left, muted shouts and screams of men, and Warren stared at the soldiers still coming, step by slow step, could suddenly hear their music, the fifes, the rhythm of the drums. Every part of him was shaking, sweat soaking his clothes, and he felt himself pressing against the dirt wall. Calm yourself. Concentrate! The drums were louder now, white legs moving with the rhythm, and he could see that they marched in three lines, each close behind the other, perfect order, pushed along by the drums. His mind was flooded now by the drumbeat, and he felt the rhythm in his own heart, could feel himself drawn forward, pulled closer to the soldiers stepping closer to him. Now he could see their faces, some of them glancing away toward the sounds that rolled up from the left. He could hear their officers, short clipped commands, cool voices, holding the line tight, the steady advance, closer, the buttons on the jackets reflecting the sunlight, the glint of the bayonets.

Prescott again: "Not yet! *Don't fire . . . till you see the whites of their eyes!*"

Warren gripped the musket hard, blinked through sweat again, his heart racing, his mind one hard scream, the entire hillside, the entire world, all of creation, every space in his brain now filled by the great mass of red and white. He tried to steady his hands, the drums still pulling him closer, and suddenly his mind fixed itself on one man, moving as they all moved, but this soldier's bayonet was pointing at *him*. He could see the man was young, pale white skin, could see he was shorter than the fellow beside him, saw every detail of the man's uniform, the black boots shiny at the top, covered with mud at his feet. Warren moved his right hand slightly, his thumb finding the hammer of the musket, and slowly he pulled it back, the hard click blending with the drumbeat, his eye sighting down the long barrel. He tried to hold the gun still, but it was shaking, jumping, bouncing about with the drums, the damned drums, and the end of the barrel was moving all over the man's body, his chest, his stomach, no, too low, now the head, the young face . . . freckles . . . and he saw the man's eyes . . .

"Fire!"

The wall erupted into one blast of flame and smoke, and thirty yards away the British line collapsed into bloody screams. The smoke blew straight down the hill, hiding the soldiers who still stood, and all around him, men were already reloading, the snap and click of muskets, other sounds, men's voices, some cursing, others crying, the emotion breaking free with the volley from the muskets. Warren was still aiming, still gripping the musket, staring hard into the smoke, tried to see the man . . . the boy . . . but the smoke was drifting away, clearing, revealing the extraordinary horror, a great mass of soldiers down in the grass, some moving slowly, twisting, some trying to crawl, and behind them, what remained of the red and white line was backing away, some running down the hill, the order gone, the drums silent, erased by the sounds from dying men.

THE SHOCK DID NOT WEAR OFF, AND THE MEN STAYED BEHIND THE wall, staring at the slow writhing of the men all across the ground in front of them. Warren felt a cold sickness, could see blood on the uniforms, the white shirts ripped apart, could hear moans, screams. Beside him, one man said, "My God . . . we killed them."

Another man began to shout, shaky bravado, "Come on back, you cowards! Come get some more!"

Prescott was moving quickly behind them, responded to the man, "They'll be back soon enough! Check your ammunition, clear your muskets! No misfires! If you haven't reloaded, do it! This is not over!"

Warren turned away from the awful sight in front of him, looked along the wall, saw the men at work, most loading their muskets, some sitting, their backs against the dirt, empty stares. He had a sudden burst of panic: Reload! I don't have any musket balls, no powder! He saw the man beside him reaching into his pocket, retrieving a lead ball, dropping it into the barrel of his musket, then the quick jab with the ramrod.

"Excuse me," Warren said, "I don't have any ammunition."

The man next to him said nothing, no smile, no acknowledgment. He completed the loading of his musket, poured powder from a horn into the pan, snapped the pan shut. Then the man said, "Not much left." He reached out, handed Warren the powder horn, a round lead ball, watched as Warren poured powder into the barrel, said now, "Not too much. Don't want to break your shoulder. That's it."

Warren felt embarrassed. "Thank you, sir."

"Thank *you*, Doctor," replied the man, still unsmiling. "If you hadn't come up here, half these men would have been gone already. Maybe even me."

"I don't understand, sir."

"I'm not up here to die for some old goat like Artemas Ward. We volunteered to come here because we believe in what you've tried to do, the things you write about. But when a man stands up with a musket in his hand, sometimes it's hard to remember all that. When I saw you, when you picked up that musket . . . well, you honor us, sir. I'm privileged to be fighting beside you."

He didn't know what to say, the man now tending to his musket, and Warren said, "Where are you from, sir?"

"Connecticut. The coast, little place you never heard of. I'm a weaver, nets mostly, for fishing. Most of Colonel Prescott's men are from down that way. These others, I don't know. Some are yours, some from New Hampshire, Rhode Island, I guess. Yesterday we heard that some Maryland men marched into Cambridge, New Yorkers, too. I suppose until the lobster-backs decide to kick up a fuss somewhere else, these boys'll come to where the fight is."

The man turned out to face the wall, and Warren looked down at the musket in his hands.

"Thank you, sir. God bless you."

The man stared out down the hill, said, "Name's Johnson, sir. Rafe Johnson."

"Pleasure to meet you, Mr. Johnson." The words sounded silly, and Warren raised the musket, rested it on the dirt wall. What *pleasure* is in any of this? He could still see movement from some of the fallen British, many more very still. He closed his eyes, lowered his head, the word again rising in his mind: *general*. Glorious titles. Glorious war.

Prescott's voice broke into his thoughts.

"Up, gentlemen! No time to rest now!" Prescott was close to him now, shouted, "Where are the field guns? Send a message to General Putnam! We need those cannon up here now!"

Warren saw a man scrambling out through the rear of the earthwork, saw another man running in through the opening, out of breath, gasping to Prescott, "Sir! Colonel Stark reports that the enemy has retreated on the left flank. We drove them back down the shoreline, sir."

"Return to Colonel Stark and tell him to prepare for another assault! They're already re-forming. Tell him, fine work!"

The man was quickly gone, and Prescott was beside Warren now, said, "Good man, John Stark. New Hampshire. A lot of good men here, Doctor. We'll need them all before this day is through. Too many green men, untested. We must hold tight here, keep these men from panicking! I will need your help, General!"

"Yes, of course, Colonel. I wonder . . . should I be checking the wounded?"

Prescott managed a short smile.

"We have no wounded, General. The redcoats never got off a volley. That will change, though. Before this is over, we may have to deal with the bayonet."

Prescott moved away, and Warren watched him, thought, I meant *their* wounded. Prescott was talking to officers now, adjusting the men, shifting strength. Reports came in from all along the line, and Prescott responded to each one, no hesitation. Warren watched him, saw the others along the dirt wall doing the same, one word now in his mind. *Leadership*. And he thought I came out here to tell *him* what to do. *He* should be the

general. When this is over, I'll do what I can to see that he becomes one. This is the kind of man we need.

Just then, men began to shout along the wall, and he turned,
his heart suddenly jumping in his throat. He could see the British
in line once more along the base of the hill, their perfect rows
again. His mind was a jumble of thoughts: Already? So quickly?
It's been barely fifteen minutes. They began to advance again,
and he studied the line, thick and wide, as though men had
simply appeared from nowhere, no effect from the loss of all
those who still lay in the grass so close to the wall. So that's why
we don't tend to their wounded. There isn't time.

The muskets came up again, and Warren heard the hard clicks
of the hammers, the men already prepared for the next volley. He
sighted down the barrel again, heard Prescott call, "No firing!
Wait for my order!"

Warren felt the sweat in his eyes again, his heart beginning to
beat in time with the drumbeat. He waited as they all waited,
could see that the line was perhaps not as wide this time, that the
angle was slightly different, more of the soldiers coming toward
the earthwork itself. He tried to clear his mind, tried to think,
knew that Prescott was in motion everywhere behind him. That's
what a commander must do. *General* Warren . . . how ridiculous.
I am barely fit to hold a musket. He could hear the drums clearly
now, the rhythm rolling up the hill, could see the white legs in
motion. He brushed at the sweat on his face with a quick wipe of
his hand, then gripped the musket hard. He ignored the slight
quiver in his hands, the hard knot in his gut, his mind becoming
colder, focused on nothing but the march of the troops, the legs
moving, boots stepping through grass, the drums filling his
mind. The soldiers reached the bodies of their own men, stepped
past, some looking down, a slow waver in the line. Warren began
to feel an icy chill, wanted to shout at Prescott, Too close!
They're already too close! The calm in his mind was gone now,
and he suddenly remembered the aim, found one man, then
moved, another one, the man staring ahead with a look of raw
terror, and Warren put the end of the barrel on the man's chest,
the man still coming. Too close . . . my God . . .

"Fire!"

The muskets erupted again, and as soon as he had squeezed the trigger, Warren backed up a step, expected them to come right at him, straight over the wall. The man beside him suddenly grabbed his musket, poured powder in the barrel. Warren did not look at him, stared into the great cloud of smoke, all sound now. There were small flashes of musket fire in front of them, scattered response from the British soldiers, but the noise of the shooting was drowned out by awful screams. The musket was in his hands again, loaded, and Warren did not look down, leaned on the wall again as the smoke began to clear, waiting for a target, another uniform, another face.

"Fire!"

The gun kicked against his shoulder, and he was furious, had not aimed at anything, just pulled the trigger. He looked to the side, saw Johnson still aiming. Johnson fired his musket, backed away, reloaded quickly, handed Warren his musket.

"Here! Aim low!"

Warren turned, raised the musket, Johnson's words in his mind: *aim low*. He sighted down the barrel, scanned the ground in front of him, saw red motion, his finger on the trigger, but the man was on the ground, suddenly rolled over, blood on his chest. Warren raised his head, fought to see farther through the smoke, and now it began to disperse in the breeze. The soldiers were gone, and he thought, So fast? They must have run. Now he could see across the open ground, a thick carpet of red and white, hands and arms and fallen muskets in one solid mass all down in front of the line. Men were down right in front of him, ten yards away, and he could see the man he had shot, a new horror, not just a soldier, a uniform, but the man's face, wide-eyed, staring past him, past nothing at all. He turned away, saw that men were down in the earthwork, only a few, from the British response, some of the soldiers returning fire. He leaned the musket against the dirt, moved quickly, bent low over one man, blood on the man's head, a sharp gash. The man grabbed Warren's arm.

"They killed me!"

Men were gathering, and Warren said, "A rag! Cloth! Tear his shirt!" Hands obliged, and Warren wrapped the dirty cloth around the man's head, took the man's hand, placed it on the makeshift bandage, telling him, "Hold it here. Tight. You're not dying. Just a bloody headache."

He scurried away from the man, saw another, men gathering, and he shouldered between them, bent low, saw another bloody face, a neat hole in the man's forehead. He stood, looked at the others.

"Pull him back. We'll bury him later."

Prescott was talking to an officer now, and Warren moved that way, heard Prescott say, "Where are those damned cannon?"

The other man was filthy, drenched with the sweat of a man who has done his work.

"Sir, I heard General Putnam order Major Gridley to bring his guns forward. The next thing we knew, Major Gridley was high-tailing it to the rear, guns and all. Didn't even say anything, just turned and ran away! Old Put was pretty mad, sir."

Prescott was furious.

"Damned town square militia!" He shook his head, looked at the man again, said, "What about ammunition? Is General Putnam planning on joining us up here? We need the reserves! We need powder and shot!"

"Sir, he's been ordering men to come up here, said to tell you he's pushing 'em as best he can."

"Pushing them? Has he thought perhaps he should *lead* them?"

Warren moved away from the two men, felt that small stir of panic again, moved toward his place at the wall. He looked for the musket, saw it was gone, picked out Johnson now, holding one gun, the other on the ground behind him. Johnson saw him coming.

"No more powder, sir. This one's ready. But that's all we got, sir." Johnson held the loaded musket out to him, and Warren shook his head slowly.

"No, Mr. Johnson. You're the better shot, I'm certain. I'll make do. What about the others?"

Prescott was suddenly beside him.

"One shot per man, maybe. We can't hold up if they charge us. They're not going to just run away every time we give them a volley. They have bayonets, they'll use them." Prescott bent down now, picked up the empty musket, handed it to Warren.

"I'd keep this if I were you, General. Make a good club."

Warren took the musket, looked out across the sea of uniforms, muskets lying scattered.

"Colonel . . . what about . . . we can take powder from the British."

Prescott glanced out over the wall.

"You fancy the taste of a bayonet, General? A good many of those fallen men can still put up some kind of fight. We go scavenging among 'em, we'll have a mess we don't want. No time, anyway. They're lining up again."

The men settled in against the wall, and Warren stayed back, turned the musket around in his hands, held the barrel, felt the heft of the stock. A club indeed. He moved up behind Johnson, could see the wide rows coming again, the same scene repeated, thought, How can they do that? They know it will happen again, we will slaughter them again. He looked around him, saw some men standing back, as he was, clutching empty muskets, one man with only a small sword. The annoying panic began to fill his mind again. Yes, of course, that's why they do it. We cannot stand up to them after all. We have the men, we have the ground, we have the spirit for the fight. But we don't have the ammunition.

He could hear the drums again, had to see, moved close to the wall, saw Johnson cock the hammer on his musket, and Warren felt the sweaty grip on his own musket, said under his breath, "Aim low, Mr. Johnson."

The British lines reached their own fallen men, the soldiers picking their way carefully, the march wavering again, but they did not stop, driven forward by the drums, by the hoarse shouts of officers. Now they were closer still, some now dropping down to one knee, breaking their formation. Some began firing their muskets into the earthworks, ignoring the shouts of their officers, the discipline erased by the sight of their enemy.

The volley came from the wall again, ragged, uneven, no

order needed from Prescott. The sounds in front of the wall were different this time, and Warren felt himself backing up, heard the voices rising, men in red suddenly emerging from out of the smoke, reaching the wall, bayonets first, some climbing up and over. The men along the wall began to swing their muskets, clubbing down the men in red, some grabbing for the bayonets, pulling the British soldiers into the works. He saw fists now, men punching and grappling, more bayonets, soldiers now climbing in from all sides of the earthwork. The muskets were silent at last, the only sounds the voices and struggles of men. Prescott's men were backing away, some staying close to each other, a solid wall of fight still, but now the British soldiers had targets, were firing, reloading their own muskets, more coming over the wall. Warren saw Prescott, shouting his men back, waving a short sword, and Warren understood: We cannot stay here, we must pull back, the other hill. Prescott was grabbing men now, turning them around, trying to keep them orderly, fighting the panic. Warren could still see some of his men lunging forward, defying the musket fire, the hand-to-hand fighting now all through the works. He tried to back toward the rear of the works, the opening that would give the men escape, Prescott shouting, "Fall back! Keep good order!"

The British officers were shouting as well, holding their men back, breaking up the chaos, ordering their men to organize, muskets reloading again. British officers were up on the wall, directing their men out beyond the earthworks, fresh musket fire coming from along the fence line. Warren still gripped the musket, saw an officer coming over the wall closest to him, and Warren made a sound, animal-like, the raw fury of the fight, raised the musket, made a wide swing, turned himself nearly full around, the British officer seeing him now, trying to jump down. With a loud grunt, Warren swung the butt of the musket hard into the man's knees, sweeping him back off the wall. He looked for another target, his mind hot with rage, but the wall was now alive with men, a fresh line of red uniforms and bayonets, and Warren backed away farther. He could see Prescott's men filing quickly out of the rear of the earthworks, saw Prescott motioning them that way, unable to make himself heard. The musket fire was all around now, nearly all of it from the British, and Warren pushed his way to the opening, shouted at Prescott, "Go! I'll hold here, guide them out! You should lead them back to Bunker Hill!"

Prescott handed him the sword, shouted close to his face, "I will not leave you, sir. We must keep them in good order! I have sent word to the reserves on Bunker Hill. If they will come forward enough to hold the enemy back, it will cover our retreat. The enemy will not pursue. We must pull back in good order, without panic."

The words flew past him, and he dropped the musket, felt the sword in his hand, a new sensation, looked for a target, raised the sword. Come closer, damn you! He saw men still grappling, one man on the ground, the British soldier above him, the bayonet coming down, saw now it was Johnson, the man's clothes bloodied, the bayonet pointed at his heart, and Warren screamed, began to rush forward, the sword raised, *I will kill you. . . .*

He felt a hard punch in his head, and the sounds were suddenly gone, dull thunder rolling through his brain. He found himself on his back, could feel the ground under him, tried to move his arms, lift himself up, lift the sword, but he was completely numb, even his back, the ground beneath him soft, no pain. He could see light, shadows, movement above him, felt someone pulling him along, his head raised, could see a mass of shadows now, all close to him, but no sound, no voices, hot wetness on his face. Now the light grew faint, darker, the shadows moving away, and he wanted to say something, but the thought slipped away, the images drifting, dissolving into quiet calm, and now his mind was silent, no shadows, no memories.

ON THE HILLS ABOVE BRAINTREE, THE PEOPLE HAD GATHERED, AS they had gathered on hilltops for miles around, the roll of thunder from Boston bringing them out of their homes. They could see the smoke, the destruction of Charlestown, a quiet town so much like their own, engulfed and destroyed by this new and awful war. One woman had brought her eldest son, the boy now seven, held him close to her as they stood alongside their neighbors. Soon the black smoke gave way to a new sight, the peninsula just visible above Boston Harbor alive with something none of them had ever seen: patches of white fog from the silent bursts of musket fire.

As she held her son close, the letter to her husband was already forming in her mind, and she knew she would tell him of this terrible day, the first time any of the people around her had ever actually seen a war. When the sounds and the smoke grew dim with the setting of the sun, the people left the hilltop, returned to their farms in grim silence to await the first real news. She took her son by the hand, spoke gently, in that soothing sweet voice only a mother can summon, the voice that banishes the demons from nightmares, "Come, John Quincy. It is time to go home."

She did not yet know the incredible cost, did not yet know that the British had left a thousand men on that ground, did not yet know that the king's gallant marine, Major Pitcairn, had not survived the day, did not yet know that her good friend Joseph Warren had on this one day been a soldier.

PART THREE
THE FLAG
UNFURLED

34. WASHINGTON

FOR DAYS AFTER HIS APPOINTMENT, HE HAD CONTINUED TO SEEK out the support, the kind handshakes from the members of the congress. Despite all the celebrations in his honor, the lavish dinner parties around Philadelphia, he could not escape his own doubts, suffered through long sleepless nights haunted by visions of failure. It was more than just his selfish pride, though he still felt that the job he had been given with so much back-slapping optimism was far beyond his talents. Even his appointment to the Second Continental Congress had been accepted reluctantly, despite the convictions of Virginia's House of Burgesses that his good service in Williamsburg made his attendance in Philadelphia a foregone conclusion.

He had assumed that his attendance at the second congress would not require as much time as he'd given the year before. As important as the duty was, and as clearly as he accepted his role as delegate, both journeys to Philadelphia had taken him away from a home life that had become more and more fulfilling to him. His sixteen-year marriage to Martha, his development of the land around Mount Vernon, and his dedication to farming were his true loves. Mount Vernon had become the one place where he could allow himself to feel pure joy, with none of the chaos of politics.

He had worn the old uniform because he had thought it was a necessary symbol, a sign that Virginia was prepared to meet any challenge. His friend Richard Henry Lee had understood this without Washington explaining it, knew that Washington was not a man to glorify himself, to elevate his reputation by the empty parade of a grand uniform. But Washington's service had been very real and, to Virginians, very accomplished. To his former superiors in the British army, he had been an annoyance, a colonist who expected to be treated with the same respect as the British were, given the same opportunity for command and advancement in an army that made no secret of its prejudice against Americans. Both during and after the French and Indian War, his superiors had overlooked his leadership on the American frontier as trivial, and yet to the settlers whose greatest concern was survival against the danger of the Indians, Washington had established himself as a dependable protector. The British required a certain number of colonials to serve in those positions the British officers themselves found repugnant. Washington had fulfilled that role, and when he expected some recognition for it, the reality had been demonstrated with brutal clarity. In the army, he was and would always be an outsider.

The buff and blue uniform was of the Virginia militia, the source of the colonel's commission he still carried. He had been embarrassed at the reception he had received from the delegates, especially when word had begun to circulate that his quiet dignity and his experience of command had so caught the eye of the other delegates that he might be the very man to command the new colonial army.

In the days after his official appointment, the congress had named his subordinate commanders, and immediately there had been more conflict. Artemas Ward, who held senior command around Boston, was given the commission of major general and would be Washington's second in command, a move thought certain to satisfy those in Massachusetts who would react with outrage because a Virginian was now in charge of *their* fight. Below Ward, another major general's commission was given to Charles Lee, an expatriate Englishman regarded by some as the man who was more qualified to have Washington's job. Lee was now referred to as a Virginian, but considered himself a citizen of any place where he could slake a thirst for adventure. Besides service to the British in the French and Indian War, he had distinguished himself in mercenary service to the king of Poland, and was actually granted a commission as a major general in the Polish army. But Lee had sensed a new opportunity in the colonies and settled in Virginia, doing what he could to spread word of his own vast accomplishments. Besides his military skills, Lee became known as much for his unfortunate personal habits, an amazing disregard for personal hygiene and his tendency to keep company more with dogs than with humans. Relishing the center stage, Lee was disappointed when Washington was named commander in chief. But his commission as third in command satisfied many who believed this loud, crude, and profane character was an essential addition to the army and might certainly become a colonial hero.

Washington's uncertainties had prompted him to convince the congress to name an old friend as his aide-de-camp, with the rank of brigadier general. Horatio Gates was another expatriate Englishman who had settled in Virginia close to Washington's home. The two men could not be more different, Gates a short, round man with poor eyesight, who seemed, except to Washington, completely devoid of any likable qualities. Congress accepted Washington's plea, and Gates had joined the command as the familiar face and confidant Washington felt he needed.

Bowing to the uncertain political climate in New York, the congress appointed Philip Schuyler as a fourth senior commander, to rank as major general below Ward and Charles Lee. Schuyler was descended from one of New York's most aristocratic families, had given commendable service in the French and Indian War. The congress and Washington understood that having a New Yorker on the command staff would go a long way toward bringing many in that colony closer to the patriot cause, who might otherwise choose to avoid any involvement altogether.

The journey northward had begun on June 23, had taken ten days, and Washington could not avoid the convoy erupting into a celebrated parade as they passed through both farm communities and larger towns. Word spread quickly, and the group was met by cheers and salutes from the citizens who knew from the first view of the line of carriages that these were the men who would command their army. When they reached New York, the scene had been much the same, but on a far grander scale. The outpouring had been more official, the New York Assembly voting a salute that would have infuriated their royal governor, William Tryon. But Tryon had been across the Atlantic, and though his return was expected at any time, the New Yorkers, who were notorious in their lukewarm support for the Continental Congress, took the most pragmatic route: They gave their enthusiastic support to the leader who happened to be there at the time.

When the men resumed their journey, one man stayed behind. Washington made his first command decision, placed Philip Schuyler in command of what Washington himself labeled the Northern Department, with authority for any military operation that might involve activity toward the Canadian border.

Washington had been in New England only once, nearly twenty years before, tried to recall the details of Boston, assumed that much had changed, even beyond the obvious that the town was now little more than a British camp. But as the convoy rolled closer, through Connecticut, Rhode Island, the celebrations became more military, militia companies falling in behind, riding in support for a few miles beyond their town, some preparing to join the general's command at Boston.

He had hesitated to write to Martha, had not felt anything like a burst of pride, the gushing need to tell his wife all about the grand appointment, the honor granted to him by that extraordinary gathering of men. But as the days passed, as the necessity of leaving Philadelphia on the long road to Boston had grown close, he realized that the clamor around Philadelphia would soon be clamor in Virginia. She might very well hear about his new responsibility from someone else. *That* was unacceptable. After staring at blank paper for several nights, the words finally came, apologetic, concerned for her feelings. He wished he could have seen her, truly revealed his thoughts, his apprehensions. He wanted to make her understand why it was so important, why he had accepted this amazing challenge, why he would not be home quickly after all. He could not bear to think of her in sorrow, mourning his absence. If only he could explain why this was necessary, she would accept it, as he was trying to accept it himself. But he would not see her, could not rely on some gift of eloquence he knew he did not have. Instead he could only relate the extraordinary events in ordinary words, pass the news through the coldness of ink on paper. He had not made a copy, didn't have to, the first words still hard in his mind.

My Dearest, I am now set down to write you on a subject which fills me with inexpressible concern, and this concern is greatly aggravated and increased when I reflect upon the uneasiness I know it will cause you.

Would it after all? She would miss him, certainly, but he was beginning to understand that she was home, surrounded with the familiar, the comfortable. It was her husband who was making this journey toward the thoroughly unknown.

All along the journey, he had passed the idle hours mostly in silence. The others most definitely did not, particularly Charles Lee, who filled every resting moment with ever louder and more spectacular tales of grisly and frightening adventure, and Schuyler, who before he gratefully departed in New York had not hidden his distaste for the crudeness of everything Lee represented. Washington had tried to avoid both men, but he could not avoid what they represented. The contrast between these two might reflect the greatest problem he would confront: convincing very different people from very different worlds that they should fight and possibly die for each other, for one cause that was important to them all.

Each day, as he rode closer to his new command, farther from the familiar, from all that he loved about home, his doubts still nagged him, more of the letter to Martha in his mind.

It has been determined in Congress that the whole army raised for the defense of the American cause shall be put under my care . . . as it has been a kind of destiny that has thrown me upon this service, I shall hope that my undertaking it is designed to answer some good purpose.

As the carriages drew closer still to his new headquarters, he began to understand that the soothing words, the explanations weren't just for her.

CAMBRIDGE, MASSACHUSETTS, JULY 1775

A MASS OF SHELTERS LINED THE STREETS OF THE TOWN AND BEyond, the camp spread out over rolling hills, filling pastures and small clearings around patches of woods. The shelters were a blend of every kind of color and shape, tents of canvas, some made with sails taken from ships. Some of the men had built small fortresses of brick and mortar, complete with smokestacks. Others had constructed wooden shacks, with a variety of skill, some merely huts made of straw and brush, with flat, peaked, or sloping roofs of planking, cloth, straw, anything that would hold the weather away.

The convoy rolled up into the square, among the buildings of Harvard College. Washington held himself in the carriage for a long moment, waited for the others to emerge, enjoy the reception. He had hoped all along there would not be a great fuss, but he scolded himself, No, they should treat us as they see fit. We are visitors after all. Let them pay their respects. Finally he climbed out, stood on the low step, then jumped down to the ground. He looked for the official reception, the quick gathering, the great anticipation finally realized. But the men he saw were mostly tending to their own affairs, some working idly on their shelters, others sitting in small circles playing cards, a number sleeping on the grass, some minding small campfires and coffeepots. There were some glances toward the carriages, brief displays of idle curiosity. The other commanders had moved away from the carriages, had begun to question the scattering of guards or others who stood close to the larger buildings, an effort to find someone in authority, to find the proper place to make an introduction. Washington still did not move, tried to see something, anything that resembled an army, something to remind him that he was in command and not just one more visitor to an odd assembly of bored men.

"Sir!"

He looked to one side, saw Horatio Gates at the open doorway of a tall brick building.

"Sir! In here."

He felt relief. Well, all right. We shall do this inside. He began to move that way, long loping strides, climbed up short steps, turned, looked out across what he could see of the town and of what was supposed to be his army. He felt angry at himself for having had some expectation of a grand reception. They know less about you than you know about them. That may be the first challenge, to convince them you truly are in command. He looked toward Gates again, impatiently waiting for him, the small man scowling at him through thick glasses.

"I'm coming, Mr. Gates."

He strode into the building and saw Lee already talking to a small gathering of men, Lee's loud voice echoing in the large entranceway.

"Thousands of them. Every town, every stop we made. Muskets held high. Inspiration, that's what it was. A dirty job, for sure. But the men are there, willing to slit the throats, rip through the soft bellies of the red hordes!"

Washington moved up behind Lee, scanned the faces of the man's somewhat rattled audience, said to Gates, "Is this the headquarters?"

Now another man emerged slowly into the wide foyer, short, round, gray-haired. He stared at Washington with obvious annoyance.

"This is *my* headquarters, yes. Might I assume you to be General Washington?"

Washington made a quick bow.

"Indeed, sir." He expected a formal greeting, some introduction, but the man turned, suddenly disappeared back through the doorway. Now the man's voice rolled out: "In here."

Washington glanced at Gates, who shrugged.

"I'm not sure, sir."

The other men simply moved away, disappeared down a long hallway, back to whatever duties were more of a priority than greeting some new foreign commanders.

Lee did not hesitate, followed the man's words into the other room, and Washington felt strangely alone now, said to Gates, "I suppose we should go in."

Gates moved to the door, and suddenly Lee reappeared, a deep frown.

"He wants to see you. Just you. Rude bugger."

Washington winced, said under his breath, "Careful, Mr. Lee. Let's not offend these people any more than we seem to have done already." Lee sulked away, and Washington passed through the doorway into an empty outer office, saw another doorway, open, and he stepped toward it, stood at the entrance, saw the older man sitting behind a desk, scowling.

"Oh, do come in. Let's make this brief, shall we?"

Washington was feeling annoyed now.

"We have not yet been introduced, sir."

"Artemas Ward, General. There, that a sufficient introduction?"

Ward seemed to busy himself with papers on his desk, and Washington waited for more, felt clearly like an intruder. Ward said nothing for a long moment, and Washington moved closer to the desk, glanced back behind him, saw the office still empty, no eavesdroppers.

"General Ward, would you prefer I make this official?"

"Save you the trouble, General. I hereby acknowledge your arrival and turn over command of this army to you. God help you, sir."

Washington removed a paper from his pocket.

"I have your commission, sir. Are you aware—"

"Yes, yes. Major general of your Continental Army. I am now subordinate to you. I'm not sure what you expect here, General, but these men are not necessarily celebrating your arrival. We've done mighty well on our own, without anyone from Virginia or anywhere else telling us what to do."

Ward was still shuffling paper, and Washington felt his patience draining away, took a long breath.

"This is not a position I sought. But the congress has appointed me."

Ward looked up at him now.

"Congress? And just who is the congress, General? And what happens to your command when the congress decides to go home? From what I hear, some of those people down there are still sending sweetheart letters to the king. They can't agree on anything. Any day now, one of them goes into some blue-faced fit about something, and the whole lot of them might just up and go home. For all we know, it might already have happened. And I'm supposed to believe that sending you up here is going to give us something to crow about? To start with, *sir,* why don't you tell me what you know about our fight on the Charlestown peninsula?"

"I have received some details. If they are accurate, then you have every right to feel extremely proud. Your men performed with gallantry and inflicted extraordinary losses on the British."

"Aren't you going to tell me how regrettable it is that we were so defeated?"

Washington was beginning to comprehend. Of course, the retreat.

"General Ward, what your men accomplished is far more important than who now occupies that piece of land. If the numbers I received are accurate, your men inflicted something on the order of forty percent casualties, with much lighter losses on your side. I hope you appreciate that what you did goes far beyond a tallying of acreage. You showed General Gage that a direct confrontation with our troops will cost him more than he can afford. They will be very hesitant about mounting another assault."

Ward stared at him, seemed to digest Washington's words, the scowl softening.

"I hadn't thought of that, actually. You're right about the numbers. I assumed the word had gotten to Philadelphia that we were just pushed back. Gage accomplished his purpose, cleared us off the peninsula."

"And where is General Gage now?"

"They're still holed up in Boston. And the Charlestown peninsula."

"I wish you had a few more peninsulas around Boston, General. General Gage can have all the land he wants if he's willing to pay that kind of price."

Ward stood now, the scowl returning, put his hands on his hips, paced slowly behind the desk.

"It's a wise thing you can do, General, if you let these men know that news of what they did out there has spread beyond Massachusetts. Most of these men, even the ones from outside, don't really believe anyone from down south will support them. For all the ho-de-do about a congress, when it comes down to it, it's the men out there holding the muskets who will decide this mess. You coming here doesn't really change anything."

"I am aware of that, General Ward. You're telling me I have to prove I'm worthy of their respect."

Ward laughed.

"Respect comes later. First you have to convince them they should listen to a single word you have to say. Your first job is to give them one good reason why they should even *obey* you."

HE BEGAN TO MAKE REGULAR INSPECTION RIDES THROUGH THE camps, was still amazed by the lack of sameness. Everywhere he rode, he saw the display of individuality in both the men and their campsites. Gradually he met the officers, saw the same uniqueness, men who blended with their commands, who considered themselves no different from the men who took their orders. It was something he had heard from John Adams, the hard core of democratic spirit in New England, what Adams had called the great "leveling" of class. He could see it now, the army a blend of equals, managed by the common agreement that one man in your company would give the orders, and the others would obey. If the orders became unpopular, the officer would be removed, his replacement voted on by the rest of the men. If the orders were unpopular enough, the men might just decide to go home. That the army had put up such an extraordinary fight on Breed's Hill was amazing enough. But Washington was quickly coming to realize that despite the pride of the men, and despite Ward's warnings that his authority was tenuous, these men were yet to be an army at all. The men themselves, the raw materials, were there. But his first duty was, in fact, creating the Continental Army from scratch.

As he rode through the camps and met with the officers, he began the sensitive job of instruction. One characteristic of the camps that was apparent from the first visit was the smell. Little attention had been given to sanitary conditions, no effort to coordinate the placing of latrines. It was a problem soon dealt with.

The supplies for the men were abundant, a blessing Washington did not take for granted. New England had sent more than its men, it had sent its bounty. Food was not a problem, even if the methods of distribution and preparation were as diverse as the men themselves.

Ward continued to accommodate him officially, but there was little enthusiasm from the man whose overall authority had been stripped. The more junior officers did not seem quite as threatened by the arrival of the Virginian, and Washington quickly sought to put their minds even more at ease. Even if a Virginian was in overall command, it was crucial to the organization and morale of the army that the men who commanded beneath him were familiar to their troops.

As hygiene was addressed, and the instruction of officers, Washington began to focus on what was ultimately the most important part of his job: the confrontation with the British. The lines as constructed by the colonists were flimsy at best, and if Gage was staying tight in his base in Boston, it might only be because he did not realize how weak the American positions were.

Washington directed much of the labor himself, the men understanding that the lines could be greatly improved by the addition of felled trees, fence lines of rock and timber. Charles Lee was contributing his expertise as well, and Washington was pleased to find that this colorful character had such a talent for attracting the attention of the troops that his instructions were impossible to ignore. As the troops learned more about the men who came northward to lead them, Washington and his deputies began to learn the lessons as well. Washington had come to appreciate that what Ward's men had accomplished on Breed's Hill was even more significant than they had realized. Gage's inactivity had given the Continental Army precious weeks to pull itself into an effective defense.

HE HAD BECOME NUMB TO THE STACKS OF PAPER, REQUESTS, COMplaints, copies of orders on all levels, some dealing with the uncomfortable challenge of discipline. Lee had been to the far right flank, improving the defensive structures down near Dorchester. Washington could hear the sudden eruption of sounds outside the office, knew by now the commotion that Lee caused on his arrival. Lee burst into Washington's office now, his usual display of bluster, two large dogs scampering in behind him. Lee dropped himself heavily into the chair in front of Washington's desk, the man's familiar aroma flooding the room. Washington knew that anything on his desk would have to wait, leaned back in his chair.

"How did it go?"

Lee nodded vigorously.

"They're getting it. Slow sometimes, but I get out there and swing the axe a few times, and they get the idea."

Washington smiled.

"I imagine it has an effect, seeing a major general doing manual labor. Nothing like that in the British army, for certain."

"Can't agree with you, George. It wouldn't matter if I was the bashaw of Turkey, they'd expect me to do my share of the work. Very damned strange, George. I rode into one camp, saw a man repairing boots, asked to see their captain. He said, 'You're talking to him.' Said, 'I been a shoemaker, I'm still one now. Being a captain don't change that. The men need their boots fixed.' "

The dogs were lying beside him now, and Lee stretched down to scratch a pair of black ears.

"Not sure it's going to work. No army's ever been run this way. Not without—"

"An officer corps? You're right. As much as there is to admire about the way these people ignore position, we cannot command an army like a town meeting. I'm not sure how we break through that."

"Never seen an army that encourages their men to go home if the mood strikes them. A whole company from somewhere—Salem, maybe, I don't know—anyway, they up and left. Missed their wives. Fellow told me, 'Oh, don't worry, they'll be back.' "

Washington ran his hand over one stack of paper.

"Can't deny they can fight. Gage found that out. They believe in their cause, that's a strong tie. They seem to respect their officers, most of them. But they're still militia." He said the word with a twist to his mouth. "Twenty years ago, I had my first taste of local militia. They were expert at conducting drunken parties around their campfires, but when the Indians arrived, most every man I had took off for home. Lock one in the guardhouse, the rest of them tear the place down. They never showed any concern about why they should fight together, why they were a part of something larger. They served, sacrificed, if it was convenient."

"Not sure it's the same here," Lee replied. "These people know they're a part of something. The more talk I hear about Breed's Hill . . . they know. An awful lot of them believe that if they'd had better leadership, they'd have driven the British into the harbor. It's certain that if General Ward had paid any attention to getting them ammunition, they might have killed every damned redcoat Gage sent up that hill."

Washington shook his head.

"They still don't understand what it means to be an army. I think about Adams, his caution about this Yankee spirit, his warning not to push them too hard. He might as well have meant don't *offend* anybody if you want them to fight for you. How do you implant discipline in people like this?"

Lee laughed.

"Hang a few deserters. That should get the message to them."

Washington shook his head.

"Can't. Not in this command. The congress authorized lashes, confinement. We can whip a few people, but no hanging, no executions. It's very unpopular to suggest harsh measures down there when the support for the command is lukewarm to begin with."

Lee rubbed the dog's head, said something to the dog, nonsensical words. He lifted his gaze to Washington.

"You receive the reports of munitions? The supply?"

Washington raised a paper.

"Very encouraging, actually. We have over three hundred barrels of powder on hand now. Three hundred eight, to be exact."

Lee's hand lifted from the dog, and he stared at Washington for a moment.

"Who told you that?"

"Right here, part of General Ward's reports."

"You seen 'em? The barrels?"

Washington began to feel uneasy, knew that for all Lee's eccentricities, he was not a teaser.

"Well, no. But it says here—"

"George, *I've* seen them. Before that fight on Breed's Hill, they had plenty, probably just what it says there. *Before* Breed's Hill. I saw what's left. There might be thirty, forty barrels. That's it. I've never been too keen on mathematics, but I think that comes out to about nine rounds per man. Of course, if the men keep going home, that leaves more rounds for the rest of us."

Washington felt stunned, said, "Are you quite certain? I have the report. . . ."

"Tell you what, George. I'll write you a report that says the British have surrendered and gone back to England. Then we can all go home."

Washington looked at the paper in his hand, felt a flood of anger, crumpled it up, threw it aside. He slumped in the chair, stared silently at the desk, his mind a swirl of despair. He could hear Lee playing with the dogs again, the man bent over, hidden by the desk. Washington looked past him to the far wall, where a pair of square windows was open, letting in the slow drift of a warm breeze. Thoughts jumbled in his mind: the congress, Adams, Ward, soldiers sleeping in piles of hay, officers repairing boots, Martha . . .

No, he would not think of Martha, would not fall into the misery of missing Mount Vernon. He focused on Lee again, the man still crooning to the dogs, and now Gates was there, seemed out of breath, excited, unusual for the man most around headquarters had come to know as permanently sour.

"General! New arrivals, sir!" Gates seemed impatient, motioning Washington outside. "Sir, you have to see!"

Lee ignored him, still occupied with the dogs, and Washington tried to shake the dreariness from his thoughts.

"What is it, Mr. Gates? You look like you're bursting out of your skin. How many? They bring any powder?"

Gates seemed deflated by the question.

"I would think so, sir. All they can carry, I suppose. But it's been a long journey."

Washington forced himself to ask, "How far? New Hampshire?"

Gates swelled up again.

"No, sir. A bit farther than that. They're from Virginia, sir."

Washington's brain swept the misery away, and he stood, the chair clattering behind him. Lee's dogs suddenly barked, Lee getting to his feet as well, the dogs running outside, just ahead of Washington. He stopped on the steps of the building, saw them now, a ragged line of men, but a semblance of a uniform, the men all in white frock shirts and buckskin pants, most wearing wide-brimmed hats. Lee was beside him now, the dogs barking in manic rhythm; Lee shouted something, a sharp command, and the dogs fell silent. One of the men came forward, and Washington began to smile, saw the familiar stride, a big man, nearly as tall as Washington, lean, wide shoulders, the hat coming off. The man stepped close to him, made a low bow.

"General Washington, sir. It has been a while."

The man's words were a slight mumble, coming through a toothless smile.

"Daniel . . . my word, this is a surprise."

"Come up here from the Shenandoah Valley—near six hundred miles in three weeks, General. Didn't lose a man. Ninety-six rifles. We expect you might have something useful for us to do."

Washington felt Lee nudging him.

"General Charles Lee, I am pleased to introduce an old friend, Daniel Morgan. We served with Braddock together."

Morgan was still smiling, unembarrassed by the great wide abyss between his gums.

"Weren't much to serving with Braddock. Much more just to *survive* Braddock. That we did. Forgive my lack of meat chewers, General Lee. What Colonel Washington's rations couldn't do, the Indians did. A lucky shot, came in right here." He pointed to a dark scar on his neck. "Shot my teeth clean out of my mouth."

Washington glanced at Lee, saw a wide smile, the crude commander recognizing a kindred spirit. Morgan reached into his shirt, retrieved a piece of paper.

"By the way, sir, those fellows in Philadelphia give me this here piece of paper. Says you may address me as *Captain* Morgan. These men are now officially under your command as the Virginia Rifles." Morgan looked around, and Washington was suddenly aware of a growing crowd. "These be your army, General?"

"They would be, yes."

"Motley-looking group. I hear they put up a fight."

The line of Morgan's men was slowly engulfed, surrounded by the curious men who approached them, greetings, conversation beginning from both sides. Lee was looking over Morgan's shoulder, the long musket draped across the man's back.

"Excuse me, Captain, but what manner of musket is that? Don't recall seeing one with so long a barrel."

Morgan rolled the gun off his back, held it out to Lee.

"It's a rifle, sir. The barrel is engraved inside in a coil. Spins the ball. That and the long barrel make for a much more accurate shot."

Lee held the gun up to his shoulder, sighted down the barrel.

"How accurate?"

"You got any squirrels around here, I'll show you. Knock off their heads at three hundred yards."

Lee lowered the gun.

"You're joking, Captain."

Morgan cast a glance back to his men.

"We got another one, boys." He turned back to Lee again. "We're kinda fond of wagering, General. If General Washington don't mind, I'd be happy to have a little contest with any of your fine soldiers here."

Washington was laughing now, said, "I wouldn't, General Lee."

Lee handed Morgan the gun.

"Not sure I understand. What kind of contest?"

Morgan glanced at Washington, who had seen this before, was still chuckling.

"Why, a little contest of marksmanship, General."

THE ADDITION OF THE VIRGINIA RIFLES SEEMED TO INSPIRE A RISE in morale all through the camps, the first visible and very boisterous sign that someone beyond New England was rallying to their cause. But if the Virginians' shooting skills quickly became legendary, and somewhat exaggerated, they did nothing to help Washington's problems with discipline. Morgan's men were as rough as their appearance and made abundant use of alcohol. Fights were common, almost a scheduled event, and did not confine themselves to the limits of Morgan's camp. When one of the most violent offenders was hauled into a makeshift stockade, a drunken group of Morgan's men burned the stockade to the ground.

Washington had ridden far out to the right flank, climbed the tall hills known as Dorchester Heights. He could see the British works that sealed off Boston Neck, the great forest of ship masts, some of the vessels bringing reinforcements from England, others carrying the supplies necessary for Gage's growing army. He had paid special attention to the great men-of-war anchored in a tight arc all around the town, the power of the big guns that would keep any force away from the shoreline. As he rode back toward Cambridge, he felt the strange pride again, the despair replaced by a new feeling, something beginning to take hold in his mind. This was becoming his army, this amazing collection of militiamen and simple volunteers, shopkeepers and frontiersmen who had so convinced the mighty British army to seal themselves into a siege mentality. He thought of Gage. What goes through his mind? What he know of us, really? We certainly know less of him, and that must change. We need information, spies, someone to tell us what they are doing down there. There can be no surprises, no great eruption of British troops suddenly marching up here. If he finds out how little powder we have . . .

He felt a cold shock in his brain. Of course, he may know already. He certainly has *his* spies. But spies can be useful no matter which side they're on. Information can go both ways, even bad information. He stopped the horse, the staff coming up close behind him, and he turned, said in a loud voice to Gates, "General, be sure the powder is distributed evenly. I don't want eighteen hundred barrels of powder sitting in one place. A fire could prove embarrassing."

Gates looked at him blankly for a moment, his confusion obvious, and Washington held in a smile.

"Sir?"

"Mr. Gates, I want the word spread all along the line, to every commander. We have a problem. With so much powder, with such an abundance of ammunition, the men simply cannot carry it all. Be sure the word goes out everywhere. Eighteen hundred barrels of powder is simply too much. If we're fortunate, the British will come out and give us a chance to use some of it up. Am I clear?"

Gates lowered his head, peered up over his glasses now, and Washington nodded slowly, the smile escaping slightly, and Gates suddenly jolted upright, as if struck by hot iron. He glanced around, toward the men camped nearby, said loudly, "I will handle it, sir. Eighteen hundred barrels . . . my God, that is far too much powder, sir."

Washington cut him off with a small motion of his hand. All right, not too much. Spies are not necessarily fools. He slapped the horse with the reins, began to move again. If I had someone in town, I'd learn pretty quickly if this worked. Sometimes the more unbelievable a rumor is, the more believable it becomes. Of course, that doesn't mean we don't have a desperate need that is very real. That search will be much more discreet, however.

He passed a heavy row of timbers, more men working, axes and shovels. They stopped for a moment, watched him pass, some calling out, recognizing the tall man in the saddle.

The instruction to the officers was beginning to work, the companies and regiments beginning to recognize that they were part of more than their own individual fights. Washington had spent long hours talking to the officers, showing patience and tolerance, probing their sensitivities, hearing their complaints. It was subtle, had to be, the slow tilting of the level ground about which the men had so much pride. As the officers themselves began to understand how they fit into the larger army, they began to have pride in their own units, in the behavior and deportment of their own men, in their own ability to *command*. They began to understand how discipline was of value after all, not just for convenience, but for each officer's own value to the army. Washington's instructions were having an effect.

As he passed more camps, the shouts came again, and he remembered his ridiculous introduction to Artemas Ward, his assumption that the men would simply *give* him respect. But now he was beginning to hear it, and if he felt that he still had not done enough, that the work of building an army was far more daunting than he believed he could accomplish, the men were telling him otherwise.

He could see the brick buildings of the college, the light beginning to fade, a long day in the saddle wearing him down. He could smell food now, the camps preparing the evening meal, suddenly heard a roar of voices down the hill below the town. Behind him, Gates said, "Morgan's men. Their afternoon ritual. Beat each other to a bloody pulp."

Washington stopped the horse, could see men running toward the tumult, a crowd growing along a fence. The din was louder than what he usually heard from that camp, and he felt an anger growing, the stiffness of the saddle draining his patience.

"I've had about enough of this."

He spurred the horse, left the staff scrambling to catch up, galloped down the long hill. He jumped the horse over a narrow trench, past men who were still moving toward the great commotion. Beyond the fence, he could see the fight, only two men, a great audience around a clearing just wide enough for a roaring brawl. He was beginning to feel furious now, the

THE SIEGE OF BOSTON

N

0   0.5   1 Mile

Noddles Island

Boston Harbor

Castle William

Dorchester Heights

Nook's Hill

Mystic River

Bunker Hill

Breed's Hill

HOWE

Charlestown Peninsula

Charlestown

Boston

GAGE

Boston Neck

Back Bay

Cobble Hill

WASHINGTON

To Lexington

Cambridge

Charles River

To Braintree

attention of the men so captured by this absurd violence when the real violence was yet to come, would catch them all unprepared if they did not stop this foolishness. He dug his heels into the horse, galloped toward the fence, men suddenly ducking away, and jumped the horse high, clearing the fence, right over the heads of the surprised men. The horse landed in the dusty cloud of the fight, the two brawlers startled, paralyzed by the sudden appearance of this big man on the horse. He reached down, grabbed one man by the collar, then the other, pulled both of them up off the ground, held each one hanging helplessly against a flank of the horse. The crowd of men around him was suddenly quiet, and he saw the stunned surprise on their faces, began to feel it himself, the weight of the men pulling hard on him. He released the men, each dropping in a heap in the dust, and as he turned the horse slowly, scanning the men, he said aloud, "This fight is over. I expect this army to spend more energy preparing to fight their genuine enemy."

He guided the horse toward the fence, the men giving wide berth, and he jumped the horse back over the way he had come. He began to move up the rise, Gates and the staff waiting for him, wide-eyed, quiet. Behind him the sounds returned; he snapped the reins, thought, Not again, not already, he spun the horse around, saw them now. They were not cheering for anyone's drunken fight. They were cheering him.

35. FRANKLIN

PHILADELPHIA, JULY 1775

HE HATED THE SILENCE, MOVED ABOUT THE HOUSE WITH SLOW footsteps, peering into every empty room. There was too much that was unfamiliar, from the furniture to the trinkets on countless shelves. There were the things he remembered, of course, some of them his own gifts to Deborah, mostly chosen by the hand of Mrs. Stevenson. But no matter how many times he stood in each doorway, he would soon discover something new, some object, a small bit of someone else's life, something he had missed before. And then would come the pain, another reminder that though this was his house, designed by him and built under the stern gaze of his wife, in many ways it would never truly be a home for him at all.

He glanced at his watch, moved slowly into his study, the one place in the house where so much was his very own. Even that came from a special consideration from the Continental Congress, allowing an import from England to reach the wharf at Philadelphia. He had expected to lose it all, all his books and papers, a necessary sacrifice to the boycott of English shipping, but there was kindness in those men, and he did not have to ask more than once, just one favor, to allow his personal goods to be landed.

He studied the shelves, his own treasures, great files and boxes, all the evidence of what had made him famous, accounts of experiments, diagrams of inventions, and the letters from kings and all manner of celebrities. But they did not seem to matter as much now, did not inspire the grand memories, did not carry him back to those wonderful days in London, his visits throughout Europe. They are, after all, just *things*, he reflected. Like the other things spread throughout this house. All the pieces of a life of which I was not part.

His moods were always worse when the house was silent, empty, the rest of them out on some trip to the market or the park. His daughter and her husband, Richard, had lived in the house since their marriage, and now they were four, two boys, six-year-old Benny and two-year-old Willy. He never would admit it to his daughter, but he would actually wait for them, sometimes standing quietly by the door, lost in some thought that was merely an exercise in killing time. Then would come the glorious sound of his grandchildren, and they would never disappoint him, their voices carrying far down the street, giving him time to prepare his nonchalance at their return.

He had thought often of Mrs. Stevenson, received letters from her sweet hand. He knew she wanted to come to America, and though she would never say it, and certainly never hint of it to him, there would be no shame in becoming Mrs. Franklin. He had not truly given another marriage serious thought, but in the quiet moments, he missed her care, her frittering about the house scolding him for all his indelicate habits. If she came, it would be the beginning of a new life, and he was feeling his age, real- ized that the only thing new in his life was that so much of his time alone was spent doing nothing at all, his mind begging for rest, taxed by his dedication to his work in the congress.

He had been surprised to hear snippets of gossip around town, amazed to discover that to some in Philadelphia, his relationship with Mrs. Stevenson had been something of a scandal, an annoy- ance that was brought home to him by the supposed friends who came to call. They came to the house wearing their sympathy, proclaiming such sadness that Franklin had not been there to hear his wife's final breath, the exhaustion of a life alone taking its toll on the poor woman. The little performances of melo- drama came mostly from people Franklin barely knew, inspired by the gossip from visitors who had been in London, some he may actually have met, or more likely, people he had never seen at all. If he carried any guilt for his absence from Deborah's life, it was not because of any infidelity. Once he began to hear the talk, he knew she had heard it as well, hushed speculation about his life in London. It pained him to think she had endured that, and he became more and more angry, began to choose his visi- tors with care.

It was the sincere well-wishers who left him with the most sadness, people he had known well, whose friendship with Deborah had certainly been a wonderful help to her in his ab- sence. There were often tears, and they would speak of her with affection, but there would not be unspoken judgments, no critical comment of him hidden in their kindness. Her loss had been felt by a great many people, and so many of her friends spoke of her spirit, that she had given so much to the house, to their business, that she must surely be watching over him, so proud of her famous husband. Despite the genuine words of comfort, and despite how many distractions he created, when he stood alone in the dark hallways, silent rooms, he could feel the emptiness. But the worst times came in that quiet place in his mind, where he had always imagined speaking to her, bright conversations in the middle of the night, lying in his bed in London telling her of all the amazing events of the day. No matter how hard he tried to bring that back, to stare into darkness and talk to her about his voyage home, about the congress, she would not come, he could not see her face. If sleep came at all, it was shrouded by the dark sadness that she was truly gone.

THE CONGRESS HAD BEGUN TO CONFRONT THE REALITY OF WHAT was actually needed to pay for an army. Besides his position as postmaster general, Franklin had been appointed to oversee the printing of paper money, a logical choice both because of his reputation as an honest man and because of the fact that his printing business was close at hand, run now by his son-in-law, Richard Bache.

The congress had been informed that the Continental Association had failed to make any impact on Parliament, but what was more disturbing to the radicals was the failure of the economic measures in the streets of London. Those who had proposed the boycott of British goods, whether now or four years earlier, had believed that the loss of both the raw materials and the marketplace the colonies provided England would be devastating to the British economy. It was naturally assumed that as their business dried up, pressure from beleaguered British merchants would have some impact on Parliament. In fact, the British were making great strides in opening markets in other parts of the world, the great power of British shipping proving to have a healthy influence on British trade to Asia, Africa, and even South America. To the radicals, this was unfortunate news. To the conservatives, it was further ammunition for the argument that colonial protest was ultimately toothless, strengthening their determination for following the only sensible path out of the crisis. Led by John Dickinson, many in the congress still held to the belief that peace and tranquility would come only by making another appeal directly to the king.

The debate had gone on for three days, men exhausting themselves in yet another turn at convincing each other that the course they were following was either preordained by God to be successful or destined to condemn the colonies to a hell of their own making. Franklin had listened in silence, as was typical for him. He focused on each man individually, tried to measure the man's response to the opposing points of view. Some required no measuring at all, men whose allegiance to Dickinson was clear. He had been surprised at the apparent split in the Virginia delegation. From the beginning, Richard Henry Lee and Patrick Henry were certainly in loud support of the cause of Massachusetts, joined by the intensely quiet young man, Thomas Jefferson. But there were dissenting voices as well, Peyton Randolph certainly, aligning with Dickinson's conservatives.

He had tried to tally some kind of count, but the numbers were lost in the haze of talk. It didn't matter anyway, for no vote on anything that might put all their necks in a noose would be decided by a simple majority. The mundane decisions were made mostly in committee. Others were simply made by whoever had the expertise, such as Franklin himself designing the Continental currency, deciding on the complex uniqueness of vegetation, a different tree for each denomination, as a means of discouraging counterfeiting. But in the great chamber, the debate continued over Dickinson's proposal to offer one last appeal to the king, what he still referred to as the Olive Branch Petition. A simple majority would not do. They all had to agree. And if they did not agree, it was entirely possible that the congress would simply dissolve, the delegates confronted by an intractable difference that no amount of oratory or backroom negotiation could overcome.

Franklin could sense the mood of the chamber, frustration more than anything else, men leaning with exhaustion toward seeking some compromise as a means of putting a conclusion to all the talk. Even John Adams had seemed to mellow a bit, his latest oration lacking the fire that Franklin had come to expect.

Dickinson was up at the speaker's rostrum now, and Franklin pulled himself up in the chair, knew it was nearly four o'clock, the usual time for concluding the session. He studied Dickinson, the thin man appearing more sickly than usual. Of course, he's like the rest of us. He's becoming worn out. Well, perhaps he will lead us out of here today on a note of oratorical glory.

The room grew quiet, and Dickinson said, "Gentlemen, I am witness to our colonies embarking on a journey of utter destruction. But lest you believe that I am merely speaking out against what so many of you consider essential to our survival, to those of you who insist that our greatest villain in this crisis is King George, I beseech you. Consider that for all our differences and disagreements, His Majesty is still the only force that can stop this catastrophic flow of events. No army, no parliament, no Lord North, no General Washington can with a simple decree answer all the challenges we face. But King George can. With a stroke of his pen, he can eliminate the Port Bill. With a stroke of his pen, he can call home the army from Boston. With a stroke of his pen, he can bring these colonies back into his family."

He paused a moment, let his head drop, seemed to search for energy. Franklin was suddenly concerned, leaned forward in his chair, but Dickinson lifted his chin again, continued.

"I have no respect for those who make a reputation preaching destruction. I do not refer to men in this room, I refer to men in that other great hall in London. I believe a visitor there would discover that while we debate the future of our very survival, in England, no one dares be tardy at the Newmarket races. No minister or member of Parliament dares to miss their evening recital of the latest celebrated opera. I am reminded of Emperor Nero, fiddling while Rome burned around him. Now the British Empire is afire. Consider please, what might occur if the empire is torn apart the way some of you prescribe. For centuries, France and Spain have waged war with England over supremacy of the seas. An England weakened by the loss of America will invite more war. Is our best interest served by the rise to power of a king of Spain? Will not America find itself suddenly set upon by any foreign power who values our resources, who sees us as we see ourselves, a doorway to the riches of North America?" He paused again, and Franklin was glancing at the others, no one talking, some nodding in agreement.

"The hour is late. I will not go on. I only ask you to consider that waging war is a simple act. It requires no great intelligence, no great abilities other than assembling a means of killing your enemy. It appalls me. Can we not make one more effort? There is time enough for chaos; can we not attempt reason? The king has refused to hear us, because he has been convinced that we are an illegal assembly. Then let us address him as individuals, speaking on behalf of the people of our own colonies. Surely he cannot deny us that. If we remove the aura of hostility, if we demonstrate that we have the interests of peace at heart, surely, *surely* he will respond."

Dickinson left the rostrum to applause, loud shouts of approval. Franklin was surprised, looked toward Adams, who returned the look, shook his head. The chamber was dismissed, and Franklin pushed himself slowly up out of the chair. He began to struggle a bit, pain in both knees, the stiffness holding him tightly, felt a hand under his arm.

"Allow me, sir." Adams helped him up, commenting as he did so, "We have a substantial lack of backbone in this room, I'm afraid."

Franklin looked past him, saw Dickinson standing close behind, staring angrily at Adams, reacting to his words.

"Mr. Dickinson, a fine speech, sir," said Franklin.

Adams seemed suddenly embarrassed, did not look behind him, nodded quickly to Franklin, moved away toward the entrance. Franklin saw Dickinson following Adams, began to follow himself. My God, let's not have a duel. He slipped through the crowd of delegates, making polite acknowledgments left and right, still keeping his eye on Dickinson. The man was gone now, following Adams out of the hall. Franklin reached the door, could see them both, heard the taller man call out, saw Adams turn, a look of surprise. Franklin moved closer, heard Adams say, "My apologies for my indiscreet remark, sir. However, I am certain you are aware of my sentiments."

Dickinson seemed to explode in Adams' face.

"What is the reason, Mr. Adams, that you New England men oppose our measures of reconciliation? Why do you hold so tightly to this determined opposition to petitioning the king?"

Franklin heard other men gathering behind him, filling the entranceway, Dickinson's volume drawing them. He could see Adams glancing at them and then saying, "Mr. Dickinson, this is not an appropriate time. . . ."

"Mr. Adams, can you not respond? Do you not desire an end to talk of war?"

Adams seemed struck by Dickinson's words, looked at him for a long moment.

"Mr. Dickinson, if you believe that all that has fallen upon us is merely talk, I have no response. There is no hope of avoiding a war, sir, because the war has already begun. Your king and his army have seen to that. Please, excuse me, sir."

Adams began to walk away, and Franklin could see Dickinson look back at the growing crowd behind him, saw a strange desperation in the man's expression, and Dickinson shouted toward Adams, "There is no sin in hope!"

THE OLIVE BRANCH PETITION WAS APPROVED, A COMBINATION OF faith and optimism from the conservatives and a concession by the radicals to appease the fragile passion of John Dickinson. The petition left Philadelphia signed by the members of the congress as individuals, no mention of the Continental Congress anywhere in the document. It was carried by Richard Penn, who was already known in London as a devout Tory, a descendant of the man who had founded Pennsylvania. Even the radicals had become convinced that in a search for peace, it cost them nothing to make an appeal to the king, that the worst of London's policies had already been enacted. Even if they disagreed with Dickinson's hopefulness, few could argue with his logic that it was only the pen of George III that could bring the crisis to an immediate conclusion.

PERTH AMBOY, NEW JERSEY, AUGUST 1775

HE WAS IMPRESSED. IT WAS THE FIRST TIME FRANKLIN HAD VISITED his son's new home, a grand estate befitting the royal governor of New Jersey. He sat in silence, waited in the carriage for the footman to open the door, gazed out across the wide yard, studied a finely tended garden, occupied his mind with naming the flowers, a feeble exercise in stemming his nervousness. He had last seen his son in their friend Joseph Galloway's home in Philadelphia. Galloway had never recovered from the humiliation handed him by the defeat of his plan by the First Continental Congress, had not returned as a delegate for the Second. Franklin had persuaded Galloway to invite William to Galloway's home as a means of bringing William to a meeting with his father. It had been tense and awkward, and ultimately had concluded with a note of hostility that had punched Franklin as hard as any fist.

He could not just allow the strain in their relationship to settle into permanent silence, had grabbed at the excuse to offer transportation to William's son, Temple, who was to attend school in Philadelphia. All the way across New Jersey, Franklin had felt more of the lonely despair of a man who has lost some piece of himself. It was difficult enough to live in a house that did not feel like home, but it was just as painful for him to try to accept that he might have lost his son as well. Sally seemed to understand how difficult his return from England had been, had made it a point to invite her father to join her family in all activities involving the grandchildren. But Sally was not close to her brother either, could do little to help the older man bridge the void between father and son.

HE WAS MET AT THE DOOR BY ELIZABETH, HIS DAUGHTER-IN-LAW, A pleasant and pretty woman, who seemed immune to the differences between her husband and her father-in-law.

"Papa! Welcome!"

"Hello, my dear." He kissed her cheek, still felt the nervousness, sensed her arm on his as they moved into the grand foyer.

"Was your journey comfortable? I was so afraid of bad weather."

He smiled at her flow of chatter, could not help but look around the room, her touch everywhere in the stylish decoration. She led him into the main sitting room, still chirping at him like some social canary. Elizabeth was well suited for life as a royal governor's wife. She had a great affection for the shops of London, for bringing finery and elegance into her home. But she did not carry that unpleasant air of the aristocrat, had made great effort to fit in comfortably with Franklin's family, had been closer to Deborah than William had been. She was telling him about some new lace she had bought, and he was nodding politely, absently looking at a portrait on the wall: King George, of course. She was suddenly silent, catching him by surprise, and now she hugged him.

"Oh, Papa. We miss her so."

She backed away, and he could see tears, realized suddenly she was referring to Deborah.

"Yes, my dear." He was caught off guard by her emotion, didn't know what else to say. She wiped at her eyes with a small handkerchief.

"I'm sure you are anxious to see William. He is in the library, I believe. Temple is out somewhere—you know the energy of a fifteen-year-old. We are all so happy you have come!"

She had slipped into the hostess role, and he could not avoid glancing at the portrait of the king, hanging high just behind her. He nodded, unsmiling, thought, Yes, well, we'll see.

"Please don't disturb Temple in his activities. I will have plenty of time to spend with him on the journey back. I suppose I should visit my son. Could you perhaps guide me to the library?"

She took his arm, silently led him past extraordinary cabinets of silver, glassware, more portraits of former governors and their wives as well. She suddenly released him, held out her hand toward the dark wood door, said nothing, the smile fading. He could tell she was already withdrawing, and she said, "He's in there. He requested . . . a knock. Oh, Papa . . ."

"It's all right, my dear."

He faced the door, held up his fist, hesitated a brief moment, then rapped. He heard a voice call, "Enter."

He sighed, thought, Well, my son, already you are rude. He opened the door now, let it swing wide, caught the smell of old oak and cigars, the musty scent of books. William stood at a tall bookshelf, his back to Franklin, running his finger along the spines of several books. Franklin stepped into the room.

"It is not necessary to convince me you are too busy to open your own door."

William's hand dropped, and still he faced the bookshelf. Franklin continued, "How many of these have you actually read?"

William turned now.

"Not as many as you, certainly. Enough for the requirements of my position."

It had begun already, and Franklin felt the nervousness even more now. William pointed to a chair, dark red leather.

"Would you care to sit, Father?"

He moved to the chair, let himself down slowly. William noticed, asked, "Your knees?"

"And everything else. Even walking around the block has become its own challenge."

William sat in his own chair.

"I've thought a great deal about that, Father. There is no reason why a man of your age should be so . . . involved. Have you not considered retiring? Surely you have earned some peaceful years."

There was no softness in William's words, and Franklin replied, "I would draw no amusement from sitting around listening to my knees creak. There is much work yet to do."

"Work? Your work was in London. It was concluded when you left. You gave admirable service to the colonies as their agent. Why must you continue to immerse yourself in these dreadful affairs?"

Franklin sat back in the chair, shifted his weight on the fine leather. The silence was thick in the room until Franklin inquired, "So how is your friend Strahan?"

William seemed to jump at the opportunity to change the subject.

"He is quite well. He complains of the same infirmities you do. You should both be retired."

"I've not heard from him in a while. He's a member of Parliament still, I believe. Still supports his king, prints all those decrees and such. I'm afraid we don't have much in common anymore."

"He is still your friend, Father. He misses you a great deal."

Franklin thought of Strahan, all the playful intrigue.

"He misses all the turmoil I caused. I amused him, gave him something to tell his cronies."

"Some things don't change, Father. I hear you are causing turmoil again."

"No, not that I'm aware. In fact, all the congress has done lately is send the king a request to pay attention to the mess he's caused." It was casting bait, and Franklin instantly regretted it, did not want to dive into all the causes of their disagreement. He wished to apologize, to stop this before it started, but William had taken the bait completely, said in a slow hiss, "The *congress* . . . how dare you use that word in my home. Your so-called congress is no more than a gathering of disloyal protestors who draw strength from their own numbers. It is illegal, and frankly, Father, it is extremely unwise."

He knew the advice that was coming next, *stay away from those who will get you hanged,* had heard it all before.

"Actually, not all of them are so disloyal. Surely you know that; some of them are still friends of yours. I'm sure you receive your timely reports on all the dissension. Some of them would be right at home with a royal governor. The rest of us have quite a time with that bunch." He tried to laugh, to inject some lightness into the mood, but the effort was feeble. William did not respond, stared at the floor between them. The thick silence came again, so Franklin changed the subject.

"How is Temple? He prepared to endure the lectures of his grandfather? It's my prerogative, you know, set him straight." Franklin tried to smile.

William looked at him coldly, his own expression still grim.

"You would do that? You would turn my son against me as well?"

"I only meant . . . school, life . . ."

"How dare you, Father. Is it not enough that you violate the law, violate the very spirit of everything I stand for? You would poison the mind of my son?"

Franklin was beginning to feel overwhelmed, the space between them widening, a gulf over which no reason could reach.

"I am capable of speaking to my grandson about more than politics."

William was still fuming.

"I insist you do not discuss your . . . other activities."

"For example?"

"Oh, Father, torment me! Must I describe everything you do? You have taken part in obliterating every legitimate principle of government. You have made mockery of the British constitution. . . ." He paused, seemed flustered. "If you have grievances, there are legitimate avenues for addressing them. We are all Englishmen. You should respect what that means. It grieves me no end to see how your people delight in destroying what history has created. It will only end with bloodshed, Father. Your petty tyrants, those whining jackals in Massachusetts, those rum-drinking cowards, could all end up at the point of the bayonet."

"That would include me as well. Though rum is not exactly to my taste."

"Father, can you not take me seriously?"

William had shouted the words, and Franklin saw the red-faced anger, his son growing emotional now. William arose, seemed to gather himself, paced slowly around the library.

Finally Franklin said, "If I have failed to take you seriously, it is because . . . perhaps you have failed to take yourself seriously as well. You have allowed yourself to be purchased, paid in full, by . . . all of this. Look around you, your grand house, your baubles. All that is required of you is that you bow to your king, nod obediently when he speaks, and accept as gospel truth anything that he or his people tell you."

"I am proud to serve my king."

"Oh, I am quite sure of that. You have spent so many years bowing to King George that it is the very definition of who you are. You are the royal governor. But that is all you are. Your own thoughts, your own beliefs, the words around you in all these books—none of that matters to you. You are merely the conduit through which flow King George's policies . . . and his abuses and his mistakes. You speak of seriousness? You have spent so many years belittling anything American that you are making the same mistake they are making in London. It is you who do not take *us* seriously. There are some in England who spout with great authority that this problem will simply be erased if your army performs just as it has. I heard it myself, too many times. Just kill them all. In General Gage's clumsy attempt to eradicate all disagreement, his soldiers have killed perhaps two hundred Americans. While you may delight in that mighty blow against your enemies, since this mess began, it is a good estimate that nearly sixty thousand children have been born in America. It is simply beyond you to comprehend, you and your king. You may be an Englishman. But I am not. Every child born here is born American, shaped by the great differences in this land, in the culture, the beliefs, in the way their parents have learned to survive and prosper. They are growing up in a world far beyond the understanding of your king and his government. Do you not comprehend the significance of that? Can you not grasp that America has *already* moved beyond the control of England, of its corruption and its petty concerns?"

William was on the far side of the room now, his temper cooled.

"Father, I will not debate you. However, I insist you do not speak of these things to Temple. You do not have the right to preach revolutionary doctrine to my son. You may condemn all I stand for, but I will not lose his respect because you have chosen to fall in with those who would only serve themselves by the destruction of the empire."

Franklin stared at his son, saw William avoiding his eyes, avoiding everything Franklin had said. So now you will not even hear me.

"The empire is destroying itself from within, William. Most in the congress have already accepted that. That's why there is so much work to be done. If your king does not accept the Olive Branch Petition for what it is, if he is so blind as to dismiss what we are asking of him, then . . . we are at the dawn. If there is to be a revolution, bloody or not, something must follow afterward. Whatever shape or form, whoever takes the helm, we will have learned from your mistakes. And we will not repeat them."

William sniffed.

"You sound as though independence of the colonies has already occurred. I have seen very little evidence that the king's army has given up their fight, or that any one of your cherished delegates has figured out how to convince three million people to agree to such a dangerous course. I don't see them outside my home. No one has come to New Jersey and started any great revolt against *me*."

Franklin did not respond, was exhausted now. He had not wanted this, had believed they could somehow move past the great abyss between them. He could hear voices now, from beyond the library, young, excited, knew it was his grandson, the boy's tumult filling the house. He could not look at William, understood now that with Deborah gone, Temple was their only link, the only reason they might ever have to meet. He glanced up, saw William averting his eyes, felt despair. I am not a father to this man; I have nothing to give him, no legacy that he will accept. He experienced a vast wave of sadness now, wanted to leave this house, fulfill the duty, carry Temple back to Philadelphia, be gone from this grand mansion with its grand loyalties to the king he had come to despise. Yes, there will be independence, and I will do everything left in my being to bring it about. And, my son, if I have to, I will fight *you*.

36. GAGE

HE REFUSED TO RIDE, WALKED UP THE LONG RISE IN THE SWELTER-
ing heat, followed by his staff. It was unusual for him to venture
out so far from his office, but there was very little to do, at least
very little he enjoyed doing. He had given himself the excuse of
going up to the Charlestown peninsula to inspect the works, to
see General Howe, to oversee the progress on strengthening
their lines.

He had not taken the route that would carry him first over
Breed's Hill, the remains of the rebel earthworks. Except for the
British officers, most of the dead of both sides had been buried
there, close to where they had fallen. He did not require the
reminder, did not feel any need to step over freshly dug graves.

Howe had stayed up on the peninsula since assuming command of that position, and it was not by accident that Gage's office had become a much quieter place. In the weeks after the
battle, the three major generals had begun to keep their distance
from him, the natural response when a military man knows his
commanding officer's days are numbered. Howe had been particularly grateful to be out of Boston, accepted the duty commanding the new fortifications on the peninsula they had "won."
Gage could see him now, sitting on a fine horse, self-consciously
directing the construction, Howe's orders booming, the voice
carrying down the hill. Of course he knew I was coming. So he
will make a good show of it, for my benefit. At least he is not like
Burgoyne. I can count on him to handle the job and keep his ambition to himself. But he knows, as they all know. Breed's Hill
was my disaster. And in London, no explanation matters. There
must always be one scapegoat, someone who must bear the

burden of blame. He knew Burgoyne had sent a letter to someone, was never one to exercise discretion, had stated his view that Gage was unfit for his present position. That will be publicized, certainly, received with absolute glee by some. More than one of those blind fools in the ministry are positively giddy about what happened on these hills. They have been so public, so noisy about condemning my weaknesses, my timidity, as though anyone else would have solved this crisis with such ease. Well, we were not timid here. And the price . . . was horrible.

He reached Howe, who looked at him with feigned surprise, and Gage anticipated the question.

"I thought I would walk, General. My horse is back there somewhere."

Howe dismounted, a courteous gesture, saluted Gage.

"Sir, we are nearly complete here. This position cannot be assailed with any hope of success."

Gage made a show of looking along the fat rows of cut trees, fence rails, mounds of dirt. All along the crest of Bunker Hill, gun pits had been dug, cannon placed, all pointing west, toward the narrow neck of the peninsula. Gage looked again at Howe, saw confidence, and Howe asked, "Would the commanding general care for a tour of the line, sir?"

"Thank you, no, General. I am confident your men have done exceptional work." The words were for the onlookers, the men who still held axes, shovels. Gage lowered his voice.

"Do you mind walking a bit, General?"

Howe was beside him now, followed his lead, and Gage moved back down the hill, could see out over the ruins of Charlestown, the harbor, the warships at anchor.

He saw more of Howe's men closer to the blackened streets of the town, more work, charred rails piling up. I wonder if he believes this is all truly necessary, if he, or anyone else, believes the rebels will fight to regain this land. The question faded from his mind. No, he will certainly protest, and I really don't care for a lecture right now, his declaration of how efficiently everything has gone, how important this place is.

He looked off to the east, toward Breed's Hill, then down toward Boston.

"We never should have fortified Boston. We never should have stayed here."

Howe said nothing, and Gage looked at him now, continued, "It was just one more monumental mistake. We send in troops when hostilities are guaranteed. We should have occupied this place years ago, when the first protests began. The people would have become used to the presence of the army, keeping the peace, good order. There would have been no mobs, no violence, no Sons of Liberty."

"Really, sir, I'm not certain the ministry would have seen the value of placing such a large force here for no good reason."

"Well, we have reason enough now, don't we? And yet Lord Dartmouth informs me not to expect any more reinforcements until after the winter. They are ignoring all I have asked for. Now they have a full-bellied crisis, and still they don't respond."

Howe seemed uncomfortable.

"Sir, forgive me, but I must say, I don't agree. My very presence here is evidence that the ministry takes quite seriously the problem facing us here. They have continued to send every available regiment."

"General Howe, even with the reinforcements we have just received, we can put less than four thousand troops in the field. Your garrison here requires a significant percentage of them."

"How can that be, sir? We have well over—"

"You should visit Boston sometime, General. The wounded are still occupying every available bed, every available space in every barracks. You put that many men together in that kind of situation, and one certainty is the spread of disease. We have as many men on sick call as we lost on that bloody damned hill."

Howe said nothing, and Gage regretted the outburst. I do not have to tell him about what happened there. He saw most of it firsthand. Gage looked back toward Breed's Hill, his eyes fixed for a long moment, could not escape the sadness.

"We will never recover from what happened here. Not the army, perhaps not England herself."

"Our success was dearly bought, sir. But it was a success. We must take consolation from that."

Gage did not feel consoled, thought of Pitcairn, carried off that hill to die in the arms of his own son. No, men do not forget days like that.

He had wanted to discuss a new strategy for several days now, had thought of calling a council, but he had no enthusiasm for listening to another debate from the generals. At least when I talk to them like this, alone, they keep their debate to themselves.

"General Howe, I believe we should begin making preparations to leave Boston, remove the army to a more useful position." He expected protest, a sputtering response to the perceived insult. Howe thought for a moment.

"I quite agree, sir. Despite the strength of our line here and in the city, this army can do no good here."

Gage was surprised.

"Thank you for agreeing with me, General. I have considered the alternatives, and I believe we should propose to Lord Dartmouth that once the adequate number of transports can be assembled, we transfer the bulk of our strength to New York. The loyalist population there is very strong; we are not likely to be regarded with such animosity there."

"There are a great many loyalists here as well, sir. We would hear quite a howl from their lot, I'm certain. I suppose we could transport them to New York as well, or perhaps Halifax, until the crisis plays out."

Gage stared across the strip of harbor toward Boston, felt a weary disgust.

"No matter what happens now, this town will always be a stain on the empire. We should burn the place. Every home, every shop, every last timber. Pull the army away from here and leave these people a wasteland."

HE HAD SAT ALONE IN THE SILENT OFFICE FOR A LONG WHILE, staring mostly at the letter on his desk. It had arrived from London, as so many had before, on gilded paper, carrying the official seal of Lord Dartmouth, presented with the flourish of the government courier, who enjoyed the responsibility. Gage had not yet broken the seal, but he knew what the letter said. He had been expecting the official response to his reports of the disaster on Breed's Hill, was only surprised that it had come so quickly. Well, of course, their minds were made up a while ago. Breed's Hill was simply the final indignity.

He had sent everyone out of his office, would allow himself the private moment to read the order, would not have to hide his response, keep up his decorum for his staff. He knew the sentiment in London, had begun to receive letters from friends, cautionary, sympathetic, telling him what he expected, that most of the powerful voices in London who supported him had diminished to near silence. After Lexington and Concord, there had been the typical race for the reporting of the events, and the rebels had won by nearly twelve days, London reading of the alleged barbarity of the British troops. But after the fight on the peninsula, there did not have to be subversion of the facts by the rebel interests, there had been no ridiculous contest to see whose version of the truth would have the most dramatic impact. No one could disguise that what had happened on Breed's Hill had been a stunning, disastrous loss for the British, both in men and in prestige. Reports had gone back to London from all the senior commanders, and only Burgoyne insisted on emphasizing the glory they had achieved, as though the capture of a great dirt pile could justify the loss of so many fine officers and such a large number of soldiers.

The mood in the taverns had changed a great deal after the awful fight on the two hills, and Gage had felt the attitude from even the junior officers, the men who had lost so many of their own, so many friends. They did not share the detached pomposity of official London. Their loss was personal, their emotions had soon changed to pure resentment, directed not at the rebels and their extraordinary courage, but at the man who had ordered the soldiers up that hill.

The results of that day had created one other change, and this one Gage shared with his men. No one had ever believed that the rebels would put up a fight at all, much less hold their ground in the face of so magnificent a display of English might. All the casual boasting from the generals and from the Tories still in

Boston was now hollow, ridiculous, and large numbers chose to forget that so many of them had joked about the certain flight of the cowardly band of farmers. Gage had been told of statements by rebel prisoners, some of them wounded, those who could not escape Howe's final advance. There was no bluster and no regret. To a man they spoke of only one thing, their lack of powder, running out of ammunition. Gage had visited the hospitals, had spoken to one man, his wounds wrapped by British bandages, the man sullen, defiant. He thought of the man's words now, spoken with cold intelligence: *Had we been supplied, we would still be up there.*

Gage had returned to his office, the words etched in his mind, and he knew even now that the man was right.

And now they have a commander.

He knew George Washington well from their service in the French and Indian War. There was a time when the two men could actually have considered themselves friends. He had shared the battlefield with Washington on the awful day General Braddock's command had been massacred. Gage could remember it all, Braddock's arrogant stupidity, marching without preparation into a land where the enemy had all the advantages, Braddock not believing the scouts, those who knew the land, who knew how the Indians fought. Braddock himself had been killed, along with most of his officers, and it was a lesson that Gage had always tried to remember. Now he remembered too well. George Washington had been a hero on that day, had proven he was more than a backwoods militia leader. The men who escaped with their lives owed more to Washington than to any of the regular British officers, Gage included. Now he is right up there in Cambridge, and if we believe he is just another rebel, if we make the mistake of dismissing him as another bumbling militia commander, we will suffer many more fights like Breed's Hill.

In the quiet time since that June day, he had done very little outside the office. Howe fully controlled the situation on Charlestown peninsula. Clinton had made it a point to stay close to the men and their fortifications around the edge of Boston itself. The defenses were very strong now, but when they came to him speaking of their good work, the pride in their strong defense, Gage knew that what they were really accomplishing was strengthening the siege lines of the rebels, holding themselves more tightly in their own prison.

The food situation had become critical, fresh meat and vegetables nearly nonexistent. Much of the town was surviving on salted fish. Gage had sent his transport ships far up the coast, some all the way to Halifax, in a desperate search for supplies, but success was minimal, and relief very slow to arrive. The health of the army, already assaulted by disease, was threatened even further by inadequate nutrition. If London insisted on hearing sound arguments why the army should leave Boston, he could give them plenty. Washington is too new to command, he will be prone to caution, but surely someone up there is yapping at him, telling him to attack, drive them out, all the mindless rhetoric of bad generals. Certainly Washington knows our situation here, and he won't make that kind of mistake. He knows he shouldn't assault us here, we're too strong. And if he's patient, he won't have to.

He had received word from one of his spies, describing a visit by Washington to the illegal Massachusetts Assembly. Washington had requested in most urgent terms the need for gunpowder and shot, had called on every man to put forth an effort to bring in whatever help could be found for the rebel supply. Gage had to respect the information, even if it contradicted a report from Gage's own command. He still had the report on his desk from an officer, out on Boston Neck, the man overhearing Washington's guards talking of their huge store of powder, some even taunting the British sentries to attack. Gage glanced at the report, wondered, How much does it matter? One of them is right. Either Mr. Washington has enough ammunition to withstand any assault we make, or they are so desperately without that we could march right through them. Either way, we will not find out. Not for a long while. There is no enthusiasm from anyone in this command to embark on another Breed's Hill. So we will simply sit here until Lord Dartmouth tells us what to do next.

He looked at Dartmouth's letter again. *Perhaps he has already.* He could not help a burst of nervousness, picked up the letter, slid his thumb under the wax. He read quickly, uttered a small laugh, the mystery gone, his own instincts right after all.

You are ordered to report to the ministry in London with all possible speed. . . . General Howe will assume command in your absence.

Boston Harbor, October 11, 1775

At first he had tried to keep some order, packing the large wooden crates carefully, cataloguing their contents, books and papers, personal artifacts. As his library emptied, he could not keep the emotion away, his careful precision dissolving into bouts of anger and sadness. When the stevedores came to haul the crates away, he could not watch them, could not even be in the house as the last bits of the legacy of his command were carried to the ship.

There had been a quiet ceremony, turning over command to Howe. The order from Dartmouth stated that Gage was to be in London so that he could assist in planning strategy for a new campaign the following year. The inference was that Gage's stay in England would only be temporary, and nothing in Dartmouth's letter hinted that Gage had been officially recalled. But to Gage, and to all of his subordinates, there was no illusion about his loss of command. The phrasing of Dartmouth's letter was an act of kindness, not reality. And no one in Boston, certainly not William Howe, had any expectation of seeing Gage in America again.

The ship had sailed after dark, and he did not stay up on deck, did not wave a farewell to the small official party on the wharf, did not watch as the lights of the harbor dropped away below the horizon. He sat alone in his stateroom, thought of Margaret, knew she was probably in London already, her ship having sailed a few weeks earlier, even before he had received Dartmouth's letter. She had finally accepted his pleading that she leave the dangers of

Boston for the safety of his family's home. In the end, she had given up the protest, seemed to suddenly lose her loyalty to her friends, did not spend much time with anyone outside their home, did not speak of anyone left behind. He was relieved by that, thought of her now. She will certainly know soon that I am coming. Perhaps she will see it as a new adventure, different from the last time; perhaps she will enjoy finding a new home for the family, the children.

He knew that what Dartmouth's letter had ordered was the work of great manipulation, his harsh critics kept at bay by the influence of his powerful friends. He had been allowed to leave Boston with dignity, might even be received that way in London. He thought of the king, wondered if it was His Majesty's hand who had given kindness to Dartmouth's letter. It could still happen, the reward for loyalty, the king's gratefulness resulting in some position of prestige, some final honor in a gracious retirement.

He was already restless, could not just sit in his stateroom feeling the soft roll of the ship. He went out, climbed the narrow stairway, stepped up into a breezy chill. There was a mass of stars, a crystalline moonless night, and he moved to the rail, heard only the rush of water beneath him. He wanted to walk back to the stern, see a last glimpse, a flicker of light on the shoreline, but he stayed where he was, thought, No, it is gone.

He tried to feel the hopefulness again, retirement, Margaret accepting what must be. Perhaps it will be a long life, growing old together with the kindness that comes from recognition, smiles from a grateful nation. It will hardly matter what the duty was, or how bad the crisis. I have been a good soldier. I did all they asked of me.

37. FRANKLIN

BY NOW, ALL OF NEW ENGLAND HAD LEARNED OF THE LATEST horror of this growing war. Two small gunships had been sent northward by Admiral Graves, had reached Falmouth on October 16. The townspeople were given warning, were allowed to gather what possessions they could carry, and two days later, the ships opened fire, sending hot shot into the heart of the town in a bombardment that lasted over six hours. What did not burn quickly was dealt with in a more direct manner: Over a hundred British marines landed in the town and set fire to any structure left standing. To Graves, who had ordered the destruction without the approval of William Howe, it must have seemed an appropriate response to his own frustrations about the British inactivity in Boston. To the citizens of Massachusetts, and to the commander of the Continental Army, it was another infuriating example of British high-handed barbarism, and one more reason why their forces had to be strengthened sufficiently to drive the British away.

FRANKLIN HAD GONE TO WASHINGTON'S HEADQUARTERS AS A REPresentative of the Continental Congress, but the visit was personal as well. The trip to New England would give him the opportunity to retrieve his sister, Jane Mecom, who had escaped Boston and graciously been given sanctuary by a friend in Warwick, Rhode Island. Franklin was as close to his sister as anyone had been in their family, had written nearly as many letters to her as he had to Deborah. Together they represented the last survivors of a large family, linked by the bond of the longevity not granted to their siblings. Franklin had not thought much of that

425

before, but Jane was a fatalist, and as they both grew older, her letters had become stern reminders to him that he had a responsibility to give thanks, that his age was not an achievement or a reward for a healthy life, but a gift from God.

Jane's life had been difficult at best, she was widowed, with a son of somewhat dull wits who had found no pathway he seemed capable of following and a daughter whose disagreeable nature had isolated her completely from her mother's attentions. Franklin had heard all of this, every detail. But from the time she had been torn away from her home in Boston by the threat of a war she still didn't understand, he had begun to read a new emotion in her words: fear. This aging, fragile woman had nothing left of her long life in the town that had given her so much comfort. And what was worse, besides her illustrious brother, she had no one she could depend on to care for her.

He had very mixed feelings about moving his sister into the house in Philadelphia. Sally barely knew her aunt, and Franklin knew enough of Jane's bullheadedness, so similar to his own, to appreciate how she might be quite a disruption to the routine of his daughter's young family. But he had to consider his own needs as well, had come to miss Mrs. Stevenson terribly, her company, as well as her caring hand, something he was loath to ask of his daughter. If Jane needed his support, his solidity, to dispel her own fears, he just might need her as well.

IT HAD BEEN TWELVE YEARS SINCE FRANKLIN HAD RIDDEN THROUGH New England, but it was not so new to him. He had spent his childhood in Boston, most of his family had lived and died there, and he understood perhaps better than most why there were so many differences in the congress between the cultures of New England and everywhere else. In Philadelphia, those differences still caused turmoil; no agreements had yet been reached on so many of the issues that might yet sink the colonies into submission to King George.

When his carriage finally rolled into Cambridge, he had been impressed, soldiers everywhere—and they looked more like soldiers now, some units actually in their own brand of uniform. He had seen all of the reports that reached the congress, Washington's own frustrations from his first days in command, the chaos and squalor, but the camps did not appear as Franklin had imagined. There was order, tents in neat rows, men in formation, whole companies at drill. It was not perfect, certainly; the sharp crispness of the British routines would never be in these men. But as his carriage moved farther through the camps, he could not help feeling something new, unexpected. He had always felt a pride in the work of the congress, that despite the turmoil and dissension, good work was being done, historic, monumental. Now, as he rode through what had become the Continental Army, he felt the same kind of pride, a confidence that for all the difficulties, for all the challenges, it was actually working.

His carriage was led to Washington's headquarters by an escort of men on horseback. He climbed out, loosening the stiffness in his legs, saw that the building itself was a residence, but he could not miss the distinct sign of military command: guards in uniform, standing at attention on either side of a tall wooden door. One man reached in efficient motion, pulled the door open, and Franklin climbed the short steps, hesitated a moment, examined the man's coat, brass buttons on blue wool. He said to the man, "Thank you, soldier," and now he moved into the entranceway, saw activity everywhere, more uniforms, quick motion, men with papers, some passing by him quickly. He was impressed again, was suddenly confronted by a short stub of a man in thick glasses.

"Dr. Franklin! Welcome, sir!"

"Mr. Gates . . . *General* Gates, yes, thank you."

Gates seemed to appreciate the correction, made a short bow.

"Doctor, the general is in a meeting, but I assure you, it will be brief. If I can get you anything . . ."

Franklin could not help watching the activity still passing by him, listening to the sounds emerging from offices down the long hallway. One door now opened, they heard loud voices, and Gates said, "Oh . . . it seems they have concluded."

Franklin watched the men fill the hallway, saw dogs now, two large black hounds rushing toward him, then past, out the door. Gates seemed flustered.

"My apologies, Doctor."

Franklin laughed.

"No matter, sir. Obviously General Lee is present."

Gates grunted, and now Franklin heard an extraordinary burst of swearing, recognized the face of Charles Lee, the man moving toward him, and Lee stopped short, stared at him for a long moment, his face finally breaking out into a broad grin.

"Well, well, a lost traveler. Tell me, Doctor, do you never tire of taking journeys?"

Franklin bowed. Lee's smile was contagious.

"The adventure is in the destination, sir."

"Well, Doctor, there's plenty of adventure around these parts. Have to admit, if the congress feels they have to stick their long noses into the business of this army, at least they sent someone too old to be horsewhipped. Good thinking." Lee laughed, though Gates seemed to shudder beside Franklin.'

" 'Scuse me, Doctor," said Lee, sauntering past. "Got to make a ride."

When Lee was gone, Gates seemed to relax.

"I apologize, sir. General Lee is somewhat . . . animated."

Franklin was still smiling.

"Don't concern yourself, General Gates. You need colorful characters to keep the place lively. I've always heard that a soldier's life is defined as organized boredom. General Lee is a remedy for that."

Gates sniffed, proceeded down the hallway.

"Please follow me, Doctor."

Franklin obeyed, and Gates led him to the open door, stepped aside, made way for Franklin to enter. He glanced at Gates, nodded, a silent thank-you, moved into the large room. He saw one desk, the large man filling the space behind, writing furiously. Franklin waited a moment, until Washington signed the paper with a flourish, sat back, and at last noticed Franklin.

"Oh! Forgive me, Doctor. I didn't know you had arrived."

Franklin bowed again.

"I am honored you can make the time for me, sir."

"Nonsense, Doctor. Please, sit down." Washington held up the paper, shouted, "Staff!"

A soldier appeared immediately, saluted without looking at Franklin, and Washington told him, "Deliver this to Mr. Foutz. If he protests, remind him that we are in continuous need of latrine duty. I will leave it to *him* to decide between the musket and the shovel."

The man took the order, was quickly out the door. Franklin was curious.

"A bit of discipline, General?"

"In a manner, Doctor. What you see around you is a combination of military business and domestic concerns. The president of the college has been gracious to allow me to live here, as well as conduct the affairs of the army from this office. He still maintains his residence here, as he is certainly entitled to do. He simply pulled himself and his own affairs into one small portion of the house."

"Gracious indeed."

"I have found, Doctor, that so-called lofty command doesn't eliminate mundane annoyance. I have two cooks here in the house. You may have caught the name of one of them, Mr. Foutz, for whom that order was intended, and to whom it is being delivered about now. I am not anyone's notion of finicky, Doctor. But Mr. Foutz fancies himself quite the expert in worldly cuisine."

"It is the *Continental* Army, General."

Washington smiled.

"Yes, well, if we fed this army in the same manner Mr. Foutz has attempted to feed me, there would be mass desertion. He actually set out an elaborate dinner whose main attraction was bugs. Covered in some kind of sauce, mind you, but bugs nonetheless. I made the decision at that moment that Mr. Foutz would better serve this army by shouldering a musket. Not all of my orders are popular, Doctor; however, I am certain the entire headquarters will applaud *that* one."

Franklin had not known what to expect from Washington, was surprised by the show of good humor. He saw Washington glance at another paper, his smile fading, and Franklin thought, I am interrupting him after all. There is a war to contend with.

"General, I do not wish to occupy any more of your time than is necessary."

"Nonsense, Doctor. I can think of no visitor I would rather receive. Is there any particular question I can answer, any guidance I can offer to satisfy your mission?"

Franklin glanced at the open door; Washington caught the look, said aloud, "Staff!"

A man appeared, saluted, and Washington said, "You may close the door."

"Sir."

The man was gone, the door closing softly, and Washington seemed self-conscious.

"I'm not abusive to them, I assure you. Horatio Gates performs that task with enough zeal for both of us. I can't complain, for he has trained an efficient group. They certainly have more to fear from him than from me." He paused, looked at Franklin with total seriousness, then asked, "What can I do for you, Doctor?"

Franklin moved the chair closer to Washington's desk, leaned forward, said in a low voice, "You may be aware of both topics . . . both pieces of information I bring you. In the event you are not, I thought I had best be discreet. Few things are certain these days. One topic is perhaps good news. The other is most certainly bad."

Washington seemed surprised by the show of intrigue.

"If it's all the same to you, I'd rather you start with the good."

"Yes, certainly. Are you aware that a committee of the congress, on which I serve, has been established to open contact with foreign authorities?"

"Yes. That's not such a terrible secret, Doctor."

"Are you aware that we have in fact been contacted by an agent representing the French government?"

Washington leaned back, wide-eyed.

"That I did not know."

"I thought not. The man's name is Bonvouloir. He approached the committee in the guise of a trader seeking a market, wanting to make some arrangement for selling arms and equipment for use by the Continental Army."

"Sounds as though you don't believe him."

"After much conversation, we have strong suspicions that he

comes to us more as an agent of the French court than for his own personal profit. Certainly the French have an interest in knowing our strength, our requirements, and in what capacity we are capable of confronting the British army. If he is selling arms at all, they are probably coming directly from official sources in France."

"What does the congress intend to do?"

"The whole of the congress is not entirely aware of Mr. Bonvouloir. Thus far, his dealings have been only with my committee. It would not be wise to bring this matter to open discussion. Word of this sort of . . . intrusion would become public very quickly. It could be interpreted in London as an act of aggression. With everything else we are confronting, a British war with France, with all the complications that could produce, is not in our best interests right now."

Washington leaned back in the chair, his hands clasped together under his chin. He stared at Franklin for a long moment.

"How are you handling Mr. Bonvouloir?"

"He has been informed of the necessity of silence. He didn't require much convincing, seemed in fact more comfortable with all the nuances of duplicity than we are—one reason to suspect him of being more than he represents. We are not yet willing to reveal to him those things he so urgently wishes to know. Your troop strength, for example. The inevitability of all-out war, for another. How eager we are for foreign assistance, and so on. Until events unfold with a bit more certainty, we shall remain . . . coy."

"The French would love to take possession of Canada again. They could be very useful to us if Canada was in our hands instead of the British. You have given me one more very good reason, Doctor, why our mission to Canada must succeed."

Franklin had never been confident of the military reasoning behind the army's first real tactical assault. It had begun in New York, under Schuyler's command, but Schuyler himself had been ill, had turned the mission over to the command of Richard Montgomery. Montgomery's mission was no less than an invasion of Canada, in the hope of capturing Montreal and Quebec and thus bringing Canada into the conflict against England as essentially a fourteenth colony. Even the more hesitant members of the congress had been convinced that if Canada lay untouched, the British army could certainly use it as a staging area to invade the colonies by way of the Hudson River Valley, a route that could conceivably cut New England off from the rest of the colonies, while putting Ticonderoga and Lake Champlain back in British hands. The colonial troops had begun their march in September. Montgomery had led twelve hundred men on the waterborne route, up the Hudson Valley, accompanied by Daniel Morgan's Virginia Rifles, and a second column had begun the march overland, commanded by one of the heroes of the capture of Ticonderoga, Benedict Arnold. Franklin had questioned the strategy of mobilizing so many troops away from the British force in Boston, as well as commencing the operation when winter was not so very far away. But Franklin was not a military strategist, and surprisingly, many in the congress had seemed so baffled by any discussion of military planning, and so ill-equipped to argue its merits, that the plan had been approved.

"Forgive me, General, but is it improper to ask what progress we have made on that account?"

Washington focused again.

"It's not improper at all, Doctor. It's simply too soon. Had General Schuyler been fit to lead the operation himself, they may have begun by midsummer. As it stands now, we might not hear anything for a while yet."

There was quiet concern in Washington's voice. Franklin said nothing, and the military man responded to his silence.

"You can say the word, Doctor. Winter. We must pray for the best. Now, you might as well tell me the bad news."

"General, are you aware that King George has gone about Europe hiring mercenary soldiers?"

Washington nodded slowly.

"I have heard rumors. We have a few foreign soldiers right here. They have been receiving letters, families in Prussia, other places. I wasn't sure how much to believe."

"You may believe it, General. The king has been successful in hiring as many as twenty thousand men. We don't know what he intends to do with them, of course. He may use them to occupy British posts all over his empire, to free up English soldiers to come here."

"That's too complicated, Doctor. It's dangerous for them to scatter foreign soldiers all over British outposts. Why risk inspiring some ambitious European to make those outposts his own? Twenty thousand? Are you certain, Doctor?"

"Not entirely. But it's a topic of public discussion in London."

"Like the public discussion of our vast supply of gunpowder."

Franklin was confused, and Washington saw the expression.

"It's not important, Doctor. But if this is true, if the mercenaries have been arranged, it will take time to organize them, ship them. My God . . . twenty thousand."

"The reports say they are primarily Hessians. The king attempted to hire Russians, but Empress Catherine refused. If it is of any consolation, General, it doesn't seem to be a popular policy in England either."

"So we can conclude that the congress' olive branch wasn't well received?"

"We haven't heard officially. We know the king was to address the Parliament, to open their autumn session. It is likely that he responded at that time."

"But Doctor, if he has hired twenty thousand Hessians to deal with the colonial problem, what can he possibly say that will matter?"

"There are people in the congress to whom it will matter a great deal, General. We shall find out soon enough."

FRANKLIN HAD ASKED THE DRIVER TO STOP THE CARRIAGE ON THE heights above Boston, had walked out among the soldiers who manned the defenses. He could clearly see the British troops below, on guard in their own lines at Boston Neck.

He stood quietly, tried to bring back the memories, his brother teaching him to print, his voracious appetite for reading, his expertise at swimming. It had been a long time since he had gone on a stroll through Boston Common, longer since he had taken his habitual extended swim along the banks of the Charles. Now the Common was thick with British troops, the flow of the Charles broken by the great men-of-war.

The memories were not as pleasant as he had hoped, erased quickly by the sight he could not escape, the men in red who lined the works that severed the town from the rest of the colony. The stay was brief, and he boarded the carriage again to the kind salutes of the soldiers, his name filtering through their ranks, a commotion from men who appreciated a visit from a man so famous.

The carriage would not delay now, the afternoon growing late. He would make the last part of the day's journey to a home just below Boston, an invitation to dinner with an old friend, Isaac Smith. He had not expected much in the way of social finery, had not considered sharing someone's table, the mood of the people close to Boston so attuned to the certainty of war. But the invitation had come to him even before he left Philadelphia, and the connection with its bearer had made the visit a pleasant necessity. The invitation had come from John Adams. Isaac Smith's niece was Adams' wife, Abigail.

HE ARRIVED TO A MODEST HOUSE DECORATED IN HIS HONOR BY ALL manner of ribbons, dried flowers, brightly colored candles in every window. The reception was kinder than he could have hoped for, and the smells told him the dinner was already prepared, the house filled with the extraordinary aroma of roasted meat.

The introductions had been made, Smith naming off the gathering of family, and Franklin had greeted each one with the same grace he had expressed so often. The family still gathered around their guest, and Franklin asked Smith, "Forgive me, but is your niece Abigail not here? I had thought she would be."

"Oh, quite, Ben, she's in the kitchen, with my wife. They won't be a moment, I assure you."

Franklin reached in his pocket, retrieved a letter.

"I've been given a rather important charge, you understand. I have a letter from her husband."

There were cheerful giggles, excitement from the gathering of younger ladies, and Smith said, "Well, in that case, perhaps we should see what is detaining them. Now you all just wait here. You all will have ample opportunity to charm our guest."

Franklin went with his friend toward the rear of the house, the smells of the dinner working on him, stirring a rumbling in his stomach. Smith preceded him, blocking his view of the kitchen.

"Now, you two need to put that aside," Smith insisted.

Franklin heard a voice, familiar, Smith's wife.

"Very soon. The heat's up. Can't stop just yet."

The words were direct, stern, and Smith conceded, "Well, all right. But our honored guest has an important matter to attend to."

Smith backed up now, allowed Franklin into the kitchen. He expected to see a great flurry of food preparation, bowls, trays and platters, but the two woman were standing at the stove with a hot fire between them, Smith's wife focused on the contents of a heavy iron pot. Franklin was prepared with a lighthearted greeting, but the words wouldn't come, and he thought, What in the world . . . ? That's not food.

The women were evidently hurrying, and the younger one removed thick cloth gloves from her hands, brushed at the mess of her hair, a smudge of gray on her face, said, "Oh, my. Dr. Franklin, please forgive me. We are certainly not prepared. . . ."

"It is not a problem, madam. You would certainly be Mrs. Adams?"

She smiled now, a short curtsy.

"Yes, I would be."

"Well, then, I am pleased to give you some indication of just how much influence your honorable husband has in Philadelphia. I have here a letter for you, from his hand. You might notice that it is being delivered not in the usual custom. While I may balk at the suggestion that the mails are somewhat inconsistent, in this case, by the enormous power of your husband's persuasion, the postmaster general himself has made this delivery personally."

He held the letter out to her, could see tears now, her hand shaking, and he was surprised.

"Oh, dear lady, I did not mean to tease. Forgive me. I certainly appreciate how serious an occasion it is to receive the letter of a loved one."

She smiled at him, held the letter close, and he felt embarrassed now. You and your grandiose pronouncements. He looked at the older woman, saw her stirring the large pot, concentrating carefully, her hands protected by the heavy gloves as well.

Abigail glanced back at her aunt.

"Are you ready?"

The older woman nodded, all seriousness, one quick glance at Franklin.

"Excuse me a moment, Doctor," Abigail said. She moved quickly, put the gloves back on, reached down into a wooden box on the floor, retrieved a small handful of pewter flatware, and handed it to her aunt, who lowered the spoons and forks slowly into the heavy kettle. Abigail looked at him, wiped again at the sweat on her brow, creating another dark smudge.

"Forgive me, Doctor. We'll be finished here in a short while. We'll not delay dinner. The food's already prepared."

Franklin was watching the older woman.

"She's melting the pewter. Mrs. Adams, forgive my curiosity. What are you doing?"

"Why, Doctor, we're assisting the army. We have been told that pewter works as well as lead. We're making musket balls."

38. ADAMS

PHILADELPHIA, NOVEMBER 1775

HE HAD SPENT THE EARLY MORNING WITH SAM, A QUIET BREAKfast. Then the messenger came, carrying the letter. The name on the paper was familiar, Hiram Jones, an acquaintance Adams had made years before in some obscure legal hearing up north, somewhere around Falmouth. The letters were common now, and he had become used to the sentiment, knew to expect some message of support, the good wishes of the people back home. More often lately, there was advice, opinions, the kindly meant prodding from people who could never understand the business of this congress, the frustrations that Adams was confronting daily. He had become almost numb to his feeling of helplessness, the endless sessions in the chamber, the fading optimism that each new dawn signified nothing new at all, beyond the changing numbers on the calendar.

His sense of despair came from the news in Braintree as well, an epidemic Abigail could only describe as dysentery. Her letters, and the devastating news, had pulled his mind away from the affairs of the congress. The illness had cast a dark shroud over the entire town of Braintree, and beyond, into the countryside. But worse for him, Abigail had written of the horrible effects on his own family as well. His brother Elihu had been one of the first victims of the epidemic, and soon after, Abigail had been suddenly devastated by the loss of her mother. When her letters included the terrifying news that their son Tommy was affected, he had considered withdrawing from the congress, returning home, tending to his first responsibility. Even a brief visit would serve some purpose—at least he could be there with them, offering some comfort, some relief from the extraordinary burden his wife was enduring. As he planned his resignation from the congress, he received another letter telling him that Tommy was greatly improved, had survived what so many of the others had not. It was Sam who had counseled him to stay in Philadelphia after all, that there was truly nothing he could accomplish by riding into an epidemic and possibly succumbing to the sickness himself. The deaths were a fact he could not change, and he had ultimately accepted Sam's logic, that he could do much more for the well-being of his family if he continued his work in the congress. Though he had returned to his work in the committees, enduring more of the endless talk in the chamber, the scare was a harsh reminder that there was a world beyond the affairs of politics. All the oratory had become a bit less meaningful.

He finished his breakfast, saw that Sam was still eating. This was something new, his cousin not assaulting the plate, rendering it clean in a few seconds, the man's ebullient personality reflected in the way he shoveled in his food. Sam was clearly more relaxed now, resigned perhaps that no amount of explosive anger would accomplish anything in Philadelphia. Adams watched him examining a piece of dried fruit. Sam took a bite, struggled, the fruit resisting him. He gave up, tossed it on his plate.

"Too green. They picked it too soon. Even preserved, it's inedible."

Adams looked at his own clean plate.

"I had no difficulty. I don't think I noticed what I ate. It doesn't seem to matter."

Sam looked at him for a long moment.

"You going to read your mail? I know that name, Hiram Jones. Kind fellow."

Adams examined the letter, finally opened it, read to himself, and suddenly his casual expectations were shattered.

"My God. The British have burned Falmouth. The navy . . . just like Charlestown." He handed the letter to Sam, who scanned it quickly.

"No explanation why. No reason. He says no one was killed."

"Thank God for that."

"But . . . why burn Falmouth? There was no threat there. Even the militia had probably all gone to Cambridge." Sam read the letter again. "We must be sure this is accurate. This will have great impact on the congress."

Adams was rather surprised at Sam's reaction, had become so used to the fiery outbursts, the explosions of cursing. But quiet calm was much more often Sam's way now, and Adams said, "I don't know how to react to this. I've been so angry at all of the British mindlessness, I don't even feel surprised. Of course they would burn an innocent town. What is so unusual about this? Should we not be expecting other letters just like this one?"

"Perhaps there is more to this than one additional outrage, yet another example of British barbarism. This could very well be the king's response to Mr. Dickinson's Olive Branch Petition. This attack did not come from some rogue ship. Mr. Jones mentions two naval gunships. This was planned, the orders coming from someone in authority."

"Sam, surely the king would not be so barbaric."

"I'm not at all certain of that. This news will certainly create a problem for Mr. Dickinson's people."

Adams stared at the letter again, felt as much confusion as anger. He had found it more and more difficult to tolerate the stubbornness of the conservatives. Dickinson himself had threatened to break his followers away from the congress, form a body of their own to address the differences with the crown. Whether Dickinson could actually succeed didn't really matter. The disruption to the business of the congress likely would have caused the entire process to collapse. Adams set the letter aside.

"This will do much to unite sentiment against the king, of that there is no doubt."

Sam smiled now, a strange reaction.

"You see? There is some good in every tragedy. I have learned a great lesson through all of this, cousin. Patience. If we feel we are confronting an abyss, just wait awhile, and sure enough, our enemies will build the bridge. From the beginning of this, for years now, every time I despaired at the people losing interest in their cause, every time I exhausted myself trying to inspire the people's hostility toward the king's oppressive policies, His Majesty has done something amazingly idiotic and solved my dilemma." He picked up the lump of dried fruit from his place, held it aloft. "You cannot harvest the crop while it is still green. You must allow it to ripen. This congress is still green, but that is changing. The people cannot be pushed into accepting independence from their beloved king, they must ripen to it. What I have had to learn is that if we exercise the proper amount of patience, the king, the ministry, the Parliament, any or all of them will provide the fertilizer. They are certainly qualified on that count."

There was a knock on the door.

"Mr. Adams? Are you available, sir?"

"You may enter, yes."

The door opened, and Adams rose, shook the hand of Richard Henry Lee, who said, "I have heard of some extraordinary news from Massachusetts. Are you aware the British navy has burned your town of Falmouth?"

Sam held up the letter, and Adams said, "We heard this morning. It may be that this is the answer to the Olive Branch Petition. How very appropriate for a despotic king to communicate with his subjects through the muzzle of his cannon."

"Then you have not heard?"

Adams glanced at Sam who stood now, said, "Heard what, Mr. Lee?"

"We have received the king's decree, his message to Parliament. It arrived last night on the packet. The delegates are being sought out now. There had not been much expectation of new business before the chamber today, but that has most definitely changed. We should be convening in a very short time."

"Have you read it?" Adams asked. "Do we know yet what it says? What of Mr. Dickinson? Surely he has been informed."

Lee laughed.

"I have not read it, John. It's under the royal seal. You can be sure your Mr. Hancock is impatiently waiting to begin the show himself."

THE SESSION WAS CALLED TO ORDER, AND ADAMS COULD FEEL THE mood of the chamber, very different, the delegates in muted conversation all around him. The king's opening address to Parliament was an old custom, and usually no one had much interest in its details, including, it was said, the king himself. But this time the difference was obvious: No matter the message, it was a break in the silence from London, and certainly there would be some response to the petition.

He searched for Dickinson now, saw a cluster of the conservatives grouped in a far corner, watched as Dickinson emerged from their huddle of conversation. The man moved slowly, seemed ghostly pale, and the others now gathered behind him, some spreading out, separating themselves from the man who had led them. Adams was painfully curious. Well, certainly he must know something. This seems to be a day of momentous news.

Hancock was at the rostrum now, quieted the delegates.

"We have received a letter from Mr. Penn, the distinguished gentleman in whose charge we placed the Olive Branch Petition. Mr. Penn declares with absolute certainty that he made numerous attempts to gain audience with the king and was not successful. He further states that he made a like number of attempts at presenting the petition through the hand of others, friends of the royal court who might be more successful in reaching His Majesty. In all cases, the message returned to Mr. Penn was that the king would not consider receiving any such petition. It is the chair's view that despite opposition from many in this congress to the sentiment contained in the Olive Branch Petition as authored by Mr. Dickinson, we can be certain that though our efforts did not succeed, no one in this chamber shall bear the curse of failure."

He paused, and Adams caught Hancock's glance, expected some sort of knowing smile, but Hancock was deadly serious.

"Mr. Penn's lack of success is not the conclusion to this woeful tale. Though the king did not consent to receive our petition, he can be said in any event to have given more than a silent response. The chair considers it entirely appropriate to relate to this congress the official address of His Majesty King George the Third upon the opening of the autumn session of his Parliament. The chair is of the belief that the king's statement will put to rest any doubt as to His Majesty's regard of our kind wishes, as this congress expressed to him in the Olive Branch Petition." Hancock gazed around the chamber, and the silence was absolute. He raised a coil of paper, made a show of removing a thick purple ribbon, unrolled it, held it up, read aloud.

" 'Whereas many of our subjects in diverse parts of our colonies and plantations in North America, misled by dangerous and ill-designing men, and forgetting the allegiance which they owe to the power that has protected and supported them; after various disorderly acts committed in disturbance of the public peace, to the obstruction of lawful commerce, and to the oppression of our loyal subjects carrying on the same; have at length proceeded to open an avowed rebellion, by arraying themselves in a hostile manner, to withstand the execution of the law, and traitorously preparing, ordering and levying war against us . . .' "

Adams could feel the air in the room drawn in, one great in-haled breath by the men around him. While Hancock read aloud, Adams looked straight at Dickinson, saw the man staring ahead in a look of deathly sadness.

" ' . . . all our officers, civil and military, are obliged to exert their utmost endeavors to suppress such rebellion, and to bring the traitors to justice.' "

Adams focused on Hancock, expecting still to hear something about the petition, some reference to Dickinson's effort to appeal to the king, whom Dickinson himself still so revered. But the flow of words suddenly stopped, the text complete, and Hancock read the closing: " 'Given at our court at St. James, the twenty-third day of August.' "

So that's it. That's all of it. There is no response to us at all. He looked again at Dickinson, the man's head bowed low, the room still holding to the cavernous silence.

Hancock said, "Does anyone wish to comment?"

All eyes were on Dickinson now, and the man did not look up. The discussions began again, and Adams felt a tap on his shoulder, saw it was Patrick Henry, who raised his hand.

"Mr. President, I care not to insult this proceeding with the most obvious of observations, but I must make mention . . . the king has decreed that the American colonies exist in a state of rebellion, which will be suppressed by any means available. We are already aware that His Majesty has sought out and procured the services of mercenary soldiers. We are already aware that His Majesty's navy has shown no hesitation in bringing a destructive fire to American towns. These events do not signify the conclusion to our present state of crisis. They signify only the beginning. Despite anyone's allegiance, despite anyone's optimism, anyone's loyalty to either a king or a cause, to an empire or a colony, to God or to man, you must not fail to understand what King George has decreed. We can no longer hold ourselves to be protected by British law. We are no longer governed by British constitutions or British edicts. We have been severed from the empire by the king's own hand, and by the king's own hand, this congress has come to represent a people united, who abide now only in a state of nature."

Henry was through, and others now jumped into the fray, most expressing outrage at the king's extraordinary leap into a declaration of outright hostilities toward the colonies. Adams still watched Dickinson. Well, then, what would you have us do now? The man began to look around the chamber, and Adams could see his eyes, gazing absently, curiously, as though seeing the great hall for the first time. Dickinson looked directly at him now, the man's expression blank, vacant, and Adams wanted to respond with a look of defiance, even some shameless gloating: You fool, now where is your loyalty? Are you still so eager to grovel at the feet of your king? But there was no victory here, and Adams could see Dickinson now as a man who has had his heart ripped away, his loyalty punished, his life thoroughly altered in one terrible moment. Dickinson still looked at him, but there was no recognition, the man's mind far off in some private hell, and Adams felt his defiance slipping away, suddenly felt pity for the man. Dickinson believed it, believed with a passion that his king is a good man, that loyalty is rewarded. And no matter what he has tried to do, no matter how much valiant effort he has put into blocking this congress from its opposition, his king has not only ignored him, he has condemned him.

BRAINTREE, CHRISTMAS 1775

NO MATTER ON WHICH SIDE OF THE DEBATES THE DELEGATES HAD aligned themselves, to a man there was great apprehension for the new year. So much was still to be decided, in Philadelphia and in London, in Cambridge and in Boston. The king's decree had laid open a course that both frightened and excited, the loyalists not quite believing that the king would ignore their vulnerability, the radicals understanding that no matter how much fascinating philosophical truth might lie in Patrick Henry's description of their state of nature, without cohesion, without some hard thread to hold the colonies together, there would only be anarchy. And colonies in chaos would prove to be an easy conquest for the king's troops.

Many of the delegates had conceded that little would happen until the new year, and many had agreed that Christmas was best spent with family. They all had the need, a long slow breath, a quiet time away from the turmoil. The new year would come soon enough.

Adams was astounded to learn that he had been appointed chief justice of the Massachusetts Supreme Court, the assembly choosing the one man who not only was qualified, but would most certainly not be vulnerable to the threat of being tarred and feathered by the Sons of Liberty. At any other time, he would have accepted the honor as an extraordinary gift, the pinnacle of all his ambition. But as grateful as he was for the appointment, he felt the new responsibility was as much a burden as an honor. The assembly accepted his apology with complete understanding; the duties of the high court would have to wait, at least for a while. No matter what legal issues filled the dockets of the newly organized court, his priority was still Philadelphia, confronting the great void of government he feared for the colonies. Beyond all the debate, the specific duties of the committees, Ben Franklin's careful communication with the foreigners, the committees for subsistence and funding for the army, one question had never been truly addressed. It had caused him more sleepless nights than any harsh words from John Dickinson or threats from King George. If there was to be a full-scale war against the king's army, a revolution that might ultimately sweep away all forms of English rule and law, no one had yet come up with what would follow. No one had designed an acceptable plan for how the Americans would govern themselves.

THE HOUSE HAD BEEN A MOB SCENE, ABIGAIL COMMANDING THE preparation of a great Christmas feast. It was far more than a family event, more than a dinner for the boarders in their home. Abigail had combined her energy with the other women in the town, the food brought out from root cellars and pantries and cupboards, the neighboring farms contributing whatever could be spared. It was a show of religious spirit beyond the usual celebration of the season, a thank-you for blessed relief from the dysentery epidemic, glad tidings for the safety of those who had fled Boston. Abigail would turn no one away, not even the militia troops, whose nearby camp continued to swell with the men who had responded to the call to join General Washington's army.

With the darkness the house emptied, grateful guests returning to their homes, some simply climbing the stairs to their rooms under the Adamses' roof.

It was very late, and the house was quiet, the children long asleep, their guests in their rooms. He was in the kitchen, by himself, working a mortar and pestle, grinding a handful of small dark beans into coarse powder. He was not very good at kitchen implements, and more of the powder found the floor than stayed in the mortar. He put his finger in the bowl, testing the consistency of the powder, and her voice was behind him now, playfully stern.

"You are messing up my clean kitchen. What in the world are you doing?"

He held out the small stone bowl, showed her the dark powder.

"Coffee. I thought I would try to make it myself. I've seen it done. Why are you not asleep? I thought you were exhausted."

"I'm too tired to sleep. I wish we had some wine left. It appears they drank it all. And besides, I find little comfort anymore in retiring to an empty bed." She tried to hide a smile, took the bowl from him, reached up in the cupboard, retrieved a small cloth bag, poured more beans into the bowl. "Allow me, Chief Justice Adams. I've become quite good at this, actually. Our guests have come to enjoy it."

He handed her the pestle, watched her crush the beans with quick efficient motion, and now she looked past him to the stove.

"Where's the kettle? Didn't you heat the water?"

"Uh, I was going to do that next."

"Husband, if you begin heating the water first, it will be ready when you finish grinding the beans."

He felt foolish now, utterly out of place.

"I should know better than to attempt those jobs for which I am not qualified."

She looked down at the floor around his feet.

"Well, I know of one job for which you are well qualified. While I finish making the coffee, you can sweep up your mess."

THEY SAT IN FRONT OF THE FIRE, AND HE SIPPED AT THE STEAMING cup, his face curling with the bitterness. She was watching him.

"You don't like my coffee?"

"It's not your coffee. I'm still getting used to the taste. Some of the delegates positively gulp the stuff. I thought at first they were being patriotic, overly enthusiastic in their distaste for tea. But it has become the style, certainly in Philadelphia, served at every tavern, every dining room. I find I'm still undergoing a . . . weaning process. I don't miss the tea. I'm just not yet accustomed to the coffee."

She laughed softly.

"I have thought that if we had been weaned away from tea a long time ago, we might have saved ourselves a lot of trouble."

He chuckled at her joke, but soon grew serious.

"Your life has changed a great deal. I regret that I am not here to assume the burden."

"I have missed you terribly, John. But I have managed. If my life has changed, it is a positive thing. The people I have met, the visitors . . . I shared a marvelous dinner with Dr. Franklin. I received a visit from General Washington on one of his inspections. I have never been so surprised. I had become used to soldiers marching here and there, but I never expected to have this enormous man and his huge entourage suddenly filling our yard. Completely frightened the children, except for John Quincy, of course. He was ready to march off with them."

"We are fortunate that General Washington accepted the responsibility for organizing the army. There might never have been an army at all without his experience."

"I believe it's more than that, John. You wrote me of your favorable impression of him, but I was quite struck, not just by the soldier, but by the man . . . dignity with ease, such confidence and modesty. I was as concerned as many around here. I heard all the talk: a Virginia gentlemen, a slaveholder, no less. What can he know of our problems? But I saw it in him, the soldier *and* the gentlemen, an agreeable blend. Now, on the other hand, his General Lee . . ."

Adams laughed.

"Yes, Charles Lee. I would describe him as the absolute contrast to George Washington. Did he bring his dogs?"

"It seemed more as though they brought him. There were such differences between the two men, but similarities as well. When I first saw General Lee, looking all of the uncouth frontiersman, I did not expect eloquence in his words. He quite surprised me." She sipped from her cup, stared at the fire. "John, I never expected that I would be called upon to learn so much. It is as though the entire world has suddenly passed by this place, offering me lessons I never dreamed of. General Washington would approve, I think. I find that I have risen to my own command right here. I have become quite comfortable instructing the men to do their jobs. It is a relief to me that some of them can do my own work nearly as well as I can."

Her words dug at him, the reminder that he had left his own duties behind. He said, "It should not be like this, not at all. When Tommy was ill, I prayed that you would set everything else aside, tend only to my son. It is a mother's love that cures when nothing else will. You should not be devoting so much of yourself to those things best left to men."

She made a small sound, looked away from him now, stared into the fire, and he drank the last of his coffee, set the cup aside, waited for a long moment, then said, "I find myself sleeping less and thinking more. I am very afraid that the congress will allow this crisis to so consume our attention, we will not be prepared for the consequences of independence from England. There must be structure, there must be organization, not just for one colony, but for the union of all thirteen colonies, for the people."

"Well, being that a *man* is doing so much thinking on the subject, I'm sure only the best and most wise solutions will follow."

He was surprised by the edge in her voice, and she looked at him now, the firelight reflecting on a stern glare.

"Husband, I have been doing some thinking on the subject as well. Does that surprise you? I have had some time to myself, you know. The dysentery did not entirely ignore me. I carried my own share of this illness. I did devote as much time as my churning stomach would allow to caring for your son. Regrettably, with my mother's passing, I had only myself to care for me. I do not complain, however, lest you think I am out of my place."

He wanted to answer her, but the heat in her words held him silent.

"I am greatly curious just what all is being fashioned by your congress for the benefit of the rest of us. I am as curious as you are what form of government you create. Will it be decided by each colony's assembly? Will the congress offer a plan that applies to all colonies, or only those who allow it? What if six colonies form a union, and the other seven do not? I am more and more convinced that man is a dangerous creature, and that when given power, even the most noble find the temptation to grasp for a bit more than his share. The greatest fish swallow up the small. If there is dissension among your ranks, will the strongest simply ignore the weak? Or conquer him? And may I ask, husband, when you speak of the *people*, just whom are you referring to? In your new code of laws, can it be hoped that you will perhaps remember the ladies? Can it be within your male spirit to allow some authority to flow our way? Or are you to be as ungenerous to our gender as your ancestors? You certainly must know that all men have shown their first tendency is to tyranny. You who are brought to so much agitation by your own lack of *representation* . . . consider that there are a large number of us who might yet feel the same."

She was staring at him, and he could see she expected an answer.

"Um, well, we are recommending that each colony form its own government, such as the elected assembly here. We have considered that the election of men to their assemblies, whether in each colony or in the Continental Congress, should originate in an electorate composed of men of property. I am concerned that we not allow the mob to exercise control over this process. Power follows property, and too many men might allow themselves to be influenced by those men of the greatest wealth. By allowing anyone who owns land to vote, and by ensuring that anyone of even modest means may own land, the electorate will be brought level." He paused, and her stare did not change. "We must not discard our systems with whim. Man is, after all, not the master, but the subject of a higher law that governs us all. . . ."

She began to laugh, a small giggle at first, her hand covering her mouth. Then the sound rolled out, and he was suddenly anxious she would awaken the rest of the house. She tried to speak, but her laughter blocked the words, and she leaned back in the chair, slowly regained control, bringing out her handkerchief, wiping her eyes. He was completely baffled by her reaction.

"Oh, my dear husband. All those fancy words, and they may as well fall in a jumble over a cliff. All right, so we must be tolerant while you who are so wise decide our future course. But I must ask, does your congress presume that we are in the midst of a revolution?"

"I am certain that many of us feel that. There will still be debate, of course, some still believing that we must only succumb to whatever the king requires of us and all will be set right."

"Well, my husband, to the people around here, those who have been allowed to escape Boston with their lives left behind them, those whose homes were burned to the ground in Charlestown, there is no debate at all. There are a great number of people who have nothing in their lives but the passion to fight for your cause, who are sleeping in tents around Cambridge because they are inspired by General Washington. And if those men win this war, if your cause succeeds, then you will say to them, 'Well, then, in our *new* government, all the power shall be held tightly in the hands of *men* of *property*, that only *men* of *property* can decide what is best for everyone else.' If you attempt that, my dear husband, you will soon find there to be a second revolution. And it will have nothing to do with the king."

JANUARY 1776

HE HAD LOADED THE CARRIAGE, SAID HIS GOOD-BYES TO THE children. He was anxious to return to Philadelphia, but he could not escape the pain of leaving his family yet again. He climbed up on the carriage, a vantage point, gazed up the long hill beyond the houses, a fresh blanket of snow covering everything, the rock piles just white mounds, the trees in the orchard bowed by the weight. He saw something moving beyond the yard, could see a thick furry tail tipped in white, a red fox stalking slowly through the snow, stopping, listening for sounds of some creature close by. He thought of calling his son, knew that John Quincy would enjoy watching the drama play out, but he stayed quiet. He will have plenty of time to enjoy this. Perhaps one day I can enjoy it with him.

Behind him in the road, another carriage rolled by, the sound muffled by the snow. He heard his name, turned, saw a familiar face, a neighbor, wishing him well. He waved absently as the carriage passed, but said nothing. He looked for the fox again, saw it standing frozen, staring back at him. Now it began to run, bounding through the snow, disappearing into the orchard. He climbed down from the carriage, the snow crunching beneath his feet, and he moved toward the house, saw the door opening, saw her standing in the doorway, holding a bundle wrapped in red cloth. She looked down at the snow.

"Here. I don't have my proper shoes. I made you some muffins, and there's a jug of cider. I used up the last of those apples. We lost so many, it was truly a shame. Just rotted from the rain."

She seemed to run out of words, and he took the bundle from her hands, could see she was crying. She scolded herself in a low voice, "I will not do this. I don't want you to remember my face with red eyes."

He wiped at her cheeks gently with one finger of his gloved

hands, said, "I will return quickly this time. I am certain of it. My duties are here."

"Don't lie, John. You will come home when it's time to come home, and not before. There are more people requiring your presence than just your wife, or even the Supreme Court."

He looked down at the bundle in his hands.

"I am . . . hopeful. We may be running out of time, but I have confidence in those men. We are fortunate to have so many—Dr. Franklin, Mr. Henry, Mr. Lee. We will find a solution."

"I believe you will, John. Take strength from the prayers that will follow you there. Everything you do, every decision, every act, every law, will reflect on the people you represent. Do not forget that out here, in this little place, we may only know the truth of what is happening by your letters. I so treasure hearing from you."

He hugged her, could not speak, moved quickly to the carriage, climbed up. He looked back toward the doorway, saw her small wave, her smile, and then she backed into the house, and closed the door.

HE HAD GONE BY WAY OF CAMBRIDGE, WOULD PASS THROUGH THE camps of the soldiers, picking up the well-traveled route southward. The small carriage was traded for a better ride, and he was provided a driver, a team of two. All along the journey his mind worked, and he would make notes, details, small essays to himself on the principles he was trying to adapt to the situation at hand, to understand them himself before he could expect anyone else to understand. At night, he would be entertained by some local official, or even by the soldiers themselves, camps of militia everywhere he stopped. But then would come the dark silence of another sleepless night, and the notes and details would flow back through his mind. He began to feel a strange fear, his confidence giving way to doubt that no matter what wisdom emerged from the congress, no matter what solutions a handful of men could devise, none of it mattered if the king buried them in the deluge of war. And if it was not the British, it would be the people themselves, their amazing differences, the culture of the

Carolinas forced to compromise with the culture of New England. But much of that was just geography, and this was about so much more than land and boundaries. That frightened him the most, that perhaps John Dickinson was right, that most people had no taste for independence, that most people cared not a whit about anything the congress would decide. How many people, in the privacy of their own homes, so far from anyone else's crisis, families whose greatest concern is their own well-being, how many of them wish only that the king would sweep all of this away, all this talk of rebellion and congress and fights over tea? How many have already begun to respond to the king's decree with sorrow and regret, forgetting the abuses, the policies that brought it all about? How many have forgotten that what brought the colonies together in the first place was British arrogance and bloodshed? How many will close their doors and their minds to the greater needs of the colonies, will disregard the death of strangers and destruction of towns far from their own worlds? If we cannot keep the people attentive, if we cannot show them that they must stand united, then nothing we do in the congress will count at all. There cannot be a revolution if the people choose not to fight. There cannot be independence if, above all else, the people still love their king.

He had reached New York, another dinner, and now another quiet night. When he arrived that afternoon, his host had handed him a pamphlet, something new, sold on street corners, circulating with a hum of fresh excitement. He had regarded it with mild curiosity, put it away for later, and now, in the low lamplight of his room, he recalled it, pulled it from his bag. Perhaps it will help me sleep, a little reading to distract my mind. He held it up, saw the title, thought, Odd, rather quick to the point, and no author's name. Well, with all the attention this seems to be attracting, someone will admit to it sooner or later. He opened the cover, read the title again: *Common Sense*.

39. FRANKLIN

THE COMMITTEE HE CHAIRED WAS TO MEET THAT MORNING. IT OF-fered another opportunity for the Frenchman Bonvouloir to make some genuine connection to the colonial heartbeat. He had begun to dread these meetings, knew the routine, the Frenchman professing his innocent neutrality, then immediately launching into a grand speech about the terrible injustices of King George and the divine right of the colonists to be properly armed. The sentiment throughout the Continental Congress was that an alliance with a foreign power might be the only means for a colonial army to have any success against British might. Despite the double-talk coming from Bonvouloir, if the man was indeed a direct conduit into the court of the French king, even if an annoying one, Franklin knew that he should be kept close at hand.

The dangers of foreign intervention on their behalf were obvious. Every major colonial power on earth would prize what America had to offer. The Spanish already had possession of the southern half of the continent and would certainly welcome an opportunity to extend their influence north from Florida and Mexico. The French influence was still felt in the western wilderness, along the Ohio River, with both the Indians and the white traders. Some in the congress were advising extreme caution in allowing the French to gain a political foothold in the colonies, which might reinvigorate the power in the west that they had lost in the war thirteen years earlier. Franklin recognized as well that the main passion igniting what King George had now labeled a rebellion was a spirit of independence, something that had been nurtured by the culture of the colonies themselves. By inviting an alliance with a foreign power, there was danger that the very strengths of that alliance might lead to a new and even more loathsome dependence that no one in the colonies would accept.

The sessions in the congress had become much more businesslike again, as they had toward the end of the previous summer. Dickinson's influence had declined dramatically, and thus so had the debates. Franklin had grown disgusted with the stubborn allegiances of the Tories, both in the congress and elsewhere. Even if Dickinson had been shamed into silence by the king's condemnation, other voices throughout the colonies still declared that independence was no option, that the crisis was still only a family quarrel that could be settled by a colonial apology.

HE HAD BEEN FORCED INTO A COMPROMISE. THOUGH HE STILL ENjoyed filling his room with the refreshing chill of the January air, he no longer did it unclothed. What Mrs. Stevenson could not do, Sally could. He had only heard the lecture once, all the stern fierceness of her mother easily in evidence. There would be no nudity, not while his grandchildren were in the house. He was irked by her stubbornness, gazed out into the street, felt encumbered by the robe, stifled, as though his very body could not breathe.

He had reached his seventieth birthday, an extraordinary milestone, but his notions of celebration had changed a great deal. He still attempted the morning walks, even in the harshness of the Pennsylvania winter, but the chronic suffering in his knees was a handicap he could not escape. And though the invitations still came from the society matrons around Philadelphia, more often now he sent his regrets. He knew they would have expected him to be jovial, to hold court with his stories, to display his charm. And there was a reward for those efforts—the company of young women could make for a pleasant evening of dance and liquid refreshment. Now dancing was out of the question, and he had discovered that his capacity for port had diminished as well. One well-filled glass would no longer liven the party—now it just sent him to bed.

Sally had compromised, gave in to his insistence that the windows be kept open, though he accepted that when frost covered the carriages, the only open window was his own. But open it would stay, and as he watched the city beneath him come alive, he rubbed his nose, flexed his fingers, the bracing cold bringing him wide awake.

He had thought of writing Strahan, actually missed the old Tory. There had been hostility in the letters between them, arising from politics, of course, and Franklin had begun to concede that the anger came primarily from his side of the Atlantic. His son had been right on that count, that Strahan was a true friend, and even if Franklin poured out his frustrations about the amazing corrupt idiocy that infested London, Strahan was still responding with kind eloquence. He had actually thought of testing Strahan's stomach for venom, had written an extraordinarily hostile letter: *You have begun to burn our towns and murder our people. Look upon your hands! They are stained with the blood of your relations. You and I were long friends. You are now my enemy, and I am . . . yours.*

He had pushed the anger out onto the paper with a rare glee, striking out with his most dangerous weapon, his pen. The satisfaction had been overwhelming, but once his zeal had cooled, he had to accept that even if Strahan was a member of Parliament, he was not truly at fault, could not be held responsible for the astoundingly thick skulls that populated the British hierarchy. He had not sent the letter, had recalled his old analogy about the traveler in the fog who sees everything close to him with perfect clarity but cannot see anything beyond, and so wanders without knowing where he goes. If that describes Will Strahan, Franklin thought, he will suffer the consequences, as will they all.

He had actually been pleased that their path of communication had not been broken, Strahan seemingly willing to impart his version of news. His friend had provided Franklin with the first notice that Lord Dartmouth had been replaced as the secretary for colonial affairs. Strahan had been surprisingly candid, apparently unfearing of any government censor, relating how the king had not been satisfied with Dartmouth's handling of affairs, word circulating in London that the king would have preferred a more vigorous burning of cities.

Franklin was familiar with George Sackville, referred to now as Lord Germain. The readily accepted story in London was that Sackville had made himself somewhat indispensable to a Lady Germain, a woman of wealth and title, who possessed very little in terms of either taste or judgment, especially in her choice of men. Sackville had served in France during the war, and his performance had inspired the king's predecessor, George II, to declare him unfit to serve in any military capacity whatsoever, stopping just short of ordering Sackville to be shot for cowardice. Strahan had been careful on this point, and Franklin could read between Strahan's words, still wondered if perhaps Sackville's reputation had escaped the king's attention because of confusion about his new name. Despite the harsh teasing that London was apparently enjoying behind Sackville's back, Franklin did not have any illusions about how this man had come to power; certainly he had convinced the king that he would pursue a much more aggressive posture toward the colonial rebellion. Given the mood in London these days, Franklin reflected, it's surely the most effective way to secure a position.

He had not yet had breakfast, began to think of the time, the difficulty of the walk to the State House. He reached for his watch on the desk, nearly eight o'clock, one hour before his committee meeting. He stood now, stretched his back, raised his arms high, tried to ease the stiffness, felt the icy cold on his body, realized his robe was open. Outside, he could hear a squeal, and he saw the horror on the woman's face, one of his neighbors.

"Morning, madam."

He turned away, could not help a laugh, felt like an evil child getting away with some misdeed. He began to dress now, could hear the rest of the house coming alive, the voice of his daughter, the children up and about. Even his son-in-law seemed to accept willingly that Sally was the authority in the house, and Franklin heard her recite a sharp order, something about shoes. He reached for his own shoes, groaned through the motions of securing the buckles, the ache in his back unforgiving. I had best show myself at her table, or there will be no breakfast. I wish I could train her to provide breakfast up here. I was entirely spoiled by Mrs. Stevenson. Now I will be scolded if I am late at *her* table. How strange that a parent can grow so old that he becomes the child again.

THE LETTER WAS DELIVERED TO HIM AT THE STATE HOUSE, THE source a pleasant surprise. He unsealed it now, saw the familiar crest, adopted by the man still known as Lord Chatham. He had wondered about the old man's health, reminded himself again that Chatham was younger than he was. The letter was long and newsy, and Franklin could read past the pleasantries to Chatham's awareness that his time was truly past.

Many of the Whigs are so intent on preserving their fox-hunting rituals that they have abandoned all concerns of the government. We are a dying breed, those who dare now to oppose the policies of the crown. Mr. Burke and Mr. Barré squabble with each other, as they squabble with me. We have forgotten our purpose. And the king's ministers are only too happy to assist us in that regard. It is feared that the opposition to the king's course has become quite toothless. There is little the colonies can draw from England on their behalf. The king has prevailed. God help us all.

He was not too surprised by Chatham's message. Almost nothing had been heard out of London in response to King George's decree, and if there had been any official opposition in Parliament, it was muted by the overwhelming support the king had received. It is logical, of course; the king would embark on such a dangerous and risky course only if he knew already that his own government would not be too vocal in its opposition. He must have unity if he is going to expend the resources required to crush a rebellion. The English people are behind him, certainly, the merchants already lusting over the profits to be made from a war. With his opposition silenced, he can conduct his military plans however he pleases, mercenaries and all.

He was still alone in the committee room, could hear the other delegates arriving in the larger chamber. He thought of Adams now, wondered if the lawyer had yet returned from his temporary absence. *God help us if he changes his mind and stays home. It might be better for him, but it might well condemn this congress to uselessness.* He had begun to pay close attention to Adams' thoughts on the creation of a government, had come to appreciate the man's sense of detail. He enjoyed the orations of the Virginians, particularly the fire that exploded with such entertaining perfection from Patrick Henry. But he could not agree with Henry's idealism, his suggestion that the colonies would do well to follow the natural order, allow the hand of God to open the pathways, government by nature. *That works in an ant colony or a beehive. God has given man the ability and the intellect to create his own government, his own order. And I believe that God has provided us John Adams to show us how to make it work.*

He saw the massive figure of Benjamin Harrison, a round, fleshy Virginian. Harrison flowed into the room, greeted him as he always did, with a rousing salute.

"Doctor! We have survived another night!"

Franklin enjoyed Harrison's joviality as much as he appreciated the man's staunch support of rebellion. Harrison lowered himself heavily into a chair.

"I don't recall when I've felt so energized, Doctor!"

"It's the air, sir. I don't believe I ever had enough appreciation for the air in Philadelphia until I breathed a decade of soot in London."

"Could be the air. Could be what's *in* the air."

Franklin was confused, knew Harrison would offer some burst of explanation, saw another figure at the door, the young aristocrat from New York, John Jay. Jay seemed hesitant.

"Good morning, gentlemen. I fear I have interrupted."

Harrison bellowed, "Nonsense! Take a seat, young man. Dr. Franklin and I were merely commenting on the weather. He prefers the chill of the air. I, on the other hand, prefer the capacity of the air to bear good tidings."

Jay nodded.

"Yes, I understand. Well put, sir."

Franklin retorted, "Well, I don't understand at all. Is it an old man's failing mind, or is there something I have missed?"

Harrison explained, "Why, Doctor, surely you have read *Common Sense*."

"Yes, certainly. I have met with Mr. Paine in London, and again when I arrived here. I knew he had intended to make some written observation on the state of affairs, and he was gracious enough to deliver to me the first copy. I admit to being surprised by its reception. You can't help but read it. The pamphlet is everywhere you look. I only wish my presses had printed it. But . . . what does this have to do with air?"

Harrison laughed.

"Doctor, Mr. Paine's pamphlet is likely being read in every town in every colony. I have heard from Virginia that people are reading it aloud in public squares."

Jay added, "Yes, New York as well. Here, certainly. Thomas Paine has accomplished what this congress has either neglected or avoided. His words have reached, even embraced, the great mass of citizens. You are aware, gentlemen, that I have been hesitant to go so far as you in your fervor toward a break with England. I find that Mr. Paine has persuaded me that such a break is not only wise, it is inevitable. I must admit as well that this view is reinforced by the letters I am receiving from New York. It seems that a good many of the Tories are changing their, um, spots."

Franklin was surprised.

"I thought Mr. Paine did an admirable job, but I admit to having no idea—"

Two more men came into the small room, the rest of the committee, the quiet Marylander, Thomas Johnson, and John Dickinson. The room fell quiet, the unavoidable response to Dickinson now. There were subdued greetings. Finally Harrison broke the somber atmosphere.

"Tell me, Mr. Dickinson, have you read *Common Sense*? We were just discussing its amazing influence."

Dickinson shook his head slowly.

"Sorry, no. I suppose I should."

Franklin couldn't help feeling uneasy now around Dickinson. "When you have time, perhaps," he said. "I suppose we should get down to business. Mr. Bonvouloir has requested another meeting, to be held tonight—"

Franklin stopped, interrupted by a burst of sound at the door. Franklin saw Richard Henry Lee, the man's face a mask of shock. Lee looked at Harrison, said, "Excuse me . . . Benjamin, I just received a messenger. The British have burned Norfolk."

VIRGINIA'S ROYAL GOVERNOR, THOMAS DUNMORE, HAD BEEN AN absolute supporter of the king's policies, could count himself easily as loyal as Thomas Hutchinson. Yet Dunmore had decided on a more active role in a confrontation with the colonial rebels. Besides the typical outbursts of political tyranny, such as his dissolving the Virginia House of Burgesses, Dunmore had gone several steps further. When Virginia offered her delegates to the Continental Congress, Dunmore reacted by striking out in the manner of a petulant child. As a response to Patrick Henry's blazing oratory, Dunmore labeled Henry a criminal and put a price on his head. When the Virginia militia began to organize, Dunmore seized their store of powder, and responded to the outcry by removing himself to a British warship, from which he conducted his affairs. As his relationship with the people of Virginia continued to deteriorate, Dunmore struck out with his pen, issuing a proclamation that imposed martial law and called for Negroes to align themselves with the crown in return for arms and freedom. As if his role in Virginia's exploding rebelliousness had not yet become satisfactory to him, it was the governor himself who ordered the British warships to destroy the city of Norfolk.

FRANKLIN HAD SENT THE GRANDCHILDREN AWAY, SOMETHING HE could never do comfortably. There had been the usual protest, and he knew that they would be sulking away in their misery, *Grandpapa is too busy to play,* working on the sympathies of their mother. Sally understood his moods, knew when he required the solitude, would keep them quiet. He heard a door close, realized she had taken them outside. Thank you, my dear.

He was rereading Paine's pamphlet, had begun to see the words in a different way, imagining himself a farmer, a boat builder, a blacksmith. He had been so close for so long to all the trappings of official government, so at ease with monarchs and lords and ladies, so blithely accustomed to worldly discussions with the oh-so-very-important. And that was the problem with the congress after all, the delegates chosen because they were the highest order, the aristocrats, the wealthy, the political powers. How could any body of men with such backgrounds, so many well-bred scions of society, no matter how lofty their intellect, grasp the needs of the people they were supposed to represent? Great wordy debates over allegiance to a despotic nightmare of a king carry very little weight in a corner tavern. He adjusted his glasses, continued to read.

There is something exceedingly ridiculous in the composition of monarchy; it first excludes a man from the means of information, yet empowers him in cases where the highest judgment is required. The state of a king shuts him off from the world, yet the business of a king requires him to know it thoroughly; wherefore the different parts, by unnaturally opposing and destroying each other, prove the whole character to be absurd and useless.

He set the pamphlet down, thought, Change is rarely acceptable unless it comes complete with an alternative that people can understand. Bless you, Thomas Paine. Not only do the people understand your message, they are beginning to applaud it. For all our pride in the virtues of this congress, we have been missing one essential point. The king has done a more efficient job of uniting the colonies than we have.

To the evil of monarchy we have added that of hereditary succession. . . . For all men being originally equals, no one by birth could have a right to set up his own family in perpetual preference to all others forever, and though himself might deserve some decent degree of honors of his contemporaries, yet his descendents might be far too unworthy to inherit them. One of the strongest natural proofs of the folly of hereditary rights in kings is that nature disapproves it, otherwise, she would not so frequently turn it into ridicule, by giving mankind an ass for a lion.

He laughed. We must be sure this finds the bedside of King George. Perhaps Strahan can bring that about.

England since the conquest hath known some few good monarchs; but groaned beneath a much larger number of bad ones; yet no man in his senses can say that their claim under William the Conqueror is a very honorable one. A French bastard landing with an armed banditti and establishing himself king of England against the consent of the natives, is in plain terms a very paltry rascally original. It certainly hath no divinity in it.

He read for a long while, began to lose daylight in the room, his eyes straining against the glow of sunset on the pages. He reached the end, realized his heart was pounding. Yes, Mr. Paine, you put the rest of us to shame. But for all the good this will do, for the impact it may yet have on the mood of the people, the congress must show them something they can understand as well. We must give them a government that is worthy of the blood it will require to secure it.

40. WASHINGTON

THE CANADIAN EXPEDITION HAD BEEN A COMPLETE DISASTER. THE most obvious problem had been winter, the conditions through which the men in both prongs of the invasion had to march. For Montgomery, it had been somewhat easier, his men traveling on more established routes, mostly over water. For Benedict Arnold, the trek through the wilderness had nearly destroyed his thousand-man force, a fourth of them not even completing the journey, many of the men simply turning back, some bearing the injured and sick with them.

Montgomery had succeeded in capturing the lesser prize of Montreal, but there could be no coordination with the other prong of the assault, Arnold's men waiting in freezing despair outside Quebec for Montgomery's forces to arrive. When Montgomery's troops finally appeared, they launched a poorly coordinated assault against a fortress city that had had ample time to prepare. Montgomery himself was killed, Arnold badly wounded. The rugged Virginian Daniel Morgan had assumed command, and after a fight that had little hope of success, Morgan had been captured. What had begun in September with such raucous enthusiasm had resulted in an enormous waste of manpower and equipment. To Washington, the lesson was clear. If he had finally been able to convince himself that this army had truly taken shape, the invasion of Canada proved that he was far from prepared to carry any serious fight to the enemy. Canada was still firmly in British hands, and despite whatever strategy the British might launch along the coastline, Canada would remain a major threat to the security of the colonies, a gaping back door through which the British could march at their leisure.

Throughout the autumn months, Washington's frustrations had grown into complete despair, the doubts about his own abilities magnified into doubts about the army itself, whether these men could ever be organized and trained to function as an effective military force. He had unwisely written letters to his friends at the congress, expressing indiscreet criticism of some of the New Englanders under his command. To his chagrin, he learned that there were few secrets, that private letters were rarely private at all these days. Naturally, some of his unkind descriptions came back to haunt him, some of the fragile loyalty he was trying to construct suddenly dissolving.

Aside from the difficulty in Washington's personal relationships with the New Englanders, the army had a much more serious problem. Even though many of the companies of new troops had begun to abide by military dictates, showing some discipline and order, obeying chain of command, and participating in drill, nearly all of the army under Washington's command would have their terms of enlistment expire at the end of December. After the tumultuous experience of training these men, the reality was that by the first of the year, they might all simply leave for home and take their good training with them. Even if replacements were somehow brought to the defensive lines around Boston, the amazing struggles with discipline would begin all over again.

He had spent as much time in personal appeals to junior officers as he had on any other task. If he could somehow organize a true officer corps, to work on securing the reenlistment of the men under their commands, it might just save the army. As the winter rolled closer, it had been clear to him that the plan had only partially worked. Despite every kind of plea to loyalty and patriotism, by Christmas many of the soldiers were said to be packed and ready for their march home, some disappearing prematurely. As Washington settled into a dark hopelessness, other news had begun to reach the men. When headquarters received the text of the king's speech to Parliament, Washington ordered it read in the camps, igniting a spirit that he himself had failed to do. But the king's words did not carry the power of British action, and it was the attack on Falmouth that kindled a fire in many of these men, who began to understand that if they were ever to return to the comfort and security of their families, they might first have to settle this thing and finally confront the British face-to-face. To Washington's enormous relief, the men began to reenlist. Now it would be up to their commander to put them to their best use.

The flow of supplies had actually improved, powder and shot slowly accumulating in the American arsenals. There had been great debate among the senior officers from New England about the usefulness of the cannon seized at Fort Ticonderoga. If the British were concerned about Washington's great good fortune in seizing so much heavy artillery, what Howe did not know was that all of the firepower was still sitting in the fort. To some in Washington's command, that was exactly where it should stay, strengthening the defense of that vital part of the Hudson River route into New York. But Washington believed the greater need was around Boston, and despite the snickering doubts from many of his more skeptical commanders, one man had volunteered to lead the difficult expedition required to bring the guns to Cambridge.

He had met Henry Knox soon after the command was established in Cambridge. Knox was young, only twenty-five, a short, very plump man who had been a bookseller in Boston. Knox had proven his zeal for soldiering under Artemas Ward during the fight on the Charlestown peninsula. He had accepted Washington's authority with none of the prejudice of so many of the New Englanders, had impressed his new commander with his serious passion for learning, had already read most of the available books on military tactics. Washington rewarded the man's eagerness by naming him colonel of the Continental artillery, which caused even more stifled laughter around the camps. What few cannon could be described as Continental artillery hardly required the guidance of any senior officer. But Washington found Knox a willing volunteer for the mission to Ticonderoga, and in mid-November, Knox and a company of volunteers embarked, disappearing into the wilderness.

* * *

WASHINGTON HAD BEGUN TO PATROL THE COASTLINE MORE OFTEN, the chilly ride through roads thick with snow. Word had reached the camps about the burning of Norfolk, and the response from his army could be predicted, one great roar of outrage. He had made sure that a specific piece of Governor Dunmore's amazing statement to the Virginians be read to the troops, the extraordinary boast that Norfolk was only the beginning.

The harbor spread out below him, the open water broken by the anchorage of so many British ships. He had watched their number increase almost daily, great fat sails appearing on the horizon, soon adding to the congestion in the harbor. He had only sketchy details of what the ships brought, could not be completely sure whether General Howe was still adding to his troop strength, or if the ships simply brought desperately needed food. He scanned along the waterlines of the most recent arrivals, could see that very few of them were gunships. No, they are merchantmen, or navy transports, lightly armed. In a naval war, these are the prizes, the easy targets for the men-of-war. But we can offer little threat, and they have men-of-war enough here to do whatever they please.

He had been grateful for the congress' support of a makeshift navy, the committee headed by John Adams providing funding for the arming and equipping of privateers. By this time, Washington knew of six ships in colonial service, and he was aware they were no more than a small fleet of what the British would certainly describe as pirate ships. But their usefulness had already been established, preying upon unprotected British merchantmen. Most of the time, the cargo would be less interesting than the capture of the ship itself, which would immediately be converted to the colonists' use. But then had come the one lucky grab, a supply ship headed for Boston laden with the tools of war. Washington had been astounded at the report of the spoils, the capture of an enormous cargo of powder and ball, shot and shell, even cannon that were immediately fitted to the colonists' growing navy. No, we may never be prepared to fight them at sea. But we can certainly torment them.

He glassed one newcomer, saw activity on her deck, sails furled, men up in the rigging. He had felt a nagging curiosity that so many of the ships had arrived, only to just sit. He lowered the glass. No matter what their cargo, transports and supply ships would most certainly empty their holds and then leave. By remaining here, they must certainly contribute to the problem Howe has of feeding his people. Why are they not sailing back to wherever they came from and refilling their holds? He raised the spyglass again, scanned the decks of the closest ships, saw virtually no activity, no preparation, no one preparing to sail. They're not going anywhere, not anytime soon. They arrive, and then they stay, empty ships just waiting . . .

Suddenly his mind turned in a new direction. Empty ships . . . just waiting. Waiting for what? Perhaps they are waiting for a new cargo right here. He felt a sting of excitement, clasped his hands hard around the spyglass, the lens fogged by his breathing. Perhaps Howe is making preparation to leave. They're delaying because there aren't enough ships yet for his entire force. He can't take half of them and leave the rest vulnerable to us. He has to move them all at one time.

He felt a strange panic. No, Mr. Howe, don't do it yet, not yet. If you are suddenly gone, we have gained nothing. His mind was swirling. Of course, we gain Boston, but this army will have no purpose, not here, not without an enemy in front of them. And then what? The war will simply . . . move? He spurred the horse, had no idea where he was going, the staff suddenly rushing to catch up. Is this worse than an attack? If the British suddenly leave, is that a victory? They seem quite content to assault our cities from the sea. Surely that will continue. And I cannot stop them. These men . . . we must do something *now*. The enemy is right in front of us.

He knew of the mood of the troops, that nothing deflates the enthusiasm of an army like a stalemate. Boredom was a fact of life in the military, but these men weren't military, did not expect to spend the misery of winter huddled into weatherproofed shelters with virtually nothing to do. There had been some sport, particularly in the lines closest to the British on Boston Neck, contests, proud showcases for marksmanship, some of the men winning bets by successfully picking off a British officer at long range. What was sport to the colonists became an eerie nightmare to the British, the sudden whistle and whine of a musket ball, usually missing the target, but every British officer knew who the targets were. It was one more infuriating bit of evidence that the colonists had no sense of decency, simply didn't understand how to fight a war.

Washington had calmed himself, forced his mind to think of some way of breaking the stalemate without endangering his army. He rode past low huts, smoke rising from makeshift chimneys. Men would peer out, some emerging completely, saluting him, their impatience flowing toward him in their words,

"We're ready for a fight. When can we have at 'em?"

He heard it everywhere he rode, had no good answer to give them. Until now, he had believed that the greatest threat to these men was that Howe would make a move of his own, launch a direct assault on these works. Washington had a genuine fear of that confrontation, a nagging doubt that what had happened on Breed's Hill might have been a lesson to Howe that he would not repeat. There were too many British soldiers in Boston just to remain idle. With the king's decree, Howe would certainly have all the approval he would need for offensive action. Throughout the weeks of the expiring enlistments, Washington had prayed every night that Howe's intelligence not be reliable, for if Howe knew of the chaos in Washington's lines, certainly the British would take advantage. While companies and regiments had been reorganized, much of Washington's defenses had been undermanned, some of the works not manned at all. We are much stronger now, but even so, if Howe plans wisely, he can find our weaknesses—if he intends to attack us at all.

He felt utterly helpless, his brain in a great fog of doubt. He stopped the horse, realizing he was perched up on a wonderful vantage point, the view complete, all of it, Boston itself, beyond, the hills on Charlestown peninsula. He could see the British works spread over Bunker Hill, could see the awful stain of Charlestown, ragged black skeletons only partially disguised by the layer of snow. He looked around closer to him, knew he was on Dorchester Heights, a prominent hill south of Boston. All of his commanders had been amazed that Howe had not come up here to occupy the hills. There had been no good explanation, nothing from Washington's few reliable informers in the town. He had tried to see the ground from Howe's point of view, and now, surveying the length of the works up on Charlestown peninsula, it became clear. It's too much ground to protect. Howe simply doesn't have the numbers. He couldn't defend the high ground in both directions, and when Ward's men occupied Breed's Hill, we made his decision for him.

Washington had considered the value of Dorchester Heights for a while now, but many of his commanders were fearful of the effect of the men-of-war, that the British naval cannon could possibly devastate any force brought up here. His eye followed the contour of the hill. If we had our own siege guns up here, the ships would become nice fat targets. It would be a change in this stalemate that Howe would have to respond to. He might have to move the ships away . . . or possibly he would see it as an opportunity. Could he simply sail his army away from here without accepting the challenge? Washington shook his head, could not help a smile. No, he has the same dilemma we have. If he simply leaves here, what does he gain? It would be an admission of defeat. How does he explain that to London? The king wants the rebellion crushed. Well, here we sit. Come and crush us. He thought of Knox now, had heard nothing of the man's efforts. If we had those guns up here, all of Boston would be vulnerable. If Howe was not yet prepared to leave, he would have to respond by attacking us. It was the same plan Ward and his people had hoped to accomplish by manning those hills north of town. The problem for them was the same problem for us now. We may appear a threat, but without those big guns, we won't have any teeth. All we may accomplish is to bring the British out of their barracks. The men are itching for the fight, are all convinced it would be another Breed's Hill. But Howe won't make that mistake again. If he comes out, it will be with enough force to smash right through our lines.

His mind was racing now with a plan, an opportunity that was spread out right in front of him but might never come again. Henry Knox. Where are you, young man?

JANUARY 25, 1776

EVERY MORNING WASHINGTON HAD RISEN EARLY, DRESSED, AND descended into his office with the same anxious anticipation. It was his routine now, staring out the window across the open ground, the road that pointed west, a deep trough cut through a thick layer of snow. He would just stare, watching the far curve, where the road turned away into the far trees, hoping for a sudden vision of the head of a great column, some sign of Knox's success. He had studied the maps, imagined the route. It would be a challenge in the summer. But in the snow, a New England winter . . .

He had moved his headquarters, a fine stately home that had been abandoned by its owner, a Tory sympathizer named Vassal, who was presumed to be enjoying the protection of the British in Boston. His entire staff was now under one roof, the drawing room serving as his office. There was one other addition that had entirely changed his mood around the center of the tumultuous business of the army. His wife, Martha, had arrived.

She was a short, plump woman who had charmed everyone around, considerably softening the coarse politeness of the headquarters. Her journey northward had carried her through Philadelphia, to the waiting arms of a congress bursting with the need to demonstrate their social skills. She had been treated with extraordinary kindness, but there were always the society lionesses, skeptical that a soldier's wife from Virginia could exhibit the essential social graces. When she resumed her journey northward, she might not even have understood that she had passed their inspection. But in her wake, the society matrons of Philadelphia were breathless.

As she had at Mount Vernon, Martha took over the management of the household. While her smiling presence certainly brightened his moods, she also completely freed Washington from any involvement in the daily tormenting aggravation of servants, cooks, and laundry. The mood of his staff changed as well, with the casual reliance on profane language tempered considerably, and an impressive increase in proficiency in the use of table manners.

He stared out at the snow, deeper now from another storm the night before. He was beginning to become more than nervous about Knox's mission, still felt the knot of depression about the disaster in Canada. He had considered sending out scouts, employing Indians in the area to follow Knox's trail, seek out some news of what might have happened.

Breakfast had been laid out in the dining room, and the smells were reaching him now, a much more elaborate feast than he was accustomed to. He had taken to making brief visits to the kitchen, grabbing whatever might be available, a wedge of bread, a handful of nuts or dried fruit. But Martha would have none of that, and it had not taken him long to obey the same order that applied to the rest of the house. Breakfast was served.

He let out a long breath, felt his stomach knotted in one hard lump, did not feel like eating anything. He still stared out the window at the empty whiteness of the main road, still waited, as he had every morning for two weeks, for a rider, someone in a hurry, someone carrying a message, any word at all.

"Are you coming, husband?" He turned now, saw her in the doorway. He expected a stern scolding look, but she seemed more concerned, softer, asked, "Nothing yet?"

"Not a word. I am seriously concerned. We have had disaster enough for this winter. Have you ever imagined there would be so much snow? And it never melts. It just . . . grows."

She moved to him now, touched his arm.

"It's not so bad. Rather beautiful, actually."

He looked out the window again.

"There's a permanence about it. Winter arrives, and it just stays here. I cannot recall in my memory a winter in Virginia where the ground was never bare, where the snow never melted. And I inquired of the men here—this is all quite normal."

She stood beside him now, stared out with him.

"I imagine it makes people look forward to the spring, gives more meaning to the new year, the fresh season."

"Virginia teases us with winter. Snow one day, rain the next, a week of mud, then more snow. I should not complain. If we had to fight, it would be easier here. You can't very well drag artillery through the mud." He paused, then said in a low voice, "No mud in the mountains. Just Henry Knox and his ox teams. He said he could pull cannon on sleds. We may never find out."

"Where's your faith, George?"

"You do a much better job communicating with Providence than I do. The pure of heart are provided a better reception."

She had heard this from him before.

"God measures the heart. It is not for you to so easily dismiss yourself from His care."

He did not want an argument about theology, could smell the coffee now, an opportunity to change the subject.

"Best get to the dining room before the pot is empty."

He backed away from the window, expected her to move with him, but she stayed behind, still staring out the window. He went to the doorway, and she said, "Sleds, indeed."

"What?" He turned, looked out past her, saw movement in the road, a massive black cannon drawn behind a team of two oxen. The sight pulled him closer to the window, and he saw another one, emerging from the bend in the road, saw men with whips, a wagon, the wheels lashed into small flat sleds. He felt like shouting, bolted quickly away from the window, out the door of the office, thundering through the front entranceway. Behind him, voices followed, questions, men surging into motion. He stumbled, staggered through the snow, reached the road, looked back along the lengthening column, guns of all sizes back as far as he could see. Soldiers began to gather now, emerging from their shelters, some calling to him, some yelling out a cheer. He saw one man now, up in a wagon, saw a beaming smile on the broad round red face. It was Henry Knox.

"General Washington! May I present to you . . . a noble train of artillery. Fifty-nine pieces of His Majesty's finest!"

* * *

THEY HAD PUSHED AND DRAGGED AND HAULED AND HOISTED
through territory where the roads were often no more than old
Indian trails. The power came from oxen or from the men themselves, all manner of sleds and platforms fashioned to support
whatever mass of weight they could handle. The column had
pulled through towns and small villages, exhausted men grateful
for the cheers and gifts from those who came out to see this
amazing sight. In the back country, they crossed bridges that
collapsed under the weight, dropping men and machine into icy
streams. Eventually they would face the challenge of crossing
the Berkshire Mountains. Through the winding passes, the men
pulled alongside the animals, many of the heavier guns taken
apart, barrels hoisted into wagons, spoked wheels lashed together. Scattered between the big guns were smaller platforms
stacked high with crates of shot and shell, followed by thick
brass mortars pulled on sleds. They stretched the ropes in great
long climbs and dangerous descents on trails where the snow
was deeper than the tallest man. In six weeks, they had covered
more than three hundred miles, finally delivering to George
Washington's army the power he would need to take this fight
straight to the heart of the enemy.

41. WASHINGTON

FEBRUARY 16, 1776

THE MEETING HAD GONE AS SO MANY OF THEM HAD GONE BEFORE,
with great long debates about strength and readiness, exaggerated claims of British power, pessimism about everything from
weather to the amount of feed for the horses. He endured it, as he
had always endured it, but this time, he would let them spew it all

out, their disagreements, the petty business of the camps. The general surliness of the mood seemed to spring from Artemas Ward, who had a way of finding fault with any plan that was not his own. Washington had learned from experience that if the meeting was not about any particular event or strategy, if he didn't really have a distinct reason to assert his seniority, he could accomplish very little by interfering in Ward's petty assaults on other commanders.

Ward was still officially Washington's second in command, but he had been scarce around headquarters, often appearing only for the councils. Washington had developed a genuine dislike for the older man, and in quiet conversation with many of Ward's junior officers, he had not been surprised to learn that Ward was disliked by almost everyone. Ward's actual contribution to the French and Indian War had been at best a display of mediocrity, but the man had spent years creating himself in the role of a heroic son of Massachusetts. With the focus now so clearly on Washington, he had shrunk to a grumbling malcontent. Worse, few among the Massachusetts officers had much faith that Ward could lead an army anywhere. The pride the army had earned from their fight on Breed's Hill was directed toward men such as William Prescott and even the old war hero Israel Putnam. But there was no hiding the truth about Breed's Hill. While Ward's men had devastated the British advance, their commander had anchored himself safely in the comfort of his headquarters at Cambridge. It was no mistake to assume that the disastrous mismanagement of both ammunition and reinforcements had been entirely his fault.

Ward, in turn, made it no secret that he disliked Washington, though no one paid much attention to the man's reasoning. Nothing he could have said would disguise that he was still fuming at the congress for taking his command away from him. Washington had begun to accept that, sooner or later, Ward would lose more than that.

As the men and their officers had formed their judgment of Washington, the Virginian continued to form his own judgments: the men he could depend on, and those who would most likely be more noise than performance. His enormous confidence in Charles Lee continued to grow, and Washington had accepted a fatalistic view that if he himself was killed, Lee was the most able successor available, a view already held by many in the congress.

Henry Knox was still a bright light among Washington's subordinates, would continue to command the artillery. There were jokes behind the man's back, his obesity not lending much to Knox's soldierly image among the troops. Washington had little use for that kind of humor, had learned in the war with the French that the men with the quickest wit around the campfire rarely made a solid impression in a fight.

Knox had introduced Washington to Nathaniel Greene, and the man gave a first impression as unfortunate as that of the rotund Knox. Greene carried the infirmity of a stiff leg, a physical trait that had always raised doubts about his performance in the field. He had begun his military career by enlisting as a private in the Rhode Island militia, but it was the men of his regiment who saw beyond the young man's handicap and voted Greene to be their commanding officer. Congress agreed, and Greene was commissioned as another of the brigadiers in Washington's command. Greene had served his cause well in the fight on Breed's Hill, and Washington had accepted Knox's confident assurances that he would again. Greene had already shown Washington that he had a knack for strategy, and if the war was to expand beyond an area Washington could command himself, he was beginning to appreciate that Nathaniel Greene might very well be the kind of officer to manage his own command.

Another brigadier was an Irish lawyer from New Hampshire, John Sullivan, who had given up his seat as a delegate in the Continental Congress to join Washington's command. Sullivan had led a column of men up to Falmouth, too late to defend the city from the British guns, but with enough efficiency to convince Washington that he was a capable handler of troops in the field. Washington had assigned Sullivan to work closely with Greene, the initial planning of a strategy Washington had been drawing up on paper since his last ride on Dorchester Heights.

He had thought there would be a prominent place at the table for Daniel Morgan, but the charismatic Morgan was still under British guard in Canada, and likely would be for a long while. His freedom would come in one of those protracted negotiations common to warfare, a trade of one valued officer for another. Washington was aware that the Continental Army as yet had no one to trade. But if this plan was successful, if Howe's army could be pulled into an extraordinary trap, then Washington might have much more than a strong negotiating position. He might end the war.

The meeting had begun to wind down, the men already glancing toward the door—typical in so many of these meetings dominated by complaints and bickering, some of the men regarding Washington only in terms of his authority to conclude yet another waste of their time. Washington was feeling an unusual nervousness, had never made these meetings any kind of elaborate strategy session, had been hesitant all the way through the talking about doing it now. But his patience was as raw as that of the men who breathed the sooty air of their winter camps, and finally he had something specific to give them. At last he had a reason to exercise his authority over more than a defensive stalemate. He waited for a quiet moment, saw the restlessness, knew they were impatient to hear the order dismissing them.

"We have one more matter to discuss. If you will direct your attention here . . ."

There was a low collective sigh, and he ignored it, reached down into a drawer, pulled out a roll of paper, spread it out on the desk.

"Please study this, gentlemen."

They gathered close, studied the map silently. After a few minutes, Washington said, "All right, be seated. Certainly most of you know this countryside in much greater detail than I do; thus I do not intend copies to be prepared of this map. That only increases the risk that the enemy might somehow learn of our plan."

He waited for the inevitable protests, raised his hands.

"I mean no offense to anyone's pride, but I fear there may be too much carelessness in this headquarters." He paused, regretted immediately what they would all know to be an insult to Artemas Ward. Ward himself said nothing, sat in the back of the room, his arms crossed hard on his chest, wearing the same frown he always brought to these councils. There were small murmurs, but no one spoke out, and Washington was grateful for that.

"I have fashioned a plan. It has several elements, all of which must function well. We have been discussing for some time the occupation of Dorchester Heights. Like many of you, I have grown weary of riding the crests of those wonderful hills, despairing that we do not have artillery up there. That is about to change." He looked at Knox now, who was hanging on his words and seemed eager for him to continue. He had already been over much of the plan with Knox, had been pleased with the man's discretion, Knox keeping it to himself that the commanding general had so confided in him. It could have been one more source of jealous complaining.

"We will entrench on the heights, in a line as drawn on the map. I have considered the difficulty of digging into frozen ground. This is not a challenge I have faced in Virginia." There were wry chuckles, and Lee said, "I've scooped out a good mud hole, but never chopped my way through solid ice."

Washington nodded.

"Indeed. We are fortunate to have an engineer in this command, Colonel Rufus Putnam, who has devised a solution. Earthworks don't always have to be dug, nor do they have to be made of earth. I have been instructed in the art of building what Colonel Putnam calls *fascines*, stout bundles of sticks tied together. These may be placed end to end by framing them in what I imagine to resemble firewood racks. Colonel Putnam calls them chandeliers. I must admit, that is not what my wife would call to mind if you mention the word." They seemed to appreciate his humor, and he glanced around the room, saw them all hanging on his words, even Ward, who was leaning forward now. He was finally feeling confident, was grateful that there had been none of the interruptions so common in other meetings. "If this wall is then lined with stout bales of hay, I am convinced that it provides acceptable protection against muskets. And, in the manner described, I believe we can assemble the parts of this wall well beforehand, out of sight of the enemy, and then transport them piecemeal into position in a short period of time."

Lee was closest to him, the ever-present dogs under the man's feet. He leaned forward.

"You plan to construct these works at night?"

"Not only at night, General, but in *one* night."

Lee sat back.

"That's a tall order."

"Not so tall, sir."

Lee turned toward the voice, and Washington pointed to the brigadier, Nathaniel Greene.

"Go on, General."

"Sir, we constructed the main part of the works on Breed's Hill in one night. And we didn't have anything close to the number of men we have now. Or the organization."

Washington glanced at Ward, saw the old man's frown returning.

"You are correct, Mr. Greene. That is exactly what I am depending on—the same spirit in these men that was demonstrated on Breed's Hill. This time, they will carry not only shovels, but cannon. Colonel Knox's siege guns will be placed as I have drawn. When the sun rises on that hillside, I want General Howe to see what can result when thousands of colonial troops move into action. I want him to know that if he does not respond, we will blow his ships and his headquarters to rubble."

He was excited now, drawing the energy from the men in front of him. Knox was rocking slowly back and forward, and Lee was leaning close to the desk, staring at the map. From the back of the room, there was a grunt, and Ward said, "Oh, General Howe will respond, certainly. You think it will be any different than before? He'll take his army right up that hill, run your people off Dorchester Heights the same as he did on Breed's Hill. And there's a good many more of 'em than last time. All those men o' war, his batteries in the town. You won't have much chance to scare anybody."

Washington caught the word *you* in Ward's argument, thought, He doesn't even feel a part of this, believes he has no role.

"General Ward, I'm not interested in the scare. I'm interested in the response. What you are describing is exactly what I hope will occur. He cannot maintain his position in Boston and allow us to place our guns on that hill. I expect General Howe to launch an all-out assault, send out every available man in Boston to sweep us off that hill."

Ward seemed puzzled, and Washington was enjoying the moment, could see concern on the other faces. Ward went on, "He won't make the same mistakes as before. He'll make better use of his artillery this time; there's no town for him to use as target practice. He'll send all his firepower to the top of that hill, back his men up with his ships."

"I hope so, General. Because once he has mobilized his people and sent them across the water, moved his gunships into line to support them, trained all his batteries up on those heights, that's when the, uh, rest of the plan begins."

They were all silent, displaying complete confusion, except for Knox and the one other man he had conferred with.

"Mr. Greene? Will you spell out the remainder of our strategy?"

Greene stood, said, "The commanding general and I have estimated that with the certainty of the British response to our threat from Dorchester Heights, they will weaken themselves severely at their defenses in Boston. We will then proceed to move a large force of men in boats across the Back Bay and land in the town."

"In *Boston*?" Ward sputtered. "Howe has made the place a damned fortress. Every access along the water's edge has been blocked by a barricade."

Greene was looking at Washington, who nodded to him to continue.

"Forgive me, General Ward, but if there are no troops behind those barricades, it is not much of a fortress. Once we establish a force in the town itself, we can move toward the enemy's barricade on Boston Neck from the rear. It should be a simple matter to open up that access, and then the rest of our troops can enter Boston from Roxbury."

WASHINGTON'S PLAN
TO ASSAULT BOSTON

Castle
William

Boston
Harbor

Noddles Island

Dorchester Heights

Nook's Hill

THOMAS

Bred's Hill

HOWE

Barker Hill

Charlestown peninsula

Mystic River

Charlestown

Cobble Hill

Boston

GAGE

Boston Neck

Back Bay

To Braintree

KNOX

GREENE

WASHINGTON

Charles River

To Lexington

Cambridge

Ward huffed again. "And what of all those men coming at us on Dorchester Heights? You expect them all to just surrender?"

Washington motioned to Greene, who sat down. Then Washington went on, "Actually, General Ward, that is precisely what we can expect. If we have successfully occupied their base, they will have nowhere to return to. If you were General Howe in that situation, what would *you* do?"

THEY HAD LEFT THE MEETING WITH A RARE ENTHUSIASM, EACH commander instructed on the preparation of his men, the duties each unit would carry out. Knox would position the artillery, both on the heights and from the opposing direction as well, northwest of the town. Those guns would create a diversion, attract the British lookouts toward a completely different area from where the real work would begin. Washington knew that once his artillery began to drop shot into Boston, from whichever direction he chose, the message would be plain to the British: *Now we have guns as well. And you might be in serious trouble.*

He had estimated the preparation time to be about two weeks, assembling men, preparing guns and powder, constructing the fascines and the rowboats necessary to move the entire operation on schedule. It was the first time that the attention and energy of the commanders would be fixed in one direction, on one concerted effort. All along the lines, the men would be alerted that something new was happening, the boredom of the long winter replaced by the orders for work of a different sort.

He had asked Lee to remain, suspected that Lee had something he wanted to say privately. Lee was notorious in the council meetings for launching an opinion toward every suggestion, from questions of strategy to the location of beef herds. Washington had expected much more input from him this time, knew there was meaning behind the man's minimal comments. Except for the two of them, the office was empty now, a beaming Henry Knox having closed the door behind him. Lee still sat in the chair, attending to his dogs, the low silly talk Washington was used to now.

"You didn't say much, Charles. I was wondering why."

Lee still had his eyes on the dogs.

"They didn't need to hear anything else. You pumped them up pretty good. Even Ward had to hold his tongue. Fine job, George."

Washington was beginning to feel disappointment, had thought Lee would be more enthusiastic.

"What's wrong with the plan, General Lee?"

Lee scrutinized him now.

"Why don't *you* tell *me*?"

Washington glanced at the closed door.

"All right. It requires efficiency. We must move a large number of men into position quickly, without being observed. It has worked before, it can work again."

"So you build your great long line up on Dorchester Heights. General Howe wakes up, sips his tea at his bedroom window, suddenly realizes his town is under your guns. He says, 'Oh, bloody hell,' and drops his fine china cup on his Persian rug. Then he gives an order to his men. You're assuming that order will be to attack."

Washington had put this possibility far back in his mind, but it emerged now, like a bayonet pointed at the heart of his plan. He rubbed one hand on his chin.

"I don't believe they have enough ships yet to transport his entire army plus the loyalist civilians. But Howe might disagree. I admit, I could be wrong. They don't necessarily *have* to attack. Howe could just order them to their ships. They might just sail out of here."

Lee leaned down to his dogs again.

"They might indeed. Cheer up, George. *That* would mean you win. Of course, if he does attack, then what?"

Washington knew Lee was playing a game with him, making him rethink every detail. All right, there is no fault in that.

"Once we see his men cross the harbor, landing on the heights, we launch our boats across the Back Bay."

"How many men?"

"I worked on this with Mr. Greene. Four thousand or so. Enough force to land in the town and establish a strong enough foothold that Howe can't push us out."

Lee still toyed with the dogs, and Washington waited for a response. After a moment, Washington added, "It will work, Charles. I have planned for every variable. If Howe doesn't attack the heights, his position becomes untenable. The worst that can happen is he abandons the city. The best is we capture his entire army. Even if his men are successful in assaulting the heights, the cost to them in casualties would be enormous. And we would still have Boston. They would be an army without a base."

"He might burn the city."

Washington had no response, had kept that from his mind. Well, no, perhaps I have not considered every variable. He recalled the view of the wasteland of Charlestown, the town that had simply ceased to be.

"Is Howe such a barbarian? Is that what the British gentlemen bring to this fight?"

Lee looked at him.

"Just be prepared to find out."

MARCH 4, 1776

HE HAD ORDERED THE BOMBARDMENT FROM THE GUNS NORTHWEST of the town to begin three nights before. The first night was just a brief show, Knox ordered to limit the barrage to only two dozen shots. The next night, the bombardment had increased, but Knox had strict orders to conserve the powder, keep the gunners under control. The British had responded, their own artillery throwing streaks of red and white across the night sky, an amazing show that both armies could see, a thunderous display evident for miles around.

On the third night, the bombardment began again, but Knox was not close to the guns, had left discretionary orders for the men to use what powder they had, use it all, make a show that would last through the night. As the daylight ended, Knox himself had ridden south, had joined Washington behind Dorchester Heights, would now supervise the hauling of the rest of the artillery up that wonderful hill.

Washington sat nervously on the horse just behind the crest of the hill, and most of the men had no idea he was there, were consumed by the work, the labor of hauling the fascines and hay bales up the rise. They had not been told of their destination until the march had actually begun, the first order to move out timed to the setting of the sun. The orders were explicit: no sounds, no shouts, no music. The men would not carry muskets, and that was the most unpopular order of all, but Washington understood that these men would not do the fighting. Their job was to build the defensive line, and any man who might accidentally fire a musket could jeopardize the entire operation.

He could see the wall going up, the engineer's design working perfectly, the four-foot-long fascines set down into the frames of the wooden chandeliers, the hay stacked behind. On the near side of the hill, an orchard of small fruit trees had been cut and dragged out in front of the line itself, the branches pointing down the hill to where the enemy would come from, another obstacle Howe's men would have to confront. He would not ride up close to the laboring men, forced himself to stay back, could not risk a spontaneous cheer. The low sounds rolled down the hill toward him, many of the men now marching back to their camps, their work done. From far back came the new sounds, ox teams pulling the larger siege guns, each creak and groan of the wheels cutting through the dark silence, knifing into him. The guns rolled past him, again with the men unaware that their commander watched every motion, nervously flinching at each indiscreet sound. Behind the guns, another column stepped into formation, and this time, the men did have muskets. From the roads that led back to all the camps, over two thousand men marched up the hill, falling into line behind the strange wall. As more of the men moved past him, he knew the necessity for quiet had passed, and now he spurred the horse, rode up to the crest of the hill, could see the dark shadows of the siege guns where Knox had placed them, could see small movements in the moonlight, the men settling into their defense. To some, it was a reminder of what they had done up there on those other hills, clearly visible now, dark mounds speckled with the light from

British campfires. There was hushed talk now, many of the inexperienced seeking out the veterans with questions, fears, asking what it was like to see the face of the enemy. They began to notice Washington now, the big man on the tall horse, moving slowly along their line, but the cheers were muffled, the men themselves realizing the need to remain undetected, imagining the enormous surprise that would greet the British when the sun finally rose.

MARCH 5, 1776

HE COULD SEE THE CHAOS IN THE STREETS, THE BRITISH SCRAMBLING to formations, officers gathering their men into line. Along the wharves, the barges had been quickly assembled, and before the earliest morning mist had burned off the still waters of the harbor, the British troops gathered on the same flatboats that had carried them to Breed's Hill. They did not yet cross toward Dorchester Heights, but instead moved slowly toward Castle William. Washington could take in the entire process, moved the horse farther forward to keep his vantage over the British deployment. As the sun rose higher, he could see the masses of red, now thick around the island fort. He could not help the knot in his stomach, the fear that it was the first step in the failure of his plan, that Howe was assembling his men at Castle William to board them on the transports with less danger of fire from the new guns on Dorchester Heights.

He still rode forward, sweating hands gripping the leather reins, Charles Lee beside him, went down through a short valley, then up to the closest view of Boston, the smaller Nook's Hill. He could see the mouth of the Charles, where the river narrowed into a tight ribbon of water, disappearing to the west, where Greene and Sullivan and the engineer Putnam waited with the troops who would land in Boston. He glassed that way, saw nothing, no movement. No, of course not, they will not be seen, nothing to give Howe any hint of what is to come.

Lee was glassing the town itself, remarked, "They're not all gone. Howe isn't abandoning the town. The barricades are still manned."

Washington focused that way, could see large clusters of red along the water's edge, much more strength than he had expected. The knot tightened again, and he turned, the staff behind him.

"Send a courier to General Thomas. I must know how many men the British have sent to Castle William."

He heard Gates give the order, a man galloping quickly away, and now Lee said, "There's a great deal of activity just below us. Those batteries along the water's edge—"

They all saw the bursts of fire, the streaks of light suddenly splitting the air above them. The shells impacted in great blasts of dirt on the face of the larger hill. Washington spun the horse, shouted, "Back! Now!"

Lee was moving close beside him, and the riders all climbed the hill at a quick gallop. Washington reached the crest, spotted a small gap in the felled trees, spurred the horse hard, the horse responding, jumping over the barricade and the heads of cheering men. He turned, expecting to see them all on his side of the barricade, saw Lee now still below, the staff as well, and Lee shouted, "Very nice, General. However, the rest of us will find the path, if you don't mind."

Washington's chest was pounding, and he was suddenly impatient, thought, We should teach them how to ride a horse, for God's sake. He did not wait for the staff, saw officers farther down the line, pulled the horse that way, slapping leather against the horse's neck. The man rode out to meet him, older, tall in the saddle. John Thomas was the most senior of all the brigadiers commissioned by the congress, but it had not been because of anything decided in Philadelphia. Thomas had been overlooked in the first batch of commissions, but as Washington became more familiar with the men in his command, he recognized that Thomas, who had served with considerable distinction in the French and Indian War, was much more deserving of the rank than most. It had been Washington's recommendation that had given the man his commission. If there were still Massachusetts officers who bristled at the Virginian's authority, John Thomas was not among them.

Thomas had been placed in command of the infantry on the heights, and he saluted Washington now, seemed to anticipate the question.

"Not more than twenty-five hundred are either en route in the barges or have already landed at Castle William, sir. The rest are holed up still in Boston."

Washington could hear cheering from his men, directed out beyond the barrier. Knox was there now, the round man carrying his wide smile.

"Sir! The British artillery can't reach us up here! Their shot is falling well short!"

The soldiers close by reacted to Knox's words with a burst of fresh cheers. Washington did not fall into the spirit of the men, inquired of Thomas, "Are we certain the barges will not return to Boston? They could still empty the town."

Thomas shook his head.

"No, sir. The empty flatboats are being tied up at Castle William. It appears they intend to keep them there."

Lee had reached him now, the staff finally making their way through the narrow breaks in the barrier. Thomas saluted Lee.

"General, a pleasant good morning, sir."

Lee returned the salute, then turned his attention to his dogs, who sat obediently on either side of his horse.

Washington said, "General Lee, can you make an estimate how many men Howe has kept in Boston?"

"Enough, sir. It'll be a fight."

He recalled Ward's warnings about Boston, a fortress. But Howe cannot have the strength in both places. He still has troops entrenched on Charlestown peninsula, and we have a reasonable estimate of their overall strength. Thomas was reading him now.

"Sir, if I may suggest . . ."

"Certainly, General."

"The enemy appears to be matching us strength for strength. Either he has a spy up here, or he's good at counting through a glass. From everything we can see, Castle William is the best

jumping-off point he has to begin the assault here. He will certainly require a high tide." Thomas looked at his watch. "It was
to be about midday."

Lee countered, "They're too late. It will have to be tonight, the
next tide. Midnight."

Thomas put the watch away.

"I must agree, sir. If General Howe intends to land his troops
on this shore, he will do it tonight."

Washington weighed the words from both men, looked again
toward the Charles River. Howe could very well know what we
have planned. But if it's in the dark . . .

"Gentlemen, I will send word to General Greene. They will
make preparations to sail tonight. Even if the British troops are
manning the barricades, we will have the benefit of surprise."

Lee let out a small laugh.

"It worked at Ticonderoga."

Washington was not in the mood for humor.

"Tomorrow morning, I expect British troops to assault this
hill. And soon after that, I expect us to have secured a landing in
force in Boston."

The troops were shouting again, reacting as more British
shells impacted below them, punching holes harmlessly in the
hillside.

"General Thomas, I would advise your men not to enjoy
themselves too much. The British guns will make adjustments. I
would like a better look at Castle William."

He pushed the horse, rode along the lines of his men, out
toward the eastern point of the heights. He reached the end of his
line, the hill falling away toward the open mouth of the harbor.
Castle William was less than a mile offshore from this point,
seemed even closer than he remembered. The sun was high overhead now, reflecting on the empty flatboats at the fort. General
Thomas is correct. They are staying put. But if that is Howe's
plan, if they assault this hill with close to the same strength we
have up here, it will be far worse for them than Breed's Hill.
Howe must know that. Or perhaps it is that same arrogance.
They line themselves up in their grand show, and we will fall

away out of . . . what? Respect? Intimidation? These men were not intimidated at Breed's Hill, and certainly we are a much better army now.

I wish I could be in both places, right here when they send their troops up this hill, and over there, at the Charles, when we launch the boats. He tried to imagine the sight, a great fleet of small boats, rowing in silent darkness toward the unprepared British sentries. Then the landing, a sudden flood of men and muskets, bursting up and over their foolish barricades. The British might not even put up a fight, might simply quit their posts, run away screaming for their boats. Even Howe will suffer the shock, the sight of a colonial army, a swarm of troops pouring through the streets of Boston, unstoppable, no British force holding them back. He was genuinely excited, ignored the men around him, stared out toward Castle William, caught up in his daydream, could see himself marching proudly into Boston, while the British scurried to their ships like rats. For the first time, the doubts had vanished, and he glanced up at the sun, anxious. Go on, move lower, end this day! Nothing more will happen now, not until tonight. Then we shall see.

There was a sharp blast behind him, a chorus of screams, and he was jolted back to the sight, men down, their perfect defense shattered by the good work of a British gunner. He stared at the scene, the broken men pulled back, one man suddenly running away, his musket left behind, the faces of the others wiped clean of the raucous cheering. He felt suddenly embarrassed, as though God Himself had heard his private display of pride, had sent the ball smashing through his men as a warning: *Who's being arrogant now?* Yes, I understand. Nothing will come easy. There will be a cost. But . . . we have done our work. We are prepared. Surely, *surely* it is a good plan.

ALL ALONG THE LINE THE MEN SIMPLY WAITED, AND AS THE SUN dropped away, each man stared out toward the dark water of the harbor for the first signs of motion, for the first sounds that would tell them the British were on the move. The men had been given a handful of food, dried beef and bread to last them the night, but as the crude meal was consumed, they began to hear a sound they did not expect. There was no moon, thick clouds rolling close overhead, and out of the total darkness, the wind began to blow, a low moan that grew to a howl, unyielding and constant. And then came the rain, hard and driving, pushing each man low against the barricade, the only protection his hat or the flaps of a coat.

On Castle William, Howe's troops had been fed as well, the orders given, the men assembled at the wharf, waiting in formation to board the flatboats for the short crossing to the base of the heights. But as the men stood suffering in the wind and rain, their officers were more focused on what they could see through sputtering lamplight. The flatboats were in motion, swaying, rocking; out past the docks, the harbor was alive with heavy waves, black water churned into a dangerous froth. The soldiers were ordered back into their barracks to wait out the storm, but the structures were crowded, no one had room to sleep.

The storm did not pass until well after midnight, the opportunity for the assault lost. As the first dull light revealed the heavy mist that blanketed the harbor, both sides took a long breath, commanders on both sides feeling frustration mixed with a strange sense of relief. Washington could see the British responding in a different way to the threat from his guns on Dorchester Heights. The navy had backed the gunships away, as well as the merchantmen, moving them out of range, closer to Charlestown peninsula. When the flatboats began to move from Castle William, they were empty, crossing the stretch of water back to the wharves in Boston. There would be no assault. Howe had his transports and his orders from London. In the days that followed, Washington could only watch as the British barges carried their soldiers to their ships, a great fleet slowly maneuvering their way out through the harbor. The men on Dorchester Heights stood alongside their commander, sharing the strangely mixed feelings, the sharp anticipation of another great fight replaced by a quiet emptiness. As the transports moved out to sea, they were led by the men-of-war, who did not pour their fire into the town, as so many had feared. One by one, as the ships reached the mouth of the harbor, Washington watched helplessly as the great sails went up, billowing out with the winds that would take the British army out to sea.

MARCH 18, 1776

HE RODE IN WITH ONLY A FEW MEN, HANDPICKED FROM THE RANKS. Nearly every one of them had the telltale scars of smallpox, pockmarks from their fight with the scourge. The rumors had reached him of disease rampant in the town, or at least enough of a presence that he dare not risk bringing a mass of his army into a place that could kill them all. He was as immune as the men who rode with him, having survived his own bout as a boy.

He had watched from the heights as the British destroyed that part of their equipment they could not take to the boats. Cannon had been spiked, some rolled right off the wharves, buried in the deep water of the harbor, to be followed by the personal trappings of wealthy command, even Howe's own gilded carriage now resting on the bottom of the bay. What they had not taken or destroyed lay scattered in the streets, some homes standing with doors wide open, contents flung about, the lives of the people who had once lived there as shattered as the mirrors and portraits that littered their floors. Hundred of Tory loyalists had sailed with the British army, and many of the homes had been theirs, showing the signs of destructive haste. Washington had observed some of it through his spyglass, families struggling with great bundles of their belongings, only to have them stripped away by the naval guards, much of the family treasures piled still on the wharves. He could see some of the homes intact, sealed up carefully, evidence of the hope that their owners would return to resume their lives, naïve optimism that nothing would be changed, all of this horror would simply pass and be forgotten.

His men scouted out carefully in all directions, down every street, and the good news began to come back to him. The British had not been able to destroy it all, and great barrels of powder, crates of shot and shell were to be found hidden in barns, stacks of muskets bound for transport but somehow left behind.

He rode the horse slowly, avoiding the destruction in the street, clothing and glassware, military bags and civilian trunks. Now he could see people emerging from their homes, the ones who had stayed put through all of it, who had endured the abuses of the soldiers, the torment of military occupation, who had even endured the artillery barrage from Washington's own guns, huddled in basements through their own private hell. Most of them were neither Tories nor rebels, just citizens of a town who had stayed because they had nowhere else to go. Now they shuffled along the streets, poking through the debris, and he saw the faces, drawn and pale, watching this grand soldier move past them, not yet understanding what was happening or why, their bodies weakened by the lack of food, their minds dazed by the months of constant torment from the army and the war that had taken their lives away.

He rode close to the British barricades, the ones facing the mouth of the Charles, the place where Greene and Sullivan would have landed their men. He stopped the horse, studied the construction, thought, They are much more formidable than I expected. He rode past several more, the streets blockaded by thick massed piles of timber, sharp steel spikes pointing out to the water. It was a shock, and he found himself saying a prayer, thanking God that the attack had not unfolded as planned. Yes, we would have killed a great many of our own, trying to break through here. Howe did certainly understand how secure he was. That storm, which we so cursed, which we saw as depriving us of our great taste of victory, may well have saved us from a disaster.

He had no real information about where the British had gone, had heard from the desperate Tories who stayed behind that most of the civilians would likely go to Halifax. But Howe had passed the word that the army was to go there as well, then on to England, a clumsy and insulting attempt at deception that Washington never believed. No, he is surely going to the one place where his men can make a foothold, safely, with the support of many of the citizens. He is going to New York. And though we cannot travel as quickly on land as he can on water, we must make a presence there as soon as possible.

He pulled the horse to the side, rode out into a wide street, climbed a hill, could see the Old South Meeting Hall, the great hall where so much of this rebellion had begun, where the great orators had planted the seeds in the people here, just the way men such as Patrick Henry had done in Virginia. He saw a few of his troops now, some kicking through the rubble, some carrying small packages, treasures of some kind. He saw one man at the doorway of the meetinghouse, his head down, his musket lying across his legs, sitting with his back to the door. Washington heard him now, could see the man was crying. He climbed down from the horse, curious, and the man saw him, said, "Damn them . . . how they used this place . . ."

The man could not speak, and Washington moved past him, pushed slowly through the door, resistance on the other side. He stepped inside, felt suddenly overpowered by the familiar smell of horses, the pungent odor of a barnyard. He stepped on straw, dirt, could see now that the place had been used as a stable, or worse, broken benches piled against the walls, empty wine bottles smashed on the floor. The floor was mostly dirt and horse manure, and he saw the stairway, began to climb up, stepped carefully over broken glass, remains of garbage, telltale signs of rats and mice. He reached the first balcony, the chairs shattered into splinters, more wine bottles, the white walls stained with dark blotches, gouged and scratched by the points of swords, initials, oaths of all kinds. He could see across, higher up, more damage on the top balcony, rags draped over the bits of railing that were not broken away. The man he had seen outside was suddenly there, had followed him up the steps. Washington had no words, and the man halted beside him, neither one thinking of rank or protocol. The soldier recounted, "I sat right here. Right in this spot. Heard Sam Adams many a time. Dr. Warren. Brought my children, so they could hear. Words enough to light a fire in your soul." The man pointed down to the main level. "The rostrum was right there. God knows what they done with it." He stepped around behind the general, and Washington could hear glass beneath the man's boots. "This place . . . this was my church. It was for a lot of us. This is where a man could bring his family to hear the truth. How dare they do this. How dare those red-coated bastards . . ."

The man began to cry again, and Washington could not look at him. The message was plain in the man's emotions. It is all right here, beyond all the talk and the politics, papers and taxes and decrees. There is more meaning in this one place than in anything any of us have done. He imagined the scene, drunken soldiers gleefully abusing this grand hall, fully aware of what this place symbolized. You hold yourself as superior, your history, your government, your culture, your damned king. And you dismiss us as a people to be subjugated and abused and dismissed in any way you find convenient. You venerate your institutions yet desecrate ours. How dare you, indeed?

He backed away from the railing, would not disturb the man, felt the man's grief deep inside himself. He moved to the stairway, stepped slowly down. There were other people coming in now, soldiers and citizens, staring at the devastation, uttering low sounds of shock and anger. He held tightly to the emotion, felt it turning, growing in him, rising in slow fury. He could not speak, stepped past the people, moved outside, back to his horse, back to the streets, back to his army.

42. ADAMS

PHILADELPHIA, MAY 15, 1776

THE CONGRESS WAS STILL A FORUM FOR CHAOTIC DEBATE, BUT NOW the delegates could not help but feel a new energy, bolstered by news of the British evacuation of Boston. Naturally the great majority of delegates saw the British move as a decisive military and moral victory for Washington. But Adams was amazed to see the influence of John Dickinson strengthening again, many of the conservatives pouring out their optimism that now the king would have to listen to reason. With the British out of Boston, the conservatives urged more caution, delay in enacting any more of the resolves that would surely have the effect of offending the king. Adams was beyond frustration that so many of the delegates were still on tiptoe in their regard for the king's policies, that even in those colonies where blood had been shed, Massachusetts and Virginia, some of the less vocal delegates, Cushing and Randolph, were still encouraging John Dickinson to lead them in his chosen course of reconciliation. But before Dickinson's people could build any momentum for their side of the issues, more blood was spilled.

General Henry Clinton had transported two thousand troops to the waters off North Carolina. Some of these troops had been part of the Boston camps, and Clinton was preparing to land them near the port of Wilmington. The mission was encouraged by the royal governor there, Josiah Martin, who had assured the British command that any rebellion in his colony would easily be extinguished, and that the large population of Scottish citizens there was fiercely loyal to the crown and would rally to the presence of the royal troops. Rally they did, seventeen hundred loyalist Scotsmen assembling and marching to welcome Clinton's landing. But the colonial militia and minutemen rallied as well, and when the Scotsmen arrived at a place called Moore's Creek Bridge, they were opposed by a thousand entrenched colonial troops. The fight was brief and totally one-sided. The Scots loyalists were completely routed, a result that sent Governor Martin scurrying to sanctuary on Clinton's warships, while Clinton wisely decided not to land his troops after all. In the congress, it was soon made clear that the delegates from North Carolina, William Hooper, John Penn, and even the Quaker Joseph Hewes, had shed any cloak of doubt about their stand against reconciliation.

The success of the fight in North Carolina was more than a piece of good news for the radicals. It was one more addition to the rapidly growing momentum to respond to the king's decree by declaring that the colonies were independent of British control. The momentum was aided by the high-handed documents that continued to flow out of London. Lord Germain declared all American seaports to be closed to all traffic, except to access by British ships. In response, congress declared in early April that all American ports were now open for trade from every country in the world *except* England. While some in the congress seemed content to play this tit-for-tat game with the British, Adams realized that the open-port decree was more than symbolic. It was a distinct message to the other naval powers of the world, most notably France, that the colonies were ready to begin conducting trade outside of the authority of any British regulations. But there had to be more than a simple decree, even if it was a thinly disguised invitation for foreign ships to confront British sovereignty in America. No foreign government would recognize the colonies as a governmental entity. The congress could not expect any formal recognition, nor would any foreign treasury extend any kind of credit to this unofficial government. Beyond the currency of gold and silver, colonial currency was simply a gesture of good faith in the form of printed paper, backed by a Continental Congress that for whatever reason might suddenly cease to exist. Until the congress could declare the colonies independent, and do so with the explicit support of the governing body in each colony, any foreign power had to treat America as British territory, regardless of the amount of passion behind their rebellion.

Even with the congress still sharply divided, Adams had quietly supported the secret sessions of Ben Franklin's committee in their contacts with the Frenchman Bonvouloir. But as Franklin had continued to have suspicions about the authority of the Frenchman, Adams had worked behind the scenes to bypass Bonvouloir and secure the delegates' approval to send their own representative to France. His name was Silas Deane, a delegate from Connecticut, and by early May, Deane was on his way to Paris, the first man chosen to represent American interests abroad.

Even the conservative delegates could not pretend that the

colonies were still governed by any legitimate structure. Most of the royal governors were either in England or exiled on board British warships. One exception was William Franklin, who had been held essentially under house arrest in his home in Perth Amboy. Connecticut's Trumbull was another exception, for a very different reason. He had long ago made his own break with the crown and generally supported the Sons of Liberty. Connecticut, like Rhode Island, had a charter that dated back to the mid-1600s, prior to the formation of the British constitution. By definition, this exempted those colonies from any possibility of control by Parliament. But even Dickinson's allies conceded that the king, in his decree, had removed the American colonies from British protection, had isolated them from British commerce, and now, in at least three colonies, royal governors themselves had engineered violent military attacks on their own people. On May 15 the congress passed a resolve that each colony should consider itself without a government and should follow the example of Massachusetts, electing its own assembly. Even Dickinson approved the resolve, understanding that it was a practical necessity, and meant only that each new assembly might eventually have to pledge its loyalty to the king. Adams understood the resolve very differently. Each colony had now taken its first major step toward independence.

WHILE THE DELEGATES CONTINUED TO WRANGLE OVER THE ARCANE issues of politics and philosophy, Adams had begun to hear from those outside of Philadelphia. In letters from friends, from Abigail as well, he began to hear that the congress itself was isolated from so many of the citizens they were supposed to represent. Beyond the walls of the State House, two strong tides were rising. Among those who either favored the break with England or were caught in the center of the issue, *Common Sense* had sparked a roaring fire. Tom Paine's pamphlet had sold well over a hundred thousand copies, offering a clearly worded explanation of why it was time for the American people to move beyond the control of an abusive, outdated monarchy.

The second tide was rolling through the ranks of the Tories,

those who still had clung tightly to the robes of King George.
When his hiring of Hessian mercenaries was confirmed, many of
the loyalists absorbed an unexpected shock. The Tories had always taken comfort in being protected by British troops, knowing that in the event of the outbreak of violence close at hand,
they could seek out safe passage or sanctuary, as they had done
in Boston. In many towns, the loudest voices in support of the
king arose from their confidence that they were ultimately protected from the wrath of the rebels by the muskets of British soldiers. But foreign soldiers were no one's ally. The reality that the
king was sending foreigners to do his fighting was a disturbing
surprise.

The colonies had readily accepted the decree from the congress that each one choose a new assembly to replace any government with direct ties to the king. It was already a fact of life in
some of the colonies, the royal governors having long ago disbanded the official assemblies. Massachusetts had been the first
to form a people's assembly, as a response to Gage's enforcement of the Boston Port Bill. In Virginia, Governor Dunmore
had made it a regular habit to disband the assembly anytime it
offered discussion on any issue offensive to the king.

Most of the new assemblies had the same faces as the former
ones, even the most devout Tories realizing that they had best
continue to participate in the governing of their own colony, no
matter how uncomfortable the debates.

JUNE 7, 1776

ADAMS SAT AT THE DINING TABLE IGNORING HIS BREAKFAST, HIS
mind having left his appetite far behind. Richard Henry Lee sat
across from him, Sam to the side, no one moving, each one
seemingly oblivious to the presence of the others. At last Sam
seemed to snap awake, moved one hand to his coffee cup, raised
it, stared into the steaming brew.

"We cannot wait. We have known this is a slow process from
the beginning. Six colonies have said yes. We will use that, em-

phasize that to the others. Surely it will have good effect. That Georgia finally consented to send delegates here, with instructions to support independence . . . I have to accept that as a sign."

Lee pushed his plate away, folded his hands in front of him, still staring downward, nodded slowly.

"Georgia, yes. Perhaps. North and South Carolina. Rhode Island, Virginia, Massachusetts. Unless you have more recent news than I, none of the other colonies have yet consented to support us."

Sam seemed to energize a bit.

"The other northern colonies will certainly send word soon. I have friends in both Connecticut and New Hampshire. They will not delay."

Adams fixed him with a look.

"But they have already delayed. What are they debating?" His words were hot with frustration, and he clenched his fists, saw Sam regarding him with an unusual helplessness. "These delays play right into the hands of Dickinson. I am astounded at the short memories of these delegates. Great catastrophic events rile them into decisive action, and then perhaps a week later, they have forgotten all about it. How many more cities must be destroyed? If I hear one more delegate suggest that this has all been some unhappy accident, that the king can't possibly know the harm his army has caused . . ." He was red-faced, taking short hard breaths, and Sam put a hand on his arm.

"John, we cannot allow impatience to cloud our purpose."

Sam's words had little effect. Adams was fighting a sickness in his gut, the months of holding tightly to decorum, politeness, gracious disagreement. He had begun to think of just leaving, packing up, riding home, returning to the farm. He knew the crops had been planted, had had news from Abigail of all the new help she had. The houses were bulging with boarders, and he recalled the Christmas dinner, how busy she had been. No time for her husband at all. He wiped his face with his hands, shook his head, tried to clear it all away, could see calm on Sam's face.

"How can you be so . . . complacent?"

Sam's expression didn't change.

"I'm not complacent at all, John. I have gone through experiences such as this for a very long time. I know I am right, I make the good argument, write the wise article, the persuasive letters. And sometimes I feel as though I am preaching to stacks of wood. People do not easily embrace change. Convincing them to turn in a new direction requires a patience and a persistence that tax everyone. It does not help matters that the course we are attempting to follow could get us all hanged."

Adams saw a smile.

"The voice of comfort."

Lee sat back in his chair, looked at Sam.

"The people who are most resistant to change are right here in this congress—men of means, men who have achieved such a level of comfort in their lives that any change is a potential threat. We have lost sight of whom it is we are supposed to represent. I assume you both are receiving letters of support, news from back home. In Virginia, the people are waiting on *us*, on this congress, to move in the right direction. Everywhere I go, even in Philadelphia, I hear the same thing, a willingness, a passion to move forward. This congress is a means to create the documents. But the people are not going to rely on us to effect the changes. Look at the impact of *Common Sense*."

Adams shook his head.

"That document causes me some considerable discomfort. Mr. Paine has fashioned the concept of a government that is too simple to work. There is a danger that people will believe he has all the answers. Many of his solutions are deeply flawed. He calls for government in one body, with no mechanism for checking its authority, no executive to manage—"

Lee raised both his hands off the table, opened them toward Adams, moved them in rhythm with his words: "It . . . does . . . not . . . matter."

Sam seemed to understand.

"He's right, John. It doesn't. No one is going to use *Common Sense* as a bible for building a new government. That, ultimately, is our job. It might even be . . . your job. But there is an enormous benefit to what he has stirred up. You know that. You hear it every day, as we all do."

Lee leaned forward, looked hard at Adams.

"What matters about *Common Sense* is that it has raised the passion in the people. It is our job now to make the best use of that."

Adams was beginning to feel better, the uneasiness loosening.

"We cannot consume so much time that we allow those passions to cool."

Lee stood up, proclaimed, "I do not intend to. I believe we should be at the State House. Gentlemen?"

ADAMS KNEW WHAT LEE INTENDED TO DO, AND IT WAS NOT JUST one man's solution to cutting past the endless debates. If anything, Lee's proposal would draw even more debate, might throw the entire congress into such a lather of indecision that it could mean the end of the whole process. Adams already had a clear notion of how much support they would have, that many of the delegates themselves were in favor of issuing some final statement on colonial independence or, like the delegates from Georgia, had been instructed by their own assemblies to push forward the issue.

The chamber was filled, and above, in the balcony, Adams saw a solid crowd, every space filled. It was unusual to have much of a public audience, but something had changed, and Adams had to accept now that Lee was probably right. Despite Adams' own doubts about Thomas Paine's understanding of representative government, Paine's impact was now clearly obvious in the gallery above him. The *people* were there.

Hancock called the meeting to order, his usual casual greeting, a quick rap with his gavel. But the hum in the audience above them continued to drone. Hancock pounded his gavel hard this time, stared upward, a stern parent to unruly children, said aloud, "I repeat . . . this session of the Continental Congress shall come to *order*." The audience drifted into silence, and Hancock still stared at them, a silent scolding. "The chair has received a request from the honorable delegate from Virginia, Mr. Richard Henry Lee."

The gallery burst into applause, and Hancock seemed truly agitated, pounded the gavel again. Adams felt a growing sense of unease but smiled at Hancock's show of formal anger. Lee moved to the rostrum, his expression a dignified calm, and Adams was truly nervous now, could feel his hands sweating, flexed his fingers. Lee waited for a long moment, glanced around the room, said slowly, "I have requested to be allowed to introduce the following resolutions, for the consideration of this congress." He paused for a moment, seemed to weigh his own words in his mind, then went on. "Resolved, that these united colonies are, and of right ought to be, free and independent states, that they are absolved from all allegiance to the British crown, and that all political connection between them and the state of Great Britain is and ought to be totally dissolved. That it is expedient forthwith to take the most effectual measures for forming foreign alliances. That a plan of confederation be prepared and transmitted to the respective colonies for their consideration and approbation."

His voice was sharp and firm, his words echoing through the chamber like the tolling of a solitary bell. Lee backed away from the rostrum, showing no emotion, and suddenly the gallery above exploded into cheers. Adams could feel the sounds rolling all through the great hall, could see some of the delegates responding as well, hands held high, the voices of the delegates mingling with the cries of the people. Hancock waited this time, would not interrupt the sounds, seemed to understand, as so many did, that Lee's resolution had sliced through the hesitancy, that the momentum toward independence could not simply be ignored or avoided by those made uncomfortable by the word.

LEE'S RESOLUTION DID NOT END THE DEBATE, BUT INSPIRED EVEN more. The words flowed all day long, and didn't end there. The resolves were considered again the following day, put aside for the observation of the Sabbath, and debated again on Monday, June 10. Despite the passionate support from the galleries above them, there could be no successful vote. Many of the delegates were concerned that their own sentiments might contradict the wishes of their assemblies, some of which were still in the process of their very creation. The conservatives proposed a delay in the vote, and the majority of the delegates agreed, accepting a three-week pause, a space of time the conservatives felt would once again calm the passions for this reckless course. To those delegates who had already received word authorizing them to vote in favor of an official call for independence— delegates from Massachusetts, Virginia, Rhode Island, North and South Carolina, and Georgia—the delay was another frustrating barrier. But Adams had to concede that the radicals simply didn't have the votes, that even with approval certain to come from Connecticut and New Hampshire, the other colonies seemed firmly opposed. In Maryland and Pennsylvania, there was even strong resistance to forming any kind of new state assembly that did not have ties to the king.

For Lee's resolve to be effective, especially in reaching out to alliances with foreign powers, for it to be meaningful, the vote had to be unanimous. Despite Adams' frustration with what he felt were the soft backbones of the conservatives, he had to accept that the three-week delay might be put to good use trying to convince the nervous assemblies, and their delegates, that this was the only course. There was nothing else he could do.

While Lee's resolution had a dramatic impact in the congress, many of the delegates realized that a document was required that would be more specific in its wording, would more adequately spell out the terms of the proposal they were being asked to vote on. As was customary now in the congress, a committee was formed to take up the task. Five men were chosen: John Adams, Benjamin Franklin, Robert Livingston of New York, Roger Sherman of Connecticut, and the quiet young man from Virginia, Thomas Jefferson.

To the relief of the conservatives, the matter seemed to have been dismissed, another issue banished to a committee where it might simply fade away. To the committee itself, the task was straightforward: create a document that would convey to the king, to the English people, and to foreign governments the message that the passion and the dedication of the American people were resolute and unmistakable. It was time for a formal declaration of independence.

43. FRANKLIN

PHILADELPHIA, JUNE 1776

EARLY THAT SPRING, HE HAD ACCEPTED AN APPOINTMENT FROM THE congress as a commissioner to Canada, along with two men from Maryland, Samuel Chase, a delegate to the congress, and Charles Carroll. Carroll was not a member of the congress but was widely known as an extremely wealthy and influential Catholic. The congress had approved a motion to send the commission to Montreal, which was still under the control of Benedict Arnold's colonial troops. The attempt would be to establish a more diplomatic relationship with the Canadians than could have been expected if the negotiations were carried out by colonial soldiers. They were to be accompanied by Carroll's cousin, John Carroll, a Jesuit priest.

The success of the journey would depend on whether they would be allowed to meet with influential Canadian citizens, who might have some motivation for making a break with England. Despite the military disaster the previous autumn, Arnold still had several hundred colonial troops under his command. In Quebec, the British royal governor, Guy Carleton, backed by British troops, held a strongly defended position that not even the optimistic Arnold believed could be assaulted. The most optimistic in George Washington's camp considered that Arnold had achieved a stalemate with Carleton. In fact, the colonial troops were woefully unprepared for the Canadian winter, had sustained themselves by raiding the pantries of the local citizenry. Having recovered somewhat from his wounds, Arnold himself knew that the only reason his small force was still encamped in Montreal was that Carleton had decided not to attack them.

Franklin's committee had begun their mission believing that their efforts might be for some good. If Canada could be convinced to break ties with England, the congress was prepared to receive Canada as a fourteenth colony. By joining in the colonial fight, it would not only add considerable power to the supporters of independence, but would possibly cut off the British invasion route down the Hudson River, which was still Washington's biggest strategic concern.

But, like every part of the Canadian operation thus far, the diplomatic effort was as farcical as the military effort. Much of what had been French Canada was Catholic, and it was no secret in Montreal that, despite the token presence of the Catholics in Franklin's committee, prejudice against Catholics in the American colonies was a fact of life. It was merely an extension of what had been ingrained into English culture dating back to King Henry VIII. Franklin knew that there was a significant population of Protestant Anglicans around Montreal, where Arnold had been encamped, who might be persuaded to join the American cause, but it turned out that the abuse Arnold's soldiers had heaped on the local civilians had doomed Franklin's mission before it began. No matter who would come calling, it was unlikely that anyone in Canada could be swayed from the belief that an alliance with the American colonies was an absurd proposition.

When the committee had begun its journey in late March, Franklin had realized that by accepting this responsibility, he might have made a much greater mistake than simply falling victim to diplomatic optimism. The harshness of the far northern springtime was nothing like he had experienced before. By the time he had reached Montreal, enduring some of the same difficulties that had afflicted the colonial troops, he was completely worn out, and suffering a variety of illnesses. Without even meeting with Carleton at all, he had appraised Arnold's situation as hopeless, and by early May, he had already embarked on his way back to Philadelphia.

JUNE 15, 1776

FRANKLIN HAD NOT BEEN TO THE CONGRESS ON MANY OCCASIONS since his return from Canada, was still suffering the effects of the foolishness of his trip. He shuffled about the house in a pair of old slippers, a reminder of London, of the comfortable times in a place that now he had trouble even remembering. It had taken him more than a week after his return before he could walk for more than a minute or two. The exposure to the harsh weather all along the trip had caused a painful swelling in his legs, the annoying stiffness in his knees expanding into a mystifying ailment that kept him on his back. He had never shown patience for being restricted, had fought his way through every illness he had ever had. But this was different, the kind of weakness he had never experienced before, a frightening reminder that no matter how much he disputed the issue in his mind, his body was telling him there was much a man his age simply could no longer do.

He moved slowly into his room, stopped at a small mirror on his wall, looked at his reflection. He grimaced, thought, It's a wonder the children even come near you. You appear to be some kind of demon. He moved to his bed, lowered himself slowly, sat, evaluated the pains in his legs. Better, not as achy. He had not thought of praying in a very long time, had rarely considered asking for anything from God. But throughout the ordeal of his return home, he had spent the quiet times talking to God, much as he used to talk to Deborah. I did ask a favor, he remembered, asked Him to just get me home safely, allow me to survive this ridiculous foolishness. When the lesson is punctuated by a reminder of mortality, an old man can learn as well as a young man. He tried to open his mind in that direction now, some expression of thanks to God: You did bring me home. I suppose You had as much to do with it as anyone. Horses and carriages and boats are, after all, Your creations.

Very long ago he had considered founding his own religion, based on the simple philosophy that though God is supreme to all things, the most effective way man can make himself pleasing to God is to do good work toward his fellow man. He tried to recall his essays, thought of the inspiration for the idea in the first place, his annoyance with those who seemed to spend so much of their time publicly announcing their connection to God, as though the louder the voice, the more secure their place in heaven. His mind wasn't helping him now, the memories blurred. He tried to recall the name of his religion, his acceptance then that all religions were apparently required to have a label. It came to him now: the Society of the Free and Easy. Yes, free of vice, of debt, of all the negatives that so infect people. God would certainly be pleased with that. Easy . . . his mind went blank. What was so easy about it, except that I could write it down on paper? If it was so easy, you'd think I would remember it. Hardly matters. There's not a single church where anyone goes to sing hymns to *my* enlightened philosophy.

He heard sounds outside his room, saw the face peering around the edge of the door.

"Come in, Temple."

The boy seemed to bound into the room like a giant spider, all legs and arms.

"Grandpapa, I have a letter from Father. I thought you'd like to see it."

Franklin looked at the folded paper in the boy's hand.

"Is he all right?"

"He says so. Says they are treating him well. He says he hears your name every day. You want to read it?"

Temple held the letter out to him, but Franklin resisted the boy's enthusiasm.

"That's good to hear. They'll not abuse him. Perhaps I'll read it later."

Temple seemed disappointed, set the letter down on the small nightstand.

"Would you like to go for a walk, Grandpapa? It's quite warm outside."

Franklin began the argument in his own mind. I'm too tired. No, get up, you old fool, it will do you some good. The boy's energy was affecting him now, the smile that never stayed gone for long. Temple held out his hand.

"Let me help you up. Come on. You should get out of this room. It has a . . . funny smell."

Franklin pulled himself up without the boy's help. Ah, yes, the frank confessions of youth. That smell is probably me.

"All right, let's go. Slowly. I'm not sixteen, you know."

The boy waited for him, led the way out of the house. Franklin was blinded by the sunshine, blinked his way into the street, the boy watching him carefully, ready to assist.

They walked a short way, Franklin feeling the effects of the warm air, opening up the dark places, easing the pains, loosening his joints. The boy began to talk, the energy of the young bursting out in chatter about all those things so important in his world. Franklin tried to concentrate on Temple's words, but the flow was beyond his mind's ability to capture it all, endless and irrelevant. The boy didn't seem to notice whether Franklin was hearing him or not, and Franklin's mind began to drift, thinking of William, of the unread letter. My grandson is going to be an adult soon. And what will he think of the two of us? How can father and grandfather be so very different?

William had been ordered arrested, the new assembly in New Jersey imprisoning him in Connecticut. He thought of Temple's words. Certainly William hears my name . . . of course he does. It's the only reason they didn't tar and feather him, or tie him up and stick him in the hold of a ship for England. It wasn't my doing; there was no way I could intervene on either side. My son must accept the responsibility.

Franklin glanced at the boy now, the burst of words breaking through to him.

" . . . the most awful hair braids, even the other girls laughing at her . . ."

He thought of Elizabeth now, his daughter-in-law's gentle soul. She is destroyed by this, certainly. She has lost everything that mattered to her. She was always sickly, fragile. I hope my son quiets his own jabbering protests long enough to care for her. Before this is over, he'll probably end up in England. He certainly won't change his allegiances. But Elizabeth . . . He swept the thoughts from his mind when he heard his name, someone passing by, a cordial greeting. He wanted to respond, but they were already gone, the boy still talking. His mind was clearing more now, the walk having a good effect. He put his hand on the boy's arm, stopping the rush of words.

"I think . . . I'd like to return home. I'm not properly dressed. I should like to attend the congress."

The boy stopped.

"All right, Grandpapa. Whatever you say. You sure you're feeling well enough?"

"That's a secondary concern, my boy. I know they are hoping for my return. There's a new committee that requires my presence."

"Grandpapa, you said you wouldn't volunteer for any more committees. Look what happened in Canada."

He was surprised at his grandson, that he would remember an old man's grumbling.

"Different this time. A bit more useful, I'm certain. And I don't have to *journey* anywhere."

JUNE 21, 1776

WORD HAD COME, AS EXPECTED, FROM BOTH NEW HAMPSHIRE AND Connecticut. Both assemblies had authorized their delegates in the congress to vote in favor of independence. But there had been a surprise as well. The same news came now from Delaware, the ninth colony to approve the resolution, a serious setback to the efforts of the conservatives to hold the middle colonies together in a firm alliance against the planned declaration.

The committee had been meeting in Franklin's absence, but it was clear that he had been missed. At Jefferson's request, they were to meet at the young man's place of lodging, the second story of the home of a German bricklayer named Graff. The four committeemen sat around a dining table, now a makeshift meeting room. Jefferson, the fifth man, was behind a closed door, in a smaller room to one side. They waited patiently, as Jefferson had urged them apologetically, as he rushed to complete the last details of the document.

Franklin felt Adams staring at him, his face stamped with a small frown.

"Is there something wrong, Mr. Adams?"

Adams seemed to snap awake.

"Oh, my, no. My apologies, Doctor. I find myself drifting to troubling thoughts."

"You are entitled, Mr. Adams. These days, there is little else."

During most of the meetings, and for their short time in Jefferson's own residence, the other two men, Sherman and Livingston, had said very little, and now Livingston stood, paced the small room.

"Did he say he would finish soon?"

"Yes. At any time now," Adams replied.

There had been very little sound from the smaller room, but now came a muffled call: "One more moment, please. I'll be right there."

Livingston grunted, still paced, and Franklin smiled at the man's impatience. He had been relieved that Jefferson, the youngest among them, had accepted the task of actually writing the first draft of the document they were charged with preparing. Franklin had been expecting to write it himself, could see from his first day in attendance that Adams had given the wording serious thought as well. The other two seemed reluctant to take an active role, and Franklin had not pushed the issue toward either of them directly. He glanced at the quiet man from Connecticut. *Mr. Sherman has the mind, but he is not a man of words.*

Roger Sherman was a Yale-educated merchant with a particular talent for both economic theory and astronomy. Any writing he had done had been arcane and academic, and his presence on the committee was a reward for his firm support of the radical cause. Sherman had made it clear from the first committee meeting that he would support any document they produced.

Livingston still paced anxiously, and Franklin avoided looking at him now, felt tired out just by the man's nervous tics. Robert Livingston was a New York lawyer and a member of one of the most prominent families in that colony. He had always been closely aligned with loyalist sympathies, was a friend of the royal governor, William Tryon. His conservative views had begun to moderate during his term in the second congress, and though Franklin was comfortable with Livingston's presence on the committee, Adams did not appear at all pleased that a man with conservative leanings should be invited to offer input to such a radical undertaking. Franklin felt more tolerance for the man's somewhat ticklish situation, representing a colony that was presumed to be firmly against independence.

The door burst open, startling Franklin, all heads turning, and Jefferson was there now, seemed to flinch under the sudden attention.

"Good day, gentlemen. My apologies. Uh . . . I have something here."

Livingston sat again, and Franklin was amused by Jefferson's nervousness.

"Please sit down, young man. You appear winded. There was no reason to hurry." He ignored Livingston, who would obviously disagree, and Jefferson seemed to calm down, slid himself into the one empty chair. Jefferson glanced at each of them.

"I worked on this most of the night. I tried to . . . explain the variety of . . ."

Adams reached for the paper, and Franklin smiled again.

"It's all right. Let the document speak for itself. No need to explain."

Adams perused the document, and Franklin watched the younger man, moving in the chair, a bundle of nervousness. He saw much of himself in the young Virginian, a man with much more talent for science and letters than anyone could suspect from his upbringing. His family had some aristocratic connections, but Jefferson himself had never taken to the role of a social lion. He had pursued a law career, graduated from William and Mary, but could not overcome a public shyness and a complete lack of oratorical skills, which made him ineffective at best in the courtroom. His reputation in Virginia had been built much more upon his talent for writing, and two years before, the young man had published a virulent attack on the crown, which had identified him, along with Patrick Henry and Richard Henry Lee, as being among the most radical men in Virginia. Franklin had rarely spoken to the young man, had on occasion observed Jefferson's uncomfortable withdrawal in the social gatherings around the congress. But Franklin had always been intrigued with the potential of the man's mind, had hoped for the time beyond the turbulent issues of the congress when they might explore Jefferson's apparent interest in science. For the time being, Franklin was as content as the other three to let the young man display his skill in drafting this declaration.

Adams handed the paper to the eager Livingston, looked at Franklin, smiled, the first break in the man's bleak expression.

"I believe our young Virginian has done us proud."

THEY DISCUSSED THE DRAFT OF THE DECLARATION, BUT IT WAS nothing like a debate. Livingston and Sherman seemed to back away, left the discussion to the other three. There was very little disagreement on the main points, and much of the discussion concerned the more precise word, the more appropriate phrase. Franklin had found himself discussing the document more extensively with Adams than with its author, and Jefferson did not object. More than once Franklin caught the look on Jefferson's face, the young man acknowledging the assistance from the other two men.

They had adjourned for the day, and Franklin felt a wonderful combination of exhilaration and exhaustion. He had emerged from the confinement of Jefferson's residence feeling every part of him reaching out for the sunshine of the late afternoon, the longer days of summer a precious gift he would not take for granted. He stood outside the house, filling his chest with the air. Adams emerged behind him, overtook him, then slowed, seemingly hesitant to interrupt Franklin's private moment.

"Do have a pleasant evening, Mr. Adams."

Adams stopped now, moved closer.

"We are very nearly complete in our task, Doctor."

"Yes. I believe we are."

"Are you aware, Doctor, that the Pennsylvania Assembly is meeting in the other gallery of the State House?"

Franklin glanced in that direction, could see the larger building a block away. There was no sign of activity, no one moving in or out of the building.

"I was not aware. I haven't been involved with them for a while. Priorities, you know. I grew rather impatient listening to the Quakers bombard us with all the reasons why God loves King George. They have an amazing capacity for emphasizing the ideal and ignoring the real. Rather like Mr. Dickinson."

Adams did not laugh.

"I don't believe Mr. Dickinson has too much to say to your assembly these days."

Franklin shrugged slightly, wasn't too sure what Adams meant.

"Old ways die hard, Mr. Adams."

Adams made a short bow, moved away, and Franklin began to follow, stopped, looked again at the State House. He could not help feeling curious. *If they are meeting this late in the day, perhaps it is something worth listening to.*

The Pennsylvania Assembly had always been dominated by the Quakers, whose staunch aversion to war of any kind translated into a political view that held tightly to allegiance to the king. While a logical argument had often been made that it was in fact the king who had created the war, the conservative tone of the governing body was absolute. Franklin had resigned several months before, to the delight of most of the assembly. And because of his journey to Canada and his subsequent illness, for a long while he had not played any role in the politics of the colony itself. He had been unaware that in mid-May the assembly had been assaulted by a public town meeting, held on the lawn of the State House. Seven thousand citizens had come together in a show of support for independence, had offered their own referendum on the spot, voting their own assembly out of existence and supporting the congress' proclamation for the founding of a new colonial government with no ties to the king. It was an outrageous show of rebelliousness that the assembly could not ignore, neither the Quakers nor the rest of Dickinson's conservatives. It was a shock for the old powers in Pennsylvania to observe that their own citizens were much more closely aligned with the radicals in the congress than with the philosophy of the Quaker founders. The assembly had been sufficiently shaken that they had finally agreed to hear debate on the matters that lay before the congress, the declaration that their own favorite son, Ben Franklin, was helping to create. Pennsylvania's absolute stand against independence was suddenly very shaky indeed.

Franklin crossed the street, moved toward the shadows of the State House, stepped into the silence of the main chamber. He could hear the voices now, muffled beyond the far wall, thought, Yes, it seems Mr. Adams is correct. He stood still for a moment, could discern the mood of the discussion from the clash of voices, and suddenly the door burst open, a flood of men coming toward him. Tempers were still hot, and he stood to one side, surprised to be ignored by several men he had known for years. The discussion rolled past him, the men moving out into the fading sunlight, and now more men emerged, and he thought, Well, obviously, their day has concluded. Several of them began to notice him now, he saw smiles, acknowledged the kindness of their greetings, and one man suddenly broke from the flow, moved sharply toward him. It was John Dickinson.

"Well, here is our Dr. Franklin! Tell me, sir, are you enjoying the spectacle?"

There was nothing kind in Dickinson's words, and Franklin could see the others sidling away. Franklin avoided Dickinson's hot stare, looked toward the others who were exiting the chamber.

"Does no one wish to intervene on my behalf? It seems my friend here has chosen himself a ripe target." It was an attempt at humor, but the others kept moving, a couple of heads shaking, obvious exhaustion from the debates that had clearly lasted all day. "Well, sir, my friends have abandoned me. The mood among the assemblymen seems to be a bit sour."

Dickinson was still glowering.

"There are no assemblymen! Your success is complete, sir! We have been superseded by the counties! The assembly is simply . . . no more."

Franklin didn't know what to say, could see Dickinson's fury blending with the man's utter exhaustion. Dickinson seemed to run out of words, turned away from him. Finally he said, "There will be a new constitution. . . . Pennsylvania is no longer to be a child of her own honored heritage."

Franklin stepped closer to him, put a hand on the man's shoulder.

"What do you mean?"

Dickinson faced him now, the fury softened into grief, the man's eyes watering, a wavering in his voice.

"There will be a constitutional convention next month . . . to begin drafting a new government for Pennsylvania. How much more explanation do you require, sir? Does this not meet with your carefully laid plans?"

Franklin ignored the sarcasm.

"I did not know anything about this. You know I have not been involved in anything of the sort."

"Well, Doctor, you may rest comfortably in the knowledge that I will not be involved as well. I am not a part of the convention. My name was not approved to be included in the *new* assembly. It seems the rising tide of your philosophy has engulfed us. *Independence.* A word that no one dared to utter a year ago is now spewed about with the perfect glee of the undisciplined mob."

Dickinson moved to a nearby chair, sat, resting his lean arms on his knees. Franklin looked around for his own chair, pulled one closer to the man, sat himself, the stiffness in his legs returning.

"John, there was a time when I agreed with you. Independence was a dangerous course, advocated by reckless men who simply did not understand the structure a civilized people must adhere to, the boundaries that hold us apart from the savage. All those high-sounding words. But John, I was there, I watched the ministry engineer their own destruction. The corruption in Parliament . . ." He stopped, saw Dickinson looking down at his own hands, wondered now if the man was hearing him. "John, independence is not a philosophy. It is a *fact.* It has come to pass by the actions on both sides of the Atlantic. England is hastening its own decay, and America is emerging into a new era. I wish I was younger, I wish I could live to see what will follow."

Dickinson looked at him now, shook his head.

"I do not share your optimism."

"No, I am quite certain you do not. But it is of no consequence, is it? Whether it is you or I who is right will not make any difference. The course is already set. Apparently the *people* of Pennsylvania know that. The people of Massachusetts, Rhode Island, North Carolina . . . name them all, the *people* have been on this course for generations. I admit, it has taken me a while to grasp that it's not even about being English. We have citizens here from every country in Europe. Each one departed from his own shore for a reason, and each one has brought something to this culture that is different from any people who have ever lived before. Every citizen of these colonies is, in so many ways, a pioneer. This is a new land. No matter how much you may fear that, it cannot just be stamped out. No matter how tightly King George wishes to hold to his power over us, no matter how many soldiers he may send, no matter what may happen in this war, it does not matter. His hold has already been broken. It has been broken by the American people. It may be that we of this congress, so consumed by our lofty debates, are the last to understand. We still believe it is our purpose to give direction to the American people. If we will take the time to listen, we will find that they are giving direction to *us*."

Dickinson was listening to him, shook his head slowly.

"The king is a wise man. He will not allow his empire to simply break into pieces. He must not. What will happen here? What do these people know about governing? What can possibly follow that will secure us, elevate us from anarchy? We might as well return to the caves."

Franklin was truly tired now, had spent his energy. He sat quietly for a long moment, knew he could not reach him after all. He pulled himself up slowly.

"John, I respect your passion. I respect your loyalty. But I am afraid we will never understand each other. I should be going home, Sally will worry." He started to move, walking slowly through the great chamber, his footsteps echoing in the silence.

Dickinson called to him, "What will happen now, Ben?"

Franklin stopped, turned slowly, rubbed one hand on the soreness in his knee.

"Don't really know, John. One step at a time. Tomorrow I'll go back to work, do what I can to assist Mr. Jefferson."

THE FOLLOWING DAY, THE NEWS REACHED THE CONGRESS THAT New Jersey's newly formed assembly, inspired by the successful removal of their royal governor, had voted to instruct their delegates to favor independence. That same afternoon, the new governing body of Pennsylvania approved a motion authorizing its delegates to vote as they believed proper, with no restriction. Now only Maryland and New York continued to command their delegates to vote against the declaration.

JUNE 28, 1776

THE COMMITTEE WAS JUST THREE NOW, LIVINGSTON HOME IN NEW York, Sherman tending to some business in the city. There had been several drafts of the document, and Jefferson had shown complete patience as Franklin and Adams applied their own hand to his words. After several days of quiet examination, all three men seemed more willing to focus less on perfection than on completion of the task.

Franklin squinted, peered through his spectacles.

"Here. 'We hold these truths to be sacred and undeniable.' A bit flowery. I would suggest . . . 'self-evident.' Cut to the point. And this one, 'deluge us in blood.' " He looked at Jefferson now, smiled. "Bit of a poet, eh? I would suggest something a bit less, um, dramatic. I'd change that to . . . 'destroy us.' Again, just a bit closer to the point."

Adams was scanning the papers.

"I have a suggestion here. . . ."

Jefferson leaped up, his words bursting out.

"I have only tried to include everything that seemed important! Forgive me for not phrasing every sentence in its most perfect form!"

Franklin leaned back in the chair, raised one hand.

"Mr. Jefferson, please sit down."

Jefferson complied, folded his arms on the table, stared down in a thick sulk. Adams looked up from the document.

"Is something wrong?"

Franklin shook his head.

"No, I don't believe so. I have been observing our young friend here. He has been extremely generous in the manner in which he has accepted our amending of his work. But we have perhaps intruded just a bit too far into his pride. My apologies, sir."

Jefferson seemed surprised at Franklin's response to his outburst, looked at both men.

"It is no matter. The apology should come from this chair, Doctor."

Franklin thought for a moment.

"Allow me to interrupt our thoughts for a moment. Anyone who offers to draft a document for public consumption puts himself at risk. I am reminded of someone I knew a while ago, a hatter. He was just opening his own business, and wished to post an appropriate banner above his store. After much thought, he constructed a sign that included the drawing of a hat, beside the words *John Thompson, Hatter, Makes and Sells Hats for Ready Money*. As he showed his creation to his friends, one observed that the word *hatter* was redundant, since he also noted that he makes hats. Another friend noted that the word *makes* might as well be omitted, because the customers would not care who made the hats. If they liked the hats, they would buy them no matter who their maker. Another stated he thought the words *for ready money* to be useless, as everyone who purchased a hat would expect to pay. The changes were made, and the sign now read *John Thompson Sells Hats*. Another friend says, 'Sells hats? Why, no one would expect you to *give* them away. And being that there is a drawing of a hat on the board, why use the word at all?' Thus the merchant reduced the sign to *John Thompson*, accompanied by the picture of a hat. He has been, I might add, rather successful."

He realized both men were staring at him with their mouths open, a show of complete fatigue. A moment later, Jefferson broke into laughter.

"Your point is well taken, Doctor. I find no fault with either of you, gentlemen. I spoke from a weakness of body, not mind."

Adams blinked at Franklin through tired eyes.

"It has been my experience that, given enough time, we may find some reason to fault every single word of any sentence ever written. It is a lawyer's prerogative, you know. Doctor, I for one am weary beyond measure. If Mr. Jefferson has lost his patience for our meddling, perhaps it is time to stop meddling."

"Oh, no, by all means—"

"He's right, young man." Franklin tossed the paper in his hand to the center of the table. "The congress will certainly have some suggestions of their own. The best we can do for our cause, and our exhaustion, is accept that what we have produced . . . what Mr. Jefferson has produced . . . is more than adequate to the task."

Adams tossed his paper forward as well.

"All right, so it is time. We should, I suppose, create one fairly clean document, with not so many scribbles. If John Hancock has to read this aloud, we should eliminate any challenges."

Franklin laughed, said nothing in reply. He cocked one eye over his spectacles, addressed Jefferson, "You're the youngest. I motion that we take advantage of the stamina of youth. Mr. Jefferson should rewrite our draft."

Adams smiled.

"Second."

"Motion carried." Franklin arose, unwound the kinks in his back, saw Adams doing the same, said, "I will report to the chamber. Awaiting only the rapidity of Mr. Jefferson's penmanship, this committee is prepared to present its document."

He moved to the stairway, saw Jefferson already at work, the pen scratching the paper in a flurry of motion. He began to move down, held himself carefully to the railing, then waited for Adams to move down beside him, said in a low voice, "Blessed are we who can rely so on the young."

Adams started down in front of him, stopped suddenly, faced by Richard Henry Lee. Lee seemed out of breath.

"Oh . . . forgive me, gentlemen. I took it upon myself to pay a visit."

Franklin made a quick motion up the stairs behind him.

"Only a moment, Mr. Lee. I believe we are ready."

"Oh, my, that is wonderful. But, um, no, that's not what . . . I mean, there is extraordinary news. It seems Mr. Chase and Mr. Carroll deemed it wise to measure the sense of the people of Maryland. They have just returned from Annapolis. It seems the mood of the people there was so adamantly in favor of independence that it has inspired the royal governor to remove himself to a British man-of-war. I am delighted to tell you that we may now count Maryland among our supporters."

Franklin looked at Adams, felt Jefferson now standing close behind him.

"That would be twelve."

44. FRANKLIN

PHILADELPHIA, JULY 2, 1776

DICKINSON HELD THE FLOOR FOR MORE THAN AN HOUR, HIS USUAL eloquence infused with what Franklin thought was a last desperate plea for a cause that was already dead. The chamber was fully charged with the expectation of great debate, the tall windows thrown wide open, as though the voices should be allowed to carry far beyond this one cavernous room.

He weighed Dickinson's words with as much care as his tired

mind would permit, the warm breeze flowing through the chamber soothing him, tempering the July heat. He had been concerned that he might fall asleep, but Dickinson's passion, the man's desperation, held his attention. He had noticed the same reaction from Adams and from several of the radical delegates. Let the man have his say.

Franklin still held Dickinson's opening words in his mind: *My conduct this day I expect will give the finishing blow to my popularity. . . . Yet I had rather forfeit popularity forever than vote away the blood and happiness of my countrymen.*

It was honest and heartfelt, and Franklin knew that despite his eloquence and the man's own bullheaded certainty about his reasoning, Dickinson was probably right about his popularity. He tried to focus on the man's words now, could sense from Dickinson's tone that he was winding down.

"If there is any pleasure in supporting war, I cannot see it here. You would ask me to vote for that which will guarantee our destruction. England has already pledged all of her resources to our suppression. And though so many of you are called upon to believe that the people of all our colonies are eager for this course, I do not believe it still. I cannot say more . . . except be prepared for what will follow. This is not a righteous course, colonial soldiers will not march en masse to the trumpets of heaven. By accepting this document, you will have laid open the pathway for civil war. And if somehow, God is to shine His light on your lust for independence, on the madness of popular fury, what then? It would be as though destroying our house in winter, before we have built another shelter. We will suffer the consequences of our own foolishness. God help us. God help us indeed."

He left the rostrum, and the room was oddly silent, no applause, none of the comments that followed every speech, the throng in the gallery above them perfectly polite. The Virginian Benjamin Harrison took the gavel now, was serving temporarily as the president of the congress. Franklin glanced over to the men from Massachusetts, saw John Hancock seated with them, a symbolic show of kinsmanship. Harrison seemed unusually nervous, the man's boisterousness replaced by a solemn gaze over the room.

"Does anyone wish to respond to the honorable gentleman from Pennsylvania?" Harrison looked toward Adams, a gesture that was almost automatic now, and Franklin watched him slowly stand up, all eyes on the man who had led so many of the debates before now. No one else had made a request to speak, not even the usual parade of orators, the men who spent more time at the rostrum enjoying the resonance of their own voices than what they were saying. But this day was different, and there was no mistaking the mood of the room, that if anyone was fit to answer Dickinson's final plea, it would be John Adams. Adams never seemed comfortable in the role of speaker, and Franklin studied him carefully, could read uncertainty in the man's movement and posture. He has yet to believe in his own talents. He is possibly the finest orator in this room, and is the only one among us who is not aware of that.

Adams cleared his throat, and there was no other sound in the room.

"I have stated with vexing redundancy, that what we are faced with is a crisis that can be solved only by . . . discipline in the army, governments in every colony, and a confederation of the whole. Today, I am forced to admit that those kinds of arguments sound more suited for the classroom." There was a sudden flash of light from outside, a hard clap of thunder. Franklin jumped, the reflex shared by everyone in the room. Adams looked toward the dark skies beyond the tall windows.

"I may have an audience to which I am not so very accustomed." There was nervous laughter, heads turning toward the windows, which were rattling slightly, buffeted by a sudden gust of wind. There was another thunderclap, and rain began to fall, the wind blowing a hard mist through the windows. Adams waited, and the sounds of the storm now settled into a solid roar. Men rose, closed the windows slightly, deflecting the rain, and the room grew still once more.

Adams continued, "I respect any man who possesses so strong a passion that he is willing to sacrifice anything dear to him to express it. Whether Mr. Dickinson has sacrificed his popularity I am not certain. But I fear that he would have us sacrifice something much more of value. He speaks of blood. A sacrifice indeed. But memories are short, it seems. How much blood has already been shed by our countrymen at the hands of others? How many cities will be burned, how many of our town squares will be trampled under the boots of a foreign army? I agree with Mr. Dickinson that we may well be embroiled in a civil war, that there are colonial citizens who will fight against their own to hold to their king. But unlike Mr. Dickinson, I do not despair over what might be. I despair over what already is. The war *has* begun. The peace has been shattered beyond anyone's ability to repair it with words and petitions. What we are debating today is not whether there is wisdom or folly in a claim of independence. We do not seek out truths. We seek only to *declare* truths. You have all received the good and sincere wishes of your own assemblies, and thus, your own people. If you would deny what your *people* want . . . is that not what began this crisis? We requested a voice in governing our own affairs. It was denied us. We have requested that King George set aside the ruinous policies of his ministers. It was denied us. We have requested in the most reasonable terms that the king's soldiers not harm us, not destroy our towns, and not endanger our very lives. It was denied us." He paused, glanced at the window, the storm still blowing, rain and wind swirling against the hall. "If we do not declare our independence, in a voice that blows against our enemies with the force and determination of this very storm, then we will suffer the fate of every people who have ever cast away their own freedom. We will wither and die under the weight of our own servility. I do not share Mr. Dickinson's call for God to help us. God does not give us strength, He rewards it. It is in the character of our citizens, it is a part of what has inspired these colonies to such a prominence, a healthy reliance on our own backs and our own hearts, a power of the *mind* that so threatens the British monarchy. We are a people who have shown the world we can help ourselves, that we have the God-given strength to *stand* for our liberty. God help us? No, sir. May God *bless* us."

Adams stepped down, returned to his chair, and the silence was broken by brief cheers, calls from the gallery above. Franklin could feel his stomach churning with nervousness, sweat in his clothes. He looked at Adams; the man had his eyes cast down, evidently drained. How much more can be said? Franklin wondered. The talk is through.

Now Harrison was at the rostrum, the big man's voice a booming contrast to Adams.

"We have a resolution before this chamber, as presented three weeks ago by the honorable Mr. Richard Henry Lee of Virginia. If there is no further debate, the chair would entertain a motion for a vote on the resolution."

Several hands rose, voices calling, and Franklin raised his own hand, joined the chorus.

"So moved . . ."

"Seconded . . ."

"I will call out the name of each colony in their alphabetical order. Signify your vote." Harrison took a long breath, seemed to say a brief prayer, and Franklin sat forward, his hands damp, the storm outside the only sound.

"Connecticut."

"Aye!"

"Delaware."

"Uh, Mr. President, I fear we are in some difficulty. The two delegates present from Delaware are divided on their vote."

All faces turned to the voice, and Franklin saw George Read, the Delaware lawyer who had always sided with Dickinson. Harrison said, "Only two? Where is Mr. Rodney?"

The door burst open in the back of the room, and Franklin saw a man stumbling in, drenched with the rain. The man removed his hat, wiped at his face, saw the eyes all focused on him, said, "Pardon me, gentlemen. Have I interrupted something of consequence?"

Read sat abruptly, and Franklin saw disgust on the man's face. He smiled, heard Harrison say, "Mr. Rodney, it seems you are the deciding vote for your delegation. The issue concerns the resolution calling for a declaration of independence."

Rodney moved toward the other two men from Delaware, and Franklin was watching Read, could see the other man, Thomas McKean, speaking to the soaked Rodney, and now Rodney stood, said aloud, "I believe the proper response is . . . aye!"

Harrison did not hesitate.

"Georgia."

"Aye!"

"Maryland."

"Aye!"

"Massachusetts."

Franklin saw Hancock stand, the man's voice booming, "Aye!"

"New Hampshire."

"Aye!"

"New Jersey."

"Aye!"

"New York."

"Mr. President . . ." Franklin saw Livingston stand now, and the man seemed embarrassed. "The delegation from New York has received no authorization from our assembly."

There were murmurs now rolling through the room, shouts from the gallery, and Franklin felt a cold lump in his chest. No, it cannot end because of that. They cannot delay us, not now, not after so much.

Livingston looked at the other men around him, and Franklin saw nods from the other New Yorkers, encouraging him to continue.

"Mr. President, in light of the sentiment expressed by this congress, it is only proper that the delegation from New York abstain from casting a vote until such time as we are instructed otherwise by our assembly."

There was sudden applause, and Franklin felt swallowed by relief. Thank God, there is wisdom to be found in the oddest places. Harrison pounded his gavel.

"The chair accepts the decision of the New York delegation. North Carolina."

"Aye!"

"Pennsylvania."

There was a hushed pause, and Franklin saw movement by the main entranceway, the door opening slightly, two men slipping out quickly, leaving the chamber. He looked around, expected to see Dickinson and the other three Pennsylvanians, saw only two men, James Wilson and John Morton. Wilson leaned forward, close to Franklin, said quietly, "Mr. Dickinson and Mr. Morris have done your cause a great courtesy. They have declined to offer a vote, leaving me a minority of one." Wilson looked at the man beside him, said, "Since I assume, Mr. Morton, that your sentiments have not changed, you and Dr. Franklin are now a majority."

Morton said in a low voice, "They have not changed, sir. I favor independence."

Franklin turned, faced the rostrum, saw the expectant stare of Harrison, saw now every face in the room staring at him as well. He said, "That would be . . . aye."

"Rhode Island."

"Aye!"

"South Carolina"

"Aye."

Harrison paused now, clearly enjoying the moment.

"Virginia."

"Aye!"

"The motion is carried . . . by unanimous vote."

Harrison's words were drowned out by the roar from the gallery, the delegates themselves now standing, hands going out, pats on the back. Franklin stood, pulled forward by the sudden release, a flood of infectious joy. He saw the Massachusetts delegation hemmed in by a crowd, Hancock's booming voice calling for a salute, Sam Adams beaming a wide smile. Franklin moved closer, saw John Adams now, the short man assaulted by the loud cheers, the kind appreciation of those he spoke for. The man seemed shaken, and Franklin pushed closer, the delegates pulling back in respect. Adams looked at him with an odd stare, his eyes glazed with emotion. Outside, the thunderstorm had passed, the windows now alive with sunlight, and Franklin saw Adams staring up that way, turned with him. The great chamber was echoing with sound, and Franklin moved closer, wanted to say something to the man, but there were no words, nothing that could measure the moment. He saw it in Adams' eyes as well, that there were no words left, the energy all in some other place. Adams still stared at the sunlight, the reflection on the tall windows, rays of new light cast through the room. The sounds began to flow outside, the word spreading out away from the State House, people in the street beyond shouting, and Adams seemed not to hear, looked at him now.

"Was I right, Doctor? Will God bless us?"

Franklin could not hold his emotions back now. He put a hand on the man's shoulder, his own head down, said in a low voice, "He already has, Mr. Adams."

THE CONGRESS STILL HAD WORK TO DO, NOW CONSIDERED THE wording of the committee's actual declaration. Changes were made, as Franklin knew they would be, clarifications, omissions, concessions to those who had voted to approve the declaration despite their own hesitation, stubborn doubts that the colonies were truly prepared for the consequences.

Jefferson had included a clause condemning the practice of slavery, and laid the blame for the slave trade squarely on the shoulders of King George. There was resistance to this theme primarily from Georgia and South Carolina, whose economies were dependent on the continuation of slavery. Jefferson had also lashed out at the English people, more of his poetic flair, the wistful sorrow that the friendship that had been so promising between the two peoples should now be laid to waste by the English obedience to their own corrupt leadership. There was a strong argument by the more conservative delegates that the best and last hope for some peaceful settlement of the crisis might yet be found in some outpouring of support that the colonists might receive from the English citizenry; thus it was best not to antagonize them directly. The clauses were omitted.

Jefferson retired to his room to complete the final draft as approved by the congress. Though the resolution calling for a declaration of independence had already passed, the final document itself must still be approved.

JULY 4, 1776

THEY SAT QUIETLY, THE GALLERY SMALL, THE CITIZENS NOT SEEM-
ing to be concerned with this last mundane bit of business
regarding the Declaration of Independence. The debates were
done, the wording changed to suit the sensitivities of every
colony. Those who were still uneasy had given up their objec-
tions, and many of the delegates had already sent word back to
their assemblies that the declaration had been approved.

A clean and final copy had been made by Jefferson, none of the
ink scratches in the margins, the crossed-out words, the scribbles
and notes jotted in every space. He had brought it first to Adams,
who had shown it to Franklin, who held it now, scanned the
wording, while around him, delegates were continuing to gather,
expectant, patient. He studied the phrasing, the precision, searched
nervously for some mistake, some addition Jefferson might have
included, yet another point they would have to debate. But the
young man had done as he was instructed, had incorporated all the
changes necessary. Franklin lowered the document, looked at
Adams.

"I believe we may now proceed."

Hancock was at the rostrum, and Adams took him the paper,
then moved to his chair. Hancock struck his gavel once.

"To order. If there is no objection, the chair will now read the
document as offered by the committee and amended by this congress." He set the gavel aside, raised the document Jefferson had
finalized, a long rectangle of parchment, read slowly, " 'When in
the course of human events, it becomes necessary for one people
to dissolve the political bands which have connected them with
another, and to assume among the powers of the earth, the separate and equal station to which the laws of nature and of nature's
God entitle them, a decent respect to the opinions of mankind requires that they should declare the causes which impel them to
the separation.

" 'We hold these truths to be self-evident, that all men are created equal . . .' "

The words reached out to each of them, the delegates, those
above in the public seats, out beyond the walls of this one simple

building. The words were carried by rider and post, copies posted in every town square, in every courthouse, every state house, every assembly hall. Like a great stone dropped into a vast deep pond, the impact of the Declaration of Independence would flow out in waves that would reach far beyond the colonies, far beyond the people who had brought it to life. The words would spread beyond the great ocean, would reach the halls and stout buildings of a government that would still not understand, would still pretend to own the spirit of these unruly people, would insist that crushing that spirit meant crushing the people and whatever sham of an army these outrageous rebels would dare to mount.

45. WASHINGTON

New York, July 9, 1776

HE COULD SEE THE WARSHIPS FAR OUT IN THE HARBOR, THEIR small shore boats in motion. Until his army had begun to arrive in New York, the British men-of-war had been anchored right along the wharves, one still serving as the official office of Governor Tryon. Once Washington's troops had begun to fortify the city, the ships had wisely sailed out beyond the range of colonial artillery, were anchored now in a position that effectively blocked anyone else from entering the harbor from the sea. Now the British sailors took their shore leave on Long Island, and most of the taverns and shops along the waterfront of the village of Brooklyn were firmly supportive of their British patrons.

Charles Lee had reached the city before Washington, and, along with Nathaniel Greene, had ignored whatever political divisiveness might still be found there, immediately beginning construction of barricades along the eastern shore of the city. Manhattan Island was densely populated at its southern tip, but northward, the vast majority of the island was mostly woods and empty pastureland. Defending the entire island was out of the question, especially since the rivers on both sides, the Hudson and the East River, were easily navigated by British warships, and for the most part were too wide to effectively plant any serious obstructions. The western shore of the island, along the Hudson, was blessedly difficult to assault, high banks along most of the waterfront. But the shores of the East River gently sloped to the water, and here Lee had his men construct defensive works, manned by sharpshooters and the first cannon that had begun to arrive from Boston.

North of the populated part of the island, Lee constructed a defensive line that spanned from one shore to the other. Preventing the British from landing on the northern half of Manhattan was impossible, but at least Lee could slow them down if they assaulted the city from above.

Washington had inspected all the new construction by now, had established his new headquarters in a house near the southern tip of the city. The people had received him with appropriate warmth, surprising him, since it was no secret that even from his shipboard office, Governor Tryon still had an influential hand in much of the colony's political power.

When Lee and Greene had arrived in Manhattan, leading the first columns of colonial troops from Boston, they had been enormously surprised that the British were not, in fact, waiting for them. From the time Howe's fleet had sailed away from Boston Harbor, they had simply disappeared, and the most hopeful among the command believed that the rumors in Boston might have been true after all. After the embarrassment of abandoning their base, Howe might simply have sailed for England. By the time Washington arrived in New York, the rumors had changed. Some of Tryon's staff had difficulty holding a secret. Washington had learned that Howe had gone to Halifax, to refit and resupply, deposit his sick and wounded, and replace them, not only with fresh British troops, but with the first of the mercenaries from Europe, the first shiploads of Hessian troops arriving in Halifax just in time to board Howe's transports for New York.

* * *

The Declaration of Independence had reached his hand that morning, opening a torrent of good cheer around his head-quarters. Washington's first reaction had been enormous relief, and he settled into a thick soft chair in the sitting room, reading the document again several times. God bless them, he thought. This required so much more than simple resolve, more than just the politics of making a protest to the king. This was an act of genuine courage. These men have placed their own necks in the king's noose.

In one small dark place in his memory, he held on to the words of Artemas Ward, the nagging fear that the congress might simply dissolve, the differences and controversies too great. But the fear was gone now, the paper in his hand sweeping it away. This has united us. No matter what our other differences, we have come together for the most important task of all. There can no longer be any argument about the interests of Massachusetts conflicting with those of Virginia. We now share much more than anything that may divide us.

He set the paper aside, had already given the order to his staff, that the troops now in the city would assemble at midday, would hear this document read aloud. He pulled out his pocket watch, said aloud, "Time to go."

The troops had gathered in the great green park that spread alongside Broad Street on a hilltop near Trinity Church. The troops had formed in a hollow square, a formation the British had used in combat for centuries. As the men tightened their ranks, the officers sharpening the corners of the square, Washington had already wondered if these troops would ever use it in combat at all.

He climbed the steps of the platform, built just this morning, stared out at his army, seven thousand men from six different colonies, an extraordinary variety of dress, some clusters of similar uniforms, other appearing to be civilians, groups of men who might as well be attending a town meeting or some sporting event. But despite their differences, they had one distinct simi-larity. Nearly all of them had muskets now. And as they stood in line under the noonday sun, shoulder to shoulder, Washington felt what they all were feeling now, could see it in the faces, all focused on their commander. By God, we are an *army*.

To one side, a corps of musicians was playing, the sharp roll of the drumbeat blending with the high-pitched song of the fife, the rhythm wrapping around the troops, holding them neat in their formation. Beyond, the citizens had gathered in thick lines as well, surrounding the park, the social elite standing with the rabble of the street, as much a blend of finery and common homespun as the soldiers they admired.

The time had come, the staff now in place behind him, Lee, Greene, Knox, many of the officers close in front of the platform. He turned, nodded to Gates, who stepped forward, raised a short sword. It was the signal to the musicians, and abruptly the music stopped. There was a roll of applause from the civilians, and Washington could see Gates react with mild horror. Washington wanted to tell him, It's all right, you can't control the civilians, too. Gates seemed to accept his fate, stepped back into line behind him. Washington looked out across the crowd, suddenly realized the focus was on him. He turned to the side, nodded to the young officer close by, the man selected both for his ability to read eloquently and for the volume of his voice. Washington now handed the officer the document, a tight roll of paper, could see nervousness in the man's face.

"Whenever you are ready, Mr. Brown," said Washington.

The man slowly unrolled the paper, glanced at the general, and Washington turned, inclined his head toward Gates again, who said aloud, "The army will come to attention. As ordered by the commanding general, this army will now hear the Declaration as approved by the Continental Congress on July fourth, the year of our Lord seventeen seventy-six."

The young officer now stepped forward, began to read. Washington saw the words in his mind, so much of it now permanent inside him. He could see their faces in that great chamber, had already imagined hearing them debate, the confident certainty of Richard Henry Lee, the emotion of Patrick Henry, the pure clear logic of John Adams. He tried to focus on the faces in front of him now, saw no one looking away, the entire sea of soldiers and civilians attentive to the young officer's words. There were shouts now, a few responding to certain phrases, some men cheering the charges against King George.

" ' . . . for quartering large bodies of troops among us: for protecting them, by a mock trial, from punishment for any murders which they should commit on the inhabitants of these states . . .' "

There were more cheers now, others straining forward to hear.

" ' . . . for imposing taxes on us without our consent . . .' "

There was a thunder of approval, and Washington glanced toward Brown, saw the man pause, waiting for the noise to subside. Washington nodded his approval, and the man continued to read. The cheers seemed to grow again, slowly, gradually the spirit of the entire audience rising as the power of the Declaration reached into each one of them. Washington was still reciting the words silently as the officer read them, closed his eyes now, knew it was near the closing.

" ' . . . that these united colonies are, and of right ought to be free and independent states; that they are absolved from all allegiance to the British crown, and that all political connection between them and the state of Great Britain is and ought to be totally dissolved; and that as free and independent states, they have full power to levy war, conclude peace, contract alliances, establish commerce, and to do all other acts and things which independent states may of right do. And for the support of this Declaration, with a firm reliance on the protection of divine Providence, we mutually pledge to each other our lives, our fortunes, and our sacred honor.' "

Washington opened his eyes, saw the young soldier staring at the paper, tears on the man's cheeks. Brown lowered the paper now, and the crowd understood, the low roar beginning to grow louder, the pitch and the volume rising with the hats that began to fly. The soldiers held their muskets high, and Washington was smiling, shared the emotions with all of them. He could hear some men calling his name, others standing quietly with their hands in the air, more tears. Beyond the formation of soldiers, the townspeople began to move, accompanied by new cheers, words he couldn't hear. They began in one long flow, moving to the south, down Broad Street, past Trinity Church, down the long hill toward Bowling Green.

* * *

THEY BROUGHT ROPES, AND A FLOOD OF MEN BEGAN TO CLIMB UP
and over the iron picket fence, the ropes slung high, draped over
the gold statue. Men jumped up on the statue's base, reaching
beneath the belly of the horse, some climbing higher, securing
the ropes into fat knots around the golden figure of the rider. Out
beyond the picket fence, the crowd around the green continued
to grow, the cheering and shouts unceasing. The men inside the
fence began to line up along the taut ropes, one man shouting
above the din, directing them. The ropes grew tighter, and the
massive golden statue suddenly moved, fueling a new roar from
the crowd. It rocked slightly, shifting on its base, then, as the
men gave one final pull, the great golden horse and rider toppled,
gouging heavily into the soft earth of the green. The cheers were
deafening now, and one man pounced on the head of the rider,
the golden face of King George, the expression immobile, oblivious, the cold metal unchanged. But the man had a saw, knelt
down, began to cut, the skill of a craftsman, a man who has done
this kind of work before. Around him, the men with the ropes
urged him on, the man cutting with a feverish energy. When the
head was severed, the man held it up high to the mass of people,
the sounds exploding again.

   As the man carried the severed piece of metal in a parade
around the green, another man stood close to the statue, saw the
hollow place where the man had cut. The gold was only gilt, a
thin plating over a massive piece of metal. The man knelt down,
knew something of metal and weapons, and now he smiled, realized something that the great throng around him might not yet
know. His hand touched the metal inside, soft and gray. *Lead.*
There was more value to this statue than simply as a symbol of
the fallen power of England. It could be melted into musket
balls.

BROAD STREET WAS STILL PACKED SOLID WITH THE CELEBRATION,
but Washington had prepared his horse to be close by, knew if he
stayed near the people, they might mob him. He had made this
ride each day, a routine that would have been a pleasant diversion had the purpose not been so very serious. He wound the

horse quickly through the narrow streets, followed closely by his guard, the handpicked men who accompanied him everywhere he went now. They rode out away from the park, turned northward. He could still hear the sounds from the great crowd, but quickly they faded away behind him. He guided the horse up a long rise, followed a trail that ran toward the Hudson. There were trees here, but he knew they would quickly give way, the bluff along the river bare, the vantage point he had come to know so well.

He stopped the horse, saw the Hudson bathed in the afternoon sun, a glow of golden fire, the clean surface unbroken, no boats, no sign of any traffic at all. The guard knew his routine by now, stayed back behind him, in silent formation. He climbed down from the horse, reached into his saddlebag, pulled out the spyglass.

The rumors had come to him for several days, colonial privateers sending word of the approach of the great fleet. He scanned the horizon to the southeast, the mouth of the harbor, saw the familiar British warships at anchor, the same pattern as before. He lowered his view to the East River, across to Brooklyn, no change, nothing new. He began to feel relief, could hear his own breathing, looked again to the southeast, toward the mouths of the two rivers, the tip of the island, could see the mass of people still around Bowling Green, the government buildings, what had once been Gage's headquarters. He raised the glass, saw clouds to the south, along the horizon, suddenly lowered the glass. He wiped the eyepiece with his shirt, raised the glass again, stared toward the south, Staten Island, could see now the clouds were not clouds at all. They were sails.

He felt his heart begin to pound, a hard anticipation growing in his chest, could see it clearly now, the fleet gathering around the far end of Staten Island. It was another indefensible place, the land mass too large for the troops he had, the island surrounded by water too deep and too open for him to obstruct. He had expected that Howe would understand how useful that place could be, a staging area, large enough to assemble whatever size force Howe was bringing with him. He tried to count the ships, but the sails were massed together, and he lowered the glass, could see them with his eyes now, thought, Yes, of course he understands. And no matter the importance of this city, we cannot truly defend this place. But I cannot just withdraw. If we are so much weaker than they are, we cannot concede that, announce our weakness by just marching away. The people would not receive that well, and neither would the congress.

He looked out now to the west, the sun settling low, the Hudson still a glorious show. He thought of the congress, wondered how they would respond to Howe's arrival. Certainly there would be some sense of relief, putting the rumors to rest that Howe might suddenly appear at Philadelphia. He had never believed that, knew the value of New York, the river below him the crucial artery splitting the colonies in two. No, the congress is safe for now. Howe will focus right here. It's what I would do.

He thought of the assembly in the park, his soldiers standing tall, hearing the words from the Declaration. He tried to see the faces of the men in the congress again, wished he had been there for the vote, the raw power of that moment, something no one there would ever forget. Those men have done all they can do. They have spoken with one voice, they have given this . . . *nation* a beginning, a point in time from which all else will follow. But it will only mean something if we can *win*.

He raised the glass again but did not look, knew already what he would see. There is an army out there, with one mission. So now it will be up to us, to all these men who are learning to call themselves soldiers. Now we will learn if we can fight a war.

AFTERWORD

"It is, as they say, a wise country that knows its own father."
PHILIP GUEDALLA, HISTORIAN, 1924

"We are in the very midst of a revolution the most complete, unexpected and remarkable of any in the history of nations."
JOHN ADAMS, JUNE 9, 1776

"I know not what course others may take; but as for me, give me liberty or give me death!"
PATRICK HENRY TO THE VIRGINIA CONVENTION, MARCH 23, 1775

LIEUTENANT GENERAL THOMAS GAGE

UPON HIS RETURN TO LONDON IN NOVEMBER 1775, THE MINISTRY, by its lack of attention to him, confirms what he already knew to be true. But Lord Germain allows Gage to languish as a commander with no command until April 1776, when he is finally notified by Germain that his status as army commander in chief is terminated. He is still, however, the royal governor of Massachusetts, and as do so many of King George's governors, he reigns in exile. The post provides him a respectable salary however, sufficient to maintain a comfortable, though modest household for his family.

Still regarded with respect by King George, in 1781 he is asked to supervise a potential defense of England from a rumored invasion by the French, which never materializes. When the Revolutionary War draws to an end and Germain is removed from power in 1782, the king facilitates Gage's promotion to full general. He never serves in any official military capacity, and suffers from failing health, dies in 1787 at age sixty-eight.

He is regarded by most of his contemporaries and by history as a competent military commander and an otherwise decent man who by extraordinarily bad fortune is thrust into the forefront of one of Britain's most complex and devastating military calamities. While history may cast harsh judgment on his actions, no one has yet concluded who, of all those commanders then available, would have performed the duty with any more positive results for his country.

In the 1850s, a portrait of the colony's last royal governor is donated to the state of Massachusetts by Gage's youngest son, then an admiral in the British navy. It now hangs in the state capitol.

The debate about Margaret Gage's role in the military activity

around Boston is unsolved and uncertain. There continues to be
pointed speculation that she had ample motive and means to
provide the Sons of Liberty with crucial information, as con-
trasted by the argument that no loyal wife of that time would
commit such an abominable offense. There is only sketchy evidence for either view. After her husband's death, she remains in
England with her family. She dies in 1824, at age ninety.

GOVERNOR THOMAS HUTCHINSON

HE REMAINS IDLE IN ENGLAND, ALWAYS NAÏVELY HOLDING TO THE
belief that when the war is settled, he will once again return to
his native Massachusetts and resume office. He seems to those
around him to be possessed of desperation, hanging on every
word of the progress of the war.

His daughter, Peggy, the namesake of his late much-beloved
wife, is stricken with a lengthy illness and dies in 1777, at age
twenty-three. Her death is a blow from which he will never recover. He is a tragic man in many ways, destined to die and be
buried in exile, roundly despised by the people of his home state.
He endures the final years of a lonely life by focusing on his
writing, publishes several historical works, including a critical
study of public sentiment, titled *The Witchcraft Delusion of
1692*. Suffering a stroke, he dies in June 1780, at age sixty-nine.

*He was born to be the cause and the victim of popular fury,
outrage and conflagration . . . he was perhaps the only man in
the world who could have brought on the controversy between
Great Britain and America, in the manner and at the time it
was done.*
JOHN ADAMS, JANUARY 1781

Governor Hutchinson is dead.
OBITUARY, *THE BOSTON INDEPENDENT CHRONICLE*,
JANUARY 1781

Samuel Adams

His greatest mission in life now successful, his signature
on the Declaration, the man to whom Jefferson refers as "truly
the man of the Revolution" now finds himself in a role to which
he is not only unaccustomed, but ill suited. With no controversy
to stir, and no longer a populace to inflame, Sam settles into his
position in the congress, but quickly becomes bored. Without
the turmoil of behind-the-scenes intrigue, he creates his own,
alienating many in the congress who had formerly rallied behind
his cause. He serves until 1781, returns to Boston, and nearly
fades into obscurity, barely survives financially by managing the
family business, a noted brewery, which he had inherited from
his father. He runs against John Hancock for the governor's seat,
fails against Hancock's inexplicable popularity, serves instead
as lieutenant governor until Hancock's death in 1793. Finally
elected on his own accord in 1794, he serves for four years. He
dies in 1803, at age eighty-one.

John Dickinson

The most ardent opponent of the Declaration of Independence continues to serve in whatever capacity his people will
support, including service on the committee that drafts the Articles of Confederation. In a move that would surprise his enemies in the congress, in 1777 he responds to the escalation of the
Revolutionary War by enlisting as a private in a Delaware regiment, and participates in the Battle of Brandywine. His explanation reflects his sensitivity to the public criticism he has
received: "I can form no idea of a more noble fate than . . . to resign my life . . . for the defense and happiness of those unkind
countrymen whom I cannot forbear to esteem as fellow-citizens
amidst their fury against me."

He eventually serves as a colonel and then a brigadier general,
but does not see further military action. He settles in Delaware,
continues to serve in the congress from that state, then returns to
Pennsylvania, and in 1783, founds Dickinson College. Though

in his later life he holds no political office, he continues to write in a political vein, publishes several articles, including a passionate call for a continuing alliance with France.

Always frail and sickly in appearance, he nonetheless outlives many of his political rivals. He dies in Philadelphia in 1808, at age seventy-six.

ROYAL GOVERNOR WILLIAM FRANKLIN

LABELED BY THE NEW JERSEY ASSEMBLY "AN ENEMY TO THE LIBerties of this country," he is imprisoned in a private home in Connecticut, where the confinement is more imagined than restrictive. He continues to act on behalf of loyalist interests, corresponds openly with General Howe in New York. George Washington loses tolerance for William's open disregard of his circumstance and orders him jailed in Litchfield, Connecticut. All during this period, he never again sees his wife, Elizabeth, who has been escorted by British troops to the safety of New York. Lonely and in fragile health, she dies in mid-1777 and is buried at St. Paul's Church.

In 1778 he is exchanged, freed, and remains around New York, serves as president of the Associated Alliance of Loyalists. The alliance proves to be much more a band of vigilantes than any political organization, and under severe pressure from George Washington, they are disbanded in 1782. William goes to England, and two years later attempts to reconcile with his father, who is now in France. Ben Franklin responds to his son's request for a renewal of their relationship with a terse though positive response. They meet briefly in France, but their relationship is never truly restored, and when the father dies, William is angrily disappointed by his inheritance, which amounts essentially to nothing and includes this final note from his father: "The part he acted against me in the late war, which is of public notoriety, will account for my leaving him no more of an estate he endeavored to deprive me of."

Bitter and unpopular in England, William spends the rest of his life in unwise property speculation, and dies alone in 1813, at age eighty-two. It is his son, Temple, who preserves and subsequently publishes much of Ben Franklin's written work.

MRS. MARGARET STEVENSON

BEN FRANKLIN'S LANDLADY IN LONDON COULD BE DESCRIBED AS one of the true loves of his life. Though she never sees him again after his departure from London in 1775, the two continue an exchange of letters that demonstrates their affection. When Franklin goes to France, her letters follow him, and there is much talk of her making a visit, which never occurs. Her financial and physical health both begin to fail, and she is forced to leave London for the British countryside and move in with her daughter, Polly, who had been the object of another of Franklin's most cherished relationships. Mrs. Stevenson continues to plan for the day when she might again fritter about the house of her famous tenant, and writes him constantly to expect her visit: "Don't be surprised if I pack myself up." But she is betrayed by her health and dies on New Year's Day 1783. In mourning the loss of one so close, Franklin writes, "This has begun to take away the rest, and strikes the hardest."

Despite all the rumors of impropriety that surrounded Franklin and Margaret Stevenson, and in fact have continued to follow Franklin for two centuries, there is no evidence to show that their relationship was anything beyond that of the dearest and most affectionate of friends.

RICHARD HENRY LEE

HE SERVES THE CONTINENTAL CONGRESS UNTIL 1780, CONTINUES his friendship with both Sam and John Adams. He returns in 1784 and is elected president of the congress. As the new United States Constitution is being created, Lee takes a hard stand against the potential abuses of a strong federal government, and is instrumental in helping create the Bill of Rights. Despite failing health, he accepts the urgings of John Adams and Patrick

Henry and is elected by Virginia to the new United States Senate, where he serves until 1792. He dies in his home state in 1794, at age sixty-two.

WILL STRAHAN

EVEN BEN FRANKLIN CONCEDES THAT STRAHAN, THE KING'S royal printer and member of the British Parliament, is and always has been his best friend, for the many years they both live. During the war, their correspondence is sparse, and though Strahan maintains his affection for Franklin in their letters, Franklin does not respond in kind, still resentful that Strahan continues his unwavering loyalty to England and its cause. In spring 1776, upon learning of Franklin's ill-advised journey to Canada, Strahan writes, "I wish your great talents had found other employment."

Strahan continues to be a good friend and supporter of William Franklin, uses his influence to some effect in having the imprisoned governor released. After the Revolutionary War, Strahan urges Ben Franklin to "return home" to England, but Franklin is in France and far from a peaceful retirement. Strahan's health begins to fail him, and unlike his friend, he loses the strength for long journeys and is nearly blind. In 1785, as Franklin begins his final journey back to America, the two men plan to meet in Southampton, England. Strahan dies two weeks before Franklin arrives. He is seventy-six.

MAJOR GENERAL ARTEMAS WARD

HE NEVER RECOVERS FROM WHAT HE PERCEIVES AS THE SLIGHT BY congress to his military abilities, and after the British abandon Boston, Ward will not accompany the army as it marches to New York. He instead offers his resignation from the Continental Army in April 1776. It is accepted in the congress with no debate. Washington writes an indiscreet criticism of Ward, describing his resignation as Ward's willingness to serve as long as he was not called upon to stray far "from the smoke of his own chimney."

Ward continues to serve as commander of militia around Boston, continues to show no skill in the position, finally incurring the wrath of the Massachusetts Assembly, the very body that had once championed him for overall command of the army. He dies in 1800, at age seventy-three.

JOHN HANCOCK

HE SERVES IN THE CONTINENTAL CONGRESS UNTIL 1777, THEN RE-ceives his much-cherished commission as a major general of militia. But his service in the field is consistent with the mediocrity of his civilian accomplishments, and he sees little action.

In September 1780, he becomes the first governor of the state of Massachusetts, serves until ill health forces him to resign in 1785. Elected to the Continental Congress that year and chosen as its president once more, he holds office for two years without ever actually attending a session. In 1788 he serves as president of the Massachusetts convention to ratify the new United States Constitution, is stricken with health problems again, resigns. When the debates stalemate, he is called upon by other delegates who recognize that his name still carries great influence, and he is discreetly provided a list of compromises to break the deadlock. Presenting them as his own creation, he thus receives considerable and undeserved prestige as a statesman. He is elected again as the state's governor, serves six years until his death in 1793, at the age of fifty-six.

PAUL REVERE

WIDELY REGARDED TO HAVE BEEN ONE OF THE "MOHAWKS" WHO participated in the Boston Tea Party, he is ultimately of more service to the revolutionary cause for his abilities as a political cartoonist and metallurgist than as a soldier.

He serves Washington's army by supervising the manufacture

of powder and shot in Massachusetts, eventually receives a military commission as a major of militia, commands the colonial garrison at Castle William. In 1779, he participates in the Penobscot Expedition, a naval battle of disastrous consequence for the colonists, and is brought before a court martial, but since he is a junior officer and the blame lies more with senior command, the court exonerates him.

After the war, he assumes a small role in the creation of the United States Constitution, continues his career as a noted silversmith. He improves his skills in the manufacture of more heavy implements, including cannon, and his company produces much of the metal used in the construction of the USS *Constitution* ("Old Ironsides"). He develops a system for rolling copper into sheets, and contributes to the manufacture of inventor Robert Fulton's first steam-powered boat.

His skills extend to the manufacture of false teeth, and thus is born the legend that he supplies the dentures used by George Washington. But there is no evidence to support the entertaining anecdote. His engraving talents bring him to create the first seal of the state of Massachusetts, which is still in use today.

His first wife dies in 1773, and he marries again, has a total of sixteen children. He outlives his second wife, and dies in 1818 at age eighty-three.

Relatively unknown and unremembered after his death, it is Longfellow's *The Midnight Ride of Paul Revere*, written in 1863, that creates the aura around his most historically memorable accomplishment. Longfellow is thus responsible for not only elevating Revere's works of silver to extraordinary value, but keeping the name of Paul Revere alive in the lore of the United States that every child learns in school.

WILLIAM PITT, LORD CHATHAM

THE MAN WHO HAD SAVED KING GEORGE'S THRONE BY HIS HEROism in the Seven Years' War with France still carries so much animosity toward the French that when France is rumored to be entering the Revolution in an alliance with the colonies, Chatham shifts his political position. In 1778, there is a proposal debated in the House of Lords calling for extreme effort at peace with America, because of nervousness about the potential risk to England if France does indeed join the war. Chatham, who supported colonial success at the expense of English pride, now reverses course, cannot stomach a loss of English pride by showing a fear of the French, whom he has already bested in war. In May 1778, participating in the spirited debate on the floor of the House of Lords, he collapses and dies suddenly, apparently of a heart attack, at age seventy.

THOMAS PAINE

THE MAN ARGUABLY THE MOST RESPONSIBLE FOR UNITING THE American people behind the theme of independence spends the rest of his life in an attempt to duplicate the glory and notoriety he earns from *Common Sense*. He serves briefly in the Continental Army with no distinction, continues to write long and thoughtful essays on the state of man. Despite the enormous circulation of *Common Sense* in 1776, it is another virtually unknown article, *The Crisis,* that contains the single line for which he is best remembered: "These are the times that try men's souls."

As a government bureaucrat in England, he had struggled to keep a position. In America, he soon establishes a reputation as a disagreeable, slovenly man who shows no patience for argument. His writings become long-winded and hostile attacks on what most people consider the accepted order, including an assault on religion titled *The Age of Reason*, described by many as the "atheist's bible."

He returns to England in 1787 and would have been accepted for the reputation of his writing, but his personal conflicts with those of powerful influence result instead in his arrest for treason, the ministry's revenge for *Common Sense*. Allowed to leave for France, he is arrested yet again, this time in Paris, after he voices loud support for the political party that is in disfavor at the time.

In 1796, one of his final essays is published. The *Letter to George Washington* is a brutal and highly inappropriate assault on the aging man who is clearly the nation's most revered hero. The essay is a stark contrast to his *The American Citizen*, which includes an exposition of yellow fever that Thomas Jefferson calls "one of the most sensible performances on that disease that had come under my observation."

Paine returns to America in 1802, settles in New Jersey and New York City, destroys his own health by a combination of excessive drinking and a grotesque lack of personal hygiene, and dies in June 1809, at age seventy-two. His admirers are many, and for the next two centuries his writings will inspire revolutionary and radical movements in Europe and America. From Napoleon to Walt Whitman to the founders of the American labor movement, his theories are toasted and venerated. While his words survive and continue to influence, there is wonderment that this man who so changed history would be himself so unremarkable.

The Declaration of Independence

The document voted to final approval on July 4, 1776, is signed that day only by the president of the Continental Congress, John Hancock. The unanimity that the congress had so valued comes finally on July 9, 1776, when, possibly inspired by George Washington's rally in the great park, the New York Assembly finally votes its approval. The final and official document is not written until July 19, and is signed by the delegates beginning on August 2, 1776, when approximately fifty signatures are affixed. Six more are added in the weeks that follow, the latest possibly in January 1777. For the protection of the signers themselves, the signed document is not released publicly until January 18, 1777.

Several of the Declaration's staunchest opponents ultimately sign the document, including Morris of Pennsylvania and Rutledge of South Carolina. Signatures notably missing include, of course, that of John Dickinson, but also that of Patrick Henry, who is not in attendance at the time.

The original document is on public display, housed permanently in the National Archives in Washington, D.C.

AND FROM THIS STORY

JOHN ADAMS, ABIGAIL ADAMS, BENJAMIN FRANKLIN, TEMPLE FRANKLIN, GEORGE WASHINGTON, MARTHA WASHINGTON, NATHANIEL GREENE, HENRY KNOX, BENEDICT ARNOLD, HORATIO GATES, CHARLES LEE, WILLIAM PRESCOTT, DANIEL MORGAN

AND

RICHARD HOWE, WILLIAM HOWE, JOHN BURGOYNE, KING GEORGE III

For six years, these men and women will endure the tragedies and consequences of a war that will rage across the colonies, a desperate struggle between old and new, between a government led by a monarch who holds mightily to the preservation of his empire, opposed by an extraordinary force the like of which the world has never seen, a people united and inspired to fight above all for their own individuality. The best-trained and most disciplined military force in the world will confront an opponent whose greatest asset is their spirit and their passion for their cause. The outcome will change the history of the world. But that is a story for another time.

THE KILLER

ANGELS

by Michael Shaara

Published by Ballantine Books.
Available in bookstores everywhere.

The *New York Times* bestselling
Civil War novel and
major motion picture

GODS AND
GENERALS

by Jeff Shaara

"Brilliant does not even begin to describe
the Shaara gift."
—*Atlanta Journal & Constitution*

Published by Ballantine Books.
Available at bookstores everywhere.

The *New York Times* bestselling novel
and compelling conclusion to the legendary father-son Civil War Trilogy

THE LAST FULL
MEASURE

by Jeff Shaara

"POWERFUL. . .A worthy companion to
The Killer Angels."
—*Chicago Sun-Times*

The national bestselling novel that takes us back thirteen years before the Civil War to another momentous conflict

GONE FOR SOLDIERS

by Jeff Shaara

"Shaara, as usual, is at his best in action and confrontation and in evoking how it felt to be there."
—*The Philadelphia Inquirer*